I0611813

Golden Age

III

The Outer Satellite Insurrection

By Michael Robert von Blucher-Altona

01-August-2025

Library of Congress Control Number: 2024920286

ISBN:
    Hardback   978-1-7637277-7-9
    Paperback   978-1-7637277-6-2
    Kindle   978-1-7637277-5-5

First published 2025

Books by Michael Robert von Blucher-Altona

ForkBraid
Book 1: ForkBraid   – The Price of Peace
Book 2: ForkBraid II – The Cost of War
Book 3: ForkBraid III – Just Rewards

Golden Age
Book 1: Golden Age   – The Unexpected Conflict
Book 2: Golden Age II – The Great Explosion
Book 3: Golden Age III – The Outer Satellite Insurrection

Time does not simply pass; it watches.

It watches as nations rise and fall,
as names are changed and then forgotten,
as treaties are signed with shaking hands
and then torn apart with fire.

Time is not memory, nor is it judgement,
it is the loom upon which memory
and judgement are woven.

And it doth not forgive,
although sometimes,
just sometimes,
it permits healing.

For Time observes and Space abides.

Time and Space are not what you think!

Folcrom Tafazah. October 15th, 2046

Table of Contents

1. Announcements.

The Earth's President had spent weeks at Colonial Central Command in Cis-Lunar L-Five. The Venusian President had also flown in, all the way from Venus aboard his Presidential Space Yacht. Discussions about past achievements, new achievements and future possibilities were all on the table. Now, however, those discussions were over and the announcement was to be made.

The press room was a large room and it was full of reporters, all eagerly awaiting the announcement. There was a large podium at the front of the room and the three Presidents marched through the side door and stood behind its central lectern. This was a surprise for the reporters. It was so very rare to see all three Presidents of the inner solar system standing together in one place, especially the Venusian President, who was a long way from home.

President Dieter Reinhardt of the Cis-Lunar Colonies stood in the middle. On his right was President
Guang Hui of Earth and on his left was President Bradly Klein of the Venusian Republic.

President Dieter Reinhardt tested the microphone and began, "Good Morning, Ladies and Gentlemen. I expect everyone in this room knows who I am and most of you probably know who my guests are. For those who don't, I have Madam President Guang Hui of Earth and President Bradly Klein of the Venusian Republic", he gestured to each in turn as he introduced them.

President Reinhardt gestured to President Hui, who began speaking. President Guang Hui began speaking in a powerful voice, which seemed quite odd for her diminutive stature. Her English was also very clear and precise, although her Chinese accent was readily apparent.

President Guang Hui began with a history lesson, "Good Morning, Ladies and Gentlemen. As some of you may be aware of history, around a century ago, the Earth undertook a twenty-year project to convert all coal-fired power stations into geothermal power generation facilities. At that time, we used plasma drills to bore deeply into the Earth's crust, tapping the Earth's own internal heat to create geothermal wells. Those wells enabled us to convert all of the coal-fired power stations to geothermal."

President Guang paused and looked around the press room, "That was a highly successful project. On Earth, we have just recently completed another twenty-year project. This project has also been highly successful."

Reporters began raising their hands, but Madam Guang continued, "All of the Earth's atomic fission power stations have been converted across to safe, clean nuclear fusion powered generation facilities. On Earth, we no longer use atomic fission reactors for power generation. They have been phased out."

Reporters raised their hands to ask questions, but their questions were premature, so President Reinhardt raised his hand and stated, "Yes, we understand that you have lots of questions, but please let us continue", and one by one, the reporters lowered their hands.

President Reinhardt addresses the reporters, "President Guang has provided us with the latest designs and blueprints for fusion power generation reactors. The most efficient designs in existence", he looked around the room and then continued, "We, here in Cis-Lunar Space and across the whole of Earth's orbital zone and its colonies are embarking on our own twenty-year project to convert across to clean, safe fusion reactors for our power generation. All of our atomic fission reactors will be phased out!"

President Bradly Klein chimed in, "We in the Venusian Republic will also be embarking on the same twenty-year plan to phase out atomic fission power generation. In twenty short years, everything in the Venusian orbital zone will be either solar powered or fusion powered."

All of the reporter's hands raised to ask questions once more.

President Reinhardt picked a reporter at random, a young woman who asked, "Mr President. There are literally thousands, perhaps tens of thousands of fission reactors across the Earth's orbital zone. Are you certain that twenty years will be enough time?"

"Yes, our engineers assure us that this is achievable", President Reinhardt replied, noting, "Our manufacturing facilities at Cis-Lunar L-Four are gearing up for fusion reactor production as we speak."

President Reinhardt picked another reporter at random, a tall, thin man, who asked, "President Klein. Does the Venusian Republic even have the manufacturing facilities to build fusion reactors?"

President Klein smiled and replied, "Not at present, however, we will begin constructing those manufacturing facilities upon my return to the Republic. Until those manufacturing facilities are up and running, we will be importing fusion reactors from Cis-Lunar L-Four."

President Reinhardt chose another reporter, who, being smaller than the rest, had trouble making her raised hand easily seen.

The young lady asked, "Madam President. Why? Why did the Earth phase out fission reactors?"

President Guang smiled, "We haven't phased out all fission reactors, just those used for power production. There are still a handful of reactors in place for other specialised purposes. As for why? Atomic waste. On Earth, we have nearly two hundred and fifty years worth of highly radioactive atomic waste and we have decided that we simply don't want to keep generating it. We intend to phase out uranium mining, almost completely within thirty years."

The same young reporter asked, "What about the colonies beyond Earth's orbit? The further out you go, the more reliant the colonies are on fission power generation."

President Guang looked to President Reinhardt, who replied, "Well, the Martian orbital zone will be converted from fission power production over to fusion power by our own engineers here in Cis-Lunar L-Five. Beyond the Martian orbital zone, things do become a bit more complicated."

The other reporters in the press room turned to the diminutive lady who'd asked why and she asked another question, "It seems to me that the colonies beyond Martian orbit are critical. The further out, the less sunlight and the more reliant on fission power generation. Surely you have a plan?"

President Guang Hui replied, "The Earth will continue to produce uranium fuel rods for export to the colonies in the Asteroid Belt and the Outer Satellite Colonies. Our uranium mines will remain open and fuel rod production will continue until all fission reactors have been replaced."

The same diminutive young reporter noted, "Madam President. You did mention closing the uranium mines in thirty years, so you do have a timeline and an action plan?"

President Guang noted, "This phase-out of uranium will benefit both the Belters and the colonies of the outer solar system. Instead of being reliant on Earth for their uranium fuel rods, they will be able to use clean hydrogen sourced from their own regions. Water, a source of hydrogen, is quite prevalent in the Asteroid Belt and the orbital zones of all of the outer planets and their satellites. They will have far less reliance on Earth and greater power generation autonomy."

The diminutive reporter persisted, "Thank you, Madam President, however, you have not divulged your actual action plan."

President Guang looked to President Reinhardt, who replied, "Everything beyond Earth's orbital zone comes under the purvey of the Colonisation Committee of Sol, situated at Eros, in Earth's Trailing Trojan Point. We have sent the Committee the full details of our plans to phase out uranium and the Committee has agreed to send emissaries to the Belter Colonies and the outer planets, the Jovian Realms, the Saturnian Demarchy, the Uranian Federation and the Neptunian Commonwealth."

President Guang Hui chimed in, "We will provide them all with all of our blueprints, designs and technical specifications, everything they need to make the transition."

President Reinhardt stepped back in, "Cis-Lunar L-Five will even send them our own engineers to help them, and if necessary, we will build and export fusion reactors to them. I assure you all, that no colonies will be left behind."

The diminutive reporter seemed satisfied by the answers, however, another reporter, a rather portly man, chimed in, asking, "What about Pluto and the Kuiper Belt colonies?"

President Reinhardt was slow to answer, "The last we heard from the Kuiper Belt colonists was from the interplanetary push ship, Chaosia, en route to the Dwarf World, Chaos. That was in twenty one seventy six, just two years ago. We've heard nothing from the Kuiper Belt colonists since then."

The portly reporter remarked, "So the Kuiper Belt colonies aren't in your action plan then, Mr President. So much for no colonies being left behind."

The diminutive reporter frowned and chimed in, "So much for your assurances, Mr President."

The Venusian President, Bradly Klein, stepped in, "The Kuiper Belt colonies were not set up in the same fashion as the other outer solar system colonies. Prior to the Kuiper Belt, when each orbital zone was colonised, the initial colonies were manufactured here in Cis-Lunar L-Four and then hauled out to their final target location using space tugs."

President Reinhardt stepped back in, "That is correct. Apart from the fact that we don't know if any of the Kuiper Belt colonists successfully made it to their destinations, their colonial foundation model was very different. They were to build their colonies in situ, using locally sourced materials."

President Guang Hui chimed in, "We have no uranium fuel rod export arrangements with the Kuiper Belt colonies, none whatsoever."

Another reporter at the back of the room offered, "If I may. I covered the mystery of the loss of Kuiper Belt communications. The Dumas Corporation didn't like their plans and only agreed with them because the ten colonial groups involved signed waivers to absolve them of any liability should things go wrong. Even the Dumas Corporation considered their plans too dangerous."

"Yes!", President Reinhardt agreed, adding, "They all took orbital mining, ore processing and manufacturing stations with them, but they had no prebuilt colonies waiting for them at the other end of their journey. Their push ships were designed to be repurposed into colonial infrastructure and they only took two push ships to each of the Dwarf Worlds."

The same reporter at the back of the room noted, "They took colony plans with them as well. Plans that had been released into the public domain earlier this century. The Dumas Corporation gave them plans for advanced fast breeder fission reactors and thorium reactors as well. They were supposed to build those in situ themselves."

President Guang Hui chimed in, "And that was the point I was making. The Kuiper Belt colonies were designed to be independent of the Earth. They were supposed to seek out their own sources of uranium and thorium. Processing those as necessary to be used in reactors that they were going to build themselves.

As they have no reliance on Earth for uranium fuel rods, they are completely irrelevant to our uranium phase out."

The diminutive report nodded, "So, we only need to consider those colonies that are reliant on Earth for their uranium fuel rods?"

President Guang agreed, "Yes. And once the fission reactors are all replaced with fusion reactors, no colonies will be reliant on Earth for their energy production. They will be energy independent!"

President Klein commented, "Hydrogen can be obtained from any number of sources. They can use water electrolysis, they can mine the atmospheres of their gas giants and even search for pockets of hydrogen gas under the crusts of their planet's moons. Water and hydrogen are everywhere in the outer solar system."

"Which, as I have already stated, will make the outer colonies all energy independent", President Guang Hui reiterated.

Another female reporter put up her hand and was quickly acknowledged, she asked, "Can emissaries be sent out the Kuiper Belt? If we are going to send emissaries to the other planets, then surely we can send them to the Kuiper Belt as well?"

President Reinhardt answered, "The Dwarf Worlds are so far out and so scattered across the Kuiper Belt, that it would take our emissaries ten years or more to get there. That's a long journey and it would require a lot of supplies, with no guarantees of arrival or return. And remember, we have no idea if those colonies are even out there. They may have failed."

President Reinhardt paused before continuing, "The emissaries that travel to the outer planets will travel from one gas giant to the next. First, Jupiter, then Saturn, then Uranus and finally Neptune. Each leg of the journey will also be a refuelling and resupply stop. Even then, we expect that round trip to take up to a decade and a half."

President Klein chimed in, "I'm actually glad you asked that question", he commented, looking at the reporter, "We will set up laser based communications directed to each of the Dwarf Worlds and transmit to them, the blueprints, the designs and the specifications. If they are there, they should be able to receive them", he was thinking on the fly, as none of this had been discussed.

The female reporter nodded, seemingly satisfied.

Another reporter who had been raising his hand, but not acknowledged, raised his hand again and stood up on his tip toes, President Reinhardt pointed to him.

The short, balding reporter asked, "You mentioned two hundred and fifty years of radioactive atomic waste. Exactly what will be done with all of that waste?"

President Guang Hui fielded the question, "All of the radioactive waste on Earth will be collected and transported to a storage facility on the far side of the

Moon, at Mare Moscoviense."

President Klein quickly added, "Not just all of the Earth's radioactive waste, either. The radioactive waste from the Venusian Republic as well."

President Reinhardt stepped in, "All of the radioactive waste from across the entire inner solar system and the Asteroid Belt will be accumulated at the facility at Mare Moscoviense."

"And then what?", the same reporter asked.

President Guang replied, "Once we have accumulated all of the radioactive waste in that one facility, we will then deal with it permanently."

"Permanently, Madam President?", the same reporter questioned.

President Guang explained, "We will use special transports, to transport all of the radioactive waste into intercept orbits with the Sun and allow the Sun to absorb it. That will be our final solution."

Now, there were murmurs amongst the reporters in the press room.

President Reinhardt raised his hand, "There is absolutely nothing to worry about. Our Sun could swallow a planet sized chunk of radioactive waste and it would have no effect", he assured them.

The diminutive reporter quickly asked, "What about the radioactive waste from the colonies in the other solar system, beyond the Asteroid Belt?"

President Guang Hui commented, "I don't believe we need to worry about their radioactive waste. Our understanding is that they currently dump their radioactive waste into their Gas Giants."

The diminutive reporter replied, asking, "That may work for gas giants like Jupiter and Saturn. They are planetary behemoths after all, but is that safe for Uranus and Neptune?"

President Reinhardt chimed in, "The radioactive waste would have little effect on Jupiter or Saturn, as you have correctly assumed. As for Uranus and Neptune, their mantles are mostly made up of frozen water, ammonia and methane ices. Compressed radioactive waste has a tendency to be very dense and very hot. It would likely sink very deep into their mantles, perhaps even to their respective cores."

President Klein added, "Not that anything would change anyway. It is their current disposal method and has been since their colonies were founded."

The diminutive reporter nodded once more but noted, "I guess that the Kuiper Belt colonies will have to deal with their radioactive waste in their own way."

President Guang Hui nodded and replied, "Yes. They are so far out, that they will need to work out their own disposal methods themselves."

The meeting ended and the three presidents made their way back to President Reinhardt's office.

President Reinhardt remarked, "Well, our education system must be working. I wasn't expecting anywhere near that many questions."

President Klein agreed, "They certainly wanted answers, didn't they."

President Reinhardt chuckled, "I should find out the name of that little reporter. I should offer her a job and put her on my own team."

President Guang smiled, "Lots of questions, that little one. She likes details."

President Klein commented, "A bad idea, Dieter, she would become a whistleblower."

"Very true, Bradly, very true", President Reinhardt nodded in agreement.

"Especially considering that our final radioactive waste disposal plans don't necessarily include the Sun at all", President Guang Hui commented dryly.

President Reinhardt placed a bottle of wine and three glasses on the table before them, then handed document folios to the other two presidents.

"We have some scientists who are unhappy with the current progress of the Mars terraforming process", he noted, adding, "They are unhappy that it didn't include the mitigation of Martian atmospheric stripping by the Sun's solar wind, nor the mitigation of cosmic ray exposure."

"Dieter, I heard that the new Martian atmosphere is coming along very nicely. We just have to wait for the toxic compounds and exotic gases to wash out. Just a matter of time", President Klein replied.

"Oh, Bradly, the new Martian atmosphere is cooking along very nicely", President Reinhardt agreed, noting, "It's the lack of a global Martian magnetic field that our scientists are pointing out."

"I've seen this already, Dieter", President Guang Hui noted, "It reads like science fiction. They actually want to try and kick start the Martian core and create a new global magnetic field?"

"Science fiction or madness, Hui. I'm not sure which to be honest", President Klein replied.

They all stared at their copies of the folios and the documents within them. On one page was a diagram of Olympus Mons, the tallest known volcano in the solar system. The diagram showed detailed scans of the deep throat of Olympus Mons. It was deep, ridiculously deep. At the very bottom of the throat of Olympus Mons was a vast, hollow, empty magma chamber, sixty kilometres deep within the crust of Mars.

"So, these scientists of yours, they want us to pack up every nasty bit of radioactive waste into sub-critical packets and simply drop it all into that magma chamber, then just let it all melt down", President Guang Hui asked incredulously.

President Reinhardt shrugged, "I don't know the math. Apparently, the boffins do. They tell me that the accumulated mass of two hundred and fifty years worth of atomic waste, could, could mind you, heat up and melt its way down through the Martian mantle. All the way to the Martian core!"

"Dieter, do they really think that that will kick start the Martian core and create a new dynamo effect?", President Klein asked, he, too, was incredulous.

"Well, they don't really know for certain, Bradly, but they do believe that all of that accumulated radioactive waste, might just add enough heat to the Martian core to have some permanent effect", President Reinhardt explained, adding, "Any global Martian magnetic field is better than none", and then he took a sip of his wine.

"Dropping all of our radioactive waste into a deep, empty magma chamber at the bottom of Olympus Mons would certainly be safer than how it is currently stored on Earth", President Guang commented.

The other two presidents both agreed.

2. The Enforcers.

High Prince Albert sat in his operations room, in his gold-gilded operations throne. The long rectangular table stretched out before him. To his left was one of his personal body guards, his enforcer, Roberta Nummus and on his right was another of his personal body guards, his other enforcer, Aurange Sheergibbon. Together, they were the most highly trained and deadliest operatives in the solar system.

The enforcers both wore tactical body armour. On their utility belts, they each carried a pulse laser pistol and a long sabre sword and on their backs, they carried a kukri sword. They had other smaller knives strategically placed at various points about their body armour. They both carried high-powered, rapid-fire pulse laser rifles, partially supported by shoulder straps. Roberta Nummus also carried a long bladed Katana strapped across her back, it was named, *the Harōingu,* or the Harrowing, in English.

The High Prince's enforcers were loyal beyond belief, like savage guard dogs fully imprinted upon their master and willing to carry out his every command. That loyalty cut both ways.

Aurange Sheergibbon was a tall, thin, wiry redhead with hair the colour of a carrot. He had once been nicknamed, *"The Carrot Top"*, but all who dared to use that nickname were now dead by his hand. Aurange was not someone to insult and he would violently eliminate anyone who did so. He may have been tall and thin, but he could snap a man's neck with just one hand in the blink of an eye.

Violence was in his nature and he relished in it.

High Prince Albert's Father, Albertus, had nicknamed, in private of course, Aurange Sheergibbon as, *"The Orange Shitgibbon"*, although he never used it to his face. That would have been dangerous!

The High Prince remembered that nickname and was always mindful not to use it.

The High Prince's other enforcer and Aurange's partner was Roberta Nummus, who was at least three inches shorter. Roberta was well built for a woman, quite curvaceous and also exceedingly top-heavy. In private, High Prince Albert's Father, Albertus, had a habit of calling her *"Booby Num Nums"*, although, as with Aurange, he would never say it to her face. Roberta had certain sensitivities!

The High Prince also remembered that nickname and was equally mindful never to use it. Roberta was known to kill a person for simply staring at her breasts for too long. There was no understanding as to what *"too long"* actually was. Was it a long stare or a fleeting glimpse? Nobody knew, so nobody dared to look. When in the presence of Roberta Nummus, it was safest for one to avert one's eyes.

The pair of enforcers were *"talented"* pieces of work and had numerous kills to their credit. Many of them did not need to die, they were simply dispatched for the pleasure of killing. Aurange and Roberta had once been in the Military, in the Colonial Defence Forces. They had been Special Operatives and, of course, were highly skilled through years of hard training. Much of this took place in a three-gravity training cylinder. However, there was far more to their story.

During their time in the Military, they had both volunteered for *"experimental"* enhancements. These enhancements included physical modifications, genetic enhancements, genetic elixirs, neurological modifications, and psychological programming. There had originally been twenty four volunteers in that *"experimental"* training program.

They had become physically much stronger, much faster and had a sharper focus of mind. They had, of course, become completely psychotic as well. Their genetic changes meant that they also aged much slower than most people, ageing at a rate so slow that people could not notice them age at all. The Military authorities had wanted them locked away for good, as they were far too dangerous to have *"wandering"* around. As a result, the volunteers were all placed in confinement.

Of course, that did not agree with Aurange and Roberta. They had slaughtered their way out of confinement and later killed nearly all of the people associated with the *"experimental"* military enhancement program. No one really knew how old they were, but it was believed that they were over a hundred years old, even though they both looked no more than thirty years old.

One by one, High Prince Albert's Ministers were let into the operations room. One by one, they took their assigned seats. When the last of the Ministers was seated, Aurange Sheergibbon walked out of the room's entry door. He opened it, checked the hallway, nodded to the two guards standing station in the hallway outside the room, then closed the door once more and locked it. Aurange Sheergibbon took his station by the door on its right-hand side. No one was coming in and no one was going out. At least, not until the High Prince closed the meeting and dismissed his Ministers. That was procedure!

Aurange Sheergibbon looked at Roberta Nummus and their eyes met. He smiled at her. Roberta loved Aurange's smile. It took her back down memory lane. To a time many years ago. A time when their training was completed, their assessments had been finalised and they had been imprisoned by their own creators. Naturally, they had rebelled. Naturally, their Military Commanders had responded.

Roberta's memories flowed. They had both broken out of their containment cells as planned, at the same time in the middle of the night and immediately began slaughtering their way to freedom. Their Commanders were taken by complete surprise and the death toll was mounting. So they promised the other twenty two contained *"experimental"* volunteers, that the ones who brought Aurange and Roberta to heel would be released unconditionally. Those twenty two enhanced super-soldier volunteers took up the challenge.

Outnumbered eleven to one, Aurange and Roberta took on their former comrades. Roberta Nummus remembered Aurange deftly slicing one man with his tactical knife about the shoulder, his name had been Keith. Then, using both hands and his right foot, he tore Keith's arm out of its socket. Seconds later, Aurange was beating Keith to death with his own severed limb, it took twelve bloody, bludgeoning strikes. Keith should not have called Aurange Carrot Top. That was an egregious and unforgivable offence. That caused their other former comrades to pause.

Without a moment's hesitation, Aurange had dived into the fray, swinging Keith's bloodied limb like a bludgeon. Aurange beat two more of their former comrades to death before discarding the now ragged limb. What followed was a dance of death, with Aurange slicing and carving his way through their former comrades with ruthless efficiency. Naturally, Roberta had to joined in, not wanting to miss out on any of the fun.

Fighting together, back to back, the odds quickly dropped in their favour and before long, their twenty two former comrades were all dead. Their battered, bruised and in some cases dismembered bodies lay strewn all around them. Aurange rolled his neck around on his shoulders with an audible click to release the pent-up rage and tension.

This macabre dance of death was not over as they moved through the Military Facility, slaughtering everyone who crossed their path. Technically, they were targeting the leadership, but the collateral damage was high, extremely high. Once their Military Commanders were all dead, they slaughtered their way to the facility's docks, then commandeered a shuttle and fled into the depths of space. There had been hundreds of personnel in that military facility and by the time Aurange and Roberta had left, there were perhaps only three dozen left alive.

Battered, bruised and covered in everyone's blood but their own, they were finally free. Aurange set their course for a Cis-Lunar L-Five colony, one of the smaller ones. He had picked it at random, not really caring which one it was, only that it was *"out of the way"*. It just happened to be one of the three Horridian Corporate O'Neil-style twin-cylinder colonies. It could have been any other colony, but that is where the universe just happened to send them. Unfortunately, that was the one place where their unique skills would truly be appreciated.

Aurange and Roberta then let the shuttle coast to its destination while they enjoyed each other's company with wild, savage abandon. Roberta smiled at the memories, her eyes closed slightly and then she bit her lower lip, ever so gently. She was feeling warm all over and very, very wet. Aurange continued to smile at Roberta, thinking to himself, *"Later, my Love. We are still on duty"*, he knew the effect he was having on her.

It was not unusual for Roberta Nummus to sexualise death or even murder for that matter. Roberta had even beaten targets senseless and then finished them off by smothering them with her own rather large breasts. Roberta was going through some sort of phase at the time, giving her targets, what she had considered to be, a beautiful send-off.

The interesting part was that it was Roberta herself who decided whether her target received a beautiful send-off or a quick twist of the neck. It was her choice and hers alone. Even her partner, Aurange himself, could never tell how Roberta chose which method she would use to finish off a mark. Roberta Nummus could be unfathomable at times. It was her way!

No one noticed Aurange and Roberta silently communicating through little more than simple eye contact. That was their way, they never spoke. They only used non-verbal kinesic gestures. No one knew why and no one dared to ask why.

No one noticed Roberta's little trip down memory lane and the effect it was having on her. Roberta had literally had a silent orgasm in full view of the room and yet, no one had noticed at all. All of the Ministers were doing their absolute level best not to look at either Aurange or Roberta, especially Roberta. The sheer fear they generated was palpable and both Aurange and Roberta relished that smell of fear. The operations room was ripe with it. High Prince Albert smirked, he fully understood.

Health Minister Elaine Haynes was a recent appointment and had been in the position of Health Minister for only three months. Being female was no protection, she too avoided even glancing at Roberta or anywhere near her direction. Her predecessor had once glanced at Roberta during a meeting, lingering too long on her breasts. Once was enough! Roberta had grabbed him by the hair and taken off his head with her kukri sword before anyone could blink!

Elaine had been told that the High Prince had not even been angry about it, just disappointed that he was not quick enough to prevent it. His enforcers were both hair-triggered and volatile. One had to be quick to tell them no and High Prince Albert had missed his cue. Instead, he had gently chastised Roberta, telling her that it would take a couple of months to find a replacement. Roberta had nodded in acceptance and had simply returned to her station, with the Minister's head still in her hand!

At that meeting, the High Prince reminded his remaining Ministers that Roberta Nummus was sensitive and that they needed to treat her with absolute respect. High Prince Albert was as loyal to his enforcers as they were to him.

That meeting had continued, with a headless corpse slumped over the table, bleeding out, right there where Elaine was now sitting and with the former Health Minister's head still clutched by the hair in Roberta's left hand. More than a few Ministers had met their fate that same way. It was considered an occupational hazard! The rule of thumb was very simple, never, ever look at Roberta Nummus because the High Prince won't have your back!

The Minister of Defence, Peter Macron, had noticed the fear and tension in the room. It was far greater than usual and so he asked cautiously, knowing his fellow Ministers would say nothing.

"Your Majesty. Are your personal bodyguards really necessary for these meetings?", he enquired.

The High Prince replied smugly, "I don't know, Minister Macron. Emperor Julius Caesar of Rome, might have liked to have had his personal bodyguards around him on the ides of March when his Senators knifed him to death."

The Defence Minister lowered his head and replied, "My apologies, Your Majesty. I did not mean any offence."

The High Prince waved his hand dismissively, "No offence was taken, Minister Macron."

The Defence Minister raised his head once more and noticed that Aurange Sheergibbon was re-sheathing his sabre. His question could have been fatal had the High Prince taken offence.

The Communications Minister, Albrecht Dire, accidentally glanced in Roberta's direction, then quickly closed his eyes and looked down at the table in front of him, thinking to himself, *"Please, God, let me live!"*

Roberta had not noticed, or if she had, his gaze had been quick and not caught her ire.

Communications Minister Dire, ever so cautiously commented, "Your Majesty. I have no wish to cause offence, but it is so hard to function in these meetings with the constant fear of death that your personal bodyguards present. It is very hard to think straight, Your Majesty."

High Prince Albert sighed, then took on a reasonable, conciliatory tone, "Minister Dire, fellow Ministers, none of you have anything to fear. All you have to do is not look at either Aurange or Roberta, not offend your High Prince and just get on with our business."

"My apologies, Your Majesty. I was there when Minister Haynes's predecessor was beheaded. It still gives me nightmares", Minister Dire replied honestly, in a low, equally cautious voice.

The High Prince looked around the table at his Ministers, the level of fear on their faces was palpable. High Prince Albert stood up and turned to his left.

"Roberta, would you be able to refrain from killing my Ministers?", the High Prince asked.

Roberta tilted her head slightly as if in thought, then she nodded in the affirmative.

The High Prince then turned to Aurange, "Aurange, would you be able to refrain from killing my Ministers?", he asked.

Aurange nodded in the affirmative.

"Thank you. If anyone needs to be killed, always await my decision first. It is so tedious to have to replace my Ministers at such short notice. No one seems to want their jobs, no matter how much I pay them", the High Prince told them both, then he turned back to the table and asked, "Does that satisfy you all? Now, can we get back down to business?"

All of his Ministers answered in the affirmative, although none of them were truly satisfied.

A ballsy Miles Morton, the Minister for Security, took a risk and looked deliberately towards Roberta and commented, "Ms Nummus. When people look at you, it is not in disrespect. They do so because you are strikingly beautiful. They do not mean to offend you."

Roberta actually smiled at his remark, it appeared that Minister Morton would keep his head, except, of course, for the slow sound of Aurange sliding his sabre from out of its scabbard.

"Shit! I nearly forgot that one", Minister Morton thought to himself and then he quickly turned to Aurange, "Mr Sheergibbon. A person may admire beauty and compliment it, without crossing a line."

Aurange let his sabre slip back into its scabbard, but from now on, he would keep a close eye on Minister Miles Morton.

The High Prince smiled a wry smile, "Thank you, Minister Morton", then he addressed the other Ministers, "You see, my bodyguards are just sensitive people. If you treat them with respect, they will do likewise."

"Yes, Your Majesty. Everyone in this room both respects and admires your bodyguards. Mr Sheergibbon's and Ms Nummus's particular talents are assets that protect the six Jovian Realms. Personally, I wish that I had such skills", Minister Morton was quick to reply.

The High Prince nodded in agreement.

The fact of the matter was that no one wanted to be a Minister in the High Prince's Cabinet. When the positions were advertised, there were no applicants. No one wanted to be anywhere near the Orange Shitgibbon and Booby Num Nums, they were simply too unpredictable, to volatile. Even the High Prince's Court was small for the same reasons. With the High Prince's enforcers in the same room, death was always only a heartbeat away.

The High Prince chose his Ministers from out of the relevant bureaucracies, always picking the most talented bureaucrats. Those appointees often saw their appointments as Ministers, as a death sentence. As a result, most bureaucrats did their best to appear to be mediocre and without significant talent. Being the tall poppy got you the job that no body wanted. The risk-to-reward ratio was simply not worth it!

The exception, of course, was the Military and Security appointments, where the High Prince required people with entirely different skill sets and talents.

The High Prince's Minister of Defence and his Minister of Security rarely complained about Aurange Sheergibbon and Roberta Nummus. Instead, they saw them as valuable and talented assets. Volatile assets, yes, but nonetheless talented. It was all about how you navigated that volatility.

3. The Jovian Reaction.

Health Minister Elaine Haynes stood up, she nodded to High Prince Albert, "May I, Your Majesty?"

High Prince Albert was intrigued, he nodded and replied, "You may, Minister Haynes."

Elaine Haynes approached Roberta Nummus. She was extremely cautious and very careful not to look at or even glance at her breasts. Elaine did her best not to show any fear, although that was almost impossible and she was pretty sure that Roberta Nummus could smell it all over her.

Once Elaine was directly in front of Roberta Nummus, she looked her in the eyes, smiled, held out her right hand and spoke in a friendly voice, "Friends?", it was a question.

Roberta was flummoxed!

The last time anything even remotely similar had happened was over eighty years ago when she had entered the colonial military. That was even before she had been trained as a Special Operative and certainly before her *"experimental"* military training.

Roberta automatically averted Elaine's gaze, turning her head slightly and looking to Aurange for guidance. Aurange smiled, it was a different kind of smile and he simply shrugged his shoulders.

Roberta frowned, then she looked back to Elaine, slowly reached out her hand and took Elaine's hand in hers. Elaine's hand was warm and soft, with a slight sheen of sweat from fear. Roberta was gentle.

Elaine's smile broadened, "I think we'll be great friends, Roberta."

Roberta smiled back and simply nodded. She then let her high-powered rapid-fire pulse laser rifle hang from its strap, reached out with her left hand and wrapped Elaine's hand in hers.

There was something about Elaine's eyes that Roberta noticed. Roberta's smile broadened and she squeezed Elaine's hand ever so gently but enthusiastically. Then, ever so slowly, Roberta withdrew her hands, took control of her pulse laser rifle once more and stood to attention.

Elaine smiled once again, "Coffee, Roberta. On one of your free days, yeah. I'll call you."

Roberta looked at Elaine once more and then nodded.

Elaine then walked back to her seat, and as she did so, Aurange looked at her, smiled and nodded.

Aurange thought to himself, *"Roberta could do with a real friend."*

High Prince Albert smiled and remarked, "Well then, that was unexpected. Now, Roberta, you have a friend, please don't kill her. Your High Prince would find that very upsetting."

"Okay then. I understand that we have a situation?", High Prince Albert questioned.

Communications Minister, Albrecht Dire, replied, "Yes, Your Majesty. We have been quarantining the latest news feeds from the inner solar system, from Earth and Cis-Lunar L-Five. Both myself and Security Minister Morton thought we should discuss these latest developments."

"So, Minister Morton. What are we looking at?", the High Prince enquired.

"Your Majesty. The Earth has shut down all of its fission power generation stations. They've replaced them all with new fusion power generation facilities", Miles Morton informed him.

The High Prince thought for a moment, letting the information sink in, "That must have taken them quite some time."

Communications Minister Albrecht Dire added, "Your Majesty. It was apparently a twenty-year plan and they finished converting across to fusion power very recently."

The High Prince nodded, "Okay, so the Earth no longer has fission power generation. Just how does that affect us?"

Miles Morton replied, "The Earth is phasing out uranium mining and uranium fuel rod production."

Now the penny dropped, "Wait a minute! We are completely reliant on uranium fuel rods from Earth for our own fission reactors", the High Prince was now alarmed.

Albrecht Dire quickly noted, "Your Majesty. The Earth is implementing a thirty-year phase-out period, during which time all of the colonies will be converting across to fusion power generation."

"Okay, so they are phasing out uranium mining and fuel rod production. I want details, people", the High Prince demanded.

Miles Morton quickly responded, "Your Majesty. The Presidents of Cis-Lunar Space and the Venusian colonies have both agreed to implement twenty-year plans to convert all of their territories across to fusion power. That pretty much covers everything from Venusian orbit to Martian orbit."

"Minister Morton, you said that everything from Venusian orbit to Martian orbit is covered by these twenty-year plans. What about beyond Martian orbit? What about us?", High Prince Albert questioned.

Miles Morton responded, "Your Majesty, everything beyond Martian orbit is being handled by the Colonisation Committee of Sol, at Eros in Earth's Trailing Lagrangian point."

"So the Colonisation Committee is handling the fusion reactor conversion beyond Martian orbit?", the High Prince asked for confirmation.

"Yes, Your Majesty", Albrecht Dire confirmed, adding, "The Colonisation

Committee is coordinating the entire process beyond Martian orbit."

High Prince Albert steepled his fingers together and considered what he'd been told, "I very much doubt that the Venusians or anyone in the Martian orbital zone could build fusion reactors."

Defence Minister Peter Macron quickly commented, "Your Majesty, my understanding is that the latest fusion power station blueprints, designs and schematics have been made freely available to facilitate the process of converting across to fusion power generation. The colonial construction yards at Cis-Lunar L-Four will be manufacturing and exporting fusion power reactors for any colonies that can't build them themselves."

"Your Majesty", Communications Minister Dire caught his attention, "The Colonisation Committee is going to send emissaries to the Belters and the outer satellites. We here at the Jovian Realms, the Saturnian Demarchy, the Uranian Federation and the Neptunian Commonwealth. They intend to officially hand over the fusion power station blueprints, designs and schematics and then discuss our options for the crossover. Everything we need, they say they will provide."

Elaine Haynes, the Health Minister, chimed in, "Your Majesty, this is actually to our advantage."

High Prince Albert was still in thought mode, he asked, "How so, Minister Haynes?"

"Sire, fusion reactors are powered by hydrogen and hydrogen is readily available in the Jovian Realms. We can source it from Jupiter's moons, Jupiter's atmosphere and even from Jupiter's Trojan asteroids. More importantly, if we convert across to fusion power, we won't need Earth's uranium fuel rod exports at all. The Jovian Realms will be energy independent, Your Majesty."

Science Minister Peter Patronis, who had been sitting quietly, confirmed, "That is correct, Your Majesty. Elaine has nailed that one perfectly. We will become completely energy independent."

High Prince Albert turned around to look at Roberta Nummus, "You see that, Roberta. Elaine's a keeper. She is also your friend. Your High Prince likes this one"

That made Elaine Haynes very happy, it definitely increased her chances of survival. Perhaps her gambit would pay off. Elaine glanced over at Roberta and smiled. She had to admit to herself, for all of Roberta's violent tendencies, she was an incredibly attractive woman. Roberta smiled back at Elaine, it was a cautious, almost hesitant smile.

"So, we have a pro! Energy self reliance", High Prince Albert announced, then he noted, "I do, however, see a few cons!"

"Cons, Your Majesty?", Defence Minister Peter Macron enquired.

The High Prince smiled, it was a devious smile, he announced to his Ministers, "I do not like the Venusians or the Belters having fusion reactor technology and I most certainly do not want the Saturnian Demarchy, the Uranian Federation or the Neptunian Commonwealth to have it either! That technology should belong to the Jovian Realms and the Jovian Realms alone!"

High Prince Albert delivered that pronouncement in a harsh tone that was almost a snarl.

Defence Minister Macron cautiously replied, "Sire, I have seen the quarantined news feeds. The Venusians cannot make their own fusion reactors, however, they will be stepping up their manufacturing capabilities to do so. Cis-Lunar Space already has that technology. The window to prevent the dissemination of this knowledge is closing very rapidly, Sire."

Security Minister Morton agreed, "Minister Macron is correct, Your Majesty. At the moment, manufacturing capabilities for these fusion reactors lie with Earth and Cis-Lunar L-Four. Once the Colonisation Committee starts sending out their emissaries, that technology will quickly spread."

Communications Minister, Dire noted, "Your Majesty. We could preempt the Colonisation Committee. Before they officially notify us, we could send a communique to them. We could recommend that they send their emissaries to the outer satellites via a *'Grand Tour'*. First, the Jovian Realms, then the Saturnian Demarchy, followed by the Uranian Federation and then finally, the Neptunian Commonwealth. We could frame it as the safest method, using each orbital zone as refuelling and resupply stops."

It was Defence Minister Macron's turn to smile deviously, "Once the Colonisation Committee's emissaries have been given our hospitality and have reported back to their superiors about how wonderful and cooperative we've been, they'll be on their merry way to the Saturnian Demarchy. However, they don't actually have to arrive there. In deep space, things can go horribly wrong!"

Security Minister Morton chuckled, "Your Majesty. Perhaps Aurange and Roberta might enjoy playing with the emissaries after they leave our Jovian Realms?"

High Prince Albert smiled, "I am absolutely certain that Aurange and Roberta would love to play with the Colonisation Committee's emissaries. Communications Minister Dire, send our preemptive communique with precisely that suggestion. No one beyond the Jovian Realms will have the Earth's new fusion reactor technology!"

Communications Minister, Dire replied, "Your will shall be done, Sire."

Aurange Sheergibbon and Roberta Nummus smiled at each other across the room.

Defence Minister Macron noted, "It is a good plan, Your Majesty. However, it does not address the fact that the Belters will be receiving this technology. The Colonisation Committee will likely send emissaries to at least the thirteen major Belter Colonies."

"Good point, Minister Macron", the High Prince agreed and then he asked, "What is your estimate of Belter technology? Can they build these fusion reactors themselves, or are they reliant on the Cis-Lunar L-Four construction yards, just like the Venusians?"

Peter Macron did not actually have an answer, so he very slowly crafted one.

"Your Majesty, we don't really know what the Belter's capabilities are", Peter Macron began, "They are a highly resourceful lot. Of the original thirteen Belter Colonies, I'd say that the largest six are the most capable. The remainder of their thirty plus colonies are much smaller operations and unlikely to be capable of doing so."

It was not the answer that High Prince Albert wanted, he frowned and that was never a good sign.

"Minister Macron, how do they compare to our Trojan Realms?", he demanded.

Again, Peter Macron was cautious, "The six biggest Belter Colonies would be far more capable than our Trojan Realms, Sire. The other seven of the original thirteen, not that far behind their brethren. The remainder would be reliant on the others."

Elaine Haynes could see Minister Macron was floundering, "Your Majesty, Minister Macron's area of expertise is Defence, perhaps Science Minister Patronis has a more useful answer."

Science Minister Patronis glared at Elaine momentarily, he did not want to be in the spotlight! None of the Jovian High Ministers did!

"Your Majesty, we cannot make a judgement about the Belter's capabilities until we see the new fusion reactor specifications, the detailed blueprints", Peter Patronis replied cautiously, adding, "Perhaps, when Minister Dire sends his preemptive communique to the Colonisation Committee, he can also request that they send us the fusion reactor blueprints. We can then study those blueprints in advance of their emissary's arrival."

Peter Macron chimed in, "We need to study those blueprints, Your Majesty. Until then, we can't be sure that we can manufacture those fusion power reactors either."

Albrecht Dire agreed, "Your Majesty, I can make that request. I agree with Minister Macron and Minister Patronis, we do need to study those reactor blueprints."

"Make it so, Minister Dire. Get those damned blueprints", High Prince Albert commanded.

"Yes, Sire", Albrecht Dire replied, then he commented, "Your Majesty, we do monitor the Belter's communications. I can state unequivocally that all of the Belter Colonies, big and small, work together for their greater good. They all behave more like a family diaspora than scattered colonies, Sire."

The High Prince was unhappy with the answers thus far, but there was nothing to be done about it.

"For now, I will assume that the big six Belter Colonies have the capabilities to build the new fusion reactors", he looked around at his Ministers, "Our real problems are the points of dissemination. The Earth, Cis-Lunar L-Five, their construction yards at Cis-Lunar L-Four and, of course, the Colonisation Committee of Sol, at Eros."

High Prince Albert looked around at his Ministers once more, making sure they all understood and then he issued an order, "Minister Macron. Put together a *'mitigation'* plan for all of the dissemination points I've just mentioned. If necessary, I'd like to eliminate them."

"A hot or cold strategy, Sire?", Defence Minister Macron enquired.

"Prepare plans for both, Macron. I want all options on the table", the High Prince commanded.

Defence Minister Peter Macron understood, he nodded, "Yes, Your Majesty."

"Sire, we may need a pretext", Security Minister Miles Morton commented.

"A pretext. You're right, Minister Morton. We do need a pretext. I can't get the other outer satellites on board if I don't have a *'valid'* pretext", the High Prince agreed, "Options, people?", he asked.

Elaine Haynes made a suggestion, "Your Majesty. We could use last year's assassination attempt."

"Yes, yes. Thank you, Elaine. Still a keeper, I see. Last year's assassination attempt", the High Prince replied, then turned to his Communications Minister, "Dire. Those two sorcerers we hung last year. The two who came here to assassinate me. Have you allowed that footage to go beyond our networks?"

"No, Sire. That entire event is only internal to our Jovian Realms. The other colonies have not seen any of that footage", Minister Dire replied.

"Excellent", the High Prince clapped his hands together, "Dire, keep that footage handy. After the Colonisation Committee's emissaries have come and gone, we'll wait a few days, perhaps a week and then we'll release it across the entire solar system. That will be our pretext, Ladies and Gentlemen. Everyone will think that the assassins were delivered to us by Eros's Colonisation Committee emissaries. They will be seen as complicit. Just make sure that you adjust the timestamps in the metadata accordingly. They have to reflect our timeline perfectly."

"Brilliant, Sire. I'll make it so", Minister Dire replied as he took down some notes.

The meeting had ended and High Prince Albert's enforcers were now off duty, their tasks were taken up by less capable operatives. Twelve of them were required.

Roberta noticed a ping on her communicator. It was from Elaine Haynes, her new friend.

The message read, *"Coffee? At the Cafe on the Hill at four pm?"*, it was a well-known cafe in Ganymede Prime's northern end cap.

Roberta smiled, it was a genuine smile, perhaps, just perhaps, Elaine would become a good friend.

Elaine sat at a picnic table at the top of a hill in Ganymede Prime's northern end cap. The Cafe on the Hill was fifty meters behind her. Elaine had purchased two cups of coffee, the kind she liked, cappuccinos with one sugar. Roberta approached the table, rounded it and sat down opposite Elaine.

Elaine passed Roberta a cup of coffee, "I wasn't sure what coffee you liked, so I got you the same as mine. A cappuccino with one sugar."

Roberta took the cup and then began typing on a virtual keyboard on her data tablet, then sent the message to Elaine's communicator.

"Aurange and I normally just drink black coffee, but this will be fine. Thank you, Elaine", then she smiled a true genuine smile.

"I've never seen you unarmed before, Roberta", Elaine noted.

Roberta smiled and almost laughed, something that she could not do, she typed into her data tablet, *"I am a weapon, Elaine. I am never truly unarmed. Even now, I am armed with throwing knives and throwing stars, and even my kukri sword is strapped to my back. It's just more concealed and not so easily noticed."*

Elaine read the latest message and nodded, "Always armed? I guess that makes sense, given your background. The military really did turn you and Aurange into weapons?"

Roberta nodded and typed in a single word, then transmitted it, *"Yes."*

"You and Aurange don't speak?", Elaine cautiously asked.

Roberta typed the answer into her data tablet and sent it, *"We don't vocalise. We were conditioned to be non-verbal. All two dozen of us. It makes interrogation very difficult if we can't speak. Although we are exceedingly adept at reading non-verbal cues. Aurange and I can transmit volumes of data to each other just by eye contact alone. Just with a look or even just a glance."*

"Wow! I can see that being useful", Elaine had to admit.

Roberta typed and sent another reply message, *"It has its moments and its limitations"*, she held up her data tablet as an example.

"I see", Elaine replied and then cautiously asked, "We've never noticed either you or Aurange age?"

Roberta smiled and typed in another message, *"We age, just very slowly. Since our experimental training and conditioning, we age perhaps one year in eight, perhaps, as little as one year in ten."*

"Wait! Roberta. That means if you lived to be one hundred", Elaine did the math in her head, "You'd actually be six hundred and sixty years old?"

Roberta typed in her reply, *"Your math is fairly accurate. Although, neither myself nor Aurange have any idea how long we'll actually live."*

Elaine reached out and placed her hand on top of Roberta's, "Your life sounds like it's been so horrible", she truly felt sorry for her.

Roberta placed her other hand on top of Elaine's momentarily, then lifted it back off, typing another message, *"It certainly has been different. Neither good nor bad, but always lucrative. We are paid exceedingly well. We both could live the next thousand years on what we have squirrelled away."*

It was a simple, pragmatic answer, without any reflection of what might have been, nor the lives lost and taken along the way. Roberta Nummus and Aurange Sheergibbon were unapologetically what they were. Elaine instinctively tried to pull back her hand, but Roberta held firm, looking into her eyes with the collective sorrow of scores of decades.

When Roberta finally let go, she quickly typed a message, *"Please, Elaine. Please, don't be afraid of me. Everyone is so afraid of me. I cannot help being a monster! It is what I was made into!"*

Elaine's heart was pounding, her fear was palpable and Roberta could smell it.

Roberta quickly typed another message into her data tablet, then reached out for Elaine's hands and took them both into her own, *"Elaine, I will never hurt you. I promise. I will always keep you safe."*

"Roberta, you beheaded my predecessor right there in the operations room. He bled out over the table! I now sit in a dead man's chair!", Elaine replied, her heart still pounding.

Roberta let go of Elaine's hands, tears welled in her eyes and she began typing another message, *"I know. I know. Sometimes, my conditioning just takes over. When men stare at my breasts, it just triggers me. I become death incarnate."*

Elaine looked at Roberta's freely flowing tears. They were genuine tears. Roberta knew that she was a monster. She knew that she was easily triggered. Elaine could see that Roberta Nummus was one fucked up mess. She actually felt sorry for her.

"Roberta, how can I be sure that I won't trigger you?", Elaine enquired.

Roberta wiped her tears away and typed, *"You are neither a target nor a male. You are my friend."*

Then Roberta did something that would normally seem absurd, but knowing her history, it made perfect sense in a weird sort of way. Roberta unzipped her jacket and allowed her ample cleavage to show. Her nipples were clearly visible within the confines of her bra.

Elaine looked at Roberta's breasts, she could not take her eyes off of them. Nothing happened. Nothing at all. Roberta Nummus remained untriggered.

"You see, Elaine. You don't trigger me. Only men do!", Roberta typed in a new message, then re-zipped her jacket.

Roberta keyed another message into her data tablet, *"I know that this will sound really weird, Elaine, but are you a lesbian?"*

"What the fuck, Roberta? What kind of question is that?", Elaine questioned.

"Aurange!", Roberta quickly typed in, *"If I have a relationship with a man, Aurange will kill him, automatically. If I have a relationship with a woman, Aurange will be triggered sexually."*

"So, Aurange could be a threat to me?", Elaine enquired.

Roberta typed into her data tablet, *"Not if you're a lesbian. Lesbians don't trigger him that way."*

Elaine ran her fingers through her hair, "What the fuck, Roberta! What the fuck!"

Roberta's next message came across, *"I'll just tell him you're a lesbian. It's safer for you that way."*

"Exactly how safe will I be around Aurange, Roberta?", Elaine asked, she had serious concerns.

Roberta frowned and typed in another message, *"Trust me, if Aurange thinks you're a lesbian, we could fuck right in front of him and he'd walk off and watch the news feeds. He'll have no interest in you whatsoever. Aurange's psychoses triggers are very different from mine."*

What the fuck kind of friendship had Elaine struck up!

The really ironic thing was, that Elaine, was in fact a lesbian. Unfortunately, in the Jovian Realms, controlled by High Prince Albert von Horridian, with its Jovian High Church, that was something that would not be tolerated. It was something that Elaine Haynes had to keep deeply buried. There was no coming out of the closet in the Jovian Realms! They were a Feudal Principality and Theocracy, with the Jovian State and the Jovian Church, tightly entwined. The punishment for *"deemed"* aberrant behaviour was death, and the onus of proof of innocence was placed upon the accused.

What's good for one is good for the other, "So Roberta. What about you?", Elaine asked.

Roberta typed in another message, *"When I was younger before I joined the military,*

I enjoyed the company of both men and women. I wasn't partial to one or the other", she openly admitted.

So, Roberta Nummus was, as a young woman, bisexual.

Elaine leaned in really close across the table. Roberta followed suit until they were just inches apart.

Elaine admitted softly in almost a whisper, "Roberta, you cannot tell anyone this. I am a lesbian! No one else can know! Not ever! You cannot tell anyone!"

Roberta typed in a new message, *"I still need to tell Aurange that you are. That will keep him disinterested. It will keep you safe!"*

"Roberta, what if His Royal Majesty finds out?", Elaine enquired, "Have you considered that?"

"Yes, of course, I did, Elaine", Roberta typed back, adding, *"If the High Prince does find out, I'll explain to him that I told Aurange that to prevent you from being raped. The High Prince will probably find that amusing. You will be able to hide in plain sight."*

Elaine palm-faced herself with one hand while running her other hand through her hair. Somehow, somehow, she really needed to emigrate away from this place.

It was at that point that Elaine realised that Roberta was broken, yes, but not only that, Elaine herself was also broken. They were two broken women. One had been broken by the Colonial Marines eighty-plus years ago in the past, the other had been broken by Jovian society in the present. Both of them had been discussing their relative levels and degrees of brokenness across a picnic table on a hill, in the Ganymede Prime mega colony's northern end cap.

Elaine wasn't entirely sure how it had happened, but somehow, both she and Roberta ended up in her apartment. Roberta stayed the night and Elaine was completely taken by surprise at how gentle the psychotic warrior woman could be. This Roberta, her Roberta, was a completely different woman.

It was still in the early hours of the morning when Roberta slipped quietly out of Elaine's bed. Elaine was still fast asleep, snoring almost imperceptibly. Roberta got dressed, checked her weapons systems and then silently, like a thief in the night, she left Elaine's apartment and disappeared into the dark.

When Elaine finally awoke two hours later, she found herself alone in her apartment. There was no sign that Roberta Nummus had even been there. Elaine checked her communicator. All of Roberta's messages were gone. Every single one! Not just missing, but completely gone. It was as if Roberta's messages had never been sent in the first place.

Had Elaine Haynes hallucinated everything that had transpired since four pm yesterday?

Did yesterday afternoon even happen?

Did last night even take place?

Had Roberta Nummus, Assassin Extraordinaire, really stayed the night, or was this just some kind of strange and weird dystopian dream?

Sadly for Elaine, it was all too real and her coffee dates would never be the same again!

It must have been a Tuesday!

4. The Sendarans.

Professor Maria Corbel, Central Speaker of the Colonisation Committee of Sol, sat in her office in her comfortable chair. It was an impromptu meeting triggered by a legal communique from Cis-Lunar L-Five, specifically from Dumas Legal Incorporated Ltd.

The communique was digitally signed by the current head and Chief Executive Officer of Dumas Incorporated Industries, Connor Dumas. Connor's younger Brother, Daniel Dumas, the Chief Operating Officer of Dumas Incorporated Industries had also signed it.

Sitting across a coffee table were the other two Colonisation Committee Speakers, the Left Speaker, Professor Lyra Banks and the Right Speaker, Professor Stephen Terrell. In between the two Speakers was the current Security Council of Sol's liaison to the Colonisation Committee, Ms Sone Dharma.

Professor Corbel began, "The current Ceresian Administrator, Harlequin Moon, has contacted Dumas Legal Incorporated. Administrator Moon has obtained a court injunction against our Colonisation Committee from taking any further action concerning the phasing out of fission power generation reactors and their subsequent replacement with fusion reactor technology."

"That is ridiculous!", Ms Sone Dharma spat out, remarking, "Those Belters are making fools of us, yet again! You all know what I mean. There are more than thirty Belter colonies out there and yet, somehow, somehow, they have only managed to register just one twin-cylinder colony with your Colonisation Committee and the Security Council!"

"Yes, Sone. We are fully aware of that. They have us over a barrel", Professor Terrell replied, noting, "As long as their colonies are not officially online, they are exempt from registration."

"And that is tied to their final financial loan repayment", Professor Banks chimed in.

"You do all understand that they are paying those final loan repayments out at one credit per year forever", Ms Dharma replied, adding sarcastically, "At that rate, they will never come under our jurisdiction. Not ever!"

"Yes, Sone, we are fully aware of that as well. All thanks to the Granddaughter of the Ceresian colony's founder, Harmony Moon. She pulled that rabbit out of her hat when she was just twelve years old. One damned clever child!", Professor Terrell replied.

"Harmony Dumas", Professor Corbel corrected.

"Harmony Dumas?", Professor Terrell queried.

"Yes, Stephen. Harmony Dumas", Professor Corbel confirmed, "Harmony Moon married Stuart Dumas's Grandson, Daniel, Connor Dumas's younger brother. She is now a Dumas, not just a Moon."

"Oh, God help us. With those two families united, we'll never get out from under their legal loopholes!", Ms Sone Dharma exclaimed.

"Sone. We could spend hours going around and around in circles on that one issue, best to let it lie and just move on", Professor Corbel recommended.

Ms Dharma simply nodded. It was just so frustrating.

"Okay. The good news is they're not saying no. They just want to change our format for the discussions", Professor Corbel announced, explaining, "We were going to send thirteen emissaries, one for each of the major Belter colonies. They want us to send just one emissary to Ceres Central Command. One and only one. They also want to see the fusion reactor blueprints in advance, so that they can have their engineers assess them."

"I can understand them wanting to see the fusion reactor blueprints, but only one emissary?", Professor Banks questioned.

"Yes, Lyra. One emissary", Professor Corbel confirmed, adding, "They have an Icelandic kind of setup in the Asteroid Belt."

"Icelandic?", Professor Banks inquired.

"Yes, it's called the Belter Althing", Professor Corbel confirmed, explaining, "Back in old Iceland, the Althing would meet around mid-summer to discuss 'All Things'. The Belters have something similar, which they also call the Althing. Their Althing commences on January first each year and continues for two weeks. Representatives from all thirteen of the original Belter colonies attend."

"And this all happens at Ceres?", Professor Terrell enquired.

"Ceres was the first Belter colony and it holds what they call 'Non-Sovereign Primacy'. All dealings with Earth, Cis-Lunar L-Five and even us here at Eros are channelled through Ceres."

Ms Sone Dharma noted, "There are more than thirty Belter colonies", then asked, "Why only representatives from the original thirteen?"

"A very good question, Sone. The original thirteen colonies were the founding colonies set up by Stuart Dumas and Harrison Moon. All of the other Belter colonies are themselves dependent colonies, set up by the original thirteen founders. Ceres, for instance, governs four of its own dependencies. All of the other founders have at least one or more dependant colony."

Ms Dharma nodded. This was quickly getting complicated, but then again, the Belters were a complicated bunch!

"There is another complication", Professor Corbel announced, noting, "Dumas Legal Incorporated has sent out a legal team to Ceres Central Command."

"A legal team?", Ms Dharma queried.

"Yes", Professor Corbel confirmed, adding, "A thirteen-person legal team. One representative for each of the thirteen founding colonies. And Dumas Legal personnel, they are all smiling sharks!"

"And we only get to send one emissary!", Ms Sone Dharma exclaimed, throwing her hands up in the air in disgust.

"Yes, that is the case, Sone", Professor Corbel again confirmed.

Professor Banks commented, "Whoever we send, better be our best diplomat."

Professor Corbel nodded, then confirmed, "Our people are going through a list as we speak. We will definitely be sending our best diplomat."

Sone Dharma shook her head, "Between those smiling sharks from Dumas Legal and those clever Belter bastards, our emissary is going to need a lot of luck!"

Professor Corbel smiled, "It gets even better. The Belters are getting all of this legal support '*gratis*'. It's a long-standing agreement that Harrison Moon set up with Stuart Dumas, that his Son and his Grandsons have carried forward."

It took seven weeks for Dag Talleyrand, the Colonisation Committee's emissary, to fly from Eros at Earth's Trailing Trojan Point to Ceres. He watched curiously as his transport ship approached the Ceres Central Command colony. It was a typical O'Neil-style twin-cylinder colony capable of housing over fifty thousand Ceresians.

As Dag's keen eyes scanned the region around the Ceres Heptaluna L-Five Trojan region, he noticed several other smaller twin-cylinder colonies. Each was capable of housing over twenty thousand Ceresians and was in a halo orbit around the Ceres Heptaluna L-Five Trojan gravitational sweet spot. All but one of these Ceresian colonies had eluded registration with the Colonisation Committee and the Security Council. It was the first of the Ceresian colonies, constructed and registered before the legal loophole had been found. It was originally named Ceres Central, however, the Ceresians had renamed it, insultingly, to *"Eros can have it"*.

Only one emissary from the Colonisation Committee had been allowed to attend the Belter Althing at Ceres Central. However, there was no mention of Secretaries, Researchers or, for that matter, the Security Council's liaison officer to the Colonisation Committee, Ms Sone Dharma. So Dag had organised two Secretaries and two Researchers to accompany him.

Ms Sone Dharma's eyes scanned the orbital zone as they approached the Ceres Central Command colony, her keen eyes looking for the first Ceresian colony.

"There. That's the one. Their first colony", Ms Dharma pointed out, "When they renamed it, the new name they gave it was an egregious insult!"

The Security Council had insisted that their Liaison Officer accompany Dag to the Belter Althing. Dag, of course, considered that to be a mistake. Dag considered Ms Sone Dharma to be far too reactive.

Dag's transport ship docked at Ceres Central Command's northern docking ring. Dag and his team were quickly processed through Ceresian customs and their luggage was automatically routed to their hotel suites. The first thing Sone Dharma noticed was the gravity, it was all wrong, so very wrong and she quickly mentioned it.

"What the hell? This isn't one standard gravity. It's far too low", Sone announced.

"You should have done your research, Sone. The Belters have not only managed to avoid colony registration, they don't follow the gravity laws either", Dag informed her.

"That is ridiculous!", Sone exclaimed, she reminded Dag, "For all colonies, that derive their gravity via artificial methods, i.e., centrifugal force, that artificial gravity shall not deviate from one Earth g, by more than plus or minus ten percent as applied to the colony's main living surface. That is the law!"

Dag frowned, "Sone. The Belters don't adhere to our laws. They have their own laws and those laws set the lower limit to point three five gs. Hell, they even have permanent colonies on Ceres itself."

"Permanent colonies on Ceres?", Sone questioned rhetorically, noting, "That's even more ridiculous! Ceresian gravity is so low, it may as well be non-existent! They'll all evolve into jellyfish!"

Dag and his team were at Ceres Central Command colony for the two weeks of the Belter Althing and a week on either side of it. It was going to be one long month.

A week before the arrival of Dag and his team, the team of thirteen lawyers from Dumas Legal Incorporated had arrived at Ceres Central Command, along with their Secretaries and Researchers. Travelling with them was Daniel Dumas and his Wife, Harmony. Daniel's older Brother, Connor, had asked them to accompany the legal team, to ensure that the Belters got the best possible outcome from the phase out of the fission power reactors. Harmony was exceedingly happy with this, as it had been several years since she had visited her Ceresian cousins. It was not just a business trip, it was a family visit, a reunion and a working holiday. Harlequin Moon, the Administrator of Ceres, was Harmony's first cousin and they corresponded quite often.

Via his hotel suite's compucomm, Dag requested access to the Althing Hall, where the Althing was to meet. Dag did not elaborate on his reasons, only stating that he wanted to get a feel for the space. Within ten minutes, his access had been granted and his entry permit was sent to his personal communicator. Dag left his hotel suite with his Secretaries and Researchers. Sone had chosen to remain in her hotel suite. She said that needed extra time to acclimate to the lower gravity in Ceres Central.

Using a built in function of his personal communicator, Dag accessed Ceres Central's information system and using that, located the Althing Hall. Instructions downloaded into his communicator and Dag followed those to the Hall. It was, like the hotel in which they were staying, in Ceres Central's northern end cap. After a short stroll from their Hotel, they found themselves before a large, ornate circular building topped with an equally ornate dome. It was a beautiful, ornate building, stunning!

They entered the building through large, open, arched wooden double doors. Dag held up his communicator with its screen showing his credentials and his entry permit. The guards within the foyer waved Dag and his team through. They followed a long corridor to the Althing Hall's central chamber. There was only one entry point and its doors had been left open. The central chamber was large, round and the interior of the building's dome was clearly visible above them. Everything was white marble, and not just any white marble, it looked like imported Italian white marble from Earth. The white marble walls appeared to be inlaid with large, clear quartz crystals at strategic locations around the chamber. These, too, appeared to have been imported from Earth.

On one side of the room was a large semi-circular stone desk, it looked like obsidian, with thirteen well spaced chairs. Behind each chair at the table were two more chairs.

Dag considered the extra chairs, thinking to himself, *"Advisers, legal representation?"*

There were name plaques on the desk in front of each chair. In front of the central chair was the name plaque, which read, Ceres: Sendaran, Administrator: Harlequin Moon.

The six name plaques on the right read, Vesta: Sendaran, Mr Ansel Zeffirelli, Hygiea: Sendaran, Mr Goren Halvek, Davida: Sendaran, Mr Jarik Solvyn, Sylvia: Sendaran, Ms Tessa Yorin, Eunomia: Sendaran, Mr Orris Delmar and Bamberga: Sendaran, Mr Karl Dravik.

The six name plaques on the left read, Pallas: Sendaran, Mr Kantian Velstro, Interamnia: Sendaran, Mr Calder Minos, Europa: Sendaran, Mr Brenner Ione, Euphrosyne: Sendaran, Ms Selin Andorran, Juno: Sendaran, Mr Rutan Thales and Psyche: Sendaran, Ms Savanna Strafe.

Dag looked to one of his two Researchers.

He pointed to the name plaques on the right-hand side of the desk, "Record every name, including Administrator Moon."

Dag looked to his other Researcher, he pointed to the name plaques on the left-hand side of the desk, "The same deal. Record every name."

While his researchers were recording the names of the Sendaran, Dag instructed, "When we get back to the hotel, find out everything you can about each of those individuals. And someone find out what the hell Sendaran means."

One of Dag's Secretaries noted, "Over here, Mr Talleyrand."

It was a smaller stone desk made of the same material in the form of an arc. Had the arc continued, it would have joined the main semi-circular desk. Behind this desk were six chairs. The two chairs in the middle had name plaques in front of them. Eros: Colonisation Committee: Sendaran, Mr Dag Talleyrand and Eros: Security Council: Sendaran, Ms Sone Dharma.

Dag nodded his head, "Well then, it looks like Sendaran means representative or something similar, perhaps ambassador. Six seats, one for each of us!"

The other one of Dag's Secretaries called him over to the other side of the chamber. It was another arc-shaped desk made of the same material, equal in size to the one Dag had been looking at. Likewise, had the arc continued, it would have joined the main semi-circular desk. All three stone desks sat along the circumference of a perfect circle. The black obsidian of the desks contrasting with the while marble walls and the clear quartz crystal inlays. It was a chamber not designed to be opulent, but more for form, function and ceremony.

Dag had walked over to the third desk. Curiously, there were only three chairs.

The name plaque on the left read, Cis-Lunar L-Five Dumas Incorporated: Sendaran, Mr Daniel Dumas. The name plaque on the right read, Cis-Lunar L-Five Dumas Incorporated: Sendaran, Mrs Harmony Dumas nee Moon. The plaque in the middle had no name, just the title, Ceres: Non-Sovereign Primate, First Among Equals."

Dag thought to himself, *"Daniel and Harmony Dumas, a Husband and Wife team, representing Dumas Incorporated Industries, but who is this middle person. Who is this Non-Sovereign Primate? What is a Non-Sovereign Primate? The term was an oxymoron. More questions and no answers!"*

Dag looked around the Althing Chamber and used his personal communicator to record the entire scene before instructing his team, "Let's get back to the hotel and try and figure out what we're dealing with here. We have thirteen representatives from the thirteen original Belter colonies, we have ourselves and the Dumas's and a mystery person. And why is this place steeped in Icelandic mythos?"

Dag took one more look around the Althing Chamber before leading his team back out the way they'd come.

On the first day of the Belters Althing, Dag, Sone and the team strolled towards the Althing Hall.
Dag asked one of his Researchers, "What do we know about the Sendaran?"

"It's a multipurpose word with Icelandic roots, Sir", the Researcher replied.

"More information, please", Dag requested.

"Well, Sir. First, there's Sendinefnd, which means delegation or envoys. There's also Sendiráð, which means embassy or diplomatic mission, and then there's Sendimaður, which means ambassador or envoy. Sendaran is kind of like a combination of all three and yet, it's not", the researcher replied.

"So, let me see if I've got this right. The Belter Sendaran are what, ambassadors? We, as Sendaran, are emissaries and the Dumas's, as Sendaran, are representatives? Administrator Moon is a Sendaran because he represents Ceres. That one word covers them all?", Dag enquired

"Yeah, that's pretty much it, Sir", the Researcher confirmed.

Dag asked for confirmation, "So, the Belter Sendaran are ambassadors from the other twelve colonies that are stationed here, in Ceres Central?"

"Yes, Sir", the Researcher confirmed.

"And this Icelandic connection? Where does that come into it?", Dag asked.

The other Researcher chimed in, "The Moon family's ancestry is Icelandic and Norse, Sir."

"Ha, well then, I guess that explains a lot", Dag commented.

"And the Italian marble? The quartz crystal and obsidian?", Dag queried.

"An aesthetic preference, perhaps, Sir. Nothing more", the first Researcher answered.

As they approached the Althing Hall, Dag asked, "What about that Non-Sovereign Primate?"

"We aren't certain, Sir. We think that it may be the position of speaker, perhaps moderator, mediator or even tie breaker. Perhaps even all of them", the second Researcher commented, adding, "We aren't really sure about it, Sir."

As Dag and his team entered the Althing Hall, their credentials were checked, then double-checked and they were handed name badges. As they entered the Althing Chamber, they found all of the other participants milling about in the central space. The doors were closed behind them, as everyone was now present. The doors were then locked.

The Ceresian Administrator, Harlequin Moon, quickly introduced Dag's team to the other participants. As the introductions were made, Dag noticed that he had guessed correctly, each Belter Ambassador had his own adviser and a Dumas Legal Incorporated provided lawyer for legal advice.

There was, however, an exception, Harlequin Moon's adviser was his Wife, Helena, although he did have a Dumas-provided lawyer as well.

Harlequin Moon announced to the chamber, "Data tablets have been provided for every Sendaran and their advisers. Please turn off your personal communicators and devices and put them aside."

"Is that necessary?", Dag asked.

Harlequin replied, "Yes, Mr Talleyrand. Each of the data tablets we have provided has the same specifications, the same functions and the same access to the data. The data tablets are all equal. No one has any advantage."

"Administrator Moon. Are these data tablets capable of recording and documenting these proceedings?", Dag enquired.

"Yes, of course, they are, Mr Talleyrand. The software suite is fairly standard. At the end of this Thing, any documents you've created will be accessible to you on your own devices", Administrator Moon confirmed, then he requested, "Okay, Friends, Ladies and Gentlemen, let us take our seats."

After which all of the participants began moving towards their assigned seats.

Once the participants had taken their seats, Harlequin Moon remained standing in the centre of the Althing Chamber. Harlequin looked around the chamber.

"Friends", Harlequin announced, then he turned to Daniel Dumas and his Wife, Harmony, "Family", he then turned to Dag and his team, "Honoured Guests", then finally back to the Belter Ambassadors, "Ladies and Gentlemen. It is now time to select our Primate to preside over this Thing."

One by one the Ambassadors began activating the data tablets that had been supplied to them. The Dumas's, Dag and his team activated their data tablets as well. One by one, a list of names appeared on the screen. There were twelve in all. Some of the names were the names of the ambassadorial advisers that were present in the Althing chamber, while the others names were of people not actually present.

Harlequin Moon reminded the Ambassadors, "Remember, Ambassadors. The person you nominate must be present within the Ceres Central Command colony. If they are elected, we must be able to bring them to this chamber by midday."

Harlequin Moon had not nominated his preferred candidate, instead he allowed his adviser, his Wife, Helena to submit the name. Then the thirteenth name appeared on the data tablet screens, Harmony Dumas nee Moon. Several Belter Ambassadors through up their hands. One by one, the other candidates were all removed from the list. Within minutes, Harmony's name was the only name left. Harmony Dumas nee Moon, was the only nominated candidate remaining.

Harlequin smiled, nodding to himself, "It appears unanimous", he turned to his Cousin, Harmony, "Cousin Harmony. Will you do us the honour of being our Primate for the duration of this Thing?"

Harmony stood up and moved from her seat to the central seat at her desk. As she did so, she moved her name plaque across, placing it next to the plaque that listed just the title, Ceres: Non-Sovereign Primate, First Among Equals.

Harmony addressed the Chamber, "Friends, Family, Honoured Guests, Ladies and Gentlemen. I accept the position of Non-Sovereign Primate, First Among Equals, for the duration of this Thing and will perform my duties to the best of my abilities", then she sat down and took her new seat.

Harlequin Moon nodded to his Cousin, bowing slightly, before slowly walking back to his seat.

Ms Sone Dharma was confused and piped up, asking, "Wait a second! I thought there was going to be a vote?"

Sendaran, Mr Ansel Zeffirelli of Vesta, replied, explaining, "Ms Dharma. Many of us here know Harmony personally. For those of us who don't, Harmony's reputation precedes her."

Sendaran, Ms Selin Andorran of Euphrosyne, added, "It was Harmony Moon who created the very loophole that keeps us out of your Security Council's jurisdiction and the jurisdiction of the Colonisation Committee. Harmony came up with that solution when she was just twelve years old."

Sendaran, Ms Savanna Strafe of Psyche chimed in, "At only eighteen years of age, it was Harmony who created the Althing system that you see before you. We are not a federation, nor a confederacy, nor a commonwealth. We are all sovereign nations unto ourselves and yet, we have this supranational political structure, this Althing, that brings us all together in mutual cooperation for the benefit of all."

Sendaran, Mr Goren Halvek of Hygiea affirmed, his voice forceful, "There is no one, no one in this chamber who is more qualified than Harmony Moon!"

For once, Ms Sone Dharma was getting a handle on the mindset of the Belters and their resistance to overarching jurisdiction and oversight. They were fiercely independent and united in purpose through the Althing Assembly. They were, in essence, the Thing itself and all it represented. Sone's head was beginning to spin with all of the implicit implications. They would never bow down to oversight! Not ever!

Ms Sone Dharma placed her hands firmly on the desk, she was definitely feeling vertiginous.

Dag asked quietly, "Are you alright, Sone?"

Sone replied equally quietly, "Yes, Dag. I'll be fine. I've just had an epiphany. An overwhelming epiphany. We have everything backwards and the Belters have everything right. We have no business dictating to them at all. I was, I was wrong!"

Sone stood up and asked, "If I may ask. What is the function of the Non-Sovereign Primate, the First Among Equals?"

Harmony stood up to reply, "Yes, Ms Dharma, you may. Your question is very valid. During this Thing, I will serve multiple functions. I have the position of Speaker, Moderator, Mediator and Tie Breaker. I am responsible for maintaining order and decorum. Should discussions become overly heated, I moderate. Should parties become entrenched in an argument, I mediate. If a vote is tied, I cast the deciding vote. I hold Primacy over this chamber as the First among Equals and yet, I have no power, except for that which they, the Ambassadorial Sendaran, have granted to me."

Dag enquired, "There are thirteen Sendaran Ambassadors. How can a vote become tied?"

"In some votes, there will be Ambassadors who have an inherent conflict of interest and they must abstain from voting. In which case, there may be an even number of voters and the possibility of a tied vote. I then cast the deciding vote", Harmony explained.

Harlequin chimed in, "You should also be aware that the Primate is responsible for the Althing Chamber's security as well. Should a Sendaran, perhaps more than one, become disruptive, the Primate has the power to call in security and have them ejected from this chamber."

"Yes, there is that as well. I do have a gavel and a gavel block", Harmony tapped the gavel to its block twice in demonstration and then announced, "Shall we get on with the proceedings then? This Thing is now in session!", it was more of an instruction than a question.

The provided data tablets displayed a screen of the day's itinerary and Dag's team scrutinised it. It contained mostly mundane things pertaining to the Belter colonies. There was no mention of the phasing out of fission reactor power production and its replacement with the new fusion power reactors. There was also no mention of the phasing out of uranium fuel rod manufacturing or uranium mining and no mention at all of the disposal of two and a half centuries worth of radioactive waste.

Dag stood up and asked, "At what point during this Thing do we get to the reason for us being here? The cutover from fission power production to the new fusion power generation?"

Harmony Dumas nee Moon, replied, "Mr Talleyrand, today is merely day one of this Thing and this is just the schedule for today. The proposed phase-out of all things fission is probably the most important point of discussion, as such it will be scheduled last so that we can allow sufficient time to cover all of its ramifications."

"Mrs Dumas, this Thing is scheduled to last two weeks", Dag noted in reply.

"Yes and no, Mr Talleyrand", Harmony replied, explaining, "We schedule two weeks for the Althing, however, it may be shorter, or it may be longer. It all depends on the number of topics we have to cover, how long each topic of discussion takes and the efficiency with which we deal with each topic."

"Might I suggest, that if my team is not required until our topic of discussion comes up, that my team be called into attendance at that point in time", Dag suggested, commenting, "It seems inefficient for us to be present for discussions for which we are not actually required."

Harmony frowned, "That is not how the Althing works, Mr Talleyrand. All participants, all Sendaran, are to be present from day one of the Thing until its final day. You will be here each morning when those doors open and you will leave at the end of the day when those doors close. The only exception would be those Sendaran ejected for being disruptive. A disgrace, I assure you. Is that understood?"

"Yes, Mrs Dumas. We fully understand", Dag replied, trying not to show his frustration.

Harlequin Moon stood up and chimed in, "Trust me, Mr Talleyrand. Even though you might have little or nothing to add to the other points of discussion, you will find this Thing to be both informative and instructive. It will be a learning experience for all of you, I assure you."

Dag Talleyrand, Sendaran and Emissary from the Colonisation Committee of Sol, nodded in reply.

It appeared that this was going to be a very long two weeks.

5. All Things Belter.

The Althing continued, following the scheduled points of discussion for the day. Most of the points were quite minor things. Some were requests for clarification of the finer points of previously made agreements, while others were discussions about food production and internal Belter trade.

Once Ambassador, Sendaran, Mr Karl Dravik, had even put forward the suggestion that all given names should be compiled into a register, which would then be used as a list of *"acceptable"* given names and that parents would only be allowed to choose their child's given names from that register. That suggestion, although not unusual in Nordic countries back on Earth, was quickly struck down.

That same Sendaran also put forward another suggestion, that if a citizen changed their surname by deed poll, some surnames should be restricted for historical reasons. That no one should simply be allowed to change their surname to a historically significant name. Strangely, that suggestion had gained traction. There were some Sendaran that were in favour of it and there were others that were not. The sticking point was what surnames were historically significant. Discussion on what one would have thought was a fairly mundane point dragged on for well over an hour.

Dag felt the need to lower his head onto the desk in front of him, but did his best to resist the urge.

The surname renaming restriction was passed, eight to five, with the recommendation that a committee be set up to decide which surnames ought to be on the restricted register. That list would be made available to all of the Belter Colonies for internal discussion, with the final vote on the issue to take place at the following year's Althing.

Dag and his team were more than happy when at one pm a bell chimed, signifying a break for lunch. The chamber doors opened and lunch was served. Even then, the Thing did not stop and all of the Sendaran worked through lunch. By the end of the day, Dag and his team felt exhausted. They left the Althing Hall and returned to their hotel suites, knowing that tomorrow would be the same.

That evening, Ms Sone Dharma wrote an email to the Security Council of Sol, back at Eros in the Earth's Trailing Trojan point. In the email, Sone described the Belters, explaining that their more than thirty colonised asteroids were effectively thirteen sovereign nations based upon the original thirteen founding colonies. Sone explained the oxymoronic situation with Ceres, the first of the Belter colonies. Ceres, by being the first, was accepted as having *"non-Sovereign Primacy"* over all of the others. A contradiction in terms, if ever there was one.

Sone then went on to describe the reverence that the Belters held for the Dumas and the Moon families. This was largely due to Stuart Dumas and Harrison Moon being responsible for the very existence of the Belter Colonies. That and the continued assistance that the Dumas and Moon families provided. That the Dumas and Moon families had earned their trust, respect and admiration.

She then delved deeper into the equally oxymoronic annual Belter Althing Assembly, where all participants, no matter their station or job title, were Sendaran. All of equal voice and standing and yet, they'd elect a *"non-Sovereign Primate"*, who had no real power, except that which they'd yielded to them for the duration of the assembly, the Thing.

Ms Sone Dharma finished off with a recommendation, *"We cannot push our jurisdiction onto the Belters, it is an anathema to them and they will resist us at every turn. Both the Security Council of Sol and the Colonisation Committee of Sol must work with the Belters as equal partners. They must never be treated as anything less. All of our dealings with them must be fair, clear and transparent and above all things, any agreements we make with them must be kept to the letter. We may offer them help, we may offer them suggestions, perhaps even guidance, but we must never push our rules or decisions upon them. Doing so will simply push them further away. To bring the Belters closer to us, we must treat them as equals and with all due respect. We must earn their trust and respect. These things are not a given, they are earned. The Belters will come to us if we meet them halfway.*

Sone Dharma signed the email as "Ms Sone Dharma, Sendaran", carbon copied in all of the Belter Ambassadors and Administrator Moon and then sent off the email.

The second day of the Althing, Dag and his team arrived at the Althing Hall as usual. As with the day before, their credentials were checked, then double-checked and they were handed their name badges. They all walked down the hallway and entered the Althing Chamber, noting that all the other participants, the other Sendaran, were already present and seated.

Before Dag and his team had even reached their desk, Harlequin Moon and the other Belter Sendaran, the Ambassadors, all stood up and made their way over to Ms Sone Dharma. One by one, they shook her hand and thanked her, before they all returned to their seats.

Dag asked Sone, "What did you do?"

"Oh. Didn't I copy you in?", Sone replied, she'd sent the email to the Ambassadors, but had forgotten Dag, "I sent out an email yesterday evening. I'll send you a copy", which she did after taking her seat.

Harmony Dumas nee Moon, stood up and addressed the Chamber, "A certain email sent yesterday evening by Sendaran, Ms Sone Dharma, has caused quite a stir. The thirteen Belter Sendaran and I convened an emergency external session to discuss this email."

The Ceresian Administrator, Sendaran, Harlequin Moon, stood up and continued, "We will, as a group, be following up on Sendaran, Ms Dharma's email. We will be informing the Security Council of Sol and the Colonisation Committee of Sol, at Eros, in Earth's Trailing Trojan point, that we will be appointing an Ambassador to Eros before this month is out. This will occur outside of this Thing."

Sendaran, Mr Ansel Zeffirelli of Vesta stood up and chimed in, "We will recommend to Eros that they send us an Ambassador to be stationed here, in the Ceresian colonies. As it will take time for the Security Council and the Colonisation Committee to appoint an Ambassador, in the interim, we will accept, Sendaran, Ms Sone Dharma as the interim Ambassador from Eros. We will include that recommendation in our communique."

Harmony smiled and congratulated Sone, "Well, Sendaran, Ms Sone Dharma. Congratulations are in order. Welcome, interim Ambassador."

Then all three Sendaran sat back down.

As Dag and his other team members looked at Sone in surprise, she stood up and replied, "I must decline your offer. I am not qualified for this honour."

Harlequin Moon stood up, "The email you sent to Eros yesterday clearly shows that you are. Ms Dharma, you may not feel qualified, but we can assure you, we have more faith in you than perhaps any other choice that might come from Eros."

Sendaran, Ms Savanna Strafe of Psyche stood up, "Ms Dharma, this is all new to you, we understand that. It is also perhaps quite an unexpected shock. You will grow into this new position, your new role. You will excel at it."

Sone was quiet for a moment in thought and then she replied, "Okay. I will accept the position as interim Ambassador on one condition."

"And your condition is?", Savanna Strafe enquired.

"Is there anywhere within the Ceresian colonies with one standard g of gravity? I find point three five gs just a little unsettling", Sone replied honestly.

Savanna Strafe smiled, "I can understand that. It does take time to get used to our lower gravity."

Harlequin chimed in, "We do have one twin-cylinder colony with its rotation set for one standard g."

"You do?", Sone enquired.

"Yes, our very first colony. The only Belter Colony that was ever registered with the Colonisation Committee and the Security Council. It was registered before we came up with our loopholes. It adheres to the gravity laws", Harlequin informed her.

Sone Dharma suddenly realised and she smiled a wry smile. It was poetic. The one colony that the Belters had, that complied with the gravity laws, was the original Ceresian colony, *"Eros can have it"*.

The original Ceresian Central colony was renamed by the Ceresians as an insult to Eros and now Sone would be living there, she shook her head at the realisation before answering, "I accept!"

Not a lot happened over the next few days. Most of the issues being dealt with in the Thing were quite mundane. Dag and his team were quite bored and at one point, he caught one of his secretaries playing pong on his data tablet. Dag just rolled his eyes and shook his head.

Sone, on the other hand, had her dramas. The Security Council had been pleased to receive her report and recommendations. They were, however, rather peeved that Sone had copied in the Belter Sendaran. Sone explained to them that it was done in the interests of transparency and fostering trust.

The Security Council punished Sone by making her their official Ambassador to the Belters permanently. The Colonisation Committee concurred. Ms Sone Dharma, Sendaran, was now the official Erosian Ambassador to the Belter colonies. The Security Council would have the contents of her apartment packed up, placed into a shipping container or two and on its way to Ceres before the Althing was over.

On the fifth day of the Thing, an issue cropped up that caught Dag's ear. His whole team sat with intense fascination. Two Belter colonies had a dispute over sovereignty over one of their own *"satellite"* colonies. The newer Asteroid colony, forty-eight Doris, or simply Doris, as it was being called, was just another rock in the Asteroid Belt, albeit a large one, at two hundred and nineteen kilometres in diameter.

The Hygiean Belters had colonised Doris and currently held sovereignty over it. The Pallasian Belters contested the Hygiean's sovereignty, claiming that Doris was in their backyard and therefore came under their sovereignty and jurisdiction. It was turning out to be a heated debate. Both sides were entrenched in their positions. Neither side was willing to budge, their positions were fixed!

Sendaran, Mr Kantian Velstro of Pallas stated with authority, "Doris lies within Pallasian space. Practically in our orbital backyard. It is just point zero two two AU away from Pallas. Hygiea is nearly sixteen times further away. Its natural sphere of influence is clearly Pallasian. This is a matter of gravitational domain and common sense. Sovereignty is ours by simple proximity."

Sendaran, Mr Goren Halvek of Hygiea had countered with equal authority, "Doris was colonised, developed and governed by Hygiean settlers. We have maintained a continuous presence and governance. It was our credits spent, our resources expended, our colonists and our efforts that created the Dorisian colony. Sovereignty belongs to those who plant roots and settle the rock, not to those who simply hover nearby."

The two Sendaran were shouting at each other and the Non-Sovereign Primate, Harmony Dumas nee Moon, was forced to step in, "Silence!", she shouted and she slammed her gavel down on its block several times.

Harmony stood up and asked, "Does proximity establish legitimacy, or does stewardship and historical investment hold primacy? That is the question that must be decided."

Dag found himself rising to his feet, much to the astonished looks of the other Sendaran in the chamber. What could Sendaran, Mr Dag Talleyrand from Eros possibly have to offer on this issue?

Dag spoke clearly and forcefully, "There is a historical precedent!", he announced, before explaining, "In the twentieth century, the Earth saw a parallel situation: the Falkland Islands. They were claimed by Argentina due to proximity, but they were first discovered and settled by Britain and Britain held sovereignty. Twice they were invaded, in eighteen thirty three and again in nineteen eighty two. Twice they were reclaimed. The last time was through a bloody seventy-four-day war. The deciding factor? It was not their geography, but instead, it was the self-determination of the Falkland Islanders themselves. The question here is not where Doris is, but what the Dorisian peoples want. What is the will of the Dorisian people?"

The Belter Sendaran Ambassadors were all gob-smacked. They had not expected Dag's interjection in what was clearly an internal Belter matter.

Sendaran, Mr Goren Halvek of Hygiea quickly chimed in, "Since the Pallasians began contesting our sovereignty, we have held two referendums on this very subject. The results are in the records. In both referendums, the Dorisian people chose, overwhelmingly, to remain under Hygiean Sovereignty!"

Sendaran, Mr Kantian Velstro of Pallas slammed his fist onto the desk and shouted, "Enough of this nonsense. The asteroid, forty-eight Doris, is far closer to Pallas, therefore, it is Pallasian. We will not accept your ridiculous referendums. Your people, voting for your sovereignty! It is simply ridiculous!"

Sendaran, Mr Kantian Velstro's actions had most definitely upset the decorum of the chamber. Harmony Dumas, nee Moon, slapped her gavel down on its block twice and rose to her feet.

"Strike that desk one more time, Mr Velstro and I will have you ejected from this chamber", Harmony warned him.

She had used his name, minus his title, Mr Velstro was skating on thin ice and he knew it. More importantly, the other Sendaran in the chamber all knew it as well.

Harmony asked in a softer voice, "So, Mr Velstro. You and your people won't accept the Dorisian referendums? The will of the Dorisian people?"

"No! Never! We will never accept the results of sham Hygiean referendums!", Mr Velstro replied.

Harmony Dumas, nee Moon, nodded and frowned, then she asked, "Mr Velstro. Will you accept the will of this chamber? The will of your fellow Sendaran?"

Sendaran, Mr Kantian Velstro looked around at his fellow Sendaran. Surely he would win the vote.
The asteroid, forty-eight Doris, was far closer to Pallas than Hygiea. They would surely see the logic.

Sendaran, Mr Kantian Velstro replied, "My people and I will accept the will of the Sendaran", he stated it clearly for the record.

"Good then. We will vote on this matter. Sendaran, Mr Goren Halvek of Hygiea. Sendaran, Mr Kantian Velstro of Pallas. You both have a conflict of interest in this matter. You will be recorded as non-voting abstentions", Harmony announced.

Then the vote began. There was no further discussion on the matter and the result was very quick. The vote went eleven to zero in favour of Hygiea. The Sendaran had chosen self-determination over proximity. All eyes in the chamber turned to Sendaran, Mr Kantian Velstro of Pallas.

Kantian Velstro was stunned, the vote had gone unanimously against Pallas. He did not want to accept. He knew his people would be incensed. He also knew that to defy a vote of the Sendaran was unheard of. A defiant Pallas would be automatically sent to Coventry, ostracised by all of the other Belter colonies. No trade, no communications, no immigrants, nothing, just pure silence.

Sendaran, Mr Kantian Velstro of Pallas, stood up from his chair.

He looked around the chamber and then replied, "We, the people of Pallas, will accept the will of the Sendaran. We will no longer contest the sovereignty of forty-eight Doris."

Harmony Dumas, nee Moon, replied, "Good then. Let it be recorded thus. Let this vote also become a new Belter precedent. Proximity does NOT convey sovereignty. Self-determination does."

Dag received a message on his data tablet. It was from Daniel Dumas, who had been silent throughout most of the Thing.

The message simply read, *"And you thought you were wasting your time here, Dag Talleyrand. You have just helped create a new Belter legal precedent."*

The days dragged on during the Thing. Harmony Dumas, nee Moon, as the Non-Sovereign Primate, had a large part to play, as did the Ceresian Administrator Harlequin Moon and the twelve Ambassadorial Sendaran. Dag and his team, on the other hand, were like added extras, waiting until their moment in the Sun. Dag's two Researchers busied themselves, learning about the Belter society and culture. Dag's two Secretaries jotted down notes into their data tablets, recording interesting points in the proceedings, in between playing games of pong and solitaire.

Sone Dharma had somehow managed to access a three-d schematic of her future Ambassadorial apartment in the O'Neil-style twin-cylinder colony, *"Eros can have it"*. Sone's apartment was in what was designated the northeast end cap. It was large, spacious and already furnished. Sone used her time trying to figure out how her belongings and furniture were going to fit in and where to place them.

The colony, *"Eros can have it"*, was extremely underpopulated. Not because it had a weird name, but due to it having one standard g of gravity. Most Belters preferred living in point three five gs, so few Ceresians wanted to live there.

Capable of comfortably housing well over twenty thousand people, it currently housed only around six thousand. As a result, there was much more open space and parkland than in most colonies. There was also a shortage of skilled workers and high-paying jobs in the colony were plentiful. Prospective employees simply had to be happy to live in a one-g environment.

Sone spent quite a bit of time looking at photographic images of the colony's interior. It was quite a beautiful colony. Each end cap had seasons that were a quarter of a year out of sync. So you could have a change of seasons by simply travelling to another of its four end caps.

Sone's new home didn't have the artificial, sculptured mountains that Eros had, however, it did have bulkheads in between the end caps and the main cylinders proper and each was sculptured with *"end cap mountains"* on either side. Sone was actually looking forward to her new digs.

Around day ten, something interesting came up. One of the smaller colonies, Juno, smaller by size and mass, was having issues obtaining rare earth elements, which are crucial for colony construction. Sendaran, Mr Rutan Thales of Juno, had stressed the need to resolve the rare earth element supply issues quickly. He explained that their population was expanding and that their new colony construction was being held up by the supply issues surrounding rare earth elements.

Without even being asked, Sendaran, Mr Ansel Zeffirelli of Vesta and Sendaran, Ms Savanna Strafe of Psyche, stepped in and offered assistance. Not all asteroids in the Asteroid Belt were equal. Some were rich in volatiles, while others were rich in minerals and metals. Vesta and Psyche were both rich in the latter two and were able to provide for Juno's shortfall of rare earth elements.

A usually quiet Daniel Dumas had also chimed in, noting that one of the companies under the Dumas Incorporated umbrella was Mars Trojan Mining Ltd and that they had excess stocks of rare earth elements. Daniel informed, Sendaran, Mr Rutan Thales, that they could ship directly to Juno from either of the Martian Trojan points on an expedited basis if the need was that urgent.

Dag was actually impressed at how quickly the Belters came together to help each in a pinch. He was equally impressed at how quickly the Dumas family stepped in to help out. The Belters and the Dumas's worked together like hand in glove.

When the discussion moved on to the costs involved, Daniel Dumas waved his hand dismissively and stated, *"We'll work all of that out later. A special deal, mates rates. It's all good!"*

It was the fourteenth day of the Thing and Dag's team was excited. Today was the day they'd get to explain the phaseout of uranium fission power generation and everything that it entailed. All of the other Sendaran were present. Dag sat down at their desk and picked up the provided data tablet. A look of disappointment quickly came across his face. The uranium power generation phaseout was not on the itinerary for the day.

Dag stood up and was about to enquire about the day's schedule, but Harmony Dumas, nee Moon was already standing and began speaking.

Harmony looked towards Dag and his team, "Friends", then she looked to Daniel, her Husband, "Family", then across to the Ambassadorial Sendaran, "Ladies and Gentlemen. We have had a lot to cover over the past two weeks, however, we are not done. There are more items to discuss. As a result, this Thing is to be extended by two days. All current participants are expected to be present."

Dag sat back down and slumped in his chair. As much as he was impressed with the Althing, at times it was like bureaucracy on steroids. Dag Talleyrand and his team resigned themselves to two more days of this Thing.

The grinding Thing continued on, as if never-ending, the topical minutia continued. Then right when Dag's team felt like they were going to shit themselves from sheer boredom another interesting issue cropped up. It was unusual, something that none of Dag's team had heard of before.

Sendaran, Mr Calder Minos of Interamnia, brought up the subject of something called the Black Blight! No one on Dag's team had ever heard of it!

"We have two main cylinders in one of our new colonies infested with the Black Blight", Mr Calder Minos had stated, "It hasn't yet spread to any of the four end caps or any of the our other colonies, but it is only a matter of time. We have evacuated the whole colony."

Sendaran, Mr Dag Talleyrand of Eros, found himself standing on his feet and enquiring, "Please forgive my ignorance, Sendaran, but what is the Black Blight?"

Mr Calder Minos replied, "Mr Talleyrand, Sendaran, the Black Blight is a kind of fungus. You would know it as Black Mould. It is highly toxic, full of mycotoxins. Once it infests the soil in our main cylinders, nothing can grow in it. It is a blight of the severest magnitude!"

Sendaran, Ms Tessa Yorin of Sylvia chimed in, "We had a problem with the Black Blight last year. It contaminated an entire twin-cylinder colony before we managed to eradicate it. It took a lot of effort."

Mr Calder Minos enquired, "Ms Yorin. What method did you use? Which methods worked?"

Tessa Yorin frowned, "We had to irradiate every square millimetre of the entire colony. Everything! Then once the Blight was eradicated, we had to remove all of the soil from the colony and replaced it."

"That sounds like a lot of work, Ms Yorin", Mr Minos replied.

"It was. It took the best part of a year and was very expensive. We also had to order in a colony's worth of new processed regolith", Ms Yorin explained.

Dag was curious and asked, "What did you do with the contaminated soil?"

"Even though we had eradicated the Blight, we took no chances, Mr Talleyrand. We worked the contaminated soil away into Astcrete radiation shielding and relegated it for use to the exterior of ore processing stations", Ms Yorin explained.

Mr Yorin turned to Mr Minos, "Calder, the only way to treat the Black Blight is to irradiate it, remove it and then treat what's left of it as suspect forever after."

Calder Minos considered that information and then replied, "I will forward your remarks to my people, Tessa. Fortunately, this was a new colony and we caught it before it spread anywhere else."

"Interesting, Calder. Our colony was also new, however, we were not so lucky, it spread quickly and was everywhere before we caught it", Tessa Yorin replied.

Dag was curious, he asked, "How did this infestation begin? I mean, where did this Black Blight come from?"

Tessa Yorin frowned, "We have our suspicions, Mr Talleyrand", then she turned to Sendaran, Mr Calder Minos, "Calder. Where exactly did you source your processed regolith? Your soil?"

Mr Calder Minos replied, "From the Jovian Realms, as usual, of course, their Leading Trojans."

Tessa's frown grew tighter, "Goes to pattern, Calder. Goes to pattern. So did we!"

Tessa stood up and walked around the main desk at which the thirteen Belter Sendaran sat and addressed them, "Sendaran. Before the annexation of the Jovian Trojan colonies by the Jovian Realms, we had no issues with their processed regolith. We had no Black Blight! Now, since their annexation, we have two infestations of the Black Blight and more than likely, it came from their processed regolith. I am putting forward that this was not accidental. The Black Blight severely affects our production of crops. The very food that we and our livestock rely on. Our food security is at risk. That puts us all at risk", and then she turned to Harmony Dumas, "Just what are the Jovians playing at?", before she returned to her seat.

Harmony Dumas, nee Moon, stood up, "Ms Yorin, Sendaran. Those are serious accusations. Do you have actual proof?"

"No, Mrs Dumas, however, it is one hell of a coincidence, wouldn't you say?", Ms Yorin replied, then she told her fellow Sendaran, "Whether this contamination was deliberate or unintentional is largely irrelevant. I'm recommending that we switch to using internally processed regolith instead of the imported Jovian Trojan product. We simply cannot afford to have any Black Blight infestations."

Daniel whispered something to Harmony, then he stood up and noted, "Mars Trojan Mining Ltd produces high quality processed regolith for the Martian orbital zone. We can step up production and export to the Belter colonies if you need more than your local production can supply. We've got this."

Harmony stood up and called for a vote, "Okay. So let's decide, shall we? We currently source our processed regolith, our soil, from the Jovian Trojans. Are we to switch to our own internal supplies, augmented with supplies from Mars Trojan Mining Corporation? A simple yes or no answer."

The votes quickly came back, unanimous, thirteen to zero. No one trusted the Jovian Trojans for their processed regolith suppliers anymore.

Once bitten, twice shy, twice bitten, contracts cancelled!

That was the Belter way!

A message came through on Dag's data tablet. It was from Harmony Dumas, nee Moon.

Harmony's message read, "*We have scheduled the uranium fission power production phaseout discussion for tomorrow and have allocated up to two days. That was why we placed it last. Tomorrow might be a short day, or it may spill over into the next, perhaps even another after that. Belter folk are pragmatic and phasing out reliable fission reactors for an unknown future is likely to be a contentious issue with a lot of push back. Good luck.*"

6. The Crux of the Matter.

Dag and his team entered the Althing Chamber, hopefully, to finally get down to the very crux of the matter. Their very reason for being there. The previous evening, Dag's Secretaries emailed all of the Ambassadorial Sendaran copies of the nuclear fission phaseout documents. Dag wanted to make sure that they were all well-informed about the project. They had been sent these same documents in the weeks leading up to the Belter Althing, but Dag wanted them to have the information fresh, in front of them and readily at hand.

The Ceresian Administrator, Harlequin Moon, had already been sent the same documents as well, along with the blueprints and specifications for the new fusion power generation reactors in the months leading up to the Althing. Everything was set, the i's dotted and the t's crossed. Nothing had been left to chance. Dag had made sure of it.

Dag noticed that each Ambassadorial Sendaran had folios on their desks in front of them, no doubt, the same documents that had been sent to them the night before. Dag stood in the centre of the chamber as his team took their seats at their desk. Dag looked to the Non-Sovereign Primate, Harmony Dumas, nee Moon, and she nodded for him to begin.

"Friends, Ladies and Gentlemen, fellow Sendaran", Dag began, "Today we are hear to discuss the phasing out of uranium fission power generation reactors and their replacement with the latest, the most advanced, fusion power generation technology."

Dag looked around the chamber, making sure he caught each eye as he continued, "Earth has already cut across to fusion power generation systems. Earth's uranium fission power generation systems have already been shut down and dismantled. Over the next twenty years, the governments of Cis-Lunar Space and the Venusian Republic are embarking on a project to replace all uranium fission power generation systems with the latest fusion power generators. The entire inner solar system is converting to fusion power."

The Ambassadorial Sendaran had already read about this, nonetheless, there were plenty of murmurs.

"The aim is simple. Two decades from now, the entire inner solar system will have transitioned to fusion power generation systems. As part of this process, the Earth's government and the government of Cis-Lunar Space, are sharing their fusion power generation technology with every colony across the entire solar system", Dag paused before letting the penny drop, "The Earth's government intends to shut down all uranium mining and uranium fuel rod production on Earth in thirty years!"

Now the murmurs picked up in earnest, so much so that Harmony had to bang her gavel several times to bring order back to the chamber.

"Thank you, Madam Primate", Dag commented as the chamber fell silent once more.

Sendaran, Mr Karl Dravik of Bamberga stood up and noted loudly, "Mr Talleyrand! We here in the Belt, all of us, all of our colonies are dependent on uranium fuel rods exported from Earth!"

"Mr Dravik. We understand your concerns, that is why the Earth's government and the government of Cis-Lunar Space are sharing their fusion technology with you", Dag responded.

Then Dag explained, "Once you have transitioned to fusion power generation, you can use hydrogen sourced locally from within the Asteroid Belt to generate fuel your reactors. The aim is not just to phase out uranium, it is also to provide the colonies, all of the colonies, with power generation independence and autonomy."

Sendaran, Ceresian Administrator Harlequin Moon stood up, he remarked, "Our engineers have already studied these fusion reactor blueprints and specifications. They can run on any hydrogen isotope, they can even run on helium. It is not stated in the documentation, but they can even burn lithium as a fuel. My concern, however, is fiscal. Who is going to bear the costs?"

That had caught Dag by surprise, he had considered the technological sharing, the power generation autonomy, even whether the Belters could build these fusion reactors. He had not consider the costs.

Sendaran, Daniel Dumas of Dumas Incorporated stood up and replied, "Dumas Colonial Financial can provide any necessary finance and we will do so at our usual low 'preferred customer' rates."

Harlequin Moon replied, "Thank you, Daniel. We do appreciate our friends in the Dumas family, however, my concern is why we Belters should bear the costs at all. This entire project is driven by the troika of Earth, Cis-Lunar Space and Venus. It is their project, surely it is their responsibility to bear the cost burden, not we Belters."

Harlequin Moon, ever the pragmatist, gave Dag a simple lesson in mathematics, "When we looked into the costs, Mr Talleyrand, you will understand what I mean", he paused, looked around the chamber and then began his lesson, "Say it takes us ten credits to manufacture a uranium fission powered reactor. It takes us twice as much, say, twenty credits, to manufacture a fast breeder fission reactor. If we instead decided to build a thorium reactor, it would cost us fifteen credits. Your fusion reactors, on the other hand, would cost us fifty credits. Yes, we would have fusion reactor fuel autonomy, but at a very high price. Too high!"

"Understood, Mr Moon. Understood", Dag replied, quickly returning to the main point, "Is not fusion reactor fuel autonomy and independence from Earth and its fuel rod exports worth the price?"

"Mr Talleyrand, this is your first trip to the Belt and it shows. You need to understand how we Belters think. Here in the Belt, we live on the raggedy edge of existence. Credits are a resource that we do not squander lightly", Harlequin replied, noting, "It would be far cheaper and simpler for us to open up our own uranium mines and produce our own uranium fuel rods here in the Belt."

Dag admitted, "I did not know that was an option", and then he enquired, "Do you actually have uranium resources here in the Belt?"

Helena Moon stood up and rattled off a list, her voice was soft, almost sweet, "Psyche, Vesta, Pallas, Hygiea, Davida, Interamnia, Europa and even Lutetia all have untapped uranium and thorium deposits, Mr Talleyrand. We just haven't needed to open up those deposits until now."

"Thank you, Helena", Harlequin smiled at his wife and then he continued, "We could mine our own uranium, build our own refinement and enrichment plants, even build our own fuel rod production facilities. The costs would be far lower than cutting over to fusion power production."

"Noted, Mr Moon", Dag replied, then he asked, "Costs aside, you can see the benefits of transitioning to fusion power production, yes?"

"Yes, of course, we can, Mr Talleyrand, however, costs are indeed a major consideration", Harlequin Moon replied.

"Then it is a consideration that we need to take into account, Mr Moon", Dag replied, smiling.

"Mr Moon, if we ignored the cost issues, could Ceres construct those fusion reactors?", Dag asked.

"I have been informed that we could, yes. We would need to clarify some of the finer points, but yes, we could build them", Harlequin confirmed.

Daniel Dumas chimed in, using his diminutive, "Harley, Dumas Colonial Constructions and Himmelstaff Interplanetary Constructions can provide you with any expertise you might require. Himmelstaff Interplanetary Constructions is also active in the Martian orbital zone, so they would be the closest. I can organise a few calls if you like."

"Thank you, Daniel. Please do, even if we don't build them, we'd still like to be across the designs", Harlequin replied and then he asked, "Daniel, how are your people familiar with these new fusion reactor designs?"

"Oh, Harley", Daniel Dumas began, "Dumas Colonial Constructions and Himmelstaff Interplanetary Constructions have been contracted to build the fusion reactors for the entire inner solar system. We've even been contracted to help the Venusians develop their own fusion reactor construction facilities. We are well-positioned to help you. We can help all of the Belter nations, in fact."

"Wait! Mr Dumas, your companies are the contractors?", Dag asked, he had not been informed.

"In Cis-Lunar Space, no one else has the construction facilities for this kind of work", Daniel informed Dag, noting, "The only other facilities are planetside on Earth. And, of course, here in the Belt. It was a natural choice. We have the economies of scale and the efficiencies to keep the costs down as well."

It seemed that Dag was receiving one revelation after another.

Sendaran, Mr Brenner Ione, of Europa, asked, "Mr Talleyrand, if we do as you suggested and assume cost was not an issue. How the hell is this going to work? We must have close to a thousand fission reactors across the Belt and your inner solar system must be close to twenty times that number."

"I can't speak to your numbers here in the Belt, Mr Ione, however, your numbers for the inner solar system are pretty close to the mark", Dag confirmed, then he turned to Daniel Dumas, "Mr Dumas, your companies have the contracts. Do you have a handle on their capacities?"

"Funnily enough, as the Chief Operating Officer of the Dumas Incorporated Industries, I do, Dag", Daniel replied, he was in his element now, "Both Dumas Colonial Constructions and Himmelstaff Interplanetary Constructions are building up capacity as we speak. When they are up and running at peak production rates, we can expect fifty fusion power reactors per month rolling off the assembly lines. That's fifty per month per company. We do, of course, have to take into account future colony construction and growth as well."

Dag was stunned at how casually Daniel Dumas talked about fusion power reactors rolling off of the assembly lines, he did the math in his head. Twenty four thousand fusion reactors over twenty years!

Dag turned to the Ambassadorial Sendaran, "Well then, it looks like Dumas Incorporated Industries has got production covered, at least for the entire inner solar system", he did his best not to look like a stunned mullet!

Daniel commented to Harlequin as he would with a family member, "Harley, if you guys go ahead, my people will help you scale up production. We will help you with whatever it takes."

Harlequin Moon nodded and smiled at Daniel, "Thank you, Daniel, but we have not decided yet and we do have three decades until the Earth's uranium fuel rod production ceases."

Dag Talleyrand looked around the Althing chamber. This was not how he'd expect the day to proceed. The biggest sticking point was the costs involved in replacing up to a thousand perfectly functional Belter fission reactors. Dag had to admit to himself that the Belters were right. Colonial Central Command and the President of Cis-Lunar Space may have been pleased to replace their fission reactors and bear those costs. The Venusian President was also pleased to bear the cost of replacing their fission reactors. Neither of them had considered that the Belters, living precarious lives at the raggedy edge of existence, would not want to bear those same costs and why should they?

What was Dag's next move?

Dag was still formulating a response when Daniel Dumas stood up once more, he addressed Administrator Moon, "Harley, your cost estimates, they are based on your current manufacturing facilities, aren't they?"

"Well, yes, of course, Daniel. What else would I base them on?", Harlequin Moon replied.

"Harley, Harmony and I visited your manufacturing complex at Heptaluna L-Four", Daniel informed him, then stated, "Your reactor manufacturing facilities can only build one reactor at a time. They are not geared up for mass production. Even if you were to proceed with the phasing out of fission power production, you couldn't easily do it. Not without reworking and retooling your manufacturing facilities. I would expect the other Belter manufacturing facilities to be in exactly the same boat."

A few of the other Ambassadorial Sendaran nodded their heads as Harlequin replied, "Well, yes, Daniel. Obviously, that would be another major issue."

"I would recommend upgrading your reactor manufacturing capacity, Harley. Engineers from Dumas Incorporated can advise and assist with the design work. Retool the factory to be able to manufacture multiple reactor types and designs. Run the factory more like an assembly line than a bespoke one-off assembly plant", Daniel suggested.

Dag caught on quickly and chimed in, "Economies of scale", he remarked clearly, then added, "If you upscale your factories and run them as an assembly line, you will be able to reduce your costs."

Daniel pointed to Dag, then he pointed to Harlequin Moon, "Precisely where I was heading. If we pull this off, you could reduce the cost of production per unit by at least fifty percent".

Daniel was a Dumas and in his element. His old Brother, Connor, would be proud of him.

"Hmm", Harlequin moon frowned, he commented, "Even if our costs reduced by fifty percent per unit, for a fusion reactor that is still quite a cost impost."

"Yes, it is, but remember your previous math, Harley. Do a quick recalculation", Daniel reminded.

Harlequin Moon did a quick reassessment, "A uranium fission reactor becomes five, a fast breeder reactor becomes ten, a thorium reactor becomes seven fifty and a fusion reactor becomes twenty five."

"You see, Harley", Daniel confirmed, "A factory upgrade, with retooling cuts costs overall. It's a win-win proposition, Harley."

Harlequin Moon rubbed his chin, his Wife Helena placed her hand on his shoulder. Harlequin's Cousin-in-law was right. There were definite cost benefits involved.

"Thank you again, Daniel. I'll have my people run the numbers. If you are right and you usually are, we will move ahead with the upgrade and retooling", Harlequin Moon replied, he was now smiling.

Harlequin Moon stood up and addressed the chamber, "My fellow Sendaran. If this pans out as a beneficial proposition, then I will recommend it. I will keep you all in the loop."

Then Harlequin Moon turned back to Daniel, "This will reduce overall costs, yes, however, the cost burden of cutting over to fusion power production still falls on us."

"Yes, Harley, but please remember, I can only solve one problem at a time", Daniel replied.

Dag Talleyrand was still standing in the centre of the Althing Chamber. While Daniel and Harlequin both talked, he had been formulating a possible plan. Dag Talleyrand had an epiphany!

Dag reminded everyone, "Sendaran, Ladies and Gentlemen. In three decades, the export of uranium fuel rods from Earth will cease. We need to come up with a plan and it is better to be on top of the wave than under it, crashing upon the rocks", he used a surfing analogy to evoke a vivid image.

Sendaran, Mr Karl Dravik of Bamberga, quickly asked, "Do you actually have any suggestions, Mr Talleyrand? We can ill afford these cost burdens!", his tone was sharp and straight to the point.

Dag nodded, then replied, using Mr Dravik's first name, "Karl, I, in fact, do have a plan."

That caught everyone's attention. Up until now, Dag had come across as just another useless Erosian twat, not that anyone would say so out loud. The Belter way wasn't to insult people directly. Negative opinions were internalised and rarely spoken. Their very existence was predicated on cooperation.

Sendaran, Mr Rutan Thales of Juno, replied, "Then, Mr Talleyrand. Dag, let us hear it."

"Three irons in the fire, Ladies and Gentlemen, Sendarans all", Dag announced, he'd caught their attention and then he went with it, "The export of uranium fuel rods will cease and you all need to be ready for that moment."

Dag looked around the chamber, catching the eyes of every Ambassadorial

Sendaran, "Your first iron", he announced, expounding, "Open up your own uranium mines, tap them! Build uranium refineries and enrichment plants. Manufacture your own uranium fuel rods. This is an imperative. You must all be energy independent when the gate comes crashing down!"

Dag's rhetoric was deliberately full of metaphors, "Your second iron", he announced, once more looking around at the Sendarans, then continuing, "Diversify. Open up your own thorium mines! Build thorium reactors. Ensure that you have at least two viable systems to ensure energy independence!"

The chamber was quiet now, they were hearing words that made sense, a practical plan that they could move forward with. Dag was gaining newfound respect and with the Belters, respect was always earned, it was never, ever given. To the Belters, respect was everything!

Once again, Dag looked around the chamber, then announced, "Your third iron", then he paused, just for dramatic effect, "With the upgrading and retooling of your reactor manufacturing plants, costs will come down. As existing fission reactors reach the end of their lives, one by one, replace them with the new fusion reactors. Which, as I have been informed, can be fuelled with hydrogen, helium and even lithium. This ensures both energy independence and that you have full control of the latest power generation technologies! You can have your cake and you can eat it too!"

That last sentence caught the Belter's attention and a round of applause and cheering began. Harmony Dumas, nee Moon, had to bang her gavel onto its block several times before order was restored. However, she was smiling as she did so.

Dag Talleyrand, Sendaran from Eros, had them, he finished off with, "Those are your three irons in the fire. Those three irons will lead you to energy independence on your terms!"

Once again, Harlequin Moon stood up, "I call for a vote!"
Sendaran, Mr Ansel Zeffirelli of Vesta, also stood up, "I too call for a vote!"
Sendaran, Ms Savanna Strafe of Psyche, stood up, "We must vote on this now, while the iron is still hot!", using one of Dag's own metaphors.
The Non-Sovereign Primate of the Thing, Harmony Dumas, nee Moon, stood up, "So be it! You will all vote on Sendaran, Mr Talleyrand of Eros's Three Irons Strategy!"
The vote was held and all Ambassadorial Sendaran voted for it, thirteen to zero, it was unanimous.
Harmony Dumas, nee Moon, stood and announced the results of the vote,

"The vote is unanimous in the affirmative. Sendaran, Mr Dag Talleyrand of Eros's Three Irons Strategy will be carried forward as official Belter policy. Post Thing, all Ambassadorial Sendaran in this chamber will form a committee to formulate how this new policy is to be implemented", she smiled, "You all have your work ahead of you", it would be a major planning task.

Sendaran, Sone Dharma of Eros, liaison from the Security Council of Sol and now Ambassador to the Belter Colonies, stood up and walked over to Dag.

Sone whispered into Dag's ear, "What will the Colonisation Committee and Security Council make of your Three Irons Strategy?", and then she casually walked back to her seat.

Dag smiled as he watched Sone return to her seat, then, in the interests of transparency, he announced, "Sendaran, Sone Dharma, has just reminded me that I work for the Colonisation Committee of Sol. I am, of course, their Emissary. So, what will my superiors at the Colonisation Committee make of this new Three Irons Strategy?"

Sendaran, Mr Jarik Solvyn of Davida, replied, "The Colonisation Committee of Sol is irrelevant, Mr Talleyrand. They have no say in this matter whatsoever!"

Dag pointed to Jarik Solvyn, replying as he then looked to Sone, "And that is the answer. The Colonisation Committee has no control over Belter policy, no control over Belter decision making and that is the way it should be. The Colonisation Committee can suggest, they can give advice, they can share information and they can share their data, but they cannot, however, tell you what to do. The Belter Colonies have their own agency and I intend to remind them of that."

Sone Dharma watched as the Ambassadorial Sendaran applauded Dag once more, he was on a roll.

"Order! Order", Harmony Dumas, nee Moon, shouted as she banged her gavel several times.

Dag brought up one final point of discussion, "Can anyone here tell me what you do with your radioactive waste?"

Sendaran, Mr Orris Delmar of Eunomia, replied curiously in a soft voice, "That's an odd sort of a question, Mr Talleyrand. Do you mind explaining why you need to know?"

"It has to do with the uranium phaseout, Orris. This whole phaseout is precisely because of the radioactive waste issue", Dag replied, noting, "On Earth, they have close to two and a half centuries worth of radioactive waste and they are now starting to deal with all of that accumulated waste."

"Precisely what does that entail, Mr Talleyrand? This dealing with waste?", Orris Delmar enquired.

"Well, Orris. The Cis-Lunar Space colonies have a storage facility on the far side of the Moon, at Mare Moscoviense. All of the radioactive waste from the Earth, the Venusian and Martian orbital zones is going to be transferred to that facility. Pretty much all of the radioactive waste from across the entire inner solar system", Dag explained.

Sendaran, Ms Selin Andorran of Euphrosyne, enquired, "To what end, Mr Talleyrand?"

"Once all of the inner system's radioactive waste is accumulated at that facility, specialised transport ships will be constructed to send that radioactive waste to its final destination", Dag informed her.

"And that final destination would be?", Selin Andorran queried.

"The Sun, Selin, the Sun!", Dag replied, explaining, "The ships carrying the radioactive waste will be placed into solar intercept orbits. The Sun will swallow the waste, lock, stock and barrel!"

"Which then brings us back to my original question, Mr Talleyrand", Orris Delmar commented.

"Well, Orris. If we are going to deal with all of the inner solar system's radioactive waste, then why not deal with all of the Belter's radioactive waste at the same time?", Dag explained.

Mr Orris Delmar enquired, "Is there are cost involved for this, this disposal service?"

"Not that I'm aware of, Orris. Your people would be responsible for delivering your radioactive waste to the facility at Mare Moscoviense. My understanding is that it then becomes Colonial Central Command's responsibility from that point on", Dag replied, adding, "Being that we are talking about radioactive waste, I would expect that all shipments would be registered and all necessary security procedures put in place."

Ms Selin Andorran chimed in, "We accumulate our radioactive waste into accumulated radioactive masses and place them into a solar orbit. Orbits that closely match the orbits of our home asteroids. We, too, have our own radioactive waste problems."

Dag was quiet for a few moments. Ms Andorran's revelation about how the Belters handled their radioactive waste was not what he expected. It bordered on pure recklessness.

"Ms Andorran, Selin. You do understand, don't you, that treating radioactive waste in such a cavalier fashion is a strategic liability?", Dag cautiously enquired.

Another Sendaran, Mr Ansel Zeffirelli of Vesta, concurred, with honesty, "Yes, Mr Talleyrand. We are well aware of our recklessness concerning how we handle our radioactive waste."

Ms Savanna Strafe, the Sendaran from Psyche, commented, "It isn't like we have a huge gas giant to just drop the radioactive stuff into like the Jovians or the Saturnians. We have far fewer options."

Dag nodded, "I understand, but this is a major problem. You literally have big balls of radioactive waste in co-orbit with your home asteroids and that is a major liability. We need to address this sooner rather than later. I recommend direct dialogue with Colonial Central Command on this issue. Dealing with that radioactive waste needs to be given a priority."

Mr Karl Dravik, the Sendaran from Bamberga, suggested, "Why don't we just throw it into the Sun? Colonial Central Command was planning to do that anyway."

Now that horrified Dag, who responded, "Mr Dravik, Karl! It is a far cry from transferring radioactive waste from one place to another via specialised space transports and hurling large masses of radioactive waste around the inner solar system, hoping that it finds its final target. Transport ships provide precisely targeted trajectories. Tossing balls of radioactive waste around is not recommended."

"Which is why we haven't done so in the past, Mr Talleyrand", Ms Andorran replied, while at the same time glaring at Mr Dravik for his ridiculous suggestion.

Belters, if anything, were supposed to be far more cautious and pragmatic by their very nature!

Sone Dharma stood up and chimed in, "That thirty-year timeline for the phasing out of uranium is also tied to the radioactive waste issue."

Dag nodded, he was appreciative of that reminder, "Sone is correct. The architects of the uranium phaseout envisaged that in thirty years, there would be no more fission power generation. That all power generation would be fusion-based. That all of the fission-based radioactive waste would be accumulated at Mare Moscoviense within that timeline. That is the point at which their final solution for the radioactive waste was to be implemented."

Harlequin Moon stood up and he remarked, "That means we still have a thirty-year deadline! We still need to cut over to fusion before that thirty years is up!"

"Not necessarily so, Mr Moon, Harley, but we do need to let the Colonisation Committee and Colonial Central Command know about the Three Irons Strategy. You may well be able to deliver your current radioactive waste to Mare Moscoviense in a timely fashion, however, it is likely you will still be producing atomic fission waste after that thirty-year deadline is up. Their 'Sun Dive' strategy might have to wait another decade or perhaps take into account 'straggler' waste", Dag explained.

Harlequin Moon nodded, "We need to dialogue with Colonial Central, sooner rather than later. I'm calling for a quick vote on this."

The motion was supported by two other Ambassadorial Sendaran and

Harmony Dumas, nee Moon, formalised the vote. The results also came back unanimous.

Harlequin Moon announced to the chamber, "I will personally put together a communique to Colonial Central Command as soon as this Thing has finished. I will, of course, copy in Dumas Colonial Legal to ensure that they are in the loop", and then he nodded to Daniel Dumas.

Sone Dharma stood up once more and commented, "Mr Moon, please copy in the Colonisation Committee and Security Council. Eros does not like to be left out of the loop. Going directly to Cis-Lunar L-Five and Colonial Central Command will be seen as going over their heads."

"And that would result in?", Harlequin Moon enquired.

"This is Dag's show. They'd hold Dag responsible and probably sack him", Sone replied.

"Hmm. Sone is correct. If we don't keep the Colonisation Committee and Security Council in the loop, they will see that as my failure and call for my scalp", Dag confirmed.

"Pish-tosh and poppy-cock!", Harlequin Moon exclaimed, and then he smiled, "If they sack you, Mr Talleyrand, I'll give you a job out here in our colonies. We are going to need someone to manage that Three Irons Strategy of yours, not to mention this radioactive waste management issue. How'd you like to wear those two hats? We would, of course, remunerate you appropriately."

"I might take you up on that offer, Harley. I am certainly having my own doubts about my current employers", Dag Talleyrand replied with a wry smile.

The Ambassadorial Sendaran all laughed, Dag's Belter assimilation was almost complete.

After the Thing ended, Sone Dharma stayed on at Ceres. She moved into her Ambassadorial Apartment in the northeastern end cap of the O'Neil-style twin cylinder colony named *"Eros can have it"*, with its low population and abundance of open spaces. Sone's belongings from her apartment at Eros were shipped to her in two shipping containers and delivered in quick order. Sone Dharma, the new Erosian Ambassador to the Belter Colonies. A collective of Sovereign Belter Nations, with a Non-Sovereign Supranational Assembly, the Althing.

Dag and his team returned to Eros. His bosses did not sack him. They needed him to finalise his reports and provide critical advice about the Belters, their cultural and political systems. The Belter political system was something that both the Colonisation Committee of Sol and the Security Council of Sol found unfathomably oxymoronic.

What the fuck is a Non-Sovereign Primate?

Dag had heard that question so many times.

How the hell can Ceres hold Primacy and yet be Non-Sovereign?

That was another one that kept coming up. Their confusion was never-ending.

Both the Colonisation Committee and Security Council tried to relate the Belter supranational political structure to that of the European Union, which currently embraced all European nations, excluding the United Kingdom, Turkey, Kazakhstan and Russia.

However, even though nations under the European Union were all sovereign, the European Union itself held primacy over their collective member states. It was itself quasi-sovereign and called the shots on many matters. Ceresian primacy was on the surface similar and yet completely non-sovereign. Ceres did not call the shots! Ceres was simply a part of the dialogue!

Five months after his return to Eros, Dag Talleyrand emailed in his letter of resignation, politely giving the Colonisation Committee one month's notice. Then, just after six months from the date he returned to Eros, Dag emigrated to the Ceresian colonies, taking up the head managerial positions for the Three Irons Strategy and the Radioactive Waste Disposal issue.

Dag's new apartment was large and spacious. It, too, was in the northeastern end cap of the Ceresian colony, *"Eros can have it"*. It was also in the same building as Sone's Ambassadorial apartment. Dag and Sone even became great friends, more than great friends in fact. They soon became a couple.

7. Outer Satellite Emissaries.

When Elaine Haynes, Jovian Minister for Health, arrived at the operations room, she found all of the other ministers waiting in the corridor outside. Both of the High Prince's Enforcers, Aurange Sheergibbon and Roberta Nummus, were guarding the door and not allowing anyone to enter the room.

Upon spotting Elaine, Roberta walked up to Elaine and took her by the arm. Roberta's grip, although strong, was remarkably gentle at the same time. Elaine was led to the operations room's door. Aurange Sheergibbon opened the door as they approached. Roberta led Elaine through the door. High Prince Albert von Horridian was seated upon his gold-gilded operations throne. The High Prince beckoned Elaine forward. Roberta Nummus remained inside the room, guarding the door.

"Ms Haynes. Roberta has told me something that I find hilarious", the High Prince informed her.

"Hilarious, Your Majesty?", Elaine asked in a low voice.

"Yes, Ms Haynes. Absolutely hilarious!", the High Prince reiterated, commenting, "As you are now Roberta's friend", he gestured to Roberta and Elaine's eyes followed his gesture, "Roberta tells me that she needed to take action to protect you from Aurange. As you are now Roberta's friend, Aurange might be triggered to, how do I put this?", then he just spat it out, "Rape you!"

Elaine had already discussed this with Roberta during their *"coffee date",* and she did her best to feign ignorance, "Your Majesty?", she replied questioningly.

The High Prince explained to Elaine some of his enforcer's history, "During their experimental training and conditioning, certain triggers were installed into both Aurange and Roberta. However, the genetic enhancement elixirs they were given had deleterious effects on them. It did create a certain degree, a high level, in fact, of psychopathy. That, in turn, affected not only the *'military'* triggers that were installed, but it created new, uncontrolled, psychopathic triggers. Multiple psychoses, in fact."

Elaine turned and looked at Roberta with both new understanding and deep compassion. Roberta remained unflinchingly impassive, not reacting in any way. Not to Elaine's gaze nor the High Prince's words. Roberta was the epitome of an enigma that was wrapped in a riddle. She was simple, yet complex, easily understood, yet unfathomable. Capable of great gentleness and yet equally capable of immense violence. Elaine smiled at Roberta before turning back to the High Prince.

When Elaine's gaze met the High Prince's once more, he noted, "We did not create Aurange and Roberta. When they fell into our laps all those decades ago, my Father merely adopted them. He gave them purpose. They have both been exceedingly useful ever since."

"Sire, you mentioned that Roberta had to take action?", Elaine cautiously enquired.

"Yes, yes, Elaine. Roberta had to make you unattractive to Aurange. She had to *'turn off'* one of Aurange's triggers", the High Prince replied, he was smiling and most certainly amused by it.

"Your Majesty?", Elaine questioned, again feigning ignorance, "How did Roberta *'turn off'* one of Aurange's triggers?"

High Prince Albert smiled, then he chuckled to himself before replying, "Roberta told Aurange that you were a lesbian. Isn't that hilarious? Aurange is turned off by lesbians!", he laughed.

Elaine feigned looking surprised, she glanced at Roberta once more, before replying, "Yes, yes, Your Majesty. Absolutely hilarious", she lied.

Elaine had had this conversation with Roberta on their *"coffee date"*. It was a necessary ruse, a very necessary one. It also ran a very fine line because it was also very true!

"Sire, Roberta and Aurange communicate using text messages. Is that their only way to communicate with us?", Elaine enquired, wondering if that was truly the case.

"They are conditioned not to speak, Ms Haynes. So to communicate with us, they must use technology. Messaging is just one technological method they use. They even have their own personal sign language, it is so subtle", the High Prince confirmed, noting, "Although, in over six decades, I have actually heard them speak. Only the once and that was at my coronation."

"Thank you for that confirmation, Your Majesty", Elaine replied, then enquired, "Roberta's messages disappeared after they'd been read, as if they'd never even existed. I did not know that was even possible, Your Majesty."

The High Prince frowned, "It isn't, Ms Haynes. My experts tell me that it isn't possible. That there are always logs, always traces and metadata left behind after a message or email deletion. And yet, Aurange and Roberta simply do what I have been told is impossible. It is one of their mysteries."

Elaine glanced at Roberta once more, then she looked back at the High Prince and nodded.

"Now, Ms Haynes. Please take your seat and Roberta will let the other ministers in", the High Prince commanded.

Roberta opened the operations room door and nodded to Aurange before she turned and walked quickly to the other side of the room. Roberta stationed herself at the left-hand side of the High Prince's throne. Aurange then entered the operations room and took up his position, precisely where Roberta had been stationed. Only then did Aurange allow the ministers to enter the operations room.

The High Prince's enforcers were, as usual, heavily armed with weapons overtly visible and others unseen. Their laser pulse pistols and sabres at their sides, kukri swords sheathed on their belts behind their backs and high-powered, rapid-fire pulse laser rifles hung on straps around their necks, held firmly in their grip. Roberta's katana was sheathed and strapped across her back. The mere presence of the High Prince's enforcers had more impact on the room than the High Prince himself.

As all of the ministers filed into the operations room, during the confusion as they made their way to their seats, Roberta glanced at Elaine, caught her eye, smiled and winked. It was quick, perfectly timed and the High Prince had not seen nor noticed. Aurange had not seen or noticed. Nobody had, except for Elaine. It was at that point that Elaine realised that everything that had taken place since she had entered the operations room had been manipulated and orchestrated by Roberta herself.

Roberta Nummus was the High Prince's left-hand of darkness and Aurange Sheergibbon was the High Prince's right hand and roving sword of retribution, but who, who really was in charge of the Jovian Realms?

"My Ministers", High Prince Albert greeted, then asked, "The emissaries from Eros. When are we expecting them to arrive? Surely they must be close?"

Foreign Affairs Minister, Mr Tarant Durant, replied, "Sire, the Erosian emissaries should be here in seven or eight days."

Science Minister, Mr Peter Patronis added, "I'm not so sure we need them, Your Majesty. They have sent us the technical specifications and the blueprints for their new fusion reactors. Our scientists and engineers are across them and they assure me that we can manufacture these fusion reactors ourselves. We don't really need their help, Sire."

Mr Tarant Durant added, "Your Majesty, they are just coming to wave their Colonisation Committee and Security Council flags. As Minister Patronis has stated, we have their blueprints. We also have their documents explaining the entirety of their fission reactor phaseout. I agree with Mr Patronis, we simply don't need them, Sire."

Defence Minister, Mr Peter Macron chimed in, "Your Majesty, we could just blow them into cosmic dust. Accidents happen in deep space all the time, Sire."

"No, Minister Macron. We need them to come here first and then leave for the Saturnian Demarchy safely. What happens to them after they leave, on the second leg of their journey in deep space, is another matter entirely", High Prince Albert informed his ministers.

"You have something in mind, Your Majesty?", Security Minister Miles Morton enquired.

The High Prince glanced at Roberta Nummus, then he glanced at Aurange

Sheergibbon, before confirming, "Yes, Minister Morton. You could say that."

"On another matter, if I may, Your Majesty", Commerce Minister, Mr Devlin Dervish requested.

"Yes, Minister Dervish. You may", the High Prince allowed.

Commerce Minister Dervish nodded and commented, "Our Belter initiative has not succeeded, Sire. The Belters have cancelled all of their contracts for our Trojan Realms processed regolith exports."

"Hmm, so they were quickly on top of the Black Blight, were they?", High Prince Albert enquired.

"Yes, Sire", Mr Devlin Dervish confirmed, adding, "We managed to infest only two colonies, Sire."

"How unfortunate. I was hoping to wreak havoc with their food production. Make them dependent on food aid from us", High Prince Albert noted dryly, adding, "It seems they got on top of things far too quickly and identified the source of infestation far quicker than we thought."

"Yes, Your Majesty. That does appear to be the case", Mr Dervish agreed.

"So, we won't be getting those contracts back then?", the High Prince enquired.

"No, Sire. They sent us the following, *'Once bitten, twice shy, twice bitten, contracts cancelled'*. I think they've seen straight through us, Sire", Mr Dervish admitted.

The Minister for Agriculture, Mr Mauricio Velly, chimed in, "Your Majesty, that also means we won't be getting those lucrative grain contracts either. If the Belters can't trust our regolith, they certainly won't trust our food produce either."

Communications Minister Albrecht Dire quickly commented, "Our communications intercepts inform us that the Belters are going to source their processed regolith internally and from Martian exports, Sire."

"Martian exports?", the High Prince questioned.

"From Mars Trojan Mining Ltd, Your Majesty. They are now exporting processed regolith", Commerce Minister Dervish explained.

"Hmm, so our plan was found out far too quickly and now we've lost some very lucrative processed regolith contracts. It appears the Dumas's have stuck their noses into our business yet again!", High Prince Albert noted, adding, "Well then, we won't be leveraging food aid over Belters any time soon."

The ministers remained quiet at that point, allowing the High Prince the last word on the matter.

The ambassadorial space vessel, Sleek Runner, was still ten million kilometres out from Jupiter and its destination, Ganymede Prime at Ganymede L-Five. The ship was long and sleek, with its hull skinned in silver, it was bright and easily detected. The Sleek Runner was chosen for this task because it was the fastest interplanetary ship in the Colonisation Committee of Sol's Ambassadorial fleet.

An image of Ganymede Prime came up in a window on the ship's bridge main screen, the ship's scanners showing the mega cylinder colony in great detail.

Ambassadorial Emissary, Ms Sonia de la Cruz, enquired, "How big is that thing?"

Captain Thames Barker checked his data feed, "It's easily as big as Colonial Central Command. Twenty four kilometres long with a main cylinder diameter of four kilometres. The same basic design, just much, much thicker radiation shielding."

Helmsman, Douglas Damson chimed in, "I'm detecting another three mega colonies, Captain. Their pings come back as Callisto Prime, Europa Prime and Io Prime. And they are all just as big."

"Io Prime?", Captain Barker asked rhetorically, "Jupiter's radiation belts in that orbital zone are ridiculously intense!", he exclaimed

"Yes, Sir", Helmsman Damson confirmed, "I'm also detecting another, smaller, mega colony in Amalthea's orbital zone as well. Amalthea Prime, according to our ping data."

Captain Barker turned to his Helmsmen, "Are you sure? That's a hell of a lot closer to Jupiter than even Io Prime."

"Confirmed, Captain, confirmed", the Helmsman replied.

A perplexed Helmsman, Douglas Damson, asked, "How are they surviving? Do they have Slayers and Eramis technology?"

Captain Barker checked his data feeds, "They have both Slayers and Eramis technology. Generation one. Although I must be honest. Where the hell did they get that from?"

Emissary, Ms Sonia de la Cruz, frowned, "They stole it. Nearly seventy years ago."

"Stole it?", the Captain questioned.

"Yes, Captain. They stole it", Sonia de la Cruz confirmed and then noted, "They stole the technology from Dumas Incorporated's research and development division. If I remember correctly, they murdered twelve people in the process."

"And that's where I'm taking you?", Captain Barker asked incredulously.

"Sadly, yes, Captain", Sonia de la Cruz confirmed, explaining dryly, "The Horridian Corporation fled to the Jovian Republic in disgrace. They changed their surname to 'von Horridian', a small change, yes, but it was enough to obscure their identity. Albertus Horridian took over the Jovian Republic and then his Son, Albert, took over from him. Albert consolidated his power and then disbanded the Jovian Republic, replacing it with his Jovian Realms, self-styling himself as *'High Prince Albert von Horridian'*. A farce, yes, I know, but we still have to deal with him nonetheless."

The young Diplomatic Intern, Miss Lina Mitchel, had been standing in the bridge's doorway, "What are the Slayers and Eramis technologies?", she enquired.

Helmsman, Douglas Damson, explained, "SlaReS, Stackable Layered Radiation Shield Plating and E-RaMiS, Electromagnetic Radiation Mitigation System. It's radiation shielding and mitigation. The Jovians have the first generation of the technology. Our ship, the Sleek Runner, has the sixth generation of the same technology. Our shielding is far more effective and much thinner."

Captain Barker noted dryly, "Which is why their radiation shielding is so incredibly thick. It's the first generation and having stolen it, they weren't capable of improving upon it."

Emissary, Ms Sonia de la Cruz, frowned once more, "Captain, we don't want them stealing any technology from this ship. Keep an eye on any of their personnel who come too close to the ship."

"That is a given, Ambassador", Captain Barker agreed, adding, "My crew will stay close to the ship at all times and we will triple-check the fuel and supplies they provide as well. Make sure everything is kosher, so to speak."

"Make sure you do", Ms Sonia de la Cruz agreed, noting, "We sent them everything in advance, so I don't expect we'll stay here long. Maybe just a few days if I can get away with it."

The Captain nodded in agreement. No one trusted the Horridians.

The Sleek Runner was directed to dock at Ganymede Prime's northern end cap docking ring. Captain Barker had wanted to dock at an external docking port, instead, Ganymede Prime's flight controllers directed them to an internal docking port.

"Negatory on that Ganymede Prime flight control, the Sleek Runner is just a tad too large for your internal docking ports. Please redirect us to an external docking port. One that allows for ventral docking with both crew airlock and cargo docking facilities", Captain Barker lied convincingly.

"Understood, Sleek Runner, Captain Barker, please proceed to external docking port six", the Ganymede Prime flight controller redirected.

"Thank you, Ganymede Prime flight control. Sleek Runner is on approach to external docking port six", Captain Barker confirmed.

"An external docking port?", Ms Sonia de la Cruz enquired.

"They can't easily approach and study the Sleek Runner if she's surrounded by a vacuum. Especially in the radiation-rich environment around Ganymede

Prime", Captain Barker explained, noting, "In an internal docking bay, they'd be able to walk straight up and sample the hull directly. That is not something either of us wants."

"Agree, Captain, agreed", Ms Sonia de la Cruz responded.

As soon as the Sleek Runner had docked at external docking port six, Captain Barker organised fuel and supplies for the next leg of their journey to the Saturnian Demarchy. Captain Barker ordered his crew to check the fuel quality and all of the supplies as they were being loaded through the docking port's secondary cargo umbilicus. They maintained the strictest of security while the resupplying of the Sleek Runner was taking place.

High Prince Albert had commanded Elaine Haynes to escort Ambassadorial Emissary Sonia de la Cruz and her team to their first meeting. Ms Haynes was chosen because she was the only female minister in the High Prince's court. Something the High Prince thought would keep them at ease.

Ms Sonia de la Cruz's team consisted of just three others, her Diplomatic Secretary, Ms Gena Richter, her Diplomatic Aide, Mr Goren Zither and her Diplomatic Intern, a young Miss Lina Mitchel, who was quite young, at only sixteen years of age.

The meeting place was actually in High Prince Albert von Horridian's throne room. High Prince Albert sat on his ornate, gold-gilded throne, wearing his finest regal uniform. In front of the throne and to the left was a desk, at which some of the High Prince's ministers sat.

Foreign Affairs Minister, Mr Tarant Durant, Defence Minister, Mr Peter Macron, Security Minister, Mr Miles Morton, and Science Minister, Mr Peter Patronis. There was an empty chair with the name plaque, Health Minister and Hostess, Ms Elaine Haynes. In front of the throne and to the right was a second desk with five seats. One for Emissary Ms Sonia de la Cruz and one for each member of her team. There was also one extra seat at the table.

As Elaine led Sonia and her team to their desk, Sonia took in the throne room and the seating arrangements. Only the ministers who were required for the discussions about the phase-out of uranium fission power generation were present. There was an extra seat at their own desk. Perhaps they thought that the Sleek Runner's Captain would be present.

Sonia looked at the High Prince. Apart from sitting on his throne, Albert looked so much like the photographs of his Father, Albertus, who had passed away in twenty one sixty seven. The High Prince was a man of average height, his hair was grey and short-cropped. Albert looked to be about seventy five years of age. It was known that Albert had four sons, none of whom were present.

There were two other people that Sonia recognised from both their reputation, their dossiers and their wanted posters. Aurange Sheergibbon and Roberta Nummus. It was quite the surprise. Their wanted posters were from more than six and a half decades ago and yet, neither of them had aged at all!

Aurange Sheergibbon and Roberta Nummus were both heavily armed, pulse laser pistols, heavy pulse laser rifles, knives, at least two swords and that was just what Sonia could see. No doubt they had more weapons that were not so easily seen, hidden about their person.

Sonia and her team took to their seats, as Elaine crossed the floor to her desk and her own seat.

Before the High Prince could even open the meeting, Emissary Sonia de la Cruz stood and boldly addressed High Prince Albert, "Mr Horridian, we all know you are not a Prince, High or otherwise. I have no interest in your theatrics. I am only here to ensure that you and your people fully comprehend the uranium fission power generation phaseout and how it affects your so-called Jovian Realms", she paused momentarily, then continued, "I should also like to point out that your two bodyguards are both wanted felons. Murderers in fact!"
Surprised gasps arose from the ministers sitting at the other desk.

Roberta Nummus gave an almost imperceptible wink to Elaine Haynes, as if to say, yeah, that's us.

The High Prince raised his right hand to silence his ministers and then he replied, chuckling, "It seems, Ms Sonia de la Cruz, that you have more balls than any single one of my ministers. Except perhaps, Elaine. I like Elaine, she is ballsy", then he paused, "As an outsider to my Jovian Realms, you have no requirement to treat me as Princely, although, I will point out, my subjects do", reinforcing that to his ministers with a single glaring look.

High Prince Albert continued, "I admit that my bodyguards are indeed wanted felons and murderers. However, I will also point out that my bodyguards are also under Jovian jurisdiction and protection."

During the High Prince's reply, neither Aurange nor Roberta showed any overt signs of noticing.

"How is it that neither of them has aged?", Ms Sonia de la Cruz asked.

High Prince Albert laughed, "Don't ask me! Ask your Colonial Armed Forces. They created them. Suffice it to say, they simply do not age! At least not in the way that we do."

Ms Sonia de la Cruz was shocked, *"What were the Colonial Armed Forces hiding?"*, she asked herself and more importantly, *"How did the Horridians acquire them?"*

These two internal questions were largely irrelevant for the purposes of Ms de la Cruz's mission.

The High Prince then took control of the discussion, "Well then, Emissary, you are here to discuss the phasing out of uranium fission-based power generation, so I suggest that we all get on with it."

"Yes, Mr Horridian. Let's get down to brass tacks, shall we?", the Erosian Emissary, Ms Sonia de la Cruz, agreed.

High Prince Albert von Horridian then nodded to his ministers to begin discussions.

Minister for Science, Mr Peter Patronis, kicked off, "Ms de la Cruz, our scientists and engineers have studied the new fusion reactor blueprints and specifications that were provided to us in great detail. They are impressive, or so I am told. I have also been told that our engineers are fully across them, that we should be able to build these new reactors without any trouble at all."

Foreign Affairs Minister, Mr Tarant Durant, chimed in, "Yes. Our people have also studied all of the other documentation that has been provided. We have a good understanding of the uranium fission-based phaseout as well."

Finally, Security Minister, Miles Morton, chimed in, "Which makes us wonder. Why are you here at all? We could easily move forward with building and rolling out fusion reactors for our power generation without your help."

"Well then, Ministers. If that is the case, then our only purpose in being here is a polite, friendly discussion or two and the resupplying of our ship for transit to the Saturnian Demarchy. If your people are already across everything, our meetings should proceed very quickly", Erosian Emissary, Ms Sonia de la Cruz replied.

As the discussion began, one of Sonia's team members, her Diplomatic Aid, Mr Goren Zither, happened to glance at Roberta Nummus. Goren's eyes lingered just a little too long on Roberta's chest. Roberta's right hand reached behind her back and grabbed her kukri sword by its hilt, then she unclipped its catch with her thumb and her right foot stepped forward.

Roberta was triggered!

Goren Zither was about to die!

Elaine Haynes stood up from her seat and walked across the throne room to Sonia de la Cruz's team.

As Elaine did so, she looked directly into Roberta's eyes and mouthed the words, *"No!"*.

Roberta Nummus froze mid-trigger! Roberta began blinking, her mind in complete turmoil.

Elaine whispered into Goren's ear, "Do not stare at Roberta's chest. It's one of her psychopathy triggers. It can get you killed!", then she got back up and returned to her own seat.

Goren Zither gulped audibly.

The High Prince turned to his left and looked at Roberta, realised what was happening and commanded, "Roberta! Stand down!"

Roberta's thumb reengaged her kukri sword's catch, removed her hand from its hilt, moved her foot back into place and stood to attention once more.

Sonia de la Cruz enquired, "What just happened?"

The High Prince smiled and replied, trying to hide his embarrassment, "It is best not to stare at my bodyguards. They are both... Sensitive. Better yet, don't even look at them."

High Prince Albert then turned to look at Elaine Haynes, "Thank you, Elaine. You were right to act."

Emissary, Sonia de la Cruz suggested, "Perhaps, Mr Horridian, we should adjourn for the day and meet again tomorrow at the same time. During the interval, I can better prepare my staff", she glared at Goren, then continued, "And perhaps, your ministers can ask their people if they have any questions or points of discussion for tomorrow. Anything that we might be able to clarify while we are here."

"Yes, Ms de la Cruz, yes. A great suggestion. I'll talk to my bodyguards about their sensitivities and how they react to perceived infractions", High Prince Albert replied.

The meeting then broke up to be continued the next day.

As they walked out of the throne room, Sonia spoke to her Diplomatic Secretary, Gena Richter, "Find out what you can about Roberta Nummus!"

Several hours later, Gena Richter, Diplomatic Secretary, passed her data tablet to Sonia, who began reading the information it contained on both Roberta Nummus and Aurange Sheergibbon.

Gena highlighted, "Our own defence forces created them. Something went horribly wrong and they both became psychotic. They were then contained for safety and security reasons. Of course, they escaped. There were originally twenty four of them. Aurange Sheergibbon and Roberta Nummus are the last two that are still alive."

As Sonia flicked through the data, she asked, "What happened to the other twenty two?"

Gena hesitated, then replied, "Aurange and Roberta slaughtered them, along with a lot of other personnel. Hundreds of personnel. They are really dangerous.

The details are a bit further down."

After several minutes, Sonia passed the data tablet back to Gina, her eyes wide in shock, "Those two are walking time bombs. How the hell did the Horridians get hold of them?"

"That is unknown, Ma'am", Gena replied.

The Captain entered the room with Elaine Haynes in tow, "This one came to talk to you", he stated.

"Yes, Ms Haynes. What do you want to discuss?", Sonia enquired.

"Roberta Nummus", Elaine replied, then she informed her, "Roberta is my friend. I understand her to some degree. At least more than most people do."

"How the hell did you end up with a psychopathic murderer for a friend, Ms Hayes?", Sonia asked incredulously.

Elaine was blunt and straight to the point, "Survival, Ms de la Cruz, survival. Roberta protects her friends and she slaughters her enemies. There is no middle ground. None whatsoever."

"So you made friends with a psychopath for protection?", Sonia was completely incredulous.

Elaine put up her hands and began explaining, "Neither Roberta Nummus nor Aurange Sheergibbon were born the way they are. They were both made into killing machines, made into monsters. The Horridians didn't do that, your people did! When you are around them every day, like I am, then understanding them means survival. Being Roberta's friend keeps me from dying."

"Okay, okay, understood. So what advice do you have for me?", Sonia asked.

"Tomorrow, leave Goren Zither on your ship. Women don't trigger Roberta, men do. Mr Zither nearly died today. Roberta would have taken his head. So, heed my words and leave him behind", Elaine explained and then she asked, "How old is your Intern?"

"Lina? She's almost seventeen, still a teenager. Why?", Sophia queried.

"Lina's still a teenager, still a child. I'll tell Roberta that. It will help protect her", Elaine told her, explaining, "I don't think Roberta would kill a child, even if ordered to do so. Oddly, for all of her psychoses, Roberta can actually be quite sweet."

"Okay then, Ms Haynes. Tomorrow, I'll leave Goren with the ship", Sonia replied, then as Elaine turned around to leave the ship, she asked, "Who was the extra seat for?"

"We thought your ship's Captain was going to be at the meeting", Elaine replied as she left.

The meeting the following day had only three representatives from Eros, the Diplomatic Aide, Mr Goren Zither, having been told to remain on their ship, the Sleek Runner.

Upon entering the throne room, Sonia de la Cruz walked up to Roberta Nummus, stood before her and stated clearly, "I instructed Mr Zither to remain on our ship, so as not to upset your sensitivities."

Roberta's eyes gazed upon Sonia and she nodded ever so imperceptibly, thinking to herself, *"I like this one. I hope the High Prince does not order me to kill her."*

Sonia then turned about and sat in her seat with the rest of her team.

The discussion that followed was not what Sonia and her team had expected. Science Minister Peter Patronis had spoken with his chief engineers and scientists. They had all informed him that they understood the fusion reactor blueprints and specifications and that they could have a working prototype ready in under three months.

"Three months, Mr Patronis?", Sonia enquired, "That does sound ridiculously fast."

"Ms de la Cruz, we started work on our prototype before you even left Eros", Peter Patronis responded, noting, "Our construction facilities at Ganymede L-Four are first class. When we finally scale up production, we'll churn out fusion reactors much faster."

Foreign Affairs Minister, Tarant Durant asked, "Ms de la Cruz, how long did it take to construct Colonial Central Command?"

"Close to twenty years or so, I believe, Mr Durant", Sonia replied.

"Yes, well, we here in the Jovian Realms have built equivalent mega colonies. One Prime every five years over that same period of time", Tarant replied, adding, "Never underestimate our capabilities."

"Yes, that is impressive, Mr Durant. We saw those Primes on our approach. Very impressive", Sonia had to admit, simply because it was.

The remainder of the meeting was full of questions, but not the sort of questions that Sonia was expecting. The Ministers wanted to know why now.
Why was uranium fission power generation being phased out now?
Sonia had explained how nearly two hundred and fifty years of radioactive waste had built up. The radioactive waste had to be dealt with once and for all. The Earth's government was phasing out both uranium mining and uranium fuel rod production and exports. The Earth had already completed its phaseout and the phaseout was being replicated across the entire inner solar system. Upon completion, all of the colonies would have energy independence via fusion-based power generation.

The Minister for Commerce, Devlin Dervish, noted, "Energy independence. Yes, that is desirable, Ms de la Cruz. We do have abundant reserves of hydrogen. Dare I say it, we will achieve energy independence well ahead of the inner solar system."

"That is good to hear, Mr Dervish", Sonia was happy to hear that, it was what they'd wanted, the Jovian Realms were on board with the uranium phaseout and cutting across to fusion power generation.

Sonia's Diplomatic Secretary, Ms Gena Richter, commented, "We weren't aware of your technical prowess, Mr Dervish. We had thought your people would have far more questions."

"Ms Richter, when our High Prince and his Father had commissioned the building of the Primes, we had a large influx of highly skilled immigrants from the inner solar system", Devlin Dervish explained, noting, "We already had a skilled workforce to begin with. The new immigrants brought with them even more skills and our capabilities quickly expanded."

High Prince Albert chimed in, "Back then, I was merely the President. It turned out that building our mega colonies, the Primes, was exceedingly popular."

"Yes, Your Majesty. So much so that we requested that you be our High Prince", Defence Minister, Peter Macron lied.

Security Minister, Miles Morton, chimed in and piled on more lies, ingratiating himself, "It was most gracious of His Royal Majesty to accept our request."

"Yes, it was", High Prince Albert agreed, his ego knew no bounds.

At the end of the mission, Sonia and her team returned to their ship, the Sleek Runner. It has been decided that, as the Jovians were across all aspects of the uranium phaseout, there was no need for any further meetings. Captain Barker had organised refuelling and resupply of all of the ship's stores and they could be on their way at any time that they wished.

"Ms de la Cruz, Ma'am. The fuel they provided was of top quality. No funny business going on that we can detect", Captain Barker had assured her.

Helmsmen, Douglas Damson chime in with, "Our crew has triple-checked all of the other supplies as well. It's all kosher. No surprises. Everything is of top quality. It is, as Captain Barker stated, no funny business going on that we can detect."

"Good then. Notify Mr Horridian that we will be departing before the day is out", Sonia instructed, refusing to call Albert the High Prince, she added, "Make preparations for the next leg of our journey, the Saturnian Demarchy. I want us all out of here and on our way!"

While they'd been docked, no one had expected anyone to approach the outside of the Sleek Runner. After all, she was docked at an external docking port. The Sleek Runner was in the vacuum of space, within Ganymede's orbital zone at Ganymede L-five and the radiation outside of the mega colony and the ship was quite deadly.

Aurange Sheergibbon had put on his space suit, with its enhanced radiation shielding. Then, he had gone for a simple space walk. Aurange exited Ganymede Prime at an airlock that was close to external docking port six. Aurange's mag-boots activated, he casually strolled over to the Sleek Runner, approaching it from the rear.

Aurange carefully tampered with the Sleek Runner's rear scanner array, reprogramming the array to go into a loop when it was fifty million kilometres out from Jupiter. Should any ship approach the Sleek Runner from the rear, it would not be detected.

Next, Aurange strolled over to the Sleek Runner's ventral airlock system. The very airlock through which Sonia's team had accessed Ganymede Prime. Aurange tampered with the airlock's security systems, reprogramming them to recognise his own ship, the Dark Angel, as not a security threat. Indeed, the changes Aurange put in place meant that there would be zero notifications should the Dark Angel dock.

Aurange was not quite finished, so he next moved over to the Sleek Runner's ventral cargo dock. Aurange made adjustments to the cargo dock's security. When Aurange had finished, he'd programmed the Sleek Runner's cargo dock to allow his ship, the Dark Angel, to use it as a stable connectivity point. The Dark Angel would be able to connect to the Sleek Runner and travel beneath her undetected.

Aurange smiled at his handy work and casually strolled back to the airlock from whence he'd exited Ganymede Prime. His task was completed.

8. Provocations.

As the Sleek Runner flew swiftly on its way to the Saturnian Demarchy, Ms Sonia de la Cruz made a detailed report to Eros, with a copy sent to Colonial Central Comment at Cis-Lunar L-Five.

Sonia's report detailed how the Jovians were moving ahead with the crossover to fusion-based power generation systems. Eros was informed that the Jovians had started work on their first prototype reactor even before she, herself, had left Eros.

Sonia had also noted how the Jovian ministers had very few, if any, real questions and that they had stated that they were across every aspect of the uranium fission reactor phaseout. The Jovians seemed completely unconcerned and her team had only had two meetings with them before departing on the second leg of their journey to the Saturnian Demarchy.

On a darker note, Sonia had informed the Security Council and the Colonisation Committee, both situated at Eros and Colonial Central Command at Cis-Lunar L-Five, that the two fugitives, Aurange Sheergibbon and Roberta Nummus, were indeed in the Jovian Realms.

Sonia informed them all that self-declared High Prince Albert von Horridian was using them as bodyguards. This was added confirmation that the pair were responsible for the theft of the Dumas Incorporated Slayers and Eramis technologies and the murders of twelve Dumas personnel. Sonia also provided further information about their lack of ageing and their apparent psychoses.

As Sonia transmitted her report, she instructed Captain Barker to send daily progress and status reports to Eros. Even if there was nothing to report, except to say that all was well. Captain Barker agreed and also included the ship's telemetry data, along with crew and passenger health.

It was one week after the Sleek Runner, with its crew of ten and its four diplomatic passengers, had left Ganymede Prime on the second leg of their journey to the Saturnian Demarchy. Communications Minister, Albrecht Dire, showed High Prince Albert the video to be released into the external news feeds across the entire solar system. The same video had been played across the internal Jovian new networks one year earlier, over and over, for a full week. This would be the very first time that it was to be released externally.

"Have you altered the metadata?", the High Prince enquired.

"Yes, of course, Your Majesty", Albrecht Dire confirmed, smiling as he noted, "It will look like it happened just yesterday, Sire."

High Prince Albert smiled, "Beautiful. This is just what we need."

It was the year twenty one seventy seven and High Prince Albert had just been proclaimed High Prince of the six Jovian Realms. Two operatives of the Council of Shadows had jaunted from Earth to Ganymede Prince to observe the rapidly devolving situation after the fall of the Jovian Republic and the rise of the feudal principalities, the six Jovian Realms. The Council of Shadows was a covert, occult organisation within the Earth's Psi Corps. Even Psi Corps itself had no idea that they existed. The Council of Shadows were the shadowy, silent watchers who watched over the Psi Corps.

Tina and her Cousin, David, jaunted into existence in a quiet part of the northern end cap of Ganymede Prime. They had been here many times before, but this time, things had changed. The pair were to blink into the High Prince's palace grounds, under the cover of their psychic obscuration fields and observe what was happening. The Council of Shadows required further information before any decision could be made on what action to take.

Tina and David blinked into the palace grounds completely unseen, their psychic obscuration fields in place and working perfectly, or that is what they thought. The new High Prince was a paranoid man and he employed Doberman Pinscher guard dogs as part of his security. Doberman Pinschers, all dogs in general, could see straight through any psychic obscuration field. Psychic obscuration fields only worked with fully sapient beings.

Within minutes of their arrival, both Tina and David were set upon by four Dobermans. They were knocked to the ground and mauled savagely by the dogs. Their psychic obscuration fields dropped immediately under the onslaught of jaws and fangs. Minutes later, six security guards joined the attack, while four dog handlers dragged off the Dobermans. Tina and David had been badly mauled, savaged and now they were being severely beaten by security guards with batons and steel-capped boots. It was not long before they were both beaten unconscious and lay limp on the ground in severely bruised and bloodied messes. They were almost unrecognisable.

The High Prince's paranoia had other aspects. In another section of his palace grounds, a gallows had been built. High Prince Albert had expected pushback against his coronation and he fully intended to publicly hang people five at a time from his gallows. He even had the cameras all set up and ready to roll. There were to be no trials, no jurisprudence, these were to be extrajudicial executions.

Tina and David were both dragged unconscious to the gallows. A guard on either side of them was holding them upright. They stood there unconscious in hooded robes of shimmering black like the feathers of a raven, now all bloodied, torn and ragged. Their faces were almost unrecognisable, beaten, bruised and bloodied beyond recognition.

Executioners placed the rope nooses around their necks and placed the knots to the side of their necks, so that their necks would snap when they dropped. Then the executioners took up their positions, while two guards snapped vials of smelling salts under their noses.

Tina and David both snapped into consciousness, not knowing where they were or what had happened to them. Their brains were addled with pain and confusion. Then, just as they realised what was happening, they dropped to their deaths, their necks snapping with audible cracks!

The entire scene at the top of the gallows and the finality of the pair swinging below it, captured in high-definition video! Complete with that sick, audible cracking sound as their necks snapped. The entire episode from the moment Tina and David had been attacked by the Dobermans had also been videoed by multiple palace garden security cameras. Ironically, that was the only time that the gallows were actually ever used and the people executed, were just there to observe!

The old spin was that Psi Corps had sent assassins to murder the new High Prince. The assassins were sorcerers or demons in human form. The Earth and Cis-Lunar L-Five were implicated by association. Their execution and the spin were originally for internal Jovian consumption.

That was in twenty one seventy seven, it was now a little over a year later in the year twenty one seventy eight. The new spin was that the assassins were there to murder the High Prince. That had not changed. They were still labelled as sorcerers or demons. That had not changed. Now, however, it was stated that the assassins were delivered to the Jovian Realms and to Ganymede Prime by the ambassadorial ship, the Sleek Runner. That the assassins had been delivered by the Ambassadorial Emissary, Ms Sonia de la Cruz, herself!

The allegations were that the Psi Corps, the Earth's Government, the Government of Cis-Lunar Space at Colonial Central Command at Cis-Lunar L-five, and even the Colonisation Committee of Sol and the Security Council of Sol, both situated at Eros, were all implicated. That it was an inner solar system conspiracy to murder the High Prince of the Jovian Realms and, by implication, an attack on the entire outer solar system, the outer satellites.

That was the new spin!

Captain Thames Barker and Ambassadorial Emissary Sonia de la Cruz watched the video for the second time. It has been sent to them from Eros, from the Colonisation Committee of Sol.

Sonia read the message that came with it for the third time, *"The Jovians have released this video into our networks. It depicts an alleged assassination attempt on High Prince Albert and their response. Note: They are saying that the assassins were delivered to Ganymede Prime on your ambassadorial transport ship, the Sleek Runner. That this was an attempt, a conspiracy, by the Earth, Cis-Lunar L-Five and Eros to assassinate their High Prince."*

"Captain, send the following reply, *'The alleged attempted assassination, as you are all well aware, had nothing to do with us. The ship's crew complement of ten and its four passengers, my team, arrived at Ganymede Prime alone and left Ganymede Prime alone. We stayed for only two days. Just long enough for two meetings and the ship's resupply. We had a feeling that they were up to something, however, we did not know what. Now we know'.* Send that message straight away and Captain, don't let young Lina have access to this. I don't want her seeing something that violent", Sonia de la Cruz instructed the Captain.

Adjutant Colonel John Johnson led Lord Folcrom Seamus and Lady Folcrom Larissa into General Maxwell Beckonwolf's office. The matter had been deemed urgent, so urgent that Seamus and Larissa had been flown in all the way from the Flinders Island Psychic Academy on Flinders Island, near Tasmania in Australia, to Los Angeles on the east coast of the United States. Seamus and Larissa were shown to their seats.

"Thank you both for coming, Lord Seamus, Lady Larissa. You've probably already seen the video I'm about to show you on the news feeds. What I'm about to show you is the full unedited version.", the General greeted them.

"Direct and straight to the point. I like that, General", Seamus remarked.

"General, please call us Seamus and Larissa. Our titles are not required here", Larissa advised.

"As you wish, Lady Larissa", the General replied, then ordered, "Colonel, play that video clip."

The video clip played in all of its brutality. Two people, a man and a woman, dressed in black shimmering hooded robes, were being mauled by savage Dobermans. The same couple was then beaten within an inch of their lives by Jovian palace guards. The same couple was then dragged unconscious to a gallows and while still unconscious, had nooses placed around their necks. Then the smelling salts, their regaining of consciousness, their sudden comprehension, the quick drop to their deaths and the audible snapping of their necks. Larissa gasped in horror. Seamus stared wide-eyed and angry.

As both Folcrom turned to the General, he explained to them, "The Jovians are saying that those two were sorcerers or demons sent by Psi Corps on an Erosian Diplomatic vessel to assassinate their High Prince", then he asked, "What is your take on the matter?"

"We have both seen the news feeds, General. Heavily redacted as they were and we are fully aware of the allegations by the Jovians. This is all over the news feeds after all", Seamus replied.

"Yes, Seamus, but what were two of your Psi Corps operatives doing on Ganymede Prime?", the General asked, he was looking for answers.

"The quick answer, General. They weren't Psi Corps operatives", Seamus replied.

"And the long answer?", the General asked.

Larissa chimed in, "When we first saw that video and the allegations, General, we immediately checked our data. The whereabouts of every Psi Corps member, globally", she informed him.

"And the results?", General Beckonwolf enquired.

Seamus chimed in, "Every Psi Corps member is accounted for, General. Whoever that pair was, they were not Psi Corps members."

"And you can be certain of that, how, Seamus?", the General asked, he needed to be certain.

"General, it is very rare for psychics to go off-world. Very rare", Seamus informed him, explaining, "When a psychic goes off-world, they lose all of their gifts, their abilities. A psychic off-world is just the same as any other mundane, just the same as you and the Colonel."

"Even the most powerful psychics?", Colonel Johnson questioned.

Seamus snorted as Larissa chimed in, "Seamus is the head of the remote view teams. That position is held by the most powerful of us. The most powerful psychic on Earth", she explained.

"And even I cannot use my gifts off-world, General", Seamus admitted, noting, "I have been to Colonial Central Command up at Cis-Lunar L-Five. It was the most uncomfortable experience in my entire life. I had never felt so vulnerable in my life. I did that once and only once, never again."

"If those two weren't Psi Corps operatives, then who were they?", the General enquired.

"They can't have been psychics, General. Off-world, beyond the Earth, there are no psychics", Larissa announced unequivocally.

"No psychics off-world?", the Colonel enquired.

"None, Colonel. Not a single psychic has ever been born off-world", Seamus confirmed, noting, "We are all tied to the Earth and its biosphere. Off-world, no psychics", he gestured with his hands.

"Then who the hell were they?", the General questioned.

Seamus was blunt, "My opinion on the matter, General. They were two random Jovian citizens dressed up to look like psychics. Then they were used in a brutal, false-flag setup for propaganda purposes. Simply put, a false-flag snuff movie."

General Beckonwolf was in deep thought for several minutes and Colonel Johnson chimed in, "General, that would explain the anomalies, Sir."

"Anomalies?", Larissa quickly enquired.

General Beckonwolf explained, "The first instance of this video that appeared in the news feeds had metadata that reflected the timing of the incident as being shortly after the Ambassadorial vessel, the Sleek Runner, departed Ganymede Prime. Roughly one week after their departure. A second instance of the video dropped into the news feeds within hours. It was exactly identical except for the metadata. The metadata in this new version was from over a year ago. The timestamps between the two conflict. So there is an issue as to when this incident actually occurred."

"So, it's possible that this happened over a year ago and the first drop was a copy of the video with its metadata altered for propaganda purposes", Colonel Johnson summarised.

As the General, his Adjutant and the two Folcrom discussed the video, a trio of unseen *"visitors"*, stood at the side of the office along the wall. All three had the psychic obscuration fields up and they were unseen and undetected, even by Folcrom Seamus, who was a high-level nine psychic.

Folcrom Freyja, telepathically noted to her companions, *"That second drop of the video. That was my copy from last year. I thought releasing it into the news feeds would disrupt the Jovian propaganda machine. Give the authorities some clarity on when those murders actually took place."*

Folcrom Gideon Reas replied, *"Smart move, Freyja, smart move."*

Folcrom Sandra Danker noted, *"Lucky you took the time to make a copy, Freyja."*

"I find it interesting that after all of these many decades, Psi Corps still has no idea that the Council of Shadows exists", Gideon noted.

"Yeah, it is kind of quaint, isn't it?", Freyja questioned rhetorically.

The attention of all three unseen Folcrom picked up when the General placed a folder on his desk.

The General opened the folder and took out a report. It was an older report, from the twenty one forties, more than thirty years earlier. The report was from one Commandant Colonel Strong from the Deimos Military Base on the Martian moon Deimos.

General Beckonwolf read directly from Colonel Strong's report, *"We had a visit today from Doctor Gideon Reas, the Aries Colonial Administrator and Martian Terraforming Overseer, along with Ms Sandra Danker, the Martian Terraforming Team's Head Engineer. The manner in which they arrived indicates that they are both top-level Psi Corps operatives operating in High Martian Orbit."*

General Beckonwolf then noted, "That's all we have from Colonel Strong's report. This report is thirty three years old. It indicates that two Psi Corps operatives were working and fully functional in High Martian orbit thirty three years ago. That contradicts everything you have just told us."

Freyja glared at Gideon and Sandra, telepathically asking, *"How exactly did you let that happen?"*

Sandra glared back at Freyja, *"Gideon was heavily overworked and Orpheus kept dragging us into Council of Shadows business. What did you expect, Freyja? Of course, we made mistakes!"*

Gideon chimed in, *"It was over thirty years ago. One report without clarification or evidence!"*

The three continued observing silently, still unnoticed.

Seamus took out his data tablet and began a search, "Doctor Gideon Reas", he read out the name as he entered it into his search.

The data came up on the data tablet's screen and Seamus summarised the result, "Doctor Gideon Reas. This confirms that Doctor Reas was indeed the Aries Colonial Administrator and Martian Terraforming Overseer. Two very busy hats I see. He was a very accomplished administrator and scientist. It says here that he is retired and that his current whereabouts are unknown. Perhaps he immigrated to the outer colonies. Ah, here we go. Gideon Reas was born in Cis-Lunar L-Five. In a typical O'Neil-style twin cylinder colony."

Seamus gave his objective conclusion, "Doctor Gideon Reas could not possibly be a Psi Corps member, let alone an operative. He was born off-world. There are no psychics off-world."

"What about Sandra Danker?", Larissa enquired.

Seamus performed another quick search, "Sandra Danker", he read out as he keyed in the name.

Two results came back, "We do have a Sandra Danker in Psi Corps. She was born in Dusseldorf, Germany and is currently a fifteen-year-old student in the Icelandic Psychic Academy. That does not sound like your Sandra Danker, General."

Seamus moved on to the second result, "We do have another Sandra Danker, although this one is not a Psi Corps member. This is your Sandra Danker, General, born in the Colonial Central Command mega colony in Cis-Lunar L-Five. Again, born off-world. Most definitely not a psychic."

Larissa noted, "They're both in their seventies now and likely in retirement somewhere in the outer colonies. If we have no record of them in our Psi Corps databases, then they simply cannot be psychics, let alone Psi Corps operatives."

"Then how do you explain Colonel Strong's report?", the General demanded.

Seamus shook his head, "An error. Your Colonel Strong must have seen something and completely misinterpreted it. That is the only possible explanation. There are no psychics off-world, General."

Gideon concentrated on the General, gently pushing his mind towards acceptance.

Sandra did the same to Colonel Johnson, noting telepathically, *"Better late than never."*

Freyja sighed, *"There were always bound to be a few loose ends."*

General Beckonwolf replied, acceptingly, "I suppose the good Colonel could have been mistaken."

There was an ever-so-slight, imperceptible shimmer and all three interlopers jaunted out of the General's office.

The General shivered slightly and requested, "Colonel, turn up the thermostat a notch or two."

Gideon, Sandra and Freyja jaunted back into existence in a large cavern about fifty kilometres from the township of Coober Pedy in the Australian state of South Australia.

A town that was largely built around underground dugouts. Even the pubs and hotels of Coober Pedy were underground. The meeting place was a huge underground complex, where the Council of Shadows lived, ate and slept. Their meeting hall was a huge underground cavern, which, like the rest of the complex, was literally carved out of the sandstone.

The Martian woman, Winchilly, tall and thin, with golden-yellow hair, golden-hued skin and impossibly bright emerald-green eyes, had been waiting for their return with fear and trepidation.

Winchilly ran up to her Sister Wives, Sandra and Freyja and hugged them tightly. Ever since the brutal murder of Freyja's two Cousins, Tina and David, at the hands of the Jovians, Winchilly had been afraid for her family whenever they jaunted out on Council of Shadows missions.

After hugging her Sister Wives, Winchilly grabbed her Husband, Gideon, hugged him and kissed him deeply before placing her forehead to his and allowing him to share his memories of their mission. Winchilly smiled, all had gone well, all was on track, her family was back with her and safe.

Winchilly turned to look at Orpheus, the Head of the Council of Shadows. He was old, well into his nineties, his wizened old face, wrinkly old skin with its liver spots and what was left of his wispy grey hair, showed his time on this Earth was short and would soon be coming to a close.

Winchilly, being a non-verbal telepath, as all Martians were, announced telepathically, *"My family is back. Gideon and my Sister Wives have seen into the mind of General Beckonwolf. He knows the murders took place more than a year ago. He knows that the murders were nothing more than the murders of innocents. The government of the Earth will push back against the false allegations pushed by the Horridians. The truth is already out!"*

Orpheus was tired, he had been performing his duties as a Council of Shadows operative since he was a teenager. He simply nodded as Winchilly informed him of the latest developments.

Freyja chimed in, "Cousin Orpheus. I know that vengeance is not our way, but surely, this evil bastard, Albert von Horridian, cannot be allowed to get away with murdering our Cousins."

Orpheus smiled, "Freyja, my time in this world grows shorter by the day and yet, I see more clearly now than I have ever seen before. I assure you, Albert von Horridian's time is even shorter than mine. His own decisions will bring him undone."

Sandra chimed in, "Orpheus? How can you be so sure of that?"

Orpheus coughed briefly, then resumed smiling, "As I approach my sunset, Sandra, I see more now than I have ever seen before. It is not Albert von Horridian who will be the problem, but rather his eldest Son, Godric. He is the one who will bring on the burning times and the death of Dolphins."

Gideon transmitted a private telepathic message to all three of his Wives, *"Albert's Son Godric? The burning times? The death of Dolphins? I think old Orpheus might be becoming a little bit senile."*

"Perhaps", Winchilly replied telepathically in private to her family, *"Remember this, however. Martian elders of advanced age had prophesied the Martian liberation from the Tarlaks with the aid of the Humans from Earth, for many, many generations before it actually happened. That the visions born of senility sometimes come to fruition is something that you should always keep in mind."*

Winchilly turned to Orpheus and politely, as all Martians were, replied telepathically, *"Thank you, Orpheus, for your wisdom. We shall await the unfolding of your visions."*

Then Gideon took Winchilly by the hands, Sandra and Freyja placed their hands on Winchilly's shoulders and then they all jaunted across that vastness of space to their home inside the Saturnian ice moon, Mimas, under its internal Northern Mountain peak. The transition from Earth to Mimas was close to instantaneous.

The Earth's Government, along with the Government of Cis-Lunar Space at Colonial Central Command at Cis-Lunar L-Five, put out a joint video broadcast. In the broadcast, they refuted the claims that the Ambassadorial Emissary ship, the Sleek Runner, had been used to deliver assassins to the Jovian Realms, to Ganymede Prime.

They pointed out that there were two conflicting releases from the Jovians. One timestamped in its metadata as having occurred six days after the Sleek

Runner had left Ganymede Prime. The second had timestamped metadata, placing the incident more than one year earlier. In the broadcast, the Jovian accusations were labelled as a false-flag propaganda operation.

The Governments of Earth and Cis-Lunar Space accused the Jovian regime of fabricating the entire incident and of murdering two of their own citizens in a brutal and disgusting snuff movie designed to create hatred toward the inner solar system and distrust and instability across the entire solar system.

They even went so far as to accuse the Jovian regime of being illegitimate and called for the restoration of the former Jovian Republic and behavioural normalcy. As if the Jovian regime was simply barbaric in its very nature.

High Prince Albert was incensed and wanted to know how the unadulterated copy of the incident had found its way into the external news feeds. His ministers had no answer for him and High Prince Albert was having none of it. Someone was responsible, someone was to blame, someone had fucked up and the High Prince wanted a head!

The Jovian Realm's Communications Minister, Mr Albrecht Dire, became the scapegoat.

High Prince Albert called out his Communications Minister for sheer incompetence and with a simple nod to Aurange Sheergibbon, Albrecht Dire, lost his head, then and there, right at the operations room table. Aurange Sheergibbon had been swift and with one clean, deft slice of his sabre, the Communications Minister's head was rolling along the table, blood flicking in every direction, while his body slumped forward and bled out on the table in front of his seat.

The remaining ministers copped the spray from Albrecht Dire's severed head, while the High Prince himself walked out of the operations room, with Aurange and Roberta following closely behind. All of the remaining ministers sat there in stunned silence.

Some of the ministers had even shit themselves.

Not a single one of them wanted to be there. They all hated their jobs.

Elaine Haynes sobbed quietly to herself, her own piss pooling on her seat beneath her and she was sitting in it.

"I have to get out of this place! The High Prince is insane!", Elaine thought to herself.

For when evil has nowhere else to turn, it turns inward unto itself!

The operations room was quiet the next day as the High Prince gave out his orders. The room had been cleaned during the night and Elaine Haynes found herself wondering.

How had the cleaners felt, mopping up the blood, the gore, the shit and the piss?

How had the cleaners felt, disposing of the ministerial head and the corpse?

This place, this room, was not meant for any sane person. Every minister in this operations room was insane, because they were too impotent to do anything else but sit and suffer in their own filth!

High Prince Albert doubled down!

Truth has quality, lies have quantity!

If the High Prince could not control the truth, he would bury it with lies!

High Prince Albert insisted that their propaganda be pushed out on a daily basis, reinforcing his false narrative that the Ambassadorial Emissary, Ms Sonia de la Cruz, had delivered two sorcerer assassins to the Jovian Realms, to the very seat of power, to Ganymede Prime itself.

Earth's government and the government of Cis-Lunar Space countered, by posting the evidence refuting the Jovian allegations into the public domain for all to see and referring to it every time the Jovian Realms pushed out their bullshit. And so it went on, tit-for-tat, until finally the High Prince took his bullshit one step too far and it was the Belters who finally refuted the High Prince's new allegations.

High Prince Albert placed another propaganda claim into the external news feeds. This new claim from the Jovian Realms was that Ambassadorial Emissaries from the Colonisation Committee of Sol, at Eros, had poisoned numerous Belter colonies with the Black Blight.

A toxic black mould that infested soil, ruined crops and poisoned livestock and the entire food chain. The Jovians even went so far as to claim that this had been done to lay the blame on the Jovian Realms and disrupt Jovian trade. They declared it to be ecological and economic warfare! It was, of course, patently and demonstrably false.

For once, the Belters were angry. They did not have a Cock in this fight and yet, here they were being dragged into a propaganda war between the Jovian Realms and the inner solar system. Worse still, they had proof positive that not only was the Jovian narrative demonstrably false, but that the source of the Black Blight infestation was deliberately contaminated processed regolith from Jupiter's Trojan Asteroid colonies. Two of High Prince Albert's very own six Jovian Realms.

Harlequin Moon stood in front of the lectern, on his left were six Belter Ambassadors, on his right were another six Belter Ambassadors. All together, they represented the thirteen sovereign Belter nations. Mr Calder Minos, the Ambassador from Interamnia, stood immediately on Harlequin Moon's right, while fellow Ambassador, Ms Tessa Yorin of Sylvia, stood on his left.

Harlequin Moon greeted his audience, "People of the solar system. I am here to refute these ridiculous allegations from the Jovian Realms. We have no place in this propaganda war between the Jovian Realms and the inner solar system. What I can tell you, however, is that these allegations that the Emissaries from Eros infected our colonies with the Black Blight are patently false."

Mr Calder Minos stepped forward, "I am the Ambassador from the sovereign nation of Interamnia. No emissaries from Eros have ever set foot in our nation. We suffered an outbreak of the Black Blight, which we now have under control. This was at a very high expense. We have scientifically traced this outbreak to processed regolith exported to us from the Jovian Trailing Trojan Realm. That is an undeniable fact!", he then stepped back into line with the other Ambassadors.

Ms Tessa Yorin stepped forward, "I am the Ambassador from the sovereign nation of Sylvia. No emissaries from Eros have ever set foot in our nation either. Over a year ago, we suffered an outbreak of the Black Blight. We managed to get it under control and eradicated it at great expense. We, too, have scientifically traced the outbreak to processed regolith exported to us from the Jovian Leading Trojan Realm. This, too, is an undeniable fact!", she then stepped back into line with the other Belter Ambassadors.

Harlequin Moon took over, "Thank you, Ambassadors", he nodded to them and then he continued, "Only one Emissary has come from the Colonisation Committee, from Eros. That Emissary, Mr Dag Talleyrand, arrived at Ceres Central, stayed at Ceres Central and left Ceres Central to return to Eros. At no point in time, did he ever travel to any other Belter nations. Mr Dag Talleyrand is the only Emissary from Eros to ever visit our nations."

Harlequin Moon let that sink in, then he continued, "I have seen the evidence for the source of the Black Blight outbreaks. It was, without any shadow of a doubt, contaminated processed regolith from the Jovian Trojan Realms. Under our Belter norms and conventions, *'Once bitten, twice shy, twice bitten, contracts cancelled'*, all Belter trade with the Jovian Realms has now ceased. That is the result of Jovian duplicity! Not Erosian interference!"

Harlequin Moon paused, he wanted that to really sink in before continuing, "Yes, duplicity. We have intelligence that proves that the contamination of the Trojan processed regolith was deliberate. It was the Horridian regime's attempt to destroy our food supply and make us Belters dependent on the Jovian Realms for our food security. As a result, we now only trade with the inner solar system and those outer realms beyond Jupiter. Good Day", there was a long pause and then the transmission ended.

The Belters replayed that message over and over from each of their thirteen sovereign nations every thirty minutes, flooding the new feeds with their truth and drowning out the Jovian lies.

The rule of thumb was simple, *"Never, ever piss off the Belters"*, they are very, very unforgiving!

High Prince Albert was livid, but who could he blame?

None of his ministers had said anything more than, *"Yes, Your Majesty"* or *"Your will be done, Your Majesty"*, since the beheading. They were all lily-livered!

They had merely implemented his own orders and commands to the letter. The High Prince had done this all to himself!

"Get out of my sight! All of you!", High Prince Albert screamed at his ministers and they all left the operations room quickly, lest they end up on the wrong end of the High Prince's wrath.

The Propaganda war ended after that and the High Prince turned inward, seething in his own anger.

High Prince Albert's pretexts were in tatters!

It was not long after that that High Prince Albert von Horridian sent his Orange Shitgibbon and Booby Num Nums on their mission to intercept the Sleek Runner. Not that he used those nicknames, mind you, the High Prince might have been insane, yes, but clearly he was not crazy.

Aurange Sheergibbon and Roberta Nummus sat on the bridge of their ship, the Dark Angel, a heavily armed Tristar Interplanetary Stealth Ship. The Dark Angel's hull was coated and skinned in midnight black. In space, the Dark Angel was virtually invisible, you'd only notice it if it occulted a celestial object in the background. The Dark Angel was shaped like a spear tip, long and sleek with a pointed nose and a tapered tail.

Aurange and Roberta waited for the Sleek Runner to reach the fifty million kilometre threshold that Aurange had so carefully set up in the Sleek Runner's rear scanner array. Once the Sleek Runner crossed that threshold, Aurange launched the Dark Angel in pursuit.

The Dark Angel was a fast ship, however, they did not plan to overtake the Sleek Runner quickly. Instead, the interception point was set for six weeks in the future. The Sleek Runner would not detect them approaching. The Sleek Runner's crew would not see them coming.

Roberta was feeling conflicted and did her best not to show it. Roberta actually liked Sonia de la Cruz, but worse than that, Elaine had spoken to her on the morning of the second meeting. The Diplomatic Intern, Lina Mitchel, was only sixteen years of age, just a child and yet, everyone, without exception, on the Sleek Runner was a mark. And all marks must be terminated!

9. Ghost Ship.

The Ambassadorial ship, the Sleek Runner, was well on its way to the Saturnian Demarchy when Aurange's and Roberta's ship, the Dark Angel, finally caught up. Sleek and dark against the inky blackness of the void, the Dark Angel approached undetected and unseen from the rear. The Sleek Runner's rear scanners had been surreptitiously sabotaged back at Ganymede Prime seven weeks prior.

The Sleek Runner had just sent its daily communications check back to Eros. All was well, or so they believed. This was the time. No one would know what had happened until the next communications check failed to arrive and that would be the following day.

Roberta spun the Dark Angel one hundred eighty degrees along its longitudinal axis as it approached the Sleek Runner and both ships oriented their ventral hulls to face each other. With absolute precision, Roberta Nummus lined up the Dark Angel's ventral passenger portal with the ventral passenger portal on the Sleek Runner.

Slowly, gingerly and with skilled hands at the navigation controls, Roberta docked the Dark Angel to the Sleek Runner. No alarm had been raised, as the docking portal on the Sleek Runner had also been surreptitiously sabotaged back at Ganymede Prime. No one aboard the Sleek Runner knew that the Dark Angel had docked. The Sleek Runner and Dark Angel flew through the void locked together in perfect sync and none of the Sleek Runner's crew were aware.

Aurange and Roberta checked the Sleek Runner's ventral docking portal's security. Aurange's overrides were still in place. Aurange smiled broadly. This was too easy. Together, the duo crossed through the docking portal and entered the Sleek Runner. Roberta made some very subtle gestures with her fingers. It was their personal sign language and Aurange understood Roberta's message.

"Ten crew. We deal with them first and leave the passengers till last", Roberta was the tactical one.

Like eerie shadows, they moved through the ship. Aurange snuck silently up on the first crew member and, without a moment's hesitation, snapped his neck. He stuffed the corpse into a maintenance locker so that it would not be discovered. Roberta's tally began just as quickly, as the first crew member that she found had an ice pick slammed into his ear. He stared silently at Roberta, eyes wide in terror as his brain slowly shut down. Roberta passed the corpse back to Aurange, who quickly stuffed it into the same maintenance locker.

Aurange signed to Roberta subtly with his fingers, *"Nice work, Roberta. Eight more crew to go."*

Aurange and Roberta snuck silently through the Sleek Runner, killing crew members swiftly and silently. Aurange with a snap of the neck, Roberta used a combination of neck-snapping and ice picking. Bodies were stashed and concealed quickly, leaving no overt signs of their presence. One by one, the crew members died.

Aurange finally signed Roberta, *"Eight down, two to go. They'll be in the ship's bridge."*

Roberta nodded and the pair silently made their way to the bridge.

The ship's bridge door was closed when they came to it. Aurange looked at Roberta and they nodded in unison. One, two, three, then they opened the door and burst in.

Captain Thames Barker died quickly. All it took was a single, powerful blow to his nose. Aurange's uppercut sent the fractured bridge of Barker's nose straight into his brain and he crumpled to the ship's deck. Roberta's strike was just as quick. Helmsman Douglas Damson found a pair of ice picks shoved deeply into his eyes. Damson reflexively raised his hands to his head and then he collapsed to the ship's deck. Roberta then closed the bridge's door.

Roberta signed to Aurange with subtle finger movements, *"Capture the Diplomatic Team alive. Bind them and take them to the ship's dining room."*

Aurange nodded in agreement.

With equal efficiency, Aurange and Roberta rounded up the Diplomatic Team. Roberta had selected two targets, the Ambassadorial Emissary, Sonia de la Cruz and the Diplomatic Intern, Lina Mitchel. Aurange was left to target Diplomatic Secretary Gena Richter and Diplomatic Aid Goren Zither.

Roberta had selected her targets with purpose. Roberta liked Sonia and would spare her if she could, but that was highly unlikely. Sonia was their primary mark and Aurange would most certainly not let her live. Lina Mitchel, on the other hand, was still a child and Roberta simply could not kill a child.

Aurange and Roberta were methodical, moving from cabin to cabin. Each victim was rendered unconscious using simple, dosed needles. The Diplomatic team was rendered unconscious even before they could register what was happening. When the Diplomatic team awakened, they were lying on the ship's dining room deck, with their hands bound behind their backs with plastic zip ties.

Sonia woke and realised her predicament immediately, "What is the meaning of this? We have diplomatic immunity!", she told her captors.

Aurange began keying a message into one of the ship's data tablets, then he held it up in front of Sonia, *"Your diplomatic immunity has been revoked by High Prince Albert."*

Sonia was shocked, that was not how diplomatic immunity worked, "Your so-called High Prince has no power to revoke diplomatic immunity."

Aurange shrugged and typed in another message, he held it up to Sonia, *"That is not our problem. High Prince Albert was very upset when he gave us our orders. High Prince Albert wants us to torture you slowly and then kill you. He wants us to take our time and make it as painful as possible."*

Sonia looked around the room at her colleagues, her eyes lingered on Lina and then on Roberta, "You can't! That goes against all diplomatic conventions! You simply can't!"

Aurange shrugged and simply began sharpening his knife.

Roberta noticed Sonia's eyes linger on Lina and then on herself, she caught Aurange's eye and began signing with her fingers, the movements far less subtle, *"We cannot torture these people, Aurange!"*

Aurange began signing back, *"You are shouting at me, Roberta. We have our orders and the High Prince was very specific. He wants this woman to suffer and suffer she must!"*

"The High Prince's orders are conflicting", Roberta signed back, this time, her finger movements were back to their usual subtlety.

"In what way?", Aurange sign back, questioning.

Roberta moved her fingers subtly, *"Our instructions are to leave no trace, Aurange. No trace. How are we going to leave no trace after a major torture session? The cleanup will take far too long."*

Aurange thought about that. Torture is a messy business. That much was true and they didn't have a *"clean room"* set up. Cleaning up after a major torture session does take a lot of time.

"Okay, okay. I'll just tell the High Prince we tortured them. Satisfied?", Aurange signed back.

Then he picked up Goren by his throat, forced him against the wall and knifed him in the heart. Goren Zither collapsed to the ship's deck.

"This should make you happy, Roberta. He did stare at your breasts after all", Aurange signed.

Sonia and Gena looked at the crumpled body of Goren Zither in shock. Lina did her best to move herself along the deck, to distance herself from the scene. She left a trail of urine behind as she did so.

Aurange moved to Gena next and took her by the hair, dragging her violently to her feet. He tilted his head to the left and then to the right, looking at Gina.

Aurange thought to himself, *"Pity we're on a schedule. I could have had fun with this one"*, then he knifed Gena in the heart as well.

Gena Richter's body dropped to the deck in a crumpled mess like Goren's.

Roberta crouched down in front of Sonia, who was now in a sitting position, she silently mouthed the words, *"I am so sorry, Sonia. I cannot control, Aurange. You will be next."*

Sonia knew her time was short, "Please, Roberta. Please save my Niece, my Lina", she implored.

Roberta frowned and silently mouthed, *"I will protect your Niece, Sonia. I will protect your Lina as if she were my own"*, she promised.

Sonia's eyes welled with tears and she nodded to Roberta, "Make it quick. Please make it quick!"

Then Roberta gently reached out and snapped Sonia's neck. It was quick. It was painless.

Aurange approached Roberta as she stood back up and he signed, asking, *"So, are you doing this one, or am I?"*

"No one is doing this one. Lina Mitchel is under my protection", Roberta signed back.

"Under your protection? That's not how this works, Roberta. Everybody aboard this ship is a mark. They must all die. There are no exceptions", Aurange signed, he was genuinely becoming confused.

"Lina is a child. I do not kill children!", Roberta signed back in a shouting retort.

"That is irrelevant, Roberta. We are paid a lot of money to eliminate marks. Lina is a mark. It is that simple. Lina Mitchel must die!", Aurange explained, signing in reply.

Roberta signed back, *"It is not that simple, Lina is a child, she is not a mark"*, then she reached out and grabbed Aurange by the throat forcefully and silently mouthed the words, *"Lina is under my protection. You will not touch her!"*

Aurange put up his hands in mock surrender.

Roberta released him and he signed to her, *"Okay, okay, but I don't know how the High Prince will respond to your assertions. He may not be pleased."*

Roberta smiled back at Aurange, then she signed, *"All those years ago at that military facility. They not only turned me into a monster, Aurange, but they also took away my ability to have children. If the High Prince complains, I'll tell him that I'm adopting Lina, that she is family."*

"Now, I know you're insane, Roberta", Aurange signed back and then scratched his head.

"No more than you are, Aurange, no more than you are", Roberta signed in reply.

Roberta looked at Lina and then signed to Aurange, *"You start on the cleanup, I'll look after Lina."*

Aurange nodded in agreement and started on the clean-up. They were not to leave any trace of their having been there.

Roberta crouched down beside Lina and silently mouthed the words, *"No one is going to harm you. You are now under my protection, Lina."*

Lina looked back with fearful eyes as Roberta placed her left arm around Lina's back and her right arm under her legs. Ever so gently, Roberta picked Lina up and cradled her in her arms. As Roberta carried Lina back to her ship, the Dark Angel, she sniffed. Lina had soiled herself. Roberta had a cleanup of her own to perform.

The Dark Angel was a much smaller vessel than the Sleek Runner. It only had three cabins, two were used by Aurange and Roberta and the third cabin was largely unused, except occasionally for storage. Currently, it was empty.

Roberta carried Lina into the empty cabin and sat her down on the cabin's deck. Roberta left the cabin to grab some necessities, bedding, towels, other toiletries and a data tablet. When she returned, Roberta made the bed and placed the toiletries in the cabin's en-suite.

Once that was done, Roberta helped Lina to her feet and undressed her. Lina was then helped into the cabin's en-suite shower, where Roberta washed her, washing away the piss and shit. When Roberta was finished washing Lina, she dried her off and then led her to the cabin's bed. Roberta placed Lina in the centre of the bed and covered her with the sheets and blankets.

Roberta picked up the data tablet and began keying in a message and then she held it up to Lina so that she could read it, *"I am so sorry, Lina. Today has been truly horrible for you. Now, however, you are safe. I promised your Aunt Sonia that I would protect you and look after you. No one will harm you. You are under my protection."*

Once Lina had read the message, Roberta typed in another, *"I have to help Aurange with the clean up. Please try to sleep and try not to think about what's happened. I will check in on you soon."*

Then after Lina had finished reading that message, Roberta placed the data tablet on a nearby desk, picked up Lina's soiled clothes and left the cabin, locking the door behind her.

Roberta returned to the Sleek Runner and quickly made her way to Lina's former cabin.

Methodically, Roberta gathered all of Lina's belongings and piled them on her former bunk. Then Roberta went to Emissary, Sonia de la Cruz's cabin. This time, she went through Sonia's possessions and piled them onto the cabin's bunk. Roberta bundled all of Sonia's possessions together using the bunk's blankets and then carried the bundle back to Lina's former cabin.

Then Roberta bundled all of Lina's belongings together in the same fashion using her blankets. Once this was done, Roberta carried the two bundles back to the Dark Angel and plopped them down by Lina's new cabin door. The task took two trips and upon completing the second trip, Roberta carried the two bundles of possessions into the cabin and placed them by the bed.

Roberta looked at Lina, she was still awake, gripping the blankets up around her face, her eyes staring out in fear.

Roberta picked up the data tablet once more and typed, *"Lina, I know that this day has been truly horrible. I know that you are scared. It will take time for you to accept what has happened and adjust. I will help you, Lina."*

After Lina had read that message, Roberta typed another, *"I have gathered all of your belongings and also your Aunt's belongings. They are in two bundles by the bed. You can go through them when you are ready."*

Once Lina had finished reading the message, Roberta placed the data tablet back on the desk once more, then silently mouthed the words, *"I'll be back soon"*, and then she left the cabin, again locking the door behind her.

Aurange had been extremely busy. He had dragged all of the corpses from where they had been stashed and lined them up along the Sleek Runner's main corridor, close to the ship's dorsal airlock. Aurange had grouped the corpses of the crew into two groups of five and the corpses of the diplomats into a separate group. Aurange had tied all of the corpses in each group together tightly by their ankles using tether lines. Three groups, three tether lines.

Roberta joined Aurange in the Sleek Runner's main corridor and then they went about the business of cleaning up any sign of their presence. They followed their assault path precisely, scanning with their eyes for any sign of their presence or the victim's blood or any other bodily fluids. They methodically cleansed the Sleek Runner of their presence. Their last stop was the Sleek Runner's dining room.

Aurange spied the pool of piss and traces of shit on the deck and he signed to Roberta, *"That's yours. You kept her alive. You clean up her shit!"*

Roberta looked at the pooled blood and bloody streaks on the deck and then signed back, pointing, *"Fine, Aurange. Then you can clean up your fucking mess!"*

Once they had finished their clean-up duties, Aurange went back to the Dark Angel and put on his space suit. He then returned to the three lines of bodies in the Sleek Runner's main corridor. Roberta helped Aurange place the corpses into the dorsal airlock. It was only large enough for eight people, so they had to perform the task three times.

Once sealed inside, Aurange cycled the airlock, opened the outer hatch and unceremoniously pushed the corpses out into the vacuum of space. He tied the tether line off to one of the outer hull's external tether points. This was done three times, five crew corpses first, three diplomatic corpses next and then finally the last *"string"* of five crew corpses.

Aurange exited the dorsal airlock hatch and stood on the outer hull, his mag boots holding him firmly in place. He looked briefly as the three tether lines with their accompaniment of corpses drifted at the rear of the Sleek Runner. Aurange knelt down and fed more tether line through the external tether point so that the corpses hung in space well behind the ship.

Aurange then walked down the hull towards the ship's rear, eventually stopping in between the Sleek Runner's two main thruster nozzles. Aurange spied what he was looking for, another external tether point. He took a carabiner from off of his utility belt, placed the three tether lines through it and then clipped it to the external tether point. This had the effect of placing the three strings of corpses in the direct line of the ship's main thrusters. Aurange smiled to himself, this would be clean, very clean.

Aurange turned up the power on his mag boots, making sure he was firmly held in place, then he tethered himself to the external tether point.

Aurange sent a message to Roberta, *"The stage is set. Perform a long burn for thirty seconds"*, and then he braced himself.

Roberta was on the ship's bridge. She set the main thrusters for a thirty-second burn and then activated them. The Sleek Runner's plasma thrusters sparked into life, the twin plasma torches leaping rearward and cremating the thirteen corpses.

Aurange had watched with morbid fascination. Three strands of corpses, all strung out like dead human sausages. The plasma torches struck them with an intense fury and in mere seconds, the thirteen corpses were all turned to ash! They were gone! Erased from existence!

At the thirty-second mark, the main thrusters cut out. Aurange knelt down and retrieved his carabiner, then casually sauntered his way back to the dorsal airlock. Aurange knelt down once more, untied the tether lines and cast them adrift into space.

Then Aurange climbed back into the airlock, closed the outer hatch, cycled the airlock and re-entered the Sleek Runner. Job done, a broad smile of satisfaction on his face.

Aurange and Roberta were not yet finished. The ship had been cleansed, the corpses disposed of, yet there were a few more tasks to be performed. Aurange reversed the sabotage he had conducted on the Sleek Runner's rear scanners, placing them back into normal operations.

Then he reversed the security changes he'd made to the Sleek Runner's ventral passenger docking portal and the changes he'd made to the ventral cargo portal. All signs of sabotage were removed and no one would ever know that they'd been there.

For Roberta's part, she disabled the remote pilot access systems, making sure that the Security Council of Sol, at Eros, could not override the ship's navigational console. Remote navigational access was locked out! Then Roberta checked one more thing. The ship's internal security cameras and sensors. They were all operating. Roberta deleted the video and sensor logs, removing any signs that they'd been there and then set the cameras and sensors to kick back on one hour after they'd left.

The final thing Roberta did before she and Aurange left the Sleek Runner was to ensure that the Security Council could remotely access the security camera and sensors, all of them. Roberta smiled, the Sleek Runner would become a ghost ship, the Mary Celeste of deep space and worse. The Security Council of Sol would be able to see it in visceral detail.

The Sleek Runner's security camera feeds, all of its sensor feeds and forever wonder, what happened to its crew and passengers. A mystery forever more!

Roberta sat down in the pilot's seat on the Dark Angel. With practised precision, she disconnected the Dark Angel from the Sleek Runner. Her ship coasted along as the Sleek Runner slowly coasted farther and farther ahead. Roberta watched, monitoring its trajectory for nearly ten minutes and then checked the results of her calculations.

Roberta signed to Aurange, *"The Sleek Runner is way off course. She should overshoot Saturnian space midway between Saturn and its leading Trojan colonies."*

"Exactly what we wanted", Aurange signed back, noting, *"She's so far off course that not even the Uranian Federation could intercept her, let alone the Saturnian Demarchy."*

Roberta performed several controlled burns of the Dark Angel's control thrusters, reorienting the ship for a return trip to Ganymede Prime. Then she calculated the correct burn time and fired up the ship's three main plasma thrusters. After the set length of time, the burn was complete.

"We will be back at Ganymede Prime in around seven weeks", she signed and announced.

Aurange smiled and then signed back, *"Roberta, you'll make a monstrous mother!"*

"Really, Aurange, really. If you had children of your own, you'd murder them in your sleep", Roberta signed in retort.

Aurange grinned and signed back, *"Hahahaha! You know me too well, Roberta Nummus!"*

The day's events had led Roberta to a revelation. The *"special"* military training at the hands of the Colonial Defence Forces, with its training, psychological conditioning, genetic enhancement elixirs and serums, had made her into a monster. Aurange, however, when she thought back to before their *"special"* training, had always been a monster. In Aurange's case, the *"special"* training had simply enhanced what was already there. While Roberta was a monster by design and manufacture, Aurange was a monster since birth.

To keep Lina safe, Roberta was going to have to watch Aurange like a hawk!

Once again, a familiar scene unfolded. Professor Maria Corbel, Central Speaker of the Colonisation Committee of Sol, sat in her office in her usual comfortable chair. It was another impromptu meeting triggered, this time, by the Security Council of Sol.

Sitting across a coffee table were the other two Colonisation Committee Speakers, the Left Speaker, Professor Lyra Banks and the Right Speaker, Professor Stephen Terrell. In between the two Speakers was the current Security

Council of Sol's liaison to the Colonisation Committee, Mr Carl Stavros, who had replaced Ms Sone Dharma, their current Ambassador to the Belter nations situated at Ceres.

The main office screen displayed natural scenes of Earth, cycling through each image at ten-second intervals. Carl Stavros passed Maria Corbel a data stick.

"That is what this meeting is all about, Maria", Carl noted.

Professor Corbel placed the data stick into a device on the coffee table and the office's main screen sparked into life, displaying a list of files. Carl picked up the remote control and opened the first file.

An image depicting the solar system appeared. It clearly showed the orbits of the outer gas giants. The position of each gas giant and the positions of its leading and trailing Trojan points were shown.

There was a green line depicting an orbital transfer trajectory from Jupiter to Saturn. This green line split into two, the new branch, in red, showed a trajectory that led into deep space. The green and red lines were labelled *"Sleek Runner trajectories"*. There was a small yellow dot on the red trajectory line, it was labelled *"Sleek Runner"*.

Professor Lyra Banks quickly understood what they were looking at, "Why is the Sleek Runner so far off course?", she asked.

The Sleek Runner was the fastest of the Colonisation Committee's ambassadorial vessels. It was well known to the three Colonisation Committee speakers. They had sent the Sleek Runner, its crew of ten and a four-person Ambassadorial team as Emissaries to the outer system colonies.

The Sleek Runner was supposed to be en route to the Saturnian Demarchy and the capital colony, Titan Central Command, located at Titan's trailing Trojan point. That their ambassadorial vessel was so far off course and headed into deep space was completely unexpected!

Mr Carl Stavros replied almost impotently, "We don't know."

Professor Corbel was extremely concerned, their Emissary, Ms Sonia de la Cruz, was a personal friend of hers.

Maria had personally picked her for this very mission. Sonia was well known for her particular brand of no-nonsense diplomacy. Sonia never messed about, a spade was a spade and a shovel was a shovel, she was quick to call people out when they tried to mess around. Sonia was perfect for the mission. Sonia de la Cruz had even taken her young niece, Lina Mitchel, with her as a Diplomatic

Intern.

"What do we know, Carl?", Maria asked, her face showing her concern.

"We received the Sleek Runner's last check in transmission at eleven twenty am yesterday. The Captain of the Sleek Runner, Captain Barker, sent that message at around ten am. We failed to receive today's check in transmission, so we decided to check our tracking and telemetry data", Carl replied, then he gestured to the image on the screen, "That is what we found."

Professor Stephen Terrell noted, "That tells us how you knew they were off course, Carl. It doesn't tell us why."

"We don't have a why, yet, Stephen", Carl admitted, noting, "We have tried to communicate with the Sleek Runner. We aren't getting any replies, not even a signal receipt confirmation."

Professor Terrell commented, "Carl, all of our diplomatic vessels have remote control navigation capabilities. Have your people attempted to take control of the Sleek Runner?"

"We tried that as soon as our communication signal receipt confirmation failed", Carl responded, frowning, and then he informed them, "The remote control navigation appears to be locked out!"

Professor Lyra Banks asked, her voice showing her shock, "Locked out? How?"

Again, Carl Stavros replied, "We don't know why", then he added, "We can only speculate."

The Colonisation Committee speakers were all in shock, there was disbelief in their eyes. That a modern-day ship like the Sleek Runner should be in such a predicament was unfathomable.

Carl Stavros speculated, "We think that maybe Captain Barker locked out the remote control navigation when they entered Jovian space as a precaution. He may have kept it locked out on their way out of Jovian space as well, however, why he didn't reactivate it when they were far enough away, we just don't know."

Professor Maria Corbel enquired, "So, Carl. Where are they headed? Can the Sleek Runner be intercepted? Do we have any options there?"

Carl rubbed his chin, his five o'clock shadow seemed somehow to have come early, "Maria, the Sleek Runner is headed for deep space. The ship will cross Saturnian orbit midway between Saturn and its leading Trojan point. We have contacted the Demarchy and they tell us that the Sleek Runner will be well outside of Saturnian orbit before they can intercept it. We also understand that to be the case."

Lyra Banks asked, her eyes wide with concern, "What about the Federation? The Uranian Federation? Can they help?"

Carl picked up the remote control and rolled the image forward in time as an active simulation. The gas giants and their Trojan points moved in their orbits. The Sleek Runner's trajectory continued, the trajectory line changing to yellow in colour. Carl stopped the simulation at the point where the Sleek Runner crossed Uranus's orbit.

Lyra Banks frowned, Uranus, with its Federation and its Trojan colonies, were on the opposite side of the solar system, "Well then. I guess the Uranian Federation can't help us."

Stephen Terrell stared at the screen, "Carl, roll that forward. I want to see what happens."

Carl clicked on the remote control and the simulation carried forward in time once more. The gas giants and their Trojan points moved in their orbits. The Sleek Runner's yellow trajectory line continued on, getting farther and farther into deep space. Then they all noticed, based upon the simulation, the Sleek Runner would make its way straight into the Neptunian Commonwealth's colonies in Neptune's leading Trojan point.

Stephen Terrell enquired, "Carl, how accurate is that simulation?"

"I don't really know, Stephen. I knocked it together rather quickly. This is the first time I've played it further than Saturnian orbit", Carl admitted and then he commented, "I'd expect it to be better than ninety five percent accurate, though"

Maria Corbel chimed in, "Carl, have your people contact the Commonwealth. Let them know what's happened and request that they intercept the Sleek Runner when it arrives. Give them its trajectory in detail. Assuming that they can do so, ask them to perform an investigation. I want to know what went wrong. We need to know."

Professor Lyra Banks then stated the obvious, something that no one wanted to mention, "The Sleek Runner does not have the capacity to hold enough supplies for such a long journey. They were supposed to travel from one gas giant to the next, refuelling and resupplying as they went. By the time that ship reaches the Neptunian Commonwealth, the Sleek Runner will be coasting and its passengers and crew will more than likely all be dead."

Professor Corbel ran her hand through her hair nervously, "This is all my fault. I sent them all on this mission. I should never have sent them!"

"It's not your fault at all, Maria", Lyra replied, noting, "We had to send someone and well, you can't predict what happens in deep space. We don't have any idea what went wrong either."

"About that", Carl interjected, "We couldn't access the Sleek Runner's remote control navigational console, however, we were able to access the ship's internal security cameras and sensors."

Carl brought up a series of images onto the screen, which were images from the Sleek Runner's internal security cameras. Sixteen image windows appeared as boxes on the screen. Each and every image displayed an empty section of the ship.

Lyra Banks stammered questioningly, "No one's on board?"

Carl confirmed, "These camera feeds don't change. That ship is empty. No one is on board the Sleek Runner. The internal sensors all confirm it as well. There's no motion detected, no oxygen being used, no carbon dioxide being produced. The atmospherics are perfect, there's just no one there to breathe it. The Sleek Runner is completely empty!"

Maria Corbel quickly chimed in, asking, "Life pods?"

"All of the life pods are present. Not a single one has been launched", Carl responded, then he noted, "Some three hours after their last transmission, the Sleek Runner performed a thirty second burn of its main thrusters, which is why it's so far off course, but the whereabouts of its passengers and crew remains a mystery. They are simply not on the ship."

"How is that even possible? People don't just disappear?", Lyra questioned.

Carl frowned deeply, he sighed, "I have no answers for you, Lyra. The Sleek Runner is empty, there is no one on board. It is as I said, a mystery."

And it was, the Sleek Runner was now a ghost ship, the modern-day Mary Celeste of deep space.

Even if the Neptunian Commonwealth intercepted and captured the ship, what would they find?

An empty ship, no crew, no passengers, not even a single corpse.

The Sleek Runner itself was now a ghost ship!

The Mary Celeste of Deep Space!

10. Simmering Tensions.

Carl Stavros sent a message to the Neptunian Commonwealth, its content was simple enough, *"Erosian Ambassadorial vessel, Sleet Runner, is off course on a heading into deep space. Based on its current trajectory, the Sleek Runner should intercept Neptune's leading Trojan point. Note: Remote internal surveillance shows the ship to be empty. The diplomatic passengers and the ship's crew are missing. Please intercept and investigate."*

Carl included complete details of the Sleek Runner's trajectory and an estimate of when it would arrive in close proximity to Neptune's leading Trojan point. Carl copied in the three Colonisation Committee speakers.

It was a full twenty four hours later when the reply came back from the Neptunian Commonwealth.

Carl read the reply, *"Message receipt confirmed. Trajectory data confirmed. Estimated time of arrival confirmed. We have the Sleek Runner on our long-range tracking. We will intercept the Sleek Runner on its approach to Commonwealth Trojan space. We will investigate the ship as requested. Please confirm that the diplomatic passengers and crew are missing?"*

That last sentence showed signs of disbelief at the Neptunian end.

Carl forwarded the reply to the three Colonisation Committee speakers before sending off the requested confirmation that the diplomatic passengers and crew were missing. Neptune's leading Trojan colonies were four and a half billion kilometres from Earth's orbital zone and for now, the mystery was in the Neptunian Commonwealth's hands. There was no telling what they would make of it!

Roberta quietly entered Lina's cabin, hoping that she had fallen asleep. Lina was indeed asleep, although Roberta could not tell if her sleep was full of nightmares or not. Quietly, Roberta placed a stack of MRE packs, meals ready to eat, on the cabin's desk. Each pack contained a different meal, none of which could be considered tasty, but they were nutritious. Alongside the MRE packs, she placed a selection of protein bars, each with different flavours. On the Dark Angel, those were the only food stocks available. Pretty much just military supplies.

As Lina began to stir, Roberta picked up her data tablet from the desk and then sat down on the edge of Lina's bed, waiting for her to awaken. Lina awoke to see Roberta sitting on her bed and immediately pulled the bed covers up over her eyes, hoping that the *"she monster"* would simply vanish and that the previous day's memories were just a horrible nightmare. Sadly for Lina, yesterday's memories were all too real. They surfaced with all of their horrific detail. Lina Mitchel screamed!

Lina pulled the bed covers down and peeked out, the *"she monster"*, Roberta, was still sitting there, "Go away! Go away! Get out of here!", she shouted.

Roberta typed a message into the data tablet and held it up for Lina to read, *"I'm sorry, Lina. I can't do that. I promised your Aunt Sonia that I'd look after you and protect you."*

Lina snapped back angrily, "You murdered my Aunt Sonia!"

Roberta typed in another message and held it up, *"Yes, Lina and I'm sorry, very sorry, but I had to do it. The alternative was Aurange and his instruction had been very clear. Very unpleasant!"*

Lina's horrific memories resurfaced in graphic detail. Aurange picked up Goren by the throat and stabbed him through the heart. Aurange picked up Gena, staring at her like a hungry predator and then stabbed her through the heart as well. They were her friends, her colleagues.

Watching Lina carefully and noting she was in deep thought, Roberta typed in another message, *"Aurange had been ordered by the High Prince to torture your Aunt Sonia to death and to do so as slowly as possible. I know Aurange, he would have taken hours. That was the alternative. Your Aunt extracted a promise from me to spare you and protect you. I fully intend to keep that promise. It was your Aunt's final request. That and a quick end for herself."*

Lina read the message and realised the implications. Roberta had murdered her Aunt Sonia, yes, but Aurange, what he would have done would have been barbaric in the extreme.

Lina replied softly, questioning, "It was a mercy killing?"

Roberta nodded and then typed, *"Your Aunt Sonia knew she was next on Aurange's list and she asked me to be quick, to make it painless"*, a single tear ran down her right cheek.

Lina saw the tear and thought to herself, *"Monsters don't show remorse. Monsters are remorseless."*

Roberta turned her head away as the tears began to flow freely.

Roberta reached around and grabbed the data tablet once more and typed in, *"You need to eat. I put a selection of MRE packs and protein bars on the desk. They aren't much, but they are the only food supplies we have on board"*, then she reached back around and handed to data tablet to Lina.

Lina read the new message, noticing that several tears had fallen onto the data tablet's touch screen, *"Monsters don't shed tears"*, she thought to herself once more.

Lina then got out of bed, she was naked, but noticed that a dressing gown had been draped over a nearby chair. She put it on and then walked around the bed to the cabin's desk.

Lina picked up three protein bars and put them in her dressing gown's pocket.

Lina turned to face Roberta, crouching down in front of her, "I understand why you killed my Aunt. The alternative was, as you said, Aurange, but don't expect me to forgive you. I never will!"

Roberta's tears were still flowing as she nodded in understanding.

Lina looked at Roberta and noted questioningly, "My Aunt Sonia extracted a promise from you to protect me and look after me?"

Roberta nodded once more, wishing she could actually talk and say something more.

"I will accept your protection, Roberta Nummus", Lina told Roberta, adding, "Better to have the monster on my side than against me."

Another burst of tears welled in Roberta's eyes and she covered her face in shame of what she was, a monster, as Lina walked around the bed and climbed back in.

While Lina opened up one of the protein bars, Roberta typed another message for Lina to read, *"I'll leave now, but I'll be back later to see if you need anything."*

Roberta got up and placed the data tablet back on the desk and started for the door.

Lina remarked, "Roberta, you probably should wash your face. I'm assuming that Aurange would see your tears as a weakness."

Lina was right, Aurange would see tears as weakness, so Roberta went to the cabin's en-suite and washed her face and eyes before leaving the cabin.

A diplomatic protest was sent from Eros to the Jovian regime. It basically accused the High Prince of ordering the *"sabotage"* of the Sleek Runner and the *"disposal"* of its passengers and crew, even though they had no proof. They had nothing more than the fact that the diplomatic vessel's last port of call was Ganymede Prime. The fact that the passengers were diplomatic emissaries and had diplomatic immunity was also noted. The protest was worded strongly, even forcefully.

High Prince Albert himself sent a simple two-word reply, *"Prove it!"*

Neither the Colonisation Committee of Sol nor the Security Council of Sol could. They had no evidence whatsoever.

Roberta tended to Lina's every need over the following weeks without complaint and Lina slowly became appreciative of her attentiveness. Her *"monster"* was exceedingly polite and attentive. Their interactions became less strained and Roberta even began teaching Lina her and Aurange's personal sign language. Lina found it difficult to learn at first due to the subtle nuances of each finger movement or even their subtle twitches.

The intensity of a discussion was controlled by the pronouncement of each finger movement. The more pronounced the movement, the *"louder"*, or as Aurange would call it, *"shouting"*. Whereas, the most subtle movements were considered *"whispering"*. As it was, even in normal use, the finger movements were subtle enough not to be noticed by ninety nine percent of people. It took time, but Lina slowly, gradually became fluent. This was something they kept from Aurange. He did not know!

Lina never left her cabin, fearing that any encounter with Aurange could be fatal. Roberta had deemed that wise and even changed her cabin's lock code. To prevent Aurange from accessing the lock code, Roberta applied a polynomial-encrypted lockout to the maintenance system controlling that specific cabin door. Once Roberta locked the cabin door, only Roberta could open it, although Lina herself could open it from the inside if it became necessary.

The Dark Angel was only one week out from Jupiter and Ganymede Prime when Aurange confronted Roberta. Lina Mitchel was an undead mark and that was problematic for both of them.

Aurange signed, *"We need to discuss little Miss Not Dead Mark"*, to Roberta.

Roberta signed back, shouting, *"Her name is Lina Mitchel!"*

"Whatever! Your Lina Mitchel is supposed to be dead!", Aurange signed, shouting in reply and then signing more softly, questioning, *"What am I going to tell the High Prince?"*

Roberta smiled and signed, *"Tell the fucking High Prince that I spared her life!"*

"He'll have your fucking head, Roberta!", Aurange signed back.

"No, he won't, the High Prince will be amused", Roberta signed in return.

"Are you fucking mad! He will most certainly not be amused!", Aurange signed, shouting.

Roberta smiled again and she signed, *"Tell the High Prince that I'm adopting Lina. Tell him that she is now part of my family."*

That took Aurange aback, he ran his fingers through his carrot red hair and signed, *"No! No! No! Are you fucking insane? I will not tell him that!"*

"Yes, you will, Aurange", Roberta signed back, remarking, *"Remember, Aurange, you were supposed to torture Sonia de la Cruz to death, slowly. High Prince Albert gave you that order, not me. And you disobeyed that order. Not me!"*

"What the fuck, Roberta! You told me to disobey that order", Aurange shot back, signing.

"You are the one who disobeyed, Aurange, not me", Roberta signed with a smile.

Aurange was quiet and for many long moments in deep thought before he responded, *"I have a plan, Roberta, or at least the concepts of a plan"*, he announced, signing with urgency.

"Okay, Aurange, let's hear it", Roberta requested, signing back.

"I'll report back to the High Prince that you tortured all three senior diplomats, including Sonia de la Cruz. That I delegated the work to you while I dealt with the other ten bodies", Aurange signed, explaining, *"That should make the High Prince very pleased with you. You'll be in his good books."*

Roberta was surprised, it would actually work, the High Prince would love that, she signed with fast-moving fingers, *"And I'll tell the High Prince that Lina is a child and that I don't kill children. It is a part of my conditioning. And being a child, she is superfluous anyway, she has no real agency. When I tell him that I'm going to adopt Lina, his amusement will know no bounds."*

"And you're sure that will work?", Aurange enquired, signing back.

Roberta smiled a wry smile and signed, *"His Monster becoming a Mother. Of course, it will and if it doesn't, I'll take his fucking head and the heads of his Sons. No one, no one, is going to hurt my Lina!"*

Aurange was suddenly shocked, that was bold even for Roberta, he signed back, *"Let's hope it doesn't come to that. I kind of like my job and it does pay very, very well."*

The Dark Angel docked at external docking port thirteen, its usual docking port, at the northern end cap of Ganymede Prime. This particular docking port was used exclusively for the Dark Angel and the port master knew not to use it for any other ship. His predecessor had found out the hard way that Aurange liked the number thirteen. They found the man's head sitting on his desk, but his body, they never found it.

Speculation was that Aurange had unceremoniously tossed it out of an airlock, or that perhaps the Dark Angel had its own crematorium. Amongst all of the docking crews and maintenance workers, Aurange Sheergibbon was known as the *"head taker"*, and the *"corpse maker"*, and they all kept well clear of him.

During the last week of their journey back to Ganymede Prime, Roberta had filled Lina in on how she and Aurange were going to manipulate the High Prince into keeping her alive. Lina did not know which was more ridiculous. Either Roberta would formally adopt her, making Lina family and thus placing her under protected family status, or she and Aurange would tell the High Prince that Roberta had tortured Lina's Aunt and colleagues to death, even though none of it had actually happened.

It all hinged on the High Prince's perverse and macabre sense of enjoyment. Thankfully, Roberta spared her the details of the torture that never happened, as they would tell the High Prince that she was locked in her cabin at the time. There was a disconnect in Lina's mind, she had actually been present when her Aunt and colleagues had been murdered. Something that still gave her nightmares.

Roberta had also told Lina to never mention that Ambassadorial Emissary, Sonia de la Cruz, was her Aunt, as the High Prince did not know and it would go against her. Roberta stressed that point, making sure it sank deeply into her psyche. It was all about Lina's survival and, strangely enough, Aurange Sheergibbon was complicit.

Once docked, Roberta requested that Lina stay in her cabin for her own safety, until she came back to collect her, then she left, locking Lina's cabin door as she did so. The docking master received the usual request from the Dark Angel for refuelling and resupply. The list was exactly the same as their last request, it never deviated. Dock workers diligently refuelled their ship while Aurange and Roberta observed their progress, as always, unseen. Once the task of resupply was completed, Aurange secured the Dark Angel's ventral cargo docking portal.

Roberta sent a detailed message to her friend, Elaine Haynes, filling her in on all of the details of their plan. When Elaine read the message, she replied to Roberta, telling her it was dangerous, even reckless and highly unlikely to succeed. Roberta assured Elaine that her plan would work.

"Elaine", Roberta typed, *"I have been manipulating Albert and his Father, Albertus, for decades. I have the High Prince's measure. This will work."*

Then, as always, their messages vanished from their devices as if they'd never been.

Aurange and Roberta left their ship, the Dark Angel, activating its security systems as they did so. No one would approach their ship during their absence, everyone knew better. Aurange and Roberta made their way to the High Prince's palace and his throne room for an audience. Fully armed as always, the pair made their way, citizens moving well clear of them, knowing not to block the path of High Prince Albert's enforcers. Elaine Haynes was on her way to meet them at the palace.

Elaine met Roberta and Aurange at the palace gates, "Roberta, if this goes south, please make sure my death is quick and painless", she whispered.

Roberta stopped, held Elaine by the shoulders and mouthed the words silently, *"I've got this!"*

The throne room was empty, except for the High Prince himself and his twelve *"ordinary High Prince's Guards"*, all waiting in the antechamber outside. They were actually highly trained, elite Jovian Shock Troopers, yet compared to Aurange and Roberta, they were little more than playful puppies. All twelve guards stepped back out of the way and stood to attention, six abreast, as Aurange, Roberta and Elaine approached. Even the palace guards, elite shock troopers though they may be, knew better than to trifle with the High Prince's Enforcers. Two guards opened the ornate throne room doors and let the trio into the High Prince's throne room.

Once the trio were inside the throne room and the doors closed behind them, one of the High Prince's guards enquired, "If push came to shove, how many of us elite shock troops would it take to bring down those two?"

The senior guard answered gruffly, "Shut the fuck up, man! A hundred of us would be no match for those two. Just asking that question could get us all killed and the High Prince would enjoy the spectacle as entertainment."

As the trio approached the High Prince, sitting on his ornate, gold-gilded throne, he greeted them, "Ah, my two favourite enforcers", and then he asked, "Why is Ms Elaine Haynes here?"

Roberta typed into her communicator, *"Elaine is my friend, Sire and her presence is necessary for this debriefing."*

The High Prince replied flippantly, "Okay, I'll allow it, although I have no idea how Elaine has anything to do with fourteen dead marks."

Elaine had her data table out and was reading Roberta's messages. She was aware that Aurange and Roberta had been on a mission for almost fifteen weeks, she was also aware that it was an ambassadorial assassination and that everyone on the Sleek Runner was supposed to be dead. Still, the number shocked her, as did how casually High Prince Albert spoke of it. Dead marks!

"That will come to light in due course, Your Majesty", Roberta messaged in reply.

High Prince Albert nodded, then asked Aurange, "How went the mission, Aurange?"

"It went well, Sire", Aurange keyed into his communicator, noting, *"The Sleek Runner is now a ghost ship heading into deep space. We have cleansed her, Sire."*

Good, good. And my orders. Did you send off the Ambassador as I requested?", Albert enquired.

Aurange typed in his reply, lying, *"I delegated that task to Roberta and she carried it out with alacrity, Sire. She really enjoyed herself. I could not have done better myself."*

"Roberta? I gave that order to you, Aurange", High Prince Albert frowned.

Roberta chimed in, lying and typing, *"Your Majesty, we had a lot of corpses to dispose of and a very short timeline. Aurange is very good with cleanup duties and I have a certain flair with torture."*

Aurange chimed in, typing and lying, *"While I disposed of the crew's corpses, Roberta set up a clean room and flayed the Ambassador and her staff alive. It was, I believe, exquisitely painful and a very, very slow, drawn-out process. It was beautiful in its brutality!"*

High Prince Albert smiled and laughed, "Yes, yes, of course, it was. Thank you, Roberta!"

The High Prince was most pleased.

Elaine, on the other hand, even though she knew everything to be a fabrication, still felt like puking.

The lie embedded in the High Prince's mind, his pleasure centres now triggered, Roberta began to deliver the dangerous news, the information that could bring them all undone.

"Sire, I did have to deviate from the planned operation slightly", Roberta typed and announced.

"Deviate, Roberta? That is so unlike you", the High Prince questioned.

"Yes, Sire. The Ambassador's diplomatic intern is a child", Roberta carefully typed, adding, *"I cannot kill a child. It is a part of my conditioning, Sire. The killing of children is forbidden."*

That was something that Albert did not know, he'd thought that his enforcers could just kill anyone.

"What about Aurange?", the High Prince questioned.

Aurange carefully typed in his reply, *"I can kill anyone, Sire. Children included, however, Roberta was triggered and she had no choice but to protect Lina Mitchel. I acquiesced to Roberta's trigger to maintain mission harmony. Disaster would have certainly followed otherwise"*, he was honest.

Aurange and Roberta were both very careful to make it sound like they were acting under involuntary triggers, which governed their joint behaviour.

Roberta typed into her communicator, *"Sire, Lina Mitchel is a child, she has no value as a mark. A child has no agency whatsoever. I am conditioned to protect children, Sire."*
"And where is this child, this Lina Mitchel, now?", the High Prince enquired.
Roberta keyed in her reply, *"Sire, Lina Mitchel is safe. I must protect her."*
High Prince Albert sighed, "Must you, Roberta? Really, must you?"
Roberta typed in, *"Yes, Sire. If necessary, I will adopt her. Treat her as my own child. Even train her and teach her to be an operative just like me."*
That piqued the High Prince's interest, "Adopt her, Roberta? After what she has seen?"
Roberta typed in her next lie, *"The child has seen nothing, Sire. I locked her in her cabin on the Sleek Runner before we started our work. Lina Mitchel has seen nothing, Sire."*
"Nonetheless, Roberta, you murdered the ship's crew and tortured her colleagues and friends, flaying them slowly to death. How is this adoption going to work?", the High Prince questioned.
Roberta frowned falsely and typed, lying, *"Yes, Sire. It will be difficult, however I am confident that I can condition her to respond positively. Lina Mitchel is showing signs of Stockholm Syndrome, exactly as I have planned. Five years from now, you will have another enforcer, Sire. "*
That was the clincher, another possible enforcer.

High Prince Albert was quiet for an overtly long length of time. That had

Roberta worried. Then the High Prince's demeanour changed

High Prince Albert let loose a low chuckle, slowly it grew louder, before long he was laughing and eventually he was belly laughing so loud it seemed ridiculous.

Roberta smiled, the High Prince was amused to the point of acquiescing to her wishes.

Albert pointed to Roberta, "You! A Mother! Oh my God, Roberta! That is just too much!", he blurted out between bursts of laughter, he even had tears of joy, or were they tears of madness, streaming down his cheeks.

Albert pointed to Elaine and asked, "What about you, Elaine? Is this hilarious or what?"

Elaine feigned laughter convincingly and replied, "Yes, Your Majesty. The whole concept borders somewhere between the absurd and the ridiculous", then she asked falsely, "How long will it be before Roberta slaughters young Lina. Your Majesty, you could even take bets."

That cracked up the High Prince and he laughed even more loudly. So loudly, in fact, that his Imperial Guards in the antechamber could hear him.

Roberta kept a straight face, internalising a smile, thinking to herself, *"Thank you, Elaine, you just pushed him in the right direction."*

Several minutes later, the High Prince finally composed himself, "Roberta, just how is this adoption going to work? You are an operative. You and Aurange are always out and about. You know, you are both always killing someone here or there. A bit of espionage. That sort of thing. So just how will this work?", to Albert, it was becoming a matter of practicality.

"Well, Sire", Roberta began typing, *"I will ask Elaine Haynes to take in Lina Mitchel in the interim, at least until I have her conditioned enough to trust me. Then she can move in with me. Whenever Aurange and I go on a mission, Lina will stay with Elaine. It is actually quite simple, Sire."*

Elaine feigned ignorance perfectly, "Sire, I could, in theory, take Lina in. I do have a spare room."

"And what is to stop Lina from talking?", the High Prince enquired.

Elaine answered, "The same thing stops every Jovian citizen from talking, Sire. No ordinary Jovian citizens can access the external communications network. No one outside of Ganymede Prime will ever know that Lina Mitchel is even still alive."

The High Prince sat silently considering everything he'd been told, then he spoke, "Roberta, your petition to adopt Lina Mitchel is granted. Elaine, help Roberta with the paperwork and I will notarise it myself", then he added, "And Elaine, no betting pools. That suggestion, although hilarious, was just plain crass."

The High Prince then smiled, and noted, more to himself than anyone else, "Roberta Nummus, the Monstrous Mother!"

Roberta didn't care, she'd just played the High Prince like a fine violin.

Aurange made a request of the High Prince, he typed, *"Your Majesty, if I may. Roberta and I have been in space for nearly fifteen weeks. Perhaps we could have a few weeks off. We would be on call, of course, in case of emergencies, but we do need some downtime, Sire."*

The High Prince was in a good mood and feeling generous, "Yes, yes, Aurange. You and Roberta, take four weeks off, on call twenty four seven, of course."

"Thank you, Your Majesty", Aurange typed in reply.

The audience with the High Prince ended and the trio left the throne room. The twelve imperial guards waited in the anteroom, watching as the trio crossed the room to the far side. Aurange and Roberta were still heavily armed with their high-powered rapid-fire pulse laser rifles, their pulse laser pistols, sabres, katana, kukri swords and other knives. The guards all knew that what they could see was just scratching the surface. Their High Prince had been laughing raucously, he was happy with his enforcers. A good thing too, the imperial guards had no wish to go up against either Aurange Sheergibbon or Roberta Nummus. That would be suicide!

Aurange went about his own business. Roberta and Elaine made their way to external docking port thirteen. Once on board the Dark Angel, Elaine noticed an almost metallic taste in the air.

Roberta knew that look and typed in a message, *"Nigh on fifteen weeks in space leaves that taste in the air. It will settle down once the scrubbers are fully auto-cleaned and new fresh air is cycled in. It will take a few days for that to take place."*

Elaine nodded as they made their way to Lina's cabin. Roberta opened the door and Lina ran up to her and hugged her. It was an awkward moment, Roberta was still heavily armed.

"I thought you weren't coming back. I was so scared!", Lina exclaimed.

Roberta was surprised. Lina had never hugged her before.

Elaine introduced herself, "I'm Elaine, Elaine Haynes, Roberta's friend. You are safe now, Lina."

Roberta stepped back and typed a message into her communicator.

Elaine read out the message, *"Relatively safe, for now."*

Elaine explained the situation to Lina, "You'll be moving into my apartment, Lina. I've prepared my spare room for you. Roberta has officially adopted you and that makes you a part of her family. It's a layer of protection. Anyone who messes with you is messing with Roberta. No one messes with my Roberta. I know it probably sounds weird, but it should keep you 'relatively' safe."

Roberta mentally took note of the phrase Elaine had used, *"My Roberta"*, but said nothing.

It was weird, Roberta was the monstrous beast woman that had murdered her Aunt Sonia and Lina replied, "It is weird. Roberta murdered my Aunt, yes, but she does protect me. Roberta may be a monster, but she is my monster."

Roberta smiled and typed a new message, Elaine read it out, *"A lioness protects her cubs. Always!"*

Roberta typed in a longer message, it took her quite a while and then Elaine read it out, *"Lina, leave all of your things here. If anything goes wrong, this cabin will be your bug-out bag and the Dark Angel will be our escape ship. Anything you need in Ganymede Prime, I'll provide it all brand new."*

Lina joked, "What if I have expensive tastes?"

Roberta smiled and messed Lina's hair, then typed in another message, Elaine read it out, *"I have more credits than I know what to do with."*

When they arrived at Elaine's apartment, Lina walked in, noticing straight away that it was spacious, beautifully furnished and looked more than comfortable.

"Lina, your room is over yonder, on the left", Elaine pointed to an open bedroom door, then added, "I've already filled your wardrobe with clothes. Roberta told me your size. I hope I got the styling right. Please let me know if I didn't."

As Lina ran to her new bedroom, Roberta relaxed, placing her pulse plasma rifle in a corner and hanging her utility belt with its multiple swords and pulse laser pistol from a coat rack. Roberta rolled her head around her neck and it clicked and popped, releasing her pent-up tension.

Elaine stood in front of Roberta, placed her hand on Roberta's waist and then leaned in real close, whispering, "I really, really missed you, my love", then she planted a lingering kiss on Roberta's lips.

Roberta wrapped her hands around Elaine and returned the kiss with gentle ferocity.

"Your styling is perfect, Elaine", Lina shouted out as she came back out of her bedroom, then upon seeing Roberta and Elaine kissing, "Guys. You really need to get a room."

Elaine smiled, her face slightly flustered with embarrassment, "We have one already, Lina. It's the bedroom next to yours."

"I'll leave you guys to it", Lina replied and then returned to her room, her face ever so slightly red.

Elaine locked her apartment door and then walked over to her bedroom, on the way asking Lina to make herself at home.

Roberta collected her pulse laser rifle and utility belt and followed Elaine. Roberta would never allow herself to be far away from her tools and she placed them inside Elaine's bedroom on her dresser.

Roberta messaged Elaine, *"I thought we, us, were just friends. You needed my protection. Friends with benefits. That was all. I am confused."*

"Absence makes the heart grow fonder, Roberta", Elaine replied and then noted, "I didn't realise it was love until you were three weeks out of space dock."

Roberta chuckled slightly and messaged back, *"That cuts both ways. I love you as well, at least as much as a monster can love."*

Elaine closed her bedroom door, *"You are not a monster to me, Roberta. Once yes, but not now."*

Elaine and Roberta spent several hours of intimacy in Elaine's bed, until Lina knocked on the door, "I've cooked supper. Are you guys hungry?"

And that was the beginning of one highly unusual family.

Over the following months, Elaine explained Roberta's and Aurange's back stories to Lina, which did match some things that she had already known. Elaine filled in the gaps in her knowledge and Lina began to comprehend her protective monster much better.

Roberta came over to Elaine's apartment quite often, staying overnight, but always disappearing before morning. Roberta completed Lina's training in the secret finger language that she and Aurange used and began to teach it to Elaine as well. Elaine learned it very quickly.

During the day, Roberta took Lina to the private gym where only she and Aurange trained. It was here that Roberta taught Lina how to defend herself, but later that changed. Self-defence was first, yes, but offensive fighting techniques and skills quickly followed. Roberta did not want Lina to become a monster like her, but she did want Lina to know how to protect herself, even if that meant killing an assailant. Roberta explained to Lina that a dead assailant does not get a second attempt at your life.

There were days when Roberta would get emotional, lamenting the fact that she was a killer and she would tearfully describe herself as a monstrous mother replacement, not worthy of having children. Lina could see the inner hatred that Roberta had for herself and what the military, all those years ago, had made her into.

It was during one of these emotional displays of depression that Roberta mentioned that she could never have children of her own. Her *"special"* training with its conditioning and the genetic enhancement serums and elixirs had robbed her of ever being a real mother. Gradually over time, in Lina's eyes, Roberta somehow became less of a monster and more of a fierce warrior woman protector.

Time passed slowly in Ganymede Prime, but it still passed and a few years later, it was the year twenty one eighty one. Little had happened in the intervening three years and life seemed almost normal for a family made up of a Health

Minister in the High Prince's cabinet, one of the High Prince's two deadliest enforcers and a young woman, now nineteen, who had once been targeted for elimination. Someone who, by all logic, should not be alive.

Roberta appeared to have much better control of her *"triggers"* and no more heads had been *"taken"* during the High Prince's cabinet meetings. High Prince Albert himself was becoming senile and he was not sending Roberta and Aurange on external missions anymore. Along with High Prince Albert's senility came paranoia and he wanted his two best enforcers close at hand.

Roberta saw that as a worrying sign and secretly ensured that the Dark Angel was always ready and prepared for launch at a moment's notice. The High Prince was becoming unstable and erratic, he could, under the right, or perhaps more correctly, the wrong influence, turn on them and Roberta could see where that influence would come from.

High Prince Albert had four Sons, Princes Godric, Aluric, Emeric and Friederic, and none of them trusted Aurange Sheergibbon or Roberta Nummus. All that they needed was a solid pretext to turn their Father's twisted mind down a path towards their downfall.

All four Sons considered Lina Mitchel, still being alive, the mark that lived, to be an anathema. Someone who should not exist and the fact that Roberta Nummus spared her, in their eyes, made her a traitor. The fact that Aurange Sheergibbon was complicit, in their eyes, made him a traitor as well. It did not matter that their Father, High Prince Albert, had let the young woman live. They considered him senile and would have preferred him to step down and abdicate. Of course, High Prince Albert was not one to abdicate his throne.

Slowly, the four Sons of High Prince Albert, Princes Godric, Aluric, Emeric and Friederic, began their plotting. It started with the simple acquisition of some rather innocuous information. These were the four Sons of High Prince Albert and the Apocalypse was coming.

Far away from Ganymede Prime, on distant Earth, in a large cavern under the South Australian sandstone, fifty kilometres from Coober Pedy, an old man with crepey, old, liver-spotted skin and badly balding hair named Orpheus, mumbled in his sleep, *"His time is nigh and so is the death of Dolphins. The burning times were coming!"*

11. Betrayals.

Not a single one of the High Prince's four Sons was happy with the fact that a mark, someone who should by all rights be dead, was still alive and worse still, adopted and protected by the very woman who was supposed to kill her. High Prince Albert's second Son, Aluric, who liked to think he was the dominant Son, took matters into his own hands and sent three of his own assassins to murder Lina Mitchel during the night.

It was two twenty two am when Roberta awoke to the subtle vibrations of her wristwatch, its alarm was silent, but it was meant to be. Roberta held the watch up to her face and activated the backlighting. Hmm, external sensors that Roberta had planted surreptitiously in the hallway outside of Elaine's apartment had triggered the silent alarm. Roberta sat up in bed and Elaine stirred in bed beside her.

Roberta placed her index finger on Elaine's lips and mouthed, *"Shhh."*

Roberta got out of bed and walked over to the dresser where she removed two ice picks from her utility belt, leaving her sabre, katana, kukri swords and pulse laser pistol behind. Elaine watched, frightened and fascinated at the same time, as her naked lover left the bedroom and closed the door behind her. Roberta had moved with a smooth, subtle grace that belied her true nature.

Roberta silently moved across the room towards the apartment door. She stepped back along the wall, checked the screen on her wristwatch and waited. Two of the figures in the hallway were approaching Elaine's apartment door, the third stayed back, a watchman. All of a sudden, the apartment door was kicked in and the two men entered. The door itself swung inwards towards Roberta's position and rebounded off the wall, shielding Roberta from their sight.

Roberta swung into motion, slammed the door shut and within a split second jammed her ice picks in the first assailant's ears. As the assailant collapsed to the floor, Roberta took the pulse pistol from his right hand and lined it up on the second assailant. The assassin turned around, only to find Roberta naked and holding a pulse pistol aimed squarely at his chest. Veeeee-wack! Veeeee-wack! Veeeee-wack! Three shots to the chest. Veeeee-wack! Veeeee-wack! A double tap to the forehead. The assailant collapsed to the floor.

Roberta checked her wristwatch's stop clock, three seconds, *"I'm getting slow"*, she thought.

Roberta silently moved back to her position against the wall and checked her wristwatch once again.

The third man, the watcher, was now moving forward. Roberta noted his position in relation to her sensors and moved to the apartment door.

In one fluid motion, Roberta swung open the door and rolled out into the hallway, the pulse laser pistol in her hand finding its target. Veeeee-wack! Veeeee-wack! Veeeee-wack! The pulse laser pistol fired three shots at his chest. Veeeee-wack! Veeeee-wack! And another double tap to the forehead. The third assassin, now dead, was still staring in disbelief at the naked woman who had just shot him. He fell to the hallway floor.

A neighbour of Elaine's opened her apartment door to see what the commotion was. She took one look at the armed and naked women, recognised her face and quickly closed the door again. Roberta dragged the dead assassin into Elaine's apartment and closed its door, securing it as best as she could.

Lina opened her bedroom door with sleepy eyes and saw the three dead assassins, "What the fuck!"

Elaine was standing at her now open bedroom door, "Go back to bed, Lina. We'll take care of this."

Roberta was already on her communicator and typing, *"Aurange! Wake the fuck up! We need a cleanup crew at Elaine Haynes's apartment."*

And now the troubles were beginning.

Aurange arrived with a cleanup crew within twenty minutes, he was wearing tracksuit pants and a t-shirt and quickly signed with his fingers, *"Sorry I took so long, I had to wake these lazy fuckers up."*

Aurange didn't know it, but both Elaine and Lina were fully fluent in his secret sign language, Roberta signed back, *"These were fucking amateurs. They had no idea I was even here."*

Aurange looked at Lina and then signed to Roberta, *"The undead mark was their target. She is not safe here, Roberta."*

Roberta scoffed and signed back, *"Pigs arse. Let the word out. Whoever came after my Lina, I'm coming after them. I'll line up their fucking heads up and down that fucking hallway after this."*

Aurange nodded and signed, *"I'll make it so, but be careful. This stinks of one of Albert's Sons."*

Roberta nodded. Aurange was probably right and that meant treading more softly.

Aurange supervised the cleanup crew and by six am, the bodies were gone, blood stains removed and Elaine's apartment door had been not only fixed but also reinforced.

By midday, the word had spread. Roberta Nummus was pissed off and wanted heads. Prince Aluric went to ground in Ganymede Prime's southern end cap and surrounded himself with his bodyguards.

The young Prince had right royally fucked up!

The heir apparent to the throne, Prince Godric, travelled with his other Brothers, Emeric and Friederic, from their Father's palace to Ganymede's southern end cap. Godric knew where his Brother's bunker was, where his safe house was.

"Brother Aluric! Of all the stupid things you could have done", Godric shouted at him, "You've put that bloody bitch on alert and now she wants heads!"

"Does she know it was me, Brother?", Aluric asked sheepishly.

"No, you dumb fuck! But, do you know what? She could easily blame any one of us, perhaps even all of us!", Godric admonished, shaking his head in disgust.

Prince Emeric chimed in, "We could try again. Use a better team. Perhaps take down Nummus first and then go after the undead mark", he was supposed to be the strategic thinker.

Prince Godric was about to tell him what an idiot he was when Prince Friederic chimed in, "We need an angle, Brothers. We need something we can pin on Nummus. We need to get our Father on our side first. He can order her death!"

Prince Godric pointed to Friederic, shaking his finger at him, "Yes, yes, Brother Friederic. Work on that. We need to paint that bitch as a traitor. We need Father to order her death."

All of the High Prince's Sons had access to the external news feeds and data networks. Prince Friederic worked diligently, looking for any angle on Roberta Nummus that could be used against her. It was, of course, going nowhere. Aurange and Roberta had been shadows and there was very little information about them. Most of what Prince Friederic found came across as myths and legends. The young Prince needed another angle.

Why did Roberta Nummus adopt a sixteen-year-old mark?

Who was this undead mark?

Where did she come from?

What was her background?

Prince Friederic started poking around. Lina Mitchel's Father was Darren Mitchel and her Mother was Sancia Mitchel, nee de la Cruz. That caught Friederic's attention, so he looked into Sonia de la Cruz's family details. And there it was, Sonia de la Cruz was Sancia's older Sister, older by some eight years. Friederic smiled to himself, Lina Mitchel was Ambassadorial Emissary Sonia de la Cruz's niece!

Prince Friederic was intrigued and he dove deeper into the tale of Lina Mitchel.

Lina Mitchel was five years old and she was excited. Her Mum and Dad were taking her to see her Aunt Sonia at Eros, the City within the Rock. They were going to stay a whole month. Lina's home was nice. It was a typical O'Neil-style twin-cylinder colony, but Eros, Eros was humongous. It had mountains and artificial seas, even a city and all of it, inside the hollowed-out asteroid Eros. A huge, cylindrical hollow, carefully crafted into a living, breathing world. It was so beautiful! A paradise!

The best part from Lina's perspective, Eros had real beaches, sailing boats and best of all, Dolphins and Porpoises. They were colonists just like people, just ones that swam in the Erosian Seas. Lina's Mother had promised to buy her a translator, so that she could talk to the Dolphins.

Lina was so excited.

Lina's home was a corporate colony, one of six at Earth's trailing Trojan point. Eros was in the same region, although much farther out in a far larger, higher halo orbit. Lina's Father, Darren, worked for the Earth Trojan Mining Corporation, one of the many corporations under the Dumas Incorporated Industries umbrella. Darren Mitchel was an executive. He, his Wife, Sancia and his Daughter, Lina, were on board an executive shuttle flying to Eros, a trip that should only take four hours.

Then it happened, they were just one hour out from Eros when there was a sudden, ping, ping sound. Immediately, the alarms sounded and Lina watched as the co-pilot opened the Pilot's Cabin door and reached for a cabinet. Lina was quite close and she could read the cans. One was labelled, *"Red Mist"* and the other, *"Zoosh Sealant"*.

The co-pilot sprayed the red mist with his left hand and then followed where the mist flowed. It was the starboard hull. He sprayed the zoosh sealant into the hole where the red mist was flowing and the flow stopped. Then he turned around to the port hull and followed the red mist flowing there. Again, the co-pilot sprayed zoosh sealant into the hole and it sealed.

All the while, the pilot had been on the radio, "May day! May day! May day! Corporate Shuttle Axis five en route to Eros. We have suffered micrometeor penetration, our hull has been breached. Repeat, our hull has been breached", he shouted.

The pilot repeated that message over and over and over.

Then there was another ping, ping sound this time from the Pilot's Cabin. The pilot slumped in his cockpit seat. The back of his head was missing. Then there was a sudden popping sound and the Pilot's Cabin door slammed shut and automatically sealed itself. The pilot's cabin had suffered a catastrophic breach was was open to space. The automatic distress beacon began transmitting telemetry data.

Time seemed to slow, and, ping, ping, another micrometeor smashed through the shuttle. Lina's Father, Darren, was holding his right ear, which was missing and there was blood everywhere. The co-pilot shoved a medical kit into her Mother's, Sancia's, hands and then he went about the business of spraying red mist, tracing the airflow and sealing the breaches with zoosh sealant.

The breaches happened, perhaps, three or four more times and little Lina was terrified. The co-pilot had gone through two cans of red mist and zoosh sealant and was on his third pair of cans. Each breach was sealed in rapid succession.

Then the unthinkable happened, there was a shallower, softer, ping, ping. The co-pilot sprayed his red mist and it flowed beneath the shuttle's decking plates. The breaches would not be easily reachable.

The co-pilot turned around and around, "Fuck! Fuck! Fuck!", he screamed.

The co-pilot looked at Lina, then he turned to Sancia. He pointed to the back of the passenger cabin and the luggage compartment. Sancia thought she understood and grabbed Lina up in her arms, rushing to the luggage compartment. The co-pilot was ahead of her. The compartment was already open. He threw their suitcases out onto the cabin floor.

The co-pilot spoke to Lina, "Little one. We're going to put you in here. You will be safe. When the rescue team arrives, they'll bang on the door. You need to bang back the same way that they do, okay?"

Lina nodded and replied, "What about Mommy and Daddy?"

"There's no room, sweetheart", Sancia replied and then lied, "Mummy and Daddy will be just fine."

As Sancia placed Lina in the luggage compartment, the co-pilot told Lina, "Whatever you do, little one, don't open this door. Be patient, be very patient and wait for the rescue team", and then he closed the door shut and sealed the entire thing with zoosh sealant.

Lina was locked in and completely in the dark, alone and afraid. So alone, so afraid!

The co-pilot didn't stop, he ripped open the suitcases, "Tie all the shirts, sleeve to sleeve. Then tie the jeans and trousers legs to legs. When we're done, tie the last shirt to the first pair of jeans."

Darren was holding a gauze patch to his right ear and was almost passing out. Sancia urgently did as the co-pilot had asked. Soon they had a rope of shirts, jeans and trousers. The co-pilot tied off one end of the *"rope"* next to the main cabin door on an internal handhold. Then he stretched it over the shuttle's seating all the way back to the luggage compartment. Finally, he tied the end of their *"rope"* to the luggage compartment's handle.

The co-pilot looked at Sancia and Darren and remarked, "Breadcrumbs."

The co-pilot didn't stop. He retrieved a toolkit and started unbolting and ripping up the shuttle's deck plating in a race against time to get to the last pair of leaks and seal them. Time seemed to slow, but was moving far too quickly. The fourth deck plate was removed and now he had access. He sprayed the red mist into the superstructure and located the hole. He marked it. Then he did the same on the other side of the hull.

The co-pilot leaned deeply into the superstructure and then sprayed the zoosh sealant into the breach. With one hole sealed, they were beginning to have hope. Then he moved over to the other breach and reached into the superstructure. He sprayed the zoosh sealant and the can was empty. It was empty!

The co-pilot crawled back out of the superstructure, "The can is empty", he noted.

"Grab another one", Sancia told him, "Grab another one!", she shouted.

"This was the fourth and final can", the co-pilot informed her.

Then the co-pilot reached into the superstructure one more time and, in a futile attempt to close the breach, he jammed a sock into it!

That was all he had left. It was fucking futile, but it was all they had.

Then he climbed back out of the superstructure and sat down with Darren and Sancia.

They all waited in silence, waiting for the inevitable.

The rescue ship arrived less than five minutes later. They docked with the shuttle and boarded her, three men wearing spacesuits. They found two passengers and the co-pilot sitting on the cabin floor. They were all dead. Five minutes, five minutes was all it took. Their rescuers were simply too late.

"Says here on the ship's passenger manifest that there's a third passenger", a rescuer noted.

Another rescuer saw the *"rope"* of clothes leading from the main cabin door to the rear of the cabin and the luggage compartment, "What's this then?"

The first rescuer walked over to the luggage compartment and, noticing it had been sealed shut, he tapped on the door twice. Two taps came back. He tapped again three times. Three taps came back.

The first rescuer shouted out to his colleagues over their intercom, "Fucking breadcrumbs! We have a survivor! We need to seal any remaining breaches and get air in here asap!"

And so little five-year-old Lina Mitchel survived, to be raised by her Aunt Sonia inside Eros, the City within the Rock.

Around fourteen years later, a now nineteen-year-old Lina Mitchel woke up screaming and sweating profusely in her bed in Elaine Haynes' apartment in Ganymede Prime.

And Prince Friederic had his answers. Lina Mitchel was not just a diplomatic intern. She was Ambassadorial Emissary Sonia de la Cruz's Niece and family. The mark was meant to die!

Aurange Sheergibbon stood in the centre of the High Prince's throne room. It was an unusual situation. Normally, he would be there with Roberta Nummus, however, Roberta was not in the room. There were a lot of palace guards, however, at least two dozen, perhaps even more. When the High Prince's Sons appeared from the High Prince's private chamber, things began to make sense. The more royals, the more palace guards. Still, something felt very off about the situation.

The four Princes stood by their Father's side as he sat on his throne. He was looking much older now, quite frail, he even drooled.

Prince Godric spoke first, "Sheergibbon, we need to discuss this 'Roberta Nummus' problem."

The youngest Prince, Prince Friederic, spoke up, "Sheergibbon. Were you aware that Lina Mitchel was Ambassadorial Emissary Sonia de la Cruz's Niece? Were you aware that Roberta Nummus was sparing the life of the Emissary's Niece?"

Aurange recalled that day in the Sleek Runner's dining room. Yes, he remembered Sonia calling Lina her Niece. He remembered, yes, but he decided not to divulge that information.

Aurange keyed a message into his communicator and it appeared on High Prince Albert's data table.

Prince Friederic picked up his Father's data tablet and read the message, *"Neither I nor Roberta was aware of that information, Your Highness"*, he passed the data tablet to his siblings to read the message.

"Had you been aware of this information, would Lina Mitchel have been spared?", Prince Godric asked, "or would the mark have been eliminated?"

Aurange keyed another reply into his communicator, *"It would not have affected the outcome. Roberta's conditioning does not allow the killing of a child. The outcome would have been the same."*

Aluric blurted out, "She's not a child now! Why is she still alive?"

Aurange responded with another message, *"Your Highness. Lina Mitchel is still a teenager. Lina Mitchel is now Roberta's adopted Daughter. Lina Mitchel is under Roberta's care and protection."*

Emeric chimed in, questioning, "So the undead mark will remain undead?"

Aurange's eyes were subtly looking around the throne room, he knew precisely how every palace guard was positioned. If things went south, he was fully prepared for action.

Aurange keyed in another message, *"Affirmative. The undead mark will remain undead."*

"Aurange Sheergibbon!", Prince Godric shouted, "Lina Mitchel is an undead mark! A stain upon our Jovian Realms! A loose end that cannot and must not be allowed to exist!"

Aurange typed in his reply and Prince Godric read it, *"Your Highness. The High*

Prince allowed it. The High Prince signed off on it. Roberta's adoption of Lina Mitchel was signed by your Father, High Prince Albert's own hand."

Prince Godric spat back, "My Father can always change his mind!", and then he turned to his Father, "Can't you, Father?"

High Prince Albert mumbled, "Yes, yes, of course. My mind is always changing. Always changing."

Crown Prince Godric asserted himself, "Roberta Nummus is a traitor! You are hereby ordered to eliminate both Roberta Nummus and her adopted Daughter, Lina Mitchel! The undead mark must die!"

Aurange did not acknowledge the order, the Crown Prince had no real authority over him, he typed in another message, *"Your Highness. The order must come from His Majesty, High Prince Albert."*

Crown Prince Godric smiled, "Father, do you agree that the traitor and her adopted Daughter should be eliminated, erased?"

High Prince Albert mumbled, "Yes, yes, Godric. All traitors and their families must die!"

Aurange was careful and typed in another message, *"The targets must be named, Sire."*

Crown Prince Godric whispered in his Father's ear and then the High Prince announced, more assertively, "Roberta Nummus and Lina Mitchel. Traitors and their families must die! Bring me their heads! Off with their heads!"

There was nothing more to it, Aurange had a direct order from the High Prince himself, he could not disobey, he typed in one final message, *"Your will be done, Sire"*, then turned on his heels and left.

And that was that. That was the first betrayal of Roberta Nummus by her patron, High Prince Albert.

The four Sons of High Prince Albert, Princes all, giggled to themselves.

Prince Aluric commented, "This is too easy. All we have to do is tell Father what we want."

Prince Emeric noted, "It isn't over yet. We don't have their heads!"

Prince Friederic chimed in, "We still have Aurange Sheergibbon to deal with!"

Crown Prince Godric called over the Captain of the palace guards and then he whispered in his Father's ear once more.

High Prince Albert raised his right hand, "Aurange Sheergibbon. All traitors must die. Bring me their heads. Off with their heads!", he mumbled

Crown Prince Godric looked at the Captain, "You heard my Father's orders."

"Yes, Your Highness", the Captain replied, holding back a gulp, he had just been ordered to kill Aurange Sheergibbon and that was not an easy thing to do.

Prince Friederic chimed in, "Captain. It would be best to wait for Sheergibbon to come to us with Nummus's and Mitchel's heads. Lay in wait, an ambush and make sure you have at least a hundred palace guards on hand. Any less would be ill advised!"

Crown Prince Godric confirmed, "Yes, yes. That is a good idea, Friederic. Captain, make it so!"

Then the four Princes went back to their giggles and laughter.

And that was the betrayal of Aurange Sheergibbon by his patron, High Prince Albert.

Before heading to his audience with the High Prince in his palace throne room, Aurange had sent a message to Roberta to let her know he'd meet her there. Only Roberta had not been requested to attend.

This was the first time in over eight decades that anything like this had happened. In any meeting with either Albert or his Father, Albertus, they had always both been present. Roberta saw this as a breach of protocol, one that could not be ignored.

Roberta messaged Elaine and Lina, *"Get your bug-out bags. We are leaving!"*

Neither Elaine nor Lina hesitated. They had long prepared for this very moment. They both grabbed their bug-out bags and followed Roberta out of the apartment door.

"Your ship, Roberta, the Dark Angel. My understanding is that it's an old ship", Elaine noted as they exited the apartment building.

Roberta typed in another message, *"She is, Elaine. She's a Tristar Interplanetary Stealth Ship, but don't worry. Aurange and I have upgraded the engines, weapons systems and shielding every ten years or so since we stole her over eight decades ago. The Dark Angel is old, but fast, solid and deadly."*

Elaine nodded and replied, "Good to know", as they walked towards external docketing port thirteen, taking the most circuitous route.

They were taking the back way to avoid being noticed. Roberta wasn't stupid, just cautious, she knew Aurange Sheergibbon and he would be making his way to the Dark Angel as well. It was just a matter of whether or not he was friend or foe when they finally met up.

As the trio approached the section of the northern end cap's docking ring that contained external docking port thirteen, they came across Aurange. Roberta passed her bug-out bag to Elaine. Aurange and Roberta were both fully armed. The pair stared at each other across the open space between them.

Roberta placed her right hand in front of Elaine in such a way that Aurange could not see and began signing, *"If this goes south, at the first opportunity, take yourself and Lina to the Dark Angel. Use my codes to enter the ship, you know the ones and perform a full lockdown as I've shown you. Wait there until I return. If I don't return or if Aurange or the Jovian Shock Troops turn up, launch immediately. Open up my Omega Nine file and follow the instructions."*

Roberta passed Elaine a data stick and Elaine accepted it, placing it into her pocket.

Elaine held onto Roberta's hand, caressed it and kissed it gently before replying, "I understand."

Elaine held Roberta's bug-out bag in one hand and grabbed Lina's hand with the other.

"Friend or foe, Aurange?", Roberta signed loudly, making sure he'd see her precise movements.

Aurange shook his head, he was conflicted, but he had been given orders, he signed back, *"I have been ordered by the High Prince himself. Both you and Lina Mitchel are designated marks!"*

Roberta had known that they were living on borrowed time, the High Prince had been becoming more and more erratic, far less lucid and his four evil Sons were always skulking around like vultures.

"So, foe it is then. So be it", Roberta signed back and then she enquired, signing, *"How are we going to play this out then, Aurange?"*

Aurange smiled a wry smile as he took his high-powered rapid-fire pulse laser rifle's strap from off his shoulder and slipped the heavy weapon to the ground, *"Old school, Roberta. Let's dance!"*

Roberta did likewise and soon her high-powered rapid-fire pulse laser rifle lay on the ground beside her as well.

There were quite a few dock workers in the area and when they realised what was happening, they all quickly fled the scene.

And that was that. This was the second betrayal of Roberta Nummus, this time by her long-time partner of more than eight decades, Aurange Sheergibbon.

Aurange unsheathed his sabre with an almost imperceptible audible sound. Roberta checked her sabre, but instead unsheathed her katana. It was long, impossibly sharp and its blade contained over two hundred and sixty two thousand layers of duralium steel. It was considered unbreakable.

Roberta had crafted it herself. It took her five years to make and she only ever used it in duels against worthy opponents. Aurange was a betrayer, yes, but he was nonetheless worthy of its keen, cutting edge. Elaine led Lina back away from the duelling space and eyed the area carefully for a means to access the Dark Angel.

Aurange signed to Roberta, *"Your Katana, the Haröingu. If I fall, at least it will be with honour."*

"There is no honour in betrayal, Aurange. May the Harrowing take you", Roberta signed back with a curse.

And then their dance began!

Roberta kissed her katana, then swung it out in salute. Aurange did the same with his sabre. Then they both rushed into the middle of the dockyard's open space. The clash of cold, hard steel was heard over and over, too many times to count, in blurs of motion too fast for the eyes of bystanders to see.

Then the pair had their blades pressed firmly against each other before they pushed away and retreated from each other. Elaine tried to drag Lina to the Dark Angel, but Lina refused to budge. Her monster, her Roberta, was fighting for her life. There were tears in Lina's eyes.

As Roberta and Aurange circled each other, Aurange signed to Roberta a taunt, *"I've lost count of how many times I've fucked you over the decades"*, then he took it down below gutter level, *"Today, I'm going to fuck your corpse while it's still warm and force your Daughter and Girlfriend to watch."*

Roberta did not respond, that was exactly what Aurange wanted, she simply signed back, *"Your fucking days will soon be over, Aurange! No more fucking for you!"*

Then they both rushed into the centre and the clashing of cold, hard steel began once more. The two combatants moved in swift, blurred motions with their swords slicing the air and crashing cold steel against cold steel. Tears ran down Elaine's and Lina's cheeks as they both watched in horror. Roberta could die and should she fall, so too would Lina and Elaine.

This time the clash lasted longer and when they both finally broke apart, they were covered in sweat. Roberta rolled her head about her neck with audible cracks and pops, releasing tension. Aurange stared across the dockyard space with cold fury. Then Roberta had an idea. Why not taunt Aurange back?

Roberta signed to Aurange, *"You know, Albertus Horridian had a nickname for us. His Son Albert used the same nicknames as well, but never to our faces."*

Aurange did not know this, he had not been as observant with Albertus or Albert, at least not as observant as Roberta had been

Aurange signed back, curious, rising to the bait, *"Really, how so?"*

"Well, Aurange. They both called me, Booby Nums Nums", Roberta messaged back self-deprecatingly, setting up Aurange for the release of his nicknames.

Aurange and Roberta continued to circle each other warily, as he signed to Roberta, *"That makes perfect sense. Your tits are fucking huge and from my experience, they are quite tasty!"*, he taunted.

Roberta did not take the bait, instead, she used an old nickname for Aurange, signing, *"Well, Carrot Top"*, she taunted and then piled on with, *"Albertus Horridian and his Son, Albert, both called you the Orange Shitgibbon!"*

Aurange's face went bright red, all civility was lost and angrily, carelessly, he rushed at Roberta. She was ready and their cold, hard steel clashed once more, far more urgently. Over and over, their blades clashed, Aurange with uncontrolled ferocity, Roberta with cool, calculated blocking and counterstrikes.

As their blades clashed, Roberta dropped low, slipped underneath Aurange's sabre and sliced behind herself as she walked away. Her blade had struck true. As she turned around and saw the distinct streak of red running down Aurange's back.

Aurange straightened up, arched his back slightly and screamed internally, *"Fucking bitch!"*, then he shrugged off the pain and signed back to Roberta as if it was nothing, *"Clever bitch!"*

Roberta saw her advantage and as they circled each other once more, she piled on, signing, *"What's the matter, Carrot Top? You don't like being called a Shitgibbon, do you? You have to admit, your arms are rather long for a Human, more like a gibbon or an orangutan, really. You even waddle like one!"*

Aurange could not control his rage, he rushed in once more and the clash of steel was heard across the dockyards. Roberta maintained her control, ducking here, dodging there, her Katana, *the Harōingu,* catching Aurange and nicking and cutting him. They both broke away once more and began to circle each other. Aurange took stock. A slice to his left cheek, a slice across his upper left arm and a slice across his right leg and, of course, he had blood running down his back from Roberta's original strike.

Aurange stopped still, staring coldly back at Roberta, determination on his face, he signed, *"Your taunts won't stop me, Booby Num Nums. I'm going to slice off your tits and eat them for my dinner!"*

Roberta signed back coldly, *"You've already eaten your last meal, Shitgibbon!"*, she taunted.

And then their dance continued.

Roberta and Aurange clashed once more and the sounds of combat were beginning to draw the dockworkers back out from hiding. They stood at the edges, well out of the way, taking bets. As sabre and katana clashed with Aurange using the full force of his strength and Roberta using finesse and control, Lina and Elaine looked on in abject horror and shock.

Then it happened, right at a point when Aurange was delivering hammering blows at Roberta and she was on the back foot blocking, one of the dock workers through a pipe at her. The metal pipe caught Roberta on the back of the leg and she fell backwards to the ground, landing with an audible thud.

With Roberta lying on her back, her katana held aloft defensively, Aurange Sheergibbon took full advantage and brought down his sabre. Aurange's blade shattered against Roberta's katana, the *Harōingu!* And then, before Roberta could react, Aurange had tossed his shattered sabre aside and had drawn his kukri sword.

Then, there was a sudden sound that was not often heard.

Veeeee-wack, wack, wack, wack, wack, wack, wack, wack, wack, wack, wack,

wack, wack, wack, wack, wack, wack, wack, wack, wack, wack.

Aurange Sheergibbon's chest was riddled with small, self-cauterised, pulse laser holes, which bored right through his body. Eyes wide in horror, Aurange looked slightly to his right and kneeling there was the undead mark, Lina Mitchel, holding Roberta's high-powered rapid-firing pulse laser rifle. Aurange collapsed to the ground dead. Lina was still kneeling, training Roberta's heavy pulse laser rifle on the dock workers, who then quickly dispersed once more. Damn! Roberta's pulse laser rifle was heavy!

Roberta walked over to Lina and took her pulse laser rifle from her hands, she signed, *"Why are you still here? What are you waiting for? Get to the Dark Angel and wait for me there!"*

Elaine kissed Roberta, a quick peck on the lips and then dragged Lina off towards the ship. Roberta watched them go for several minutes until she was sure that they'd be safe. Then she walked over to Aurange's pulse laser rifle and picked it up.

Two pulse laser rifles in hand, Roberta walked over to Aurange's corpse and spat on it. After which, Roberta looked up at a surveillance drone hovering nearby, above the scene.

Roberta glared at the surveillance drone, knowing who'd be watching, she silently mouthed the words, *"I am coming for you!"*

Prince Aluric looked at his Brothers, Emeric, Friederic and Godric, Princes all, "We are all fucked!"

Crown Prince Godric commanded his Brothers, "Get out of the palace and go to ground", they were slow to move, "Do it now! That bitch will be here at any minute."

Godric watched his Brothers run for the door and then he turned to look at his Father, High Prince Albert and then turned around, "Protect the High Prince", he told the Captain of the palace guards.

Godric followed his Brothers out of the throne room. They were going into hiding.

The Captain of the palace guards sent some of his men out in advance of Roberta's arrival. Roberta was fully armed and wearing her usual combat armour. Now, however, she was not only carrying her own pulse laser rifle but also Aurange's. As Roberta approached the palace, two dozen guards rushed out, past the gate and squared off against her. Roberta let loose with both pulse laser rifles.

Veeeee-wack, Veeeee-wack, wack.

Veeeee-wack, Veeeee-wack, wack.

Veeeee-wack, Veeeee-wack, wack.

It took mere seconds and two dozen elite palace guards lay on the ground, dead, riddled with neatly bored holes through their chests. The Captain of the palace guard watched the camera drone footage with trepidation. Two dozen men were cut down in seconds. The Captain crossed himself and prayed.

"Don't let that bitch into the palace", the Captain of the palace guards ordered.

Palace guards lined the windows and the main palace doors, their weapons at the ready.

Roberta entered the palace grounds. The palace Dobermans had all been set loose and they all ran straight towards Roberta. Quick bursts of the pulse laser rifles. Veeeee-wack, wack, wack, wack. Veeeee-wack, wack, wack, wack, over and over and over. Roberta was a like kill bot, a Terminator in the flesh!

The Dobermans attacked, the Dobermans died. Their many bodies were left lying where they fell on the palace lawn, steaming bags of dead meat and bone.

Roberta approached cautiously from behind the palace trees. One particular tree caught her eye. It was an ironbark, a dense, solid eucalyptus with bark and a trunk-like iron. Roberta made her way quickly behind it. The tree was just the right width for her purposes.

With one pulse laser rifle on either side, Roberta began strafing the palace, with well-practised hands honed over eight decades of missions, many of which included combat. The Veeeee-wack, Veeeee-wack, wack, wack, wack, wack, wack of her high-powered rapid-firing pulse laser rifles resonated throughout the palace grounds.

The palace windows, walls and doors erupted as the laser pulses penetrated them. Multiple screams were heard emanating from behind them. Behind those windows, walls and doors, unseen, dozens of imperial palace guards were being shredded alive. Steaming corpses littering the palace's front rooms!

Roberta paused strafing and waited. The palace guards quickly returned fire. Roberta went back into "play" mode and began strafing once more. Once more, the Veeeee-wack, Veeeee-wack, wack, wack, wack, wack, wack of the pulse laser rifles resonated throughout the palace grounds. Once more, the screams of the palace guard were heard as they were being shredded alive. Roberta repeated this procedure six times before the return fire finally died down. Not a single palace guard was willing to approach the palace windows or doors. They were places of death, of steaming, shredded Human meat and the stench was fresh and hot in the air.

Roberta approached the palace completely unscathed. She gently placed her two pulse laser rifles on the palace porch, taking note to collect them on the way back out. Roberta unsheathed her sabre, these arseholes were not fit for her Katana, *the Haroingu*. Roberta unsheathed her kukri sword from its scabbard behind her back. Sabre in her right hand and kukri in her left, Roberta entered the palace and the melee began.

"Come on, you dogs, come and get your just rewards!", Roberta thought to herself.

The air was thick, it was hot from thousands of laser pulses and the stench of partially cooked meat was everywhere, Human meat. Bodies were strewn in the hallway behind the palace doors. Off to the sides in the palace's front rooms were many more bodies. Roberta did not bother to count them. Her mathematics was far more focused on the deeper recesses of the palace.

The imperial palace guards stormed at her and with deft precision, she hacked off limbs. Arms, legs and heads went flying. Blood was spraying every which way. Roberta was virtually swimming in it. Guard after guard, Roberta sliced and diced her way through to the High Prince's throne room. The smart guards ran away, all to no avail. Roberta took them all down with poisoned throwing stars!

With a trail of countless maimed and dead behind her, Roberta finally reached High Prince Albert's throne room and then the carnage finally began.

The throne room was packed full of palace guards. The Captain of the guards stood in front of the High Prince. Roberta Nummus, who just like Aurange Sheergibbon, had rarely ever spoken in over eighty years, the last time as an affirmation of High Prince Albert von Horridian's coronation in twenty one seventy seven, finally found her voice. Her psychological conditioning was unravelling fast.

Roberta shouted out, going against all of her conditioning, "Ich bin der Blutige. Ich bringe Gerechtigkeit und Vergeltung!", it was in German.

High Prince Albert von Horridian mumbled the English translation to himself, "I am the bloodied one. I bring both justice and retribution!", and then the true carnage began.

Roberta moved with fluid motion, she was a blur of death incarnate. Her sabre sliced into torsos and her kukri sword sliced off heads. Some guards were even sliced down the middle. Try as they may, not a single guard could get a bead on Roberta with their pulse laser pistols. The whirlwind of violence continued unabated for ten full minutes and in the end, there stood Roberta Nummus, knee-deep in corpses and severed limbs, painted fully in everyone's blood but her own. The Captain had been spared.

Roberta told the Captain, "Tell your people what you saw here this day. Warn them. If you come after my family, I will come after you and leave nothing in my wake! Now go!", and the Captain left.

High Prince Albert spoke, "You seem upset, Roberta."

Roberta frowned, the High Prince was old, he was feeble, his mind was diminished, "Your Sons, I would say, have done you a major disservice, Sire", she replied.

High Prince Albert replied, "You can speak. I've only heard you speak once. At my coronation", his fleeting memories solidified momentarily.

"Yes, Your Majesty. I spoke at your ascension to the throne. Now I speak at your death", Roberta replied, then with a chop on either side of Albert's neck, she grabbed his head by its wispy hair and tore it from his shoulders.

Roberta stepped over the multiple corpses on her way out of the palace. At the palace doors, she knelt down and hung both pulse laser rifles over her neck and with Albert von Horridian's head in hand, she strolled casually back to her ship, the Dark Angel. Roberta took the main route, right out in the open for all to see and the citizens of Ganymede Prime stared in disbelief at the severed High Prince's Head in Roberta Nummus's hands. They were all agog at the spectacle.

High Prince Albert von Horridian died at the age of seventy eight by decapitation. Chop, chop, rip!

Far away from Ganymede Prime, on distant Earth, in a cavern under the South Australian sandstone, fifty kilometres from Coober Pedy, an old man with crepey, old, liver spotted skin and badly balding hair named Orpheus, mumbled in his sleep, *"His time is over and the death of Dolphins is nigh!"*

Roberta stepped aboard her ship, the Dark Angel and then closed and locked its ventral passenger portal. Once inside the ship, she unceremoniously dropped the two heavy pulse laser rifles to the deck and then carried High Prince Albert's head to the ship's crematorium. Yes indeed, the Dark Angel had a crematorium. How else were state-sanctioned murderers supposed to dispose of their victims? Roberta tossed Albert's head into the ship's crematorium and incinerated it.

It was as if Roberta were in a daze. Elaine and Lina had followed her from the ventral airlock, trying to get her attention. It was as if Roberta could not see or hear them. Finally, Roberta stopped and recognised them.

"Roberta, you're covered in blood", Lina said with concern.

Roberta replied almost robotically, "It's okay. It is not my blood. Ich bin der Blutige."

Elaine and Lina were surprised to hear Roberta speak, she normally relied on technology, messaging and sign language.

Elaine translated for Lina, "I think that she just called herself the bloodied one."

"Well, she is, Elaine", Lina replied, again with concern, "She is literally covered in blood!"

"Roberta. My love, you need a shower", Elaine advised.

Roberta nodded her head, "Not yet. We have to leave this place", then she led them to the ship's bridge, where she sat down in the pilot's seat.

Lina pointed to the blood staining the pilot's seat, Elaine whispered, "I'll clean it up later."

Roberta disengaged the Dark Angel's docking clamps and then pulled away from the external docking port thirteen. Once the Dark Angel was far enough from Ganymede Prime, Roberta fired up the ship's three main plasma thrusters. It wasn't a long burn, but it wasn't short either.

"Was that High Prince Albert's head you just incinerated?", Elaine asked.

Roberta nodded, "Yes. I've sent them a message. I even renovated their palace, just a little bit."

"What was the message?", Elaine enquired.

Roberta turned around and smiled eerily, "The High Prince's Sons may have their Father's corpse, but they don't have their Father's head!"

Elaine understood, but Lina did not, so Elaine explained it, "A corpse cannot rest if it is separated from its head. Roberta has cursed their entire family."

"Nice", Lina responded, commenting, "If anyone deserves to be cursed, it's the Horridians."

Elaine looked at the vast expanse of space on the ship's main screen, "Roberta, my love. Exactly where are we going?"

"I'll tell you our final destination later. For now, though, we are heading in the direction of Jupiter-Sun Lagrangian point two, fifty four million kilometres away on the far side of Jupiter from the Sun."

"What's out there?", Lina enquired.

"Several O'Neil-style twin-cylinder colonies, including Jovian Lagrangian-Two Central", Roberta replied, explaining, "I'm setting up a false trail."

"Okay, Roberta, my love. We are safely on course, so Lina is going to help you shower and I'll clean up the blood from your pilot's seat", Elaine commanded.

"I don't need any help", Roberta protested.

Lina chimed in, "You once helped me to shower. Remember, the day you murdered my Aunt", calling up a memory of that terrible day, then she added, "Today. I am going to help you, Mother."

It was the first time that Lina had called Roberta, Mother, since she had been adopted by her. Usually, Lina called Roberta, my monster, my protector or something to that effect. Something had changed in Lina. Something had also changed in Roberta. Their worlds were still turning, but now, somehow, they were far more in sync.

After the departure of the Dark Angel and Roberta Nummus, the Horridian

Princes came out of hiding and returned to the palace. Corpses littered the grounds outside the palace gates. The corpses of Dobermans littered the palace grounds. The front facade of the palace was torn apart and shredded.

They entered the palace and found themselves stepping over and around corpses and the pieces of corpses. The air was thick and the stench was horrid. Prince Aluric stumbled at least twice and found himself face-first in some poor bastard's guts on the second stumble.

When they finally made it to the throne room, it was even worse. There was no stepping over the bodies and body parts, they had to walk over them and on top of them! Blood was everywhere and the stench was awful. Crown Prince Godric ran to his Father's body. There was a large V cut into its shoulders where High Prince Albert's head ought to be. It was missing. It was gone!

"Find our Father's head", Crown Prince Godric shouted to his Brothers."

The Captain of the palace guards walked into the throne room, climbing over corpses and body parts.

"Your Highness", the Captain addresses Crown Prince Godric, "Roberta Nummus, she took your Father's head with her as a trophy."

"Fuck no! We can't bury him without his head", the Crown Prince replied, "He'll never rest without his fucking head."

"We have no choice, Brother. We will have to cremate him", Prince Friederic advised.

"Cremate? Are you insane? That's for Slaves and poor people", the Crown Prince protested.

Emeric chimed in, "And yet, Brother. We do not have Father's head. Roberta Nummus has stolen it!"

Aluric agreed, "We cannot bury Father without his head, Brother. Cremation is all we have left."

Crown Prince Godric glared at the Captain, "How the fuck are you even still alive?", he questioned.

The Captain gulped softly and replied, "Roberta Nummus refused to kill me, Your Highness. She wanted a living witness. Someone who watched and lived through the entire event."

Crown Prince Godric looked around the palace throne room and asked, "How many palace guards did we lose, Captain?"

The Captain gulped softly once more, "Your Highness, you did suggest we station a hundred palace guards. We considered that insufficient, so we stationed two hundred and fifty of our best, most elite Jovian Shock Troopers."

"How many did we lose, Captain?", the Crown Prince asked once more.

The Captain slowly answered, "Your Highness, we have found about ten survivors, including myself, of course."

Crown Prince Godric just shook his head in sheer disbelief.

The Captain of the palace guards chimed into the silence, "Forgive me, Your Highness", then he stood to attention and shouted, "The High Prince is dead, long live the new High Prince. High Prince Godric, for the throne must never be empty", then he bowed, "Your Majesty."

The new High Prince replied dryly as he cradled his Father's headless corpse, "The fucking throne is soaked in fucking blood!", he screamed.

12. Ascensions.

The palace in the northern end cap of Ganymede Prime was a shambles. Its front facade was all but destroyed, its hallways and throne room strewn with bodies and body parts. The cleanup was ongoing and the repairs would take months. It was even suggested that the palace should be rebuilt, or if not, at the very least, everything from the throne room to its front.

The new High Prince, not yet crowned, sat on his other gold-gilded throne in the operations room. Being further to the back of the palace, it was one of the places untouched by the carnage. Godric's three Brothers sat on their own smaller *"Thrones"* on his right-hand side in the order of their birth: Princes Aluric, Emeric, and Friederic.

The long operations room table was largely empty. The Captain of the palace guards occupied one seat, and three ministers sat in theirs: the Science Minister, Peter Patronis, the Defence Minister, Peter Macron, and the Security Minister, Miles Morton.

The Captain of the palace guards reported, "Your Majesty. We lost another three guards last night, Sire. That makes two hundred and forty three."

High Prince Godric glared back, "How? Just how did one woman do all of this?", he scowled.

Security Minister Miles Morton fielded the question, "Your Majesty, a lot of the damage was done by those high-powered rapid-firing pulse laser rifles. Nummus wielded both hers and Sheergibbon's."

Prince Friederic queried, "I've only ever seen two of those weapons and only in the hands of Nummus and Sheergibbon. Why is that?"

Defence Minister Peter Macron shifted uncomfortably, "Your Highness, they made those weapons themselves. They were never meant to be handheld weapons. They are designed to be mounted on Infantry Fighting Vehicles and Interceptor craft. Nummus and Sheergibbon crafted them themselves."

The Captain of the palace guards chimed in, "Your Highness. They are extremely heavy weapons as well. I doubt that any of my guards could even wield one of them, let alone two."

High Prince Godric glared back, "That bitch wielded two of them! If they are so fucking heavy, how the hell did she do that?"

"Sire", Science Minister Peter Patronis cautiously began, before explaining, "Nummus and Sheergibbon were originally elite special forces with Cis-Lunar

Space's Colonial Armed Forces. They were given three years of *"specialised, experimental"* training in a military facility with the gravity calibrated to three gs. They were also conditioned both mentally and neurologically, and given genetic enhancement serums and elixirs. They are unnaturally strong and fast."

High Prince Godric had to agree, "Yes, yes, Patronis. I saw the raw video feed from the surveillance drone. Sheergibbon's and Nummus's dockyard fight. Unnaturally strong and fast is an understatement. I've never seen anyone move so quickly! They were like blurs of motion! However, one has to ask, how that undead mark managed to wield one of those fucking heavy weapons and kill Sheergibbon!"

Science Minister Patronis replied cautiously, "Sire, when you watch that video again, you'll notice that Lina Mitchel was kneeling at the time with the pulse laser rifle resting on her right knee. Your Majesty, the undead mark was barely able to lift it and yet, somehow managed to fire the shot that took down Aurange Sheergibbon."

Security Minister Miles Morton played the duel on the operation room's main screen. The four Horridian Princes had seen the footage before, nonetheless, it was still disturbing.

Prince Aluric commented, "The video is so much clearer now. It was so hard to see properly the first time with all of that interference. Damn, they are fast, aren't they!"

Security Minister Miles Morton replied, "Your Highness. That wasn't interference. That was just how quick Roberta Nummus and Aurange Sheergibbon move. To us, they look like a blur of motion. I'm actually replaying this back at one tenth speed."

Next, Security Minister Miles Morton replayed the security video from the throne room massacre. The new High Prince, Godric, sat there, eyes glued to the screen, refusing to look away. His Brothers had to occasionally look away from the displayed carnage. It was more than disturbing, limbs and heads flying every which way, bodies cleaved in two, intestines and other bodily organs spilling out onto the palace floor. There were even rivulets of blood flowing and pooling into macabre little lakes.

There were several points in the video where Roberta Nummus was clearly running along the throne room walls, taking off heads as she did so. Laser pulses impacted the wall behind her as she moved in a fluid blur of motion, the palace guards unable to get an accurate bead on her.

Prince Aluric stared in disbelief, "Is that even possible?"

Prince Emeric also stared at the depicted scene, "No, Brother Aluric. That should not be possible."

Prince Friederic replied, "And yet, Brothers. There it is. Captured on video for all to see."

"Fucking great! Now that fucking bitch defies gravity!", the High Prince exclaimed dryly.

After ten long minutes, the bloodletting subsided and then there were only three living people left in the throne room. The Captain of the palace guards, High Prince Albert and now, a much calmer Roberta Nummus. She spared the Captain and told him to leave and then she spoke to the old High Prince. It was in German and the old High Prince translated it, mumbling.

The new High Prince, Godric, repeated the translation, "I am the bloodied one. I bring both justice and retribution!"

Then, as they watched, chop, chop, rip and the old High Prince was beheaded. Roberta Nummus left the throne room with Albert's head clutched by the hair, her trophy!

Prince Friederic commented, "Perhaps, just perhaps, we should never have provoked that woman."

There were well over a hundred dead palace guards in that one large throne room alone.

The new High Prince stood up and looked a Prince Friederic, "What's done is done, Brother. Now, where has the bitch gone? Where is Roberta Nummus?"

Defence Minister Peter Macron fielded the question, "Roberta Nummus, her 'Daughter', Lina Mitchell and Elaine Haynes are on the Dark Angel, Your Majesty. The Dark Angel is a stealth ship and she's very hard to track, Sire. However, based on their ship's last burn, they do appear to be heading for Jupiter-Sun L-Two."

Prince Aluric enquired, "Jupiter-Sun L-Two? What's Jupiter-Sun L-Two?"

Prince Emeric replied sarcastically, "Brother Aluric, sometimes you can be such a moron. Jupiter-Sun L-Two was one of the three original colony zones of the old Jovian Republic."

Prince Friederic chimed in, "Yes, that is correct, Brother. They were Jupiter-Sun L-One and L-Two, and Himalia L-Five. The people who built the original Jovian Republic. The Jovian Dream Consortium didn't have the required radiation shielding to colonise anything closer to Jupiter."

Prince Aluric replied to his Brother, Prince Emeric, "I don't like it when you call me a moron, Brother! Why is it that I don't know these things, Friederic?"

Prince Friederic shook his head and closed his eyes momentarily before replying, "Aluric. You simply need to read more. You are going to be named Prince of Callisto, so you need to know your future domain."

Prince Aluric asked, "What's Jupiter-Sun L-Two got to do with Callisto?"

Prince Friederic replied as if speaking to a small child without being overly condescending, "Brother Aluric. Both Jupiter-Sun L-One and L-Two are governed from their main colonies, L-One Central and L-Two Central. Both of those governing bodies are subordinate to Himalia Central Command, which in turn is itself subordinate to Callisto Prime. All three are a part of your future Jovian Realm!"

High Prince Godric shook his head, "Enough of this nonsense. Someone can explain all of that to Aluric later. He will be given advisers. Now, why are they going to L-Two Central?"

Prince Friederic piped up, "They are not, Brother. L-Two Central is one of our territories. It is far too close to us, only fifty four million kilometres away. Whatever Roberta Nummus is, she is not stupid. The woman knows that we'll come after her."

High Prince Godric looked at his Defence Minister, Peter Macron, who replied to the look, "Your Majesty, that is what their last ship's burn indicated, however, it may not be their final destination."

Prince Friederic scoffed, "It's a feint, Minister Macron. They are not going to L-Two Central."

The new High Prince chimed in, "Brother, Friederic. Where are they going? What's your opinion?"

"Brother Godric, they are heading outwards from our orbital zone", Friederic replied, then turned to the Defence Minister, "Defence Minister Macron. Continue scanning along the Dark Angel's last known trajectory."

"What are we looking for, Your Highness?", Defence Minister Peter Macron enquired.

"If I'm right, you should expect to detect another ship's burn, a long burn this time", Prince Friederic smiled back.

"Brother Friederic?", High Prince Godric sought clarification.

"They are heading to Saturn, Brother", Prince Friederic informed, adding, "To the Demarchy!"

High Prince Godric took that in, it made sense, he nodded and responded, "Defence Minister Macron, do as my Brother suggested. Keep scanning their trajectory. If my Brother, Friederic, says it's a feint and expects you to detect a long burn, then it will happen. My Brother is very rarely wrong."

"Your will be done, Your Majesty", the Defence Minister replied.

High Prince Godric noted, "If they are going to the Saturnian Demarchy, we won't be able to intercept them."

Prince Emeric replied, "Brother, Nummus has slaughtered her way through the palace and brutally assassinated our Father. We cannot let her get away with this!"

Prince Friederic chimed in once more, "We won't, Brother. We will send a message to the Demarchy denouncing Nummus and her crimes, and then issue arrest warrants. Three warrants, one for Roberta Dumas, one for Lina Mitchel and one for that other traitor, Elaine Haynes. Why not let the Saturnian Demarchy do our work for us?"

High Prince Godric smiled for the first time since their Father's death, "The Saturnian Demarchy has always cooperated with us in the past. They have always been good trading partners as well. They will do this thing for us, I am certain. They certainly won't want a ship full of traitors and assassins within their Realms."

Prince Emeric also smiled, "We do have extradition treaties with all of the outer colonies. The Saturnian Demarchy is no exception. They'll capture the traitors for us and hand them over in chains."

Prince Aluric questioned, "What if Roberta Nummus kills them all?"

Prince Emeric rolled his eyes and replied, "They are in a spaceship, numb nuts. The Saturnian Demarchy can blow them all to smithereens for all I care."

Prince Aluric responded angrily, "Will you stop calling me that?", and then he asked his elder Brother, "Brother Godric, tell Aluric to stop calling me that."

High Prince Godric pinched the bridge of his nose before responding, "Brother Emeric, no more antagonising your Brother, Aluric. That's my first official commandment. Now, apologise to Aluric."

Prince Emeric replied formerly, "Yes, Your Majesty", then to his Brother, Prince Aluric, "I am sorry, Aluric. I will try not to upset you in the future."

Prince Friederic sent his Brother, Godric, a message with his communicator, "Brother Godric. Aluric's mind is soft. Under Jovian law, as the second son, he will become Prince of Callisto. Aluric will be in charge of our outer defences. You will need to assign him the best possible advisers."

High Prince Godric replied to the message with one of his own, "Yes, Brother Friederic. I am well aware of that. In addition to first-class advisers, I am considering giving you oversight of all of his decisions as well. I need you in charge of Callisto, not Io, which is your principality by Jovian law."

Prince Friederic leaned forward slightly and nodded to his Brother Godric.

The Dark Angel was still ten million kilometres from L-Two Central, at Jupiter-Sun Lagrangian point two, when Roberta detected their reception. Two squadrons of six standard Star Fire fleet fighters on an intercept course. A total of twelve.

"Elaine, it appears that the new High Prince, Godric, has organised a reception for us", Roberta informed her lover, before noting, "Cheap bastards, they could have sent a baker's dozen."

Elaine looked at the images on the long-range scanner screen, "What are we going to do, Roberta?"

"We do what I always planned to do", Roberta replied as she adjusted some settings on her navigation console, "There we have it. Our new course is locked in", then she punched the controls.

The Dark Angel's control thrusters fired up and reoriented the ship for its new course. The ship's three main plasma thrusters fired up for a long burn. One minute later, the main thrusters cut back out and the Dank Angel was on an entirely new course.

Lina had entered the ship's bridge and enquired, "Where are we going?"

"Saturn, Lina. We are going to Saturn", Roberta replied, smiling, "I bet you've always wanted to see Saturn's rings, Lina."

"Roberta, I have concerns", Elaine commented, noting, "Won't the new High Prince send word to the Saturnian Demarchy? Won't we just find another reception waiting for us?"

"True enough, Elaine, very true, but you know what? Those ships that L-Two Central sent to intercept us were top-of-the-line Jovian fighters and they would have had trouble detecting our ship, the Dark Angel. The Saturnian Demarchy's ships are even less capable. Not much more than a police force, really. It is unlikely they'll even detect us", Roberta reassured her.

"Hmm, Roberta, we still have to land somewhere in the Demarchy", Lina noted and then commented, "Even if we are just passing through, we'll still need to stop for supplies."

Roberta smiled at Lina, "If I were ever to be able to bear a child, Lina. I would want it to be you."

"A very nice sentiment, but not an answer, Roberta. What have you got up your sleeve?", Lina enquired, placing her hands on her hips.

"Well, my young Lady, we are not going to the Saturnian Demarchy", Roberta announced, explaining, but not fully, "We are going to Saturn, yes, and you will be able to see those glorious rings up close, but there is a lot more at Saturn than just the Demarchy."

Elaine chimed in, "Roberta, what else is at Saturn?"

Roberta bit her lower lip, "Sanctuary, my loves, sanctuary, or at least, I hope so."

High Prince Godric and his Brothers were staying in another building, an apartment close to their palace in the northern end cap. The badly damaged palace was being demolished and rebuilt. The occupants of the apartment building had all been relocated. Not by choice, of course, they were all forcibly removed and relocated to less salubrious accommodations.

Defence Minister Peter Macron was let into the apartment block's penthouse apartment. The Minister had some bad news, but also some good news.

Peter Macron delivered the bad news first, "Your Majesty, we ordered two squadrons of fighters to intercept the Dark Angel. They did not, however, even manage to detect them. The Dark Angel is a stealth ship after all."

"Okay, so give us the good news, Minister", High Prince Godric replied.

"Your Brother, Prince Friederic's assessment was correct, Your Majesty", Minister Macron replied, informing the four princes, "We detected their plasma torch, their long burn. We've calculated the Dark Angel's new trajectory."

Prince Friederic smiled, he was now curious, "And their destination, Minister Macron?"

Minister Macron replied, "Just as you determined, Your Highness. They are now heading for the Saturnian system, the Saturn Demarchy!"

High Prince Godric commanded, "Minister Macron, inform the Demarchy that they have assassins and terrorists heading their way. Inform the Demarchy of their crimes, as we have discussed. Tell the Demarchy that the assassins arrived on the diplomatic vessel, the Sleek Runner, from Eros and that they will repeat there what they have done here. Then issue those three arrest warrants."

Prince Emeric smiled, "Brother. If we tell them that, the Demarchy will shoot first and talk later."

High Prince Godric chuckled, "Brother Emeric. That was the general idea."

Elaine asked Roberta, "This sanctuary of yours, Roberta. Whereabouts is it exactly?"

Roberta bit her bottom lip, "Elaine, you won't believe me if I told you."

Elaine smiled, "Roberta, I will believe you, I promise, but you are not giving me a choice."

Lina chimed in, "We can't make a decision one way or the other without knowing."

"Okay, okay", Roberta agreed, then began, "Do you guys remember the Great Disaster?"

Elaine looked surprised, "The Great Disaster of twenty one forty two? Surely everyone remembers that. It's something that's taught in every school."

Roberta looked at Lina and Elaine, "Guys. The Great Disaster of twenty one forty two never happened. It's all a lie. A complete sham!"

"Roberta, that's not possible. Everyone knows about it. At least fifty thousand people were killed by those interstellar micrometeor swarms", Lina replied, adding, "We learned all about it at school."

"They were not interstellar micrometeors!", Roberta informed them both.

Elaine took hold of Roberta's hands, "My love, if they weren't interstellar micrometeor swarms, then what were they?"

Roberta bit her lower lip once again, "Elaine, it was a War. A brutal War. It started in the year twenty one forty and finished in the year twenty one forty two. Over fifty thousand civilians and millions of Colonial Troopers died! Millions!"

That caught both Elaine and Lina by complete surprise. It was not the answer they'd expected.

Lina asked, "How, Roberta? How does a brutal two-year conflict, a War, get erased from history?"

Roberta replied, "I'll tell you what I know. What I remember. What Aurange remembered."

Roberta recounted from memory, "I'll start at the beginning. The first battles were fought on Mars. At that point in time, there were rumours about Martians. Thousands of Colonial Troops were involved and our side won, however, the details were never released", she stopped to gauge their reactions.

Roberta continued, "The next phase started in the Saturnian Demarchy. A new mining station on the ice moon Mimas was destroyed mysteriously. Then, unknown forces from inside Mimas attacked the big twin-cylinder O'Neil-style colony at Titan L-Five and destroyed it. Then, later, an identical colony at Titan L-Four was attacked and destroyed. Both of those colonies were new. They had not even received official names. The death toll was up around forty thousand", she paused once more to let it all sink in.

"So, they were attacks, not micrometeors?", Lina questioned.

"Yes, Lina and the attacks continued", Roberta replied, adding, "The forces from Mimas also attacked the twin-cylinder colonies at Saturn L-Five and Saturn L-Four, although the death toll was much lower. The colonists had more warning and far more time to evacuate. At that time, the old Jovian Republic took in around a hundred thousand refugees. It was a decade after the War's conclusion that the last of the refugees finally made their way back to the newly rebuilt Saturnian colonies."

"Who were the attackers, Roberta? Who were they?", Elaine enquired.

"They were aliens, Elaine, aliens", Roberta replied, hoping that Elaine would not think she was mad.

"You think I'm mad, don't you? That my psychoses are making me delusional?", Roberta asked with a worried look on her face, "I should never have told you and just let us find what we find at Saturn."

Elaine gently squeezed Roberta's hands and then leaned in and kissed her, "I believe you, Roberta. Now, tell us, where did these aliens come from?"

"I can only tell what I know and what I remember, Elaine", Roberta replied and then she continued, "It turned out that Mimas was hollow. Kind of like Eros, but spherical inside. Inside, it's huge, much, much bigger than Eros, three hundred and twenty kilometres across and it was made with alien hands. It also turned out that Mimas was a generation ship and that its massive crater Hershel and its central mountain peak were an enormous ion engine", she stopped once more to gauge their reactions.

Lina was listening with keen interest, "Please continue, Roberta", and so Roberta did.

"Mimas broke orbit from Saturn and travelled into the inner solar system. The Earth and Cis-Lunar L-Five had to rapidly develop new ships and build a huge armada. When Mimas was within striking range of Earth and Eros, they began launching attacks", Roberta informed them, pausing slightly, then adding, "Eros was damaged, as were over two dozen twin-cylinder colonies at Cis-Lunar L-Five. The colonial forces beat them back."

Elaine noted, "Twenty seven. There were twenty seven damaged colonies at Cis-Lunar L-Five, although my understanding of history says they were damaged by interstellar micrometeor swarms."

"That appears to be the 'cover' story, Elaine", Roberta replied and then continued, "The Colonial Armada attacked Mimas and the Colonial Troops managed to get inside and defeat the enemy. That is where the millions of Colonial Troops were killed. Now, where it gets confusing is, the aliens were all wiped out. My understanding is that it was genocide. After which, Mimas was flown back into Saturnian orbit. Mimas's precise original orbit!"

"Roberta, that last part sounds kind of convenient", Lina remarked, noting, "I'm not saying that I don't believe you, just that the generation ship leaves

Saturnian orbit and returns to Saturnian orbit, perfectly. The exact same orbit."

"I know, it does have a whiff of weirdness about it and I have no answers for that part", Roberta admitted honestly.

Roberta stared into the bridge's main screen, staring out into deep space, into the direction they were travelling, towards Saturn.

"After the War concluded, everyone remembered what Aurange and I remembered. Precisely the same. Then one day, people started to forget the War and instead, they started remembering this thing about interstellar micrometeor swarms. It started with the leaders first, political and business leaders and it quickly spread. The Jovian Realms were still the Jovian Republic back then. It was before Albertus von Horridian became the President. Over time, it spread. More and more people just forgot the War and they only remembered stories of interstellar micrometeor swarms", Roberta recounted, adding, "There were even times when Aurange and I would forget and we'd believe in interstellar micrometeor swarms as well, only for our real memories to resurface the very next day."

"Wait! So you and Aurange also forgot?", Lina enquired.

"Yes, Lina. We'd forget, but unlike everyone else, the following day, we'd remember", Roberta confirmed, and then she speculated, "Aurange believed it was our genetic enhancements. Our memories are eidetic, we never forget and as our neural enhancements are artificial, whatever was affecting everyone else was only temporarily affecting us."

"That bit right there, Roberta, makes it all the more believable", Lina remarked, explaining, "That your memories are inviolable, that they cannot be altered or adulterated, is very compelling."

"I have to agree, Roberta", Elaine chimed in, "Whatever was affecting everyone else's memories only had a temporary effect on you and Aurange.

It was quiet on the bridge for some time after that, then Roberta gave them more information about Mimas. Something that clashed with both her memories and typical colony sovereignty.

"Our destination is actually Mimas and this is for two reasons. The first is a mystery that's been eating away at me for forty years. The second is Mimas itself", Roberta paused, still staring into the bridge's main screen, "Mimas is a *'private'* colony. It is not under Demarchy jurisdiction at all."

"No, Roberta, that can't be right. The first colony in an orbital zone holds sovereignty. That's a long-standing rule", Elaine corrected, explaining, "The Saturnian Demarchy colonised the entire Saturnian orbital zone. They hold absolute sovereignty over that zone."

"So you'd think, Elaine", Roberta replied as she pulled up a document.

"I've been digging into this mystery for forty years. Have a read of this", Roberta recommended.

Elaine and Lina both read the document that was displayed on the screen in front of them.

Elaine looked at Roberta, "This can't be right. It makes no sense, Roberta. According to this document, Mimas was colonised thirty years before the Saturnian Demarchy even got there. That, under interplanetary law and convention, gives Mimas primacy. That, by extension, gives Mimas sovereignty over the whole Saturnian orbital zone!"

"Yep! And yet, that Mimasian *'private'* colony does not exercise that sovereignty. Which is why we are going there", Roberta concluded.

"Roberta, this directly conflicts with your memories of the War. Mimas can't be an alien generation ship and be the original Saturnian colony at the same time. It makes no sense", Elaine commented.

"Yeah, tell me about it, Elaine. Mimas is both an independent sovereign Human colony and an alien generation ship", Roberta agreed, adding, "Which is why we need to go there. We need to find out!"

Lina smiled. She understood that whatever Mimas was, it was outside of the Demarchy's jurisdiction. It was quite possibly a sanctuary.

Prince Friederic von Horridian was the smartest of his Siblings. They had a problem. Their Father's headless corpse could not be buried. The headless dead could never rest if buried without their head. The corpse lay in the morgue under guard, lest anyone should confirm the rumours that former High Prince Albert's head was carried off by Roberta Nummus. His head had been seen, carried through the streets of Ganymede Prime's northern end cap like some grotesque trophy. The Horridian Brothers, nonetheless, must control the narrative.

Then it came to Friederic, an idea, "Brother Godric", he called out to the new High Prince, "The Jovian Realms were only declared in twenty one seventy seven. It is now twenty one eighty one. Father's reign as High Prince was quite short. Just four short years."

High Prince Godric turned angrily, "That matters not, Brother. Father was still the High Prince!"

Prince Friederic raised his hands placatingly, "Brother, if you let me finish, it will all make sense."

High Prince Godric nodded, "Continue, Brother."

"Father was the first High Prince of the six Jovian Realms. That makes him unique. Father is literally the bedrock upon which our Horridian Dynasty stands", Prince Friederic noted.

High Prince Godric was listening intently as Prince Friederic continued, "Bedrock, Brother. Think of that. Your palace has been raised to the ground. The rubble has been cleared away and your new palace will be raised in its place."

"Friederic. My patience is growing thin, where are you going with this?", the High Prince asked.

"My Brother, we cannot bury our Father without his head. So we are left with cremation as our only option. The poor man's option, the Slave's option. So we dare not do that, unless", Prince Friederic left the question hanging just long enough, "We turn our Father's ashes into the bedrock of our future."

High Prince Godric was not following and Prince Friederic was being cautious, he continued slowly, "I propose that we do cremate Father, yes, but that his burnt remains be ground up and incorporated into a memorial block. The first block, inscribed and dated accordingly, becomes the first block laid for your new palace. Our Father will become quite literally, the block upon which our dynasty stands."

High Prince Godric chuckled softly, then he smiled, "Father's block would have to be prominently placed, very visible", and then he slapped his knee, "We could have a magnificent ceremony, perhaps even a feast of foundation and remembrance! Father, High Prince Albert, our foundation stone!"

And so it came to pass. Former High Prince Albert's ashes and ground-up bones were mixed into the astcrete that became the new palace's first foundation stone. The memorial block was inscribed:

High Prince Albert von Horridian.
Born : 2102   Died : 2181
Reigned : 2177 to 2181
The 1ˢᵗ High Prince.
The bedrock upon which all von Horridians stand!
Betrayed and murdered by the one he trusted the most.
Never Again!

What followed was three days of celebration, feasting and pageantry. Even the poor and the Slaves were allowed to participate, just so long as the memory of High Prince Albert's head being carried through the streets of Ganymede Prime was forgotten.

While the four Horridian Brothers were recovering from their hedonistic, debauched revelry, the new Communications Minister, Mr Temu Trump, entered the room. The Captain of the palace guards started kicking the Prince's naked entertainers, all women, out of the room. The Captain's boots in the sex Slave's butts had a quick effect and the room was quickly cleared. The naked women left the room, both bruised and abused. Bleary-eyed, the four Princes were awoken to the Communications Minister's news. The Captain threw the Princes their robes and they quickly put them on. The Horridian Princes all had Wives, but Wives were for State, Wives were for Children, Wives were long-suffering, sex Slaves were for fun. Their orgy was over and business was now at hand.

"Hey, bring those bitches back", Prince Aluric shouted, "I was having fun", and he had been, he was awake and busy when the Captain's boot started swinging.

Prince Emeric was still half asleep, "Shut the fuck up, Brother! Why do you have to be so loud!", he was hungover and still drunk from the night before.

Prince Friederic awoke more quickly, he had drunk in moderation and treated his Slaves somewhat more gently, "Captain. We need food and hydration. Send word to the kitchens."

High Prince Godric sat up on his floor mat, "Well, that was fun", then he looked up at Minister Trump, "Really, Temu! Don't you think it's a bit early for business?"

"Your Majesty. It is one pm, Sire", the Communications Minister replied.

The High Prince looked at the wall clock, "Holy fuck! So it is", and then he smiled to himself, remembering his night of wanton debauchery.

The Communications Minister cautiously replied, "Your Majesty, if I may give you some advice, although I doubt you want to hear it. Sire, you are the ruler of an empire, the six Jovian Realms and they do require your complete attention. Spending your days", Temu looked around the room, "thus, it endangers your rule, Sire."

High Prince Godric scowled, but Prince Friederic stepped in, "Minister Trump is right, Brother. You do need to focus more on the Realms. This", he looked around the room, "we are far too distracted."

"Okay, okay. Minister Temu Trump, today's business? Let's hear it?", the High Prince commanded.

"Sire, we have sent word to the Saturnian Demarchy and they have replied", the Communications Minister informed him.

"Look, Temu. My head's a bit slow at the moment. Remind me what we told them", High Prince Godric asked.

"Your Majesty, we have informed the Saturnian Demarchy of the following", the Communications Minister replied and then he started rattling off the main points, "High Prince Albert has been assassinated. Three of the assassins, Roberta Nummus, Elaine Haynes and Lina Mitchel, are en route to Saturn in a stolen spacecraft, the *'Twilight'* Angel."

"Wait! Temu, Nummus's ship is the Dark Angel, not the *'Twilight'* Angel", the High Prince noted.

"Yes, Sire. It took a strategic liberty. I've had the Dark Angel's registration changed in our ship's registration database", the Communications Minister explained.

Prince Friederic chimed in, "Smart move, Minister. Should the Dark Angel manage to make port anywhere in the Saturnian Demarchy, they'll use the ship's name in their port logs. The port officials on the Demarchy's side will do a registration check and the names won't match. Bingo! A red flag!"

"Precisely, Your Highness", Minister Trump confirmed.

High Prince Godric smiled, "Smart move, Temu. Smart move!", he agreed.

"There is more, Your Majesty", the Communications Minister informed.
"What are you waiting for, Temu?", High Prince Godric asked.
"We have informed the Saturnian Demarchy that the assassin's accomplice, Aurange Sheergibbon, was neutralised by our Jovian security forces whilst attempting to escape", Temu Trump continued and then he followed on, "Along with the crime of regicide, the assassination of your Father, I took the liberty of adding the mass murder of around four dozen palace guards."
"Hmm, the last I heard, Temu. Those numbers had reached two hundred and forty five", the High Prince corrected.
"Yes, Sire. Your numbers are accurate. They are just inconvenient. Giving the Saturnians a lower number is more realistic and downplays Roberta Nummus's prowess. Four assassins taking down four dozen guards simply sounds more reasonable. Stating two hundred and forty five will have a negative effect", the Communications Minister explained.
"Smart move, Temu", Prince Friederic chimed in, "We don't want them to know what Roberta Nummus is really capable of. Not until they're knee deep in blood and gore at least."
High Prince Godric nodded, between his Communications Minister, Temu Trump, and his youngest Brother, Friederic, he did have fair counsel.

High Prince Godric then requested, "Come on, Temu. I know there's more.

You always have more goodies for us. So, bring out the steak knives."

"Yes, Sire. Indeed, I do. I always try to please, so I left the *'steak knives'* for last. Kind of like a pleasant little cherry bomb", the Communications Minister replied, informing the Princes, "I have informed the Saturnian Demarchy that the assassins, Aurange Sheergibbon and Roberta Nummus, were delivered to Ganymede Prime by the Erosian Ambassadorial ship, the Sleek Runner, by Ambassadorial Emissary, Sonia de la Cruz herself. I have even *'evidenced'* this assertion by noting that the Emissary's Niece, Lina Mitchel, was one of the assassins, so delivered."

"Oh, oh, that is just so cherry!", Prince Friederic chimed in.

Communications Minister Trump continued, "Yes, quite, Your Highness. I took the liberty of stressing that should the *'Twilight'* Angel arrive in Saturnian Demarchy space, they will do there, exactly what they did here. That their purpose is to decapitate the outer colony power structures. I did, of course, warn them that both the ship and the assassins are heavily armed and highly dangerous."

Prince Emeric was now fully awake and he chimed in, "The Demarchy will blow them out of the void on sight!"

"Oh my god!", High Prince Godric exclaimed, "That is just brilliant. Temu, you are still my favourite Minister. Seriously!"

Then Prince Aluric chimed in, because why not, "Okay, the meeting is over. Now, can you bring back my bitches? I wasn't finished."

Both High Prince Godric and Prince Friederic rolled their eyes, both thinking to themselves that Prince Aluric the Simple was going to become the Prince of Callisto and that he would be in charge of the Jovian outer defences.

As the Communication Minister began to leave, the High Prince gave him one final instruction, "Temu. Should the Saturnian Demarchy manage, by some weird quirk of fate, to actually capture our three fugitives? Make sure that they understand that we want them extradited back to Ganymede Prime. Tell them that we want to exercise our justice."

"Yes, of course, Your Majesty. Should I also take the liberty of providing the same information to the Uranian Federation and Neptunian Commonwealth?", the Communications Minister enquired.

"Oh, most definitely, Temu. We certainly can't leave them out of the loop, can we now? They both need to be forewarned of Erosian duplicity", High Prince Godric replied with a wry smile.

High Prince Godric and his Brothers were seated in four gold-gilded thrones in the Jovian High Church's Cathedral in Ganymede Prime's northern end cap. The Cathedral was packed with carefully selected loyalists, who were all seated in the nave of the Cathedral. In the centre between the seating, the nave was left clear and open. Each of the audience members was carefully checked for weapons as they entered. Off to the sides in the aisles were no fewer than two hundred fully armed Jovian Shock Troops to ensure that the ceremony proceeded without incident. A Cardinal dressed in red passed the Pope of the Jovian High Church a crown.

Then the Pope of the Jovian High Church held the crown high above Prince Aluric's head as he declared, "By the powers invested in me by God almighty, I hereby declare, Prince Aluric von Horridian, Prince of the Jovian Realm of Callisto and all of its domains", and then he slowly placed the crown upon Prince Aluric's head.

Then the Pope of the Jovian High Church moved on to the next Horridian Prince and the Cardinal dressed in red passed him the next crown.

The Pope of the Jovian High Church held the crown high above Prince Emeric's head as he declared, "By the powers invested in me by God almighty, I hereby declare, Prince Emeric von Horridian, Prince of the Jovian Realm of Europa and all of its domains", and then he slowly placed the crown upon Prince Emeric's head.

The Pope of the Jovian High Church moved on to the next Horridian Prince and the same Cardinal passed him the next crown.

The Pope of the Jovian High Church held the crown high above Prince Friederic's head as he declared, "By the powers invested in me by God almighty, I hereby declare, Prince Friederic von Horridian, Prince of the Jovian Realm of Io and all of its domains", and then he slowly placed the crown upon Prince Friederic's head.

Finally, the Pope of the Jovian High Church moved on to the next Horridian Prince and the same Cardinal passed him a different crown. The other three crowns had been simple crowns of gold, this crown, however, while still being gold, was far more ornate. It was magnificent.

The golden crown glinted softly in the Cathedral's candlelight. Its polished gold surfaces caught every glimmer, flickering like fire. The circlet, thick and heavy, was shaped in a flawless ring. Along its rim rose eight spires of great elegance, tapered, regal, each crowned with a gleaming gemstone: deep red rubies and cold white diamonds alternating in perfect harmony.

Between each spire curled delicate golden filigree, twisting like vines, etched with patterns too fine to trace. At its centre sat a soft velvet dome, rich and deep crimson, glimpsed between the arches and bordered with a thin trim of the purest, whitest fur.

To call it magnificent was an understatement.

It was beyond magnificent.

The crown commanded a presence all its own.

The Pope of the Jovian High Church took a deep breath, he could not mess this up.

The Pope held the ornate crown high above Crown Prince Godric's head as he declared, "By the powers invested in me by God almighty, I hereby declare, Prince Godric von Horridian, Prince of the Jovian Realm of Ganymede and all of its domains", then he paused and took another deep breath, "High Prince of the six Jovian Realms of Ganymede, Callisto, Europa, Io, the Leading Trojans and the Trailing Trojans", and then he slowly placed the crown upon Crown Prince Godric's head.

The Pope stepped to one side and the entire Cathedral erupted in applause. The Horridian Princes had all been officially crowned and the Jovian Realms now officially had a new High Prince.

The entire Cathedral began shouting, "Long live High Prince Godric", and they did so over and over.

Long after the ceremony was over and the four Princes were back in their *"confiscated"* penthouse apartment, High Prince Godric reminded his Brothers of their responsibilities.

"Brother Emeric. As the Prince of Europa, you are responsible for our inner defences. I fully expect you to cooperate with your Generals to ensure our inner defences are rock solid", the High Prince instructed him and then he made a request, "Brother. Europa? What's under that ice? Emeric, I want you to find out. Get your people working on what's under Europa's ice."

Prince Aluric asked, "What are my responsibilities, Brother?"

This was a difficult question. Prince Aluric was thicker than blue stone.

"Brother Aluric. As the Prince of Callisto, you are, ostensibly, responsible for our outer defences. It is a very challenging task. I'm not sure that you will enjoy that kind of stress. I need you to listen to your Advisers and your Generals, and follow their advice and decisions", the High Prince instructed him and then he added, "If you're not sure of something or uncertain of anything and you feel your advisers cannot help, I want you to talk to Friederic or me. Can you do that?"

"I think so, Brother Godric", came Prince Aluric's reply.

Next, High Prince Godric turned to his Brother Friederic, "Brother, your realm is the innermost realm. The main responsibilities you'll have will be the Amalthean and Ionian mines. I feel certain you'll manage those responsibilities with ease."

"Not a problem, Brother Godric. That is right up my sleeve", Prince Friederic replied.

Emeric and Aluric moved off to go about their business. Emeric went to the kitchen to order some food. Aluric, of course, had other appetites and went looking for his favourite four sex Slaves. Godric and Friederic rolled their eyes as Aluric left the room. They knew exactly where he was going.

"Friederic. Honestly, I don't care what Aluric does. He can drink himself to death, he can eat himself to death, he can even fuck himself to death. Whatever keeps him happy, I don't care. Just make sure his Advisers are the best you can find", High Prince Godric instructed him.

"I'm already on it, Brother. His Advisers will be better than mine", Prince Friederic replied.

"Well, that makes perfect sense. You probably don't need any", replied the High Prince, he then added, "I will personally instruct Aluric's Generals that Aluric has absolutely no authority over them. If they are in doubt, they will be under orders to come to you or me, whichever of us is available."

Prince Friederic laughed, "Could you imagine Brother Aluric in charge of a fleet of Dreadnoughts?"

High Prince Godric chuckled while shaking his head, "Gods no, Brother Friederic. Let's not even think about that. He'd probably turn the flagship into a fucking space brothel!"

"Yes, Brother. With a flashing red light on its main airlock, to boot", Prince Friederic laughed.

13. My Sanctuary is My Palimpsest.

Roberta called Elaine and Lina to the ship's bridge, "I've been monitoring official communications between Ganymede Prime and the Saturnian Demarchy", she informed them both.

Elaine commented, "I thought all diplomatic communications were encrypted."

Roberta smiled her wry smile, "They are, but it was Aurange and I who set up the Jovian Realm's encryption protocols. So it's not that difficult for me to decode them."

Elaine smiled and then asked, "That's good to know, Roberta. So, what have you found out?"

Roberta frowned, it was one of her, I should have told you, but withheld the information, kind of frowns, "I actually picked this up weeks ago, but I didn't want to upset you both."

Lina chimed in angrily, "Roberta, you have to stop doing that. We are not children!"

Roberta smiled back at Lina, "I know, sweety, I know, but I don't know how else to protect you both from this kind of shit."

Elaine asked, "So, why are you telling us now, Roberta?"

"Because we are getting close to Saturn, we're only a week out and at this point and you both need to know", Roberta informed them.

Roberta brought up the communications from Ganymede Prime to the Saturnian Demarchy on the main screen. It popped up in a window, completely decrypted. As Elaine and Lina read the communications on the screen, Roberta summarised the details.

"Basically, the new High Prince, Godric, has told the Demarchy that we are all assassins and terrorists. That we have committed regicide and mass murder. Better yet, Lina. Apparently, your Aunt Sonia delivered Aurange and me to Ganymede Prime on the Sleek Runner", Roberta informed them both, noting, "The irony of their bullshit. Aurange and I worked for the Horridians for more than eight decades. The ungrateful bastards!"

Elaine replied, with hope in her voice, "None of that is true. I'm sure I can explain everything to the Saturnian Demarchy when we arrive."

"It gets even better, Elaine. My ship, the Dark Angel, they're calling her the Twilight Angel in their communications", Roberta remarked.

"How does that make things worse?", Elaine enquired, not sure how the name of the ship mattered.

"It's a failed attempt at creating red flags", Roberta replied and then explained, "Wherever we make port in the Saturnian Demarchy's domain, we have to register my ship's name at the port's office for their records. Dark Angel won't match up with Twilight Angel on the Jovian Realms ship's registry. That would have been an instant red flag. The idiots didn't think I'd crack their communications."

Lina continued reading the communique, "Roberta, we won't even get close to any Saturnian ports. Based on what I'm reading, they'll intercept us first, probably with guns blazing."

Roberta brought up the Saturnian Demarchy's reply. Elaine and Lina read it. The Demarchy's reply confirmed Lina's suspicions that they were planning to intercept and destroy, not capture.

Looking at Elaine's and Lina's faces, Roberta commented, "Yep. That little cunt, Godric, has the whole Demarchy in panic mode. They are going to come at us hard."

Lina's eyes welled with tears, "They're insulting my Aunt's memory", she paused for a short moment, "I'm no assassin and I don't want to be killed for something I didn't do! Murdered for a lie!"

"It won't come to that, Lina", Roberta assured her, commenting, "The new High Prince is not very clever. He's arrogant, pompous and inconsistent, and that plays in our favour."

Elaine chimed in, "Roberta, you're doing it again. What are you not telling us?"

Roberta smiled. She played a video that was released into the new feeds, the external solar system-wide news feeds. The video showed a section of cleared ground and the laying of a foundation stone, which was inscribed with High Prince Albert's name, his details and a short epitaph.

Roberta informed Elaine and Lina, "We are all being blamed for the destruction of the High Prince's palace as well. Sorry about that, that was my bad."

Lina enquired, a confused expression on her face, "How does this help us?"

"Read High Prince Albert's epitaph, Lina. Most importantly, read the second-to-last line", Roberta explained, she had a broad grin on her face.

Lina read out the second-to-last line of the epitaph, "Betrayed and murdered by the one he trusted the most", then exclaimed, "That's you, Roberta!"

"And that is where Godric's arrogant, pompous, lying little arse is laid bare for all to see. He allowed that to be transmitted externally, across all of the news feeds. If Albert was murdered by the one he trusted the most, then how could she have arrived on an Ambassadorial Emissary ship from Eros? Inconsistencies, as I said ", Roberta explained.

"That blows their narrative right out of the void!", Elaine remarked.

"Perhaps, assuming they'll believe it", Roberta replied and then she smiled broadly once more.

"Oh, Roberta, there's more, isn't there? What have you done?", Elaine enquired.

"I have sent the President of the Demarchy and the Saturnian Administrator a copy of that video, including a few stills highlighting that section of the epitaph as well. I've admitted to killing High Prince Albert and informed them that it was only after the High Prince had ordered my death. I have explained that I did not arrive on the Sleek Runner and that I have been employed by the Horridians for many decades", Roberta divulged and then she turned to Lina, "I explained to them that the Sleek Runner was only in dock for two days and that Lina Mitchel was a sixteen-year-old child at the time, not an assassin or a terrorist."

Lina threw her arms around Roberta and hugged her.

Roberta's eyes brimmed with tears, "I may not be your biological Mother or even your Aunt, Lina, but I will always do my best to keep you safe. I am your Monstrous Mother, but only Monstrous to those who would be stupid enough to even try and harm you."

"Will it work, Roberta?", Elaine asked.

"Potentially, but there is no guarantee. I'd be lying if I said that everything would be okay", Roberta admitted, remarking, "I have admitted to regicide. I will also be seen as a mass murderer as per Godric's narrative. I've admitted to being in the Horridian's employment for decades. That alone could be reason enough for the Saturnian Demarchy to move against us."

"Do me a favour, Roberta. Send a copy of that video, the still frames you've highlighted and anything else you can to Eros. To the Colonisation Committee and Security Council. I'm pretty sure that Godric's narrative will be generating diplomatic protests from the Saturnian Demarchy. Perhaps even the Uranian Federation and the Neptunian Commonwealth as well", Elaine requested.

"That was actually next on my list, Elaine", Roberta informed her.

"So, we could still have an armed reception waiting for us when we arrive?", Lina questioned.

"Yes. I would say that is highly likely", Roberta admitted.

"It's actually not as bad as it looks", Roberta noted, trying to be more cheerful, "The Dark Angel is a stealth ship and she won't be easily detected. Even if they do detect us, my ship is using enhanced Slayers and Eramis technology."

Lina commented, "I know about those. SlaReS, Stackable Layered Radiation Shield Plating and E-RaMiS, Electromagnetic Radiation Mitigation System. Just how is stolen Dumas Incorporated technology going to help us?"

Roberta smiled, "You know about that then?", then she nodded before explaining, "The Jovian Realms have the original versions and every ship in Jovian territory, by law, has to have Slayers and Eramis shielding installed. The version used on the Dark Angel is enhanced. Aurange and I made some interesting tweaks", she paused for a moment, then divulged, "We had all of the original specifications because we were the ones who stole the technology."

"Interesting tweaks", Lina enquired.

"Yep. Our versions are great for radiation mitigation, but are equally good at neutralising laser beams and particle beams. So, even if the Saturnians can detect my ship, unless they throw some really big weapons at us, they can't do a whole lot", Roberta explained, adding, "Even if they do detect us."

"And they won't detect us, will they, Roberta?", Elaine chimed in and asked.

"Elaine, we are travelling really fast. I mean, seriously fast. I'm going to have to perform a reverse burn with orbital corrections if we are going to aim for orbital insertion around Mimas. The minute I do that, the Saturnians will be able to detect us", Roberta noted, adding, "The Dark Angel's reverse thrusters and manoeuvring thrusters are not something that I can hide. They will be like a light show that the Saturnian detection systems will not miss."

Three days later, Lina and Elaine were on the Dark Angel's bridge watching Roberta make course adjustments. The Dark Angel was slowly being lined up for an intercept of the ice moon, Mimas, the seventh moon from Saturn. Roberta carefully fired the ship's manoeuvring thrusters for the alignment.

Then Roberta performed a long burn of the Dark Angel's reverse thrusters, slowing her ship down significantly. Roberta aimed to slow down the Dark Angel enough to prevent overshooting the Saturnian system entirely, but at the same time, she still wanted the Dark Angel to come in fast and hot. Something that seemed contradictory. The next thing Roberta did was to perform a precise burn of the Dark Angel's three main plasma thrusters, placing her ship on a Mimasian orbital intercept trajectory.

"Okay, guys, the Saturnian Demarchy will definitely have detected us", Roberta announced, noting, "They know that we're heading for Saturn's inner lunar system, but they won't know exactly where. At least, not until I perform our final reverse burn and course adjustments."

Elaine looked at the ship's settings, "Roberta, we are still on a fast approach."

"Yes, we are, Elaine. I want them scrambling, confused and wondering what the hell I'm doing", Roberta explained, noting, "We are still four days out and falling rapidly into Saturn's gravity well. I want them throwing small, fast interceptors at us. Nothing bigger."

Lina chimed in, grinning, "You're manipulating their response."

"Yes, I am, Lina, yes I am", Roberta admitted with an even broader grin.

The Dark Angel was much closer now and a squadron of twelve Saturnian Demarchy light interceptors appeared on the short-range scanners. Roberta had already noted their presence.

The lead pilot hailed, "Twilight Angel, Twilight Angel, slow your approach and prepare for interception. Repeat: prepare for interception. You will be encircled and escorted to Titan L-Five Central Command under guard."

Roberta snorted, "Stupid bastards are trying to box us in."

Roberta keyed her comm, "This is the Dark Angel, repeat, the Dark Angel. That's a negatory on your interception. We've got other plans. Go away and stop bothering us."

The same voice came again, "Twilight Angel, Twilight Angel. Prepare for interception. You will be"

Roberta cut him off abruptly, "Check your scanners, Squadron Leader. Your weapons systems are no match for the Dark Angel's shielding. You may as well be pissing on a fire. Dark Angel is a Tristar Interplanetary Stealth Fighter and is heavily armed. Repeat, heavily armed. If you continue with this ill-advised approach, we will respond with main force. Would you like to see the Dark Angel's fangs?"

The Dark Angel's gun ports slid open, revealing high-powered lasers, particle beams, plasma turrets, and rail guns. The Dark Angel bristled with advanced weaponry.

"We have your whole squadron on weapons lock", Roberta added coldly, advising, "One button. One shot. Twelve kills. No survivors. The choice is yours to make."

There was a long, silent pause.

Then came the chatter, "Squadron Leader to all pilots, break away! Break away. Stay out of range of the Twilight Angel. Repeat: break away and hold position!"

Roberta smirked. "Smart choice. And it's the Dark Angel by the way. Get it right next time."

The Dark Angel was still falling fast into Saturn's gravity well. The squadron of Demarchy light interceptors was quickly dropping away. They were fast little ships, but not fast enough to keep up with the Dark Angel. The Demarchy's interceptors were now well behind the Dark Angel and being monitored on the ship's rear scanners. Roberta made a judgement call.

"Lina, Elaine, take to your seats and strap in. This could be a little rough", Roberta ordered.

Roberta glanced at Lina and Elaine. They'd both taken to their seats and had their seat belts fastened. Harnesses over both shoulders and fastened across their laps. Roberta smiled and fired up the Dark Angel's reverse thrusters at full throttle.

The Dark Angel shuddered violently, it rattled and groans and moans were coming out of the ship's superstructure. The ship's inertial dampers failed and several loose objects in the ship's bridge slammed forward against the bridge's wall plating. Roberta began manipulating the ship's manoeuvring thrusters.

The small ice moon Mimas appeared on the bridge's main screen. It was still small in the distance, yet approaching swiftly. Ever so slowly, the Dark Angel's groaning and shaking stopped. The inertial dampers re-engaged. Mimas was growing larger now, but at a far more reasonable pace. Roberta had pushed the Dark Angel's reverse thrusters hard and the reverse burn had lasted a little over fifteen long minutes. All three were feeling the effects. Roberta, not so much. Elaine and Lina, much more so.

"We are on target for Mimas orbital insertion. We are in the pipe, five by five", Roberta announced.

And then Elaine threw up! Her lunch was now coating the console in front of her.

Roberta double-checked that the Dark Angel was indeed on course for orbital insertion and then unstrapped herself. She turned to her right and took note of Elaine and the vomit-coated console.

"Sorry about that, Elaine", Roberta apologised and then she turned to her left to check on Lina.

Lina was sitting quietly, biting her lower lip. She wasn't saying anything at all and then Roberta realised why when she noticed the wet patch on the deck beneath her seat. Lina was rather embarrassed by her predicament.

Roberta reached out and gently held Lina by the arm, "I am so sorry, Lina", and then she remarked, "It seems I gave you guys one hell of a rough ride. I should have given you both more warning."

Roberta stood up and then helped a shaky Elaine and equally shaky Lina from their seats, "You guys go and get cleaned up. I'll take care of this."

By the time Elaine and Lina had both showered and redressed, Roberta had already cleaned up the ship's bridge. The Dark Angel was now in orbit around Mimas and Roberta had already started detailed scans. The bridge's main screen was showing a multiple split-screen display.

Mimas was being displayed in real-time in the top half. The bottom half on the left showed older historical images of Mimas compiled into a rotating globe. Images taken before the twenty second century. The bottom right-hand side of the screen showed a global composite being built with new scans as of now.

As Lina and Elaine entered the bridge, Roberta announced, "And there's our proof positive that there was a War. The globe on the left is based on images compiled from the last century. The globe on the right is compiled from my latest scans. See how different they are. You can see how someone blew the bejesus out of that Moon's surface. I am detecting a patterned strike of a hundred major weapons. Military strike patterns. Nuclear weapons! I expect that would have been the final devastating strike before the Colonial Troops got access to the Mimasian interior", she explained.

Elaine stared at the screen, "You're right, Roberta, the old and the new look completely different."

Roberta felt vindicated, her memories and Aurange's were being validated in real-time.

Roberta rolled the right-hand image of Mimas on the screen showing, Hershel Crater and its central rebound mountain peak, "And that, my darlings, is the biggest fucking ion drive I have ever seen!"

The Dark Angel's orbit was allowing complete scans of Mimas. Roberta brought up high-resolution side scan images of a specific region of Mimas. These were scans of the opposite side of Mimas to the Hershel Crater. Roberta studied them intently as she magnified and enhanced the images on the screen.

"Well, would you look at that? Under those thin layers of water ice and surface frost", Roberta commented and then she got excited, "Those are fucking ships. Old Colonial Troop Transport ships!"

Lina looked at the scans, "Are you sure, Roberta?"

Roberta brought an image up on the screen of a single, alleged Colonial Troop Transport. It was as clear as day. It was a ship, definitely a ship. There was no doubting it!

Roberta instructed the Dark Angel's computer, "Computer. Identify the artefact."

The computer responded, *"Troop Transport, Vanguard Class, Ship name, CTT-VC-515. Capacity one thousand Colonial Troops, not including pilot, co-pilot, navigator, engineers and kitchen staff. Cis-Lunar Colonial Armed Forces. Operational: Twenty one forty two. Lost: Twenty one forty two."*

Elaine stated the obvious, "The ship recognises it, even knows its classification."

Roberta smiled, "Yes, our ship's database goes back a long way. Based on my scans, there are one thousand of them", she then paused to let that sink in and then brought more images up on the screen.

The deep-side scan images of the same region showed that underneath the Troop Transports were a series of tunnels leading deep into the Mimasian ice shell. Sadly, the scans could only see so deep.

Roberta checked her long-range scanners and frowned, "We've got company", she announced.

"Company?", Elaine questioned, her face taking on a worried look.

"Nothing to worry about, Elaine, my love", Roberta assured her, then pointed out, "There are two Saturnian dreadnoughts in Epimetheus's and Janus's orbital zones. Those are co-orbital moons on the inside of Mimas's orbit. There are also another pair of dreadnoughts in Enceladus's orbital zone. These are very new. I was unaware that the Saturnian Demarchy even had dreadnought-class ships."

Elaine quickly asked, "Are they a threat?"

"No, no! They're nothing to worry about at all", Roberta assured her, explaining, "Remember, Mimas is a private colony and actually holds primacy over the Demarchy."

Lina chimed in, "You told us that already, Roberta. How does that protect us?", she too, was worried.

"The law. Under Saturnian Demarchy law, no ship is allowed to approach within twenty five thousand kilometres of Mimas", Roberta assured them both, explaining, "Mimas holds primacy, but does not exercise its sovereignty over the Saturnian Demarchy. Sending in the Saturnian Armed Forces would violate that law and upset a very delicate balance. They won't be willing to do that."

"Roberta. That is a complete contradiction.", Elaine pointed out.

"What? Mimas holding primacy and sovereignty but not exercising it?", Roberta questioned.

Lina quickly caught on, "No, Roberta, that's not what Elaine meant. Mimas, Aliens, Generation ship. The Mimasian War. Those are your memories, even your ship's memories and from what we can see, those memories are very real. So, how in the hell can Mimas be a Human colony that predates the Saturnian Demarchy? It does not make sense at all!"

Elaine chimed back in, "Lina's nailed it in one. The current situation is completely at odds with your memories and the evidence of your scans, Roberta."

Roberta smiled, it was a wry smile, a broad smile, almost a Cheshire grin, "So, we have a mystery to solve, yeah. Everybody loves a mystery, right?"

Roberta flew her ship, the Dark Angel, in a loop above the region where the Colonial Troop Transport ships lay buried under thin layers of water ice and surface frost. Close surface scans were being taken, mapping the region in great detail and Roberta was looking for something very specific. The most advantageous point of ingress into the interior of Mimas. Just as Roberta had suspected, it was in the very centre of the region.

Most of the Colonial Troop Transport ships were sitting above deep tunnels bored into the ice shell of Mimas. They were, based on the scans, docked with those very tunnels. Each transport's docking umbilicus was perfectly locked into place. Sadly, ninety nine percent of those tunnels had been blocked off not far below the surface. However, Roberta found what she had been searching for, those few tunnels that remained open for ingress. There was one central tunnel and nine others around it. Those ten tunnels were all still open and each had a Colonial Troop Transport ship docked right above it.

Carefully and cautiously, Roberta flew the Dark Angel down to the central Colonial Troop Transport ship. She adjusted the ship's manoeuvring thruster nozzles downward and used them to clear away the layers of water ice and surface frost. Slowly, the Colonial Troop Transport ship became clear of ice and frost and its dorsal docking ports became visible.

Roberta picked the most appropriate docking port, lined up the Dark Angel's ventral docking port and slowly, carefully docked with the Colonial Troop Transport. The Dark Angel's computer systems showed the designation of the Colonial Troop Transport as *"CTT-VC-001"*, and it was listed as the command ship of one, General Tilos T. Brennan-Chives, who was designated as MIA.

Roberta led Elaine and Lina through the ship's ventral docking port into the ship below, the *CTT-VC-001*. Roberta was overly cautious, not knowing what they would encounter, she dressed appropriately for the occasion. Full battle armour, a full utility belt with her swords, pulsed laser pistol and knives. She had many other nasty little weapons, poison-coated, secreted on her person. Just to be absolutely sure that she was ready for anything, she also had both hers and Aurange's high-powered rapid-firing pulse laser rifles hanging by their straps around her neck.

Elaine looked at Roberta, rolled her eyes and just said, "Really, Roberta?", questioningly with her hands on her hips.

Roberta answered by passing both Elaine and Lina utility belts, each containing a Kukri sword, a long Bowie-style hunting knife and a pulse laser pistol.

"Put these on. We are not taking any chances", Roberta told them both, "I've seen pictures of the Mimasians. They are supposed to be extinct, but you never know."

"What do they look like?", Lina enquired.

Roberta smiled, "Did, honey, did. They are supposed to be extinct, remember?", then she paused and added, "They were supposed to look like a seven-foot-tall cross between an angry gorilla and an angry winged gargoyle. Horns, fangs, claws, the works. Even a pointy, prehensile tail."

Both Elaine and Lina looked shocked. Then they both quickly drew the pulse laser pistols and checked their power charge packs and operability before returning them to their holsters. Then they checked that they had extra power charge packs on their utility belts. They did, Roberta was thorough.

The trio entered the Colonial Troop Transport ship with Roberta in the lead. Roberta's upper arm muscles bulged from carrying the weight of the two pulse laser rifles, her veins clearly visible. How she managed to carry the pair of heavy weapons was a wonder that Elaine and Lina marvelled at.

The Colonial Troop Transport ship was lined with seats, lots of seats. Enough seats to seat a thousand Colonial Troops with all of their weapons and equipment. They did not hang around. Roberta led them straight over to the ship's ventral docking portal. The trio descended through the connecting umbilicus on a scissor lift to the ice tunnel below. Even after all of these decades since the War, the Colonial Troop Transport ship and the umbilicus were still full of air. That too was surprising.

When the trio reached the ice tunnel, Roberta led them through a bulkhead that contained an airlock, which blocked the entrance from the tunnel proper. The air in the ice tunnel had a crispness to it, not exactly cold, but certainly not warm. What caught their eyes straight away were three Segways parked against the ice tunnel's wall.

For the first time since they'd left the Dark Angel, Roberta spoke, "Well, well! Three of us and three Segways! Now, isn't that interesting?"

"Surely no one could possibly know that we're here, Roberta?", Elaine questioned curiously.

"Elaine, I chose the Colonial Troop Transport ship that was in the very centre simply because it was in the centre and underneath it, the ice tunnel was open and clear", Roberta explained and then she admitted something that she had not told her companions, "That Colonial Troop Transport and the ice tunnel beneath it were the only ones that still had air. And here we are, three of us and three Segways."

Lina squatted down beside one of the Segways and felt its battery container, "Roberta, this is still warm. It was left here very recently."

"Less than an hour ago, more than likely", Roberta agreed and then she told them, "It's ten clicks until we hit the rock shell. We should make use of these", and she pointed to the Segways.

Roberta climbed aboard the closest Segway. She balanced her heavy pulse laser rifles on the handlebars and began leading the trio down the ice tunnel. Elaine and Lina understood from Roberta's posture and bearing, if anyone came from the other direction, she would turn them into minced meat. That gave them both a feeling of safety and dread in equal measure.

They rode those Segways for what seemed like forever, however, it was only about two hours. Every minute of their trip filled Lina and Elaine with growing apprehension and existential dread. Eventually, the end of the ice tunnel changed from a straight line into a gradual spiral, which told them that they were close to its end. When they finally arrived at the rock shell, they entered a huge circular cavern.

There were ten tunnel entrances in the cavern wall set equidistantly apart. About fifty metres in front of each ice tunnel, there was a large desk. The kind of desks you might find in an immigration centre. Ten tunnels, ten *"immigration"* desks. Their ice tunnel opened up in a central position and they rode their Segways to the nearest desk.

The trio climbed off their Segways and approached the desk. There was a large card on the desk propped by a thermos of hot coffee, which was surrounded by precisely three cups. The card had English writing on it, handwritten. Elaine picked up the card and read it out aloud.

"Welcome to Mimas Customs and Immigration. Sorry about that lack of immigration and customs staff, but we rarely have guests these days and you are all armed to the teeth. It has been a long ten-kilometre journey, so please accept this coffee and relax. It is white with just a touch of sugar."

Elaine shook her head in disbelief, "What the fuck is going on here!", she exclaimed.

Roberta's head was on a swivel as she kept watch over the entire cavern. Lina took the card from Elaine and began reading the rest of the handwritten note.

"We've been watching your progress since you left Ganymede Prime. The 'mess' that Roberta Nummus left behind at Ganymede Prime has created quite a stir."

That caught Roberta's ears, "Wait! They know who I am?", she questioned rhetorically, noting, "That means that they likely know who you are as well."

Lina continued reading, *"Once rested and when you are ready, please proceed to the central orifice. Gravity will adjust as you enter the funnel. We have the most excellent gravity plating here on Mimas. Once you are beyond the inner bulkhead and airlock, you will find a jeep. Please leave all of your weapons behind and proceed along the tunnel to the interior of Mimas. The distance to your final destination is twenty five kilometres."*

Roberta tried the coffee, "Not too bad", she noted.

Elaine slapped the cup from her hand, "It could be poison, Roberta!", she shouted.

"Elaine, if they want us dead, we'd already be dead", Roberta replied reassuringly and then noted, "Besides, my love. I'm immune to ninety nine point nine percent of all poisons and toxins."

After around two hours, the trio found themselves at a junction in the rock tunnel. The tunnel in front of them branched to the left and to the right. A sign fixed to the opposite wall pointed to the right. The sign was very old and covered in dust. There was some degree of corrosion clearly visible on the sign. It was definitely very, very old, decades old.

Roberta, who was driving the jeep, stopped in front of the sign, with the jeep facing in the direction that the sign was pointing. Roberta checked that Lina and Elaine, sitting in the back seat, were both okay. They had finished the coffee and were feeling somewhat more relaxed. Then Roberta checked her two pulse laser rifles sitting on the seat beside her. She would be ready for whatever came next.

In English were the words, *"New Arrivals. Turn Right."*

There were other words written above the English words in a script that was unknown to either Lina or Elaine. It did not look like any script or language that they had ever seen before. Roberta recognised the language from her *"experimental"* training more than eighty years ago. It was an ancient script that operatives learned to use for quick and simple coding of messages.

Roberta looked at the script, then back at Elaine and Lina, "It says *'New Arrivals. Turn Right'* in a script called *'Angelic'*. It's an ancient Earth script."

As Roberta started driving down the new tunnel, Lina remarked, questioningly, "Your description of the Mimasian was kind of like devils and now we have angels?"

Roberta had no real answer and simply replied, "Angels and Devils are recorded in history in equal measure. Our history is full of these references."

A hundred meters further down this new tunnel, they came across another junction. A sign was fixed to the opposite wall. The sign looked almost identical to the previous sign. It was equally old and equally dust-covered. It had instructions again written in both Angelic and English, only this time the sign pointed left and read, *"New Arrivals. Turn Left."*

Roberta turned the jeep to the left and followed the new tunnel to its end. It took around thirty minutes to reach the end of the tunnel and it opened up into a large cavernous space. The cavern had ten more tunnels leading away from it, not including the one they'd come in on. There were no further instructions, so Roberta stopped the jeep in the centre of the cavern and decided to wait there at that point. Roberta climbed out of the jeep and then picked up her two heavy pulse laser rifles. Elaine and Lina climbed out of the jeep as well. Then the trio waited. Just who would come for them?

The trio did not have to wait long. From out of a tunnel on the opposite side from the tunnel they'd entered from, appeared five people. The trio had never met or even seen them before. One of them was male and the other four were female. The man and two of the women were obviously Human. The other two women had the appearance of being Human but were different.

They were both very slender and around five feet ten in height. What made them different, though, was their skin tones, which could only be described as golden, their hair, which was golden-yellow blond and their eyes, which were bright, emerald green. Their appearance was quite striking.

The man and the two more Human-looking women looked to be around seventy years of age, perhaps a little older. The older of the two golden women looked about ten years younger and the younger one looked to be about twenty years younger than her. Their facial features were very similar, perhaps a Mother and her Daughter.

A soft voice entered the trio's minds, *"You are safe. Please do not be afraid"*, the message appeared to be sent from the older of the two golden women.

Roberta shouted out, "Who are you?", and then she paused, thinking and added, "What are you?"

The elder golden woman replied telepathically, *"I am Winchilly. On my left are my Sister Wives, Freyja and Sandra, and our Husband, Gideon Reas. On my left is my Daughter, Weehalani. My Daughter and I are both Martians."*

The younger golden woman corrected, *"Please get it right, Mother"*, and then she transmitted to the trio, *"I am a hybrid, half Earth Human and half Martian Human. Gideon Rheas is my Father."*

The trio all looked at each other, confused. Gideon's name was a household name. He was the man in charge of the Martian terraforming project for over forty five years.

The pair of Humans on the right began slowly walking forward. They stopped when they were only about twenty feet away. Roberta's grip on her heavy pulse laser rifles tightened.

Sandra spoke politely, "Why have you brought your weapons?", she asked rhetorically and then she continued, "We did ask you to leave them at customs and immigration. Seriously, I even said please."

Elaine quickly answered, "Roberta had concerns. It is not her way for us to go somewhere unknown without the ability to defend ourselves."

Roberta nodded in agreement. Elaine could not have said it better.

Sandra replied bluntly, "You came here seeking sanctuary, seeking political asylum. You cannot enter the Mimasian interior with your weapons. They must be relinquished!"

Roberta raised her two pulse laser rifles ever so slightly, "Not happening. Where my Wife and my Daughter go, I go and my weapons go with me."

Gideon replied clearly, "Roberta Nummus. You do not have a choice in this matter", then he sent a telepathic message to his Wife, Sandra, *"Ready?"*

Sandra gave Gideon a telepathic nod and then she raised her right hand up with its palm open and facing Roberta. Sandra closed her right hand sharply and Roberta gasped, every muscle in her body froze except her diaphragm and eyelids. Roberta could not move. She was immobilised!

Gideon pointed to Lina Mitchel and whispered the word, "Sleep", and then pointed to Elaine Haynes and did the same, "Sleep."

Lina Mitchel and Elaine Haynes slowly slumped to their knees and slipped gently to their sides, lying on the ground fast asleep. Roberta could not move, she was helpless. Try as she might, her muscles refused to work.

Gideon approached Roberta and he gently stroked her left cheek with his right hand, "I am sorry, Roberta Nummus, but you must let go of your weapons, you must let go of your past. Do not be afraid, Lina and Elaine will be fine, they are just sleeping. Now, Roberta, you must also sleep."

And that was when Roberta Nummus slowly slumped to her knees and gently slipped to her side, lying on the ground fast asleep, her heavy pulse laser rifles lying on the ground beside her.

Roberta stirred to the sound of giggling children. She felt someone climb into the bed beside her. Her mind was still waking and she automatically thought it would be Elaine. It was. Elaine laid down beside Roberta and gently stroked her cheek.

"Wake up, sleepy head", Elaine whispered softly as she leaned close and planted a kiss directly on Roberta's lips.

Roberta, still half asleep, returned the kiss, then after a few seconds pulled back and sat up in bed.

Roberta looked around the room, startled, then quickly awakened into an alert state, "Where am I?"

Elaine sat up in bed as Lina explained, "This is your new bedroom, Roberta. Yours and Elaine's", she gestured to the room around them.

There were children in the bedroom, lining the room, giggling and whispering to themselves.

"They've been watching you sleep, Roberta", Elaine informed her, explaining, "They think you're some kind of Warrior Queen."

"Where are my weapons?", Roberta questioned, looking around the room and not seeing them.

"Gideon took our weapons away. He said he was going to put them in a secure weapons locker", Lina explained, adding, "He did say that if the need was ever to arise, he would give them back to us."

Elaine noted, "He did make one small exception", and then she pointed to a wall.

There, sitting across a pair of mounts on the wall, was Roberta's Katana, *the Harōingu.*

'Gideon said that your Katana, the Harrowing, had deep spiritual significance", Elaine informed her.

Roberta looked down at what she was wearing and a silent voice in her mind explained, *"My Mother and I changed you, Roberta Nummus. Dressed you in night attire. We thought it would be more appropriate than your military battle armour"*, it was Winchilly's Daughter, Weehalani.

"I don't think I've ever slept so deeply. What's wrong with me?", Roberta questioned, more of herself than anyone else in the room.

Weehalani's voice entered Roberta's mind once more, it was soft and soothing, *"My Father made you sleep so that we could disarm you. He made sure you slept deeply. You should be feeling refreshed."*

A small wee voice entered Roberta's mind, it was a child, a small female Martian child, she enquired, *"Why are yours so big? My Mummy's aren't even close to half that size"*, she was just a curious child.

The other children all giggled and Weehalani shooed them away, *"Go, go. Go out and play"*, chasing them out of the room.

"Sorry about that. They're just curious children. Most Earth Humans that come here aren't as formidable as you, Roberta", Weehalani explained and then she sat down on the end of the bed.

Lina sat down on the end of the bed as well and excitedly noted, "You were right, Roberta, you were right all along. There was a War and there were Aliens. There are even Martians living on Mars!"

Both Lina and Elaine had awoken a little over an hour earlier and Weehalani had explained everything to them both over breakfast. Gideon had told them that Roberta would sleep longer and that he'd done that purposely. He wanted Lina and Elaine to be fully across the situation so that they could bring Roberta up to speed themselves. Given Roberta's history, they deemed it to be safer that way.

Lina explained to Roberta that Mimas was once home to the Aliens, only that they were called Tarlaks, not Mimasians and that they looked exactly like Roberta had described.

"Over ninety thousand years ago, they conquered Mars, destroying the Martian biosphere in the process. The Martians became Slaves and were liberated during the Mimasian War by the Colonial Marines from Earth", she told her.

"Then why are they here now, inside Mimas?", Roberta had asked.

Lina explained, "At the War's conclusion, the Tarlaks had been slaughtered. They were extinct. This place, inside Mimas, was all desert and semiarid landscape. Gideon, Weehalani's Father and his other Wife, Sandra, altered the environmental settings to make Mimas a paradise and then handed Mimas over to the Martians."

Weehalani chimed in with her soft, silent telepathy, *"My people assessed Mimas as suitable and the Great Exodus began. Two and a half million Martians moved to Mimas and took up residence. It was almost the entire Martian population. They used the abandoned Colonial Troop Transport ships."*

The question that had been at the back of Roberta's mind for forty years surfaced, "Why does nobody remember any of this?"

Weehalani answered the question in her usual telepathic way, *"The Council of Shadows"*, she began and then continued, *"They are a powerful group of psychics from the Earth. Freyja, Gideon's other Wife, is a member by birth. Gideon and Sandra were both inducted into the Council of Shadows just after the Martian Exodus. To cut a long story short, the Council of Shadows have been jaunting across the solar system rewriting people's memories, archives and computer records. They've been concealing the Mimasian War and using the Great Disaster as a cover."*

"Why? Why would they do that?", Roberta demanded to know.

"Roberta, you still remember the War", Weehalani replied, her voice soothing and comforting in Roberta's mind, *"You remember the fear and the chaos. There was sheer panic across the entire solar system. I wasn't even born then, but my Mother, Winchilly, has shared her memories with me."*

Roberta replied almost angrily, "That does not make it right!"

Winchilly was standing in the bedroom doorway, her telepathic reply entered Roberta's mind, *"Weehalani left out the other reason. The Colonial Marines from Earth slaughtered the Tarlaks. It was genocide. What would become of us Martians if the whole of Humanity knew we existed? Another genocide, perhaps?"*, the question was rhetorical, *"The Council of Shadows could not take that risk."*

Roberta had to admit that it could have been a real possibility, "I understand. Concealing the War conceals your people. They are protecting you."

"Yes, amongst others. There are more than just we Martians living here. Other victims of the damnable Tarlaks", Winchilly informed her, then in a strict, yet Motherly tone, *"Get dressed. Shower first. You need to eat"*, she pointed to the wardrobe, *"You will find suitable clothes in there."*

Roberta looked at Winchilly, she had no fear of her. Winchilly, an older, almost frail, tall, thin, wisp of a woman and yet Winchilly had no fear of the beast woman, Roberta, in their midst.

Winchilly picked up on the thought, frowned and replied, *"I was born a Slave to the Tarlaks. They were brutal and being raped by those demons was a regular hazard. A mind in fear is a mind frozen."*

Roberta looked at Winchilly with new eyes, the Martian woman was a survivor.

Lina chimed in, "I forgot to mention. The Martians can't speak. They are all non-verbal telepaths. It will take a little getting used to."

Elaine showed Roberta to their kitchen and dining room. It was a large space on the lower level of the two-story structure.

"This house has four bedrooms upstairs with bathrooms and toilets. The living space is all downstairs", Elaine informed Roberta, explaining, "It is a flat pack pop-up. Self-founding and self-levelling. Gideon organised it for us to live in."

"Those children? Whose are they?", Roberta enquired.

"Well, some of them, the older ones, are Gideon's Grandchildren. The younger ones are his Great-Grandchildren", Elaine explained, noting, "He does have three Wives and they apparently had four children each. All of them are now grown up. Weehalani is Gideon's eldest Daughter via Winchilly."

"Complicated", Roberta noted, smiling, she was conditioned to be protective of children.

"The little one that enquired about your", Elaine faltered for the right word and then just settled on, "your breasts. She is Weehalani's Granddaughter. A precocious little thing."

Elaine and Roberta sat down at the dining table and Lina came in from the kitchen with a plate of food. Lina placed the plate on the table in front of Roberta.

"The Martians are all vegetarian, even the hybrids, but their food is really, really good", Lina told Roberta, she even sounded convincing.

Roberta stuck her fork into a piece of the food and tried it, "It's actually quite good", she noted.

"Much better than MRE packs", Lina remarked dryly about the rations on board the Dark Angel.

Winchilly, Freyja and Sandra sat down at the table. They had thought that Roberta would have lots of questions. They were right. Freyja also had questions of her own.

Roberta stopped eating and asked, "Those direction signs? I can understand the English directions, but what's with the Angelic script?"

Winchilly looked completely perplexed, *"Angelic?"*, she transmitted questioningly, looking confused and then she clarified, *"That is not Angelic script. That's Martian script. High North Martian, to be more precise, although these days, we just call it Martian."*

"Okay, so what we on Earth call Angelic script is actually Martian script", Roberta surmised.

"I can only assume so", Winchilly agreed and then she noted, *"I have never seen it used on Earth, so I cannot be one hundred percent certain. If it is used on Earth, it would simply be Earth Human languages transliterated, not truly Martian."*

"Now, here's a question for you", Roberta announced, questioning, "Mimas was the Tarlak's home world, their base of operations. So, how on Earth did Mimas manage to obtain Primacy over the Saturnian Demarchy? I have seen the documentation. Mimasian Primacy predates the Demarchy by thirty years or more and we all know that is impossible."

Freyja laughed out loud, "That was Orpheus's handy work. Orpheus is my Eldest Cousin. He runs the Council of Shadows, although now he's really old. Nearly ninety eight from memory. That document, it really looks so convincing and it has other *'foundational'* documents to back it up", she paused for theatrical amusement, "The whole thing is a carefully crafted fallacy, a fraud", she admitted.

Winchilly explained, *"It is a well-crafted and necessary lie to keep we Martians and our friends safe. It keeps prying eyes away from Mimas, our home and we have friends on the outside to facilitate this."*

Roberta noticed that Winchilly had her hand on Freyja's forearm, stroking it gently.

Winchilly noticed that Roberta had noticed, so she sent Roberta a private telepathic message, *"I'm keeping my Sister Wife, Freyja, calm. Your former employer, Albert Horridian, did something horrible to two of her cousins back in twenty one seventy seven and I don't want Freyja lashing out and lobotomising you. Freyja is a Folcrom and she is quite powerful. She is also still upset, still grieving."*

Roberta was well aware of the event in question. It had happened when she was on a mission with Aurange shortly after the declaration of the disbandment of the Jovian Republic and the rise of the Jovian Realms. At that time, both Aurange and Roberta were at Jupiter's Leading Trojan point, at the Hector Central Command twin-cylinder colony.

They were putting down a short-lived rebellion after the annexation of Jupiter's Trojans. It was one of three rebellions that she and Aurange had put down. Two at the Leading Trojans and one at the Trailing Trojans. Upon their return to Ganymede Prime, they'd viewed the footage. Neither of them knew what to make of it at the time. Now, Roberta had powerful inklings about it.

Roberta saw this as a knife lodged deep in the ribs that needed removal, she stated boldly, "Back in twenty one seventy seven, when Aurange Sheergibbon and I were in Jupiter's Leading Trojan point, breaking up rebellious dissent, a couple of people were brutally murdered. Hanged by High Prince Albert's palace guards. Were they Council of Shadow members?", she asked.

Freyja's eyes went red with rage and Winchilly had trouble keeping her calm.

"They were my Cousins!", Freyja screamed out loudly as she stood up.

Sandra Danker placed her hand on Freyja's other forearm and between her and Winchilly, they maintained control.

Freyja sat back down, tears flowing down her cheeks, "They were my Cousins, Tina and David. They just went there to observe the situation. They were not assassins! Tina had such a gentle, beautiful soul!", she looked distraught.

Lina and Elaine sat there with wide eyes. Why did Roberta deliberately bring this up now?

Roberta noted calmly, "Everyone involved in their deaths is now dead. Everyone, from the palace's Doberman Pinschers to the palace's Royal Guards themselves, right down to High Prince Albert von Horridian himself", she informed Freyja.

Freyja was almost pleased that the culprits had met their just rewards, but nonetheless questioned, "How can you be so sure of that, Roberta Nummus?"

"The High Prince made the mistake of trying to kill my family. It was a fatal mistake on his part. I personally killed his dogs, both Canine and Human and then I took his fucking head and incinerated it to curse his fucking Sons",

Roberta admitted and then she looked at Freyja, "If ever you wanted revenge, Freyja, they have met it by my hand. They all deserved what they got!"

Freyja stood up, this time less angrily. She leaned across the table, taking Roberta's cheeks gently in her hands. Then she leaned in closer and touched her forehead to Roberta's.

A message entered Roberta's mind, *"Show me their deaths, Roberta Nummus. I want to see their deaths"*, and for the first time in her life, Roberta felt what it was like to telepathically share her memories with another person.

When Freyja finally pulled back from the sharing, she looked Roberta in the eyes, "Chop, chop, rip!", she stated and then continued, "Albert Horridian deserved that. Thank you, Roberta Nummus, thank you. For this thing you have done, I name you my friend!"

Winchilly sent another silent message to Roberta, *"Freyja will be a powerful friend. A wise move."*

Winchilly, Sandra and Freyja led Lina, Elaine and Roberta out of their new house and into the interior of Mimas. Freyja had taken her newly declared friend, Roberta, by the arm and walked side by side with her. Elaine was feeling just a little jealous and Winchilly picked up on it.

Winchilly took Elaine gently by the arm and then sent a private message to her, *"Don't worry, Elaine. Freyja does not swing that way."*

As they walked, Freyja informed Roberta, "You know, Roberta, back in the forties, we tried to alter your memories, yours and Aurange's. It never worked. Your memories kept coming back the very next day. They simply resurfaced. I think Gideon, Sandra and I each tried at least a dozen times before we finally gave up. Gideon said at the time that we obviously weren't meant to change your memories."

Roberta said nothing, she was feeling a little giddy and lightheaded from sharing her memories with Freyja. It had created a gob-smacking sense of closeness that she could never have expected. Their new *"pop-up"* house was just inside a tunnel in the side of a mountain. It was well sheltered and as they walked out onto a broad ledge and into the open, the sight was awe-inspiring.

The air was crisp and clean, neither hot nor cold, quite pleasant in fact. Gravity inside Mimas appeared to be around point four gs, slightly above Martian Gravity.

The broad ledge sat on the flanks of a well forested mountain. The trees were tall and majestic, reaching well above three hundred feet, perhaps even a hundred feet higher. Before them was a circular sea, or at least it appeared to be circular from their vantage point, arcing to both the left and the right.

Beyond the circular sea appeared to be a ring of mountains. From their vantage point on the broad ledges that looked to be easily five kilometres high. Beyond the ring of mountains was hill country, followed by hummocky terrain and eventually broad plains flowing all the way to a broad central sea and the same pattern appeared to be duplicated on the other side of the Mimasian interior. Forested woodlands and sweeping grasslands were clearly visible. It looked like paradise!

What made the vista all the more awe-inspiring was that this was all on the interior of a sphere three hundred and twenty kilometres in diameter, with the horizon curving upward in every direction. Unlike either Earth or Mars, the horizon was concave, not convex and in the very centre was an artificial Sun. It, of course, was not a Sun. It was a controlled plasma fusion reaction and that was the source of both light and warmth inside Mimas.

Winchilly remarked telepathically to them all, with barely concealed pride, *"Sandra and Gideon transformed this place from the Tarlak's desert world into a paradise and then they just gave it away!"*

As Roberta, Elaine and Lina stood there looking out over the magnificent vista before them, they heard the sounds of trilling, clicking and soft barks coming from around the flanks of the mountain. From out of the tall trees flew half a dozen Humanoid shapes.

Roberta automatically went into defensive posture, "Don't worry", Sandra assured her, explaining, "They are our friends. They've just come to visit."

A half dozen newcomers landed on the broad ledge only about fifty feet away. They were only about five feet tall and they looked very Human in every way, except, of course, they were not. Their skin was alabaster white and they had great leathery wings which were of a creamy colour. Their hair was white blond and their eyes were a deep purple. They had a long, prehensile tail with a rounded, manipulative tip. Their hands had six fingers, set in three pairs, with the outer pair being opposable. Their feet reflected the same arrangement.

Lina noted, "They're beautiful. They look just like Angels", an amazed look was upon her face.

Winchilly added, *"They are Thols! Thols not only look like Angels, they behave like Angels as well. They are very gentle beings with very gentle souls. They live in the forest canopy, in tree houses."*

The female Thol in the lead trilled, clicked and barked.

Winchilly translated, *"That is Yareenah, the Daughter of Yarule, their matriarch. She is saying, 'Welcome new friends, welcome.' Thols are very friendly."*

Sandra smiled and noted, "Yareenah's Mother, Yarule. She is a very old friend of mine. You guys will love her. I'm certain of it."

Freyja noted, "Our Thol friends are another reason why we had to hide the Mimasian War. We aren't just protecting the Martians here. We are protecting the Thols as well. They are an endangered species and so very few in number."

Roberta Nummus replied, "We came here seeking sanctuary, seeking hope. Everything is based on lies! The most glorious of lies! My sanctuary is my palimpsest."

Elaine took Roberta's hand and squeezed it gently, "No, Roberta, our sanctuary is our palimpsest!"

Lina joked wryly, because it was definitely opposites day, "And those glorious lies have set us free!"

14. The Litany of Lies.

Once again, a familiar scene unfolded in the office of Professor Maria Corbel, Central Speaker of the Colonisation Committee of Sol. She sat in her usual comfortable chair. It was yet another impromptu meeting, one of many, triggered once again by the Security Council of Sol.

Sitting across a coffee table in their usual seats were the other two Colonisation Committee Speakers, the Left Speaker, Professor Lyra Banks and the Right Speaker, Professor Stephen Terrell. In between the two Speakers was the current Security Council of Sol's liaison to the Colonisation Committee, Mr Carl Stavros.

"Professor Corbel, the situation is reaching preposterous levels of ridiculousness", Carl Stavros informed her, noting, "I've had complaints come in from the offices of the President of Earth and the President of Cis-Lunar space. President Guang Hui and President Dieter Reinhardt are not happy. We and by that I mean, your Colonisation Committee and my Security Council, are being accused of not doing our jobs!"

"Not doing our jobs? In what way are we not doing our jobs, Carl?", Professor Corbel enquired, her tone borderline angry at the accusation.

"Both President Guang and President Reinhardt have received no less than three official diplomatic protests from the outer solar system colonies", Carl Stavros informed them, noting, "From the Saturnian Demarchy, the Uranian Federation and the Neptunian Commonwealth. All three bypassed us entirely and went straight to the highest offices on Earth and in Cis-Lunar space."

"Carl, that is serious. They wouldn't have bypassed us, bypassed Eros, unless it was something really, really big. Big and bad!", Maria Corbel replied, wondering what was going on out in the outer colonies.

"I'll start with the small stuff first", Carl began and then continued, "Remember the Sleek Runner. The Neptunians are demanding the access codes to the Sleek Runner's internal sensors and cameras. They want to check that our ghost ship really is a ghost ship and not a trap."

Professor Lyra Banks almost spat in her coffee, "Trap!", she exclaimed, "What are they on about?"

"Someone has told them that the Sleek Runner delivered assassins to Ganymede Prime. So now they want to verify everything we've told them about the Sleek Runner", Carl explained.

Professor Stephen Terrell enquired, "Who the hell told them that?"

"The information came from the Jovian Realms, from Ganymede Prime itself", Carl replied.

Stephen Terrell then asked, "Who are these alleged assassins?"

Carl replied, "Aurange Sheergibbon, Roberta Nummus, Elaine Haynes and get this, Lina Mitchel."

"That's ridiculous, Carl. Sheergibbon and Nummus were already at Ganymede Prime working as High Prince Albert's most trusted bodyguards. Sonia de la Cruz confirmed that herself. And Lina Mitchel was her Niece and only sixteen years old at the time. Everyone aboard the Sleek Runner is missing, presumed dead, including Lina Mitchel. It is a ghost ship!", Maria Corbel replied incredulously.

"Yes, Maria and we have no idea who this Elaine Haynes is either. She was not onboard the Sleek Runner. Not a crew member and certainly not a member of your Ambassadorial team", Carl replied.

Maria Corbel decided, "Send the Neptunian Commonwealth the Sleek Runner's access codes. At least they'll be able to see that the Sleek Runner has no one on board", then she paused, "Now, Carl. Obviously, there's a lot more to this nonsense, so tell us everything."

Carl nodded, "We've already sent the Neptunians the Sleek Runner's access codes, Maria", and then he opened his briefcase and passed three folios across the coffee table.

The three Colonisation Committee speakers read through the documents contained in the folios. There were copies of the official diplomatic protests. Everything they read was either a blatant lie or carefully crafted distortions of the truth. The source of this *"truth"* in every case went back to the same source, the Jovian Realms and Ganymede Prime.

"Oh my God!", Lyra Banks exclaimed and then remarked, "This is pure propaganda. Seriously, it's like the kind of rubbish a nineteen-forties Nazi would be proud of!"

"You can see that, can you?", Carl replied, noting, "Apparently, Sheergibbon, Nummus, Haynes and Lina Mitchel committed regicide and killed four dozen palace guards in the process. Read a bit further and you'll find the damage they caused required the High Prince's palace to be demolished and rebuilt."

"And none of it could be remotely true", Stephen Terrell chimed in, commenting, " Sheergibbon and Nummus were both Horridian operatives. Haynes is a complete unknown, as far as we know. Lina Mitchel went missing on the Sleek Runner at sixteen years of age, three years ago. Whatever happened at Ganymede Prime had nothing to do with us."

"And yet, they are blaming us anyway", Maria Corbel noted with incredulity.

Maria Corbel gave Carl some verbal instructions and he started taking notes.

"First, we need to inform Earth and Cis-Lunar space that the Jovian Realms are playing the propaganda game and that means that they're up to something. Something big. Carl, make sure that President Guang Hui and President Dieter

Reinhardt both fully understand that there were no assassins on board the Sleek Runner. Point out that Aurange Sheergibbon and Roberta Nummus are known operatives working for the Horridians and that they have been for eight decades or more. Include hyperlinks to their internal dossiers. We have no idea who Elaine Haynes is. Make sure that they are aware of that as well. She is a complete unknown to us."

"Okay, I've got all of that noted down, Maria", Carl nodded and then enquired, "And what about our friends in the outer satellites?"

Maria replied thoughtfully, "Send them the dossiers we have on Aurange Sheergibbon and Roberta Nummus. Make sure that they fully understand, Sheergibbon and Nummus were both existing Horridian operatives", she then paused and finally added, "Send them the details of the missing crew members and Ambassadorial passengers of the Sleek Runner. Make sure to highlight that Lina Mitchel was only sixteen years of age at the time that they went missing. Oh, don't forget, Elaine Haynes is unknown to us. Mustn't forget that. We have never heard of her."

"There isn't much more that we can do, except counter the Horridian lies with the truth. Give them the correct information and let's hope that it sinks in. The Horridian are playing them like a fine fiddle", Lyra Banks commented.

"They're not stupid, Lyra. Give them the truth and they should be able to see through the Horridian lies", Maria commented, although she was not so sure that they would.

"Did you get to the demands section?", Carl asked, noting, "The Horridians have twisted the uranium fission power production phaseout as well."

The three Colonisation Committee speakers read further into the documents. Professor Corbel ran her right hand through her hair. It was not looking good.

"Damn them!", Maria Corbel spat out, "They are spinning the uranium fission phaseout as a deliberate ploy to leave the outer colonies without uranium fuel rods. The Horridians are making them believe that they are going to be left without power production and completely vulnerable. Ripe for a military takeover by the Earth and Cis-Lunar space. They are demanding an end to the uranium fission phaseout, especially the end of uranium mining and fuel rod production on Earth."

"This is bad, Maria", Stephen replied, explaining, "If I didn't know any better, I'd say they are trying to convince the Demarchy, the Federation and the Commonwealth to mobilise. It's not mentioned explicitly, but if they think we're taking away their power production, well, what options are they going to be left with?"

Carl chimed in with four simple words, "A preemptive military strike."

Maria pointed out their dilemma, "We have no idea how long the Horridians have been playing this game and we are just catching up!"

Lyra Banks asked, "Why, though? Why would they even entertain that idea? The Earth has never threatened them in the past."

"No, Lyra. They haven't", Maria confirmed, but then noted, "All of the colonies beyond the Martian orbital zone were not created by Earth or by Cis-Lunar space. They weren't even created under our Erosian auspices. The entire colonisation effort of the outer solar system was privately driven and enabled by Dumas Incorporated and Himmelstaff Consolidated Industries. To them, we are all outsiders and they have never really trusted us."

"And you have to remember that fiasco with the colony registration requirements and the punitive fine regime that was put in place at the beginning of the century", Stephen recalled, noting, "That was draconian stupidity at its best and they have never forgotten that. Like or not, we are the bad guys, or that is what they're thinking."

"Stephen, that is ridiculous. That was nearly eight decades ago", Lyra protested.

"Yes, it was, Lyra and it gets even better", Stephen confirmed and then he noted, "Way back then, the late Stuart Dumas predicted this very situation. It was back before Jupiter or even its Trojans had been colonised. Our predecessors had been aggravating the Belters and so, the Belters kept coming up with loopholes and clever schemes to avoid compliance. Stuart Dumas predicted way back then that if Eros didn't change its ways, the animosity between the outer colonies and Eros would grow and there would be open rebellion and eventually War."

Stephen's words sank in and then Lyra enquired curiously, "What was Stuart Dumas's timeline? You know, for his prophecy?"

Stephen replied, "Stuart Dumas predicted this kind of situation would come about in a century or less in his future at that time. So roughly about now, I guess."

Carl Stavros chimed in, "We cannot waste time arguing about the misdeeds and inadequacies of our predecessors. We have a current situation to defuse."

"Carl's right", Maria Corbel agreed and then instructed, "We need to send the Saturnian Demarchy, the Uranian Federation and the Neptunian Commonwealth the full blueprints and specifications for the new fusion reactor technology. We also need to stress the point that the uranium fission power generation phaseout is about providing them with a viable alternative. Clean hydrogen fusion power generation and their eventual energy independence. They can source their hydrogen for their new fusion reactors locally! No need for Earth's exports."

Carl replied, noting, "I'll send them the message about the fusion reactor technology and hydrogen energy independence first and then I'll follow up with the full blueprints and the specifications. I'll also request that they send us a return message confirming receipt. I will use tight beam laser comms to ensure integrity and security."

Lyra chimed in, "Tell them that if they need any assistance manufacturing the new fusion reactors, we can arrange to provide them with engineers from Cis-Lunar L-Four to assist them. If necessary, we can even have the fusion reactors built at the Cis-Lunar L-Four construction yards and shipped out to them. We will help them transition to fusion power generation."

Stephen Terrell chuckled and Lyra asked, "What's so funny, Stephen?"

Stephen replied, grinning, "Sorry, Lyra. It's just that Dumas Colonial Constructions and Himmelstaff Interplanetary Constructions are the contracted manufacturers of the fusion reactors and of course, Dumas's Cis-Lunar Haulage does the shipping. The Dumas family have their hands in every pie."

"Then, tell them that, Carl. Not the pie thing, the other stuff. They all trust the Dumas family", Maria Corbel interjected.

"Carl?", Maria Corbel caught his attention, "Lina Mitchel was noted as an assassin. The girl has been missing, presumed dead, for three years. So, just how did that come about?"

"Well, this is where things take a really weird turn, Maria", Carl started, before explaining, "We have the Saturnians to thank for this information. Aurange Sheergibbon is dead. He was, according to the Horridian regime, one of the assassins and he was killed while attempting to escape Ganymede Prime by the Jovian Security Forces. If we are to believe what the Horridians have told the Saturnians, Roberta Nummus, Elaine Haynes and Lina Mitchel fled Ganymede Prime on a ship, the Twilight Angel, en route to Saturn."

"Wait! Carl, Lina Mitchel was on the Sleek Runner when it veered off course and its crew and passengers went missing. That was three years ago!", Maria reminded him.

"Did I mention that really weird turn?", Carl remarked questioningly.

Carl continued from his rhetorical question, "Maria, we have over seven weeks, a full fifty days of daily check-ins from the Sleek Runner. Every crew member was listed as being present on board. Your full Ambassadorial team was listed as present on board, including Lina Mitchel. We even have their daily biodata updates. And then on the forty-ninth day, the Sleek Runner's thrusters fired up, she veers off course and everyone goes missing. Lina Mitchel was definitely on board at that time!"

"And yet, three years later, Lina is somehow involved in an assassination and fleeing to Saturn", Maria Corbel continued, "Carl! None of this makes any sense."

Lyra Banks chimed in, "Wait now. Is it possible that somehow the Sleek Runner's crew and passengers ended up back at Ganymede Prime? If Lina was there during the last three years, perhaps the others were too? They may all still be alive?"

Stephen Terrell noted, "That's not the Horridian's style, Lyra. Do you remember their last round of propaganda back in seventy eight? The Sleek Runner was one week out from Ganymede Prime and the Horridians released a video of alleged assassins being mauled, beaten and hanged for the attempted assassination of High Prince Albert. They tried to blame that on Ambassador de la Cruz as well."

Carl Stavros agreed, "Stephen's right. Based on that alone, if they did end up back at Ganymede Prime, they probably would all be dead."

"And yet, apparently, Lina Mitchel is alive and on her way to Saturn", Maria concluded.

"I did say something weird was going on, Maria", Carl remarked.

They had another mystery on their hands.

The ghost ship, the Sleek Runner and now, the ghost of Lina Mitchel.

Mr Quintus Malbeck, the Saturnian Demarchy's current Parliamentary Prime Minister, was sitting in the office of Ms Swenna Goodchild, the Administrator of the Saturnian system and liaison to the Colonisation Committee of Sol situated at Eros. Swenna was in charge of the Saturnian bureaucracy.

"Ms Goodchild, it is simply unacceptable that these fugitives, these assassins have taken refuge at Mimas", the Prime Minister complained, "It is simply unacceptable. That Roberta Nummus woman has confessed to regicide and mass murder."

"And yet, Prime Minister, the Mimasians have taken them in and given them all sanctuary and political asylum. All three of them are out of our reach", Swenna Goodchild replied, adding, "We have zero jurisdiction over the Mimasian colony."

"Why? Why have they done this?" the Prime Minister rhetorically asked, noting, "Surely they know that they have three assassins in their midst."

Swenna responded, "I have used the hotline to speak with them, Prime Minister. The Mimasian Administrator tells me that, while Roberta Nummus did commit the crimes, it was her conditioning that forced her to do so. Roberta Nummus is the product of military experimentation and conditioning. They say that they are working diligently to deprogram her."

"Deprogram! And what if she leaves Mimas? What if she leaves and goes on a rampage?", Prime Minister Malbeck asked.

"Prime Minister, the Mimasians have assured me that that can't happen and I trust them", Swenna Goodchild replied and then noted, "We have a pair of dreadnoughts in Epimetheus's and Janus's orbital zone, and another pair of dreadnoughts in Enceladus's orbital zone. They are matching Mimas's orbital position at all times, boxing them in. Should Roberta Nummus try to leave Mimas, she will have four dreadnoughts pouncing right on top of her."

"That ship of hers, the Twilight Angel. It's fast and heavily armed", Prime Minister Malbeck noted.

"And no match for four of our dreadnoughts, Prime Minister", Swenna Goodchild assured him and then clarified, "Roberta Nummus's ship, she calls it the Dark Angel, not the Twilight Angel."

The Prime Minister caught that last statement, "What difference does that make?"

"The Horridians tell us her ship is called the Twilight Angel. Roberta Nummus calls her ship the Dark Angel. Scans of her ship's hull clearly show the ship's name decaled as, Dark Angel, Prime Minister. Something does not add up, Sir", Swenna Goodchild explained.

"What if we just sent our dreadnoughts to Mimas? Mimas is a smallish colony and our Colonial Marines could probably take it over very quickly. In a matter of hours, certainly less than a day", Prime Minister Malbeck queried.

This was one of those queries that Swenna had been trained to handle, "Mr Prime Minister, our own laws clearly state that no Saturnian Demarchy ship, state or civilian, is allowed within twenty five thousand kilometres of Mimas. That little ice moon, Mimas, holds Primacy over the Demarchy, Sir."

"Yes, yes. I have seen the documents. And yes, I have had them investigated. They are backed up by other founding documents as well. It's all very kosher", Prime Minister Malbeck admitted and then he asked, "Why then, do the Mimasians not exercise their sovereign rights over our Demarchy?"

"Choice, Prime Minister, choice. As is their prerogative", Swenna Goodchild replied, being careful to add, "If we, the Demarchy, invade and annex Mimas, and make no mistakes, that is what you just implied, Mr Prime Minister. We will have the Uranian Federation and Neptunian Commonwealth looking down at us with snake eyes. We will lose their trust."

"The Jovian Realms annexed their Leading and Trailing Trojans and no one batted an eyelid", the Prime Minister countered.

"Not so, Prime Minister. Here I am double-checking, triple-checking and validating every single thing they tell us. I don't trust the Horridians at all, Sir", Swenna Goodchild responded, noting, "You can guarantee that the Federation and the Commonwealth are doing exactly the same. The Jovian Realms are a military power and the Horridians are conquerors, and we are all very wary of them."

"Then you don't agree with invading Mimas, Administrator?", the Prime Minister asked.

"I do not, Sir. Invading Mimas would open up a can of worms. A big can of worms, Sir. There is no guarantee of success. We know very little about the Mimasians, just that they keep to themselves and that is just the way that they want it", Swenna Goodchild carefully responded.

Prime Minister Malbeck scoffed, "So, you don't think that four dreadnoughts and our Colonial Marines can take that one tiny moon!"

"Mr Prime Minister, with all due respect, it is not about whether we can or not. It is about whether we should even make the attempt. We are the Saturnian Demarchy, Sir. We are not an imperialistic power like the Jovian Realms, Sir", Swenna Goodchild countered.

Prime Minister Malbeck considered that. It was true, they were a Demarchy.

"Yes, you are right, Administrator. An invasion is an act of War and that would have to go to a full plebiscite", he concluded.

"Yes, Sir. The people would have to be consulted and they would never agree", Swenna confirmed and then she showed the Prime Minister something that he had never seen before.

Swenna Goodchild showed Prime Minister Malbeck a series of photographs of Mimas. They were simple photographic scans taken from a legal distance.

The Prime Minister wasn't sure what he was looking at, "So, what am I looking at here exactly?"

"Prime Minister, that is Mimas", Swenna replied simply and then explained, "According to all of our records and documentation, Mimas was colonised at least thirty years before the Saturnian Demarchy group came here to colonise Saturn."

"Yes, Administrator. I am fully aware of that", the Prime Minister responded.

"Yes, Sir. I don't show these photographs to just anyone, Sir", Swenna informed him and then she explained the photos, "You see those regular pock marks, craters in the Mimasian surface?"

"Yes, I see them. What about them?", Malbeck enquired.

"Prime Minister, they are nuclear blast craters and they are still radioactive", Swenna informed him.

Prime Minister Quintus Malbeck was taken aback, "No. That can't be right!"

"It is entirely correct, Prime Minister", Swenna confirmed and then she explained, "We know that Mimas was colonised more than three decades before we arrived out here. We know that something, something very bad happened to Mimas. We have no idea what that something was", she lied and then continued, "but one thing is very certain, Sir. The Mimasians managed to fend off a nuclear holocaust and they survived it."

"Why haven't I been shown these photographs before?", Prime Minister Malbeck demanded.

"Prime Minister, if you check the regulations, this information only becomes available to you, when you need to know it", Swenna explained, adding, "You need to know it now, Sir. The Mimasians keep to themselves because they went through something horrible and they survived it. We have no idea what it was", she lied once more, "but I would not want to put them to the test by attempting an invasion. It looks like they've already fended off one and anything that we could do would pale in comparison. So, Prime Minister, let's not go there."

Prime Minister Malbeck looked at Administrator Goodchild incredulously. If what he had just been told was true. Attacking Mimas would be a very, very bad idea indeed.

"It's a mystery, Prime Minister. An enduring mystery and we have no answers for it", Swenna told him, again lying, then she gestured to the hotline to Mimas, "And the Mimasians aren't saying what it was either, Sir. They are very coy on the subject."

As this slowly sank in, Prime Minister Malbeck mumbled, "I think we should leave the Mimasians alone. I don't think that can of worms needs opening."

"Prime Minister, Sir. This is a state secret. No one else can know of it", Swenna explained.

Prime Minister Quintus Malbeck nodded in understanding.

The meeting ended and Swenna Goodchild smiled. She had just stopped yet another Saturnian Prime Minister from overstepping their authority, from overreaching. Swenna knew exactly how the hundred nuclear craters on Mimas's surface got there. Swenna had full memories of the Mimasian War that had engulfed the solar system back in the early forties.

Swenna was a part of the cover-up that buried the War deeply, turning a terrible War into the Great Disaster caused by interstellar micrometeor swarms. Tens of millions of memories had been subtly altered and the entire conflict was buried under layers upon layers of shared trauma.

Swenna, just like every Saturnian Administrator before her, worked with the Council of Shadows to keep the Martians and Thols living inside the interior of Mimas safe. The Great Conceal as it would one day be known would continue, until centuries into the future, when Humanity was ready and then there would be the Great Reveal.

Communications Minister Temu Trump entered the operations room. He straightaway noticed the presence of fellow Ministers, Peter Macron of Defence and Miles Morton of Security. High Prince Godric sat in his gold-gilded throne. To the High Prince's right were three lesser, gold-gilded thrones. Sitting in the furthest throne from the High Prince was Prince Friederic. In the next closest throne sat Prince Emeric. The throne beside the High Prince's was empty, that was Prince Aluric's throne.

Minister Trump enquired, "Will Prince Aluric not be joining us, Sire?"

Instead of High Prince Godric answering, Prince Friederic fielded the question, "Temu, you do remember the last time Prince Aluric attended a meeting, don't you?", it was entirely rhetorical, he continued, "Our Brother, Prince Aluric, stood around with his cock hanging out complaining about why his *'bitches'* had been kicked out."

High Prince Godric stepped in, "We thought it better to leave our Brother, Aluric, to his own devices. Please, take a seat, Temu."

"I see, Your Majesty", Minister Trump replied, then to Prince Friederic he enquired, "Your Highness, your Brother's responsibilities. They are being supervised, yes?"

"Yes, Temu. I have my people dealing with Brother Aluric's responsibilities and I receive regular updates", Prince Friederic replied, noting, "I keep our Brother, High Prince Godric, informed of any important matters."

"Yes, Temu, based upon your advice, we keep our Brother, Aluric, on a very short leash", High Prince Godric informed him and then he asked, "Now, Temu. Why are we all here?"

"Your Majesty, we have received word back from the Saturnian Demarchy", Minister Trump announced straight away.

Security Minister Miles Morton stepped in straight away, "Ah, excellent, Temu.

Are they extraditing the fugitives here themselves, or do we need to collect them?"

Minister Trump turned to Minister Morton and replied, "Miles, your question is premature", then he turned back to the High Prince, "Your Majesty. The fugitives have not been captured. They have", he paused, looking for the right words, "found sanctuary and asylum on a small inner moon of Saturn, Sire. Mimas, I believe it is called."

High Prince Godric looked incredulous, "And why can't they just send in their Colonial Troops to, I don't know, capture them? They are fugitives from justice after all."

Defence Minister Peter Macron commented loudly, "If their Saturnian Troops don't have the balls to do the job, we can loan them some of our Jovian Shock Troopers."

Minister Trump frowned before addressing the High Prince, "Your Majesty, Mimas is not under Saturnian Demarchy jurisdiction. The Demarchy has no authority there, Sire."

"How is that even possible, Temu? Mimas is a part of the Saturnian system", the High Prince noted.

"Apparently, Sire. The Mimasian colony predates the Demarchy's arrival by more than three decades. The Mimasians hold Primacy over the entire Saturnian orbital zone, yet they do not exercise their sovereignty. Instead, they refuse it. It is most unusual, Your Majesty", Minister Trump explained.

"Easily rectified, Temu", Defence Minister Macron replied, commenting, "We just send a few of our own dreadnoughts and take what we want. A little shit of a colony like Mimas won't stand a chance."

Minister Trump frowned once more, hawks had short fuses and even less common sense, "Peter, sending in our dreadnoughts would be an act of War. I doubt very much that the Demarchy would distinguish between our warships being in Saturnian space or Mimasian space. In either case, to get to Mimas, you must first cross Saturnian space."

"Temu's right", Prince Emeric chimed in, "We want the Demarchy on our side as allies. We most certainly don't want a War with them."

Prince Friederic was steepling his fingers and Minister Trump noticed, "Your Highness, you have a thought or two perhaps", the youngest Prince was well known for his ideas.

"Nothing that will help, Temu", Prince Friederic replied, explaining, "I was just gaming a War with the Demarchy in my head. We would win, yes, but it would set back Brother Godric's plans by at least five years. That would be a significant delay and our Realms would be weaker at its conclusion."

Godric nodded in agreement, he often deferred to Friederic's judgement, "Yes, agreed. No delays. I want the Demarchy as allies, not enemies. We can conquer them later on down the track. Once we have the full resources of the inner solar system under our control."

Prince Friederic commented, "We could always make a request of the Demarchy. We could ask them if they would be willing to let us intervene in their Mimas problem and extract the fugitives. They will, of course, say no, but the fact that we asked and then accept their refusal would play in our favour."

"Request. Request denied and then we accept their refusal", Minister Trump considered, he smiled and added, "Your Highness, that would have a very subtle psychological effect. I would recommend that after their refusal, we should respond with pleasantries and a promise to aid them in the future should the need arise."

High Prince Godric smiled and chuffed, "Make an offer of future aid now and later, later we turn it into a future alliance perhaps. Well, Temu, I guess we need to start the wheels turning at some point."

"Yes, Your Majesty. I'll make the necessary overtures straight away", Minister Trump replied.

The High Prince looked to Defence Minister Macron, "Peter. Finesse first, brute force later."

Defence Minister Macron nodded in agreement, "Yes, Your Majesty."

Professor Maria Corbel, the Central Speaker of the Colonisation Committee of Sol's intercom buzzed, her secretary was on the line, "Professor Corbel. Mr Carl Stavros is here to see you. He's also requesting that Professors Banks and Terrell be called in. Mr Stavros says it's urgent."

"Thank you, Taylor. Show Mr Stavros in and then call Professors Banks and Terrell to join us", Professor Corbel instructed.

Taylor showed Carl Stavros into Professor Corbel's office and Maria gestured for him to take a seat by the coffee table.

"I take it you have some information, Carl?", Maria enquired as she also took a seat by the coffee table, noting, "It must be important if you didn't schedule a meeting."

"It is something that you need to see, Maria. You personally and the other Colonisation Committee Speakers", Carl replied, noting, "This is important. Very important."

Taylor opened the office door and showed Professors Banks and Terrell into Professor Corbel's office. Maria gestured for them to take their seats by the coffee table without standing.

"Carl says this is important", Maria announced as Lyra Banks and Stephen Terrell sat down.

Carl took a data stick out of his pocket and passed it to Maria, "Play this video recording."

Maria placed the data stick into the receptacle sitting on the coffee table and picked up her office screen's remote control.

"This came in less than an hour ago from the Saturnian system on tight beam laser comms", Carl commented and then he clarified, "It is not from the Saturnian Demarchy. It was sent from Mimas."

"Mimas?", Lyra Banks enquired.

"Yes, Mimas", Carl confirmed and then he explained, "They are an independent colony within the Saturnian system. They are not under the Demarchy's jurisdiction. Strangely, the Mimasians were the first to build a colony within the Saturnian system. So they hold Primacy over the Demarchy, but they don't exercise the sovereignty that comes with Primacy. Their choice, I expect."

Stephen Terrell stepped in, "Not that strange really, Carl. The Belters also have an unusual concept of Non-Sovereign Primacy. Ceres holds that title as well, except that it's purely by Belter agreement", he informed the others.

Maria clicked play and her office screen kicked into life. They all turned to watch the video.

A woman's face appeared on the screen. It was a pleasant face to look upon, yet showed a thinness to it, as if the woman had very little, if any, body fat. Then the image panned out and more of the woman became visible. Indeed, the woman had very little body fat. She was muscular, much more so than one would expect from a typical woman. The muscles of her upper arms appeared strong and ropy, giving the impression of steel cable strength. What stood out the most was her chest, the woman was heavily endowed in the breast department.

Professor Maria Corbel's eyes opened wide in shock. She knew this person. She was in their files. A wanted fugitive from justice.

"Roberta Nummus!", Maria exclaimed, informing the others in her office.

Roberta Nummus's reputation preceded her.

The woman in the video spoke, "My name is Roberta Nummus and I am here to expose the truth!"

"There are few people who know me. Some know me by reputation. Others who do not know me at all", Roberta Nummus commented, before continuing, "For those who do not know me, I am the product of experimental military training, conditioning, adaptation and genetic augmentation. Myself and others like me. There were twenty four of us originally. We all trained for three years in a high-gravity military training cylinder at three gs in Cis-Lunar L-Four."

"The genetic augmentation, the elixirs and serums, they worked, yes, but at the cost of psychoses and our sanity. We subjects became dirty little secrets to be locked away or eliminated, but instead, we broke free. Our nightmare began nigh on eighty five years ago. Three years later, two of us escaped that military training facility. Aurange Sheergibbon and I, Roberta Nummus. The Cis-Lunar Colonial Armed Forces created us. "

"She's giving everyone her back story", Lyra Banks noted.

Roberta had paused, apparently for people to take her words in, "After we escaped, we found ourselves at the Horridian Corporate colonies in Cis-Lunar L-Five. From that moment forward, we both became agents in the employment, first of Albertus Horridian and then later his Son, Albert, the former High Prince of the six Jovian Realms. For more than eighty years, Aurange and I, both loyally served the Horridian family."

Stephen Terrell noted, "Eighty years plus as a Horridian agent. That blows the Horridian's *'arrived on the Sleek Runner'* lie straight out of the void!"

Roberta's video confession continued, "Three short years ago in seventy-eight, Aurange Sheergibbon and I were ordered to eliminate what High Prince Albert considered a *'threat'*. The crew and Ambassadorial Emissaries aboard the Ambassadorial ship, the Sleek Runner. Aurange Sheergibbon tampered with the Sleek Runner's systems while the ship was docked at Ganymede Prime so that we could approach it in deep space undetected. Aurange and I then followed the Sleek Runner for seven weeks. On the fiftieth day, we boarded the Sleek Runner and murdered its crew. Aurange murdered Diplomatic Aide, Goren Zither and Diplomatic Secretary, Gena Richter. They died quickly, a knife to the heart. Aurange Sheergibbon had been personally ordered by High Prince Albert himself to kill Ambassadorial Emissary, Sonia de la Cruz, slowly. Aurange was ordered to torture her to death."

Both Maria and Lyra had placed their hands to their faces in shock as they took in the cold, matter-of-fact confessions. Roberta's words sank deeply into them.

Roberta Nummus continued with her confession, "Sonia de la Cruz made two final requests of me. The first was that I spare her Niece, Lina Mitchel and that I look after her and keep her safe. The second was that I make her own death quick and painless", tears welled in Roberta's eyes as she continued, "I honoured both of Sonia's requests. Sonia de la Cruz died quickly and painlessly. Lina Mitchel is alive to this day and under my protection", her face was streaming with tears, genuine tears.

Carl paused the video confession at that point, "Roberta Nummus's conditioning must have been breaking down, otherwise, Lina would not be alive today and we would not have this confession."

"Lina is alive, Carl. Sonia de la Cruz was my friend. I knew both her and Lina personally", Maria replied with tears streaming down her cheeks, "It's a miracle!"

Stephen passed Maria his handkerchief as Carl pressed the play button on the remote control.

Roberta Nummus's confession continued, "Aurange disposed of our victim's bodies using the Sleek Runner's plasma thrusters while I cleaned up and sanitised the crime scene. The same long burn that placed the Sleek Runner off course incinerated their corpses almost instantly."

A young woman entered the frame, she dabbed at Roberta's tears with a tissue before passing her a few more. It was Lina Mitchel.

"You're doing great, Roberta. You need to do this. People need to know. The truth has to come out", Lina encouraged, before stepping back out of frame.

"As you can see, Lina Mitchel is alive and well", Roberta continued, pausing for a long moment, not sure what to say next, "Aurange and I concocted a story to placate High Prince Albert. We told him that my conditioning did not allow the killing of children and that Lina was only sixteen and so, a child."

Roberta bit her lower lip, "In order to protect Lina further, I told High Prince Albert that I would officially adopt Lina and treat her as my own child under my protection. High Prince Albert thought that was amusing and allowed it. He thought that one of his monsters adopting a child was amusing."

Lina stepped back into the frame and dabbed at Roberta's tears once more with a tissue, "You were a monster, Roberta. That was the old you. You are not a monster now."

Another woman came into frame, she announced, "I am Elaine Haynes, former Health Minister of the Jovian Realms. Lina Mitchel lived with me in my apartment in Ganymede Prime's northern end cap for three years. We were both under Roberta's protection", the woman smiled, she had tears in her eyes, "Roberta is my lover, my partner, my Wife, my everything. She is not the same woman as the one who murdered those people."

Elaine held Roberta's arm as Roberta continued, "For three years, we lived peacefully in Ganymede Prime. During that time, High Prince Albert's mind descended into dementia. Eventually, his four Sons, Godric, Aluric, Emeric and Friederic, manipulated him into ordering both Lina's death and my death. Aurange Sheergibbon was ordered to kill us both. Aurange Sheergibbon always followed orders."

Lina took hold of Roberta's other arm to steady her.

Roberta continued with her confession, "Aurange and I fought. Aurange died", she did not elaborate.

Lina Mitchel stepped in, "I shot Aurange Sheergibbon with a pulse laser rifle. I killed Aurange Sheergibbon", she announced.

Roberta frowned, "Lina, honey. You did that to protect me. You didn't have any choice in the matter. We all know what would have happened if Aurange had survived."

Lina nodded and replied, "That may be so, but he died by my hand, not yours. You did not kill him, Roberta, I did!"

Roberta looked at the camera, "To kill in self-defence is not a crime. It is a necessity. Lina was forced to kill. She had no choice in the matter. Lina Mitchel is innocent of any crimes. As is my Wife, Elaine Haynes, she is also innocent of any crimes."

Roberta stared into the camera, "After Aurange Sheergibbon fell, I knew that the Horridians would not stop. That is their way. So, while Elaine took Lina to my ship, the Dark Angel, I dealt with the Horridian regime. I proceeded to the royal palace where I slaughtered the High Prince's palace dobermans, his palace guards and finally High Prince Albert himself, destroying his palace in the process", she stared into the camera coldly, "I took Albert Horridian's fucking head and incinerated it to curse his fucking Sons! Anyone who threatens my family, I will take their fucking heads as well!"

Lina reached up and held Roberta's chin, forcing Roberta to look at her, "Roberta, that was the old you. You don't take heads anymore. That is not you."

Roberta shook her head, "No, Lina, you are so young, so naive. My past cannot be erased. I am a monster. I will always be a monster and I deserve to die. The logic is very simple."

Lina stared back at Roberta, "Then you are my monster, Roberta and I'll not let anyone harm you."

There was a certain fierceness in Lina Mitchel's eyes as she said it.

What the people watching Roberta's confession had not been told was that during those three years in Ganymede Prime, Roberta had trained Lina in self-defence and martial arts combat techniques. Lina herself was a formidable warrior in her own right.

A fourth woman entered the frame. She was smaller than Roberta and older, perhaps in her seventies. She moved with both grace and purpose. The woman oozed power, a subtle, sublime power that one could not fully comprehend, and yet, one could not deny its existence, even through the camera's lens. The sense of power was palpable and yet undetectable all at once.

The woman touched Lina, gently, softly and then she did the same with Elaine, again gently and softly touching her. It was as if a silent exchange was occurring, one that the audience was not privy to. Finally, she touched Roberta and Roberta nodded several times as if a full, undetectable conversation was occurring. The audience, however, heard nothing. Finally, the woman stood in front of the others, almost protectively and looked directly into the camera's lens.

"I am Freyja", the woman announced, "and these three women, Elaine Haynes, Roberta Nummus and Lina Mitchel, are now under the protection of the Mimasian colony. We have given all three of them sanctuary and asylum. Roberta Nummus was not born the way she is. She was created and my people will be working diligently to eliminate her weaponised triggers and her conditioning. For anyone out there who might be considering revenge against Roberta Nummus, I assure you all that would be ill-advised."

And then the confession video ended.

Stephen Terrell commented, "This completely demolishes the Horridian's entire narrative. The assassination of High Prince Albert was an internal matter. Plain and simple."

"Yes, it does, Stephen", Maria Corbel agreed, "However, I'm more concerned about young Lina."

"Agreed", chimed in Lyra Banks, "Is she suffering from Stockholm syndrome?"

Carl shook his head, "No. Something more primal. Lina has been trapped in a world of fear for three years. Living in a stranger's house, protected by the monster who murdered her Aunt and who then adopted her. Under the constant threat that the mad High Prince would order their deaths. No. Not Stockholm syndrome, something much more primal. Lina has adapted and she has evolved. She has taken ownership of her monster and made it her own."

"That sounds so dangerous, Carl. Roberta Nummus comes across as anything but stable", Lyra Banks replied with even more concern showing in her features.

"Less than you might think, Lyra. Nummus has promised and pledged to protect her", Carl replied.

Stephen Terrell chimed in, "I'd be asking why. Why did Roberta Nummus's conditioning break?"

Carl Stavros answered with two words, a name, "Elaine Haynes."

"Elaine Haynes?", questioned Maria Corbel.

Carl elaborated, "We've always looked at the reports of the important people, like Sonia de la Cruz. I had my people look into the notes of her secretary and her aide. We needed to know who this woman was and how she fitted in."

"And what did your people find, Carl?", Stephen Terrell enquired.

"In Gena Richter's notes, we found mention of the High Prince's court and the names of his Ministers. At least those that were present during the two meetings with Sonia and her team", Carl replied, he paused a moment and then he continued, "Elaine Haynes was noted as being the Health Minister in Gena Richter's notes. Roberta Nummus was noted as standing at the High Prince's left."

"And that means what, Carl?", Maria Corbel enquired.

"Gena's notes mentioned Elaine glancing at Roberta far more than one would expect for a professional relationship. She also noted that Roberta would make almost imperceptible glances back at Elaine", Carl explained and then he remarked, "Those two were lovers long before Sonia's Ambassadorial team even arrived at Ganymede Prime. Roberta Nummus's relationship with Elaine Haynes is likely what broke her conditioning. That would be my take on the matter."

"And when Sonia asked Roberta to spare and protect Lina, it snapped completely?", Maria queried.

"Yes, quite probably", Carl confirmed, his opinion was in line with hers, "Weapons aren't meant to love or to be loved. They are purely meant to be loyal and obedient."

Lyra Banks enquired, "And what did Sonia's aide, Goren Zither's notes, reveal?"

Carl blinked, he did not want to answer, but he replied anyway, "Goren was impressed with Roberta Nummus's ample cleavage."

It was Lyra's turn to blink.

Carl quickly added, "We have to remember that these were their personal notes automatically archived to our servers by the Sleek Runner's computer systems. They were not official reports."

Lyra casually remarked, "That Freyja woman was seriously unsettling. There was something very off about her, something seriously off."

Maria asked, "Have you been to Earth, Lyra?"

"No, why, Maria?", Lyra replied.

"Well, Lyra, because I have been to Earth and I've seen that look, felt that aura before", Maria replied, adding, "It was when I was younger. I met a few very powerful psychics. Folcrom, they were called. They gave off that exact same vibe."

Stephen chimed in, "There are no psychics off-world, Maria. They never leave the Earth."

Carl added, "Yes, something about them losing their abilities off-world."

"Yes. I know all of that, but you'd have to agree with me. That Freyja woman had power oozing out of every pore of her skin and we all felt it, even on recorded video", Maria replied, remembering the vibe that Freyja had given off.

Lyra stepped back in, "So, this Freyja woman is an out-of-place psychic?"

"No, Lyra. I am not saying that at all, but I am saying that she is something else and that we should take very careful note of everything that she said. That woman is dangerous", Maria concluded, thinking to herself, *"Probably more so than Roberta Nummus."*

"Can we bring Lina back, bring her home?", Maria enquired.

Carl gave Maria the bad news, "Not with our ships, Maria. Our ships would require refuelling and resupply in the Jovian Realms and after what they did to the Sleek Runner, its crew and your Ambassadorial team, I would not recommend it."

Stephen chimed in and asked, "What about Colonial Central Command? They have ships that can bypass the Jovian Realms. They can get to Saturn without the need for refuelling or resupplying."

"You can ask, but they won't do it", Carl advised.

"Why not?", Maria questioned.

"To get to Mimas, they'd need permission to cross Saturnian space. That in itself would be problematic. Then, there is the matter of Mimasian sovereignty. No ship is allowed within twenty five thousand kilometres of Mimas. That is Saturnian law", Carl informed them all.

Stephen summed up, "So, we need a long-range ship. We'd probably have to barge through Saturnian Demarchy space uninvited, further violate Saturnian law to approach Mimas and we have no idea how the Mimasians will react when we arrive there. Are we friend or foe to them?"

"I have no answers for you, Stephen", Carl admitted, explaining, "We know very little about the Mimasians and I suspect it would be a moot point anyway. Once Colonial Central Command sees that video and Lina Mitchel's face, they will wash their hands of her. Lina Mitchel has changed and it is not in a good way. You can see it in that video. Lina is no longer the innocent young intern we sent out into deep space. Lina Mitchel has changed."

It was true. The young intern that Maria Corbel once knew had indeed changed. Lina was now the master of a monster and, by association, would be deemed monstrous herself. No one helps monsters!

Over the next few days, Roberta Nummus's confession video was analysed and classified. The full video confession would never be released to the public, however, certain snippets of it would be.

Roberta's back story, although a damning indictment of the Cis-Lunar Colonial Armed Forces, albeit many decades ago, was released. It directly refuted the Horridian lie that Aurange Sheergibbon and Roberta Nummus were delivered to Ganymede Prime on the Ambassadorial ship, the Sleek Runner.

Roberta Nummus's confession that both she and Aurange had been personally ordered by High Prince Albert himself to intercept and murder the crew and passengers of the Sleek Runner was also released. The fact that the passengers were an Ambassadorial team with full diplomatic immunity was particularly damning.

Finally, Roberta's confession that she and she alone was responsible for the mass murder and destruction at High Prince Albert's palace, including her act of regicide, was also carefully curated and released. All mention of Lina Mitchel and

Elaine Haynes had been carefully excised. That snippet alone demolished the Horridian lie that the High Prince's murder was an assassination plot by Eros. It became readily apparent that the whole situation was an internal issue within the Horridian regime itself.

When Communications Minister, Temu Trump had entered the throne room, everything had been relatively calm and quiet. Three of the four Horridian Princes sat idly on their gold-gilded thrones. They were bored and it showed on their faces. Prince Aluric, of course, was not present. High Prince Godric was more than happy to leave his *"problematic"* Brother to his own debauched devices. Temu Trump was bringing them bad news, very bad news indeed.

"Your Majesty", Temu Trump addressed the High Prince, "I, I", he stammered, "I have some bad news, Sire. Important news, but it is bad news, Sire", then he passed Godric a data tablet.

High Prince Godric watched the video feeds on Temu's data tablet. They were the confessions of Roberta Nummus in three clear, precise and curated snippets. These video feeds had spread across the entire solar system like wildfires, spreading on the ethereal winds of the news feeds. They were, of course, all external video feeds, having been blocked by the Jovian Realm's firewalls.

The High Prince watched each of the three videos multiple times and with each viewing his anger grew until finally his rage erupted. As Prince Emeric and Prince Friederic looked on in shock, Temu's data tablet flew against the throne room wall and shattered.

"Fuck! Fuck! Fuck! That fucking bitch confessed!", Godric screamed, his face was red with rage and he ran his hand through his hair, "She fucking confessed to everything!", it was so unexpected.

The Horridian Brother's carefully curated litany of lies was quickly unravelling and all High Prince Godric could do was sit back and watch.

In this matter, High Prince Godric was all but impotent.

15. Outer Satellite Alliances.

Prince Emeric and his Brother, Prince Friederic, walked into their Brother, High Prince Godric's, throne room. They both proceeded to their *"lesser"* thrones, gold-gilded nonetheless. Their other Brother, Prince Aluric, remained in his own palace in his own realm of Callisto and its mega colony Callisto Prime. Both Princes nodded to their Brother, the High Prince, before moving towards their own thrones.

Prince Friederic noted as he sat down, "Brother Godric, I took the liberty of having our Brother Aluric officially diagnosed. As you know, Brother, all of his advisers are my own people. What you don't know is that one of them is a psychoanalyst. I appointed him myself."

"Brother Friederic. Our Father always refused to have Brother Aluric diagnosed. You should have consulted me first.", High Prince Godric chided.

"Brother Godric, our Brother, Aluric, has been deteriorating", Prince Friederic replied, explaining, "If we don't understand what is wrong with him, then we cannot provide adequate care for him."

High Prince Godric nodded, "I am not angry, Friederic, just concerned. What was the diagnosis?"

"Doctor Shorthorn, a well-trained psychoanalyst, whom I've entrusted to give us an accurate understanding of our dear Brother, Aluric's condition, has diagnosed the following", Prince Friederic announced before continuing, "This is Doctor Shorthorn's analysis. *'Prince Aluric von Horridian presents a complex psychological profile defined by low cognitive ability, compulsive sexual behaviour, and severe anxiety rooted in existential dread. He demonstrates signs consistent with Mild Intellectual Disability (ICD-11: 6A00), marked by an IQ of approximately seventy five. Though this places him just above the clinical threshold, it manifests in slowed reasoning, poor impulse control, and difficulty processing abstract consequences.'*, and that is just the beginning."

Prince Friederic continued after a short pause, "Here's some more, *'His actions following the failed assassination attempt against Lina Mitchel, and the shock of witnessing the aftermath of his Father, High Prince Albert's, brutal murder by Roberta Nummus, have exacerbated his mental instability. In particular, psychological stress acts as a potent trigger, dramatically worsening his symptoms and driving erratic, sometimes dangerous behaviour in an effort to regain control or numb his internal chaos.'* Our dear Brother, Aluric, is trying to numb his pain and existential dread without having the mental capacity to understand his own actions."

Prince Friederic paused once again before continuing, "This might explain a lot. *'Aluric also exhibits symptoms consistent with Compulsive Sexual Behaviour Disorder (ICD-11: 6C72), using excessive sexual activity not for pleasure but as a maladaptive coping mechanism to suppress fear, guilt, and emotional emptiness. This behaviour ties directly to an overarching condition best categorised as Anxiety or Fear-Related Disorder, Unspecified (ICD-*

11: 6B00.Z). His dread is existential, chronic, and untethered from specific phobias, an ambient terror of death, insignificance and loss of agency. Under stress, these fears spiral into a volatile state of inner disintegration. These three conditions, (6A00), (6C72), and (6B00.Z), interact dynamically, painting a portrait of a deeply compromised prince whose mind teeters on the edge, unfit for power yet trapped within its cruel expectations.' Doctor Shorthorn has recommended treatment with suitable pharmaceuticals. Our dear Brother, Aluric, needs medication to alleviate his condition."

High Prince Godric mumbled, "Seventy five?", questioningly, and then he asked, "I know our dear Brother, Aluric, is a bit slow, but an IQ of only seventy five? How is that even possible? We three are above average intelligence and you, dear Brother Friederic, your IQ is through the roof?"

Prince Emeric chimed in, "Luck of the draw, dear Brother, luck of the draw."

Prince Friederic noted, "One high, one low and two in the middle. The universe provides balance."

High Prince Godric made his decision, "Brother, Friederic. If our dear Brother, Aluric, requires treatment, then ensure that he gets the best available. We need a stable mind in Callisto Prime's palace."

Prince Friederic nodded, "Yes, Brother. I am on top of it. Our dear Brother, Aluric, will have the best available care. I have already provided him with the best available advisers. The court of Callisto Prime will remain stable."

High Prince Godric shook his head in disbelief at Friederic's revelations and decided to change the topic to other *'domestic'* matters.

"Brother. Aluric's Wife, Princess Serenity, has been staying in my palace here at Ganymede Prime for nearly a month now. My Wife, Princess Valeria, isn't saying anything, but would this be because of our dear Brother, Aluric's condition?", the High Prince enquired.

Prince Emeric bit his lower lip and his Brother, Prince Friederic, rubbed his clean-shaven chin with his right hand. Neither wanted to get involved in palace gossip, however, in Prince Aluric's case, it was not entirely gossip, it was observed facts being spread on the grape vines of the palace servants.

"Brother", Friederic began, trying to think of the easiest ways to put it, "I had our dear Brother, Aluric, diagnosed because word of a certain behaviour reached my ears. It was an event that happened about two months ago. You might remember, Princess Serenity spent a month with Brother Emeric's Wife, Princess Chastity, in his palace at Europa Prime."

"Yes, yes. I do remember that", High Prince Godric recalled, noting, "Princess Chastity said it was a holiday. Rest and relaxation from Princess Serenity's usual palace duties."

Prince Emeric chimed in, "Brother Godric, it was shortly after Minister Trump gave us word about Roberta Nummus's confession. Apparently, when our dear

Brother, Aluric, found out about it, he became very upset."

"Existential dread?", High Prince Godric enquired rhetorically, remarking, "Roberta Nummus generates that with just the mention of her name. She's the modern-day equivalent of the boogeyman."

Prince Friederic informed his Brother, the High Prince, "In three days, our dear Brother, Aluric, will be arriving here at Ganymede Prime. Ostensibly just to touch base with us, his Brothers, more importantly, so that he can be more fully diagnosed and suitable pharmaceuticals prescribed", he paused before announcing, "The day before Aluric arrives, his Wife, Princess Serenity, will be leaving for Io Prime to stay with my Wife, Princess Minerva, for a few weeks, perhaps a month."

"You're giving me a heads up, Brother, Friederic, but without the reasons behind it", his Brother Godric replied.

"The reason goes back to the even that occurred two months ago, Brother", Prince Friederic replied, commenting, "Our dear, Brother, Aluric, has always been rough with his woman. Those Slave women who service him, yes, but now, also with his own Wife", he paused, the next part was quite unpleasant, "Princess Serenity has literally fled their palace!"

"What was this event you are alluding to, Brother Friederic?", High Prince Godric asked bluntly.

"Just after we received the news about Roberta Nummus's confession, our Brother Aluric, went ballistic", Prince Friederic informed his Brother, the High Prince.

"Define ballistic, Brother Friederic!", High Prince Godric demanded.

"Aluric tied his Wife, Princess Serenity, to their marital bed by her wrists and ankles. He then proceeded to rape her continuously for over thirty hours", Prince Friederic informed his Brother, "And then when Princess Serenity could not hold onto her bodily functions any longer, she soiled their bed."

High Prince Godric looked shocked, why had no one told him, "You have confirmation of this?", he quickly interrupted.

"Yes, Brother and it gets worse", Prince Friederic replied, before continuing, "Our dear Brother, Aluric, blamed his Wife for the mess, the soiling of their marital bed", he paused for a long moment, "Aluric beat Serenity mercilessly and then ordered his palace servants to clean up the mess."

Emeric chimed in, "While the palace servants sanitised their marital bed, Serenity's Mistress of the Robes had Doctor's brought in to provide medical assistance. It was all very discrete", the Prince paused before continued, "Within three hours, Princess Serenity's condition was stabilised and she was then transferred to my palace at Europa Prime, under the care of my Wife, Princess Chastity."

High Prince Godric's face took on a gobsmacked look. Why had he not been told?

Prince Emeric chimed back in once more, "Brother Godric, Princess Serenity nearly died!"

"Which is why I organised our Brother's careful psychoanalysis and diagnosis", Frederick noted.

The High Prince shook his head. How far had the Horridians descended?

"Why was I not told of this?", High Prince Godric demanded.

Prince Friederic replied diplomatically, "Brother Godric, since the confession of Roberta Nummus and its ramifications, you have spent most of your time in meetings. Our Communications, Defence and Security Ministers have monopolised all of your time. We have been handling these *'domestic'* issues ourselves, Brother. You had enough problems on your plate as it was."

Prince Emeric chimed in, "More correctly, Brother Godric. Our Wives have been handling these *'domestic'* issues. They have all rallied around Princess Serenity and formed their own little *'defence'* alliance. Wherever our Brother Aluric is, Princess Serenity is not. It's like a protective shell game."

"You might remember, Brother Godric. Princess Serenity used to be the life of the party. Always cheery and always happy. Now, Brother, you would not recognise her. She is quiet, withdrawn and jumps at every sound, even shadows", Prince Friederic noted, adding, "What our dear Brother Aluric did to Princess Serenity has fundamentally changed her. She is broken and might never recover."

Prince Emeric said, "My Wife, Chastity. She tells me that Princess Serenity will be barren. The Princess can no longer have children. The damage from Aluric's beating was far too great."

High Prince Godric closed his eyes and shook his head, then, when he reopened his eyes, he commanded, "Make sure Princess Serenity is looked after. As for our dear Brother Aluric, Brother Friederic, make sure he is watched at all times. Make sure he is appropriately medicated. Being rough with his sex Slaves is one thing, raping and beating his Wife, a noble Princess, is simply unacceptable."

"That was the plan, Brother Godric, that was the plan", Prince Friederic confirmed.

The throne room doors opened and the Communications Minister Temu Trump entered. He straight away walked over to his audience with the High Prince.

"Temu! You're right on time", High Prince Godric announced.

"I do aim to be punctual, Your Majesty", the Communications Minister replied.

"So, Temu. How is your spin machine going?", High Prince Godric enquired.

"We have had some success, Sire", Temu replied, noting, "We can refute most of the narrative assertions in the Nummus confession videos. We have also cleared up another issue that arose before the Nummus confession was even released."

"Well, that is interesting, Temu. Please divulge this other issue?", the High Prince queried.

"Your Majesty", Minister Temu Trump bowed before continuing, "You may remember the laying of the foundation stone and the feast of foundation and remembrance."

"Yes, I remember it well, Temu. We partied rather hard afterwards", High Prince Godric confirmed.

Prince Emeric chimed in, "It is amazing how quickly they rebuilt Brother Godric's palace."

"Yes, Your Highness. It is amazing what can be accomplished with copious quantities of Slaves and Indentured servants", Minister Trump replied before continuing, "The day after the laying of the foundation stone, the ceremony was broadcast across all of the news feeds. The very reason for the rebuilding of the palace, apart from its damage, was tied directly to the narrative we were creating."

"Yes, Temu. I remember that. I signed off on that myself, if I remember correctly", High Prince Godric confirmed, he remembered it well despite his hungover state that day.

Minister Trump frowned, "Perhaps we should have vetted that video more fully, Sire. The foundation stone's third line reads, and I quote, *'Betrayed and murdered by the one he trusted the most'*. After the release of Roberta Nummus's confession, the one he trusted the most was being attributed to her. This has unfortunately given credence to Nummus's confession, making her appear to be the trusted one who murdered your Father, Albert, the former High Prince."

Prince Friederic chimed in, "Temu, Temu. Temu! This is your bread and butter. We know you've spun this around to suit our narrative. Why do you have to drag things out? Just spit it out?"

"Yes, Your Highness", Temu agreed, noting, "I do prefer to make my communications clear and concise. You are correct, Prince Friederic, I have spun this problem to our advantage."

Prince Emeric chimed in, "You're doing it again, Temu. Just tell us."

High Prince Godric replied, "Brothers, I like the way Temu spins his tales. Stop being so impatient."

Minister Trump bowed once more, "Thank you, Your Majesty. I have publicly released that the phrase, *'Betrayed and murdered by the one he trusted the most'*, refers to former Health Minister Elaine Haynes. That the former Health Minister betrayed your Father by aligning herself with Roberta Nummus, Aurange Sheergibbon and Lina Mitchel, thus being directly responsible for his murder!"

High Prince Godric remarked, "That would definitely work. Elaine Haynes was the Health Minister. She was trusted and had our Father's ear. Our Father called her a *'keeper'* on several occasions."

"It is incomplete, Temu", Prince Friederic noted, explaining, "We need to refute that whole confession. That whole confession needs to be discredited."

Minister Trump smiled and High Prince Godric took notice, "I know that smile, Temu. You've already done it, haven't you? You've trashed Roberta Nummus's entire confession?", he questioned.

"Yes, Your Majesty. At least the part we need to, Sire", Minister Trump replied.

"The parts we need to?", Prince Friederic asked with interest, "You're being strategic, Temu?"

"Yes, Your Highness", Temu Trump replied, "Some parts of Nummus's confession are to our advantage, so we need those. Others not so much."

"Come on, Temu. Now, I'm getting impatient. Spill it, man", the High Prince commanded.

"Yes, of course, Your Majesty", Temu Trump bowed once more and began his explanation.

"Roberta Nummus's back story is useful to us, right up to the point where she escapes her military training facility with Aurange Sheergibbon. So we need that part. It paints Roberta as an operative of the Cis-Lunar Colonial Armed Forces by her own admission."

"Oh, yes", Prince Friederic chimed in, "That is so very useful to us", he agreed.

"Yes, Your Highness", Minister Temu nodded before continuing, "Everything that follows that part of her back story can simply be denied. We can label everything that follows as an Erosian fabrication."

High Prince Godric looked at his Communications Minister thoughtfully, "That is bold in its simplicity, Temu. Just how are you going to evidence this, Erosian fabrication?"

"By using Roberta Nummus herself, Your Majesty", Minister Trump replied and then he asked, "Sire, how old does Roberta Nummus look to you?"

"Roberta Nummus's age? We know that she's over a hundred years old. She only ages one year in eight, maybe even as little as one year in ten", High Prince Godric replied.

"Your Majesty, we have a rough idea of how old Roberta Nummus truly is and how slowly she ages. Sire, how old does she actually look?", Minister Trump cautiously asked once more.

Prince Friederic chimed in, "Roberta Nummus looks no more than thirty, if that."

Prince Emeric chimed in, "Yeah, I agree. A hot, maybe not quite thirty-year-old with big tits. Really, really big tits", he chuckled as he said the last part.

Minister Trump ignored the last part of Prince Emeric's response and continued, "Outside of your Jovian Realms, more specifically your court, Your Majesty. Very few people know that Roberta Nummus ages one year in eight or even one year in ten. No one would believe it if we told them. For all intents and purposes, Roberta Nummus is a twenty-nine-year-old woman."

Prince Emeric laughed, "A twenty-nine-year-old hot woman with bloody huge jugs."

"Can you not, Brother Emeric? It's bad enough when our Brother Aluric does that", High Prince Godric chided.

"Brother Godric, not a single one of us wouldn't want to sink our face into Roberta Nummus's jugs", Prince Emeric replied, "Just saying!"

High Prince Godric shook his head, "Temu, ignore my Brother Emeric. Continue."

The Communications Minister continued, "Roberta Nummus claimed in her confession that she was in the employment of your Horridian family for more than eighty years, yet she doesn't even look like she is thirty years old. Her own visual appearance flies in the face of her own assertions."

Prince Friederic stepped in, almost laughing, "That paints Roberta Nummus as either temporally dissonant, delusional or as just a straight up liar. Oh, Temu, that is so perfect. You release that into the public domain and you not only discredit Roberta Nummus, but no one will believe anything she says ever again. Everything she said in her confession will just unravel."

"That was the general idea, Your Highness, however, I do require your Brother, High Prince Godric's permission to proceed", Minister Trump replied.

High Prince Godric was quiet for a long moment, deep in thought with his fingers steepled.

"Let me get this straight. Roberta Nummus's confession paints her as a Cis-Lunar Colonial Armed Forces operative by her own admission and there will be records to back that up", the High Prince replied, pausing for a moment, "Her appearance gives the impression that her training took place less than a decade ago. So everything in her confession beyond her backstory becomes dubious, suspect and pretty much impossible. Which makes our original narrative, that Aurange Sheergibbon and Roberta Nummus arrived here on the Erosian Ambassadorial vessel, Sleek Runner, plausible once more. Do I have that right, Temu?"

"Yes, Your Majesty", Minister Trump confirmed.

"Then let it rip, Temu. Let's discredit that bitch", High Prince Godric commanded, "And Temu. Make sure you've got all of these machinations written down. They are getting really complicated."

"Yes, Your Majesty. If I may say so. Life is complicated and so is the truth. A good lie and a good narrative must be so as well. Carefully crafted and embedded within the truth. A clean, smooth flow and repetition make it stick in the public perception", Minister Trump explained.

High Prince Godric nodded in agreement. Temu Trump was still his favourite Minister.

Prince Emeric was still concerned that the trio, Roberta Nummus, Elaine Haynes and Lina Mitchel, had all been given sanctuary and political asylum by the Mimasians, deep within the Saturnian system. Especially so, as Roberta Nummus had beheaded their Father and Lina Mitchel was still the undead mark. Both had to be brought to *"justice"* or at least the Horridian's form of justice.

"What of the fugitives, Temu?", Prince Emeric enquired.

"Your Highness, I have received a communique from Prime Minister Quintus Malbeck of the Saturnian Demarchy himself", Minister Trump responded.

"And what does this Prime Minister Malbeck have to say?", Prince Emeric demanded.

"Prime Minister Malbeck has checked with his people concerning Mimas, Your Highness", Minister Trump replied, adding, "I can read out his communique if you wish."

High Prince Godric chimed in, "Do that, Temu. I'd like to hear what he has to say as well."

"Yes, Your Majesty", Temu responded as he bowed once more and began.

"Dear Minister Trump. I have checked with the head of the Saturnian Demarchy Supreme Court, our highest legal authority, Chief Justice Ms Jeannine Huxley. It is confirmed that under the laws of old Earth, Interplanetary law and the laws of the Saturnian Demarchy, Mimas does indeed hold Primacy over the entire Saturnian orbital zone. The Mimasians do not, however, exercise their inherent sovereignty over the Saturnian Demarchy. The Mimasians have made that decision and we have no wish for them to change it. This is an apple cart we have no wish to upset", Minister Trump read the communique on his data tablet, "Sire, Prime Minister Malbeck has confirmed Mimasian Primacy over the Demarchy. It is indeed a form of non-sovereign primacy and it was a Mimasian decision."

Minister Trump continued reading the communique, *"The twenty five thousand kilometre exclusion zone around Mimas is a legally instituted requirement. No ship of the Saturnian Demarchy, private, military or otherwise, may enter that zone without the express permission of the Mimasians themselves. I have spoken with my Defence Minister, Mr Bruce Mannaz and he assures me that due to the situation with your fugitives, the Mimasian exclusion zone is now being policed by no fewer than four Saturnian dreadnoughts. We have Mimas boxed in and contained. Your fugitives will not be leaving Mimas any time soon"*, he paused and noted, "Boxed in and contained, Sire. That means that they cannot leave."

"Yes, Temu. I'm fully aware of what that means", High Prince Godric replied.

Prince Friederic questioned, "The Saturnians have dreadnoughts?"

"Yes, Your Highness. It appears that the Saturnian Demarchy have at least four. Dreadnoughts are capital ships and using four of them to contain our fugitives on Mimas is overkill. They could just have easily used Corvette-class prowlers. This development alone indicates that the Saturnian Demarchy, in all likelihood, has many more dreadnoughts at their disposal", Minister Trump informed him.

"We were under the impression that the Demarchy had no dreadnoughts", Prince Emeric remarked.

"Yes, Your Highness. That situation appears to have recently changed", Minister Trump replied.

"Temu, continue reading that communique", High Prince Godric ordered.

"Yes, Sire. Prime Minister Malbeck tells us", Temu responded before continuing, *"We do have a communications line to the Mimasians. Our head bureaucrat, Saturnian Administrator, Ms Swenna Goodchild, has that hotline. Ms Goodchild has contacted the Mimasians on your behalf. The Mimasians have informed us that under no circumstances are any ships, Saturnian or otherwise, to cross into their exclusion zone. They have reiterated that Lina Mitchel, Elaine Haynes and Roberta Nummus have been granted both sanctuary and asylum. Should any ship enter their exclusion zone, they will consider it a hostile act and respond with main force. Ms Goodchild has told me that we have been warned and that we should not escalate the situation under any circumstances. I believe her."*

"Well, Temu, at least our fugitives are contained. They aren't going anywhere", Prince Emeric noted.

"Yes, Your Highness, but you have failed to read between the lines, the words. There is more to this than what was written", Minister Trump replied.

High Prince Godric chimed in, "What's your take on this, Temu?"

"Sire", Temu Trump bowed once more and began, "Prime Minister Malbeck's communique is written with fear and trepidation. It oozes that fear."

"Fear and trepidation, Temu?", the High Prince questioned, "I didn't get that impression."

"Sire. The Demarchy has boxed in Mimas with four capital ships. Dreadnoughts no less, when two Corvettes would suffice. That oozes fear and trepidation, Sire", Temu replied, explaining, "The choice of ships, the number of ships, that tells me that they not only fear the Mimasians, but that they also have a dual purpose in mind."

Prince Friederic was sitting quietly steepling his fingers, "Agreed, Temu, agreed. Brother Godric, whoever the Mimasians are, whatever the Mimasians have, it's got the Demarchy rattled. Those Saturnian Dreadnoughts are boxing in Mimas, yes, but they're also keeping us out. The Saturnian Demarchy is concerned that we might take unilateral action and cause an incident. A Mimasian incident and they fear that above all else. They fear the Mimasians! That fear is palpable!"

"Yes, yes, my Prince. Your Highness, you have nailed it in one", Minister Trump replied.

High Prince Godric noted, "Temu, we need the Saturnian Demarchy on our side as allies. Make sure that they understand, we are their friends and that we will respect their decisions and their boundaries. We will also provide them with any assistance that they might request. All and any assistance!"

"Yes, Your Majesty. I will make it so", Minister Temu Trump replied.

While Temu was writing down notes into his data tablet, High Prince Godric asked, "Temu, we need the outer satellites on our side. All of them, not just the Saturnian Demarchy, I'm talking about the Uranian Federation and the Neptunian Commonwealth as well. We need a grand alliance. How are we going on that front? "

Temu Trump looked up from his data tablet, "I do have a few ideas, Sire."

Prince Friederic leaned forward on his throne and requested, "Bring it forth, Temu. Bring it forth."

Minister Trump smiled, "Princes, Your Majesty. The new fusion reactor. Our prototype, based on the designs and blueprints provided by Eros, is working perfectly. Exactly as specified."

Prince Emeric chimed in, asking, "Temu, exactly how does that help us?"

Temu smiled his broadest smile, "Your Highness. We have the skills, we have the engineers, we have the manufacturing capacity. The other outer satellites, the Demarchy, the Federation and the Commonwealth simply do not."

"Temu, Eros has given them all the same blueprints and specifications. Even made the same promises to help them build their own fusion reactors using engineers and expertise from Earth and Cis-Lunar space. Hell, they have even offered to build the new fusion reactors at Cis-Lunar L-Four and ship them out to them", Prince Emeric responded, again asking, "How does that benefit us?"

"Your Highness, might I suggest that we tell the Demarchy, the Federation and the Commonwealth that our prototype fusion reactor, based upon the blueprints and specifications provided by Eros, turned out to be a failure, a pup", Minister Trump explained, adding, "We tell them that Eros lied to everyone. That this entire phaseout of uranium fission reactors was nothing more than a feint to weaken us all."

Prince Friederic was curious about how that would work, "Duplicity is always a good story, Temu, however, you will need to flesh it out further."

"Yes, Your Highness. I was just getting to the good part", Minister Trump replied and then explained, "We tell the Demarchy, the Federation and the Commonwealth, that the Erosian provided designs are flawed, deliberately flawed and that their fusion reactors cost twenty times as much to build and generate only one-tenth of the specified power output. That by the time they have invested time and credits in building them, it will be far too late to fix all of the problems."

Prince Friederic was leaning forward on his throne, steepling his fingers, "And then we come along and provide the solution, our engineers, our own *'tweaked'* blueprints and even offer to build the new reactors for them?", he questioned.

"Yes, Your Highness", Minister Trump confirmed, "It will paint Eros, the Earth and Cis-Lunar space as deliberately attempting to weaken us all. Making us all ripe for invasion and subjugation. Only we saw through their *'evil'* plans and *'white knight'* the situation, coming to their rescue."

Prince Emeric smiled, "Fucking hell, Temu. Were you born this shrewd, or did someone make you in a vat of chemicals?"

"Your Highness. My Mother and Father made me in the normal way", Temu Trump smiled back.

The High Prince quickly understood how this would unfold. It would not only discredit the inner system worlds, but it would paint the Jovian Realms as the outer system's saviours, while at the same time placing them in a position of extreme leverage. The Jovian Realms would control all fusion reactor technology across the outer colonies. If Temu Trump could pull this off, in the long run, the Saturnian Demarchy, the Uranian Federation and the Neptunian Commonwealth would all have to come to Ganymede Prime with cup in hand begging! They would all be locked in!

"Temu, get to work on your plan. I want to see results", the High Prince announced.

Prince Emeric smiled, "Brother Godric, Temu's scheme is so cherry. Temu deserves a reward. Might I suggest you have your Matron of Pleasures provide him with four women per night for a month."

"Yes, yes, Brother Emeric. So long as it doesn't interfere with his work", High Prince Godric agreed, "So ordered, so rewarded. Temu, my Matron of Pleasures, will be notified of your reward."

"Thank you, Your Majesty. I look forward to it", Minister Trump accepted his reward.

Communications Minister Temu Trump spun his magic, promising that the Jovian Realms had no intention of interfering in the Saturnian Demarchy's internal affairs and that all boundaries, decisions and existing or future agreements would be respected. Prime Minister Quintus Malbeck was extremely interested in the offer of all and any assistance by the Jovian Realms should the

Saturnian Demarchy request it. That led to further developments.

A formal agreement was reached, signed and ratified by both governments between the Saturnian Demarchy and the Jovian Realms. An agreement that should either the Jovian Realms or the Saturnian Demarchy be attacked, each would provide the other with material support and logistical assistance. It did not provide for military assistance, however, it was a start in that direction.

After achieving his aims with the Saturnian Demarchy concerning mutual cooperation and assistance should either be attacked, the Communication Minister went back to weaving his magic. All three of the distant outer realms, the Saturnian Demarchy, the Uranian Federation and the Neptunian Commonwealth, were notified of the Jovian Realms *"experience"* with the *"fatally flawed"* blueprints and specifications issued by Eros.

Communications Minister Temu Trump promised to send them all, *"updated"* and *"corrected"*, Jovian versions of the blueprints that would work, to replace the *"flawed"* Erosian designs they'd already received. Temu Trump planted the seeds of thought that the Jovian Realms were the masters of this new fusion reactor technology and that only they could assist the outer realms in developing this new fusion reactor technology to its fullest potential.

It was a short pause, perhaps a week before Minister Trump officially sent the Jovian *"corrected"* and *"enhanced"* blueprints and specifications. There was essentially no difference. The Jovian engineers had merely tweaked a few things here and there. Altered superficial components and designs that had no effect on the overall functionality or build quality.

At a glance, the difference between the Erosian blueprints and the Jovian blueprints was obvious for all to see and yet, the changes were meaningless in terms of construction, form and functionality. The Saturnian Demarchy, the Uranian Federation, nor the Neptunian Commonwealth had the technicians or the engineers who understood the new technology sufficiently to understand the differences.

Minister Trump also stressed that the Jovian Realms were far closer to the outer satellite realms, which, of course, was true. Temu Trump stressed that the exchange of technicians, engineers and even the possibility of whole manufactured fusion reactors would be more efficiently delivered from the Jovian Realms than Cis-Lunar L-Four, especially considering the original *"flawed"* Erosian designs.

The first on board with the new plans and blueprints was the Saturnian Demarchy, then they were followed by the Uranian Federation and finally the Neptunian Commonwealth. All fusion reactor discussions with Eros and its Colonisation Committee and Security Council had halted. Attempted further discussions initiated by Eros fell upon deaf ears and went completely unanswered.

The final nail in the coffin for Eros and its outer system diplomacy was Temu Trump's discussions about the Saturnian Demarchy's and the Jovian Realm's agreement on providing material support and logistical assistance to each other should either polity be attacked. That generated two more identical agreements between the Jovian Realms and the Uranian Federation and the Jovian Realms and the Neptunian Commonwealth.

Temu did not finish there, he already had bilateral agreements with each of the outer realms. However, the High Prince had wanted more. Temu stressed to the outer satellites the need for efficiency and four-way mutual cooperation. It was in February, twenty one eighty two that Temu achieved that goal, *"The Quadripartite Outer Satellite Agreement, QOSA."*

It was done, the Jovian Realms had built a quadripartite agreement for all four outer realms to provide material support and logistical assistance in the case that any one of them was attacked. It did not include military support. However, if High Prince Godric had been a more patient man, Temu Trump may have had time to add that into the quadripartite agreement.

Nonetheless, Communications Minister Temu Trump, Spin Doctor extraordinaire, was rewarded. Godric ordered his Matron of Pleasures to provide Temu with women anytime he requested them.

16. Even the Dolphins Died.

Prince Friederic was furious, yet doing his best to control himself. His Brother, Godric, the High Prince, had plans that he considered reckless. To make matters worse, his Brother, Emeric, was agreeing with those same plans.

"Brother Godric, if you proceed with this plan, our allies will turn against us", Friederic had noted.

"Friederic, my Brother, you worry over nothing. Once we set off the explosion on Himalia, we will have our pretext for our War. Our allies will flock to our side", High Prince Godric countered.

Communications Minister Temu Trump chimed in, "Sire, the Quadripartite Outer Satellite Agreement is not a military alliance. It is an agreement to provide material support and logistical assistance, nothing more. Perhaps we should postpone our plans for six months. I may be able to persuade our allies to upgrade the agreement into a true alliance by then. It would be a prudent move, Sire. The more cautious approach."

"Temu, Temu, Temu. Surely after our little explosion, our allies will be more amenable to such an upgrade", High Prince Godric replied.

Prince Emeric chimed in, "Yes, Temu. If they see us under attack, they'll flock to our sides, just as Brother Godric has predicted."

"Your Highness, our allies could just as easily see it as a sign that we are dragging them into a War. A War that they will want no part of", Minister Trump informed him.

Prince Friederic stepped back in, "Yes, Temu is right, Brother. They will see it precisely that way. Us dragging them into a War that they will want no part of. This *'pretext'* you are planning is one thing, but what you're planning to do next! They will all see that as an atrocity!"

"One man's atrocity is another man's proportionate response, Brother Friederic", Prince Emeric replied dryly.

"Temu? Do you see it that way? I value your opinion", High Prince Godric enquired.

"Your Majesty. I see the economic powerhouse that is Cis-Lunar space and I fear it will quickly move from civilian production to military production, Sire", Temu Trump replied, advising, "They can outproduce us by at least twenty five times over. We need more time and perhaps a different approach."

"Yes, you've mentioned that before, Temu. Move on the Belters first and then annex them, then move on to Mars. Your stepping stone approach", the High Prince replied, nodding, "My way is better, much quicker. Once our first strike is done, they will quickly capitulate. They will surrender rather than see more destruction", he turned to his Defence Minister, Peter Macron, "Isn't that right, Minister Macron?'

"Your Majesty, nothing is certain in War. Nothing at all", the Defence Minister replied, noting, "We can engineer our pretexts. We can deliver our first strike. How the governments and Earth and Cis-Lunar space react is not something that I nor anyone else can predict", he was non-committal.

"You worry too much as well, Peter", the High Prince responded, then he looked at his Security Minister, Miles Morton.

Security Minister Morton shifted uncomfortably, "Sire, there are a lot of unknowns. We recently found out that the Saturnians have dreadnoughts. Something we did not think possible. What might we discover about our adversaries in the inner system after our War has begun? What does Earth and Cis-Lunar space have up their sleeves?"

"It appears that my Ministers are all a bunch of nervous Nellies", High Prince Godric surmised.

Science Minister Peter Patronis chimed in, "If I may, Your Majesty. Your Ministers are simply being cautious. To start a War is not something to be treated lightly. There are, as Minister Morton has mentioned, a lot of uncertainties, a lot of unknowns. More time and research are appropriate, Sire."

"I appreciate caution, Minister. I appreciate honesty. I also appreciate loyalty. I appreciate loyalty above all else", High Prince Godric replied, he then glared at his Brother, Friederic, before commanding, "Our pretext will go ahead. Our plans for our first strike will be put in place. I am the law and my will will be obeyed!"

Prince Friederic held back his anger. He stood up and marched out of his Brother's throne room.

Standing in the doorway, he turned and told his Brother, "Godric, Brother. I will be leaving for Io Prime. When you come to your senses or when this War of yours blows up in our faces, call to me and I'll help you sort out the mess. Preferably the former and not the latter! And, Brother, I do remain completely loyal. I just don't do stupidity! In my opinion, your current plans are insane!"

Prince Friederic left the throne room, cursing under his breath as he did so. There was little he could do, both of his Brothers, Godric and Emeric, had taken fixed, immutable positions and there was nothing more to it. The War was coming and so was the impending disaster.

The High Prince snidely remarked, "Temu, have our Brother Aluric's Wife, Serenity, sent to Io Prime. My youngest Brother, Friederic, is only good for babysitting! His balls have yet to drop!"

There was an immense explosion above the surface of the Jovian moon, Himalia. It was immense, it was blindingly brilliant, it was clearly visible at the Himalia Central twin-cylinder colony in Himalia's L-Five orbital zone. It was just as clearly visible to all of the other smaller colonies in that zone as well.

The blast was so large that it was clearly visible across the entire inner solar system. The Saturnian Demarchy detected the explosion as an immense bright flash of blue-white light. Even the Uranian Federation and the Neptunian Commonwealth detected it, although not anywhere nearly as bright.

The calculated estimates were that the explosion, the blast, was well over one hundred megatons and it appeared to have the signature of a nuclear detonation.

The news feeds across the entire solar system were alive with the news of what appeared to be some kind of massive nuclear accident on the Jovian moon, Himalia. An explosion so large and of such power and magnitude that no one understood what could possibly have caused it.

Was it an accident?

Himalia was an ice moon. Nothing more than a rock.

Himalia was uninhabited and only used for resource extraction.

The mystery deepened across the news feeds with experts, far and wide, speculating on its cause.

And then the High Prince of Ganymede, Godric von Horridian, made his announcement.

The High Prince introduced himself, "I am Godric von Horridian, Prince of the Jovian Realm of Ganymede and High Prince of the Six Jovian Realms. As the ruler of the Jovian Realms, I must bring you news of bad tidings", then he paused for dramatic effect.

The High Prince continued, "My people! We have been attacked! A heinous, devastating attack!", then he paused once again.

The High Prince launched into his tirade, "The explosion on the surface of our Jovian moon, Himalia, was caused by a nuclear detonation well above one hundred megatons! That weapon of mass destruction was delivered to our Jovian Realms by an interplanetary stealth missile launched from Cis-Lunar space. It was a deliberate attack upon our Jovian Realms. It was a deliberate attack upon our people!", and then he paused once more for dramatic effect.

The High Prince continued, "My people, we got lucky! Very lucky! Our scientists have determined that the trajectory of the interplanetary stealth missile was on a perfect intercept course for Ganymede Prime itself. Had our Jovian moon, Himalia, not crossed its path, I would not be speaking with you today. Ganymede Prime would have been annihilated. It is only by the grace of God and the fortuitous crossing of the missile's path by our Jovian Moon, Himalia, that we here at Ganymede Prime are alive today! We were saved by both God and Himalia!", he paused once more.

High Prince Godric continued, "The governments of the Earth and Cis-Lunar space are responsible for this atrocity and by implication, the Colonial Council of Sol and the Security Council of Sol, situated at Eros, are both complicit in this heinous act! It is not the first time either. Back in seventy seven they tried to assassinate my Father, High Prince Albert. Last year they succeeded! They murdered my Father, the former High Prince. Now, they have tried to destroy the capital colony of our Jovian Realms! They did not succeed!", he shouted out the last sentence.

After a brief pause, High Prince Godric continued, "Make no mistake and mark my words, this was an act of War and it will not go unanswered. It will not go unpunished! There will be a proportionate strategic response, I assure you. We did not start this War, but by God, we will finish it. Hell have NO fury like the Jovian Realms under attack. I hereby officially declare that a state of War exists between the six Jovian Realms and the Earth, Cis-Lunar and Eros. They have started it and we will now end it!"

The broadcast cut out, it was now March, twenty one eighty two and the first Horridian War, the Outer Satellite Insurrection, had been declared. Godric von Horridian's pretext, his lie was in place.

The rebuttal came almost immediately. President Dieter Reinhardt of the colonies of Cis-Lunar space stood at the lectern upon his podium for his rebuttal.

The President began by stating his confusion, "As President of the Cis-Lunar colonies, I find myself confused as to what Godric Horridian is talking about", he refused to use Godric's title and stuck with the High Prince's, older, historical name.

The President continued, "We, here in Cis-Lunar space, have no nuclear weapons and neither does the Earth. They were banned and dismantled almost one hundred and twenty years ago. The closest thing that we might have to such a weapon would be twenty-kiloton cold fusion mining charges and those are five thousand times smaller in power. Likewise, we have no interplanetary missiles, stealth or otherwise. The things that Godric Horridian has accused us of using simply do not exist."

There was a brief pause before the President continued, "For nigh on one hundred and twenty years, Humanity has been at peace. A peace, which has ushered in our Golden Age of solar system exploration and colonisation. A Golden Age of peace that Godric Horridian appears to be intent on destroying."

"The Jovian Realms are a brutal, feudal dictatorship, run by a despotic, autocratic family. It was just five years ago that they annexed the colonies of Jupiter's Leading and Trailing Trojans. They did so with a show of military force, threatening to destroy those colonies", President Reinhardt noted.

"Since then, they have embarked on a constant propaganda War, spreading blatant misinformation, falsehoods and straight-up lies. It was just a few short years ago that Godric Horridian ordered the murder of diplomats aboard an Ambassadorial vessel. Diplomatic immunity meant nothing to the Horridian Regime. They are an aberrant force where the rule of law does not exist. The

Horridian family does as it pleases, pushing lies, falsehoods and now an obvious false flag operation with no evidence or credence to back it up", the President continued.

The President stared into the camera, "We cannot and will not ignore Godric Horridian's threats. I have spoken to Madam President Guang Hui of Earth and we both agree that Godric Horridian's threats are of serious concern to both of our societies. I hereby announce our full mobilisation. The Earth's Defence Forces are mobilising. Our own Colonial Armed Forces are mobilising. Neither of us will sit idly by while a murderer, Godric Horridian, threatens us both with retaliation for something that they themselves have perpetrated. Mark my words. Should Godric Horridian follow through with his threats, he will not like the response that we deliver in return."

The broadcast ended. The board was set. The pieces were yet to move.

Religious fervour was taking place across the six Jovian Realms with the Jovian High Churches of each realm preaching the righteousness of their High Prince's position and declaration of War. Propaganda was not just external, it was heavily internalised and the High Prince's narrative was the normal state of internal information.

It had been since the days of the old Jovian Republic, when Albertus von Horridian became President back in twenty one forty seven. Albertus's two terms as President, followed by his Son, Albert's four terms as President and the subsequent fall of the Jovian Republic into the Jovian Realms had indoctrinated the Jovian people to the point of believing nothing else.

If the High Prince said God had saved them and that God was on their side and the Jovian High Churches backed up the narrative, then the people would believe it. The citizens of the Six Jovian Realms all lived in a tightly controlled information bubble from which they could not escape.

Further out in the solar system, in Saturnian Demarchy, Prime Minister Quintus Malbeck was extremely concerned about recent broadcasts from both the Jovian Realms and Cis-Lunar space. Prime Minister Malbeck went to the one person who always seemed to have the right answers, Administrator Swenna Goodchild.

"Ms Goodchild. Just last month, we signed the Quadripartite Outer Satellite Agreement, the QOSA agreement. The ink is barely dry and now, it looks like the Jovian Realms are going to drag us into a War. A War, Ms Goodchild!", the Prime Minister commented.

"Yes, Prime Minister. I can see that. You might remember I did advise against signing anything with the Horridian regime. You did go against my advice", Ms Goodchild gently chided.

"Yes, Ms Goodchild, but we did get you to vet the agreement before we signed it", Prime Minister Malbeck noted in reply.

"And a good thing I did, too. I struck out anything to do with military cooperation. Our agreement does not allow for any military support whatsoever. I was very deliberate about that", Swenna replied.

"Yes, but if War does break out, we will still have to provide material support and logistical assistance", Quintus reminded her.

"Yes, but not military support. Stick to the letter of the agreement", Swenna advised, explaining, "The Horridians will try to push for more. They will want weapons, they will want ships, they will even ask for troops. Stick to the letter of the agreement and say no to any further requests or demands! Give them nothing more than what we have promised in the agreement. No more and no less."

"Ms Goodchild, what if we don't honour the agreement? What if we just shred it?", the Prime Minister asked, he was serious.

"Prime Minister. We live in the Saturnian Demarchy in the far reaches of our solar system. The only people farther out than us are the Uranian Federation, the Neptunian Commonwealth and whatever Kuiper Belt colonies that may survive. God help them. If we shred an agreement, even one that should be shredded, we will never get another agreement with anyone out here ever again. Especially when the ink on this one isn't even dry", Swenna advised him.

"Then we won't be doing that", the Prime Minister decided, noting, "Why are they doing this? The Horridians? War does not help anyone. There's no benefit in it."

"Prime Minister, this is no coincidence. The Horridians planned this all along. They are playing the game of empire and they want expansion, they want conquest. Pure and simple", Swenna explained.

"And you saw it coming, didn't you?", Prime Minister Malbeck noted.

"Yes, Prime Minister, yes I did", Swenna confirmed, and then she asked, "And with your permission. The advice I've just given you, I'll give that same advice to the Uranian Federation and to the Neptunian Commonwealth. I have contacts with them both and I'm absolutely certain that they do not want to be dragged into a War either."

"Yes, do that, Ms Goodchild. We need solidarity on this issue", the Prime Minister agreed.

The meeting was all but over, but before the Prime Minister could leave, Swenna asked, "Prime Minister, you do understand that everything Godric Horridian said in his speech was a lie, don't you?"

Swenna Godchild also refused to use Godric's self-appointed title and his assumed noble surname.

"Can you prove it, Ms Goodchild?", Prime Minister Malbeck asked hopefully.

"I do not need to, Prime Minister. It's simple logic, really", Swenna informed him, explaining, "An interplanetary stealth missile targeted at Ganymede Prime just happens to get blocked and intercepted by a small ice moon, Himalia. A bit convenient, don't you think?"

"Yes, I guess it is, Ms Goodchild", the Prime Minister agreed.

"An interplanetary missile with a guidance system that could not adjust for an ice moon being in its path. Seriously, we have had that technology for well over a century and a half", Swenna continued, adding, "And the sheer overkill. A one-hundred-plus megaton warhead when a mere two megatons would be enough to do the job. Not that those even exist. The inner system got rid of all of its nuclear weapons well over a century ago. There was no missile, interplanetary or otherwise, Prime Minister. It was all theatrics. It was an oversized bomb designed to produce a huge light show that the whole solar system could see and around which Godric Horridian could weave his lies. Everything that comes out of the Horridian regime is a lie or worse, something carefully crafted to look truthful, but is full of falsehoods. They are insidious! Now I understand why the Mimasians gave those three fugitives, Roberta Nummus, Elaine Haynes and Lina Mitchel sanctuary and asylum."

Prime Minister Malbeck looked at Swenna thoughtfully, "Ms Goodchild, add your analysis to that communique you're sending to the Uranian Federation and the Neptunian Commonwealth. They need to know. We have all been played like a fine violin!"

Swenna sighed, "Whatever the Horridians do next, that Quadripartite Outer Satellite Agreement, the QOSA, makes us all complicit. History is going to tar us all with the very same brush! All of us!"

Prince Friederic flew to Io Prime using his private space yacht with his Wife, Princess Minerva. When the royal couple arrived at the space yacht, they found Prince Emeric's Wife, Princess Chastity and Prince Aluric's Wife, Princess Serenity, waiting for them in the passenger cabin, their luggage already stowed away.

"We were not expecting company", Princess Minerva commented.

"We weren't expecting to accompany you", Princess Chastity replied and then explained, "High Prince Godric has commanded that Princess Serenity be sent to your palace on Io Prime. My Husband, Emeric, agreed with him. I, I stand with Princess Serenity. Where she goes, I go. If Emeric wants me back, he will have to do some serious grovelling."

Princess Serenity spoke softly, almost fearfully, "Why am I being banished? What have I done?"

Prince Friederic replied, "Serenity. Princess, this is not about you. My Brother Godric thinks he is punishing me. You, Princess, are just a pawn."

Princess Serenity asked timidly, "What did you do?"

"I disagreed with my Brother", Prince Friederic replied honestly, "Godric is going to start a War with the inner solar system. I told him to his face that it was stupidity and that his plans were insane."

Princess Chastity agreed, "That would do it. I'm really pissed at Emeric for agreeing with that craziness as well. Wars benefit no one!"

"Our High Prince believes we can win his War with one devastating strike", Prince Friederic replied and then he noted, "The Earth and Cis-Lunar space won't just fold, they'll hit back and they will hit back hard. Ultimately, we will lose. He does not see it that way and I cannot convince him otherwise."

"But why does exiling me punish you, Prince Friederic?", Princess Serenity asked, her voice still meek and soft.

Princess Minerva took Serenity's hands in her own and replied, "Serenity, honey. Your Husband, Prince Aluric, is mentally unstable. Our High Prince sees him as broken. So he makes sure that Aluric is at your palace at Callisto Prime as much as possible. After what Aluric did to you and your injuries, Godric considers you to be broken as well. He just wants you away from Ganymede Prime."

Prince Friederic stepped in, adding, "My Wife, Minerva, has summed it up well. Godric could have sent you to Princess Chastity's palace on Europa Prime, but instead, he's sending you to our palace. My Brother thinks he is insulting me. Turning me into some kind of glorified babysitter. It is just the opposite. I am more than happy to be your protector, Princess."

"We are all more than happy to be your protectors, Serenity", Princess Minerva corrected.

"And that includes me as well, Serenity", Princess Chastity chimed in.

Prince Friederic smiled, he almost chuckled, "Princess, by sending you to our palace on Io Prime, my Brother Godric has placed you in perhaps the safest place within the Jovian Realms."

Princess Serenity didn't understand, so Friederic explained, "Io Prime is the newest and most modern of the Galilean Primes. It benefited from all of the newer technologies and enhancements developed during the design and construction of the preceding primes. Io Prime is also deep within Jupiter's gravity well and deeply embedded within Jupiter's intense radiation belts. Most people don't realise, Io Prime's position gives us extreme natural defences."

Princess Minerva smiled and corrected her Husband, "There is another place even safer, Friederic. Amalthea Prime is even deeper within Jupiter's gravity well and the radiation belts there are even more intense, although it is half the size of the Galilean Primes and it is nowhere near as pretty."

"That is true, Minerva, however, I think perhaps that Princess Serenity would prefer to have her friends around her. At least for now", Prince Friederic replied.

"That is also true, dear Husband. Amalthea's orbital zone is also part of the

Ionian Realms. Maybe, just maybe, when Serenity has recovered further and is feeling stronger, we could set her up as the Mistress of Amalthea Prime. Under our auspices, of course."

Princess Chastity smiled, "Princess Serenity, Mistress of Amalthea Prime. It does have a nice ring to it, doesn't it?"

Princess Minerva squeezed Serenity's hands, "Not just yet, Serenity. When you're feeling a little stronger. When you're ready."

Princess Serenity didn't say anything, she switched seats and sat down beside Minerva, leaning in and hugging her tightly, tears welling in her eyes. Princess Minerva reached up and stroked her hair.

"It's okay, Serenity, honey. No one, no one is going to hurt you ever again", Minerva assured her.

Minerva looked to Friederic and then to Chastity with concern. The Princess they were protecting had been raped repeatedly and abused by her Husband, Aluric and then finally beaten to within a hair's breadth of life. The young Princess had nearly died. Princess Chastity was suffering from severe post-traumatic stress and it would take years for her to recover. They all knew it. They all understood.

On Eros, the Colonisation Committee of Sol and the Security Council of Sol met in a rare, combined full meeting. There were only three Colonisation Committee speakers, Maria Corbel, Lyra Banks and Stephen Terrell. They were all Professors and academics, and they ostensibly oversaw the bureaucracy behind the colonisation of the solar system. The Security Council had thirteen speakers and these were all bureaucrats, the first and foremost of whom was Central Speaker, General Ulysses Bone, retired. He was Professor Corbel's counterpart in the Security Council. He was, as his name indicated, a former military man and known for taking tough and unyielding positions on most subjects.

Neither the Colonisation Committee nor the Security Council had been effective in their respective roles of late, as evidenced by the recent propaganda wars, the murder of their diplomats and now a declaration of War. All of this had been foreseen. The late Stuart Dumas, a visionary during his day, had predicted and warned of this very situation. No one had listened to him, no one had taken him seriously and now, eight decades after his prediction, all of their chickens had come home to roost and the wolves had surrounded the coop. War had been declared and the Earth and Cis-Lunar space barely had any armed forces to field.

The discussions had been going on since the wee hours of the morning, since before *"sunrise"* within the cylindrical, hollowed-out world that was Eros. The City within the Rock was calm, its people were calm and all was well. The calm before the storm, perhaps, although the people of Eros knew it not. That, of course, contrasted entirely with the arguments and deliberations taking place behind closed doors in Eros's Central Citadel.

As Eros's artificial *"plasma ball"* Sun traversed from North to South along the central axis of Eros, everything seemed normal, everything seemed okay. It was a warm day, with scattered clouds and the artificial environment was currently set to late spring. There had been rain earlier in the morning and the air had a crisp, moist, even sweet quality to it. Life in Eros was good. It was almost a paradise.

It was Sunday, the thirty-first day of March, in the year twenty one eighty two and the people of Eros went about their weekend, enjoying themselves, while the Colonisation Committee and Security Council continued their meeting.

"Who the hell attacked the Jovian Realms?", the third speaker on Ulysses Bone's left shouted.

"As we've stated a dozen times. We do not know!", Professor Corbel threw back.

The fourth speaker on Ulysses Bone's right commented as he had several times before, "Well, someone certainly did! We all saw the explosion on the news feeds!"

Ulysses Bone stepped in, "Enough! We are circling around an event for which we have no definitive information. I can personally attest that neither the Earth nor Cis-Lunar space have any nuclear weapons, let alone something bigger than one hundred megatons. Whoever, whatever caused that explosion, it was not us. We are just being blamed for it!"

Another of the Security Council speakers, one on the far left, commented, "Nor do we have any interplanetary missiles either! Stealth or otherwise! It doesn't make any sense. A missile that could not autonomously navigate around a moon. For fucks sake! Himalia is a hundred and forty kilometres across. It's not exactly a small moon, is it?"

It had been going on like this for hours, round and round in circles. No one, no one had a clue what the Jovian High Prince had been talking about in his broadcast.

Carl Stavros, the Security Council Liaison to the Colonisation Committee, entered the deliberation chambers. His movements were rushed and hurried. He made his way to the centre of the room, dropping his files and picking them back up as he did so.

The room fell quiet as Ulysses Bone called out, "Stavros! Get your act together, man!"

Professor Corbel was less dictatorial, "Carl, take a deep breath. What do you have for us?"

Carl placed a set of documents in front of Ulysses Bone and a duplicate set in front of Maria Corbel.

"This came in from Administrator Swenna Goodchild. She's the head bureaucrat in the Saturnian Demarchy's Administration system. Ms Goodchild sent the same documents to the Uranian Federation and the Neptunian Commonwealth as well. All by tight-beam laser comms for security. She blind carbon copied us in, us, the Earth and Cis-Lunar space", he was completely out of breath and had trouble spitting it out.

Professor Corbel offered Carl her glass of water, which he took and downed with three gulps, "Carl, please give us a summary?"

"Thank you, Maria", he replied as he passed back her glass.

"Bad news, people. Just last February, the four outer satellite polities sign an agreement. They call it the Quadripartite Outer Satellite Agreement, their QOSA", Carl informed them all, noting, "It is an agreement to provide material support and logistical assistance in the case that any one of their group is attacked by an external enemy."

"Fuck!", a Security Council speaker on the right exclaimed, "So, we're are War with all of them now? All four outer satellites?", he questioned.

Ulysses Bone glared at the speaker for speaking out of turn, then commanded, "Stavros! Clarify!"

"Yes, Sir", Carl replied and then he provided more information, "Although their agreement requires the provision of material support and logistical assistance, it is not a military agreement. Ms Goodchild is informing us that they are fully aware that the Horridians have played them. Ms Goodchild is also assuring us that they will stick to the letter of the agreement and that means that they will not provide the Horridian Dynasty with any military assistance. That's the good news, Sir. They will not give the Jovian Realms any weapons, ships or personnel."

"Well, Stavros, that does temper their agreement somewhat", Ulysses Bone agreed, nodding and summing up, "Material support, logistical assistance, but no weapons, no personnel or ships."

"How is that good news, Mr Bone?", Professor Stephen Terrell enquired.

"The Horridians are limited to only their military-industrial complex, Terrell. They'll have no access to the Saturnian, Uranian or Neptunian manufacturing industries", Ulysses Bone explained, noting, "The Horridians would have been relying on that access. They've started a fight with one hand cut off!"

"There is more", Carl Stavros announced, "Ms Goodchild says that there was no missile and she has provided her analysis. It was a false flag operation to create a pretext for War, Sir."

"Well, I'd already figured that much out. Ms Goodchild is just adding confirmation", Ulysses agreed.

Before I brought this news to you I requested the latest images of the Jovian Moon, Himalia", Carl informed everyone, "If you check the documents you will find before and after images. Dumas Astro Resources came in very handy."

Professor Corbel checked her file as did Ulysses Bone, "They look almost the same, at least to my eyes", Maria Corbel noted.

Ulysses Bone scoffed, "It was a skyburst. They didn't actually want to destroy Himalia. They just wanted the *'light show'* for their pretext. Good work, Stavros!"

"So, now we know the truth, we can release it publicly. There won't be a War", a smiling Professor Lyra Banks suggested.

"We will make all of this public, Professor Banks. As to whether there will be a War, that is entirely up to Godric Horridian", Ulysses Bone replied, commenting, "Without military support from the other outer satellites and with this being released publicly, he may, just possibly may, think twice."

Lyra Banks was the voice of hope. Stephen Terrell, the voice of scepticism. Maria Corbel, the voice of concerned reason and former General Ulysses Bone, the voice with experience who understood that some people are just plain bad and Godric Horridian was one of those people.

While the Colonisation Committee and the Security Council debated their next move, outside of their deliberation chambers and outside of the Citadel of Eros, the day continued, a typical Sunday. The artificial *"plasma ball"* Sun had reached midway on its traversal from North to South along the central axis of Eros, signifying midday. The Sun shone brightly and it was a typical pleasant Erosian day inside the hollowed-out Asteroid, the World with the Rock.

There was one central sea at the centre of Eros, which wrapped around the inside of its cylindrical surface, it was two miles wide. Two long seas extended from it north and south for six miles, each being one mile wide as well. The Citadel of Eros sat on an Island in the centre where the three seas met. One hundred and twenty degrees around the cylinder were four more seas. Each being one mile wide and five miles long. They were all connected to the central sea by mile-long canals, two per sea.

In the land sections between each of the seas were low mountains that reached peaks of up to fifteen hundred metres in height. The mountain slopes were heavily forested with trees specifically chosen for Eros from the forests of Earth. The lowlands on either side of the mountains were dotted here and there with villages and the villages themselves were surrounded by farmlands and orchards.

Beneath the inner surface of Eros was a labyrinth of underground suburbs, each connected by maglev transport tubes. This was where the majority of Erosians lived and it was a Sunday. For most of the Erosians, it was a day of rest, a day of recreation, a day of pleasure. Singles, couples and families were all out and about, picnicking in the fields, hiking in the forests and on the many beaches and picturesque ports that lined the artificial Erosian seas.

Sailboats were sailing upon the tranquil waters. Canoes paddled in the seas and the artificial rivers that flowed into them. People were swimming and enjoying their Sunday. People of all species, for Eros, was not just colonised by Humans. Oh no, Humans had developed translation devices that enabled them to talk to the cetaceans, to Dolphins, Porpoises and even Dwarf Sperm Whales. They had asked their various cetacean friends if they wanted to become colonists.

It was a difficult process to explain to the cetaceans what a colony like Eros was and what being a colonist would be like. Yet after showing the cetaceans pictures and films of the interior of Eros and the many discussions about the shallow artificial seas full of fish and other life forms that all three species enjoyed eating, many of them had volunteered. And so it came to pass that the semi-sapient non-Human colonists came to colonise and live in the seas of Eros.

Humans, of course, had taken their companion animals, their cats, their dogs and even their ferrets with them, but this was different. Dolphins, Porpoises and Dwarf Sperm Whales were not companion animals. They were semi-sapient colonists! Sentient beings in their own right. There were thousands of each species enjoying the warm, shallow seas and the copious supplies of fish and food within them.

Ms Lorraine Riddle was relaxing on her beach towel. The Sun was warm and she had applied a good layer of sunscreen, not that it was truly necessary, as any really harmful UV rays were filtered out. The sunscreen was being used more to promote a healthy tan as opposed to one created by a mild sunburn.

Lorraine looked up at the sky. If she looked to the north or the south of the artificial plasma Sun, she could see the other side of Eros, a little bit more than seven point six kilometres away. Lorraine was used to this vista. She was even used to the view of Eros's concave curvature and the landscape to either side of her. Mountains reaching skyward from the other sides of the Erosian cylinder roughly one hundred and twenty degrees to either side of her.

Lorraine almost laughed at how she'd developed vertigo and vomited the very first time she'd seen such a vista when she, herself, had first come to Eros. Of course, it did not help that at that time she was pregnant with her first child, Leanna. Lorraine was on Earth, single, pregnant, unemployed and given an opportunity, a job position at Eros, the City within the Rock. Lorraine Riddle had grabbed that opportunity with both hands and she was living and working inside Eros within twelve weeks.

Leanna was born inside Eros and was now eight years old. Lorraine had lived inside Eros for eight and a half years! Eight and a half years of true paradise!

"Mum! I need the translator headset!", an urgent young voice disturbed her reverie, "Mum! Quickly, the Dolphins are here! I want to talk to the Dolphins!"

Lorraine sat up and frowned, "Leanna, darling. Do you need to shout so loud?"

"Mum, the Dolphins are playing and they want to talk. I need the translator headset", Leanna replied with an urgency that only an eight-year-old child could muster.

"Okay, okay, Leanna", Lorraine replied, passing her the translator headset, clearly stating, "Now, darling. Look after them. Leanna, they were very expensive, nearly three hundred credits."

"Of course, I will, Mum", Leanna replied as she placed the translator headset on her head and bolted for the tranquil, azure waters of the Northern Long Sea.

Leanna waded into the waters, no deeper than her waist. Two Dolphins swam up to her and greeted her with their clicks and squeaks. They were young Dolphins, not that much older than Leanna herself.

"Hoo man child! Hoo man child!", their greetings came through her translator.

One of the Dolphins nuzzled her gently with its beak and rolled onto its side, looking up at her with its left eye. Leanna smiled and automatically reached down to stroke it behind its blowhole.

"Do you have a name?', Leanna asked curiously, her translator creating squeaks and clicks.

The Dolphin pulled back slightly, raised its head and replied, squeaking and clicking, "Yes, Hoo man child, but our names do not come across well in Hoo man speech"

"That's sad", Leanna replied, "My name is Leanna", she told them.

The second Dolphin squeaked and clicked, the translator came back with laughter and, "Pretty name, Hoo man child, Leanna. Pretty name."

Leanna giggled, which, of course, was translated back to the Dolphins as laughter. Both Dolphins replied with laughter in return, clicking and squeaking.

Leanna asked the Dolphins, her translator clicking and squeaking, "Are there many Dolphins nearby? Perhaps even Porpoises and Dwarf Sperm Whales?"

The furthest of the two Dolphins nodded, squeaked and clicked back, translating as, "Long words, Hoo man, Leanna. Learn. Clip words short. We are Fins, the others are Oises and Squales."

Leanna chuckled, "Fins, Oises and Squales! You're so funny!", the translator creating Dolphin clicks and squeaks.

The closest Dolphin answered Leanna's original question, "The others swim deeper. Farther out. More Fins, Oises and Squales. Eat fish, eat food. Yummy fish. Many fish", with a long series of clicks and squeaks.

The other Dolphin added with its own squeaks and clicks, "Our Mothers will come soon. Tell us to eat. Many fish in sea. Yummy fish."

"You like to eat fish?", Leanna asked, more clicks and squeaks being created.

Both Dolphins nodded in unison and answered, "Yes. Fish good. Fish very good!"

The nearest Dolphin clicked and squeaked, "Your Mother comes soon. Tell you to eat. You want us to catch fish for you?"

Leanna smiled and answered, "My Mum buys fish in the market. We have fish at home", her translator rendering her words into something the Dolphins could understand.

"Dead cold fish, not fresh. Not good fish", one of the Dolphins clicked and squeaked back, adding, "We can catch your Mother fresh fish. Still wriggling fresh."

The other Dolphin chimed in, clicking and squeaking, "Fresh fish. Good fish", and then gestured with its beak further out to a man in a small boat fishing, "We catch fish for, Hoo man. He was very happy. Hoo man, likes fresh fish."

Leanna smiled and replied, giggling, "Maybe if my Mother comes into the water to swim, you can ask her if she wants fresh fish", the translator rendering her words into clicks and squeaks once more.

Both Dolphins nodded with clicks and squeaks, indicating they would be happy to do so. And so, Leanna, eight years of age, conversed with young Dolphins in the Northern Long Sea of Eros, with its tranquil, blue azure waters, under a golden yet artificial plasma Erosian Sun.

Eight objects hurtled through the darkness of the void. They had travelled a long way. All the way from the missile silos of Ganymede L-Four. They were long and sleek. They were coated with a deep black paint that was radar absorbent. They could not easily be seen or detected. As they approached their designated target, their target acquisition matrix scanned ahead and calculated precise course adjustments. Stealth thrusters fired up in short, precise bursts.

The eight, dark, sleek objects were locked on, travelling at high velocity and precisely staggered, twenty five seconds apart. Each contained a single two-megaton fusion warhead. Old-school warheads with chemical explosive detonators, atomic fission explosive compressors and hydrogen-lithium cores.

The first missile struck the exterior of Eros, right in the centre. The two megaton nuclear flash immediately vaporised a portion of the surface to a depth of several hundred metres, yet vitrified the Erosian shell beneath it. Beyond the region of vitrification, cracks, small at first, began to form. Cracks in the outer shell of Eros.

Inside Eros, there were massive vibrations. The Central Citadel began to shake and sway. It was as if Eros was experiencing a violent earthquake, something that was all but impossible inside Eros. People were thrown to the ground and panic began to spread. Eros, struck hard with nuclear main force, was ringing, inaudibly, like a huge bell. Inaudible to all but the cetaceans, to whom it was loud, painfully loud, their natural sonar picking it up and amplifying it.

Then, when things seemed to be calming down, precisely twenty five seconds later, it repeated. Eros rotated at zero point five rotations per minute and the second missile struck forty five degrees further around the outer shell of Eros, right in the middle. It too vaporised the surface to a depth of several hundred metres. It too vitrified the Erosian shell beneath it. It also created small cracks beyond the vitrification zone. Yet more cracks in the outer shell of Eros.

For the second time, people were thrown to the ground as the massive wave of vibrations passed through the Erosian shell. The Central Citadel continued to shake and sway, its tall spires precariously so. People everywhere were panicking. The Dolphins, the Porpoises and the Dwarf Sperm Whales were panicking. The tranquil, azure blue waters of the Erosian seas vibrated as the shell of Eros continued to ring like a huge, inaudible bell.

"What the hell is happening?", Professor Corbel shouted as the room shook and moved side to side.
Ulysses Bone answered, his voice was grim with understanding, "We're being attacked. Those were nuclear detonations. Big ones!"

Then, just like before, as things began to settle down, the third missile struck, twenty five seconds after the second and another forty five degrees further around the outer shell of Eros. The Central Citadel of Eros shook and swayed violently as the massive wave of vibrations passed through Eros.

"Another hit like that and the city will collapse", Stephen Terrell noted in alarm, there was terror clearly visible in his eyes.

The vibrations began to settle once more and the Citadel's swaying slowed. Sighs of relief appeared on the faces of the Colonisation Committee and Security Council speakers. Eros was still ringing like a bell, a vibration they could feel, yet could not hear.

And then the fourth missile struck, it too was twenty five seconds behind the third and another forty five degrees further around the outer shell of Eros. Immediately, several hundred metres of the Erosian surface vaporised and the rock shell beneath it vitrified. More cracks began to appear beyond to zone of vitrification. This detonation, however, was almost directly in line with the Central Citadel inside Eros, directly underneath it.

The Central Citadel of Eros shuddered violently as the wave of vibrations from the fourth detention flowed through it. The Citadel, with its tall, ornate spires, began to sway beyond tolerance. The swaying was drastic, it was clearly visible from one end of Eros to the other. Stephen Terrell's prescience came back to haunt him.

Carl Stavros had been thrown to the floor four times. This was the fourth time he had struggled to his feet. He finally stood up, only for the floor beneath his feet to vanish. Carl Stavros fell, disappearing into the hole as the Colonisation Committee and Security Council speakers looked on in horror.

And then it happened, the deliberation chamber's walls collapsed inward. The floor beneath them crumbled and they all fell into the open abyss as hundreds of tons of rubble piled down on top of them, as the entire Central Citadel collapsed.

The Colonisation Committee and Security Council deliberations had been cut short!

Lorraine Riddle had struggled to her feet and ran towards her Daughter, Leanna, being thrown to the ground as each missile struck. Lorraine had briefly turned to her left as she heard the sudden cracking and booming of the Central Citadel's collapse a mere two and a half kilometres away. Lorraine Riddle forced herself to her feet and lunged towards her Daughter.

Then the fifth missile hit! It was twenty five seconds behind the last and another forty five degrees around the outer shell of Eros. Once more, the outer shell was vaporised, the shell beneath that zone was vitrified and even more cracks appeared in the outer shell around it.

Lorraine was thrown to the ground just as she reached her young Daughter, Leanna, only this time she was in the shallow waters. The massive shock wave and its wave of massive vibrations began passing through Eros. The ground beneath their feet was vibrating. The waters of the Northern Long Sea themselves, azure blue as they were, were also vibrating.

Lorraine placed her arms around her Daughter, only to notice that Leanna was protectively holding two young Dolphins, both of whom appeared to be in a great deal of pain.

"Too loud! Too loud! Too loud!", the translator shouted with urgency, as the pair of Dolphins clicked and squeaked in urgent agony, their bodies wriggling and shaking in terror.

"Leanna! Leanna! We have to go! It's not safe here!", Lorraine told her Daughter with urgency.

"No, Mommy! The Fins, the Fins, they're in pain", Leanna replied, tears streaming down her cheeks.

"They'll be fine, sweety. We have to go! It's not safe here!", Lorraine insisted.

"I won't leave them, Mummy!", Leanna argued back.

And then the sixth missile struck!

Twenty five seconds behind the last, forty five degrees further around the outer shell, another section of the Erosian crust was vaporised, again the section beneath vitrified and again more cracks formed in the outer shell beyond the strike zone.

The young Dolphins still writhed in acoustically induced pain, their cries almost a continuous chorus, "Too loud! Too loud! Too loud!", the translator doing its job all too well.

Lorraine wrapped one arm around her Daughter and her other arm around one of the Dolphins, bracing them as the next shock wave, with its massive vibrations, passed through. All the while, Eros continued to ring like a gigantic bell, the ground vibrating, the sea vibrating. Everything was vibrating. They could feel it in their very bones!

"It's okay, sweety. We won't leave the Dolphins. We'll stay here and look after them", Lorraine decided, changing her mind, after all, where else could they go that was not in complete chaos?

The seventh missile struck, again twenty five seconds behind the last and forty five degrees further around the outer shell of Eros. The results were the same as the previous six. Vaporised crust, vitrified rock shell and cracks formed beyond the blast radius. Lorraine and Leanna held onto two hapless young Dolphins, caring for them as best as they could.

The Dolphins were no longer crying out in anguish, they had both gone all but silent. Their bodies still writhing in pain, their eyes still displaying terror, yet now the translator only gave off the sounds of what could only be described as children whimpering.

The shock wave and its massive vibrations passed through once more and Eros continued to ring like a bell. Lorraine and Leanna sat in the water, holding the Dolphins as the Eighth missile struck.

Twenty five seconds behind the seventh and forty five degrees further around the outer shell of Eros, the patterned strike was complete. The entire circumference of Eros has been struck by no fewer than eight two-megaton warheads. The eighth and final patch of vaporised crust, vitrified rock shell and as with the other seven before it, those cracks, those awful cracks forming just beyond the blast radius.

The shock wave with its massive vibrations passed through and Lorraine and Leanna held onto those two young Dolphins, waiting for the next strike. It didn't come. It was several long minutes before Lorraine realised that the attack was over. Eros was still ringing like a bell, but the vibrations, those horrible vibrations that only cetaceans could hear, were slowly diminishing. It was a full ten minutes before the young Dolphins began to stop shaking, before they began to stir.

Lorraine Riddle and her Daughter, Leanna, sat there in the shallows of the Northern Long Sea. They held, no, they nursed the two young Dolphins as they slowly recovered from their ordeal. Looking to their left with tears in their eyes, they both stared at the remains of Eros Central, the Citadel at the centre of Eros, the City within the Rock.

Eros Central was on an island in the middle of the conjunction of the Circular Sea, and the Northern and Southern Long Seas. It had an area of one square mile. A citadel of nine plasteel, aluminumised glass and astcrete spires, the central spire being one thousand five hundred metres tall. Now, it was a collapsed, twisted and broken mess of rubble. Broken astcrete blocks, shattered shards of aluminumised glass and great lengths of broken and twisted plasteel.

Half a million people had lived and worked in Eros Central. Lorraine Riddle wondered how many of them had survived. It could not have been very many. The devastation appeared to be total. No, very few people would have survived that devastation. Half a million dead buried under all of that rubble.

The young Dolphin in her arms began to move and she instinctively began to gently stroke it behind its blowhole, comforting it.

Clicking and squeaking drew Lorraine's and Leanna's attention towards deeper waters. A pod of Dolphins was approaching, they clicked and squeaked with urgency.

"It's their Mothers, Mummy", Leanna commented, adding, "They're just worried."

The young Dolphin in Leanna's arms squeaked and clicked, "Painful noise, painful noise. What was painful noise? Why?", it was confused.

The young Dolphin's Mother replied and Leanna's translator did its work, "Noise worse in shallows. Not as bad in deep. Little ones were in a bad place at wrong time."

The two young Dolphins swam out of Lorraine's and Leanna's arms to join their Mothers in the pod.

One of the Dolphin's Mothers approached, clicked and squeaked, "You looked after our little ones. Thank you. What was that bad noise?", then it gestured to the devastated Citadel, "Big Hoo man place. It falls down. Why did the big Hoo man place fall down?"

Leanna had no answer, so she passed the translator headset to her Mother, "Bad people did a very bad thing", Lorraine tried to explain and then she continued, "The bad people caused the big Human place to fall down. Many Humans have died!"

One of the other pod members clicked and squeaked, "Bad Hoo man people hurt our friends, our hoo men friends. Bad people hurt us. We won't share fish with bad people."

The beach had been busy before the attack and now the people were recovering from the ordeal and moving about. A commotion on the beach and foreshore behind Lorraine caught her attention. There were a number of people all talking, some screaming, some were running and many of them were pointing towards the Central Sea. Lorraine and Leanna turned around to watch the commotion and then they turned to look at where the people were pointing. The sight was so odd, it was so off. At first, it didn't make a lot of sense.

The sky above the fallen Citadel was beginning to swirl with smallish clouds. These were not the clouds that were normally seen inside Eros. Lorraine's eyes scanned the Circular Sea to the West of the Citadel and then back to the East. There were more places where smallish clouds had begun to swirl.

Finally, Lorraine scanned the entire Circular Sea, along its full length around the cylinder, all nearly fifteen miles of it. There were precisely eight regions around the cylinder, all equidistant apart, where this phenomenon was occurring. Eight patches where the sky was filling with swirling clouds. As Lorraine and Leanna watched, the swirling clouds coalesced, became thicker and developed multiple funnels that drifted downwards towards the ground. They looked like tornadoes and yet, this was Eros. Tornadoes simply did not exist inside Eros.

When it dawned upon Lorraine as to what was happening, she took on a look of terror, "Oh my God!", she exclaimed.

One of the Dolphin Mothers sensed something was wrong, something very wrong and asked with squeaks and clicks, "What is it? What are those strange clouds?"

Lorraine's eyes welled with tears. How could she explain what was happening to a Dolphin? They knew not what was outside of Eros, of space, of the void between the worlds. Perhaps, just perhaps, the ancestors of these Dolphins had once seen space through a porthole on the ship that brought them here during their transit. These Dolphins, however, had never seen or been in space.

Lorraine cupped her hands and scooped up some seawater, "This water is contained", she told the Dolphins, the translator rendering her words to clicks and squeaks.

The Dolphins all nodded in agreement, some replying with, "Yes. We understand."

Lorraine nodded and allowed a small gap to form in her cupped hands, "The container is broken. It now leaks water."

The Dolphin's eyes showed that they were beginning to put two and two together, but they were not quite there yet.

Lorraine explained, her translator rendering the required clicks and squeaks, "This world, Eros, is a container. It contains all of our air, the air we all need to breathe. It contains all of our water. The water we are all swimming in. Eros is now a broken container. The air, the water, it will all leak out."

Lorraine pointed to the swirling clouds and the funnels that were now touching the ground.

The Dolphins understood, "The air and water that sustains us, it is leaking out!", one Dolphin Mother exclaimed with a series of squeaks.

"Where does it go? Our air? Our water?", another Dolphin asked.

Lorraine's cheeks were streaming with tears when she replied, "It goes away from us and when it is all gone, we will not be able to breathe", the translator did its job and the Dolphins finally understood.

"Bad people did this. We no share fish with them", another Dolphin clicked and squeaked, "Good Hoo man friends. They fix this, yes?", it questioned.

Lorraine looked at the Dolphin, then looked at her Daughter, Leanna. She did not want Leanna to know and yet, the Dolphins had a right to know. To understand their fate.

Lorraine pointed to the fallen citadel, "Good Humans who fix things are there. All dead. Long sleep. Never wake up", the translator did its work.

The Dolphin's faces were unreadable, but their eyes showed shock and fear as they realised their predicament. The long sleep from which none wake up, death, they all understood death.

One of the Dolphins, a Matriarch, spoke, her clicks and squeaks were urgent,

"Long sleep. No wake up. All dead! We are all dead! All Fins, all Oises, all Squales, all Hoo mans. Pass words. Little bit long time left. Go! Pass words! All must know!"

Several of the Dolphins in the pod left to spread the word.

A small pod of Porpoises approached. Porpoises and Dolphins did not share the same language and they wanted to understand why the Dolphins were so excited, so frightened. They had also noticed the strange clouds and funnels descending to the ground. Lorraine adjusted the settings on her translator headset for recognition of both Dolphin and Porpoise speech patterns.

The Dolphin Matriarch clicked and squeaked with urgency. The headset translated Dolphin's speech to Porpoise, replying with squeaks and clicks that they now understood. As with Dolphins, a Porpoise's face is unreadable, only their eyes showed their understanding. They too understood, they too were frightened. When the Matriarch had finished explaining the situation, the Porpoises nodded and then swam off to warn their people. Word was spreading quickly. The end was nigh.

A spray of water in the distance caught Leanna's attention, "Mummy, Squales are coming!"

"Squales, sweety?", Lorraine enquired.

"Dwarf Sperm Whales, Mummy. Clip words, Mummy. Squales!", Leanna explained.

Lorraine and Leanna walked a little further out into slightly deeper water. Lorraine removed the headset's hydrophone attachment and held it under the water. It immediately began to pick up the Squale's whale song.

"We understand both Fin speak and Oise speak, although we cannot speak it", one of the Squales informed Lorraine, "We have seen the strange clouds and understand the situation", the translator rendered their song to English with remarkable accuracy.

"Then you know that our world is leaking air and water", Lorraine explained, noting, "You should be spreading the word to your kin folk", the translator creating a perfect whale song via its hydrophone.

"Word is spreading. All Squales will know of it", the Squale replied, motioning her head towards Leanna, "Is your little one alright? Word has spread also of a young Hoo man child who cares for young Fins", the whale song continued.

Lorraine almost choked and she sniffed, "My little, Leanna. She, we'll be okay or at least as much as we can be under the circumstances."

The Squale moved its head in what might have been a nod, "Be not afraid. The long sleep is not the end. It is the passage, the gate through which we all must pass. What comes next is beyond your comprehension. When the light comes, accept it, follow it. Let it lead you to the life beyond this life", the whale song continued.

When Lorraine's eyes welled with tears once more, the Squale continued, "You are frightened. That is understandable. You cannot see what we Squales can see. Trust us, the long sleep of death is not the end. Your people will all transcend."

Lorraine reached out and stroked the Squale as it slowly began to swim away.

The Dolphin Matriarch squeaked and clicked, "You are privileged. The Squales rarely speak to others not of their kind. They rarely reach out. Great wisdom they have", and then the Dolphin pod swam off the meet with their fate.

Lorraine Riddle led her young Daughter, Leanna, out of the water. They both sat on their beach towels on the beach. The chaos of Humans panicking behind them on the foreshore was the last thing on their minds. There were others on the beach, all resigned to their fates. They all knew they couldn't fix this. What was done was done. Panicking and running around like headless chickens was not going to achieve anything.
Eros the City within the Rock was already dead and now, Eros, the World within the Rock would soon follow. It was inevitable. Time was precious, so very precious and it was better spent with family, friends and loved ones.
Lorraine held her Daughter, Leanna, tightly and told her, "Trust the Squales, sweety. Trust the Squales. They know something that we all seem to have missed."

As the air leaked away and the atmospheric pressure dropped below that critical threshold, Lorraine and Leanna slowly succumbed to the long sleep from which none awaken. They passed away peacefully, lying together on their beach towels in their loving embrace, Mother and Daughter.
Whether resigned to their fate or rushing around in a panic, they all succumbed to asphyxiation in the end. First, the Humans had all passed and then the Dolphins and Porpoises had passed. Some had panicked, leaping out of the water in an attempt to obtain precious air.

Their sleek bodies broke the waters, seeking breath, calling out, but there was only emptiness. Alas, there was no air for them to breathe and all they could see along the seashore were their deceased Hoo man friends.

"Our friends the Hoo mans are all dead, they are all dead!", they clicked and squeaked.

"There is no air, there is no air", they clicked and squeaked.

The blue azure waters of the Erosian seas, once a cradle of promise and plenty, had betrayed them.

The Dwarf Sperm Whales, with their larger lungs, lasted a little longer. They too quietly and peacefully went into the long night with an unequalled confidence during the end times of Eros.

The World within the Rock grew quiet, except for the soft bubbling of its artificial seas. The atmospheric pressure was now too low to even sustain water in its liquid form. The water levels had lowered somewhat, as water had also escaped through the many cracks in the Erosian rock shell, along with its air. Soon, the interior of Eros would become a dry vacuum, completely devoid of air and water.

The automated systems would still continue to function until they, too, broke down and ceased to work. Broken things with no one alive to repair them. The artificial plasma ball Sun continued on it journey from north to south along the central axis of Eros, providing both light and warmth. Extinguishing at dusk in the south and reigniting at dawn in the north.

Automatically, with no one, not a single being alive to enjoy its light and warmth.

Six point five million souls gone! Ascended and transcended!

Their bodies, desiccating and mummifying, in the airless remains of Eros, the World within the Rock. The once-thriving, albeit artificial world of Eros, now rendered to little more than an enormous mausoleum, a tomb, an ossuary, a container for the dead.

For time observes and space abides, and yet, in the end, even the Dolphins died.

17. The Aftermath.

It was in the wee small hours of the morning and Freyja sat bolt upright in bed screaming. Gideon Reas, asleep on Freyja's left, awoke to the sound of Freyja's screams and attempted to console her. Winchilly, asleep on her right, awoke and did the same. Freyja, however, was still asleep, the night terror that was gripping her preventing her from awakening. Sandra Danker had been sleeping beside Gideon on his left and also awoke.

"What's happening?", Sandra enquired.

"We don't know", Gideon informed her, "It's some kind of night terror. We can't wake her up."

A short distance across the way in another house, Roberta Nummus awoke suddenly, sensing that something was wrong. Roberta leapt out of bed and grabbed her Katana, *the Harōingu,* from off its mounts on the bedroom wall and, without dressing or hesitation, rushed towards the door.

"Roberta? Where are you going?", a still half asleep, Elaine Haynes asked.

"Something's wrong at Freyja's house", Roberta replied as she headed out the door.

"At least put some clothes on, Roberta", Elaine called after her.

"No. Time. Something is very wrong", Roberta Nummus called back as she left their house and Elaine heard the front door close behind her.

Lina Mitchel peered into the bedroom, "What's happening?"

"I have no idea, Lina. Lock all the doors. Roberta says something is very wrong", Elaine replied.

Roberta quickly and quietly entered the house where Freyja lived with her Husband, Gideon and two Sister Wives, Sandra and Winchilly. When Roberta entered the main bedroom, she found Winchilly, Freyja, Gideon and Sandra all sitting up in their oversized marital bed. Freyja's night terror had broken, she was cold, clammy and sweating profusely, gasping for air as if she could not breathe.

"What's happened?", Roberta asked, standing in the doorway, katana in hand and naked.

Sandra blinked, "Roberta Nummus, could you have at least put on some clothes?", she asked.

"There was no time. I could *'feel'* Freyja's screams. It was urgent", Roberta replied.

Sandra rolled her eyes, "There's always time to put on a pair of knickers, Roberta."

Gideon chimed in, explaining, "Freyja's just had some kind of night terror", as an equally naked Winchilly climbed out of their bed.

Winchilly walked over to the bedroom's dresser and took out a nightgown, she passed it to Roberta, *"Please, put this on, Roberta"*, she transmitted telepathically.

Roberta re-sheathed *the Haröingu* and then placed it on the dresser before putting on the nightgown. As she did so, she noticed Winchilly's nakedness more clearly.

Winchilly picked up on Roberta's thoughts, *"We Martians do not have body hair, Roberta, nor do hybrids, for that matter, generally speaking."*

"Sorry, Winchilly. I didn't mean to", Roberta began to apologise.

Winchilly cut her off with a wave of her hand, transmitting *"You have nothing to apologise for, Roberta. Curiosity is not a crime."*

Freyja, who was recovering from her night terror, shouted, "They're all dead! They're all dead! A whole world, they're all dead!"

"Dead? Who's dead, Freyja?", Gideon asked with concern.

Freyja turned to Gideon, her eyes were slightly glazed, then she pointed to Roberta, "He stood right there where Roberta is now. Cousin Orpheus. He said, *'even the Dolphins died'* and then I saw it all. They're all dead! All dead! The people, the Dolphins, the Porpoises, the Dwarf Sperm Whales, the whole world is all dead! And then he died. Orpheus just died!"

Freyja was making no sense, so Gideon leaned in, touched his forehead to Freyja's and let her night terror memories flow into his mind. After several minutes of shared memory communion, he pulled back. His face was a mix of shame and horror. Shame for humanity and horror at what he had seen.

Sandra saw Gideon's face, grabbed him by the arm and demanded, "Show me, Gideon!"

Gideon shook his head, "No, Sandra. You don't want to see this. Truly, you don't!"

"To hell with that!", Sandra leaned in, kissed Gideon on the lips and then pressed her forehead to his, allowing Freyja's memories, now within Gideon, to flow into her own mind.

After several minutes, Sandra pulled back and now her visage had taken on the same expression as Gideon's, "Holy fuck!", she exclaimed, noting, "I can't unsee it! I can't unsee it!"

Sandra pounded her fists against Gideon's chest and he took her in his arms and held her tightly, "I did warn you, Sandra. I did warn you."

Winchilly looked at Freyja and then at Gideon and Sandra, *"I need to know"*, she transmitted.

Gideon replied verbally, "No. No, Winchilly. You really don't. Seriously,

Winchilly, you don't."

Winchilly gently turned Freyja's head towards her and looked into Freyja's still, slightly glazed eyes. She kissed her on the lips and leaned in to retrieve Freyja's memories, touching her forehead to Freyja's forehead.

When Winchilly finally pulled back, tears were streaming down her golden-toned cheeks, *"This cannot be! So much death! So much needless death! Why?"*, she transmitted to the others, her mind was screaming, reeling and screaming.

Roberta was becoming frustrated and she ran her hands through her hair, "Will someone please explain to me what in God's name is going on?"

Sandra, in a state of undress, stepped out of their bed and approached Roberta, who straight away noticed that she, too, lacked body hair in certain places.
Sandra picked up on Roberta's thoughts and noted verbally with complete honesty, "No, Roberta. You know that I'm not a Martian, nor am I a hybrid. My Sister-Wife, Winchilly, just prefers me this way. It's just cleaner, smoother and personally, I find it more enjoyable."
Winchilly blushed, the golden-toned skin tones of her face taking on distinct rose-gold hues.
Roberta closed her eyes and then shook her head to clear her thoughts, "I'm so sorry. I was just..."
Sandra cut her off, "Stop apologising, Roberta. You cannot control your thoughts like we can. You have yet to develop your filter. We understand that. You're neither Folcrom nor Martian", and then she asked, "Do you really want to know what's happened, Roberta Nummus?"
Roberta Nummus nodded and then replied, "Yes. I need to know. I need to know everything!"
Sandra Danker leaned in and said to Roberta, "Brace yourself, Roberta Nummus. This is truly awful on a scale that you cannot possibly imagine. It is beyond comprehension", and then she leaned in and shared Freyja's memories with her.

When the sharing had completed, Roberta Nummus pulled back, almost staggering. Her eyes were wide with horror, pure horror, something that Roberta Nummus had never experienced before. Sandra reached out and steadied her, lest she fall over and collapse to the floor. Roberta reached out and sat down at the end of their marital bed.
Sandra walked back to their bed and climbed back in, "I did warn you, Roberta. True horrors", and then she noted lightly, "Do not climb into our bed, Roberta Nummus. It's already far too crowded and our Husband, Gideon, does

not need a fourth Wife."

Roberta shook her head as she recovered from the memory sharing, her mind still trying to collate all of the data she'd received, "Noted, Sandra. I'm already taken, my Wife, Elaine Haynes, remember."

Sandra nodded in reply, "Your love for Elaine grounds you. She is your anchor. Remember that."

After a couple of minutes, Roberta spoke, her voice was cold as ice, "That little cunt, Godric Horridian has murdered six and a half million people! I should have taken his head when I had the chance, when I was still on Ganymede Prime. Eros would still be alive if I had! This is all my fault!"

Winchilly's calming telepathic voice entered Roberta's mind, *"This is not your fault, Roberta. How could you have predicted this?"*

Freyja, who had now recovered, chimed in, "Winchilly is right. Cousin Orpheus predicted this back in seventy-eight, during the Horridian's propaganda War. This was prophesied and that alone means you could not have stopped it."

Gideon agreed, "Old Orpheus made two prophecies. The first was that Albert Horridian would pass before he did and through his own actions. The second was that Godric would bring on the burning times and the death of Dolphins. Both have now come true. Eros is a dead world now!"

Sandra added, her face contorted with rage, "All of us here have been to Eros. I am deeply saddened that it is now gone. It was the most beautiful place. A paradise! There were well over sixty thousand Cetacean colonists on Eros. Pure innocents, like Children. They did not deserve this fate. Add those to the six and a half million dead Erosians and this becomes more than just a crime against Humanity. This was a crime against life itself. That little arsehole has killed off an entire world!"

Freyja interjected, "Three prophesies, Gideon, Sandra, three. I'm not so sure that the burning times and the death of Dolphins represent the same event. There may be worse yet to come."

"No, no, Freyja, let's hope that is not so. If the burning times are a separate prophecy, then that does not bode well for anyone", Gideon replied.

"I've been a monster for more than eight decades and even I cannot fathom what Godric Horridian has done. That little cunt wasn't just the master of monsters, he's turned out to be the worst monster of all of us", Roberta replied, lamenting the passing of so many souls, too many souls.

"Roberta, you haven't been a monster since you left Ganymede Prime", Winchilly assured her with her soft, calming telepathic voice, confirming, "You will never be a monster, ever again. We are all helping you to overcome your conditioning, your programming and your psychoses triggers."

Tears flowed down Roberta's cheeks, "There is no absolution for me,

Winchilly. Once a monster, always a monster. I am what I was made into. That cannot be changed!"

Freyja chimed in, replying, "You won't always feel that way, Roberta", and then she informed everyone, "You know what. It was Orpheus's one hundredth birthday yesterday and my Elder Cousin passed away at the exact same time that the last of the Dolphins took their final breaths."

That was a revelation that they all allowed to silently sink in.

Roberta was still inconsolable, *"How can I explain this to Elaine and Lina? Not taking Godric's life was my greatest failure!"*, she thought to herself, doing her best to cover her thoughts.

Roberta Nummus silently vowed never again to allow an opportunity to remove evil pass her by!

The Erosian atrocity had fundamentally changed her!

The once monster was one day to become an avenging angel.

When all communications with Eros stopped, the first reports were that Eros was suffering from some kind of communications outage or a series of technical communications faults. Nobody seemed to be overly concerned. Then, of course, the truth eventually came out, but not in the way that one might have thought. The truth kind of emerged sideways from the most obscure of sources.

Eros, the World within the Rock, was in a *"high"* halo orbit about the Earth's trailing Trojan, L-Five, gravitational sweet spot. At the centre of that sweet spot was a large accumulated asteroidal mass used for resource extraction by the Dumas Corporation's, Earth Trojan Mining Corporation Ltd.

On and about that resource mass were mobile mining stations. Further out in two orbital rings were ore processing stations and manufacturing stations. Even further out in *"mid"* halo orbits were six large O'Neil-style twin-cylinder corporate colonies. That was where the Earth Trojan Mining Corporation's employees and supporting colonists all lived.

One of those corporate colonies had a telescope continuously trained on Eros, transmitting a video feed twenty-four-seven to the rest of the solar system. It was kind of like those old twenty-first-century videos taken by cameras mounted on trains travelling on long-haul rail journeys. Only this feed showed nothing more than Eros rotating continually, serenely in space. This feed had captured Eros from the beginning of its construction and it had continued nonstop. As with all video feeds, it was recorded.

This video feed was boring, yes, but some people watched it for hours on end. Others used it as a *"peaceful, serene"* digital video backdrop on their video walls. Something calm and settling, a pleasant thing running in the background. The thing is, people actually watched it and that is where the first signs of the disaster came from.

The Horridian's attack on Eros, their first strike in their Horridian War, was videoed from the start to the finish. Each and every massive Warhead detonation on Eros's surface was captured in all of its horrific detail. The streams of escaping atmosphere and water were likewise captured, signifying the death of Eros, the World within the Rock. Communication lines began buzzing with concerned citizens urgently reporting the disaster. And for every citizen jumping on their communicator to report the atrocity, there were ten others frozen in abject disbelief and pure shock. Eros, a world had just died!

Within minutes, the news was spreading and the tranquil Eros feed quickly went viral. The news spread like a bush fire and soon the video feed became the most watched video in Human history! Within the hour, the news had spread across the entire inner solar system. Before the day was out, the news had spread to every known corner of the entire solar system. The one place this video feed was not seen was on the internal news feeds of the Six Jovian Realms, where it was completely blocked and fire-walled, only allowed to be watched by those in power.

Connor Dumas and his Wife, Carmelita Dumas, nee Alvarez, had both watched in horror. In their shared office, Eros was rotating endlessly in space, running on the office's main wall screen. It was serene and tranquil, then all of a sudden, immense bursts of blue white light, eight in all, every twenty five seconds. Eight bursts, each forty-five degrees apart, each scorching a segment of Eros's crust, no doubt causing deep crustal fracturing.

Connor Dumas did not wait, he was on his intercom within seconds, "Daniel, you and Harmony need to get over to my office asap", there was no reply.

The office door opened unannounced and Daniel Dumas and his Wife, Harmony Dumas, nee Moon, entered, "Have you seen it?", Daniel enquired.

Connor pointed to the wall screen and Daniel nodded, noting, "We have it playing on ours as well."

Connor noted dryly, "That, my dear, Brother, is Godric Horridian's proportionate response to his own false flag bullshit!"

"What can we do?", Carmelita asked with her strong Brazilian Portuguese accent and her face carrying a horrified look upon it, her Sister-in-law, Harmony, had that very same look.

"From here, not a lot", Connor admitted, adding as he watched the video feed, "Eros's crust will be breached in multiple places. There'll be cracks everywhere. By the time our rescue ships get there, it will be far too late."

"Even from our Earth Trojan Mining Corporation", Daniel added, it was not a question, it was just a very sad fact.

"They are all going to asphyxiate, aren't they?", Harmony questioned.

"Yes, Harmony. Eros's atmosphere is going to bleed out into space and it won't take that long either", Connor replied, informing her, "Even if we could get ships to them, there's just no way to evacuate six and a half million people."

"No time and not enough ships", Harmony nodded, summing up the problem.

"Nowhere near enough time and nowhere near enough ships, honey", her Husband, Daniel, corrected, noting, "What we are looking at is a catastrophic, worst-case failure scenario. There is no contingency plan for this kind of situation. The designers of Eros simply did not consider Nuclear War to be a plausible scenario."

"In their defence, Daniel. When Eros was built, Nuclear weapons had been banned and eliminated", Connor responded, noting, "War, Nuclear or otherwise, was meant to be a thing of the past."

"I remember Dad telling us about the Great Disaster of forty two", Daniel told his Brother.

Daniel was referring to the Mimasian War, which the Council of Shadows had buried under the collective Human trauma of the day, rewriting memories and altering history until it was remembered as the Great Disaster. A series of interstellar micrometeor swarms and the damage they caused.

Connor nodded, "I remember as well, Daniel. No one is going to get out of Eros, even with the ships inside their docks. And no rescuers are going to be able to get in either. Eros is now one sealed but very leaky bottle", he noted, his face displaying a grim look.

Carmelita didn't understand, "Why, Connor? If they have ships in their docks, surely, some people will manage to escape."

"Carmelita, honey, Eros has a dock at both ends and they are both going to be locked in place and completely non-operational", Connor explained.

"How can you be so sure, Connor?", Carmelita enquired, she still held out hope for survivors.

Daniel chimed in and explained, "Our Grandfather, Stuart, his company, Earth Trojan Mining Corporation, was contracted to shape Eros's exterior and hollow out its interior, forming a huge cylindrical space. After that, the outer crust and inner crust were vitrified, glassed, to give Eros structural integrity and impermeability. It was a major project and our family was heavily involved."

Connor continued, picking up at a later point in history, "After the Great Disaster of forty-two, Eros was badly damaged. Not breached, but damaged nonetheless. Our Grandfather, Stuart, personally financed the repairs. Our Father, Baron, signed off on all of the expenses himself. The biggest issue was Eros's docks. We are talking about two massive hubs. Each one is a disk a kilometre across and one kilometre in depth. They sit in receptacles at each end of Eros. As Eros rotates, those giant docking hubs remain stationary."

Harmony understood, she had a good handle on Eros's history. Carmelita, not so much.

Daniel stepped back in, "The shockwaves from those detonations will have destabilised the hubs. They will have scraped against their receptacles and friction-welded themselves in place. Add in the vibrational resonances from each of the blasts and we can expect the six external docking hubs to be trashed along with the far larger internal docking bays. Each hub has six huge petal-shaped doors to the internal docking bays and they will likely be non-functional as well. They will all be locked in place."

"What Daniel is trying to say is, we've seen this before. No one will be getting in and no one will be getting out. And to make matters worse, the Erosians will be long dead before help can even get there", Connor concluded.

"We can't just do nothing, Connor. We must try something. At least try something", Carmelita insisted, enquiring, "How long will it take to fix those docking hubs?"

Connor looked to his Brother, Daniel, who replied, rubbing his chin, "The last time. Both hubs had to be pulled out. Both of the hubs and their receptacles had to be repaired. The whole process to nearly five years for each hub. It is a huge job, Carmelita."

Carmelita sat down in despair and Harmony told her, "I'm doing the only thing we can do, Carmelita. I'm sending instructions to our Earth Trojan Mining Corporation to provide all and any assistance. What they can do, they will do. Although I don't hold out much hope."

Harmony gestured toward the wall screen. Jets of air and water were escaping from Eros. The jets were becoming visible around each of the blast zones on Eros's surface. The air was leaking out, the water was leaking out and time itself was running out.

Carmelita's eyes widened in horror and she turned away from the screen. She grabbed hold of Connor and held on as if for dear life. Daniel responded automatically and shut off the screen. It was all far too much to watch.

Connor looked at his Brother, Daniel and then he looked at his Brother's Wife, Harmony and then he looked at his own Wife, Carmelita, and then he stated, "We cannot let Godric Horridian get away with this. He has destroyed an entire world. That is a crime against Humanity, yes, but it is also a crime against life and nature itself. His crimes cannot go unanswered."

"Agreed, Connor. We cannot let this stand", Daniel agreed entirely with his Brother.

"I know what you're thinking, Connor", Harmony noted, "You want that man to swing from a rope."

"Oh, I want more than that, Harmony. I want to throw the full might of our Corporate Empire behind our government. Whatever our government needs, we will provide it", Connor explained.

"Finances, Resources, Manufacturing, Research and Development. The whole enchilada", Daniel agreed, adding, "No half measures. Godric Horridian and his regime are going down."

"Agreed", Connor replied.

"Agreed, let's do this", Harmony replied

"Agreed", Carmelita replied, adding, "Let us make that punheta bastardo pay!", and then she flicked her fiery red hair.

Connor pressed a button on his intercom, "Shelly, could you come into our office, please and bring your data tablet? We need to send an urgent email to President Reinhardt. We have a proposition to offer him."

"Yes, Sir. I'll be in straight away", Connor's and Carmelita's personal assistant, Ms Shelly Shiraz, replied.

Sone Talleyrand, nee Dharma, watched the news feed showing the destruction of Eros for the sixth time. Her eyes welled with tears and freely flowed. To Sone, this was personal, she had friends and family inside Eros. Now they were all gone. Sone's Husband, Dag, sat quietly watching the video, he, too, had cried at the destruction of Eros, now, however, he was all cried out.

Sone had once been the Security Council of Sol's liaison to the Colonisation Committee. Now, however, she was the Erosian Ambassador to the Belters, stationed at Ceres and residing in the Ceresian twin-cylinder colony, *"Eros can have it"*. An Erosian Ambassador without a world.

Dag had once been the Erosian Diplomat and Emissary to Eros and had attended a critical Althing Assembly at Ceres Central Command. Now, Dag was the manager of the Belter's Three Irons Strategy with regards to future Belter power generation and the manager of the Belter's Radioactive Waste Management and Disposal. Dag wore two very important hats.

Both Sone and Dag had friends, colleagues and family back in Eros and now they would all be dead. When they'd seen the streams and jets of air and water leaking out of Eros, they both knew it would not be long before every Erosian inhabitant was gone. Asphyxiation! It sounded like a horrible way to go. They both understood that there would be no hope!

Dag was cradling their young Son, Carter, in his arms, wondering why this tragedy was happening. It was truly horrible! It made no sense! They both realised that had they not emigrated to Ceres, they too would have been dead!

And the irony of it all, they lived in a colony named *"Eros can have it"*, as a rebuke to Erosian oversight, to Erosian jurisdiction and now, Eros was no more.

The communicator buzzed and Dag left the room to take the call. Sone had just started replaying the news feed back for the seventh time. When Dag took the call, he found the Ceresian Administrator, Harlequin Moon, his friend, on the other end, calling from the Ceres Central Command colony.

"We've been watching the news feeds, Dag. Our condolences for your loss. How are you both coping?", Harlequin enquired.

Still cradling his Son, Carter, Dag replied, "Well, as good as we can, I guess. I mean, I lost my parents and my siblings in Eros, but Sone, she's lost her entire extended family. Parents, Grandparents, Aunts, Uncles, Siblings, Cousins, Great Grandparents, Second Cousins, you name it. They're all gone! Sone's the only one left. She's lost everyone and everything! I have no idea what to do."

Harlequin replied, he was shocked but not surprised, "That's devastating", and then he asked, "Is Sone okay? I mean, how is she coping?"

Dag shook his head, "I don't think Sone's coping at all, Harley. She keeps replaying that video over and over, eyes glued to the screen and she isn't saying a word. She just sits there staring at the screen."

Harlequin looked concerned, "Survivor's guilt!", he noted and then he asked, "Is there anything we can do for you both?"

"Yeah, a couple of things, Harley. I might need a few days off to get my head around all of this", Dag requested, noting, "I'm supposed to be the strong one, you know, there for Sone and little Carter. To be honest, though, I'm barely coping myself."

"Dag, you take as much time off as you need. Look after Sone and little Carter", Harlequin replied.

"One more thing, Harley. Our colony, where we live, is beautiful. With the gardens and parks everywhere. Being heavily underpopulated has its benefits, but it also has its downside", Dag noted, then he got to the point, "We don't have any councillors over here, at least not any trauma or grief councillors. We could seriously do with some help right now."

"I can see how, under the current circumstances, that will be a real problem," Harlequin replied as he turned to his Wife, "Helena, could you track down a counsellor specialising in grief and trauma? The best that we have?" he requested.

Helena came into view, "Sure. I'll get on it straight away, Harley", she replied, before turning to the screen, "You have our condolences, Dag. Both you and Sone."

As Helena disappeared from view to organise a grief and trauma councillor, Harlequin gave Dag some news he'd received from Daniel Dumas. It was a change of topic, yet extremely relevant.

"Dag, Daniel Dumas ordered some scans of that Jovian Moon, Himalia", Harlequin informed him and then he stated, "It was all bullshit, Dag. Every bit of it."

"What do you mean, Harley?", Dag enquired.

"That so-called attack on Ganymede Prime. The interception of the stealth missile by Himalia", Harlequin Moon replied, before explaining, "Himalia was virtually undamaged. A one-hundred-megaton blast should have left a massive crater and its orbit should have been affected. No crater, no change in orbit. That blast had to be a skyburst. There was no missile!"

"No missile!", Dag exclaimed, his grief quickly turned to anger, "So this, this so-called proportionate response was for a lie. A lie that the Horridians perpetrated themselves!"

"Yes, Dag. A false flag operation to justify an atrocity", Harlequin confirmed.

"No! No! No! Those bastards can't be allowed to get away with this", Dag replied as he ran his hand through his hair, "They have to pay!", he shouted.

"And they will, Dag. They will. Daniel and Connor Dumas are furious. They are throwing the full weight of the Dumas Corporation's capabilities behind their government's response", Harlequin Moon replied, adding, "Godric Horridian has seriously miscalculated and I think he knows it as well."

"What makes you say that, Harley?", Dag Talleyrand enquired.
"We, that is all of the Belter Administrators, including myself, of course, have received a communique from Ganymede Prime. From the Jovian Communications Minister", he replied.
"A communique?", Dag questioned.
"That little snot, Godric Horridian, is asking for an alliance with us Belters", Harlequin scoffed, remarking, "He commits genocide and destroys an entire world, and then he has the gall to request an alliance! He actually thinks that we'd agree to let his military use our colonies as Jovian military bases. Use our colonies for refuelling stations and our manufacturing capacity to make his weapons and his ships. The sheer gall of the man! He is a right piece of work, he is!"
Harlequin continued, "We may not have agreed with the Colonisation Committee or the Security Council overreach, but what Godric Horridian has done is unconscionable. To kill an entire world! My God! And then to turn around and ask us to support his madness!"
"What answer did you give them?", Dag queried, his mind turning to curiosity.
"Dag, all of the Administrators have agreed. All trade with the Jovian Realms has immediately ceased. All discussion with the Jovian Realms has immediately

ceased", Harlequin informed him, noting, "We are sending the entire Jovian Realms to Coventry. Every communique they send us will be acknowledged and replied to with a single dot. They are not worth the time or effort to provide anything more. If we could spit into a digital reply to them, we would!"

That was the Belter way.

The President of Cis-Lunar Space, Dieter Reinhardt, held a press conference. He stood at the lectern with Connor Dumas on his right and Daniel Dumas on his left. President Guang Hui of Earth was included via a video link with Earth, her face showing on a large wall screen. The bidirectional delay between Colonial Central Command at Cis-Lunar L-Five was almost three seconds. President Guang Hui was mainly there for solidarity, but also for commentary of her own if required.

President Reinhardt began the press conference, "What Godric Horridian has done is an act of genocide. There is no other way to put it. The destruction of Eros, six and a half million dead, was not just a crime against Humanity, it was a crime against nature, against life itself. To kill an entire ecosystem, an entire world, is an unconscionable atrocity. I can think of no crime nor sin greater", he paused to let his opening sink in.

Dieter Reinhardt continued, he found this part galling, "Godric Horridian has sent us his terms of surrender! That's right, his terms of surrender! He expects us to unconditionally surrender, to bow to his will! Not just us here in Cis-Lunar space, either. The same terms were sent to President Guang Hui of Earth and even President Bradly Klein of Venus. Godric Horridian believes that now that he is a World killer, he can demand our surrender and that we should all bend the knee to him. Godric Horridian has miscalculated. He is wrong, very, very wrong. We do NOT bow down before a tyrant, a World killer! We will NEVER bend the knee!", he then paused once more.

President Reinhardt continued, "After Godric Horridian's pretext for War, the attack on Ganymede Prime that was supposedly prevented by the fortuitous positioning of the Jovian moon, Himalia, the Dumas Corporation's Astro Resources, took new scans of Himalia", he then gestured to Danial Dumas.

Daniel Dumas stepped up to the lectern, "Our latest scans of Himalia revealed very little surface damage. After a one-hundred-megaton blast, we would have expected a major, new crater and even orbital changes. We found neither. No new craters and no orbital changes. Our conclusion. This explosion was a skyburst at an altitude above the Himalian surface of at least twenty five thousand kilometres. In simplest terms, there was NO missile. It was a Horridian false flag operation", and then he stepped back from the lectern.

President Reinhardt took over once more, "Thank you, Daniel. The Horridian's *'proportional'* response", he air quoted the word proportional, "was for an event of their own creation. A false flag operation to create a pretext for War", he paused once more to let that sink in.

"After their pretext, we, President Guang Hui and I, together, began mobilising our armed forces. Our combined resources and manufacturing capacity are being mobilised for the defence of the inner solar system. This Horridian atrocity will not go unanswered! Godric Horridian will rue the day that he perpetrated this genocide. We will be responding with main force!", then he gestured to Connor Dumas.

Connor Dumas stepped up to the lectern, "My Brother and I are placing the entirety of our Dumas Corporate capacity behind our government's response. Our mining resources from the Venusian orbital, Earth orbital and Martian orbital zones. Our financial resources, our manufacturing capacity. Even our research and development capacity. All of it will be placed at the disposal of our Cis-Lunar government. We will not tolerate Horridian tyrants and their demands", then he too stepped back from the lectern.

President Reinhardt took over once more, "Thank you, Connor. Godric Horridian's shock and awe attack and destruction of Eros have not worked out in the way that he thought they would. Godric Horridian's miscalculations are going to bring him down. Our forces are mobilising. The Dumas Corporation's research and development division has provided us with new weapons and ship designs. Both Dumas Colonial Constructions and Himmelstaff Interplanetary Constructions have started building these new weapons and ships. Godric Horridian has started this War and it is a War that he cannot possibly win. Godric Horridian wanted War and now we will give it to him."

There was a short delay and President Guang Hui spoke, it was short and straight to the point, "The Earth stands ready. The Earth stands behind colonies of Cis-Lunar Space and the inner solar system. We have already started our recruitment drive. We have already begun constructing new weapons and ships. This Horridian atrocity will not go unanswered. The Earth is ready to respond. We will NEVER bend the knee to Godric Horridian and his totalitarian cronyism!"

And then the press conference ended. The board was set and the War was enjoined!

A familiar face walked into Swenna Goodchild's office. It was Prime Minister Quintus Malbeck and he had been expected. The Prime Minister was concerned, not only had the Horridian regime killed an entire world, but they were now demanding access to Saturnian shipyards and weapons factories. They were even demanding personnel, literally conscripted troops, to bolster their Jovian Armed Forces. Swenna Goodchild had carefully vetted the Quadripartite Outer Satellite Agreement, the QOSA, before it was signed and Quintus Malbeck needed advice on what their position should be.

"Take a seat, Prime Minister", Swenna greeted, noting, "I take it you're concerned about how far our obligations under the Quadripartite Outer Satellite Agreement extend."

"Yes, Ms Goodchild. I know you've said in the past that it does not include any military support, however, that is precisely what the Horridians are demanding", Prime Minister Malbeck informed her.

"The Horridians have made the same demands of us as they have with the Uranian Federation and the Neptunian Commonwealth, Sir", Swenna informed him, noting, I have already been in contact with my counterparts in the Federation and the Commonwealth, and we are all in agreement. We must have a unified, united front."

Prime Minister Malbeck nodded in reply, as Swenna took a folder out of her right-hand desk drawer and passed it to him, "This is what we've come up with."

Quintus opened up the file as Swenna explained, "The first document is a *'draft'* communique that my contacts and I have come up with. The Federation and the Commonwealth are going to alter it for their purposes while keeping the main points that it contains, precisely the same. You know, give it their own lilt, so to speak. We should do the same. Keep the main points, but put them into our own *'Saturnian Demarchy'* wording, giving it our own lilt. We must all be speaking with the same voice."

Quintus looked up from his perusal of the document, "Ms Goodchild, this is the most strongly worded condemnation I could possibly imagine."

"Yes, Mr Prime Minister, it is. Godric Horridian killed off an entire world and murdered six and a half million people. That was an act of genocide", Swenna reminded him, noting, "If that doesn't deserve the strongest condemnation, then I do not know what does. That draft communique reflects that. We need to let Godric Horridian understand that genocide is completely unacceptable."

Quintus nodded. Swenna was right, it had been an act of genocide and worse, Godric Horridian had now become a world killer.

"Yes. You're right as always, Ms Goodchild", he replied in full agreement.

"And the other documents, Ms Goodchild?", Quintus enquired.

"A *'draft'* copy of our refusal to provide any military assistance whatsoever. Citing references to the relevant sections of the Quadripartite Outer Satellite

Agreement", Swenna replied, explaining, "It points out their unacceptable overreach, especially considering their act of genocide and their false flag pretext. The draft also points to our obligations under the agreement and that we will provide material support and logistical assistance as stipulated and nothing more."

"I see you've included a copy of the agreement with the highlighted sections as well", Quintus noted.

"Yes, Prime Minister, I have", Swenna replied, adding, "Adjust the draft as you see fit, but try not to disturb the main talking points. We need the Horridians to fully understand our position."

"Yes, yes. I'll run these by my Cabinet Ministers and we'll make our own adjustments. Give it our own lilt, as you say", Quintus replied and then noted, "The final copies. I will bring those to you for your perusal and perhaps changes, before I officially send them off."

"Ms Goodchild, these contacts of yours? Your counterparts?", Quintus enquired broadly.

"It's a network of Administrators, Mr Prime Minister", Swenna replied.

"A network of Administrators?", Quintus questioned.

"Yes, Sir, and it goes back a long way", Swenna replied, explaining, "The network is kind of like an old-fashioned phone tree and we all keep in touch at least once a month. Always via tight beam laser comms for secure communications."

"And this *'phone tree'*, who exactly does it involve?", Quintus Malbeck was actually quite curious.

"Well, Prime Minister, as I said, the network goes back a long way", Swenna reiterated before beginning her explanation.

"The network was started by Stuart Dumas when he was building up his business empire", Swenna began, "He developed a fledgling network of administrators and contacts, starting first with Earth and Cis-Lunar Space. Then, as his interests expanded outwards, to Venus and Mars, the network also expanded. The overseer of the Martian terraforming project and administrator of the Aries colony in high Martian orbit, Doctor Gideon Reas, was also a member of the network, right up until he retired. You've probably heard of his name."

"Yes, yes, I have. He was a household name, as was Stuart Dumas", Quintus replied knowingly.

"Well, when the Dumas Corporation started enabling the colonisation of the solar system, the network expanded accordingly. First Ceres and then later, the other twelve sovereign Belter nations. That was followed by Jupiter's leading and trailing Trojan colonies, and then by the former Jovian Republic that was set up by the original Jovian Dream consortium", Swenna continued to explain, adding,

"From the outside looking in, we have contacts with the Neptunian Commonwealth and the Uranian Federation. Five separate contacts with the Federation, in fact."

"Five?", Quintus Malbeck queried.

"Yes, Sir. I have a main contact at their Federal Capital colony, Miranda Central, but I also have contacts at their sovereign State Capitals, Titania Central, Oberon Central, Umbriel Central and Ariel Central. They prefer individual representation. They will also be responding to the Horridian Regime's Erosian atrocity and demands individually as well", Swenna explained.

"You mentioned Jupiter's Trojans and the old Jovian Republic, surely the Horridians would have stamped all of that out", Quintus commented.

"Well, yes, they would, if they knew about them", Swenna replied, explaining, "Himalia Central was the old Capital of the former Jovian Republic. When Albertus Horridian became President back in twenty one forty seven, our contacts took on a low profile. Then, when the capital moved from Himalia Central to Ganymede Prime in twenty one fifty seven, the old capital started to become a backwater. As each new Galilean Prime came online, its population dropped and Himalia Central became a backwater *'niche'* colony. We still have regular contact with them. My contact there has confirmed, one hundred percent, that the detonation at Jupiter's moon, Himalia, was, in fact, a false flag sky burst."

Prime Minister Malbeck nodded and continued, "And the two Jovian Trojan Realms?", he enquired.

"Prime Minister, the Horridians may have annexed Jupiter's Leading and Trailing Trojans into their Jovian Realms, but they still keep in contact with us secretly", Swenna informed him and then she noted, "Sir, the fact that we have contacts in the Jovian Realms, treat that as a state secret. They do have families and if they are discovered by the Horridians, they will all end up on the gallows."

Quintus nodded in understanding.

"Is Mimas a part of this network of yours?", Quintus enquired.

"Yes and no", Swenna replied, "They are only connected to the network through me and my hotline to Mimas. Kind of like an offset node. It is very rare for the Mimasians to reach out to the other nodes."

"Who runs this network? Is there a central node?", Quintus enquired further.

"Well, yes, of course, there is, Prime Minister", Swenna replied in the affirmative, noting, "The central node and central repository is at the Dumas Corporation's Dumas Legal Incorporated Ltd."

"Ms Goodchild, I understand how the Federation and the Commonwealth are going to respond. I've also seen the Earth's and Cis-Lunar Space's response. Do we have an idea of how the Belters are responding?", he asked.

"Yes, we do, Sir", Swenna replied, divulging, "The Horridians made the same demands of the thirteen sovereign Belter Nations that they made of us and more. The Belters were furious. Especially after they'd killed off Eros. They have no defence agreements with them and, yet they had to gall to demand materials support, logistical assistance, manufacturing access, refuelling and even military bases within Belter territory."

"How did the Belters respond to those demands?", Quintus enquired curiously.

"The Administrator of Ceres, Harlequin Moon, tells me that they've cut off all ties with the Jovian Realms. No more trade, no more diplomacy, they've sent them to Coventry. Every overture the Horridians make to them will be replied to with a single dot! Nothing more."

"A single dot?", Quintus looked perplexed.

"Yes. That is the Belter way. They are telling Godric Horridian that he is not worth their time", Swenna concluded.

Godric von Horridian, High Prince of the Six Jovian Realms, was furious. His shock and awe tactics of destroying Eros had failed spectacularly. Godric thought that by perpetrating an atrocity so bad, so horrific, that the inner solar system worlds would all bow down in fear and capitulate to him. Rather than run the risk that he would destroy more colonies with an even greater death toll.

They had not, just the opposite, in fact, they had all galvanised together in opposition to his demands and were doubling down, mobilising and building up their military capabilities. Even the accursed Dumas Family Corporation, the bane of his Grandfather, Albertus, had thrown their full weight behind the call to arms.

The meeting took place in Godric's palace operations room. Godric hated that room, it contained a *"lesser"* throne, still gold-gilded, just not quite as ornate as the one he preferred in his throne room. Prince Emeric was there, seated on his own throne, second to the right. Prince Friederic was present, Godric having demanded his presence and so he'd flown in all the way from Io Prime specifically to be there. He was seated on his throne on Prince Emeric's right. Prince Aluric as usual was not present, the throne immediately on Godric's right was empty.

Godric looked at his Brother's empty throne, "Where is our Brother, Aluric?", the High Prince asked.

Prince Friederic frowned, "Brother, there is no point to his being here", he stated, explaining, "You know his condition. The stress will aggravate him and he will become unmanageable."

Prince Emeric agreed, "Yes, Brother Godric. Our Brother, Aluric, would not be beneficial to our discussions. He is better off at his own palace on Callisto Prime, where he can be managed."

Godric looked towards his Brother, Friederic, "How is our dear Brother's condition?"

Prince Friederic answered cautiously, "Our Brother, Aluric, is stable. I have put in place a novel solution for his condition. One in which he can be managed with minimal medication."

"Please explain", High Prince Godric requested.

"On the advice of his psychoanalyst, I have replaced his Matron of Pleasures with a Dominatrix", Prince Friederic replied matter-of-factly.

"How does that help our Brother exactly, Friederic?", the High Prince enquired.

"Aluric was harming his sex Slaves and his psychoanalyst recommended women who know how to deal with people who are difficult", Prince Friederic explained, noting, "It seems to have worked."

Prince Emeric laughed, "A Dominatrix? How the fuck does that work?"

Prince Friederic explained, "She has hired twelve women, who, like her, know how to handle difficult, troubled people. They are highly skilled and I pay them handsomely. They work in teams of four, taking care of Aluric's needs. His favourite pair, twins actually, go by the professional names of Willy and Nilly when in private. They have nicknamed our Brother, Aluric, Silly and he appears to love it. Willy, Nilly and Silly! When in his throne room and at court, they play the part of Court Harlequins using the personas of Left and Right. They amuse him with jokes and tickle him with feather dusters and fake cat-of-nine tails. It keeps him distracted, especially when they keep switching their personas. I have been told by his psychoanalyst that those two alone keep him happy and under control. The others are more there for show and servicing his other needs."

"Oh my God, Friederic. That is crazy. I have to see that. I could do with some Willy Nilly time and a good spanking as well", Prince Emeric laughed.

"A novel solution, Friederic, but if it is working, then stick with it", High Prince Godric decided.

"It was either that or have our dear Brother, Aluric, heavily medicated", Prince Friederic replied as the operation room's doors opened and the Ministers relevant to the meeting filed in.

Science Minister Peter Patronis led them into the room. He was followed by Defence Minister, Peter Macron, Security Minister, Miles Morton, Commerce Minister, Devlin Dervish, Foreign Affairs Minister, Tarant Durant, Agricultural Minister Mauricio Velly and finally, Communications Minister, Temu Trump. They all filed in and took their seats.

High Prince Godric raised both of his hands into the air, "I've seen that so-called Presidential press conference. So, why are they not capitulating? Why are they not submitting? For fucks sake, we destroyed a whole world. They should all be shitting themselves!"

"Your Majesty, while there was a chance that they would capitulate and surrender, it was always a slim chance with low odds", Science Minister Peter Patronis responded.

"Slim chance? All of you thought it was a great idea when I brought it up", the High Prince replied.

Security Minister, Miles Morton, cautiously replied, "It was a Hail Mary play, Sire. It was either going to succeed or it was not."

Prince Friederic chimed in, "Brother Godric, I did calculate the odds of capitulation at around three percent. What has happened was entirely predictable."

High Prince Godric snorted, "Well, if they can double down, so can we. Full mobilisation starts today. Conscription starts today. They doubled down and now we double down. Simple!"

Prince Friederic quietly frowned inwardly. This was not going to end well.

High Prince Godric spied his Commerce and Agriculture Ministers sitting at the operation room's board table, "Why are you two even here? These are military matters!"

"Sire, there have been developments. Developments relating to recent events", Agricultural Minister, Mauricio Velly replied, not naming the atrocity that murdered six and a half million people.

"Right, recent events. I wonder what they could be?", High Prince Godric replied rhetorically and then asked, "What developments?"

"The Belters have cancelled all of their food purchase contracts. Every Belter nation, Sire", Mauricio Velly informed him.

Before High Prince Godric could answer, Commerce Minister Devlin Dervish chimed in, "Sire. It is not just agricultural contracts. The Belters have cancelled all contracts with our Jovian Realms. All of them, Sir! Every single one. Their smugglers won't even deal with us, Sire!"

"Tarant, you're our Foreign Affairs Minister. What do you make of this?", the High Prince asked.

"Sire. We sent off your communique requesting Belter's aid. Military bases, refuelling stations, use of their manufacturing facilities, Sire", Minister Tarant Durant reminded him.

"Yes, I do remember that, Minister Tarant", the High Prince replied.

Foreign Affairs Minister Durant got up from his seat and approached the High Prince, "They all responded with this, Sir", he held out a printout.

High Prince Godric looked at the reply of the printed communication, "What is this? There's nothing here! Just a full stop!"

Communication Minister, Temu Trump, closed his eyes and sighed. It was an audible sigh.

"What do you know, Temu?", High Prince Godric demanded.

"If I might see that document, Sire?", Temu Trump requested.

The High Prince passed the document back to his Foreign Affairs Minister, who then passed it to Temu Trump, the Communications Minister.

Temu read through the document and then he explained the situation, "Your Majesty. We destroyed Eros, which caused six and a half million deaths. Most of our adversaries classify that as genocide. However, that is not my point. We then sent the Belters, all of them, a demand for military bases, refuelling stations, manufacturing plant access, material resources and logistical assistance. Sire, we did not ask, Minister Durant demanded these things of the Belters and they have taken umbridge."

"What does that mean, Temu?", High Prince Godric enquired.

"The Belters are outraged with us, both our attack on Eros and our demands. Sire, the Belters have cut all ties with the Jovian Realms. That full stop, that dot, means that in the Belter's eyes, we are not worthy of their words. Sire, they have ostracised us", Temu interpreted.

"Tarant! We demanded those things of the Belters?", the High Prince questioned.

"Yes. Sire. Your Majesty, these demands were written in exactly the same vein as the ones we made of our allies in the Quadripartite Outer Satellite Agreement. You said yourself, Sire, *'The Jovian Realms demand and all others comply'*, and that, that was the Jovian way", Minister Durant replied, his hands were shaking.

High Prince Godric responded with the realisation, "Shit! I did say that, didn't I?"

"So, speaking of the Quadripartite Outer Satellite Agreement, what have our allies said concerning our needs?", High Prince Godric asked.

Foreign Minister Tarant Durant passed his folder to Temu Trump, "Please, Temu", he whispered with urgency, "I can't!"

Communications Minister, Temu Trump frowned and then he took up the folder and opened it up, "Your Majesty, if you can please give me a moment to familiarise myself with these documents."

"Granted, Temu", the High Prince replied.

After a few minutes, Temu began his assessment, "Your Majesty, we have received seven official letters of condemnation from the Demarchy, the Federation and the Commonwealth. All very strongly worded and accusing us of genocide and mass murder. Crimes against Humanity, Sire."

"Seven? We only have three allies, Temu?", High Prince Godric queried.

"Yes, Sire. We have received one letter each from the Saturnian Demarchy and the Neptunian Commonwealth, but we have received five from the Uranian Federation. One from their Federal Polity and one from each of their sovereign States."

Temu got up from his seat and passed the seven documents to the High Prince, who, upon reading them, seemed more amused than anything else.

Temu noted, "Sire. If I did not know any better, I'd be inclined to think that there was only one original draft letter. All of the key talking points are identical, just reworded differently."

"Okay, so, what about our *'request'* for military assistance, weapons, ships, personnel?", High Prince Godric asked, with a chuckle and air quoting each request.

Temu read through the second set of documents and checked with their cross-referencing of the Quadripartite Outer Satellite Agreement. Temu sighed audibly once more.

"Your Majesty, under our Quadripartite Outer Satellite Agreement, our allies are all in agreement on one thing and one thing only. They are all refusing to give us any military support whatsoever. They are all accusing us of making this agreement knowing that we were going to start a disastrous War and drag them into it. They are stating that they will only comply with the letter of our agreement. That means material support and logistical assistance only. Nothing more."

"Well then, that could be a problem, Temu. The Belters saying no is one thing, but I was kind of hoping our allies would acquiesce to our wishes", the High

Prince replied.

Prince Friederic noted, "Brother, I told you this would happen. The Earth and Cis-Lunar Space can outproduce us twenty five times over and that was without the Dumas Corporate Empire behind them. Add the Dumas Corporation into the mix and it becomes thirty five times over."

"I know that, Friederic, I know that!", the High Prince snapped back, his demeanour changed.

Defence Minister Peter Macron chimed in, "Sire, we do have two advantages."

"What would they be, Minister Macron?", High Prince Godric asked.

"First, Sire, our military, our armed forces, are more fully developed, with the latest weapons. Second, we are higher up in the gravity well. It costs us significantly less energy to attack them than it does for them to attack us", Peter Macron explained.

High Prince Godric looked to his youngest Brother, "Friederic. Your take."

"Godric, yes, we do have those two advantages. Earth and Cis-Lunar Space will be playing catch up and being higher in the gravity well is an advantage", Prince Friederic agreed, then he frowned, "In the end, it will not save us, Brother. They will catch up, they will surpass us and we will lose. It is only a matter of time. I warned of this previously, Brother."

The High Prince shook his head, "No, Brother Friederic, I refuse to accept that!", he snapped back.

Temu Trump was reading one of the documents from the Uranian Federation. It was different from all of the others and it stood alone for its content.

"Temu! What's that document you have there?", High Prince Godric enquired.

"This, Sire. It is nothing. A minor thing", Temu lied.

"Give it here, Temu? I'll be the one to judge that", the High Prince replied.

Temu passed the document to High Prince Godric. It was an odd document with a large black image in the centre that looked like a large black dot and yet it was not completely black. It had some small sections of white within it. There was writing on the back page.

"What is this, Temu?", Godric von Horridian asked.

"It's a black dot, Sire", Temu replied.

"I can see that, Temu, but why?", Godric von Horridian queried.

"That black dot is made up of a series of words all written around and around in a circular spiral, over and over until they almost merge together, unreadable. The effect is that dot image you see on that page, Sire", Temu Trump explained.

"And these words on the back of the page, they are the words inside of that dot, yes?", Godric von Horridian enquired curiously.

"Yes, Sire, but please do not read them. It is a curse, a fourth-generational curse from Hecate Moon, Governor of the Uranian Federation Sovereign State of Oberon", Temu Trump warned him.

"Moon? What is a Moon doing in the Uranian Federation?", Godric von Horridian asked.

"Sire, there a members of the Moon family right across the entire solar system", Temu Trump replied, advising, "Please, Sire! Do not read that curse!"

"Don't be stupid, Temu. It's just superstitious nonsense", Godric von Horridian replied and then he began to read.

Godric von Horridian.
May thou be measured and thy measure taken.
May thy measure be spat upon, pissed upon and shat upon.
May thy measure be cast low into the vilest of pits, the foulest of fens and deepest of bogs.
May thy measure wither and rot.
May the foulest shades, the vilest phantasms and the wildest wights harass and take thee.
May thy seed fail you and so too, the seed of thy offspring.
May this come to pass for you and yours, until the fourth generation of your descendants.
Rot. Rot. Rot.
Thrice over and from thrice levels above thee.
The mundane, the faerie and the gods!
So mote it be!

"All that worry over nothing, Temu, over meaningless words", Godric von Horridian chided.

Prince Emeric brought his feet up onto his throne and then wrapped his arms around his legs, thinking to himself, *"Why did you read that curse, Brother? Why did you read that curse?"*

18. The Horrors That Befell Them.

The colonies in Earth's Leading and Trailing Trojan points consisted of six O'Neil-style twin-cylinder colonies at each point. These were set in mid-halo orbits around each Trojan point's sweet spot. The points that contained accumulated asteroidal mining masses. The Dumas Corporation's Earth Trojan Mining Corporation used these accumulated asteroidal masses for valuable resources extraction.

That, of course, meant that all six colonies at each of Earth's Trojan points were corporate colonies, owned by the Dumas Incorporated umbrella corporation. This same pattern was repeated at both the Venusian and the Martian Trojan points as well. Valuable space real estate for resource extraction.

Earth's trailing Trojan point was, of course, slightly different, as it was where Eros, the city and the world within the rock, orbited, in its own high-halo orbit. Under normal circumstances, it would be Eros sending out the emergency service spaceships and teams. These, however, were not normal circumstances, as Eros itself had been targeted with a fatal military nuclear missile attack!

Each of the six colonies in Earth's Trailing Trojan zone had only two emergency vehicles, one per colony cylinder. When the Administrator of the Earth Trojan Mining Corporation's Trailing Branch, was instructed to provide Eros with all and any assistance possible, they went straight to work. All twelve emergency spacecraft were immediately dispatched to Eros, each with a six-man emergency team. There was not much more that could be done. Emergency ships from Earth were nearly six weeks away and from the Earth's Leading Trojan point, twice that.

One might consider this to be Humanity's hubris, twin-cylinder colonies with only one emergency services vehicle per cylinder, but they were frontier mining outposts in deep space. Mining zones where the mining rights had been bought and paid for. Dumas Incorporated Industries, expanding Humanity's reach into deep space and living on the raggedy edge of existence in the *"cruel"* void, with ruthless operators like the Horridians farther out in the gravity well. The high ground of the void.

"Calling all Earth Trojan Mining, Trailing Zone, Emergency Response Vessels. Lead Captain Julian Whitaker speaking. Emergency service ships Eta through Mu and proceed to Eros's Northern Docking Hub. Emergency service ships Alpha through Zeta are to proceed to Eros's Southern Docking Hub", Lead Captain Julian Whitaker instructed, explaining, "We'll start with the External Docking Ports. There are six at each hub. Divide up and scan all docked ships for signs of life. It is possible that some Erosians made their way to the docked ships. If they did, they'll have air and water, although a limited supply of food. After that, we'll make our way inside the hubs and look for signs of life in the interplanetary class ships in the main Main Internal Docking Ports. Report back with your findings at half-hourly intervals."

All of the emergency services ships acknowledged their instructions.

Co-pilot Ethan Ramirez noted, "Julian. The odds are slim. Even if we do find survivors, there won't be many. Not given the sheer scale and size of Eros."

"I know Ethan, I know", Julian Whitaker agreed, then he smiled, it wasn't much of a smile as he exclaimed, "We have to have hope, Ethan!"

What else was there? It was all they had.

Darren Hicks commented, "Captain. The odds of finding survivors in those ships at the external docks are very low. If there were any survivors there, we would have received communications from them. We'd be better off making a beeline for the main international dock. That's where the big interplanetary ships and liners are."

"We still have a chance of finding survivors in the external docks, Darren. Don't discount that", Captain Whitaker replied and then he turned to his co-pilot, Ethan Ramirez, "Explain it to him."

Ethan Ramirez began his explanation, "Darren, those ships at Eros's external docks are all on communications lock. Their comms are all flowing through Eros's communications systems and Eros's communications arrays are all down. So, they can't get any communications out."

"I don't get it. Why can't they just disconnect from Eros and run their communications separately?", Darren enquired.

"That is not how docking systems work, Darren", Ethan replied, elaborating further, "When a ship docks, the docking computer interlocks with the ship's flight navigation systems. It's called DCI. Anyway, the DCI brings the ship in for perfect docking. Millimetre perfect. Once that's done, the docking clamps lock down to hold the ship in place and then the umbilicus extends up to the ship's airlock. If the ship has a cargo airlock, a second cargo umbilicus extends up to that as well. Usually, these are ventral airlocks, but not necessarily so. Once the ship is fully docked, fuel lines and communications lines automatically extend and connect. At that point, the ship is communications locked and all communications are routed through the station. In this case, it just happens to be Eros."

"Ethan, I still don't get it. Surely they can bypass the systems?", Darren responded.

"They can, once the ship is undocked", Ethan replied, explaining further, "The undocking procedure works in reverse. Almost the same. The refuelling lines withdraw, the umbilici descend and the docking clamps release. The communication lines withdraw as the docking clamps release. The communication lines are pretty much the last to disconnect to maintain communications."

"So, that means that all of the docking clamps are still in place. They haven't been released. So all of those ships are still effectively docked and their communications are routed through Eros and its dead communications arrays!", another rescue team member, Samuel Bergman, interjected.

"Bingo, Samuel, that is correct", Ethan replied and then remarked, "Not just the docking clamps either. Likely, every docking system has failed as well. Those enormous space dock hubs that Eros has and they are massive, huge mother fuckers. They will have been destabilised during the attack, ground against their receptacles and friction-welded themselves in place. That will have led to critical failures and a full shutdown situation. There won't be much of anything working in those hubs, except for emergency evacuation procedures and they all lead back inside Eros. When they built Eros, no one expected nuclear strikes and main habitat failure."

"Ethan, I get that part of it, but why do they have to reroute communications through Eros's communications systems in the first place? I simply don't get it", Darren admitted.

"For one, a direct communications link is much faster and more efficient. The second reason, it's a common courtesy. The docked ship gets full access to the station's communication systems and public data networks, all at exceedingly high speeds. Our colonies use exactly the same style of systems, only newer, through almost constant upgrades", Ethan replied.

"A courtesy?", Darren asked curiously, that statement had him baffled.

"Darren. Most of the ships at the external docks are local vessels. They're only capable of flight and communications within a million or so kilometres of Eros. The few that are capable of flying farther afield, say to Cis-Lunar space, still have the same communications limitations. In between Earth Trojan L-Five space and Cis-Lunar space, the ships simply go communications dark."

Another emergency team member, Leon Vasquez, enquired, "So when they're docked at Eros or even our own colonies, for that matter, they have full access to the interplanetary communications network?"

"Precisely, Leon", Ethan confirmed, noting, "Although not completely. Access to the entire inner system's network, yes. However, everything beyond the Asteroid Belt is chargeable. Accessible, yes, but at a cost. That does make sense, I mean, we are talking about hugely expensive long-range communications systems."

Marcus Riggs, who'd been standing at the back quietly listening to the discussion, interjected, "When everything turns to shit, those systems we all rely on, the fucking things work against you."

The southern docking hub came into view and just as Ethan had stated, they were huge, easily a kilometre across and, according to their understanding, a kilometre deep. As they had expected, the huge docking hub, which was supposed to be motionless, was now rotating along with the rest of Eros.

It had, as Ethan had expected, friction-welded itself to its receptacle. In the centre of the docking hub, the main doors to the internal interplanetary docking bays, the six *"petals"*, as they were called, were closed and likely locked firmly in place.

Each of the six Emergency Response Vessels approached its designated external dock. Lead Captain Julian Whitaker guided his ship, Emergency Response Vessel Alpha, to its designated target, Eros's Southern External Docking Complex Alpha. There were four dozen external docking bays in each of the six docking complexes.

Docking Complex Alpha had thirty six ships docked. They varied in size from small ships the size of a large Learjet to larger vessels, space yachts, smaller freight hauliers and even local passenger transport ships. Local traffic in Earth's Trailing Trojan L-Five zone between the six corporate colonies and Eros was usually very busy. Now, every ship that was docked was locked firmly in place.

As Captain Whitaker began scanning the ships for power signatures, Marcus Riggs noted dryly, "The really big ships are inside the main internal docks and they aren't going anywhere. If there are survivors in those ships, they'll have air and water, but they will be running short on food. Captain, we need to get a small team inside the internal docks to assess the situation."

"First things first, Riggs. We have to check for survivors out here. Then we'll put together a plan", Captain Whitaker replied.

Darren Hicks noted, "Thirty six ships, Captain. Just at this docking complex alone. If there are survivors inside them, there could be hundreds."

Samuel Bergman added, "If there are, they have air and water. Food? Not so much!"

Leon Vasquez chimed in, "If we can manually release the docking clamps, they can pull away and fly back to our colonies."

"If, Leon, if", Darren replied, noting, "There are thirty six ships and only six of us."

Marcus Riggs interjected, "And we haven't seen inside the main internal docks!"

Captain Whitaker responded, "Let's not get ahead of ourselves. We'll do our assessment, work by the numbers and do what we can as we can."

Captain Whitaker checked his scans and his eyes began lighting up in hope, "I am picking up power signatures. Guys, every one of these ships is powered up and running. Life support appears to be operational on all of them", he smiled broadly, "That means survivors!"

Co-pilot Ethan Ramirez smiled, "Can we detect life signs?"

"No, not life signs, but power usage, systems online, carbon dioxide scrubbers, water reclamation systems", the Captain replied, adding, "Not people, but signs of life by inference. Systems don't turn themselves on. Someone had to trigger that."

Darren Hick's chimed in, "Map the bays those ships are docked at, Captain. We can land at a nearby docking bay. I'm recommending we suit up and check each ship individually. We can access their main airlocks, tap the inner airlock door loudly and if anyone's face shows up in the airlock door's porthole, we have a winner. For every ship that has survivors inside, we can release the docking clamps manually and free their ships."

Leon Vasquez interjected, "That is a great idea, Darren, but if you don't mind, I am volunteering to get inside the hub itself. I just have to see if there's anyone inside the ships in the internal docking bays. They are mostly large interplanetary ships with porthole windows. I might actually see faces."

Captain Whitaker looked at Vasquez, "We are short on manpower, Vasquez, but you are right. I need to know as well. You will be going into the hub alone. I cannot imagine what horrors you are going to see. Are you sure you can handle it?"

"Captain, whether I can handle what I see or not, it has to be done!", Leon replied, his face fierce with determination.

Captain Whitaker nodded, "So be it. While we are checking the ships here, Vasquez will reconnoitre the hub's interior. I want you to video log everything, Vasquez, everything. At the end of this War, there will be a War crimes tribunal and everything you see will be evidence."

"You can bet I will, Captain. Those Horridian bastardos need to swing at the end of a rope and even then, that is far too good for them!", Leon Vasquez replied angrily, his Brazilian accent showing.

Captain Whitaker flew his Emergency Response Vessel to the nearest suitable docking bay, "We are going to have to do this old school. No DCI. No docking clamps and no umbilicus."

"Aye, Captain", his copilot, Ethan Ramirez, responded, recommending, "Make sure our landing gear touches down on cold, hard steel, Captain. Activating our mag-locks on glassed regolith will be less than useless."

"Thank you for that advice, Ethan. I do know what I'm doing", the Captain replied, shaking his head.

Everyone strapped themselves into their couches in preparation for a touchdown.

Marcus Riggs noted, "We can exit via one of our lateral airlocks, descend via its ladder and connect an external power conduit directly to the docking bay's external umbilicus controls. Power and cycle the umbilicus manually from our ship. That should give us direct access to the interior of the dock."

Captain Whitaker agreed, "Excellent, Riggs. Get onto it straight away once we're touched down. Don't forget to suit up!"

Marcus Riggs smiled and shook his head, "Will do. Thank you for that advice, Captain."

Leon Vasquez noted, "As soon as I'm inside, Captain, I'll reconnoitre the interior docking bays."

Within five minutes of landing, all six crew members had suited up and were ready for external vehicular activity. Lead Captain Julian Whitaker relayed his strategy for their current situation to the other six Emergency Response Vessel Captains at the other external docking complexes on Eros's southern docking hub. This was also relayed to the other six Emergency Response Vessels at the other end of Eros, at its equally huge northern docking hub.

It was quickly agreed upon that any ships showing signs of recent activity would be checked and if any survivors were detected, the docking clamps would be manually released. That would allow the ships to leave for the six Dumas corporate colonies that were only eight hours' space flight away. This was, of course, contingent on the fact that the ships could be flown.

Any ships that could not be flown for whatever reason, perhaps due to the lack of a pilot or the lack of fuel, would have the docking clamps released at a later time. Freight hauliers and tow ships would be requested to tow those ships with their survivors to the safety of the six Dumas corporate colonies. Those ships that could be flown under their own power were given priority.

A single volunteer from each of the six Emergency Response Vessels, including Leon Vasquez, was to venture into the interior docking bay. Once inside, they were to locate any of the larger vessels that contained survivors. As these ships could not leave the interior docks, it was going to create a major problem for rescuing the survivors. Air and water were not the problem, food was. If survivors were located in those ships, food and other necessities would need to be provided from the Dumas corporate colonies. The decision would need to be made. Extract the survivors from the ships or activate and open the internal dock's six *"petals"*, allowing the ships to leave. That was a complete unknown and would need to be determined by Dumas's Earth Trojan Mining Corporation's engineers.

Everyone was instructed to make video recordings of their entire excursion whilst inside Eros's southern docking hub, especially the volunteers. Similar procedures were taking place at the northern end of Eros, at its equally enormous and problematic docking hub. The sheer scale of the operation was daunting. What was found inside the docking hubs and beyond was much, much worse.

Captain Whitaker informed his team, "There's no air in the Docking Hub. So helmets on and keep tabs on your oxygen reserves."

Ethan Ramirez noted, "The system was never meant to fail that way, Captain. The bulkhead doors on either side of the Transit Ring must be open."

"They are, Ethan. The engineers considered Docking Hub breaches, but not the main Habitat", Captain Whitaker confirmed, noting, "If things were the other way around, those bulkhead doors would have closed automatically to protect the main Habitat. The failure was inside the main Habitat itself. The system wouldn't have automatically closed the Transit Ring's bulkhead doors under that circumstance and with all of the people panicking en masse, it wasn't done manually either."

Leon Vasquez noted dryly, "Had they gotten people into the Docking Hubs and closed those bulkhead doors, they could have saved tens of thousands. Even multiple scores of thousands."

Captain Whitaker noted, "That never happened, Leon and that means something very bad must have happened to Eros Central. The Central Citadel must have taken severe damage."

"I'll do a sweep on the internal docks before I make my way into the interior", Leon Vasquez noted, adding, "I should be able to see the Citadel from the spaceport's main hall and observation lounge."

"With the bulkhead doors open, access shouldn't be a problem", Captain Whitaker replied, explaining, "Upon the destabilisation of the Docking Hubs, the Transit Rings and Docking Hubs were designed to come to a full stop with all ingress and egress points in alignment."

Suited up and with helmets on, the crew of Emergency Services Ship Alpha descended into Eros's southern docking hub, via the attached umbilicus. Captain Whitaker stayed behind to coordinate the extravehicular excursion. He kept his suit on and his helmet at the ready, just in case he was needed.

Four of his crew members, Ethan Ramirez, Marcus Riggs, Darren Hicks and Samuel Bergman, had nine docked vessels to check each. They had their work cut out for them. The last member of his crew, Leon Vasquez, had volunteered to reconnoitre the hub's main internal docking bays.

The Captain's second in command, Co-pilot Ethan Ramirez's voice crackled over the intercom, "Captain. We're inside the hub, just barely and there are bodies strewn everywhere. They're all exposed to the vacuum and the process of desiccation is well underway. They'll all be completely mummified within days. We are all recording everything as instructed. It is horrific, Captain. Absolutely horrific!"

Ethan turned to Leon Vasquez, "Leon, you're going deeper into the hub. Give the Captain direct access to your video feed."

"I'm just doing that now, Ethan", Leon replied and then noted, "After I've reconnoitred the internal docks, I'll attempt accessing the interior."

"I want access to all of your video feeds in real-time. All of them", Captain Whitaker instructed.

The crew of the emergency services ship complied, and five windows appeared on the bridge's main screen. Captain Whitaker expanded Leon Vasquez's feed for greater scrutiny. Everything was being recorded as evidence, as a crime against Humanity. A War crime!

Marcus Riggs came across the first ship on his list. The docking bay's umbilicus was still firmly locked in place. Marcus used the umbilicus to access the ship's airlock and he quickly entered. Once inside, he banged as loudly as he could on the inner airlock door and then, in anticipation, switched on the airlock's intercom. At first, nothing happened, so he knocked on the airlock door loudly once again.

A face appeared in the airlock porthole inside the ship. It was a girl's face, a young teenage girl. The face disappeared and was soon replaced by an older face, a man's face.

Marcus pressed the intercom, "Marcus Riggs here. Emergency services from the Earth Trojan Mining colonies."

The man in the porthole replied, "I'm Captain Dean Collins and by damn, are we glad to see you?"

Marcus was completely honest with the man, "Don't be too glad just yet, Captain Collins. There are only four of us in this entire external dock to deal with thirty six ships. Now, Captain, is this ship of yours refuelled and flight worthy?"

Captain Collins blinked, replying, "Why yes, of course it is."

"Okay. Excellent. Now, if I manually release the docking clamps, can you fly this ship to the Earth Trojan Mining colonies?"

"I should be able to, it's only an eight-hour flight", Captain Collins replied, noting, "That was the original plan after the attack when we realised Eros was bleeding out air. We've been trying to reach the dock's maintenance crew, but no one is responding."

Marcus nodded his head, "Sadly, the dock workers are all dead", he informed him and then he added, "Your ship's still on communications lock and Eros's communications arrays are down. Once I've released the docking clamps, you'll have your communications back as well. Make sure you call ahead to let the colonies know you're on your way."

"I'll do that", Captain Collins replied.

"Captain, how many people do you have on board?", Marcus asked curiously.

"Including me, nine. Why?", Captain Collins responded.

"When you call the colonies to give them a heads up, they'll be wanting details", Marcus replied.

"Yes, yes, of course", Captain Collins agreed.

Marcus left the ship's ventral airlock and sealed the outer airlock door. He then descended the umbilicus back into the docking hub to locate the manual release mechanisms. First, Marcus triggered the manual release for the umbilicus and it slowly descended. Then he checked the refuelling line. It was already disconnected and withdrawn, showing a five hundred and twenty five credit bill.

Marcus thought to himself, *"Well, no one is alive to collect that"*, as he quickly cancelled the transaction with an override.

Finally, Marcus triggered the manual release of the docking clamps and there was a clacking sound as they withdrew. The communication line linking the ship to Eros automatically disconnected and retracted at the same time. Slowly, the ship's manoeuvring thrusters pushed it away from the docking bay and then, after a few minutes, its main thrusters ignited, sending it on course to safety.

"Marcus Riggs to Captain Whitaker. Marcus Riggs to Captain Whitaker. One ship with nine survivors on its way to our colonies", Marcus relayed to his Captain.

"Acknowledged, Marcus. Move onto the next ship and let's hope the good luck continues", Captain Whitaker replied.

"Moving on to the next ship, Captain", Marcus acknowledged, thinking to himself, *"One down, eight more to go."*

Things were far better than they'd hoped for. Ethan, Darren and Samuel were having similar results with their list of ships. The ships were all operational, refuelled and there was someone on board who could fly them. All that was required was the manual release of the docking clamps.

When Captain Whitaker checked with the other emergency response ships, he heard similar results. Straight after the attack was over, it appeared anyone inside Eros who had ships at dock made their way straight to them with family, friends and colleagues in tow. They didn't wait to confirm that Eros had been breached. They just went straight to their ships.

The number of survivors varied greatly. Some of the smaller ships had eight to ten people on board and some of the larger ships had as many as two dozen or more. At this one external dock alone, there were well over five hundred survivors. This docking hub had six external docks and was one of two docking hubs. There were going to be thousands of survivors and that was not even taking into account the big internal docks with the interplanetary class vessels.

Captain Whitaker finally had hope that their mission wasn't just to document an atrocity. There were actual survivors and if there were survivors here in an external dock, there had to be far, far more in the much larger internal docks. And then, Leon Vasquez checked in.

"Captain", Leon's comms caught Captain Whitaker's attention, "As you can see from my video feed, there are literally hundreds of dead."

Captain Whitaker had been distracted by the news of the survivors and hadn't noticed, "Sorry, Leon. I've been talking to the other guys. They have found a lot of survivors."

"I'm hoping to find a lot of survivors over here, too, Captain. There are a lot of dead bodies and it does make moving around quite difficult. In some places, I have no choice but to walk over the dead", Leon Vasquez painted a grim picture for the Captain, "However, I have accessed the flight scheduling computers. There were liners with passengers still on board when the attack occurred and other liners in the process of boarding. There is a good chance that those passengers are all still on board. Other liners that had offloaded their passengers already may have taken them back on board for safety reasons. We may have thousands of passengers alive here in the internal docks."

"That's great news, Leon. Can you get confirmation?", Captain Whitaker asked, completely ignoring the clear video of corpses lying everywhere around Leon, some two and three layers deep.

One had to focus on the living. The dead could not be helped. One could only avert one's eye.

"I have people from our other emergency response ships with me, Captain. We are just about to check the ships themselves", Leon replied, "And Captain, if we do have thousands of survivors in these internal docks, that is going to pose us with serious problemas. Logistical problemas."

"Yes, of course, it will, Leon. I'll get my head around it. Leon, you confirm the situation and get me some numbers. I'll take it from there", Captain Whitaker replied.

Before Leon signed off, he noted, "And Captain, one of our colleagues from our other emergency response ships has already tried to open the petals. That's a no-go. The six doors to the internal docks are firmly locked in place. They are not budging. So no one is flying out of these internal docks."

While Leon Vasquez went back to reconnoitring and assessing the internal docks, Captain Whitaker sent a communique to the Earth Trojan Mining Corporation's administrator in the Trailing zone.

"Administrator Zurine Zilfary. Earth Trojan Mining Corporation's Trailing Zone. There are possibly thousands of survivors trapped inside interplanetary liners within the main internal docks. The internal dock's main doors, the *'petals'*, are non-operational. Questions for our engineers: Can the *'petals'* be forced open? Space tugs perhaps? Interplanetary liner flight to safety is preferable. Or do we need to extract survivors using space suits and externally docked transports? A logistical nightmare that we should avoid if possible. Note: Our emergency response team members have documented hundreds, perhaps thousands, of dead Erosians. The interior main habitat penetration, inspection and assessment have not yet been made. More details pending further discovery. Lead Captain Julian Whitaker."

Captain Whitaker sent off the communique, knowing he would not get a response for several hours and in the meantime, he and his teams would be gathering further information to send to the Earth Trojan Mining Administrator. It was becoming a *"waiting"* game for Julian Whitaker and there were far worse horrors yet to come.

Three hours later, Leon Vasquez contacted Captain Whitaker, "Captain. I have some good news and some bad news. Which would you like to hear first?"

"Good news, Leon. It's always best to start with the good news", Captain Whitaker replied.

"We have dozens of crafts in the inner docks. Everything from big space yachts to massive freight hauliers to interplanetary liners. We even have ships in here that I'm not sure how to classify. The thing is, we have identified well over twelve thousand survivors and we are still counting, Captain!"

"Twelve thousand?", the Captain questioned.

"Yes, Captain. Over twelve thousand", Leon confirmed and then he noted, "They all have carbon dioxide scrubbers and water reclamation systems. So, air and water are not a problem. What they need is food and a lot of it. Processed food. You know, tinned food, canned food, protein bars, MRE packs and fresh fruit. We will need food shipments from our mining colonies. Enough for twelve thousand people for at least a month."

"For a month?", Captain Whitaker queried.

Leon explained, "Try as we might, we cannot get those damnable petals to open. They are effing huge and locked in place. We may have to evacuate the survivors the old way, with spacesuits and emergency transports. That is the bad news, Captain."

Captain Whitaker pinched the bridge of his nose, "Then we'll need to double those figures. The odds are that what we have here will be the same at the Northern Docking Hub. I'll have to check in with them, but I suspect they'll be in the same boat."

Leon Vasquez nodded, replying, "Captain, that is highly likely. The good news is that we have a lot of survivors. The bad news is that we cannot easily extract them and we do not have the logistics in place to feed them either."

"I'll contact Administrator Zilfary and give her a heads up. We need a solution sooner rather than later", Captain Whitaker agreed, noting, "Let's hope our engineers can come up with a way to open those bloody petals."

Leon nodded once more, "While you're doing that, Captain, we will refill our oxygen reserves and a few of us will try to access the main habitat. We need to get eyes on the interior to start recording the damage and get a feel for the situation in there. I'm not looking forward to it, though. In the rush to get out, there was a panic-driven exodus event and a lot of people got stampeded and crushed underfoot. The bodies are four, five and six deep in some places and we really do not like clambering over them and walking on them. We really don't. They are all desiccated and crunching under our boots!"

"What's the alternative, Leon?", Captain Whitaker asked rhetorically while raising his hands in the air, "Respectfully moving the bodies aside. You'll be at that for weeks and this is a time-critical operation. As you said, we need eyes on the interior. We cannot help the dead, but we may yet save the living. There is no choice in the matter."

Leon nodded again, replying, "When those Horridian bastardos are captured, I hope they pick me for jury duty. I will send them all to hell!"

Leon signed off and Captain Whitaker placed his elbows onto the workstation in front of him. He sank his face into his hands. Try as he might, he could not get the image of the victim's bodies, piled four, five and six deep, out of his mind. Captain Whitaker raised his head and shook it. He was here on the bridge of their emergency response ship, ordering his men to clamber and walk over the dead!

How the hell were his men handling these horrors when they were at the very coal face, in the thick of all of that vacuum-sealed death?

The void is like a vampire, it sucks the life out of the living and then the very essence of life, the very juices out of the dead.

Leon Vasquez and two other emergency response team members, Miriam Delmarva and Dean Morrison, from two other emergency response ships ventured deeper into the Southern Docking Hub. Their target was the Southern Spaceport's Concourse and beyond that the Spaceport's Great Hall.

A vast open space, with restaurants and gift shops at its outer extremities. It was there that the main elevators were, which were used to take travellers to the inner surface of Eros. It was also where access to the spaceport's hover bus terminus and hover taxi ranks was. In the very centre of the Hall was a large bronze statue of the late, great, Stuart Dumas, a philanthropist. The man who financed the repairs of Eros's Docking Hubs, some forty years earlier, after the Great Disaster.

When Leon and his companions reached the Transit Ring, both bulkhead doors were wide open as they had expected. Apart from the piles of corpses that they were walking on and clambering over, there was a clear path to the other side of the Transit Ring. Leon Vasquez had been to Eros before. He knew how the Transit Ring was meant to work.

"If it had been the Docking Hub that was breached, these bulkhead doors would have automatically closed to protect the main habitat", Leon informed the others, "Then the Docking Hub would have been evacuated via its secondary access points and airlocks."

"Yeah, but it was the main habitat that was breached", Miriam pointed out.

"Which is why these damned things are still open. A breach of the main habitat was considered to be impossible. Eros does have a one-kilometre-thick crust, all vitrified and glassed. They never took into account a thermonuclear attack with multiple warheads", Leon explained and then he noted, "The Transit Ring and Docking Hub were designed to line up with the main habitat upon failure. Otherwise, we'd be looking for those secondary access points and I have no idea where they are."

Dean Morrison had the jitters, he'd walked and clambered over victim's bodies and there were even more ahead of him, "So many bodies. All I can see is more and more bodies everywhere", he mumbled.

"Vasquez to Captain Whitaker. We are entering the Transit Ring. We will keep you posted", Leon reported back to Julian Whitaker.

"All go on Transit Ring ingress, Leon. I have your video feed in front of me and I'm recording all video feeds", Captain Whitaker replied.

The trio entered the Transit ring and traversed its length, the cracking of dried bone and crunching of desiccated flesh being felt through the spacesuit's over-boots. One hundred metres later, the trio stood before the Southern Spaceport's Concourse. The vast open space sprawled out before them. It was deep with desiccating corpses slowly becoming mummified in the airless space. There were thousands upon thousands of corpses, even here in this vast space and they would have to trample over the dead.

Leon pointed to his far left, "Over there, that's where the elevators to the inner surface are. I expect they'll be packed with victims as well", and then he pointed to his far right, "That's where the access to the Spaceport's hover-bus station and hover taxi ranks are."

As Leon pointed out, Miriam and Dean followed his gaze. Along both far walls, in front of the elevators and transport access, were food stalls, restaurants and gift shops, an eerie sight surrounded by all of the dead.

Leon pointed to the tall, bronze statue in the very centre of the concourse, "That was Stuart Dumas, the founder of the Dumas Incorporated Industries business empire. He was a true philanthropist. Stuart Dumas financed all of the repairs to Eros's Docking Hubs after the Great Disaster of twenty one forty two out of his own pocket", he announced.

Leon then pointed to the far side of the Great Hall, "Over there is the Southern Sky High Restaurant, behind which is the main observation lounge and deck. We can video the entire interior of Eros from that one vantage point. Make sure your cameras are set to their highest definition and maximum resolution. We want as much detail as we can get. It was an incredibly beautiful view the last time I was here. I have no idea what it's going to look like now", he finished honestly.

Dean Morrison mumbled incoherently, "So many bodies. So many dead. I can't even see the floor. There's death all around us, everywhere, we are walking on the dead. Where's the fucking flour?"

"That is what happens with scores of thousands of people trying to flee and end up in a bottleneck, Dean. The first get through and then the next get trampled underfoot. Then, more crowd in, then, more get trampled underfoot and it repeats and repeats until all of the air is gone", Leon explained, his face grim and then he commented, gesturing, "This is the result of sheer, uncontrolled mass panic!"

As if to make the vista before even more grim, several bodies only fifty feet away lifted several feet into the air before collapsing back down again.

Dean Morrison screamed, "What the fuck! Someone's alive under there. They're trying to get up!"

Miriam grabbed Dean and spun him around, "Dean! Dean! Get a grip! It's just a pocket of bodily fluids explosively sublimating into the vacuum. There is no one, no one alive out there!"

"Miriam is right, Dean. We are standing in a vacuum. No one out there is alive", Leon agreed and then with grim determination, "Let us just get over to that observation deck."

"No! No! Fuck No! Fuck that! I'm not going any further! I can't. I simply can't", Dean Morrison shouted, continuing, "I can't trample over the dead anymore. I simply can't. I won't do it, I tell you!"

Leon changed his comms frequency and reported back to Captain Whitaker, "Captain. Dean Morrison is tapping out. He's emotionally and psychologically spent. I'll have Miriam Delmarva lead him back to the internal docking bays. Have some of our people meet them when they arrive. He needs to be taken back to his ship as a matter of urgency."

"Copy that, Leon. I saw his outburst on your video feed. I'll make the arrangements straight away", Captain Whitaker replied, noting, "Leon. Dean is not the first. There have been others."

That was the toll to be paid for walking over the dead, a deep psychological scarring.

Leon switched his comms frequency back and gave out some instructions, "Miriam, take Dean back to the internal docking bays. Dean, you're going back to your ship. Miriam will help you, okay."

Dean nodded, but he didn't say a word. He was overwhelmed with a combination of grief, horror, dread and shame. All he could think of was getting the hell out of there.

"What about you, Leon?", Miriam questioned with concern.

"I have a mission to complete, Miriam. Just get Dean back to his ship. Our people will meet you both when you arrive", Leon explained.

Miriam nodded and then began leading Dean away from the southern spaceport's concourse and all of its horrors. Her own mind was also beginning to turn inward and away from all of the horrors she'd witnessed. How anyone could complete such a mission was now unfathomable to her.

Leon watched as Miriam led Dean back across the Transit Ring corridor. He waited until they'd fully crossed and then, with grim determination, he turned around and began clambering over the bodies once more. This time towards the main observation lounge and deck. They needed eyes on the interior of Eros and Leon would not stop until that task was completed.

The bodies in the concourse and the great hall were layered deeper than in the docking hub. They squished underfoot, more than cracking and crunching. No doubt that would change over the coming days as they continued to desiccate and mummify. More bodies rose and fell as bodily fluids sublimated violently into the vacuum. The vacuum vampire was extracting their juices to the fullest.

Tears began streaming down Leon Vasquez's face. He was not immune to the horrors. He simply pushed on to complete the mission. Document the atrocity, create an evidentiary video, something to be used to bring those Horridian bastardos to justice. Leon Vasquez owed the victims, both the living and the dead, that much. It had to be done and he had to succeed! There was no turning back, no stopping!

Leon Vasquez reached the observation deck and made his way to one of the special points along it. It was all aluminumised glass and gave the viewer a complete view of the interior of Eros. From beneath one's feet, to either side, above one's head and all the way out into the distance. Eros's automatic systems were all still functioning. Its artificial plasma ball Sun still rose in the north, traversed the Erosian skies and set in the south, only to repeat once more twelve hours later. Only now it illuminated a dead world, a world so different to what once was, that Leon's very heart wept.

As Leon stepped out onto the viewing platform, he checked that his main camera was on its highest definition and maximum resolution.

Leon wondered to himself, was there some other half-mad bastardos at the northern end of Eros, performing the same task that he was, documenting the atrocity from the other end of Eros?

Leon did not know. For all he knew, it was only him. Perhaps, just perhaps, only he was crazy enough to be there, recording all of those things that those Horridian bastardos had destroyed.

Leon slowly panned his camera in every direction, capturing the vista below his feet. Moving his camera counterclockwise, Leon carefully captured everything in a broad circle around the southern end mountains. Then Leon started recording the interior of Eros itself, working the camera in a clockwise spiral that culminated on the Citadel in the very heart of Eros, Eros Central.

The artificial Erosian southern long and short artificial seas, which began a mere two miles away from the southern end mountains, held no water. Their sea basins were dry and parched. The thick forests of the southern end mountains and the low mountains in between the seas were all dead. The crop fields, the orchards and the vineyards in the gradually sloping plains were all dead.

Eros Central, the Citadel, that once stood majestically at the confluence of the long seas and the central circular sea, the sea beds all dry and parched. The once proud Citadel, a metropolis of half a million souls, that had nine tall spires, the central one reaching three and a half thousand metres into the Erosian skies, had collapsed in on itself. The Central Citadel was now a collapsed pile of twisted plasteel, aluminumised glass shards and fallen blocks of astcrete. There alone were at least half a million dead Erosians. Leon Vasquez stared a Eros Central, the fallen Citadel, in sheer disbelief.

Eros, the World within the Rock, should never have failed. It was only because of the twisted ambitions of Godric von Horridian and his Brothers that it had. War had been a thing of the past, but Godric von Horridian had brought all of the horrors of War back on a grandest possible scale and Eros, a peaceful paradise, had paid the price. Out there in the vista that Leon Vasquez was recording were six and a half million dead souls!

"Captain", Leon reached out over his comms to Captain Whitaker, "Did you get all of that? Have you saved and backed up my video feed?", he enquired.

"Yes, of course, Leon. Saved and backed up thrice, in fact. Every video feed is being recorded and backed up", Captain Whitaker replied and then with concern, he asked, "Are you okay, Leon?"

"I have been to Eros many times in the past, Julian", Leon replied, his voice solemn, using the Captain's first name, a break in professional and procedural protocol.

Leon slumped against the observation platform's safety railing.

Leon continued, "I have seen the Docking Hubs in operation. I have transited the Transit Rings myself. I have walked this very concourse that is now so full of corpses. Only when it was crowded with travellers all going to and fro from one place to another. I have stood precisely where I am now and videoed this very same vista when Eros was so vibrant and alive. A vibrant living world, Julian. It was beautiful, a paradise. I had friends here, lots of friends. Hell, I may have just walked and trampled over their bodies. So no, Sir, I am anything but okay. Nothing about this is okay! Nothing about this is right! It's all so completely fucked up!"

Captain Whitaker had serious concerns, "Leon. I want you to listen to me very carefully. I want you to stop whatever you're doing and make your way back to the ship immediately. That is an order, Vasquez. Your mission is over. Bring yourself back to this ship, immediately!"

Leon sighed, his tears flowed freely, "I cannot do that, Julian. I cannot do that. What I have seen simply cannot be unseen. All I can see is hell and I cannot live with that. I cannot desecrate the dead any longer. I will not trample over the dead anymore. No, no, not again. The ship is simply too far."

"Leon Vasquez, bring yourself back to this ship. That is a direct order", Captain Whitaker ordered, using his full name in an attempt to trigger some sort of positive response.

"I am sorry, Julian. I simply cannot. Make sure those Horridian punheta bastardos pay for these crimes! These horrible things that they have done!", Leon replied and then there was the sound of air hissing, being released.

Leon Vasquez had removed his helmet, exposing himself to the vacuum of space.

The vacuum vampire had him!

"Leon! Leon!", Captain Whitaker shouted.

There was no reply.

Julian Whitaker slammed his fist down on the workstation top in front of him. He did so over and over, at least a dozen times, until his fist bled. There were only six emergency response ships at Eros's Southern Docking Hub, each with six emergency response personnel. Fully, one-sixth of his personnel were so emotionally and psychologically bereft of hope and grief-stricken by everything that they had witnessed and experienced that they'd been restricted to their ships and were in urgent need of psychological counselling. And now, one of his own team members had taken his own life.

How the hell was he going to make his next report to Administrator Zilfary?

Julian Whitaker bandaged his bleeding hand and then he wiped the blood from his workstation before making a video report to Administrator Zilfary.

"Administrator Zurine Zilfary. Earth Trojan Mining Corporation's Trailing Zone. Our emergency response teams have had significant success here at the

Southern Erosian Docking Hub. All of the ships docked at the external docks, those that contained survivors, are currently en route to our colonies. We have discovered at least twelve thousand survivors in big ships in the internal docks. The six doors to the main internal docks, the petals, as they are called, refuse to budge. They are firmly locked in place.   These ships will not be flying anywhere anytime soon. If the petals cannot be opened, then we will need to extract the twelve thousand plus survivors using space suits. Walking them through the vacuum to emergency transport ships. My understanding is that we are unlikely to have enough space suits or emergency transport ships to make this anything but a very slow process. My initial estimate is that the full extraction process will take at least three months.

The survivors have air and water, but what they do not have is enough food. We will need to bring to Eros processed foods, tinned and canned, meals ready to eat, protein bars, long-life milk and perhaps fresh fruit. What we have discovered here in the Southern Docking Hub is more than likely to be repeated at the Northern Docking Hub as well."

Captain Whitaker paused and closed his eyes, his mind still fresh on the loss of Leon Vasquez.

When the Captain opened his eyes once more, he continued, "While we have discovered thousands of survivors, we have also discovered horrors inside both the Docking Hub and inside Eros itself. My personnel have to literally trample over dead bodies to move around. One-sixth of my personnel are so emotionally and psychologically incapacitated that I have had to remove them from duties.

One of my best people, Leon Vasquez, has even committed suicide due to the horrors he had experienced. This place is harrowing. It scars the very soul and renders good people unfit for purpose. We urgently need trauma counsellors and psychologists for both the Erosian survivors and our own emergency response team members. Leon Vasquez is the one person to actually go inside the Erosian interior and he has documented everything from his first ingress into the Docking Hub right up to and including his suicide inside Eros. I will be sending you a full copy of his video recording for your perusal. Please note: It contains scenes of horror that are beyond belief. Once you have seen it, it cannot be unseen!", then he paused once more.

"Administrator, I take full responsibility for Leon Vasquez's death. I should never have allowed anyone to go into the Erosian main habitat. What was found inside the Docking Hub was harrowing enough. What Leon Vasquez recorded inside Eros was far, far worse. Administrator, Eros may have been a paradise before, but now, it is an ossuary for six and a half million souls. Signing off. Lead Captain Julian Whitaker", then the Captain signed off and sent his video report.

Captain Whitaker compressed a complete copy of Leon Vasquez's video feed from start to finish and then he sent that off to Administrator Zilfary as well, with an appropriate title.

Captain Whitaker thought to himself that it was only fair that Administrator Zilfary sees what his emergency response team members had to deal with.

The horrors that befell his emergency response team members, the survivors and the unfortunate victims, the dead, were raw and visceral and the whole solar system needed to know of it.

This was an atrocity on a whole new scale, a scale never heard of or seen before.

19. What Cannot Be Unseen.

Connor Dumas and his Wife, Carmelita, were in their shared office and had just reviewed the report from the Administrator of the Earth Trojan Mining Corporation's Trailing zone, Ms Zurine Zilfary. It was a summary of the reports from the emergency response team leaders at Eros, Captain Julian Whitaker at the Southern Docking Hub and his counterpart at the Northern Docking Hub, Captain George Saffron.

Connor and Carmelita also went through the reports from Captain Whitaker and Captain Saffron. Captain Saffron's report was written. Captain Whitaker's report, on the other hand, was a video report and quite emotionally charged. The reports were very similar in many respects, except Captain Whitaker's report came with an attached video of the one emergency responder who had ventured inside Eros's main habitat.

That responder, Leon Vasquez, had apparently taken his own life after clambering over piles of desiccated corpses to get video documentation of Eros's interior and its destruction. The atrocity and the genocide. Both Captains had reported that fully one-sixth of their emergency response team members had broken down and were no longer able to perform their duties.

Surprisingly, at both docking hubs, there were more than twelve thousand survivors, trapped behind the internal dock's six main doors, the petals, which were inoperable and completely locked in place. All of the survivors were trapped inside dozens of large ships inside the internal docks and those ships were not going anywhere anytime soon.

Connor's Brother, Daniel and his Wife, Harmony, entered the office. Daniel and Harmony had been reviewing the same reports. None of the four had yet watched the video feed from Leon Vasquez's helmet and spacesuit cameras. That video from start to finish was two shifts, sixteen hours long. All four sat down in chairs around the office's coffee table to discuss the issue. Eros was now a dead world, yes, but there were over twenty five thousand colonists still alive, trapped inside of Eros's docking hubs needing urgent assistance.

"Zurine wasn't able to get us exact figures, only preliminaries. So we know we are dealing with over twenty five thousand survivors, but it could be several thousand more", Connor summed up.

Harmony noted, "That's not including the few thousand that were trapped at the external docks at both docking hubs. We need to take them into consideration as well."

"Honey, those ships were all released. They'll be well on their way to our corporate colonies and safety by now", Daniel reminded her.

"True enough, Daniel, but it still adds to the refugee logistics crisis that Zurine needs to deal with", Harmony explained.

Daniel nodded in understanding while Connor noted, "The survivors from the external docking bays are now safe, or at least they will be soon enough. It's the survivors in the internal docks that we need to worry about. They are all still trapped."

Harmony commented with concern, "Every one of Zurine's emergency response ships and personnel has already responded. She has no one else to send."

"Zurine has told us what she needs. They have plenty of food, no problem. They can provide emergency housing, not a problem. They have spacesuits, but nowhere near enough. They have transport ships, just not enough of them", Daniel replied, summing up, "We need to send them what they need and that is transport ships and spacesuits."

Carmelita noted something else, "They will need trauma counsellors. Lots of them. Not just for the survivors, but also for their own personnel. They're emergency responders are dropping like flies. There will not be enough trauma counsellors in our corporate colonies, not for this. Not enough. Nowhere near enough!"

Connor replied, "I am taking notes down, Carmelita, my love", as he keyed notes into his data tablet.

"They are also going to need more emergency response personnel as well. Our personnel and logistics divisions can work out what's needed and how to get it to them. At the end of the day, though, it doesn't matter how quickly we act. Eros is still six weeks flight time away", Connor added with growing concern.

"Five!", Harmony chimed in, bringing up a chart of the inner solar system, highlighting the orbital zones of Earth, Venus and Mars.

Everyone turned to look at the office's main screen as Harmony explained, "The entire Martian orbital zone is too far out to be useful, but Venus, that's another matter completely. Venus is currently closer to Earth's L-Five zone and Eros than we are. The Venusians can be at Eros in five weeks if my math serves me correctly."

Daniel keyed some notes into his data tablet, "Okay, I'll write up a communique to the Venusian President, Bradley Klein, requesting aid. I will send him a complete copy of all of the reports and the videos, of course."

Connor chimed in, "Good move, Daniel. Bradley Klein is big on transparency. He will want to see everything we have", then he added, "I'll send full copies to our President, Dieter Reinhardt and Earth's President, Guang Hui, as well."

"Tell them that we are taking preemptive emergency response measures, however, we are just corporate entities and governmental responses are required", Daniel reminded his Brother, "We're helping because it's the right thing to do and because we can, but it is up to our governments to lead the way. We can only do so much."

Connor nodded, Eros as a world had been brutally murdered and both the Earth and Cis-Lunar governments needed to be across the problem and respond accordingly. They needed to step up!

Connor did, however, remind his Brother, "Daniel, we have this information first because our people are out there and on-site at the coal face. The Earth Trojan Mining Corporation comes under our corporate umbrella, so Administrator Zurine Zilfary sent these reports directly to us. With Eros dead, there is no other governance out there. Our corporate colonies are it."

Before the hour was out, communications had been sent to the Presidents of Earth, Cis-Lunar Space and Venus by tight beam laser comms. All three governments now had the same information that the Dumas Corporation had and it was time for them to act.

"This video. The one recorded by Leon Vasquez. Are we going to watch it?", Carmelita enquired.

Connor replied, noting, "Captain Whitaker and Administrator Zilfary have both warned that it is a *'once seen cannot be unseen'* kind of video. So, Daniel and I might watch it, but I'm recommending that you and Harmony don't. Whatever Leon Vasquez was exposed to, in the end, he took his own life because of it."

"Connor, Leon Vasquez was at the end of a double shift. He was in the docking hub and then finally the main habitat. So all up sixteen hours", Daniel informed his Brother, speculating, "Fatigue and overexposure to the devastation may have taken its toll on him, psychologically speaking."

Carmelita didn't hesitate and clicked the play button on the video, then quickly regretted it. The video started innocently enough, with five men entering the Southern Docking Hub via its external docks. However, it wasn't long before the bodies of the victims came into view.

Carmelita had noted, "This Leon Vasquez, his accent is Portuguese, Brazilian Portuguese."

Connor smiled at his Wife, "Just like yours, Carmelita, my love."

Then, when the desiccated bodies started to come into frame, "Bodies, dried bodies. So many bodies!", Carmelita was shocked but did not turn away, not yet at least.

When the desiccated bodies started to appear in piles and layers, Carmelita and Harmony both averted their eyes from the screen. Every time they glanced back at the screen, the video depicted worse and worse scenes. The bodies were now layered three deep and the emergency response team had been forced to climb on top of them, walking over them, to move through the docking hub.

Then, four of the response team members broke away and Leon Vasquez continued alone, trampling over bodies, walking ever deeper into the docking hub. The piles of bodies grew deeper and Leon was bracing himself with his hands touching the corridor ceiling. Carmelita winced as Leon took each step.

"How? How do bodies get like that?", Carmelita's mind was spinning with a combination of disbelief, horror and fascination, and was full of questions.

Daniel stepped in to answer, "When you have six and a half million people in a colony in space and the main habitat is bleeding air out into the void, people will do anything to survive, Carmelita. The ships at the dock all have self-contained systems. Even the docks themselves had they managed to close the bulkhead doors, they could have maintained an atmosphere."

"Yes, but layered and piled like that, four and five high?", Carmelita asked incredulously.

"Imagine scores of thousands of people all converging on the docking hubs. Some get into the ships, the rest are stuck in the docks and more people keep pouring in, trampling the people already there underfoot. Panic-driven exodus events create situations like we are seeing, although this is probably a worst-case scenario. I don't believe that there has been anything this bad, ever. The people in those docks had absolutely nowhere to go, with scores of thousands still pushing their way in, as their air was bleeding out into space", Daniel explained, adding, "I don't recommend watching this any further."

"But we must", Carmelita insisted, "We must witness what Leon Vasquez witnessed."

They watched the video as Leon reached the internal docks and came across emergency responders from the other emergency response ships. They watched as Leon and the other emergency responders accessed the dock's systems to isolate which ships had people on board. They watch multiple, frustrating failed attempts to open the internal dock's main doors, those six immense petals. They had found survivors, yes, but their frustrations mounted as the emergency responders realised that the survivors were trapped inside the internal docks and would be for many weeks at least.

Harmony noted, "This video continues for sixteen hours. We can see the issues our people had with the internal dock's systems and finding the trapped survivors. We should probably fast forward to the last two or three hours, perhaps."

"Yes, yes. These problemas with the space dock's systems and all of those trapped survivors. All those dried bodies that Mr Vasquez was forced to climb over. These things are probably what weighed so heavily on his mind", Carmelita agreed, not really wanting to see any more desiccated bodies being trampled underfoot.

Harmony issued a command to the screen's A.I. processor, "Computer, fast forward to time point, end of video minus three hours", and the computer quickly and diligently complied.

Much to Carmelita's horror, the video did not get any better. It got far, far worse.

Carmelita shifted uncomfortably as she watched three emergency responders, including Leon Vasquez, clambering over dried bodies layered six deep. Carmelita averted her eyes and winced every time one of the responders stumbled, which they did frequently. Leon's helmet camera often lined up on the dried faces of a corpse as he stumbled and fell. Finally, Carmelita could take no more and she jumped out of her chair and sat on her Husband, Connor's, lap for emotional support, yet still, she kept glancing back at the screen and the horrors so viscerally displayed on it.

Carmelita shrieked when bodies moved, lifting up and then settling back down again.

Harmony explained, "The desiccation process is ongoing. Those are collective bodily fluids violently sublimating into the vacuum. With the bodies piled up and layered like that, it's bound to happen."

"How do you know these things?", Carmelita asked, worrying that there were people still alive under the crush of dried bodies.

Harmony didn't really answer, "Knowing and seeing are two entirely different things, Carmelita", she replied with tears running down her cheeks, she noted, "I was born a Belter. We know these things."

All four watched as emergency responder Dean Morrison broke down and could not continue. They watched as fellow emergency responder Miriam Delmarva led Dean Morrison back the way they'd come. The long, slow walk over corpses back to the inner space docks. Leon Vasquez's helmet and suit cameras captured it all as the pair receded back into the docking hub's transit ring.

Then all four of them watched as Leon Vasquez continued alone, his cameras capturing every detail as he crossed the spaceport's concourse and then its great hall. Connor and Daniel both shed tears as they saw their Grandfather's bronze statue surrounded by layer upon layer of desiccating corpses.

Carmelita cried as she noted in between sobs, "I cannot see the floor! Why can't I see the floor?"

No one answered her question. They all just watched, eyes glued to the screen as Leon Vasquez, doggedly, made his way across the great hall, stumbling and falling many times as he did so. Bodies were seen in the periphery to rise and fall as bodily fluids continued to explosively sublime into the vacuum. What the eyes see, the mind will never forget!

Eventually, the video showed that Leon Vasquez had reached the observation platform. The video moved methodically. Slowly spiralling, panning and zooming, capturing as much of the interior as could be captured. Leon Vasquez's cameras held witness to the devastation of Eros, the murdered world within the rock. From the dried sea beds, the murdered mountain forests, fields, orchards, vineyards and even the collapsed and ruined Citadel of a half million souls, Eros Central City itself.

They watched as Leon Vasquez turned away from the corpse of Eros, the world within the Rock, his eyes scanning the spaceport's great hall and concourse once more. Emotionally, physically exhausted, and completely drained, Leon Vasquez slumped against the observation platform's safety railings.

Then they all listened as Captain Whitaker desperately ordered Leon Vasquez to return to their ship and Leon refused the order. Leon had said that he couldn't do it, that what he had seen could not be unseen and that he could not bring himself to trample over the dead anymore.

And then they all heard Leon Vasquez's final words, *"I am sorry, Julian. I simply cannot. Make sure those Horridian punheta bastardos pay for these crimes! These horrible things that they have done!"*, and then the hiss of air as Leon removed his helmet, followed by Captain Whitaker's urgent requests, calling Leon's name.

Leon's cameras continued recording for long minutes until Captain Whitaker cut the feed.

Carmelita Dumas, nee Alvarez, muttered, "Horridian punheta bastardos. They must pay!", tears were streaming down her cheeks, for she had seen what could not be unseen!

Connor Dumas noted to his Brother, "Daniel. We need to send another urgent message to Presidents Klein, Reinhardt and Guang Hui. This video cannot be released to the public. This video MUST never be released to the public."
"I'm already on it, Connor", Daniel replied, noting, "I started writing the communique while we were all still watching. If this video goes public, it will cause mass hysteria and trauma!"
Harmony noted, "I'll have nightmares for weeks after watching that."
Carmelita cried, "I cannot get all of those bodies out of my mind!" as Connor gently stroked her hair.
Connor explained, "That observation platform where Leon Vasquez video-graphed the interior of Eros. Where he spent his last moments. Carmelita and I have been there. We both stood almost exactly where Leon Vasquez stood, only when we filmed the interior of Eros, it was a vibrant living world. A paradise! Now, I have no words!"

This was personal for the Dumas family. It was Stuart Dumas's first company,

Cis-Lunar Haulage, that had towed Eros out of its solar orbit and placed it into its high halo orbit around Earth's Trailing Trojan point. The Dumas Corporation had shaped Eros, hollowed it out, vitrified and glassed its crust, both inner and outer, to create its main habitat. It was the Dumas Colonial Constructions corporation that built Eros's massive Docking Hubs as well.

It was the Dumas Corporation that had pulled out and repaired both of Eros's docking hubs after the Great Disaster of twenty one forty two. The Dumas family may not have constructed the interior habitats, but they had built the foundations of Eros, the World within the Rock! And now! Now Eros was rendered into Eros, the Mausoleum, Eros, the Tomb within the Rock! A world murdered, along with all of its lifeforms and its six and a half million inhabitants.

Within a single day, the Dumas Corporation dispatched ten transports loaded with the supplies Administrator Zilfary had urgently requested. Outside of Earth's L-Five zone, it was not the governments of Earth or Cis-Lunar space that answered the call first, but a private family enterprise. It was a mega-corporation, yes, but a family one nonetheless.

A day later, the Venusian government launched a small fleet of five transports bearing additional supplies. The Venusians had received help from the Dumas Corporation in the past, both economic and financial, and they were quick to pay back their perceived debt. As they departed, the Dumas Corporation followed up with a full interplanetary liner, packed full with volunteer emergency responders, trauma specialists, medical personnel and many more.

During this time, Earth's government and the Cis-Lunar authorities remained focused on bolstering their defences and expanding their military posture. It wasn't until the fourth day after Administrator Zilfary's request that they finally launched their emergency aid mission. A dozen transport ships, stocked with provisions, with the promises of more to follow.

The contrast was stark. While Dumas Personnel Ltd reached out directly to individuals in their network, those with experience, skill, and readiness, the governments relied on a broad public media campaign for volunteers. The Dumas outreach produced a rapid, precise response. The media campaign did not. It was slow and ineffective.

Too little, too late, as Connor Dumas would later tell his brother, Daniel.

After many decades of peace, the governments of Earth and Cis-Lunar Space were floundering, not really knowing how to respond. Just like fish flapping about on dry land.

Somewhere along the line, a video that once seen, could not be unseen, a video that both Connor Dumas and his Brother Daniel had recommended not be released to the public, was released. The first time Connor and Daniel knew of it was when sections of Leon Vasquez's video appeared in the news feeds. Not just any sections, either, the worst, most horrific sections.

Both Connor Dumas and his Brother, Daniel, flew from their corporate colony in Cis-Lunar L-Five to the Cis-Lunar Space government centre, Colonial Central Command. A massive twenty four kilometre long mega colony of the single cylinder O'Neil-style. The flight took them a little over three hours, but they had determined that the trip was absolutely necessary.

Secretary June Weaver buzzed President Dieter Reinhardt, "Mr President, Sir. I have Mr Connor Dumas and Mr Daniel Dumas in the lobby."

"Here? Now? I don't remember them making an appointment", President Reinhardt replied.

"They don't have an appointment, Sir. However, they are here in our lobby", June replied.

"Let them in, June, let them in", President Reinhardt replied.

The Dumas Brothers entered the President's office, greetings were made and President Reinhardt offered them chairs to sit in. Connor and Daniel unbuttoned their suit jackets and sat down.

"So, Gentlemen, what can I do for you?", President Reinhardt enquired.

Connor accessed a news feed video and handed his data tablet to President Reinhardt, who watched the news feed recording in abject horror.

Daniel explained their visit, "It is so nice to see that our recommendation, not to release that video, was so completely ignored, Mr President. Are our opinions of such little importance to you?", he asked.

"There must be some mistake. This should not be in the news feeds", President Reinhardt replied, clearly taken aback.

"Dieter", Connor addressed the President informally, "Did you view the video yourself?"

"No, of course, not. It was sixteen hours long. I handed it to my staff and let them deal with it", the President admitted.

"So, your staff released this to the media. Did you mention our recommendation, not to release it?", Connor asked.

"Yes, yes, of course, I did", President Reinhardt replied, noting, "They made it available only on a secure feed with a minimum age requirement. Not for general consumption. Only citizens twenty five years old and over had access."

Connor just shook his head while Daniel pinched the bridge of his nose.

Daniel took out his communicator and quickly accessed the *"secure"* feed that President Reinhardt was talking about. He cast his communicator screen onto President Reinhardt's office screen and showed the President the problem. Daniel quickly went through the age verification process and in less than a minute, the video was playing. Daniel then fast-forwarded the video to within fifteen minutes of the end. The most horrific sections which included Leon Vasquez's suicide. Connor Dumas stood up, walked over to the screen and then took out his own communicator. He held it up, lined up the screen, and then began recording.

Connor began explaining, "Apart from the fact that any citizen over twenty five years of age can access this video, you cannot guarantee that those present in the same room are also of that same age. There could be teenagers, younger children, in the same room. You don't know who's in the room."

President Reinhardt didn't answer. He didn't say a word. His eyes were transfixed on the screen and the sheer horrors that Leon Vasquez lived through inside Eros. The President gulped audibly as bodies lifted and fell with the explosive release of bodily fluids, subliming into vacuum. He quickly turned off the screen and Connor stopped recording.

Connor returned to his chair, held up his communicator and played his recording, "You see that, Dieter. Anyone can access that video, so long as they can get past the age restriction. They can record it just like I have with a personal communicator. Perhaps they even play that video into a file. It doesn't really matter which. Once they have their own copy, it goes into the networks and the news feeds."

Daniel chimed in, "You can now almost guarantee that someone in the news networks has their own complete copy, downloaded or screen copied exactly as Connor has described. And now, that whole thing is everywhere, Mr President. It is everywhere. That video has gone viral!"

Connor stared at President Reinhardt before commenting, "Dieter, the second that video went up, it was compromised. Word gets out and then the vultures in the news feeds copy it and promulgate it."

Daniel added coldly, "The man who videoed that, Leon Vasquez, he offed himself at the end of that recording. A sixth of his colleagues are so psychologically affected by their own experiences that they are unable to function. They are all suffering from post-traumatic stress disorder."

Connor chimed in, "Twenty two percent, Daniel. The numbers have risen somewhat."

Daniel nodded to his Brother, "Thank you, Connor", then he addressed the President once more, questioning rhetorically, "How many unprepared young adults have seen this? How many completely unprepared teenagers? How many innocent children have been exposed to it?"

"Daniel is right, Dieter. This genie is out of the bottle and you are going to have a lot of problems", Connor told him straight up, "How many people are going to commit suicide after seeing that video? How many others are going to need counselling?"

Daniel chimed in, "We made our recommendation for a reason, Mr President. Had you actually had the guts to watch that video yourself, you would have understood why!", almost spitting it out.

"You're right, of course, Daniel, both you and Connor", President Reinhardt replied in agreement, "What little I saw of that video was bad enough. I'm now seeing mass hysteria and trauma spreading across the system like a plague. I can see that now."

"We can't cram the genie back in the bottle, so what are you going to do now? That's what counts", Connor questioned.

President Reinhardt was on it straight away, he buzzed his secretary, "Ms Weaver?"

"Yes, Mr President", June Weaver's voice came back.

"That video. The Leon Vasquez video. We need to take that video down immediately", President Reinhardt instructed.

"Yes, Mr President. I'll contact our department head immediately, Sir", Jean Weaver replied.

"And, June. We need to put together an announcement. Any copies of that video, any excerpts from that video are to be taken down immediately. Any news network that plays them will be sanctioned. This is a public health and safety issue", President Reinhardt further instructed.

"Yes, Sir. I'll start to work on it straight away and have something ready for your perusal before the hour is out", June Weaver replied.

"That's a start, Dieter", Connor noted, explaining, "Your authority pretty much ends at the borders of Cis-Lunar Space."

"I'll send a communique to President Klein of Venus and President Guang Hui of Earth. I'll explain the problem and ask them to take the same actions", President Reinhardt replied, noting, "You'll be doing the same with your corporate Trojan mining zones, I expect."

"Our corporate mining zones, the Trojans, they are the one place this video won't have been released", Daniel noted, explaining, "It's all being pushed out by the Cis-Lunar news networks."

President Reinhardt nodded, "I'll have to contact the Aries colony in Martian high orbit. With the Colonisation Committee and the Security Council both gone, they'll fall back under my jurisdiction."

"The Belters will do their own thing as always", Daniel noted, adding, "Harmony says that they'll likely block all of the news feeds. I'll contact Harmony's cousin, Ceresian Administrator, Harlequin Moon, personally and let him know what's happening. Harley will coordinate with the Belter nations."

"The colonies farther out will also have their own protocols as well", Connor noted and then he advised, "We may want to send the complete video to their administrators via tight beam laser comms, with warnings about the *'graphic'* content, of course."

"Their administrators?", President Reinhardt queried.

"Yes, Dieter. The Dumas Corporation has a network of administrative contacts", Connor replied.

Daniel chimed in, explaining, "In the colonies that our Dumas Corporations have helped to set up over the decades, the first administrators were appointed bureaucrats. As the local polities developed, the appointed administrators came under the new political systems as heads of their bureaucracies. Dumas Incorporated Industries has kept in contact with the administrators via our Dumas Legal division. This network gives us back-channel access and a voice in the systems we helped to create."

"Dumas Legal is the repository of all correspondence and the central node in the network", Connor further elucidated, noting, "Of course, our Corporate colonies, including those in the various inner system Trojan mining zones, are all still under Corporate-appointed administration. And the Belters have developed their political systems around their *'elected'* Administration system. Our Grandfather, Stuart, was very insistent that we keep this network operating in the background. He always said, that while political leadership may change, it's the bureaucrats that quietly hold things together."

"Do you have contacts in the Jovian Realms?", President Reinhardt enquired.

"None that can help with the current situation", Daniel replied accurately, yet incompletely, not wanting to let loose that they did have contacts in the Jovian Realms.

Connor explained, "The Jovian Trojan colonies had a similar political system to the Belters, right up until they were annexed by the former Jovian Republic in seventy five. And our contacts in the original Jovian Republic were all sidelined when the capital was moved from Himalia Central to Ganymede Prime back in fifty seven."

Daniel added, "That was the Jovian Republic. Now they're the Jovian Realms and they are an autocratic and theocratic dictatorship. Any contact outside of the political structure is treated harshly."

"I see", President Reinhardt replied, understanding that any back-channel contacts in the Jovian Realms had likely been disbanded or worse, been eliminated.

"Does your back-channel extend into my jurisdiction?", the President enquired.

Connor explained honestly, "The network extends from Dumas Legal Ltd to the colonies that our Grandfather, Stuart and our Father, Baron, set up. So, it does not extend to Earth, Cis-Lunar Space or even Venus for that matter. Only the colonies that Dumas Incorporated had a hand in creating."

"Well, that is good to hear, Connor. Now, what can your network tell me about the outer satellites?", President Reinhardt asked.

Daniel fielded the question and replied, "The Saturnian Demarchy, the Uranian Federation and the Neptunium Commonwealth are, to say the least, pissed off with Godric Horridian."

"You may want to elaborate on that, Daniel. I thought that they all had that Quadripartite Outer Satellite Agreement, their QOSA?", the President responded.

Connor commented, "That is precisely the reason that they are pissed off. Think about it, Dieter. They all ratified that agreement in February. The Horridian regime created their false flag incident in March and then they destroyed Eros at the end of that month. They are all fully aware of what the Horridians have done and have accused Godric Horridian of deliberately dragging them into his War."

"And you have this information first-hand from your network of administrators?", Dieter questioned.

"Oh yes. We have that on the record from them, Dieter", Connor confirmed, noting, "They may be way out in the outer solar system, but they are not stupid. They fully understood that the detonation at Jupiter's moon Himalia was a false flag operation almost immediately."

Daniel chimed in, "The Quadripartite Outer Satellite Agreement is not a military agreement and any push by Godric Horridian to expand its scope is being quashed. The Demarchy, the Federation and the Commonwealth will stick to the letter of that agreement. Material support and logistical assistance. Nothing beyond that. They will do the bare minimum of what the agreement states."

Connor noted dryly, "When they receive Leon Vasquez's video, the full copy, not just what the news feeds have sensationalised, it will harden all three of them even further against the Horridian regime. That is something we can pretty much guarantee."

Daniel smiled, "We did have a message come in from one of Harmony's cousins in the Uranian Federation. A very odd message."

"An odd message?", President Reinhardt questioned.

"Harmony's cousin, Hecate. Governor Hecate Moon of the Sovereign State of Oberon and its orbital zone in the Uranian Federation", Daniel clarified, adding with another smile, "She actually cursed Godric Horridian and sent the curse to him."

President Reinhardt blinked, "Cursed!"

"Yes. Cursed", Daniel confirmed.

Daniel smiled, "From Venus to Neptune, the Moon family is everywhere throughout the solar system and they all have their little *'quirks'*. Hecate's quirky. They are one very big, colourful family."

Prince Friederic von Horridian and his Wife, Princess Minerva, watched the video in abject horror. Minerva was firmly entrenched on Friederic's lap, watching the video in short glances. Their friend Princess Chastity, the Wife of Prince Emeric, sat in a nearby chair, glancing at the screen intermittently.

Friederic noted, frowning deeply, "My Brother, Godric, did not want me to see this. I can understand why. He doesn't want me to see the results of his actions. This evil thing that he has wrought! I discovered this while viewing the external news feeds. He hid all of the internal copies, even from me!"

Princess Chastity replied through sobs and tears, "My Husband, Emeric, he had a hand in this!"

Minerva remarked, her eyes also full of tears, "My Husband, Friederic, he was the only one who advised against this", and yet, she still turned to Friederic accusingly, "How could your Brother, Godric, do such an evil thing? Could you not have stopped him?"

"How, Minerva? Just how?", Friederic replied questioningly, "Should I have severed his head, as that Roberta Nummus woman did to my Father?"

Chastity agreed with Friederic, "This is on Godric and Emeric. They must bear the blame."

"And Prince Aluric?", Minerva questioned.

"My Brother, Aluric, he has no idea that this has even happened and he must never know of it", Friederic replied, explaining, "My Brother, Aluric, is mentally ill, knowing of this", he paused, "Aluric does not handle stress well. It will just make him worse!"

Chastity chimed in, "Princess Serenity cannot be told either. She is still far too fragile. What your Brother, Aluric, did to her. It will take years for her to recover."

Friederic nodded in agreement, "You're right, Princess. We must never tell Serenity of this."

"I cannot watch any more of this, Husband", Minerva told Friederic, her eyes red raw from crying.

"Neither can I", Chastity added, in firm agreement with Minerva.

Friederic's face hardened, "And yet we must", he gently turned Minerva's face back to the screen, noting dryly, "We three may be the only ones to witness this atrocity, this genocide, in the whole of the Jovian Realms. I know with absolute certainty that Godric and Emeric will not watch it and neither will any of his Ministers. We MUST bear witness. The dead themselves are crying out for justice!"

Minerva sobbed, "I will have nightmares for the rest of my life."

Chastity agreed, "As will I, dear friend, Minerva, as will I."

Friederic frowned, "We watch this because we must. Someone in our Jovian Realms must bear witness, for the heavens know, the dead cannot. It is up to the living to bear the burden of what our brethren have wrought. And so we must!"

And so they did, all three watched all sixteen hours of Leon Vasquez's video from start to finish. Just as Minerva and Chastity had stated, they did suffer from nightmares nightly as a result. Their Mistresses of the Robes were on hand each night to comfort them as they awoke screaming and soaked in their own sweat.

They trembled uncontrollably with their eyes wide and white in terror. It was not uncommon for their beds to be wet and even soiled. Their Mistresses of the Robes consoled them as best they could. The piles of desiccated dead filled their dreams and turned them into zombie nightmares.

Over the next week, Prince Friederic watched Leon Vasquez's video from start to finish several more times. It was becoming a sick fixation. Friederic needed to understand how his Brother, Godric, had stooped so low, to such a low level of depravity, that he should kill an entire world. Friederic could not make sense of it. Why did his Brother not listen?

And in the end, having watched Leon Vasquez's video and seen it, it could not be unseen.

Leon Vasquez's video burned into the minds of all who watched it, like a screensaver burning into the cathode ray tubes and plasma screens of old.

Once seen, never to be unseen, an indelible mark, a stain upon one's very soul.

20. Double Tap.

High Prince Godric von Horridian and his Brothers, Princes Emeric and Friederic, entered the operations room in the palace on Ganymede Prime. Prince Aluric was left to his own devices in his palace on Callisto Prime. As they all sat down on their gold-gilded thrones, Prince Emeric winced as he sat down.

"Are you all right, Brother?", High Prince Godric enquired.

Prince Friederic smirked and noted in reply, "His Wife, Princess Chastity, kicked him in the nuts."

Prince Emeric explained, "My Wife was upset with me. Her response was very unpleasant."

"Why would your Wife kick you in the nuts, Brother Emeric?", High Prince Godric asked.

Emeric turned to his Brother, Friederic, in a silent request for him to answer his Brother Godric.

Prince Frederic explained, "Brother Emeric is embarrassed, Brother. Princess Chastity has seen that Leon Vasquez video. She watched it from start to finish, all sixteen hours of it. The Princess is not happy being associated with someone who has committed mass murder and genocide. For that matter, neither is my Wife, Minerva and to be entirely honest, neither am I."

"I see, Friederic. Mass murder and genocide are very strong words", the High Prince responded.

"Strong words or not, Brother Godric, it is what it is", Prince Friederic replied, standing his ground.

Godric knew his Brother, Friederic, was not one to back down, a spade was a spade and a shovel was a shovel. If Prince Friederic used words like mass murder and genocide, he was simply being precise and accurate. It was Prince Friederic's way.

High Prince Godric changed the topic back to Prince Emeric's nut kicking, "So, exactly how did this turn into a nut kicking?"

Prince Emeric found his voice at last, "I disagreed with Princess Chastity's use of the words mass murder and genocide and insisted that she return to our palace on Europa Prime. My Wife refused. I may have manhandled her just a little and then she slapped me and kicked me where it hurts", he explained as he rubbed his sore balls.

"So, just where is Princess Chastity going to stay?", High Prince Godric enquired.

Prince Friederic replied on his Brother, Emeric's behalf, "For the moment, Princess Chastity and my Wife, Princess Minerva, will be staying with Princess

Valeria at her apartments. When Minerva and I return home to Io Prime, Prince Chastity will be coming with us."

"Is that wise, Brother Friederic?", High Prince Godric enquired as he looked at Prince Emeric.

"Wise or not, Brother Godric, it is Princess Chastity's choice", Prince Friederic replied.

"And Bother Emeric, you agree with this?", the High Prince asked.

"It is for the best, Brother. My Wife needs time to calm down", Prince Emeric noted sheepishly.

"And what of Princess Serenity, our Brother Aluric's Wife?", the High Prince enquired.

"Princess Serenity is a guest at my palace on Io Prime", Prince Friederic noted, adding, "The Princess is in a delicate state of mind. She is in the care of her Mistress of the Robes."

High Prince Godric nodded. The situation was not good. At the very time when the Horridian Brothers and their families needed to be united, they were fragments and at odds with each other.

High Prince Godric sat on his gold-gilded throne reading through the latest long-distance surveillance reports of Cis-Lunar L-Five and L-Four, as his Ministers filed into the operations room. The Ministers of Defence, Security, Science, Foreign Affairs and Communications all quietly took their seats and waited patiently until called upon.

The Cis-Lunar L-Five zone looked as it always had, busy, yes, but busy as usual, with an increase in defensive posture. Not much of a concern in that regard. The Cis-Lunar L-Four zone, however, showed significant activity of the kind that the High Prince did not like.

Both Cis-Lunar Lagrangian zones had been ringed by what Jovian military analysts had determined to be missile intercept platforms. That was to be expected after the Jovian missile attack that destroyed Eros, the World within the Rock, however, it was the other changes in the Cis-Lunar L-Four zone that were of a far greater concern.

Prince Emeric had the same reports on his own data tablet and was reading them as well. High Prince Godric had called in his other, youngest Brother, Prince Friederic, all the way from Io Prime and he too was reading through the same reports. This was the only reason why Prince Friederic was on Ganymede Prime at all. The High Prince needed his assessment.

Prince Emeric asked, "I'm not sure I understand. I mean, these new defensive platforms make sense, but what's all this other activity our people have noted in the Cis-Lunar L-Four zone?"

Prince Friederic translated their military analyst's notations, "Brother Emeric, if you look carefully, you will notice that Dumas Colonial Constructions has slowed down their production of fusion reactors for the Uranium reactor phase out. They are redirecting their efforts elsewhere."

"Elsewhere?", Prince Emeric enquired.

"Yes, elsewhere, Brother Emeric", Prince Friederic confirmed as he highlighted a section of the surveillance and shared it with his Brothers, "The Dumas Corporation is constructing ships. Lots and lots of ships at their L-Four construction yards. Warships!"

High Prince Godric chimed in, noting with confusion, "They haven't stopped production of fusion reactors completely, just slowed production down."

"Yes, Brother Godric. They've slowed down production of fusion reactors in favour of building warships", Prince Friederic replied, explaining, "Any fusion reactors that they produce are going to go straight into those new warships. The Cis-Lunar government's own shipyards are in overdrive as well and I cannot even think about what's happening on Earth itself. The Earth will be a charnel house of weapons production. I did warn you, Brothers. You should have listened. What did you expect?"

High Prince Godric frowned. This is not what he expected. He was expecting a swift capitulation.

"Minister Trump!", High Prince Godric shouted out and then he asked, "Temu! Why have the Earth and Cis-Lunar Space not capitulated?"

Communications and propaganda Minister Temu Trump stood up, bowed slightly and replied, "Your Majesty. Our first strike on Eros was always going to be a Hail Mary, shock and awe tactic. It was either going to succeed or it was not. The outcome was entirely unpredictable."

Prince Friederic shouted out, "You lying sack of shit, Trump! It was always going to fail! Look at the Bombing of London during World War Two, it didn't work for Hitler, did it? Look at the Ukraine War, the bombing of civilian targets and cities did not work for Putin either, did it? Perhaps, you should take some fucking history lessons. Attacking and killing civilians hardens resolve, always!", he turned to his Brother, Godric, "Use this idiot for propaganda by all means, Brother, but for God's sake, do not rely on him for tactics. This moron has dragged us into a War we simply cannot win!"

"Brother Friederic, you speak out of turn!", High Prince Godric screamed out.

"Do I, Brother, do I?", Prince Friederic asked rhetorically, adding, "You are listening to yes men, who only tell you what you want to hear. When you come to your senses and actually want to hear what you need to know, then call upon me.

Until then, I'm going back to Io Prime!"

Prince Friederic stood up and walked out of the operations room with High Prince Godric calling out for him to stop. Prince Friederic ignored him completely,

Prince Emeric muttered, "Well, that could have gone better", and it was an understatement.

While the High Prince's meeting continued, Prince Friederic collected his Wife, Princess Minerva and his Brother, Emeric's Wife, Princess Chastity and the three of them quickly prepared to fly back to Io Prime. On Io Prime, Prince Friederic's people were loyal to him and should his Brother, Godric's, sanity drop even lower, he would at least be prepared.

Prince Friederic explained to his Brother, Godric's Wife, "I'm sorry, Princess Valeria, but my Brother, Godric, is leading us all on the path to destruction and he only listens to fools and charlatans."

Princess Valeria replied with tears in her eyes, "I know, Friederic, he won't even listen to me."

Princess Valeria hugged and kissed her friends, Minerva and Chastity, as they said their goodbyes.

To Prince Friederic, she noted, "I too have watched that Leon Vasquez video. All of it. My nightmares will never end. They will never end. My Husband is a mass murderer and a terrorist!"

Prince Friederic nodded in reply and then led his Wife, Princess Minerva and their friend Princess Chastity to his private space yacht. Before High Prince Godric's meeting was over, they were well on their way to Io Prime.

With Prince Friederic no longer present, High Prince Godric's meeting continued.

"I need a plan, people! I need to bend these insolent, quisling peasants to my will!", High Prince Godric shouted, his Ministers shifting uncomfortably as he did so.

Defence Minister Peter Macron suggested, "We could target Colonial Central Command, Your Majesty. That would certainly put them firmly in their place."

The High Prince shook his head, "We need that mega colony intact, Minister Macron and besides, if we destroy the seat of the Cis-Lunar government, who the hell will capitulate? Any other options!"

"We could strike the Earth itself, Sire", suggested Minister of Security, Miles Morton.

"Premature, Minister, premature. We don't want to strike the Earth unless we have to", High Prince Godric responded, noting, "Until that Martian terraforming project is completed, we only have one habitable planet in our system. I'd like to take to Earth intact, without destroying its biosphere."

"We could strike one or two of the smaller colonies in Cis-Lunar-Five or perhaps their shipyards in Cis-Lunar L-Four, Your Majesty?", Defence Minister Macron put forward as his next suggestion.

"Check your data tablet again, Minister Macron", the High Prince recommended, noting, "The first thing they did was ring the Cis-Lunar colony zones with missile defence platforms."

"How about we strike Cis-Lunar L-One or L-Two, Your Majesty?", suggested Science Minister Peter Patronis, noting, "They will likely have fewer defences, Sire."

"By the time our missiles get there, they'll be protected by missile defence platforms as well", High Prince Godric replied, remarking loudly, "Check your data tablets! The work is already in progress!" and then he snorted, "My Brother, Prince Friederic, kindly highlighted that for me. The bloody shit!"

Communications Minister Temu Trump chimed in, "Sire, we could always strike Eros again."

"For fucks sake, Temu. Eros is dead. We've killed it already!", High Prince Godric responded.

"A second strike, Sire. A double tap", Communications Minister Trump recommended in his most persuasive voice, "It would show them all how merciless and serious we are."

"How would that work in practice, Temu? The fucking thing is a hulk, it's dead", the High Prince enquired, but his communications Minister had piqued his interest.

"Sire, we would hit the survivors and emergency responders in Eros's stricken docking hubs", Communications Minister Trump replied, noting, "Our brutality will not go unnoticed. They will think twice about any reprisals against us."

"Or", Prince Emeric began, "They'll harden their resolve even further, like, Brother Friederic says."

High Prince Godric turned to his Brother Emeric, his face contorted into a snarl, "I've heard enough from naysayers of late, so watch your tongue, Brother!"

The High Prince asked his Defence Minister, Peter Macron, "How quickly can we double tap Eros? Both docking hubs. I want total destruction."

Peter Macron rubbed his chin before replying, "Sire, we do have some Missile Cruisers on the inside of Martian orbit. We could probably hit Eros with a second strike in perhaps three weeks or less."

"That's beginning to sound like a plan", High Prince Godric replied, nodding his head.

"Are you sure, Sire? Eros is a dead rock. We could easily take out two of the Dumas Trojan Mining Corporation's residential cylinders", Defence Minister Macron suggested.

High Prince Godric scoffed, "Nobody gives a flying fuck about mining residences, Macron. Nobody! Emergency responders and trapped survivors, that on the other hand will put the fucking fear of God into them", High Prince Godric grinned as he told them, "And that is what I want! Make it so!"

Communications and Propaganda Minister, Temu Trump, smiled his most fake smile.

Aboard Prince Friederic's space yacht, the Ionian Wanderer, less than an hour out from Ganymede Prime, Princess Chastity enquired, "Why are your brothers like this? I mean, I know Prince Aluric is mentally ill, but my Husband, Prince Emeric and High Prince Godric, why?"

Prince Friederic frowned. He had explained this to his own Wife, Princess Minerva, some time ago.

"You can blame our Grandfather, Albertus, for that and, of course, our Father, the first High Prince, Albert, for not debunking his bullshit", Prince Friederic replied.

"It is an interesting, albeit twisted story", Princess Minerva commented.

Prince Friederic explained, "Our Grandfather, Albertus, would tell us stories all about our von Horridian greatness. It was all a pack of lies, of course, but we were all children at the time and couldn't tell. Kids be like that."

Princess Minerva interjected, "Some Grandfathers tell harmless stories. My Friederic's Grandfather told pure propaganda dressed up as history."

Prince Friederic nodded, "Grandfather Albertus told us all about this vast *'corporate empire'* that we *'von Horridians'* controlled and of our *'royal family'* status."

Friederic did a lot of air quoting before he continued, "Albertus said that we were *'deposed royals'*, deposed by a rebellion that created the Colonial Central Federal Government. He said that we fled Cis-Lunar Space, fearing for our lives, into exile. He also drove it into us that we were destined to retake Cis-Lunar Space and regain our rightful place as the true *'Sovereigns of Sol'*. The *'Horridian Imperium'* as Grandfather Albertus like to call it."

"But you never believed it?", Princess Chastity questioned.

"Ah, but that is where you are wrong, dear Chastity, very wrong", Prince Friederic admitted, "I too, believed in his lies. Lock, stock and barrel. I was but a child and children believe what they are told."

"So, how did you figure out it was all lies?", Princess Chastity enquired.

Princess Minerva chimed in, "My Friederic has always been a bookworm."

Prince Friederic chuckled, "That is correct. I was always the bookworm in my family. Godric, Aluric and Emeric would always play together, as I was the *'little'* one, they tended to tease me more than play with me. So I turned to books. My thirst for knowledge was noted and I was given online access."

Princess Minerva squeezed her Husband's hand and chimed in again, "They didn't realise how smart my Friederic is. They gave him online access and he extended that to external online access himself."

Princess Minerva was beaming with pride, or was it simply a form of sapiosexual attraction, perhaps a combination of both?

Prince Friederic smiled, "Correct once again, Minerva, my love. One of the very first things I did was to check into our family's history and what I found was completely at odds with every story that Grandfather Albertus had ever told us."

"So what did you find out?", Princess Chastity was leaning forward, her head cradled in her hands, showing keen interest.

"Well, I must admit it was an eye opener", Friederic announced, then he plunged into an exposé, "Royalty? Nope? Deposed. Nope! Corporate empire? Nope! Fleeing in exile? Yes, but only because the Horridian family were criminals running from justice. Even our surname is fake, von Horridian? No, just plain old Horridian. Grandfather changed our last name so that our disgraced surname would be harder to find in surname searches. We are not even German! Although I must admit, we were all taught to read and speak German fluently. Apparently that was important. It was all a part of our sick internal *'indoctrination'*, of course!"

"Oh my God, that is so weird. You must have been so shocked", Princess Chastity replied.

"Yeah, you could say that. It was even more shocking when my Brothers refused to believe me. They said I was making it all up. That, of course, was compounded when my Father promptly told me to stop speaking about the matter. Trying to live up to a bullshit legacy is probably what broke Aluric's mind", Prince Friederic noted, "Honestly, I wish I had a normal Grandfather who told us stories about fishing and the big fish that go away. It would have been preferable."

Minerva chuckled, "My Friederic actually has stocked one of the lakes in our palace gardens with fish. Perhaps one day we should go fishing."

"That actually sounds like fun, Minerva. We could bring Serenity along with us. I'm sure she would enjoy the outing", Princess Chastity replied with a positive suggestion.

Prince Friederic finished up by summarising his family's sad history, "We Horridians once owned three corporate colonies. One was relatively normal, in the second, we had Christian workers who were held under indentured servitude and in the third, all of the workers were non-Christian Slaves. In Cis-Lunar Space, that was completely illegal and the very reason for our family's disgrace and our exile."

"And your Father, Albert, the first High Prince, he's done exactly the same thing here in the Six Jovian Realms. Indentured servitude of Christians. Check. Non-Christian as Slaves. Check", Princess Chastity noted and then remarked, "History happens in cycles and here in the Six Jovian Realms, history is repeating itself."

Minerva reached out and held Chastity's hand and gently squeezed, "Check!"

Candida Noreaga, Captain of the Jovian Missile Cruiser, Jovian Lance, read the communique. It was the third time she'd read it and she was not at all happy with her new orders. The Jovian Lance had been patrolling deep space within Martian orbit, positioned in such a way as to surveil Eros and the Earth's Trailing Trojan zone.

Candida Noreaga was a woman of honour and considered the Jovian attack on Eros, a civilian structure, to be a War crime. Her own people had committed that War crime, the Erosian mass murder and genocide. Now this, her new orders. They were egregious and unconscionable. The kind of orders that were completely unlawful in any civilised realm. Yet here she was, faced with the choice of performing her duty or refusing her orders, for which she and any of her crew who also refused would certainly swing from a rope. Refusal of orders literally meant death by gallows.

"You've read these orders, haven't you, Lieutenant?", Captain Candida Noreaga enquired.

"Yes, Ma'am. I have indeed read those orders", First Lieutenant Corbel Dyson replied and then he noted, "They are unlawful, Captain. If we comply with those orders, we will be committing a War crime. Of that, I have no doubt, Ma'am."

"Yes, Lieutenant. That is also my own take on the matter", Captain Noreaga agreed, noting, "However, if we refuse these orders, we will all swing from the gallows for our disobedience!"

The Captain was wedged firmly between a rock and a hard place.

Captain Noreaga took her orders upon herself, refusal meant death for every one of her crew members and yet she could not taint her crew with this crime. The Captain dismissed her tactical officer, asking him to go get a cup of coffee and not to come back for fifteen minutes. Candida Noreaga sat herself down at the tactical station and brought two missiles into operational mode.

Captain Noreaga read her orders once again and then noted, "Lieutenant. Make sure no one interferes or assists in this matter. All repercussions will be on me and me alone."

"Aye, Captain", Lieutenant Dyson replied.

Captain Noreaga set the coordinates for both missiles. Eros, the once World within the Rock, now a tomb to six and a half million souls. Intercept time, almost three weeks at maximum velocity. Then the Captain set individual A.I. targeting instructions. The first missile was targeting Eros's Southern Docking Hub. Specifically, the centre point of its six internal docking bay doors, the petals. The second missile was targeting Eros's Northern Docking Hub. Again, the centre point of its six internal docking bay doors, the petals. Those damnable petals that kept the survivors from being rescued.

Captain Noreaga knew that there would be survivors trapped in the internal docking bays inside ships and that emergency responders would already be on site. That was what made her orders so unconscionable, so egregious and yet, if she did not carry out those orders, her crew would all be hanged for disobeying them. The Horridian Regime was very big on that kind of discipline.

"Lieutenant Dyson. If I push those two buttons, the missiles will fly. If I fail to push them, we will all hang", Captain Noreaga announced and then she added, "This is all on me. All of it. No one else!"

Captain Noreaga pushed the first button and the first missile launched. Then, after waiting three minutes, she pushed the second button and the second missile launched. Given that the second missile had to overshoot Eros and then turn about to target the Northern Docking Hub, it would strike five minutes after the first.

The two missiles, each with a two megaton cold-fusion warhead, were flying and on their way!

Over five hundred survivors had been released from each of Eros's External Docking Hubs, six in the north and six in the south. With the external docking bay clamps disengaged, those trapped ships had managed to fly to the safety of the nearby Dumas corporate mining colonies. In total, more than six thousand people had escaped that way. They were the lucky ones.

But well over four times that number remained trapped within the internal docking bays, on far larger ships. Both the northern and southern docking hubs had larger internal docking bays, allowing for far larger interplanetary vessels. Everything sealed tightly shut behind the internal docking hub's massive docking bay doors, their *"petals"*.

At each docking hub, well over twelve and a half thousand souls, twenty five thousand plus in total in total, were slowly being evacuated slowly through the vacuum of space in pressurised suits, inching their way to transports that were externally docked. It was a process of desperation and attrition.

The emergency response teams could only extract one hundred and seventy-five people per day. They had neither enough suits nor enough vessels. The rescue was slow, arduous and emotionally devastating. It was expected to take up to five months, unless the relief ships arrived from Venus, Earth, and Cis-Lunar Space to alter the calculus.

For three weeks, Captain Candida Noreaga let her First Lieutenant, Corbel Dyson, run her ship, the Jovian Lance. The Lieutenant maintained the ship's course inside the orbit of Mars, closely surveilling Eros in its high halo orbit in Earth's Trailing L-Five zone. For three weeks, Captain Candida Noreaga drank heavily. Her nights were filled with nightmares of the atrocity yet to come. Her atrocity! The Horridian's atrocity! She was responsible!

Each time she drank a shot of tequila, she would toast, "Que esos Horridian bastardos se pudran en el infierno", may those Horridian bastards rot in hell.

On the eventful day, a dishevelled Captain Noreaga made her way to the ship's bridge. The Captain stood on the bridge, adjusted her uniform and took over command.

"Put the missile telemetry and optical streams on-screen", Captain Noreaga commanded.

Her communications officer complied with the command and then the telemetry and video from the two missiles appeared on the bridge's main screen, side by side.

"Captain, Ma'am. We have a three-minute delay from Eros. What you're seeing is three minutes in the past", her communications officer informed her.

"Thank you, Lieutenant", Captain Noreaga replied.

As the bridge crew watched, the first missile bore down upon its intended target. Closer and closer it came until the petals looked like they could be touched by simply reaching out. Then that missile's feed went completely dead. The second missile, three minutes behind the first, videoed the blast. A brilliant burst of blue-white light and then destruction as the Southern Docking Hub was swept clean of all of its outer infrastructure.

The six outer docking hubs were all gone, everything was gone and as the blue-white light dissipated, they could see a gaping, huge hole where the petals had once been. Everything inside the Southern Docking Hub's internal docking bays had been consumed by fire. Everyone in or on the docking hub was dead!

The communications officer threw up at his station.

The second missile overflew Eros and then came about, locked onto the Northern Docking Hub's petals and bore down. The petals grew closer and closer and then the telemetry and the video feed went completely dead, along with all of the survivors and emergency responders.

Tears streamed down Captain Noreaga's cheeks and she wiped them away, "You have the bridge, First Lieutenant", she commanded and then she walked slowly back to her cabin.

Captain Candida Noreaga, a once proud, resourceful and honourable ship's officer, was now rendered an emotional wreck. Candida sat in her cabin and began to write her daily log. It was written as formally as she could make it. It was a confession! If only she'd had a priest at hand to absolve her.

"Personal log: Captain Candida Noreaga. Captain of the Jovian Missile Cruiser, Jovian Lance. Three weeks ago, I was ordered to perform a nuclear second strike, a double tap, on Eros. This strike was specifically targeting civilian survivors and emergency responders. The orders were sent explicitly from the Royal Court of High Prince Godric. They were sent by High Prince Godric himself. These orders constitute a crime against Humanity, another War crime, just like the murder of Eros itself", Candida paused and necked down another shot of tequila.

Candida continued, *"I alone carried through and implemented these criminal orders. I alone set the missile parameters. I alone sent them on their way to their targets. My crew took no part in this War crime. I absolve my crew of all responsibility. I alone am responsible for the carrying out of these unlawful orders. The Horridian High Prince is responsible for ordering the second strike double tap!"*

Tears began to flow down Candida's cheeks, she wiped them away and sniffled, before necking down yet another shot of tequila.

Candida continued, *"This War crime took place on the twenty-eighth day of April in the year twenty one eighty two and I alone am responsible for carrying out the unlawful orders. May God have mercy upon my soul, for nothing, nothing at all will save High Prince Godric von Horridian!"*

Candida signed off with the toast she had made quite often over the past three weeks, *"Que esos Horridian bastardos se pudran en el infierno! Sincerely yours, Captain Candida Noreaga."*

Candida transmitted a copy of her log to Ganymede Prime in the Jovian Realms and another copy to Colonial Central Command in Cis-Lunar Space. After which, she printed out a copy, folded it neatly, placed it in an envelope and pinned the envelope to her uniform jacket.

Candida sighed and spoke to herself, "Today I killed well over twenty one thousand people who did not deserve to die", and then she took out her service revolver, stating "May God have mercy on my soul", before putting the gun to her right temple and pulling the trigger, blowing her brains out.

The gunshot caused an alert on the ship's bridge and First Lieutenant Corbel Dyson quickly rushed to Captain Noreaga's cabin. What he found there was gut-wrenching. Captain Candida Noreaga had taken her own life in shame of her actions.

21. Double Down.

One of the Dumas Earth Trojan Mining Corporation's colonies in Earth's Trailing Trojan mining zone had a telescope continuously trained on Eros. It was live feeding the serenely rotating asteroid, Eros, the World within the Rock. This live feed had existed since the very beginning of Eros's transformation from asteroid to hollowed-out colony. The live feed had even shown the construction of Eros from its very beginning over a century ago. People had watched the feed and used the feed as a background on their wall screens. Eros, the World within the Rock, was a hub of thriving Human activity.

This video feed of Eros serenely rotating in space had captured the original attack with the eight nuclear warheads exploding around Eros's midsection, fracturing its crust. The people who'd watched this happen had flooded the emergency lines to report the attack. That video feed had not been stopped. The video feed continued, showing Eros still rotating serenely in space, albeit now, a dead world full of six and a half million desiccated, mummified corpses. Eros, the Tomb within the Rock.

People had been watching the emergency response, relief and rescue efforts. Watching and wondering how the survivors would be extracted from behind those six huge docking hub doors, known as the petals. They were jammed firmly in place on Eros's two enormous docking hubs.

Now, this video feed had captured the second strike, the Horridian's double tap. Two nuclear warheads detonated one after the other against Eros's Southern and Northern Docking Hubs. The Horridian Regime's second atrocity in less than a month. The emergency lines lit up once more, flooded with people reporting this new attack.

Ms Zurine Zilfary, Administrator of the Dumas Earth Trojan Mining Corporation's Earth Trailing Trojan mining zone, had been watching the ongoing rescue efforts as well. She looked at the screen in abject horror as the enormous docking hubs were consumed by intense blue-white light and fire one after the other. The Administrator closed her eyes as her tears began to well. There were still well over twenty one thousand survivors, including children, still trapped in those docking hubs at that time.

The small Venusian relief fleet of five transports, which were full of emergency relief supplies, was a little under two weeks out from Earth's Trailing Trojan Lagrangian point when the ship's forward-pointing long-range scanners detected the two thermonuclear explosions. The Captain of their lead ship, the

Dawn Sun Rider, requested clarification on what they'd detected.

Captain Enrico Piccolo asked his navigation officer, "What was that, Julio?"

"I'm not entirely sure, Captain", Navigator Julio de la Vega replied, noting, "I'm checking our main computer now", he paused for a moment and then noted, "Our computer says that they were nuclear detonations. Two of them, Sir."

"And right where, Eros, our destination is?", Captain Piccolo enquired.

"Yes, Captain. Right where Eros is", Navigator de la Vega confirmed.

Communications officer, Christos Theodorakis, chimed in, "Captain, Sir. If those were a pair of warhead detonations, then that's a problem. The only things left to target would be Eros's docking hubs and that's where all of the trapped survivors and the emergency responders are."

"I am well aware of that, Christos", Captain Piccolo confirmed and then he noted, "It looks like the Horridian Regime has just perpetrated yet another War crime. That's two in less than a month!"

"Mass murder, genocide. Those Horridians are beyond evil, Sir", Christos commented,

"Agreed, Christos. Julio, keep us on course. I'll write up a report and send it off to Venus Central Command. President Klein will want to hear about this new development", Captain Piccolo noted.

While the small Venusian fleet of five ships was en route from Venusian orbit to the Earth's Trailing Lagrangian point on a Fast Hyperbolic Venus–Earth–L-Five Express Orbital Transfer, two other fleets were racing outward from Earth in the opposite direction on Fast Hyperbolic Earth–Earth–L-Five Express Transfers.

The first of these fleets, a relief fleet of twelve transports from the Dumas Corporation, was scheduled to arrive in three weeks, followed four days later by a second fleet of ten transports dispatched jointly by the Earth and Cis-Lunar L-Five governments.

They too detected the two thermonuclear explosions on Eros. They too fully understood that their emergency relief missions were now in vain. They understood that the Erosian survivors and all emergency response personnel were all gone, dead, obliterated without even a trace of them left behind.

As both emergency relief fleets continued on their course, their Fleet Captains sent their reports back to Earth and Cis-Lunar Space. Connor Dumas and his Brother, Daniel, of the Dumas Incorporated business empire, were furious. President Dieter Reinhardt of Cis-Lunar Space was furious. President Guang Hui of Earth was furious. President Bradley Klein of the Venusian Republic was furious. Everyone across the inner solar system was furious. High Prince Godric had miscalculated yet again.

High Prince Godric had thought that by using terror and cruelty, he could compel the inner solar system to capitulate and surrender through sheer fear alone. It had the precise opposite effect. All three governments were doubling down. Even the Dumas Brothers, through their Dumas Incorporated businesses, were doubling down. Ramping up ship production. Ramping up weapons production. Ramping up their defences. Ramping up military recruitment. The Horridian Regime had started the War and the inner solar system was going to bring it back to him. They would finish it!

Prince Friederic had once again hacked his way around the blocks that his Brother, the High Prince, had ordered placed on his access to the external news feeds. The High Prince wanted to keep his Brother, Friederic, in the dark. Everything that Friederic had said would happen was coming home to roost. Godric von Horridian was embarrassed not by his failure, but by the fact that his *"little"* Brother, Friederic, had predicted it all. It was humiliating!

Prince Friederic shouted out from his palace's server room to his Wife, Princess Minerva, "We have the external news feeds back online again, honey."

Princess Minerva shook her head, "Friederic, when is your Brother going to learn that you mastered this stuff before you were ten?"

"Not as long as he keeps thinking he's smarter than me, my love", Prince Friederic replied, grinning.

Princess Serenity looked surprised. She knew Prince Friederic was smart, very smart, but now he was some kind of computing and networking prodigy as well.

Princess Chastity also looked surprised, "When he was ten?", she asked Princess Minerva.

"Oh, yes, Chastity. When my Friederic was only ten, he gave himself access to every outside news feed and hid it from his Parents and Grandfather for years. I fell in love with him then and there. I was only eight at the time!", Princess Minerva explained, her heart full of both love and pride for her Husband and his abilities.

Prince Friederic climbed back out of the server room with a huge smirk on his face, "The way I've routed all of the data feeds, it will take them weeks, maybe even months, before they realise we have open access again. Godric has never understood and neither did my Father, for that matter. To me, stuff like this is just a challenge and I do love a challenge!"

When Prince Friederic was closer to his Wife, he whispered into her ear, "Minerva. Godric has done it again. He ordered a second strike on Eros, a double tap. The survivors and the emergency responders are all dead. Tens of thousands of them."

Princess Minerva nodded in understanding. This was also something that they could not tell Princess Serenity. The young traumatised Princess simply wasn't strong enough yet.

Princess Minerva gave a subtle nod to Princess Serenity's Mistress of the Robes, who promptly took Serenity by the arm and enquired, "Your Highness, you must be feeling tired. Would you prefer a nap?"

The young Princess nodded, "Yes, I do feel a little bit tired. I'd like a nap, yes", and then she asked, "How do you always know? It's like you can read my mind or something."

Her Mistress of the Robes then led Serenity off to her rooms.

Princess Chastity noted softly, "I take it there's information you don't want Serenity to see."

Princess Minerva confirmed, "Sadly, my Brother-in-law, Godric, has screwed up again."

Prince Friederic nodded, "Yes, Godric's attacked Eros again and killed off everyone inside Eros's docking hubs. I caught glimpses of some of the responses while I was rerouting the news feeds. The entire inner system is doubling down. Sadly, I know my Brother. Godric will double down as well."

"Godric will see those responses, won't he?", Princess Chastity enquired.

"Yes, Chastity, he will and that is precisely why he will double down", Prince Friederic replied, explaining, "My Brother has never understood that anger trumps fear and when anger overrides fear, then fear can no longer be used as a tool of control. We are already well past that point."

"What do you think your Brother will do next?", Princess Chastity enquired.

Prince Friederic frowned, his shoulders slumped as if defeated as he sat down, his reply was simple, "Something worse. Something far worse."

High Prince Godric was sitting in his operations room's gold-gilded throne once again. His Brother, Prince Emeric, sat in his less ornate, yet nonetheless, gold-gilded throne, two seats to Godric's right. The thrones for his other Brothers, Prince Aluric and Prince Friederic, were both empty.

The High Prince was watching the operations room's main screen, flicking from one news feed to another, each equally disappointing.

In one, Connor Dumas was speaking, explaining the depths of Godric Horridian's depravity. Connor Dumas did not use Godric's title. He did not even use the Uradel prefix on Godric's surname. Connor Dumas was being deliberately demeaning, treating the High Prince like a fraud and he did so with a righteous and indignant fury.

"Godric Horridian is not a Prince, High or otherwise!", Connor Dumas had shouted.

"Godric Horridian lacks all nobility!", Connor Dumas continued.

"Godric Horridian is nothing more than a genocidal murderer!", Connor Dumas had denounced.

Connor Dumas explained something about the emergency relief response that everyone, but he, had overlooked, "Godric Horridian's depravity knows no bounds. The number of babies and children murdered by Godric Horridian was disproportionately high. They were trapped, more than twenty five thousand innocent souls. They had to be extracted through the vacuum of space to transport ships. There were no children or baby-sized space suits. Babies and children had to remain trapped, their parents with them, refusing to leave them behind. The required space suits were less than two weeks away on Venusian emergency relief transport ships. Godric Horridian double-tapped Eros with his second strike and murdered the survivors, families, parents with babies and young children."

There was a long pause and then Daniel Dumas stepped in, angrily, "I name Godric Horridian a mass murderer, a genocidal maniac, a murderer of babies and small children. Godric Horridian, baby killer!"

High Prince Godric was furious and he immediately changed channels.

Prince Emeric murmured, "Whoa. That was harsh", although he thought to himself that it was true.

The High Prince's Ministers all remained silent in their complicity.

Every channel and news feed that the High Prince switched to was the same. President Guang Hui of Earth was vehemently denouncing Godric Horridian in both English and Mandarin. She, too, refused to use his assumed title and Uradel honorific. Guang Hui's English was flawless and scathing. Her Mandarin was even more so. More than once, Godric had thought that she had actually cursed him. He wasn't sure. His own Mandarin was certainly not very good.

President Bradley Klein of the Venusian Republic was equally scathing. He called Godric an ignoble faker who had usurped the Jovian Republic and turned it into a feudal hellhole run by psychopaths and religion nutters. Bradley Klein had declared that the Jovian annexation of the Jovian Trojan colonies was illegal and called for their liberation. He too refused to use Godric's title or Uradel honorific. He, too, called Godric a bay killer. Then, at the very end, President Bradley Klein went one step further. President Klein labelled Godric Horridian an illegitimate leader and a disgraceful little cunt. It was the first time in living memory that a political leader had called another political leader such a term.

President Dieter Reinhardt of Cis-Lunar Space was equally as scathing of the High Prince as the others. Not only did he not use Godric's title or Uradel honorific, but he also called for his arrest and actually had arrest warrants issued. The charges, mass murder, crimes against Humanity and genocide. Two counts of each, all of which, if convicted, would lead to the death penalty. A punishment not delivered in over a century. Then, of course, out came that label of baby killer once more.

The worst one of all, however, was not from any President, nor the Chief Executive Officer or the Chief Operating Officer of any mega-corporation. The worst of all came from a General at a military parade ground somewhere on Earth. A red-haired female General with a scar running down her left cheek. The scar sliced through her eyebrow and down her cheek. It had quite clearly almost taken out her left eye.

Her eyes were green, sharp and cold. General Camilla Brennan-Chives stood on a high dais overlooking a very large military parade ground. The news ticker stated clearly that before the General was over, one hundred and fifty thousand recruits who had recently completed their military training.

With her arms opened wide, General Brennan-Chives addressed the new recruits, her voice booming across the parade ground from perfectly placed speakers.

"Godric Horridian has, for a second time in a month, committed an act of mass murder and genocide. For a second time, he has committed a crime against Humanity. And yet, even before we had time to register the loss of so many lives, Godric Horridian once again demands our immediate capitulation and surrender", the General looked over her recruits, scanning from left to right across the entire parade ground and back again.

Then the General shouted out, her voice booming, "To Godric Horridian, that unworthy piece of filth. We will not capitulate! We will not surrender! Instead we will give Godric Horridian and his forces our Iron and Steel!", and then she repeated, "We will give them our Iron and Steel!", and then repeating iron and steel over and over and over again.

One hundred and fifty thousand marines all chanted in unison, "Iron and Steel! Iron and Steel!", over and over. And as Godric watched, the news ticker continued ticking over, only this time, it gave out the numbers to call for the Earth Defence Force's and the Cis-Lunar Colonial Force's recruitment offices.

It would have been awe-inspiring for the people of Earth and the inner solar system, but for High Prince Godric, it reinforced one thing. The entire inner solar system was doubling down!

Communications Minister, Temu Trump stood up, "Sire, if I may", the High Prince nodded and Temu continued, "Our second strike against Eros was carried out in person by the Captain of our Missile Cruiser, Jovian Lance."

"The Jovian Lance's Captain did a good job. Perfect, in fact", the High Prince replied in appreciation of an order carried out perfectly as instructed.

Minister Trump frowned, "Sire, Captain Candida Noreaga wrote in her personal log that she had been ordered to carry out an illegal and unlawful nuclear second strike, a double tap against Eros, a civilian target", he paused, "Captain Noreaga described it as a War crime and a crime against Humanity. She stated clearly that the orders came directly from you, Sire. The Captain accepted responsibility for her part in the second strike, but laid the blame and overall responsibility directly onto you."

"Hmm. Captain Noreaga's personal log and her opinion are irrelevant", High Prince Godric snarled.

"Sire. Captain Noreaga sent us a copy of her log entry and another copy to the Cis-Lunar Space's Presidential Offices. President Dieter Reinhardt has a copy, Sire", Temu Trump informed him.

Prince Emeric chimed in, "Brother Godric. Captain Noreaga's log entry is both a confession and an indictment. One that is now in the hands of the inner solar system authorities."

"That treacherous bitch, I'll have her hanging from a gallows", the High Prince declared.

"That will be hard to do, Sire. Captain Noreaga has committed suicide", Temu Trump replied, noting, "Before doing so, she pronounced the following in Spanish, *'Que esos Horridian bastardos se pudran en el infierno'*, it means, *'may those Horridian bastards rot in hell'*, Sire."

"What is it with all of these damned curses?", the High Prince spat out rhetorically, a question that no one even tried to answer.

There was an uncomfortable quiet in the operations room before the High Prince demanded, "Temu! Why aren't they surrendering? They know we can strike them and strike them hard. They know that I'm willing to destroy civilian infrastructure. Why are they not capitulating?"

Communications Minister Temu Trump was quiet for a long moment and then Minister of Defence, Peter Macron, stepped in with an answer.

"Sire", Peter Macron began, "We previously rejected striking the Dumas

Corporation's mining colonies in Earth's L-Four and L-Five zones. They were too far out of the way and no one would care about mining colonies anyway", the Defence Minister announced.

"Yes, Minister Macron. I do remember that. What is your point?", the High Prince demanded.

"Well, Eros, Sire. Eros itself orbits in a high halo orbit in Earth's L-Five zone. A lot of lives taken, yes, but ultimately, Eros was too far out of the way as well", Peter Macron explained, before surmising, "Sire, we need to strike against the Earth itself! That will force them to take notice, Sire."

High Prince Godric shook his head, "Peter Macron! I rejected that as well. We only have one habitable world in this solar system. We need the Earth. I do not want to destroy it!"

Science Minister, Peter Patronis, chimed in, "Sire, I do believe our Defence Minister was suggesting a limited strike. Not destroying the Earth. If we burn a single large city, their morale will collapse. They will capitulate, Sire. Once they realise that we can glass their cities with such ease."

Communication Minister, Temu Trump, stepped back in smiling, "Yes, Sire. We could give them a light show before burning one of their cities. A big one that's out of the way, perhaps in the Southern Hemisphere. Give them seven skybursts and a grand finale. A definitive show of raw power and fury."

Security Minister, Mile Morton, smiled a wry smile, "Put the fear of God into them, Sire! Surely that will get them down on their knees and begging us for mercy."

High Prince Godric was quiet and in thought. It was many minutes of truly uncomfortable silence before he finally made his decision.

"Do we have any assets close enough to make that kind of strike?", the High Prince enquired, "and not the Jovian Lance. That ship is tainted. I may yet hang its entire crew."

Defence Minister, Peter Macron replied, "Sire, the Jovian Lance is well within Martian orbit, shadowing Earth's L-Five zone. Its Sister-ship, the Jovian Scythe, is in a similar orbit, shadowing the Earth itself. That is the ship that I would choose, Sire. It can strike Earth in as little as three weeks from its current location."

High Prince Godric nodded, "Good, then. I'll leave the details up to you, Minister Macron. Give those unruly peasants seven skybursts and then glass one of their cities as a demonstration of our power. They will bend the knee to me or they will burn!"

"I'll make it so, Sire", Peter Macron replied with a broad grin on his face.

High Prince Godric was going to show the inner solar system powers that he, too, could double down and that they would submit to his demands.

High Prince Godric von Horridian's hubris knew no bounds!

Prince Emeric von Horridian sighed an internal sigh. His Brother, Prince Friederic, had been right.

22. Flash Bang.

The Jovian Scythe's communications officer passed the new transmission to his Captain. The Captain read the transmission on his station's screen. It was a new order from Ganymede Prime. Captain Tapio Makela looked at his screen with displeasure. He was being ordered to launch eight nuclear warheads targeted at the Earth. Using two megaton warheads to destroy an opposing military vessel or even military stations was one thing, but the Earth was another entirely.

The order stated that this was a show of force and that the warheads were all to be detonated as skybursts above the South Atlantic Ocean. His orders stated clearly that they were a demonstration. A sequence of skybursts to demonstrate both technical weapons capability and resolve. Captain Makela was pleased to read that part, but he had his reservations. The High Prince had previously targeted Eros, the World within the Rock. The High Prince had murdered an entire world. He had form!

The Captain's orders came with explicit instructions for each missile. The missiles were equipped with cold-fusion warheads and they were each to be set to ramp up to two-megaton yields. The precise coordinates for each strike in the South Atlantic Ocean were provided. Each was to strike and detonate forty minutes apart at an altitude of fifteen thousand feet. Captain Tapio Makela passed the orders to his tactical officer.

"Jimmy, I've sent you some orders", the Captain announced, explaining, "Prepare eight missiles. Set the warheads to ramp up to two megaton yields. The target is the Earth. Use the precise coordinates as provided in the orders."

"Captain, Sir. The Earth?", Jimmy Madison questioned.

"Yes, Jimmy, the Earth", Captain Makela replied, before explaining, "If you read our orders in full, you'll see that this is only a *'demonstrative'* strike. The High Prince is delivering them a warning."

"Captain, hasn't the High Prince delivered them two warnings already?", Jimmy enquired.

"Yes, he has, Jimmy", Captain Makela confirmed, "However, it seems that our High Prince has decided to deliver yet another warning."

James (Jimmy) Madison, the Jovian Scythe's tactical officer, nodded in understanding as he prepared the eight missiles.

Captain Makela frowned. Jimmy didn't really understand and none of his bridge crew did.

Captain Makela announced to his bridge crew, "This new strike is unlikely to achieve the results our High Prince wants. When fear turns to anger and fury, fear fails to persuade. Our enemies have already passed that point. This *'demonstration'* will likely harden their hearts, their resolve even further."

"Captain, all eight missiles are prepared and at your disposal", tactical officer, Jimmy, announced.

Captain Makela double-checked the settings that his tactical officer had put in place for all eight missiles. It was a habit of his, check, check and double-check. Then he stared at the two launch buttons. Once for each missile launch tube. These weren't launched from pylons, no, these missiles were all internally stored and fired out like torpedoes.

The Captain pressed both buttons simultaneously and the first two missiles launched. The next pair of missiles automatically moved into position. Then he pressed the buttons once again and the next two missiles launched on their way. A third and a fourth time, he pressed those same two buttons.

All eight missiles flew on their way towards the Earth, with their cold-fusion warheads each ramping up to two-megaton yields. Sixteen megatons of raw power and fury. Sixteen megatons to be unleashed in the skies above the Earth's South Atlantic Ocean. Sixteen megatons of pure overkill! Their estimated time of arrival, three weeks.

Captain Tapio Makela gave out further orders, "Jimmy, track those missiles to target", and then he turned to his communications officer, "Henry, notify Ganymede Prime. Orders executed as instructed."

It was blunt, accurate and straight to the point.

The orders that Captain Makela had been given had conveniently omitted the fact that the final two-megaton skyburst was to be above the South American, Argentinian, metropolis of Buenos Aires.

High Prince Godric von Horridian had deliberately withheld that information. He lied by omission.

High Prince Godric von Horridian was sitting in his operations room throne once more. His Brother, Prince Emeric of Europa, sat two seats to his right in his own, although less ornate, throne. As per usual, Prince Aluric of Callisto and Prince Friederic of Io were not present. None of that mattered. Godric was ecstatic. His missiles were on their way to Earth. The High Prince would yet see the Earth and Cis-Lunar Space bend the knee to his will. Then reality was brought home once more.

Mr Miles Morton, the Jovian Realm's Minister of Security, announced with a slight bow, "Your Majesty, we have received word from our operatives in Cis-Lunar Space, specifically from Cis-Lunar L-Five", his voice sounded ominous.

"By the sound of your voice, Minister, you appear to be about to rain on my parade", High Prince Godric replied, ordering, "Don't drag this out, Miles Morton. Get straight to the point."

Godric had been pleased, finally, something seemed to be going his way and now something else was coming up to slap him back down. He was not amused!

Defence Minister Miles Morton placed a data crystal into a receptacle and activated the operations room's wall screen. A series of images appeared on the screen and Miles Morton arranged them into a semblance of order. There were five images in all and they were all of spacecraft, military spacecraft. They all had unusual designs. Designs that no one in the Horridian regime had seen before.

Most modern space warship designs, corvettes, destroyers, cruisers and dreadnoughts all had angular shapes. Most had basic triangular, extended deltoid shapes. Many others had basic extended rectoid or even trapezoidal shapes. They were all angular with hard edges and that was the norm across the entire solar system, with perhaps the exception of the Venusians, who always did their own thing. The five images on the screen showed something completely different. Something never seen before.

Security Minister Miles Morton announced, "Our operatives in Cis-Lunar L-Five have been scrutinising the Dumas Colonial Construction's shipyards in Cis-Lunar L-Four. These are just a handful of the telescopic images that we've received. These appear to be common hull designs coming out of the Dumas Corporation's ship foundries. They are, as you can see, highly unusual."

And they were, all of the ships had stretched ellipsoidal or ovoidal designs. They were all smooth and sleek-lined, nothing like the current classes of space warships. They were also bristling with weapons pods. A close-up of a typical weapons pod was brought up onto the screen in its own window. It contained what looked like multiple batteries of not just laser-based weaponry but also particle beams. Each weapons pod contained two of each type of weapon.

The Security Minister remarked, "These high-powered laser and particle beam batteries are capable of not only working in unison but also of independent targeting, or so we believe. They are positioned along each ship's port and starboard hull surfaces. Each of these ships also has forward-facing missile launch tubes in its bow. There are also what look like multiple quad pulse plasma cannons mounted on their dorsal and ventral hull surfaces."

Everyone, except the Security Minister, in the operations room looked stunned.

Prince Emeric stood up and walked over to the screen.

He pointed to the bow of one of the ships, "What are these small outlets under the missile launch tubes?", he enquired.

The Security Minister frowned deeply, "Your Highness, we cannot be certain, but they may be electromagnetic rail guns. The way they are mounted also gives us the impression that they have a sixty-degree forward sweep."

Prince Emeric threw his hands into the air dramatically, "That's it then. We're all fucked!" as he returned to his throne.

High Prince Godric turned to his Brother, "Shut the fuck up, Emeric!", and Prince Emeric complied.

High Prince Godric stood up and walked over to the screen. He looked at each image carefully.
"Our ships are huge. These look to be much smaller, yet they are bristling with weapon pods. How is that even possible?", he enquired.

Science Minister Peter Patronis stood up, bowed slightly and explained, "Sire. Our ships all use plasma drives and those designs are at least three decades old. They quite literally take up more than half of the ship. If I were to hazard a guess, these new Dumas-designed ships will all be using the latest fusion reactor drive systems. Smaller and more efficient than anything we've ever produced", he then sat back down.

High Prince Godric stared at the images, each had a label.

The first he studied was labelled Battle Cruiser. It had five weapons pods, each with dual laser beams and dual particle beams. One was mounted on the bow and two each mounted along its port and starboard hulls. Four pulse plasma cannons, each, were mounted along its dorsal and ventral hulls. Under its forward weapons pod, there were two missile launch tubes and beneath that, were the hypothetical electromagnetic rail guns. The High Prince shook his head. This was a Battle Cruiser!

The next image that the High Prince viewed was labelled Dreadnought. It looked like the Battle Cruiser, just a lot bigger and longer. Obviously, its fusion reactor engines were bigger and more powerful. It had four extra weapons pods mounted along its port and starboard hulls and four extra pulse plasma cannons mounted along its dorsal and ventral hulls. The placement of the missile launch tubes and possible electromagnetic rail guns appeared to be exactly the same.

Godric thought to himself, *"Holy hell. What have those damnable Dumas bastards come up with?"* He did not allow his cabinet Ministers or his Brother, Emeric, to see his internal dismay.

Godric moved to the next image, which was labelled as an Interplanetary Fighter Carrier, with IFC next to the label. This was a new class of vessel entirely. Nothing like it existed in the entire solar system. Fighters were short-range spacecraft. They were designed for short-range defence and could be moved from place to place as needed by space transport ships. They were always delivered to their destinations, like the tanks of old delivered to the battlefield by trains. This new design blew that entire paradigm out of the void.

Godric could see that the IFC was based on the Dreadnought design with all of the same weapons systems, only much, much larger. The IFC appeared to have far more powerful drive systems. Fighter launch and retrieval tubes were along the four sides of its hull, in between the two forward-most and two aft-most of its weapons pods and pulse plasma cannons.

The High Prince shook his head and asked his Ministers, "What kind of fighters does this thing have and more importantly, how many?"

Defence Minister Peter Macron stood up, "Your Majesty, that would depend on the size of the fighters. If they use a two-seat fighter like the Talon class or the Gull Wing class, then perhaps twenty. On the other hand, they could use smaller classes like Bat Wings, Switch Blades or Scimitars, then based on the dimensions of that beast, perhaps forty or perhaps fifty."

Science Minister Peter Patronis chimed in, "Based on its length, I'd be inclined to say forty, Sire. It will likely be a round number. We Humans tend to do stuff like that when we design things, Sire."

"Fort rather than fifty", the High Prince repeated, thinking to himself, *"Cold comfort!"*, he then exclaimed, "They can carry their fucking fighters around as a Battle Group!"

His Ministers all said nothing.

The High Prince then viewed the next ship on the list. This one was labelled as Armoured Refuelling Craft with the tag ARC beside it. The ARC was every bit as huge as the IFC and carried exactly the same weapons systems. The major difference, it was an enormous fuel tender. No longer would fleets be limited to simply flying strict orbital manoeuvres, fuelling up before their missions and refuelling at specifically placed refuelling stations. Stations that always required protection.

That paradigm that had meant a strict, tight choreography of fleet movements, always taking into account refuelling. The need to refuel had governed all fleet manoeuvres.

Now, however, that paradigm was shattered. Using Dumas-designed and constructed ARCs, the Earth Defence Forces and Colonial Fleet Forces could carry their fuel with them wherever they went. There was no longer any requirement to consider refuelling at the end of a mission.

Godric shook his head and pointed to the image, "A fucking fuel tender!", he exclaimed.

His Ministers remained silent as Godric viewed the next image.

The next image was labelled as Armoured Supply Tender Craft, followed by the tag ASTC. It had the same dimensions as the ARC. It had the very same weapons systems as the Dreadnought. It was, however, a supply tender and a bloody huge one at that. No doubt it would hold food, water, materials, spare parts, machine shops, you name it. Everything a fleet could possibly need to stay on mission for months, perhaps even for years at a time.

Hell, the Dumas Corporation had been responsible for providing colonisation services for every Trojan zone in the inner solar system, for the Asteroid Belt and for every orbital zone beyond it. They'd even built enormous push ships to take colonists out to the distant Kuiper Belt Dwarf Worlds. Was it any wonder that they'd take that knowledge and apply it to military fleets? If the Earth and Cis-Lunar fleets could reach the nearest stars, with those ARCs and ASTCs, they could actually colonise them.

High Prince Godric looked around his operations room with fury, "How is it that not a single person in this room had the vision to foresee any of this? Fighter Carriers? Fuel Tenders? Supply tenders? Holy fuck!"

He stood there shaking his head while his Ministers remained silent.

His Brother, Prince Emeric, sheepishly replied, "Brother, People don't think of things until the need arises. Our Ministers are bureaucrats, not innovators."

High Prince Godric glared at his Brother, but he said nothing. Prince Emeric was right.

High Prince Godric stomped back to his throne, its gold gilding no longer having the same lustre that it had when he'd entered the room.

"I want options and I want them now", he demanded.

Science Minister, Peter Patronis, was the first to speak, "Your Majesty. I recommend that we embark on warship building immediately. I will instruct our people to work on converting the fusion reactor designs we acquired from Cis-Lunar Space before the War, into warship power plants and propulsion systems.

We need a lot of ships and the latest propulsion systems urgently."

"Do that, Minister Patronis", the High Prince instructed, "Now what about these IFCs, ARCs, and ASTCs? Can we build them?"

The Science Minister frowned, "Sire, that will be almost impossible to do from scratch. We don't have any base designs to work with."

"The Dumas Corporation seems to have managed", the High Prince noted.

"Sire, the Dumas Corporation has a century or more of this kind of engineering work underpinning them. We simply do not. It would take us years to come up with anything even close to those designs, Sire", the Science Minister explained.

"Then, Science Minister, you'd better get your people working on it", the High Prince commanded.

"Defence Minister! Peter Macron, what else have you gleaned from this new information?", High Prince Godric enquired.

Defence Minister Macron rubbed the stubble on his chin before answering, "Sire, apart from being armed to the teeth, those new ships also have the latest Slayers and Eramis technology. According to Minister Morton's notes that I'm just now reading, seventh generation Slayers and Eramis. That will make them all the more formidable."

Security Minister Morton chimed in, "Our operatives tell us that the Dumas Corporation has adapted their Slayers and Eramis technology to defend against energy weapons systems."

"Well, that is not good at all, Minister Morton. Have your operatives steal that technology for me?", the High Prince commanded.

"Sire, we no longer have any operatives with those particular skills available. Certainly not in Cis-Lunar Space anyway. The ones we have there are in Cis-Lunar L-Five and getting access to the Dumas shipyards in the Cis-Lunar L-Four zone will be nigh on impossible, Sire", the Security Minister admitted uncomfortably.

Godric frowned, he remembered, this was his fault, "Minister, I understand. I may have made a mistake convincing my Father to order Aurange Sheergibbon to murder Roberta Nummus and Lina Mitchel. That not only led to my Father's beheading, but now we lack the skilled operatives to carry this out. Aurange Sheergibbon and Roberta Nummus were the best we had. Now Sheergibbon is dead and Roberta Nummus is our enemy."

It was one of the few moments that Godric had realised one of his own mistakes.

His Brother, Prince Emeric, took on a shocked look at his Brother's confession, "Brother Godric, that miscalculation was on both of us", he noted.

"Science Minister Patronis. Add upgrading Slayers and Eramis technology to your list, Peter. We are going to need it", High Prince Godric announced.

"Yes, Your Majesty. I'll add that to my list straight away", Peter Patronis replied.

The High Prince took on a less commanding tone, "Peter Macron. You're my Defence Minister. Can we take out those damned Dumas Corporation shipyards?"

"Your Majesty, Cis-Lunar L-Five and L-Four are ringed with missile defence platforms. It is highly likely that they'll have other assets prowling farther afield. Our missiles don't have true stealth, Sire. They're just painted the same colour as the background of space", Defence Minister Macron replied, adding, "Any missiles we launch against those shipyards will be easily picked off, Sire."

Security Minister Miles Morton chimed in, "I agree, Sire. To hit those shipyards would require a major fleet operation."

Defence Minister Macron pointed to Miles Morton, "Exactly. Miles is absolutely correct, Sire. We need another approach. We need to get in close with a small fleet of Missile Cruisers."

Communications Minister Temu Trump stepped in, he had been quiet up until now, "Sire, we could use Mr Morton's operatives to sow confusion and terror in the Cis-Lunar L-Five colonies. Create havoc with, say, flash vaporisers, perhaps. Chaos, confusion, a population in fear, a government scrambling, hunting down shadows. It would be quite the distraction for them."

Minister Morton chuckled, "We could do that. We have people inside Colonial Central Command itself and, of course, in some of the smaller colonies. Shock and awe within the colonies themselves."

Communications Minister Trump added, "Your Majesty, if we time this for the same time as our cold-fusion warhead detonations in the South Atlantic Ocean, we will maximise the terror. Both on Earth and in Cis-Lunar Space. It should have a highly significant effect. The relief efforts alone should keep them all very, very busy, Sire."

High Prince Godric was quiet, his heart grew colder and then finally, he responded, "Miles, have your operatives do as Temu recommends. Make sure that the timing is perfect. Let's show them true shock and awe. I want them panicking like sheep being ripped apart by wolves!"

Prince Emeric closed his eyes, *'What could possibly go wrong?'*, he thought to himself.

Sometimes it was just plain sad to be one of the spares.

Three weeks after Captain Tapio Makela launched his eight missiles, the first one struck. It was early morning and the Sun was rising slowly above the Angolan landscape. Then there was a bright, blue-white flash of brilliant light in the sky twenty kilometres out to sea. The two-megaton cold-fusion warhead detonated at its designated altitude of fifteen thousand feet. First, there was the flash and then, less than a minute later, the bang, the shock wave, struck the coast.

The blast was picked up on simple weather satellites and the meteorologists looked at their video and data feeds. It was in the middle of nowhere, an air burst, surely it must have been a bolide, a meteor, breaking up in the Earth's lower atmosphere.

Then, as the world turned, forty minutes later and nine hundred kilometres downrange to the west, there was a second brilliant burst of blue-white light. It was at the same altitude and its magnitude was the same as the first. It too was caught by the weather satellites and the meteorologists scratched their heads in confusion. A second bolide? Unusual, yes, but not outside the realms of possibility. Perhaps the meteor had split into two parts and burst apart separately, or perhaps they'd been a travelling pair?

Then it happened again, forty minutes later, nine hundred kilometres farther downrange to the west. Another two-megaton blast at precisely fifteen thousand feet. Two bolides were plausible and three were not a coincidence. When the meteorologists checked their data and their satellite video feeds, their manager jumped straight onto his communicator. The Earth was under attack!

The meteorological manager fumbled, looking for the right number to call. Just who do you call?

This was unprecedented. Eventually, he called the Earth's Defence Forces via one of the recruitment hotlines that had been on the recruitment adverts in the news feeds. Time was lost as the recruitment officer did his best to calm down the meteorologist, who sounded like a stark, raving lunatic. When he did finally get the meteorologist to calm down enough to explain the situation, the recruitment officer's face went white with horror.

"Hold on, Sir. You need to speak to my superior", the recruitment officer instructed.

Within seconds, a Captain was on the line and talking to the meteorologist. He took down detailed notes and the Meteorologist's contact number.

"I've got all of that, Sir. Someone from our Central Command will be calling you back shortly", the Captain replied before hanging up the connection.

The word was out!

Central Command called the meteorological facility and organised access to the weather satellite data and video feeds. Just in time for the fourth detonation! Like a slow drum beat, forty minutes after the last, nine hundred kilometres farther to the west. Another brilliant blue-white burst of light with a two-megaton magnitude at precisely fifteen thousand feet. The detonations were slowly marching their way across the South Atlantic Ocean.

General Camilla Brennan-Chives watched the video feed, "Those Horridian bastards!", she exclaimed, before asking one of her Lieutenants, "If these continue at the same rate, what's in their path? What's further downrange?"

The Lieutenant replied swiftly, "Ma'am, I'll get on it straight away", and then he quickly left the War room to locate some maps.

Several minutes later, the Lieutenant was back, he spread the map across a table and started marking down the blast coordinates. Then he extrapolated, marking new coordinates at nine-hundred-kilometre intervals. The Lieutenant's eyes widened in shock.

"Ma'am, let's hope there are only seven of these things", the Lieutenant remarked, explaining, "Because, Ma'am, if there are eight, it's going to be directly over Buenos Aires in Argentina!"

General Brennan-Chives's eyes widened in horror, "Get me the Argentine President on the line. They have a city to evacuate and only around two and a half hours to do it."

By the time the word had reached the Argentinian President and the Argentine emergency services personnel, it was far too late. That forty-minute interval had passed all too quickly and at another nine hundred kilometres downrange, another two-megaton air burst had erupted fifteen thousand feet above the South Atlantic Ocean.

That brilliant burst of blue-white light, the flash and the shock wave, the bang! The drum beat continued.

There were only two hours left!

How does one perform an orderly evacuation of thirty million people in only two hours?

One doesn't!

No sooner than the word of impending doom hit the streets of Buenos Aires, there was chaos, there was bedlam, and the streets and highways were all blocked within minutes. Traffic ground to a halt and people everywhere were panicking.

General Brennan-Chives looked at their projections. Everything within one and a half kilometres of ground zero would be ash, with perhaps a million dead, vaporised instantly. Everything as far out as six or seven kilometres would be rubble and ruination, with another five plus million dead. Another four million plus dead out to twelve kilometres and out to twenty kilometres, perhaps another two million.

General Brennan-Chives's voice was calm but sombre, "Our projections indicate immediate deaths at twelve million. Severely injured with life-threatening injuries, another ten million. We'll be lucky to get out of this with less than twenty million dead", she closed her eyes and just shook her head.

"We may be lucky, Ma'am", the Lieutenant replied, remarking hopefully, "There might only be seven missiles, seven warheads, Ma'am."

General Brennan-Chives replied, "Godric Horridian killed Eros, an entire world, Lieutenant. Six and a half million dead and then he double tapped the survivors", and then she paused before commenting, "That bastard will have launched eight!"

One after another, at forty-minute intervals, the two-megaton, cold-fusion warheads detonated at fifteen thousand feet. Each slowly approaching Buenos Aires in nine hundred-kilometre strides. Like a giant striding across the South Atlantic Ocean, with the brilliant blue-white flashes of light and the powerful bang of its shock waves announcing its march. And General Brennan-Chives was right!

The sixth, then the seventh and then finally over the centre of Buenos Aires, the eighth. The city burned. Its centre completely vaporised, its inner suburbs reduced to rubble, its outer suburbs a collapsed and burning, tangled mass of wreckage. Survivors wandered the rubble and wreckage-strewn streets in their scores of thousands. Their skin was deeply burned by the intense heat of the blast. Many were crying out in agony and many others were simply lying on the ground, waiting to die. Those in the outer suburbs were slightly more fortunate, but not by terribly much.

Thirty million lives ruined, twelve million lives lost, snuffed out in an instant, with many more millions to die in agony over the following days and weeks. It was like a waking nightmare from which the people of Buenos Aires could not awaken.

It wasn't over yet. The cruelty of High Prince Godric von Horridian knew no bounds. As Buenos Aires burned in Argentina, planetside, the operatives of the Jovian Realms in Cis-Lunar L-Five began their awful, egregious work.

Colonial Central Command was the first of the mega colonies. An enormous colony of the single-cylinder, O'Neil-style. Its main cylinder was twenty kilometres long and four kilometres in diameter. Each end was capped with hemispherical end caps, with two-kilometre radii. The whole structure was twenty four kilometres long and it supported a population of well over twelve million people.

Unlike every other O'Neil-style colony in existence, all governance, politics, business and finance were conducted in its Southern End Cap, with everything else, including engineering and light manufacturing, conducted in its Northern End Cap. Every other O'Neil-style colony was the complete reverse, including the five mega colonies of the Jovian Realms, the Primes.

Colonial Central's main cylinder was divided lengthwise into three land sections and three window sections, each alternating at sixty-degree intervals. The three long window strips contained double-glazed panels of transparent aluminium alloy, between which was a five-foot-thick layer of water.

The three land strips, each covering a one-sixth arc of the cylinder's main body, were just over two kilometres broad. They had low artificial mountains in their centre and contained artificial streams, lakes and even small seas. The main cylinder was even large enough to generate its very own weather, with some augmentation as necessary. Life within the mega colony was idyllic.

People lived within both of the end caps, but also within the main cylinder itself. There were farms, orchards, vineyards and small stands of forest. The rivers, lakes and seas were all stocked with fish. Along with many other life forms. Aquaculture was a major industry. Slig farming was very popular.

Each of the landstrips had unimaginative generic names. A common practice throughout the colonies where each of the O'Neil-style colonies had very similar structures and so all used generic names. The land strips were simply named Alpha, Beta and Gamma. The strip windows were named after the land strip they faced. This was done so that one could go from one colony to another and still be familiar with their surroundings.

It was a typical Tuesday, a Market Day and the markets of the Alpha, Beta and Gamma landstrips were all bustling with customers and visitors alike. All of the produce and craft markets opened early in the morning, around seven am and it was now twelve thirty pm.

Luncheon, which usually ran from midday to two pm, was well underway. Crowds had gathered in the outdoor food courts, enjoying the food and the reflected sunlight shining and passing through the opposite strip windows. Happy people were everywhere enjoying good food and in some cases, good wine and then it happened. Someone triggered a flash vaporiser in the very centre of the main market in the Alpha landstrip!

There was the sound of an enormous hissing crack, then there was a brilliant flash of blue-white light. A pillar of pure blue-white light reached up one hundred metres into the sky. It hung there for many long seconds. Just hanging there in mid-air! Like it was just lolling about.

What was this?

The market patrons all stared up at it in fascination and wonder.

What is this, some sort of skyworks show?

Slowly at first, then more quickly, the pillar of blue-white light began to drop. The pillar expanded, growing wider and wider as it collapsed towards the ground. There was a high-pitched squeal that began to lower in pitch and volume as the pillar descended, until the pillar finally struck the ground with a blinding flash and a massive, immense bang!

It had expanded to about fifty feet across at ground level. There was another loud crack as the blue-white pillar of light bounced, rebounding at ground level and quickly spreading across the ground, growing wider and wider once more.

Ripples and waves of blue-white light, crackling like lightning, were visible in the expanding ring of fiery death. Everything within a one-hundred-metre radius burned and vanished, simply disintegrating! Every biological entity, right down to the smallest microbe, was instantly vaporised and at the end of the flash and bang, there was a disk of total death, one hundred metres across.

Survivors standing beyond the zone of death all dropped to their knees, looking around in shock and horror. As they sat there fearing for their own lives, on the other land strips, Beta and Gamma, there were two more brilliant flashes of blue-white light. The sound of the cracking hiss of the weapons took a few seconds to reach them. Then, when it was over, there were visible patches, disks of destruction and death, where the main Beta and Gamma markets had once been.

It wasn't over yet. High Prince Godric Horridian liked to do things in eights. A flash vaporiser was triggered on an older, smaller Bernal Sphere colony. A boutique colony, as they were known, where ninety percent of its population vanished in mere seconds.

Thousands more colonists were vaporised when four flash vaporisers were set off in another older, smaller, boutique colony. A twin-cylinder O'Neil-style colony. One flash vaporiser for each of its four end caps. The colony cylinders were only one hundred metres wide. The entire population of each of the four end caps was vaporised in mere seconds. Only people inside the colony's two main cylinders, separated by thick bulkheads, survived.

High Prince Godric von Horridian had caused mass panic and pandemonium on Earth and now he'd done the same in Cis-Lunar Space.

23. A Bitch named Payback.

The ruined city of Buenos Aires was in chaos when the emergency responders arrived. The dead were strewn every which way and the wounded were everywhere, some lying on the ground, others just wandering around in agony. Those victims too close to ground zero were gone, vaporised instantly.

Apart from the Argentinians themselves, Brazil and Uruguay were the first countries to respond. Relief efforts from countries farther afield took somewhat longer, arriving by air and landing wherever possible. The sight of what they found was eerily reminiscent of Hiroshima or Nagasaki at the end of World War II, except on a far greater level and with far greater destruction and death.

The Earth Defence Forces watched the skies above Earth, knowing that a second strike double tap could happen at any minute. Godric Horridian had already done that once before with Eros and he could easily do it again.

While the Earth contended with the ruined city of Buenos Aires and tens of millions of dead and dying, with a million-plus inhabitants vaporised in an instant, Cis-Lunar Space was contending with tens of thousands of missing people, all presumed dead. Flash vaporisers did not just kill, they erased. In both cases, there were no bodies to identify, only the complete absence of people who had once been known to exist. With the Eros attack and double tap, with the burning of Buenos Aires and the flash vaporiser attacks in Cis-Lunar Space, old Orpheus's burning times prophesy had come to fruition.

Ms Danica Thomlinson, the Head of the Cis-Lunar Bureau of Investigations (CBI), was in President Reinhardt's office, taking notes down on her data tablet with a stylus.

"Ms Thomlinson, I want these Jovian terrorists found. I want them identified and eliminated, root and branch. What has happened can never happen again", President Reinhardt instructed.

Danica nodded but noted. "My people can track them down, Sir. However, under the law, we do need to bring them before the courts. We can't just eliminate them."

President Reinhardt scoffed, "We are at War, Ms Thomlinson and after these atrocities, the gloves are coming off. My cabinet is preparing some proposed changes to your Bureau. A new 'specialised' department, one with agents that have special 'extrajudicial' powers."

"Extrajudicial powers, Sir?", Danica enquired curiously.

"Yes, Ms Thomlinson. A new Special Operations Department within your Bureau, under your auspices, of course. The new Special Agents will not only investigate crimes and arrest the perpetrators, they will also have the power under the law to eliminate them if that need arises."

"Special Agents with a licence to kill?", Danica questioned.

"Yes, but only under exceptional circumstances", President Reinhardt replied, explaining, "When the threat presents a clear and immediate danger, where inaction would lead to disaster. Basically, to prevent what happened yesterday from ever happening again. Grave threats require grave responses."

"I've noted that down, Mr President. I will read the new legislation carefully when it passes", Danica Thomlinson replied before she left his office.

As Danica Thomlinson was leaving the President's office, Connor Dumas and his Brother, Daniel, entered with General Brennan-Chives, who had arrived overnight from Earth.

Connor remarked to Danica, "Ms Thomlinson, excellent timing, you may want to hear this."

President Reinhardt directed his three guests and Danica to a series of chairs around his boardroom table at one end of his office. They all sat down and Daniel Dumas placed a folder on the table.

"One of our companies, Astro Resources, has been busy", Connor Dumas announced, explaining, "Those missile attacks on Eros had to come from somewhere, so we instructed our facilities in Cis-Lunar L-Two to study the missile trajectories based on the Eros video feed and attempt to track back to their launching sites."

Daniel Dumas stepped in, smiling, as he passed around two photographs, "This is what they found. That first photograph is a long-range telescopic photograph of a missile array at Ganymede L-Four. That's where the first strike originated."

The President and Danica Thompson both scrutinised the photograph. The General, Camilla, had seen it in an earlier presentation.

Before anyone could say anything, Daniel continued, "That second photograph. That depicts a Jovian Missile Cruiser well inside Martian orbit. It is shadowing Earth's Trailing Trojan zone. That is where the second strike, the double tap, originated. That Jovian Missile Cruiser is still on station."

Connor smiled as his Brother, Daniel, took out two more photographs. Danica looked at the two new photographs with some confusion, "Two more pictures of the same Missile Cruiser?"

"Look closer at all three pictures, Ms Thomlinson", Conner requested with a wry smile.

Danica looked more closely. Daniel provided her with a large magnifying glass that he took out of his briefcase. Danica took the magnifying glass with a nod and looked at the photographs once more.

"This second picture. The Missile Cruiser is the JRSS Jovian Lance", Danica noted and then moved to the third photograph, "Ah, now I get it, this is another Missile Cruiser, the JRSS Jovian Scythe."

Daniel nodded in agreement, "And when you check the next photograph, you'll see it's another Missile Cruiser again, the JRSS Jovian Glaive!"

"All in the same location?", President Reinhardt enquired.

"No, Dieter", Connor replied informally, "My Brother, Daniel, and I both thought, if one Missile Cruiser was shadowing Earth's L-Five zone, there'd be another shadowing the Earth's L-Four zone. Perhaps even one more shadowing Earth and Cis-Lunar Space as well."

Daniel explained, "So we asked our company, Astro Resources, to do some follow-up scans. These three Jovian Missile Cruisers have identical orbits, just at different orbital phases."

General Brennan-Chive chimed in, "That was a tactical blunder. Once one was located, it made the other two easier to find. The Jovian Lance is shadowing Earth's L-Five zone and its Sister-ships, Scythe and Glaive, are shadowing Earth and Earth's L-Four zones. We are still backtracking the missile trajectories based on our weather satellite imaging, but my money is on the Jovian Scythe as having murdered Buenos Aires."

Connor grinned broadly, "All three ships are still maintaining their current orbits. All on station."

Daniel also grinned, "We've got them by the short and curlies. We just need to strike while the iron is still hot!"

"I've spoken to Fleet Captain Nikolaidis just the other day. Nicholas tells me that we aren't ready for any deep space operations just yet. Even our base on the Martian moon Deimos isn't ready. That base has just enough smaller ships for keeping unauthorised settlers from attempting to land on Mars", President Reinhardt admitted, "While we do have some ships up here in Cis-Lunar Space and we are building more, we simply don't have enough crews for them. We currently have a manpower problem. Recruitment has been very slow going."

Daniel noted, "Even if we had capital ships out at Deimos, it wouldn't help. Mars is not in the right orbital position at this moment in time."

"Our recruitment drive on Earth has been going very well. We are well ahead of projections. We can send you some of our people once they're trained sufficiently", General Brennan-Chives offered.

"We can have Dumas Personnel Ltd launch a recruitment drive on your behalf as well. That should help in the long run", Connor also offered.

"Connor, we do have ships and we do have crews. They are private crews, not military, but they are exceptionally well trained and our new Battle Cruisers do need field testing", Daniel suggested.

"My Brother does have a point. We can have three of our Battle Cruisers engaging those Jovian Missile Cruisers in under three weeks", Connor agreed, noting, "Dieter, your government has already paid for the ships. Let's put them to use."

"Your crews are not military, Connor", President Reinhardt objected.

Daniel countered, "No, but they've had the best possible training. They know the ships and are highly professional. We could second them over to the Colonial Fleet for short-term operations."

While President Reinhardt considered the use of seconded private ship crews, Daniel pressed on, "Dieter, we can have three of our Battle Cruisers out there interdicting the threat in under three weeks. We need to move fast. Our ships can fly out, take out the enemy's Missile Cruisers and swing back home all in one loop. Threat neutralised."

Camilla chimed in, "I know you guys want to take out the bad guys and eliminate the threat, but this will be a military operation with military objectives. We need intelligence gathering, not just interdiction. Just how are you proposing to do that?"

Daniel was thinking on the fly and had the answer almost immediately, "Life pods", he muttered, explaining, "If we order our Battle Cruiser Captains to take out the enemy's Missile Cruisers without destroying them, that will give their crews a chance to get into their emergency life pods."

"Mr Dumas, your Battle Cruisers will be travelling a high delta-v. Just how are they going to collect the enemy's life pods?", Camilla enquired.

"They don't, General", Daniel replied simply, commenting, "A slower follow-up mission will rendezvous with the debris fields after our Battle Cruisers have looped back towards the Earth. Those ships will collect any life pods that might have successfully launched."

General Brennan-Chives's eyes darted from side to side as she quickly considered the proposal, "My people can have a Light Cruiser and a recovery ship at each location in about four weeks", she replied, adding, "Any Jovian survivors might be hanging about on location for a week or so, but they should still be alive. This does actually sound doable."

"So, General", Connor began, replying, "You will get your prisoners to interrogate after all."

"Assuming your crews are as professional as your Brother, Daniel, says", Camilla replied, commenting, "Just make sure your ship's Captains understand. We need prisoners alive, so they aren't to blow those Jovian Missile Cruisers all to hell."

Daniel smiled, replying, "They can use their rail guns, General. Short tungsten projectiles with delayed explosive tips. They'll punch holes through their hulls and force them to abandon their ships. Your salvage ships may even be able to tow the Jovian Missile Cruisers back here for analysis."

Connor chuckled, "We'll have three space tugs at your disposal for that possibility, General."

"Yes", Daniel agreed, noting, "Cis-Lunar Haulage was our Grandfather's first company, you know."

General Brennan-Chives nodded, "You test your new Battle Cruisers out on those Jovian Missile Cruisers. Just leave them disabled but intact. We'll send out a Light Cruiser, a recovery ship and one of your space tugs to each site", she smiled, "I'm looking at getting some good intel!"

President Reinhardt had been listening intently, "Ladies, Gentlemen. It looks like you've got this. Let's get this underway in an expedited fashion. I don't expect those Jovian Missile Cruisers will stay on station just waiting for us forever."

President Reinhardt turned to his head of Cis-Lunar Bureau of Investigations, "Ms Thomlinson, please apprise Fleet Captain Nikolaidis of this new operation and let him know that we are working on our manpower shortage. The solution is pending."

"Yes, Sir. I've just noted that down", Danica Thomlinson replied.

Within two days, the Dumas Corporation launched three of the new Battle Cruisers from their Cis-Lunar L-Four shipyards. The Avenging Angel, the Adjudicating Wraith and the Revenant Dawn. They were fully provisioned and on their way to intercept the three prowling Jovian Missile Cruisers. All three launched together, sleek-lined, stretched ovoid-shaped and skinned in radar-absorbent material with the darkest black colouring to match the inky blackness of space. They flew as a trio until they left Cis-Lunar Space and then separated. All three Battle Cruisers flew on perfectly timed schedules, set up for synchronous intercepts, one per Jovian Missile Cruiser. Their estimated time of arrival, three weeks.

The very next day, another small fleet of ships launched from the Colonial Fleet's Cis-Lunar L-Four staging grounds. Three Earth Defence Force Light Cruisers with their triangular wedge shapes, all hard angles and serious business. Alongside them flew three salvage recovery ships and three space tugs. When the small fleet left Cis-Lunar Space, they also split into three smaller fleets. One of each kind of vessel per fleet, all on synchronous intercept courses towards the three Jovian Missile Cruisers. The estimated time of arrival, four weeks and two days.

While the relief efforts continued in and around the ruined city of Buenos Aires on Earth, General Camilla Brennan-Chives of the Earth Defence Forces worked with President Reinhardt and Colonial Fleet Captain Nicholas Nikolaidis. Their purposes, Colonial Fleet mobilisation and crew recruitment. General Brennan-Chives knew the ropes, Fleet Captain Nikolaidis knew the theory and President Reinhardt knew very little concerning these things and was playing catch-up.

Camilla, with her fiery red locks, striking green eyes and her unique, long scar running from her left forehead and down her left cheek, became an unusual poster girl of sorts for the recruitment cause.

"No sooner than Buenos Aires was burned by Jovian missiles! No sooner than the Cis-Lunar Colonies were defiled by Jovian Agents! Godric Horridian sent us demands for our surrender, our capitulation", Camilla spoke strongly into the camera.

"We will not surrender! We will not capitulate! We do not bow down to tyrants! We will not bend the knee to that mealy-mouthed, self-styled pretender whose balls have barely dropped!", Camilla was deliberately insulting and then she spread her arms wide, "No, no, no, Godric Horridian. We are coming for you! With iron in our blood and cold, hard steel in our warm and bloody hands, we are coming for you, Godric Horridian! We are coming for you! There will be justice!"

Camilla pointed at the camera as pictures of the Earth mobilising appeared on the screen behind her.

"Citizens, people of the Cis-Lunar colonies. The Colonial Fleet needs Captains, the Colonial Fleet needs crews! Do you have what it takes to wipe out the Horridian menace? Step forward and step up! There are recruitment offices in all of the major colonies. The Colonial Fleet needs you!"

The camera faded out, leaving a poster of General Camilla Brennan-Chives pointing, with the caption underneath, "We need you for the Colonial Fleet", and a list of recruitment hotlines beneath it.

High Prince Godric stared at the final image on the screen. That woman, the fiery speech and equally fiery red hair. Those piercing green eyes, like cold ice and full of venom. That scar running down the left side of her face. The penultimate warrior woman.

Her words were demeaning to him, yes, but Godric could not help but think, *"Why don't I have Generals like that one?"*

The High Prince questioned, "Why are they not surrendering? Why are they not capitulating?"

Prince Emeric replied gruffly, "Because we have pushed them too far, Brother. Fear has its limits and they are beyond fear. They now have righteous fury! Our Brother, Friederic, predicted this!"

Godric turned to his Brother, thinking, *"How unusual for Emeric to speak out so strongly"*, and then he replied, admitting, "You are right, Brother Emeric, you are right."

Prince Emeric pointed to Communications Minister Temu Trump, "Brother Godric, Everything that weasel has told you was wrong. He speaks with a serpent's tongue, always with double meanings and falsehoods. Never the fucking truth! Never what you needed to know! Only what you wanted to hear. He twisted words to suit a narrative that you preferred and now look where that snake has landed us!"

High Prince Godric nodded to his Brother Emeric in understanding, his Brother was right.

The High Prince nodded to Security Minister Miles Morton, who stood up immediately.

Communications Minister Temu Trump stood up and approached High Prince Godric.

"My Liege, I beseech you. I have always acted in your best interests", Temu Trump begged and then he turned as the Security Minister approached, "Sire! Your Majesty! I have always provided advice in good faith! Always provided advice to the best of my abilities! Please, My Liege, I beseech you."

A firm hand gripped Temu's arm and spun him around. It was the Security Minister and he had unsheathed a knife, a military K-bar. Miles Morton plunged the K-bar deeply into Temu's spleen and then he twisted it. Temu stared into Miles Morton's eyes in shock as the blade was dragged from his spleen across his liver. Then Miles Morton twisted the K-bar once more and sliced downwards through the colon and intestines, a deep, sharp cut, before withdrawing the blade.

The smell of bowel arose.

Temu Trump looked down at his gut in shock. His intestines were falling out like weird sausages.

In complete shock, Temu Trump feebly reached down to push his intestines back in but failed miserably at the task. Miles Morton wiped his K-bar's blade clean in Temu's ministerial robes before releasing his grip on his arm. Miles pushed Temu backwards and he fell to the floor, writhing and twitching, still trying to hold in his guts, his intestines. Miles Morton watched Temu Trump as he re-sheathed his K-bar before returning to his seat. Temu Trump was now dead.

"What now, my Ministers? Where do we go from here?", High Prince Godric enquired.

Defence Minister, Peter Macron replied, "Your Majesty. We have no choice. We must prepare for the inevitable. A long, protracted War."

Science Minister, Peter Patronis, assured the High Prince, "Your Majesty. Our people are all working hard on our current projects. Our research and development teams are making good progress."

Commerce Minister, Devlin Dervish, requested, "Sire, with your permission. I will provide more Slaves to our production lines to support our War effort. As many as our Science Minister can use."

High Prince Godric replied, "So ordered and if our Science Minister needs even more labour, then drag in personal house Slaves, even from the Nobility if necessary."

"Yes, Your Majesty", the Commerce Minister replied.

High Prince Godric stood up and walked towards the operations room's door, commenting, "And have that mess cleaned up. It fucking stinks!"

Prince Emeric followed his Brother out of the operations room.

The Battle Cruiser, Revenant Dawn, with Captain Heinrich Zarensdorf in command, was on a fast approach to the Jovian Missile Cruiser, the Jovian Glaive. They were approaching from the rear, in the Jovian Glaive's six. They already had the Jovian Glaive on screen.

"Tactical. Have they detected us?", Captain Zarensdorf enquired.

"No, Captain. Our target is in the dark", the Tactical Officer replied.

"Good, then. Bring our electromagnetic rail guns online and set the munitions feed line for explosive-tipped tungsten bolts", Captain Zarensdorf commanded.

"Aye, Captain. Electromagnetic rail guns online. Explosive tungsten bolts are in the pipeline", his Tactical Officer confirmed.

"Tactical. Both barrels. Twelve rounds per barrel. Acquire target lock and let loose on my mark", Captain Zarensdorf ordered, noting, "We just want to disable the Jovian Glaive and force its crew into their emergency life pods."

"Aye, Captain. Everything is set. We have target lock and are ready for your mark", the Tactical Officer confirmed.

Captain Zarensdorf's face took on a severe expression, then he commanded, "Mark!"

The Tactical Officer fired the electromagnetic rail guns in rapid succession and two dozen explosive tungsten bolts hurtled at extreme speeds, north of Mach thirty, towards the Jovian Glaive.

The bridge crew's eyes were all glued to the main screen, as seconds later the hull of the Jovian Glaive was peppered with small explosions. The Revenant Dawn's long-range scanners detected twenty four precise hits.

The ship's Tactical Officer noted, "Two dozen direct hits, Captain."

"Let's keep monitoring. I want to confirm that they've launched their escape pods", Captain Zarensdorf replied as he studied to main screen, his eyes unflinching.

The first emergency pod detached and moved away from the Jovian Glaive and then another. Then a third emergency pod detached. Things were looking good. Everyone on the Revenant Dawn's bridge smiled. It looked as though they'd succeeded in their mission.

Then there was a series of electrical arcs that shot out from the Jovian Glaive's immense plasma drives. The blue and orange electrical arcs expanded, travelling up and down the length of the ship's hull. As a fourth emergency pod detached, the Jovian Glaive exploded in an immense ball of blue light. The light exploded outwards, engulfing all four of the emergency pods that had managed to launch.

When the light died down, all that was left was a tangled mess of debris.

Captain Zarensdorf shook his head, "Well, that was unexpected", he remarked, noting, "It seems we have underestimated our rail guns and overestimated Jovian technological stability."

Captain Zarensdorf turned to his Communications Officer, "Comms. We need to send an urgent message to Command and our Sister ships. Jovian Glaive was destroyed. All hands lost. Do not use explosive tungsten bolts. Repeat. Do not use explosive tungsten bolts. Use plain tungsten bolts only. Repeat. Plain tungsten bolts only. The recommended number of projectiles is twelve. Please confirm transmission receipt."

The Battle Cruiser, Adjudicating Wraith, with Captain Barry Campbell in command, was on a fast approach to the Jovian Missile Cruiser, the Jovian Scythe. They were also approaching from the rear, in the Jovian Scythe's six. They, too, had the Jovian Scythe on screen.

Captain Campbell quickly read the urgent message from the Revenant Dawn's Captain.

Captain Campbell thought to himself, *"We should have been the first to strike. The Jovian Scythe wiped out Buenos Aires."*

"Tactical! Bring our electromagnetic rail guns online with plain tungsten bolts in the pipeline. Both barrels, six rounds per barrel", Captain Campbell ordered.

"Confirmed, Captain. Electromagnetic rail guns online. Six rounds of plain tungsten in the pipeline for each barrel", the Adjudicating Wraith's Tactical Officer confirmed.

"Acquire target lock and be prepared to fire on my mark", Captain Campbell ordered.

"Confirmed. We have target lock, Captain", the Tactical Officer replied.

Captain Campbell didn't hesitate, "Fire!"

The Tactical Officer fired the electromagnetic rail guns in rapid succession and a dozen tungsten bolts hurtled at extreme velocities towards the Jovian Scythe.

On the bridge of the Jovian Scythe, there was the sudden punch and zipping sound of projectiles ripping through the ship's hull. Klaxons began to sound, red emergency lighting switched on and the ship's computer began issuing warnings.

"Multiple hull breaches detected. Multiple hull breaches detected. The atmosphere is venting out into space. The atmosphere is venting out into space", the computer warned continuously.

Captain Tapio Makela checked the ship's instruments and he frowned. The situation was dire, not something that they could fix. Their air was venting out way too fast. Their time was running short.

"All hands abandon ship. Repeat. All hands abandon ship. Repeat. All hands abandon ship", Captain Makela ordered, thinking to himself, *"What the hell just hit us?"*

As the bridge crew of the Adjudicating Wraith watched, one emergency escape pod after another detached from the Jovian Scythe and moved off to a safe distance. This time, the targeted ship did not explode. It was disabled, surrounded by life pods and the whole group was drifting under their own inertia. Cheers erupted from the Adjudicating Wraith's bridge crew.

Captain Campbell commanded his communications officer, "Comms. Notify

Command and our Sister ships. Operation successful. Repeat. Operation successful. Plain tungsten bolts at six per barrel are the sweet spot. Repeat. Plain tungsten bolts at six per barrel are the sweet spot."

The Battle Cruiser, Avenging Angel, with Captain Charles Zandar in command, was on a fast approach to the Jovian Missile Cruiser, the Jovian Lance. They were also approaching from the rear, in the Jovian Lance's six, as had her Sister ships. They, too, had the Jovian Lance on screen.

Captain Zandar had read the message from the Revenant Dawn's Captain and also the second message from the Adjudicating Wraith's Captain. As a result, his ship had been prepared in advance.

"Tactical. Are we all set to go?", Captain Zandar enquired.

"Aye, Captain. All set and ready to go. I took the liberty of acquiring target lock as we approached", his Tactical Officer replied.

Captain Zandar nodded, "That's called taking the initiative, Lieutenant. Double-check your settings and fire on my mark."

"We are good to go, Captain", the Tactical Lieutenant confirmed after double-checking.

Captain Zandar nodded and issued the order, "Fire!"

The Avenging Angel's Tactical Officer fired the electromagnetic rail guns in rapid succession and a dozen tungsten bolts hurtled at immense speeds towards the Jovian Lance.

As with the Jovian Scythe, the Jovian Lance was struck with tungsten bolts, punching in through one side of the ship and then out the other side. The punching and zipping sounds were clearly audible on the ship's bridge. Corbel Dyson, the First Officer of the Jovian Lance, now its acting Captain, had the misfortune of seeing his Communications Officer's chest have a hole punched straight through it.

The klaxons began to sound, the red emergency lighting kicked in and the computer's warnings followed repeatedly, *"Multiple hull breaches detected. Multiple hull breaches detected. The atmosphere is venting out into space. The atmosphere is venting out into space."*

First Officer Dyson checked the ship's instruments for the rate of air loss and realised the obvious.

First Officer Corbel Dyson quickly gave the order to abandon ship, "All hands abandon ship. Repeat. All hands abandon ship. Repeat. All hands abandon ship."

Within minutes, the Jovian Lance was empty and all of its emergency escape pods had launched.

First Officer Corbel Dyson reached into the internal pocket of his uniform jacket. It was still there, the envelope containing Captain Candida Noreaga's last personal log entry, along with her suicide confession and indictment.

Corbel Dyson looked out of the escape pod's porthole. He saw his stricken vessel, the Jovian Lance, drifting in space and as he watched, he caught sight of something very strange. A dark shape, long and ovoid, bristling with weapons pods and pulse plasma turrets. It was sleek, dark and ominous.

"So that's what hit us", he thought to himself as the dark ship disappeared into the deep void.

On the bridge of the Avenging Angel, Captain Zandar thanked his crew for their good work and instructed his Communications Officer to notify their Command and Sister ships of their success.

Three small fleets approached what was left of the three Jovian Missile Cruisers. They arrived at the battle scenes nine days after the Battle Cruisers had departed on their return vectors to Cis-Lunar Space. The Missile Cruisers, Jovian Lance and Jovian Scythe were hooked up to the space tugs for hauling. Dumas Corporation personnel aboard the space tugs hooked communications lines to both Missile Cruiser's computer systems and networks for data download and analysis.

The Jovian Missile Cruiser's associated life pods were collected by the salvage recovery ships. For nine days, the escape pods had drifted along with their stricken Missile Cruisers. The Jovian survivors had plenty of ration packs and water, but they were nonetheless pleased to be rescued, even if it was by their enemies.

During their initial interrogation aboard the Earth Defence Force Cruisers, the letter in Corbel Dyson's jacket pocket came to light. It was spattered in Captain Candida Noreaga's blood and contained her confession at having launched the second strike, the double tap against Eros, the World within the Rock. Captain Noreaga had described her orders as unlawful, illegal and unconscionable, laying the blame directly on High Prince Godric von Horridian. It was further evidence of his war crimes.

The third Jovian Missile Cruiser, the Jovian Glaive, was just a debris field. There was no Missile Cruiser to tow back to Cis-Lunar Space. The Jovian Glaive was just a field of debris. There were no survivors to save either. The salvage recovery ship salvaged and recovered anything it could, which was not a lot. Just the ship's two black boxes, the ship's main computer core and anything else that could be used to glean further information. Then, having completed the second part of the operation, all three fleets returned to Cis-Lunar Space, thirty days away.

General Camilla Brennan-Chives was very pleased with the results of the mission. The threat posed by the three Jovian Missile Cruisers was mitigated. Cis-Lunar Space and Earth had two mostly intact Jovian Missile Cruisers to study, complete with their computer cores full of vital information. They also had the ship's crews for interrogation and even a confession and indictment of a War crime. And the Dumas-designed and built Battle Cruisers had been tested in live action.

Camilla Brennan-Chives did something she'd always wanted to do but had never had the time. Being that the system was at War, she considered it as good a time as any to do so. After all, in the times of War, the very things you have always wanted to do might never get done. So she did it.

Camilla went to a local pet store in the Colonial Central Command colony. Camilla bought herself a German Shepherd puppy. It was young and would need a lot of training, of course, but she did have staff who were capable of training dogs, so that was not a problem.

General Brennan-Chives and President Reinhardt were getting along extremely well. They were even on a first-name basis, Camilla and Dieter. Which was no problem, as they were both single, consenting adults after all.

Camilla brought her new puppy to President Reinhardt's, Dieter's Office to show off her new pet.

"Dieter, this is my new acquisition", Camilla announced with a flick of her red hair.

"A puppy?", Dieter queried.

"A German Shepherd puppy, Dieter", Camilla replied.

"Okay, Camilla. What's his name?", Dieter enquired.

Camilla smiled a wry smile, "Dieter, her name is, Payback and Payback's a bitch."

24. Deimos.

Data from the computer systems aboard the two captured Jovian Missile Cruisers was analysed by the Dumas Corporation's analysts as soon as the data was downloaded. Godric Horridian's motivations were beginning to be understood. When this was combined with further data provided by Swenna Goodchild, the Saturnian Demarchy's Administrator, things began to get much clearer.

There were a number of people in President Reinhardt's conference room. There was, of course, President Dieter Reinhardt. The Head of the Cis-Lunar Bureau of Investigations, Danica Thomlinson, was present, as was Fleet Captain Nicholas Nikolaidis, Commander of the Cis-Lunar Colonial Fleet, such as it was.

Earth's Defence Forces General, Camilla Brennan-Chives, was present, having been seconded to Cis-Lunar Space to assist with mobilisation and recruitment. The Dumas Brothers, Connor and Daniel, were present as well. Daniel had a briefcase full of files. A German Shepherd puppy named Payback sat on Camilla's lap, fast asleep.

President Reinhardt opened the meeting, "Thank you all for coming. It is my understanding that the Dumas Corporation's analysts have gleaned some useful information from the computers on board those Jovian Missile Cruisers. So I'll hand straight over to Mr Connor Dumas."

"Thank you, Dieter. However, before I begin. Camilla, a puppy?", Connor enquired.

"Yes, Mr Dumas. A new endeavour, a new life. I named her Payback", Camilla replied as she gently stroked her new pet.

"A fitting name, considering our recent successes", Connor replied in agreement and then he requested his Brother, Daniel, to take the lead.

"A female dog named Payback. That is so poetic", Daniel noted before beginning and then he looked around the room, "We are beginning to understand Godric Horridian's motivations. Firstly, he believes his own family's propaganda, their fake history. Secondly, we actually have the man rattled."

"Fake history?", Danica Thomlinson queried, "You got that from their computer systems?"

"Ah, no, Danica. We got that snippet of information from the Saturnian Administrator, Swenna Goodchild", Daniel informed her.

President Reinhardt understood, he nodded and remarked, "The Administrator's network."

Daniel Dumas went on to explain, "As we all know, the arch assassin, Roberta Dumas, has been granted asylum and sanctuary with the Mimasians."

Fleet Captain Nikolaidis noted, nodding, "That small Saturnian Demarchy colony."

"Not quite, Captain. Mimas is an independent colony and not under the Demarchy's jurisdiction", Connor Dumas corrected, noting, "The Mimasians actually hold primacy over the Demarchy, but choose not to exercise the sovereignty that comes with it. Daniel will send you the files on that later."

The Fleet Captain nodded as Daniel continued, "Roberta Nummus has given the Mimasians a lot of information on the Horridians. All of the dirt, so to speak. Of course, the Mimasians have passed that information onto Swenna Goodchild and Swenna has kindly passed that information onto the Administrator's network, to us. So, we now all know what Godric Horridian wants."

"And what is it that Godric Horridian wants?", President Reinhardt questioned.

Daniel shook his head as he replied, "That mad bastard wants to create the Horridian Imperium and he will do anything to achieve it."

"The Horridian Imperium?", General Brennan-Chives questioned.

"Basically, the Horridian Imperium is the Jovian Realms expanded on a total pan-solar scale. The entire solar system under the Horridian Regime's banner, under Horridian Imperial control", Connor chimed in with a quick explanation.

Daniel continued, "The illegal annexation of the two Jovian Trojan Republics was their first step. The second step was converting the Jovian Republic itself into a feudal state, the Six Jovian Realms. The third step, well, that is the conquest of the entire inner solar system."

The conference room fell quiet. This wasn't about Jovian grievances, political slights or even assassination attempts. This was all about conquest and an overarching goal.

"From Roberta Dumas's lips to our very own ears. That is Godric Horridian's agenda", Daniel noted, before he continued, "Disgraced old Albertus Horridian apparently fed his Grandchildren stories about how they were deposed Royals and the 'rightful' rulers of the entire solar system. So Godric Horridian, perhaps even his other Brothers, sees the Horridian Imperium as his family's 'manifest' destiny."

"He's completely fucking mad!", General Brennan-Chives exclaimed.

"Yes, Camilla. He most certainly is", President Reinhardt agreed.

"How on Earth does he expect to achieve this, this Horridian Imperium?", Camilla questioned.

"It is actually far easier than you might think, Camilla", Connor replied, nodding to his Brother.

Daniel explained, "If Godric Horridian can conquer Earth and Cis-Lunar Space, he automatically gets the entirety of Earth's orbital zone and the Martian orbital zone. That makes the Venusian orbital zone extremely vulnerable to a hostile takeover. With the inner solar system under his belt, everything between Martian orbit and the Jovian Realms becomes ripe for the taking. So the Belters would all quickly fall. Then it becomes a matter of stepping from one outer realm to the next, like stepping stones. The Saturnian Demarchy, the Uranian Federation and then the Neptunian Commonwealth. At that point, he has the whole enchilada, the Horridian Imperium."

"Except, Godric Horridian does not have the Earth or Cis-Lunar Space", Camilla countered.

"Not for lack of trying, Camilla. Not for lack of trying", Connor noted in reply.

Daniel chimed back in, "The silly prick miscalculated. Godric Horridian thought that mass murder and genocide would cower us into submission. He failed to understand, his actions were always going to have the opposite effect."

The General nodded, "He's galvanised us into something he never expected."

"Yes, he has, Camilla", Daniel confirmed, noting, "Godric Horridian, in his haste to achieve his ambitions, has unwittingly placed himself between a hammer and an anvil."

Camilla Brennan-Chives smirked, "That hammer is going to come down hard!"

Fleet Captain Nikolaidis enquired of Daniel, "You said we had him rattled, Mr Dumas?"

"Yeah, we do, Nick", Daniel replied informally, explaining, "Godric Horridian has people here in Cis-Lunar L-Five. They have been sending the Horridians photographs of our L-Four shipyards. Photographs of our new classes of warships."

Danica Thomlinson chimed in, "Yes, the same people who set off those flash vaporisers. My people have been tracking them down and rounding them up. Four dozen Jovian spies so far. We have even confiscated two dozen of those awful flash vaporiser devices."

Daniel Dumas nodded, "There will be more, so keep up the good work, Danica", then he continued his exposé, "They have analysed photographs of our new warships. Our new Battle Cruisers and Dreadnought have them worried, sure, but it's the other new ship classes that have them really rattled. They don't have anything like our Interplanetary Fighter Carriers, Armoured Refuelling Craft or Armoured Supplier Tenders. They have nothing like those at all and they understand the implications."

The Fleet Captain nodded in understanding, "The Jovian Realms are old school. Set up a base of operations. Transport in fighters, fuel and supplies. That's basically freight haulage using civilian haulage contractors."

"And that is what has Godric Horridian so rattled, Nick", Daniel agreed, noting, "We can set up Battle Groups around our Fighter Carriers and have our Refuelling Craft and Supply Tenders following up in the rear. A single Battle Group can stay on mission for years at a time, untethered from any base of operations. They are fully mobile. Godric Horridian does not have anything like that."

General Brennan-Chives nodded in agreement, "I can see why he's so rattled."

Fleet Captain Nikolaidis also nodded, noting, "That will be why they hit Buenos Aires and triggered those flash vaporisers. They want to keep us in complete disarray, sowing fear, uncertainty and doubt."

"Which brings me to the next point", Daniel told everyone before continuing, "The Jovian Lance was ordered to second strike as in double tap Eros. We now have proof positive of that. The Jovian Scythe was ordered to strike Earth with eight cold-fusion warheads culminating with the strike on Buenos Aires. We now have proof positive of that as well, although the Captain of the Jovian Scythe was kept in the dark about Buenos Aires. He believed it was all just a demonstration."

Daniel paused for a moment, "However, it was their most recent orders that we need to consider. We got very lucky with our timing. The morning of our attack on those three Jovian Missile Cruisers, they'd received orders to converge on the Martian moon, Deimos. They were to attack our military and refuelling bases there, take control of them and then hold them until reinforcements arrived. That operation was supposed to be set in motion later in the afternoon, a mere three hours after we took down their Missile Cruisers."

"That was ridiculously fortuitous", Camilla noted, "Had our Battle Cruisers arrived a day later, our targets would have already been well on their way."

"Yes, it was", Connor Dumas agreed, commenting, "Had we delayed by just one day, the mission would have failed. We need to keep striking while the iron is hot. We must be relentless!"

Daniel noted, "We dodged a bullet by taking out those three enemy Missile

Cruisers. We could have just as easily lost our logistics bases on Deimos.

"Fleet Captain Nikolaidis nodded, expounding, "In order to project power into the inner solar system, the Horridians need bases. Deimos would have been perfect. Deimos is likely high up on their list of priority targets."

"Yes, Nick. Absolutely correct", Connor agreed, "We need to get our forces to Deimos urgently."

General Brennan-Chives frowned and noted, "We can't use our current assets in play. They are still returning from their mission to take down those Jovian Missile Cruisers."

Daniel stood up and walked around the conference room table, handing out documents. It contained a list of new ships, along with their Captains.

Motto:
We are Above You. We are Below You.
We are Behind You. We are Upon You.
We are all Teeth and Claws.

- An Interplanetary Fighter Carrier, the Indomitable Wyvern, Captained by Ms Janice Whatley,
  - with forty Bat Wing Interceptors aboard.
- A Dreadnought, the Dragon's Teeth, Captained by Mr Robert Marley.
- Three Battle Cruisers,
  - The Fearless Fang, Captained by Mr Thomas Zumwalt.
  - The Razor Claw, Captained by Ms June Shaver.
  - The Venomous Bite, Captained by Mr John Tucker.
- An Armoured Refuelling Craft, the Dragon's Blood, Captained by Mr Ioannis Milos.
- An Armoured Supply Tender, the Dragon's Forge, Captained by Mr Benjamin Blake.

"This is a new Battle Group, my Brother, Connor, and I have been assembling. It's ready and waiting for the order to defend Deimos. It's just waiting on your decision", Daniel told them.

"Why do we need to send a refuelling ship and the supply tender?", President Reinhardt questioned, noting, "Deimos has all of that on-site already."

General Brennan-Chives replied informally, "Dieter, this is a War. We cannot guarantee that those bases on Deimos will still be there when this Battle Group arrives, or, for that matter, that we will still have control over those bases. It won't hurt to have independent fuel and supplies at the rear."

"Camilla is right, Dieter", Connor confirmed, noting, "There are no capital ships at Deimos, just interceptors and runabouts. I've checked our records, two-seat Talons and Gull Wings, single-seat Bat Wings and Switch Blades, ten of each. Along with a dozen unarmed Gull Wing Skimmers. They won't last long against Jovian Corvettes or Destroyers, let alone Jovian Missile Cruisers."

President Reinhardt nodded in understanding, "Based on what Camilla has just stated, this sounds extremely urgent. I will sign off on this immediately. Launch this Battle Group as soon as possible."

"You gave the ships in the Battle Group names with Dragon motifs?", an amused Camilla asked.

"You did name your female German Shepherd pup, Payback", Daniel countered with a chuckle.

"Touche", the General replied.

Fleet Captain Nicholas Nikolaidis asked bluntly, "Where on Earth did you get captains and crews for this Battle Group? We have recruits, but none of them will be ready for at least six months."

Connor smiled and chuckled, "Nick, it has been Dumas Corporate policy since the early days. Our Grandfather, Stuart, wanted every Dumas employee to have multiple skill sets."

Daniel stepped in, "It's a good policy, Nick. It ensures that if workers are redundant in one area, we can transition them across to another area very quickly. We rarely, if ever, let anyone go unless they choose to take a package."

Connor explained, "We have an excellent personal development program. You would be surprised how many of our employees have leadership, pilot, navigation, communications, engineering and even tactical qualifications. We make a request to our division, Dumas Personnel Ltd, for volunteers and our people come to us with applications."

The Fleet Captain shook his head, "Well, I never. Perhaps I should be recruiting through Dumas Personnel Ltd."

President Reinhardt questioned, "There's more to the Martian orbital zone than just Deimos. What about your Corporate colonies in the Martian Leading and Trailing Trojans?"

"They are likely lesser targets, although still targets nonetheless", Connor noted dryly, adding, "Then again, you could say the same thing about the Belters. Godric Horridian will want forward operating bases and he may even try to occupy our mining zones or perhaps, one or two of the Belter Nations."

Daniel's face took on a stern look, "My Wife, Harmony, was born a Belter. Her maiden name is Moon. Harmony is putting together a plan to protect her people as we speak. You can guarantee that she will be thorough, very thorough."

General Brennan-Chives chimed in, "To protect your mining zones and the Belters from Jovian aggression is important. We can ill afford any of them to be turned into Jovian military bases", she turned to the President, "Dieter, we are going to need a lot more Battle Groups. At least fifteen and that is just for defence. Space is vast and if we go on the offensive, we will need more, a lot more."

Fleet Captain Nikolaidis rubbed his chin, "We have Corvettes, we have Destroyers and a handful of Dreadnoughts. Honestly, Godric Horridian timed this beautifully. We are so under-prepared. We can perhaps field a few small strike groups, but nothing like this one", he pointed to the piece of paper in front of him, "Our shipyards need to produce a lot more. We urgently need to catch up."

Connor Dumas took some notes down on his data tablet with its stylus, "I will have some of our efficiency experts pay your shipyards a visit and come up with some recommendations."

The Indomitable Wyvern strike group left for Mars the next day. Travelling at top speed, they expected orbital insertion in just over five weeks. The Armoured Refuelling Craft, the Dragon's Blood and the Armoured Supply Tender, the Dragon's Forge, being much larger vessels, were following up in the rear, expecting their own orbital insertion in a little over six weeks.

The sleek, yet massive Dreadnought, the Dragon's Teeth flew in the van, taking the lead, with the Interplanetary Fighter Carrier, the Indomitable Wyvern, not too far behind. The three Battle Cruisers, the Fearless Fang, the Razor Claw and the Venomous Bite took up flanking positions around the Indomitable Wyvern in a triangular formation.

While the Indomitable Wyvern Strike Group flew swiftly towards Mars, the shipyards of Cis-Lunar L-Four stepped up production. The new sleek, stretched ovoid-designed ships, bristling with weapons, were rolling off the Dumas Colonial Construction production lines. The more traditionally stretched, triangular-designed, equally well-armed ships were rolling off the Government production lines.

Efficiency experts from the Dumas Corporation gave the Government engineers practical advice on how to improve their production lines. Dumas Personnel Ltd began advertising for volunteers to join the Cis-Lunar Colonial

Fleet.

New flight simulators manufactured by the Dumas Corporation were provided to the Cis-Lunar Government. They were to aid in the training of the new Colonial Fleet crew members in the management and operations of the newer Dumas-designed ships. By the time the Indomitable Wyvern Strike Group reached Mars, the Cis-Lunar L-Four shipyards would be running at peak production.

The Indomitable Wyvern Strike Group was still two weeks out from Mars and its destination, the Martian moon, Deimos, when the encrypted communique came through. The Captain of the Indomitable Wyvern, Captain Janice Whatley, read the communique with concern. A Jovian task force had been detected en route to Mars. The Jovians would, if not intercepted, arrive at Mars at least a day ahead of their own task force.

Captain Whatley went to her cabin and unlocked her safe. The Captain pulled out a series of contingency orders. These were contingencies for the various possibilities that could have arisen before the arrival of the task force at its destination. As the Captain read the titles on the envelopes, she placed the ones that did not apply back into her safe.

Contingency. Deimos has been destroyed. That was not applicable, so it went back into the safe.

Contingency. Deimos has been occupied by Jovian Forces. Again, that was not applicable, so back into the safe it went.

Contingency. Deimos is under attack by the Jovian Forces. Another one that was not applicable. Captain Whatley placed it back into the safe along with the others.

Contingency. Jovian Forces on approach vector to Martian space. That was the one she had been looking for. Captain Whatley placed the remaining orders back into her safe and then opened the one she'd been looking for. The Captain read the order, memorised it and then placed the order back into its envelope, before replacing it into her safe and locking it. Then, the Captain returned to the bridge.

"Tactical. How many ships are in that Jovian task force?", Captain Whatley calmly enquired.

"Seven Jovian Destroyers, Captain. I'm searching our database for precise class and capabilities", came the Tactical Officer's reply.

"Excellent Work. We have their current position and course trajectory?", Captain Whatley asked.

"Yes, Captain", her Tactical Officer replied.

Captain Whatley closed her eyes for a moment in thought before ordering, "Communications. Get me the Dragon's Teeth on the line. I need to speak with Captain Marley. Encrypted comms."

When Captain Marley answered the call, Captain Whatley informed him, "Captain Marley, one of our contingency triggers has been breached."

Captain Marley's face took on a stern look, "Which particular trigger, Ma'am?"

Captain Whatley replied, her face looking equally stern, "Captain, we have seven Jovian Destroyers on an approach vector to Mars. Our orders are straightforward, Bob. You are to take your Dreadnought and peel away from our task force. Intercept the Jovian task force with the Dragon's Teeth and eliminate the threat."

Captain Robert Marley rubbed his chin, "Seven Jovian Destroyers against one of our brand new Dreadnoughts. This will be very interesting, Ma'am."

"I'll have my Communications Officer transmit their current coordinates and their course trajectory, along with the precise classifications and capabilities of Destroyers you'll be facing", Captain Janice Whatley replied, before remarking, "Good luck and God's speed, Bob. Over and out."

The line then dropped out and the Indomitable Wyvern's Communications Officer transferred all of the relevant information and data to the Dragon's Teeth.

One week later, the Dreadnought, the Dragon's Teeth, was approaching the small fleet of seven Jovian Destroyers. Captain Robert Marley had instructed his Helmsmen to approach the Jovians from the rear, from their six. They did so undetected.

"Helmsmen, let's keep our distance", Captain Marley ordered.

"Aye, Captain", his Helmsmen replied, noting, "You will be pleased to know, Captain. They are only scanning forward, Sir. They don't even know we are here."

"Good to know, Helmsmen. Let's keep it that way for the moment. I don't want any of them to see this coming", the Captain replied.

Captain Marley was sitting in his Captain's chair on his ship's bridge. He took a data crystal from out of his jacket pocket and placed it into a data receptacle.

"Communications. Give me control of all communications channels", Captain Marley commanded.

"Aye, Captain. Access to all communications channels is now with your station", the Communications Officer confirmed.

Captain Marley brought the Jovian Fleet up on the bridge's main screen. The seven Jovian Destroyers were all flying in a loose formation and quite spread out.

"Tactical. Those two Destroyers that are on their flanks. Target them with cold-fusion missiles", Captain Marley commanded.

"Yes, Sir", his Tactical Officer confirmed, "I have two missiles locked and loaded. I must advise, Captain, that at this distance, those warheads can only ramp up to ten kiloton yields."

"Not a problem. Five kiloton yields should be enough", Captain Marley replied, ordering, "Switch our electromagnetic rail gun feed lines to explosive tungsten bolts. Both barrels, twenty five rounds a piece. Target that Jovian Destroyer in the centre of their formation."

"Yes, Sir. Locked, loaded and ready, Captain", his Tactical Officer confirmed.

"Excellent. Now, Tactical, bring all of our weapons pods, with all dual laser beams and dual particle beams online and at the ready", the Captain ordered.

"Yes, Sir. All weapons pods online and at the ready", his Tactical Officer confirmed.

"Okay, Tactical. Do the same with all of our quad pulse plasma cannons. Bring them all online and ready", Captain Marley ordered.

"All quad pulse plasma turrets are online and ready, Sir", his Tactical Officer confirmed.

"Set all weapons pods and turrets to computer-controlled automatic targeting and firing", the Captain commanded.

Again, his Tactical Officer complied, "All set and ready to go, Captain."

"Helmsmen. Prepare our ship to punch through the enemy fleet's formation, while performing a counterclockwise barrel roll", Captain Marley commanded.

The Dragon's Teeth's Helmsmen complied, "Ready and waiting, Captain Sir."

Captain Marley brought the three pre-targeted Jovian Destroyers onto the screen. Three Jovian Nova Class Destroyers, with a known defect. Their scanners had a conical blind spot at their rear, centred around their plasma thrusters. It was a common flaw in the designs of older ships. Captain Marley studied his prey, knowing that his first salvo would be devastating and his second would be final.

"Tactical. Cold-fusion missiles. Launch on my mark", Captain Marley ordered.

"Ready and waiting, Sir", his Tactical Officer confirmed.

"Fire!", came the Captain's command.

"Firing one! Firing two!", his Tactical Officer announced, "Both missiles are tracking to target, Sir."

"Prepare to fire electromagnetic rail guns on my mark", Captain Marley orders.

"Ready and waiting, Sir", his Tactical Officer confirmed.

"Fire!", came the Captain's command.

His Tactical Officer complied, "Firing! All explosive tungsten bolts are on their way, Captain."

As the bridge crew watched the screen, the high-speed explosive tungsten rounds struck first. The Nova Class Destroyer in the centre of the enemy fleet's formation, likely the command Destroyer, was peppered with fifty small, yet devastating explosions. Blue and orange electrical arcs spread up and down its cracked and broken hull. Then, less than ten seconds later, there were two massive explosions as its plasma thrusters exploded, ripping the Destroyer apart. All that was left of the Destroyer was an expanding cloud of debris.

Then, mere seconds later, the Destroyer on the enemy fleet's left flank was engulfed in a massive fireball of blue-white light. A split second after that, the Destroyer on the enemy fleet's right flank was also engulfed in a massive fireball of blue-white light. As the balls of light dissipated, the bridge crew could see that both Destroyers had completely vanished. Completely vaporised in the thermonuclear flashes! They were erased from existence in an instant.

The Dragon's Teeth's Tactical Officer noted dryly, "Both warheads managed to ramp up to seven kilotons over that distance."

"Good to know, Tactical", Captain Marley replied as he centred the remaining four ships of the enemy's fleet on the bridge's screen, "Prepare for our second salvo."

"Helmsmen! Start rolling the Dragon's Teeth counterclockwise and increase speed. Punch us through their formation", Captain Marley ordered as he then jammed every communications channel with loud classical music.

Captain Marley played the final four minutes of Tchaikovsky's eighteen twelve overture, complete with simulated explosions over every communications channel as loudly as possible. He also played it for his bridge crew, but somewhat quieter.

"Those poor bastards won't have a hope in hell of coordinating a response, with Tchaikovsky playing over every comms channel", Captain Marley announced.

The Jovian Captains were caught completely by surprise and when they attempted to communicate with each other, all they could hear was Tchaikovsky's eighteen twelve overture played loud and clear.

The Dreadnought, the Dragon's Teeth, lunged forward like a javelin, rolling counterclockwise with all weapons pods and turrets automatically targeting and blazing away. Bright blue beams of high-powered coherent laser light lanced outwards, slicing through hulls like hot knives through butter. Bright orange beams of powerful particles lanced outwards, punching through hulls like they were made of tissue paper. Brilliant blue-white balls of pulsing plasma exploded against hulls, vaporising metal as if it were little more than ice.

One by one, the four remaining Jovian Nova Class Destroyers exploded in brilliant balls of orange fire, quickly extinguished by the vacuum of space, leaving little more than expanding debris fields in their wake. By the time that Tchaikovsky's eighteen twelve overture had finished, there was nothing left for the Dragons Teeth's tactical computer system to target.

Captain Robert, Bob, Marley sighed an internal sigh of relief as he ordered, "Damage report?"

His Tactical Officer responded, "Zero damage, Captain."

The Captain requested, "Status of the enemy fleet?"

His Tactical Officer blinked before replying, "The Jovian enemy fleet no longer exists, Captain."

Then his Tactical Officer added for clarity, "Sir, the enemy was so unprepared that they didn't even get to fire off a single shot."

Captain Marley nodded, "An extremely successful hunt. Record our successful manoeuvre in detail under the file, *'Marley Tactical Manoeuvre One'*. I may want to use that again sometime."

His Tactical Officer complied. The Marley Manoeuvre, as it became known, was used many times throughout the First Horridian War. It was simply called *"Pulling a Marley"*. Generally, the only thing that changed was the musical score used to jam the enemy's communications channels. Each ship's Captain had their own musical preferences, with many choosing hard rock over classical music. Although Richard Wagner's *"The Ride of the Valkyries"* was particularly popular and had a highly psychologically devastating effect.

"Communications. Send a message to the Indomitable Wyvern, Captain Whatley. 'The Dragon's Teeth has tasted blood. We were victorious. The Jovian Fleet has been completely neutralised. We will rendezvous with the strike group at Deimos.'", the Captain ordered.

Then he took his data crystal out of the receptacle and replaced it in his jacket pocket. Captain Marley placed another data crystal into the receptacle and played it, Swan Lake. The Captain was a fan of Tchaikovsky. His bridge crew all smiled and relaxed.

"Helmsman, lay in a course for rendezvous with the Indomitable Wyvern at Deimos", the Captain ordered and then to his Tactical Officer, "Tactical, keep scanning for threats. Head on a swivel."

"Yes, Captain", they both replied in unison.

25. Friendly Fire.

High Prince Godric was sitting in his throne room. As he sat upon his throne, a handful of his Ministers entered. There was Miles Morton, his Minister of Security, Peter Macron, his Minister of Defence and finally, Peter Patronis, his Minister of Science and Technology. All three of his Ministers had serious, concerned looks on their faces. Something was wrong, very, very wrong and their faces all showed it.

Two seats to High Prince Godric's right, his Brother, Prince Emeric, sitting on his own somewhat less ornate throne, remarked, "This looks like bad news, Brother."

The High Prince turned to his Brother, "I can see that, Brother Emeric", and then he turned back to his approaching Ministers, "Give me the bad news, Gentlemen. Out with it!"

Defence Minister Peter Macron delivered the bad news, "Your Majesty. We have lost three Missile Cruisers and seven Destroyers, Sire."

"Lost?", the High Prince questioned, "Just how do we lose three Cruisers and seven Destroyers?"

Defence Minister Macron replied, hoping that the High Prince would not have Security Minister, Miles Morton, disembowel him as he had with his Communications Minister, Temu Trump.

Peter Macron presented the facts as best he could, hoping to survive, "Your Majesty, the Missile Cruiser, Jovian Glaive has been destroyed, or at least so we believe. Her Sister ships, the Jovian Scythe and the Jovian Lance, have both been captured by the Colonial Fleet, along with their crews."

"And our Destroyers?", the High Prince questioned.

Peter Macron divulged the rest, "Sire, the seven Destroyer fleet that we sent to Mars to take the Deimos military base and refuelling stations have also been destroyed. One of our assets at Port Phobos has also informed us that a Colonial Fleet IFC Strike Group has arrived at Deimos."

"An IFC Strike Group?", High Prince Godric queried.

"Yes, Sire", Minister Macron confirmed, "A Colonial Fleet Interplanetary Fighter Carrier Strike Group, IFC, Sire. One Interplanetary Fighter Carrier, one Dreadnought, three Battle Cruisers, one Armoured Refuelling Craft and an Armoured Supply Tender. They are all new Dumas Corporate-designed and manufactured ships. All of them with the latest Dumas weapons and shielding technology. We have nothing like them, Sire."

High Prince Godric's frown was almost audible, "I think I can guess what happened to our fleet of Destroyers. Wiped out, yes."

"Yes, Your Majesty, all seven of them. They didn't even get a mayday out, Sire.

That is how devastating the attack was. One Dumas Dreadnought destroyed seven of our Nova Class Destroyers, Sire", Minister Macron confirmed.

High Prince Godric was quiet, too quiet. The silence was so *"loud"* that it was uncomfortable.

Prince Emeric broke the silence, "This is a major loss, Brother", and then he noted something that perhaps he shouldn't, "If our former Communications Minister, Temu Trump, was still here, I'm quite certain he would recommend nuking Earth back into the stone age as a reprisal."

High Prince Godric scoffed, "Yes, he would have, but we need the Earth. In case you had not noticed, Brother, we only have one habitable world in our solar system. I dare not burn it!"

While Prince Emeric nodded in agreement, Science Minister Peter Patronis noted, "Sire, that is not entirely true. The Martian terraforming project has been highly successful and the word is that Mars will be open for colonisation in perhaps a century. At the very latest, by the year twenty three hundred."

Godric's eyes opened up wide and that changed everything.

If Mars was ready for colonisation in as little as a hundred years, did he really need the Earth?

"Perhaps, just perhaps, we can afford to burn the Earth just a little", High Prince Godric mused, "Perhaps, just enough to make them think twice about attacking us here in our own backyard."

Godric had a huge smirk on his face and his Brother, Emeric, thought to himself, *"Why the hell did I open my big fucking mouth?"*

President Dieter Reinhardt was in his conference room, along with General Camilla Brennan-Chives, her puppy, Payback, Fleet Captain Nicholas Nikolaidis and the Head of the Cis-Lunar Bureau of Investigations, Danica Thomlinson. The Dumas Brothers, Connor and Daniel, were also present, along with their Wives, Carmelita nee Alvarez and Harmony nee Moon.

Their first point of discussion was the Cis-Lunar military base and refuelling station on the Martian moon Deimos, as well as the elimination of the small fleet of Jovian Destroyers.

Camilla noted, "Captain Marley's methods were unorthodox, but they were also highly effective."

Fleet Captain Nikolaidis agreed, "Indeed, they were. Captain Marley eliminated seven Destroyers before they could even fire off a single shot. If I'm going to captain one of those new Dumas Dreadnoughts, I'll need to book some time on the flight simulators. That Marley Manoeuvre has everyone buzzing. I can't imagine the looks on those Jovian Captain's faces when they tried to coordinate their remaining ships and all they could hear was Tchaikovsky's eighteen twelve overture blasting across their comms channels."

Danica Thomlinson snickered, "I bet that had them confused. I know I would have been."

Connor smiled, "My takeaway from the Marley Manoeuvre was that all of the weapons systems on our Dreadnought, the Dragon's Teeth, worked perfectly as designed."

Daniel agreed with his Brother, "Captain Marley did manage to find a way to test every system."

President Reinhardt was more than happy, one of his new Dreadnoughts was battle-tested. Better yet, the Martian moon, Deimos, had a Carrier Strike Group to defend its military base and refuelling stations. By the same token, the twin-cylinder O'Neil-style colonies in high Martian order and Port Phobos on the Martian moon, Phobos, were protected as well. It was highly unlikely that Godric Horridian would risk another fleet in an attempt to take Deimos. The risk of failure was just too high.

President Reinhardt remarked, "We need to put together more of those Carrier Strike Groups."

Harmony Dumas replied, "While Carrier Strike Groups are a requirement, we do have other concerns, Mr President. Other priorities."

President Reinhardt questioned, "Other concerns, Mrs Dumas?"

Harmony frowned, "The Horridian Regime has lost three Missile Cruisers and seven Nova Class Destroyers. They are going to want payback. Godric Horridian will want a victory."

"What are you suggesting, Mrs Dumas?", the President enquired.

"I am suggesting that while it is very unlikely that Godric Horridian will take another shot at Deimos. It is quite likely that he might take a shot at one or two of the Belter Nations. That is a strong possibility", Harmony explained and then she qualified, "I am biased. I am a Moon and I have family right throughout the Asteroid Belt and its colonies. My logic is nonetheless, tactically sound."

General Brennan-Chives chimed in, "Mrs Dumas is one hundred percent correct. The Horridians won't reattempt taking Mars anytime soon. However, one, perhaps two or more of the Belter Nations would give them multiple forward operating bases for their inner solar system operations."

Fleet Captain Nikolaidis stepped in, "It would not be difficult for the Horridians to achieve that either. The Belters don't have any military. Just mining, transport, trading and police vessels."

"I have spoken to my Cousin, Harlequin. He is the Ceresian Administrator. Harley has spoken to all twelve Belter Ambassadors on Ceres Central. They fully understand the threat. They are all amenable to any defensive measures that Cis-Lunar Space and Earth can provide", Harmony informed them.

Daniel Dumas seconded his Wife, Harmony, "The Belters see the Horridians as an existential threat."

Connor Dumas stepped in, "Whatever we decide here, I can tell you all this. The Dumas Corporation will not leave the Belters hanging in the wind like low-hanging fruit, ripe for the picking."

President Reinhardt queried, "I take it that if I decide against aiding the Belters, the Dumas Corporation will act alone?"
Daniel Dumas held his Wife's hand firmly, "The Moons are our kinfolk by marriage. The Dumas Corporation will act alone in this matter if we have to."

Connor nodded in agreement, "The Dumas Corporation and the Belter Nations are intrinsically linked. We have been since we helped them set up their colonies. If the Belters want our help, we will provide it, even if it means going against the law."

"It won't come to that, Connor", President Reinhardt replied and then he asked, "Mrs Dumas, do you have a plan?"

Harmony replied, "Yes, I have a plan, but we do have limitations. There are thirteen Belter Nations, so we need to protect each and every one of them. Our limitations are human resources and personnel, namely, Captains and crews. Dumas Personnel is hiring skilled and talented people from our employee pool. We even have employees volunteering who want to step up to the challenge, so they are undergoing fast-tracked training as well."

General Brennan-Chives noted, "Okay, Harmony. So the Dumas Corporation is working out the personnel issues", and then she asked, "What about your plans?"

Harmony took a deep breath, "First, we need a bulwark. A first line of defence. That will be the Belter Nations. Our second line of defence will be in the Martian orbital zone. Mars itself with Phobos and Deimos, but also the Martian Dumas Trojan Mining Zones. Both of these lines of defence are going to start out very thin, but we have no choice in that. The ships and their crews are not as available as we'd like."

"Okay, Harmony, how do you envisage this working?", General Brennan-Chives questioned.

"The next thirteen Battle Cruisers. Once they're crewed and Captained, we send one each out to the thirteen Belter Nations. If I'm right, the Horridians will know that their Missile Cruisers were no match for our Battle Cruisers. They will think twice before making any attempt on the Belters", Harmony explained and then she noted, "Then we move on to the offence."

"Onto the offence?", Fleet Captain Nikolaidis asked, sounding somewhat incredulous.

"Yes, Captain. Offence", Harmony confirmed, explaining, "We will build two Carrier Battle Groups. Each will be the same as the Indomitable Wyvern Strike Group. One Interplanetary Fighter Carrier, one Dreadnought, three Battle Cruisers, with Armoured Refuelling and Supply Tenders following in the rear. Initially, each Battle Group will have an extra Battle Cruiser. The two extra Battle Cruisers will be dropped off at the Martian Leading and Trailing Trojan mining zones on their way out to Jovian space."

"Jovian space?", the Fleet Captain questioned, sounding even more incredulous.

"Yes, Sir", Harmony confirmed, explaining further, "While our Battle Cruisers are on their way out to the Belter Nations. Our IFC Strike Groups will fly out to Jovian space. Two Strike Groups, one hundred and twenty degrees apart. They'll drop off the two Battle Cruisers to the Martian Trojans on their way out. That way we'll have both the Belters and the Martian Trojan mining zones covered."

Camilla Brennan-Chives nodded and she understood, "The movement of our Battle Cruisers individually launching isn't very noteworthy. Just patrol manoeuvres. The fact that they're flying out to the Belters will likely be missed. Two Carrier Strike Groups, however, that's a big deal. Any assets the Horridians still have here in Cis-Lunar L-Five will pass that information onto the Jovian Realms."

"Yes, General", Harmony confirmed, "They'll see two Carrier Strike Groups heading their way. They should be too busy to notice our Battle Cruisers positioning to protect the Belters."

"Harmony, when our Carrier Strike Groups reach Jovian space. What will they be doing?", General Brennan-Chives asked.

"Interdicting Jovian military assets in Jovian space", Harmony announced, then she shrugged her shoulders, "Giving those Horridian bastards grief, of course."

Danica Thomlinson blinked, then suddenly interjected, "Harmony, if my teams take out all of the Jovian spies, that will adversely affect your plans."

"Yes, Ms Thomlinson. If the Jovian infiltrators are a threat, then by all means, eliminate them, but we do need at least a few around to pass on the news about our Carrier Strike Groups leaving the shipyards", Harmony Dumas agreed.

Danica took down some notes on her data tablet, "Got that noted down, Harmony."

Camilla Brennan-Chives considered Harmony's mention of interdicting Jovian military assets, "We are going to need information on Jovian fleet movements within their territory."

Daniel smiled, "That detailed information will become available soon, General. When Harmony mentioned her plans to me yesterday, I instructed our company, Astro Resources Ltd, in Cis-Lunar L-Two, to perform some deep surveillance of Jovian space. There are apparently regular Jovian fleet manoeuvres between Jovian space and both Jupiter L-One and Jupiter L-Two."

Fleet Captain Nikolaidis smiled a broad smile, "Any chance of me being the Captain of one of those Strike Group Dreadnoughts?"

General Brennan-Chives smiled an even broader smile, "No chance, Nick. You're the Fleet Captain of the Colonial Fleet. Your place is on the bridge of an Interplanetary Fighter Carrier. You would be in charge of the whole Carrier Strike Group!"

Fleet Captain Nikolaidis sighed. The Fleet Captain had been tied to a desk ever since his last command and subsequent promotion. Nicholas Nikolaidis was actually looking forward to commanding a ship once more.

Nick really wanted to be a Dreadnought Captain, if for no other reason than to try his hand at the Marley Manoeuvre. Then again, is it possible for an Interplanetary Fighter Carrier to roll and fire all of its weapons at the same time and what musical score would he use to jam the Jovian communications channels? Certainly not classical music, something different, very different.

Connor's Wife, Carmelita, who had been quiet during the discussions, noted, "Harmony's plan contains more, much more", her Brazilian Portuguese accent still strong despite living most of her life in the Cis-Lunar Space colonies.

"More?", Danica questioned.

"Oh, yes, there's always more", Harmony confirmed before continuing, "You might remember, I stated that our defence lines are going to start out thinly manned. That is where the Earth's and the Cis-Lunar government shipyards come in."

Fleet Captain Nikolaidis and General Brennan-Chives both looked at Harmony curiously.

"You have Destroyers and Missile Cruisers rolling off your assembly lines", Harmony noted, and then explained, "Use the Destroyers to defend Cis-Lunar Space, but the first fifteen Missile Cruisers from each of your shipyards are needed on our defence lines."

General Brennan-Chives caught on quickly as usual, she nodded and remarked, "Thirteen a piece to the Belter Nations and two a piece to the Martian Trojan mining zones."

"Precisely", Harmony confirmed, explaining, "One Battle Cruiser at each location is a good start. We can capitalise on the psychological effects of defeating those three Jovian Missile Cruisers so easily, but those effects won't hold forever. We need to bolster our defence lines with the addition of a pair of Missile Cruisers at each location."

The Fleet Captain nodded, "And by splitting the burden across both of our shipyards, Earth and Cis-Lunar L-Four, it spreads the overall burden. Thins it out, so to speak."

"Yes, exactly, Fleet Captain", Harmony confirmed and then she smiled and noted, "Fleet Captain, you might be pleased to know. Each of our Interplanetary Fighter Carriers and Dreadnoughts has onboard flight and tactical simulators for crew upskilling. I thought you might like to know that."

Nicholas Nikolaidis smiled broadly, "Yes, yes, indeed. If I'm going to be on the bridge of a Fighter Carrier, those simulators will be extremely useful for understanding ship capabilities and manoeuvres."

Harmony Dumas, nee Moon, completed the discussions with a simple statement, "If we do this right, Ladies and Gentlemen, we can interdict anything that the Horridians send into the inner solar system. Complete active territorial denial."

Both General Brennan-Chives and Fleet Captain Nikolaidis nodded in comprehension. Harmony Dumas was a Moon by birth and perhaps the most savvy of them all when it came to tactical thinking.

Fleet Captain Nikolaidis sat in his captain's chair on his ship, the Fighter Carrier Spitting Witch's bridge. Six weeks out from Cis-Lunar Space, the Strike Group had dropped off its extra Battle Cruiser, the Dauntless, at the Trailing Martian Trojan mining zone. Its mission is to protect the colonies and mining infrastructure in that zone.

A pair of Missile Cruisers, one from the Earth Defence Forces and one from the Colonial Fleet, were expected to arrive as reinforcements four weeks later.

The Earth's Missile Cruiser bore a stretched yet stocky rectangular design, in contrast to the Colonial Fleet's stretched triangular configuration.

Both contained missiles with conventional, yet powerful warheads. The newer cold-fusion warhead designs from the Dumas Corporation had not yet been accepted for production in either government's weapons manufacturing facilities.

The Spitting Witch Strike Group then continued on its way towards Jovian space for another seven weeks. Fleet Captain Nikolaidis spent much of that time training in his ship's tactical simulators.

Motto:
Welcome to The Bubbling Cauldron of Your Doom.
We will, We will, Boil you!

- An Interplanetary Fighter Carrier, the Spitting Witch, Captained by Mr Nicholas Nikolaidis,
    - with forty Bat Wing Interceptors aboard.
- A Dreadnought, the Witch's Hammer, Captained by Mr Javier Elizondo.
- Three Battle Cruisers, the Nornia,
    - Urd, Captained by Ms Alina Dragomir.
    - Verdandi, Captained by Ms Ryoko Kanzaki.
    - Skuld, Captained by Ms Sandra Zumwalt, the Sister of Captain Mr Thomas Zumwalt.
- An Armoured Refuelling Craft, the Cauldron, Captained by Mr Gregor Mihailov.
- An Armoured Supply Tender, the Hearth, Captained by Mr Ishmael Sardesai.

Then the Spitting Witch Strike Group approached Jupiter's L-One zone. One of the original three colonisation zones of the former Jovian Dream Consortium, which later became the Jovian Republic. Now, sadly, subdued and a part of the Six Jovian Realms. There were many twin-cylinder colonies present, all of the O'Neil-style, the largest of which was Jupiter L-One Central Command. The seat of local governance for the Jovian L-One region.

Fleet Captain Nikolaidis sent an order to his Armoured Refuelling and Supply Tender craft over his comms, "Cauldron and Hearth, hang back. Proceed to rendezvous point alpha. We'll meet you there when our job is done."

The Fleet Captain waited for confirmation and then enquired, "Tactical. Where are the Jovians?"

His Tactical Officer replied, "Ten Nova Class Destroyers detected. Four Missile Cruisers detected", he then paused for a moment as if confused, "Captain, the Missile Cruisers, they're Stellar Class. They must be at least thirty years old. They are no match for us, Captain. None of them!"

"Old or not. They are the enemy and they must burn", the Fleet Captain replied, his gaze fixed on the bridge's main screen and the approaching colony zone.

Fleet Captain Nikolaidis enquired, "Fighters?"

His Tactical Officer responded, "Captain. None detected. They haven't detected us yet. I suspect that if they have any fighters, they'll be docked inside those colonies."

The Fleet Captain frowned. That was to be expected. The Jovians had no fighter carriers. It was also undesirable, placing civilian colonies at risk. Collateral damage was to be avoided at all costs.

"Helmsmen. Keep us clear of those colonies", Captain Nikolaidis instructed, noting, "We'll draw their fighters away with our Bat Wings."

"Aye, Captain", his Helmsman replied.

The Spitting Witch's Tactical Officer called out, "Captain. I'm detecting another ten Destroyers, Sir. They are of an unknown configuration. Their ship class is unknown, Captain."

"Why didn't we detect them on our first sweep?", Fleet Captain Nikolaidis questioned.

His Tactical Officer replied, "They were on the other side of the Jovian L-One zone, beyond their accumulated asteroidal mass. Beyond their primary mining resource."

"Have they detected us?", the Captain enquired.

"No, Sir. Not yet", his Tactical Officer replied, noting, "These Destroyers, they are something new."

"Twenty Destroyers, ten Nova class and ten newer ones of an unknown class", the Fleet Captain considered, before deciding, "Those four Jovian Missile Cruisers are our primary targets. We definitely know that they have cold-fusion missiles. We have to take them out first."

His Tactical Officer advised, "Captain, we should lock and load our electromagnetic rail guns with explosive tungsten rounds. Take out the Missile Cruiser with our first salvo."

Fleet Captain Nikolaidis pointed to his Tactical Officer, "Good man", then he accessed his comms and gave out his orders, "All ships. Load electromagnetic rail guns with explosive tungsten rounds. Both barrels, twenty five rounds per barrel. Lock and load. Witch's Hammer, Urd, Verdandi and Skuld, lock onto those four Jovian Missile Destroyers. Target their plasma drives for maximum damage. Be ready for when I give the order."

The Spitting Witch's Helmsmen noted, "Captain. Those new Missile Cruisers represent known unknowns. They are a major threat, Sir."

Fleet Captain Nikolaidis requested, "Please explain?"

"Captain, we know they are there, but we know absolutely nothing about them, except that they are new, bright and shiny. They could be carrying cold-fusion missiles for all we know. We should take them out first, Captain", the Helmsman explained.

The Fleet Captain steepled his fingers in quiet contemplation, "New plan crew", he announced and then he activated his comms, "All ships. Coordinated cold-fusion missile lock on the ten new Jovian Cruisers. One target, one missile. Use A.I. tracking to target. Prepare and await my command."

Fleet Captain Nikolaidis noted, "Helmsman. Excellent call."

Fleet Captain Nikolaidis ordered through his comms, "All Bat Wing pilots, prepare for launch. All Bat Wing pilots, prepare for launch."

The Spitting Witch's Tactical Officer complied, as did the Strike Group's Dreadnought and three Battle Cruisers. Five ships were ready with cold-fusion missiles locked on target, with their electromagnetic rail guns locked and loaded. They flew silently through the void, unseen, sleek, stretched ovoids of doom and death, undetected and deadlier than any viper that one could describe.

Four Jovian Stellar Class Missile Cruisers and ten new Jovian Destroyers of an unknown Class all sat in their separate formations, unwittingly awaiting their destruction. The Spitting Witch Strike Group had them under weapons lock and the remaining ten Stellar Class Jovian Destroyers would simply have to wait their turn.

Fleet Captain Nikolaidis popped a data crystal into his chair's receptacle. It contained the Greek Pontic War Dance, *"Serra"*. Nicholas Nikolaidis set the file to play as loud as possible across the enemy's communications channels and then he waited patiently for precisely the right moment for the attack to begin. The loud cacophony of drums, clapping, ear-piercing, rapid and intense sounds would surely fill the Jovians with confusion, dread and despair.

"Communications. Link up with our ships, the Witch's Hammer, Urd, Verdandi and Skuld. Activate secure networked communications", Fleet Captain Nikolaidis instructed.

"Yes, Sir", the Communications Officer replied.

"Calling all ships. Calling all ships. Tactical. Bring all of your weapons pods and pulsed plasma turrets online. Set for automatic targeting of enemy vessels. Set to auto fire on target lock", the Fleet Captain commanded and then he added, "Helmsmen. Prepare for a counterclockwise barrel roll. Tactical. Prepare for rolling broadsides at the Nova Class Jovian Destroyers."

And then he waited a few short minutes longer before he gave the order, "Calling all ships. Calling all ships. Tactical. Launch your missiles at those bright, shiny, new Jovian Destroyers. Loose!"

The Spitting Witch's Tactical Officer informed him, "Green light on missile launch, Captain. All missiles are tracking to target using A.I. tracking to target. Estimated time to targets, five minutes."

"Thank you, Tactical", the Fleet Captain replied.

Now it was just a matter of waiting a few minutes before firing their rail guns.

The time passed slowly, woefully slowly, then at precisely the right moment, Fleet Captain Nikolaidis ordered, "Calling all ships. Calling all ships. Tactical. Fire electromagnetic rail guns at the Jovian Missile Cruisers. Loose!.

The Spitting Witch's Tactical Officer informed him, "Green light on electromagnetic rail guns, Captain. All explosive tungsten rounds are on their way to their targets. A near-simultaneous first strike can be expected, Captain."

"Thank you, Tactical", the Fleet Captain replied.

And then they waited for that impossibly long last minute to pass.

The bright, shiny, new Jovian Destroyers were caught completely unaware. The first one erupted in a ball of brilliant blue-white light. Then a second, followed by a third and a fourth. In less than a minute, all ten of the new class of Jovian Destroyers were consumed in brilliant bursts of radiant blue-white heat. Then, a minute after that, there was nothing left of them. It was as if they'd never been.

Fleet Captain Nicholas Nikolaidis and the Spitting Witch's bridge crew watched their demise on the bridge's main screen. How many crew were on those Destroyers? What capabilities did those Destroyers have? They were a new class of Destroyers and they didn't know. This was War and they were targeted for elimination. That window on the bridge's screen then dropped out.

As they continued watching the screen and the four Nova Class Jovian Missile Cruisers in another window, the Spitting Witch's Tactical Officer noted dryly, "Our cold-fusion warheads ramped up to fifteen kilotons, Captain. Those ten new Jovian Destroyers have been erased from existence."

"Acknowledged, Tactical", the Fleet Captain replied as their explosive tungsten bolts struck home.

Each of the four Stellar Class Jovian Missile Cruisers was peppered with fifty deep penetrating explosive rounds. Explosions were everywhere across their aft sections. Blue and orange electrical arcs spread up and down their cracked and broken hulls. Then, less than five seconds later, there were multiple massive explosions as their plasma thrusters exploded and ripped the Jovian Cruisers apart. All that was left were expanding clouds of debris.

That window on the bridge's screen dropped out and a new window replaced it. The final ten Jovian Nova Class Destroyers appeared within it.

Fleet Captain Nicholas Nikolaidis pushed the play button on his chair and the Greek Pontic War Dance, *"Serra"*, flooded the Jovian communications channels as loudly as possible.

"Calling all ships. Calling all ships. Helmsmen. Begin counterclockwise roll and take us into firing range. Tactical. Check all weapons pods and pulsed plasma turrets are online and ready to spit fire", the Fleet Captain ordered.

His Tactical Officer checked his station, "Green light, Captain. Our fleet is on the move."

"Acknowledged, Tactical", the Fleet Captain responded.

"Captain", his Communications Officer began, "They're having severe problems coordinating. Your Greek War dance is jamming all of their channels. It has them all confused", he paused, "They appear to be seriously pissed off, Sir"

The Fleet Captain smiled, "Precisely as it was meant to", replied.

The Spitting Witch's Tactical Office announced, "Captain, I'm detecting interceptor launches from their civilian colonies."

"Type and number, Tactical?", the Captain requested.

His Tactical Officer looked confused, "Ah, Captain. They appear to be old Star Fires. I didn't know anyone used those anymore. They must be fifty or sixty years old."

"Are you sure?", the Captain queried, "Our Bat Wings will slice those up like butter!"

"Yes, Sir. They've launched eighty Star Fires. They also launched four Talons and four Gull Wings", his Tactical Officer informed him.

Fleet Captain Nikolaidis thanked his Tactical Officer and then ordered, "All Bat Wings. Launch and eliminate all enemy fighters."

"Captain, the Nova Class Destroyers have launched missiles.", his Tactical Officer announced.

"Let our weapons systems take them down on approach", the Captain replied with little concern.

"Sir, our A.I. auto-targeting systems are striking them at a distance", the Tactical Officer announced.

That was a bad omen and Captain Nikolaidis leaned forward in his chair, "Ask our ship's A.I. why it's targeting those missiles at long range?"

A few moments later, the Tactical Officer replied with a concerned look on his face, "Captain, they aren't conventional. They're using tactical nukes. Wild Weasels with two kiloton warheads."

"Are you sure? Wild Weasels haven't existed for over a hundred and twenty years", Captain Nikolaidis enquired and then he noted, "They were called Wild Weasels for a reason. They were known to literally veer off course and go wild."

"They are Wild Weasels, Captain", his Tactical Officer confirmed.

"Are our weapons systems taking them down?", the Captain asked.

"Yes, Captain", came the reply, "They are not a threat to us."

Bright bursts of orange light lit up the void in the distance between the two fleets, as the Wild Weasels burst into oblivion.

"Captain. There are over three dozen Wild Weasels way off course. They've all overflown the battle zone and passed beyond the range of our weapons systems", the Spitting Witch's Tactical Officer noted.

"Where are they heading?", Fleet Captain Nikolaidis asked with urgency.

"Captain. If these readings are correct. They've locked onto the Jovian's civilian colonies", his Tactical Officer informed him.

"The civilian colonies! Sweet Mother of God!", Nicholas Nikolaidis exclaimed as he rubbed his forehead and then he noted, "Wild Weasel guidance systems were always twitchy."

"All Bat Wings. We have three dozen Wild Weasels off course and locked onto civilian colonies. Hunt down and destroy those Wild Weasels", the Fleet Captain ordered, adding, "Civilian lives are at stake. Protect and serve!"

"They are Jovian civilians, Captain", his Helmsman commented.

"Yes, civilians and so were the people of Eros and the people of Buenos Aires. Civilians are civilians and we are NOT Horridians!", the Fleet Captain chided.

The battle proceeded quickly, with the Spitting Witch Strike Group taking out Wild Weasel missiles fired at them from the Jovian Destroyers. In the end, however, the Strike Group came within firing range and as they rolled counterclockwise, they struck the Jovian Destroyers with everything they had.

The hulls of the Jovian Destroyers were sliced open by bright blue beams of high-powered coherent laser light. Bright orange, powerful particle beams punched through hulls and brilliant blue-white balls of pulsing plasma vaporised hull metal. One by one, the ten Jovian Destroyers exploded in brilliant balls of orange fire, fire that was quickly extinguished by the vacuum of space. When it was all said and done, there were no enemy Destroyers or Cruisers left in the Jovian L-One zone.

The enemy Star Fires, Gull Wings and Talons took a little longer to eliminate. Mainly because the Strike Group's Bat Wing pilots were also hunting down errant Wild Weasel missiles protecting Jovian civilians. That was a distraction that extracted a high price.

The Talons and Gull Wings were formidable modern craft and with the Strike Group's Bat Wing pilots distracted, they actively hunted them down. The Star Fires were no match and even with odds of two to one, they were all eliminated. The Talons and Gull Wings were also eliminated, but not before taking out five Bat Wings.

Sadly, many Wild Weasels got through and slammed into the Jovian colonies with thermonuclear might. Twin-cylinder colony end caps were ripped apart and in many cases, even colony main cylinders were ripped apart as well. Even the main colony in that orbital zone, Jupiter L-One Central Command, had the northern end cap of its eastern cylinder blown to smithereens.

The situation became so bad that the Strike Group's Bat Wing Interceptor pilots flew their craft directly into the path of the Wild Weasels to protect the Jovian civilians. Many Bat Wings were lost. That was something that the defending Jovian pilots in their Star Fires, Talons and Gull Wings did not even attempt to do. When the battle was finally over, Fleet Captain Nikolaidis turned off his music. The Greek Pontic War Dance, *"Serra"*, had done its job.

The Fleet Captain requested, "Tactical. Fleet-wide damage report and civilian casualties?"

"The Urd, Verdandi and Skuld all took minor outer hull damage from Wild Weasels exploding at close range. Our Slayers and Eramis shielding technology was highly effective. The Jovians threw so many at us that our A.I. auto-targeting had trouble keeping up. We lost five Bat Wings to their Talons and Gull Wings and another ten Bat Wings were lost taking out errant Wild Weasels", the tactical Officer paused before noting, "Captain, Sir. They gave their lives to save Jovian civilians."

"Yes, and so it shall be noted in my official reports and logs", Captain Nikolaidis replied and then he asked once more, "Civilian casualties?"

"Our computer is giving us an estimate now, Captain", his Tactical Officer replied and then informed him, "Four twin-cylinder O'Neil-style colonies were completely destroyed, each with a capacity of about twenty five thousand souls. Their main twin-cylinder colony, Jupiter L-One Central Command, has lost its northeastern end cap. That's likely another fifteen thousand plus souls as well, Sir."

The Fleet Captain rubbed his forehead with his right hand, "So, perhaps as many as a hundred and fifteen thousand civilians?"

"Correct, Sir", his Tactical Officer confirmed.

Fleet Captain Nicholas Nikolaidis ordered, "Calling all ships. Calling all ships. Helmsmen lay in a course for rendezvous point alpha."

His Communications Officer queried, "We aren't going to assist the survivors, Captain?"

The Fleet Captain replied solemnly, "We are a fleet of warships. We are not equipped to provide civilian assistance and should we attempt to do so, we will just attract more Jovian forces and more destruction. If we stay in this orbital zone, our presence will make matters worse."

His Tactical Officer chimed in, "We would need at least two dozen supply tenders and probably as many hospital ships on-site to provide any meaningful assistance."

The Fleet Captain pointed to his Tactical Officer, "He understands. We don't have a dozen supply tenders and hospital ships", and then he addressed his Communications Officer, "We have little choice but to leave this to the Jovian emergency response teams."

While the sharp point of the Spitting Witch Strike Group flew to its rendezvous with its refuelling ship, the Cauldron and its supply tender, the Hearth, Captain Nikolaidis wrote up his report and sent it off to Cis-Lunar Space and Colonial Fleet Command. It contained valuable tactical information. It also contained the sad truth that this War was going to be bloody, very bloody.

26. Earth Caught with its Pants Down.

While President Dieter Reinhardt and General Camilla Brennan-Chives waited patiently in the President's office for the others to arrive for their next meeting, they began talking. The pair had grown quite close over the preceding few weeks. A small secret that they kept to themselves. Dieter Reinhardt was getting more than a little amorous and Camilla had to dissuade him.

"Dieter, not now. We have a meeting in fifteen minutes", Camilla reminded him and gently pushed him back, "And besides, Payback is watching us."

Dieter smiled and leaned in to kiss Camilla on the neck, "Payback's just a puppy, she doesn't count", he noted with a chuckle.

"Stop that, Dieter. We still have a meeting", Camilla insisted, and then she noted, "After the meeting is over, I promise."

Dieter gently stroked the scar running down Camilla's left cheek. It ran from her forehead, crossed over her eye and down her cheek. The scar was thin and showed no sign of any stitching.

"Camilla. You've never mentioned anything about your scar", Dieter noted, and then he asked, "Did you want to talk about it? I mean, you don't have to, I'm just curious as to how you got it."

"It was a long time ago, Dieter. I was a special forces operative just out of training. Still raw and untested", Camilla informed him and then she noted, "I don't like to talk about it."

"Then you don't have to", Dieter replied.

Camilla frowned, "No, Dieter, I think I do. Sometimes talking about it helps."

Dieter nodded, but he said nothing, allowing Camilla time to think and gather her thoughts. He reached out and held her hand for emotional support.

"It was my very first operation. There were piracy issues in the Straits of Malacca between Malaysia and the island of Sumatra in Indonesia. The pirate lair had been extremely difficult to locate, so we requested the assistance of the Psi Corps' remote viewing teams. They gave us all of the information we needed, precise location, precise numbers, what weapons they had, almost everything we needed", Camilla recounted, she could remember it all as if it were yesterday.

"The one thing that they could not provide was time. The pirates were mobile and were preparing to move, so our window of opportunity was closing fast", Camilla noted before continuing, "We were sent in light, undermanned and up against five-to-one odds. We prevailed, yes, but it did not go well at all."

Dieter squeezed her hand gently and enquired softly, "What went wrong, Camilla?"

Camilla smiled and chuckled softly, "I don't really know, to be honest. I copped a sword to the face in the first few seconds. I was both lucky and unlucky all at once. That sword could have cleaved my head in two. As it was, just a few millimetres closer and it would have cut deeply into bone and I would have lost my left eye. Just a few millimetres the other way and it would have sliced nothing but thin air. As I said, I was lucky and unlucky all at once."

Dieter did not reply. He just gently stroked the back of her hand and nodded.

Camilla continued, "Naturally, I hit the deck. Literally, the pirate's lair was a ship. I was in complete shock, with blood streaming across my face. We had a medic with us, a woman. I was lucky that she was there. In the midst of battle, she used a special bio-gauze laced with pharmaceuticals to staunch the flow of blood. Then she used medical-grade superglue and her own fingers to pull the sides of the laceration together. You can see she did a pretty good job. No need for stitches. In the midst of battle!"

Camilla paused, it was a long pause and then she continued, "The medic taped my wound with bio-tape, the kind that's infused with antibiotics and other pharmaceuticals to promote healing. Then, as I watched, a sword protruded from out of her chest. Just like that, some bastard stuck her with his sword", she began crying as she remembered that moment, "and then the sword disappeared. The pirate withdrew it and with a single deft stroke, he took off her head. The medic's body, she collapsed onto my chest and bled out all over me. And then someone blew the pirate's head off with a pulse pistol."

Camilla was still crying, "I passed out at that point. I don't know if it was from shock or the sedative drugs laced into the bio-tape. When I awoke, it was three days later and I was in a hospital half a world away in the United States. I still have nightmares to this day. Every night I wake in a cold sweat!"

Dieter said nothing. He simply kissed her on her teary, scared cheek and took her into his arms, comforting her. Then they sat there quietly for several long minutes.

When President Reinhardt's guests began arriving, he met them in his conference room. General Brennan-Chives excused herself from President Reinhardt's office and went to a nearby bathroom on the same level to wash her face. Her eyes were red from her previous tears. The President was seated and waiting when the Dumas Brothers, Connor and Daniel, entered. Ms Danica Thomlinson, the Head of the Cis-Lunar Bureau of Investigations, followed closely behind.

As Fleet Captain Nicholas Nikolaidis was on board the Spitting Witch, commanding the Spitting Witch Strike Group in Jovian territory, the Cis-Lunar Space Defence Minister, the Honourable Tripp Carlson, came to the meeting. He had received the Fleet Captain's report on the Jovian L-One enemy fleet engagement. General Brennan-Chives, being an Earth Defence Forces General, was not in the direct chain of command. The meeting was as much to brief her as it was to brief the President and as they were the major military contractors for the Cis-Lunar Colonial Fleet, the Dumas Brothers.

President Reinhardt went through the formalities of greeting his guests and introducing his Defence Minister, Tripp Carlson, as part of the process.

"Your Wives aren't going to be joining us today", President Reinhardt enquired of the Dumas Brothers, noting, "I found Harmony's tactical sense and ability to plan so far ahead quite fascinating."

Daniel replied with a smile on his face, "Harmony and Carmelita both wanted to freshen up before coming to the meeting. My Wife, Harmony, is rather brilliant. Her opinions are usually insightful."

Connor noted, questioning, "I notice the General isn't present?"

"General Brennan-Chives will be here shortly", President Reinhardt assured him, pointing to her chair and her German Shepherd puppy, Payback, sleeping lazily upon it.

When Carmelita and Harmony entered the bathroom, they found the General inside, washing her face. Her eyes were still red and it was obvious to the two Dumas Wives that she'd been crying.

"Honey, are you okay?", Harmony enquired.

Camilla looked up from the sink basin, "I'll be fine, Mrs Dumas. It's just a little bit of post-traumatic stress. It will pass, I assure you."

Harmony replied, "Call me Harmony, General."

Carmelita placed her handbag on the bench beside the basin, "Let's get you cleaned up, Camilla."

What followed was a quick, brief bonding session between three very capable women. Eventually, when the three women entered the conference room, no one could tell that the General had been through any emotional turmoil or relived trauma. Female solidarity at its finest.

Defence Minister, Tripp Carlson tapped his data tablet's screen twice and the Fleet Captain's report transferred directly to the other data tablets within the conference room.

"I've sent you all copies of Fleet Captain Nikolaidis's report concerning the Spitting Witch Strike Group's encounter with Jovian Forces in the Jupiter L-One gravitational zone. Please read it at your leisure. I will give you a quick rundown on what it contains", Tripp stated.

"First off, ten Jovian Nova Class Destroyers, four Jovian Stellar Class Missile Cruisers and another ten Jovian Destroyers of a new unknown classification were destroyed", Tripp Carlson informed them, adding, "We don't know the capabilities of the new Jovian Destroyers. However, we have been sent detailed data scans. The main takeaway here is that we won the day."

"Why don't we know their capabilities?", Danica Thomlinson enquired.

Tripp Carlson smiled, "Fleet Captain Nikolaidis targeted the major threats first, as you might expect. So the ten new Destroyers were taken out first, followed by the four Missile Cruisers. They were caught in a tactical first strike by complete surprise", he paused, then he chuckled, "Nick actually pulled a Marley. His Strike Group's IFC, Dreadnought and the three Battle Cruises all performed counterclockwise rolls and broadsided the ten Nova Class Destroyers with everything they had, all while blasting the Greek Pontic War Dance, 'Serra', over the enemy's comms channels."

"His whole fleet pulled a Marley?", General Brennan-Chive queried incredulously.

"All except for his refuelling and supply tender ships", Tripp confirmed.

Tripp Carlson continued, "Things did not all go our way. Our three Battle Cruisers did take radiation damage to their outer hulls. Fortunately, our Slayers and Eramis technology helped in that department. We also lost fifteen Bat Wing interceptors. Nick has provided a list of the pilot's names for posthumous accommodations."

"Losses are expected in combat situations. Did Nick report how they were lost?", Camilla enquired.

"Well. That is the interesting part. Those ten Nova Class Destroyers were apparently armed with large supplies of Wild Weasel nukes. They launched them at our Strike Group hand over fist", Tripp informed them, explaining, "They are what caused the radiation damage to our three Battle Cruiser's outer hulls. There were so many launched that they came close to overwhelming the ship's defences."

"Wild Weasels!", Camilla Brennan-Chives exclaimed, adding, "Nasty things, Wild Weasels. They haven't existed for well over a century!"

Connor quickly checked his data tablet with a search, "Wild Weasels? Ah, here we go. Small two-kiloton tactical warheads, combined with any kind of missile, short or long range, along with primitive guidance systems. Quick, dirty, inaccurate and twitchy."

Camilla replied, "Quick and dirty sums them up accurately, Mr Dumas. Cheap and easy to make by the dozens. Wild as all hell when you let them loose. Their targeting systems are woeful!"

Daniel replied while keying notes into his data tablet, "My concern is that they threw so many of those things at our ships that they came close to overwhelming our automated defence systems."

"There were other concerns, Mr Dumas", Tripp Carlson noted, "Collateral damage."

"Collateral damage", Harmony queried.

"Around three dozen Wild Weasels overflew the battle zone and locked onto Jovian civilian colonies. Twin-cylinder O'Neil-style colonies to be precise. Four were destroyed and Jovian L-One Colonial Central Command had its northeastern end cap obliterated. Nick says their expectations are around a hundred and fifteen thousand dead", Tripp noted dryly.

"A hundred and fifteen thousand dead!", Harmony exclaimed.

"That is friendly fire on steroids", Camilla Brennan-Chives noted.

"It is also how we lost our Bat Wings", Tripp noted, explaining, "The enemy had launched eighty Star Fires, four Gull Wings and four Talons. All from their civilian colonies. Our forty Bat Wings not only had to contend with the enemy forces, they had to hunt down and destroy the enemy's own errant Wild Weasels. We lost five Bat Wings to the Gull Wings and Talons. The other ten, they intercepted the enemy's Wild Weasel missiles with their own ships, protecting the Jovian civilians."

Camilla shook her head in disgust, "Wild Weasels. Launching fighters from civilian colonies. That friendly fire is all on them. All on the Horridian regime. That was another Horridian War crime!"

President Reinhardt replied, "That is not how the Horridians will spin things, Camilla. They will blame us for every civilian death."

Tripp Carlson frowned before nodding gravely, "As Fleet Captain Nikolaidis noted in his report. *'Right or wrong, in warfare, quantity has a quality all its own'*, and he's right. Our enemy is going to do this at every opportunity just to wear us down. Wild Weasels are just another problem to deal with!"

Daniel Dumas began noting, "Nick will be able to replace his Bat Wings. That is not a problem. His supply tender ship, the Hearth, can manufacture Bat Wings in bulk if necessary. The problem is pilots. Both his IFC, the Spitting Witch, and his Dreadnought, the Witch's Hammer, have flight training simulators, but it's not like they have *'spare'* personnel that they can just take out of cold storage."

General Brennan-Chives replied, "They are in Jovian space, so they are thirteen weeks out of space dock. The Fleet Captain has very limited options. Some of his crew members will need to wear new hats, pilot's hats in this case."

Daniel nodded in agreement and then noted, "They can repair their Slayers and Eramis as well. The Hearth can provide those repairs. I'll send them my own recommendation to increase the number of Slayers layers by twenty percent, assuming they have the time to do so. Still, a direct hit from a Wild Weasel with a two-kiloton tactical nuke? Nothing is going to mitigate that."

Danica Thomlinson had always wondered about something and asked curiously of Connor, "Mr Dumas. Something I don't understand. When this all started with the destruction of Eros. Your company came up with new ship designs almost overnight. I know that the Dumas Corporation prides itself on technological innovation, but how the hell did you guys pull that off?"

Carmelita gave off a little chuckle and Connor smiled broadly, "This is going to be hard to explain", he replied before pausing for a moment, "The base technology for every one of those new ship designs, the Battle Cruisers, the Dreadnoughts, the IFCs, the ARCs and the ASTCs are forty years old."

"Forty years old? How is that even possible?", Danica questioned incredulously.

Daniel replied this time, "We don't actually know that ourselves, Ms Thomlinson."

Danica stared at Daniel in astonishment and then asked again, "How is that even possible?"

Daniel looked at his Wife, Harmony, "I think you'd best answer this one, Darling."

Harmony nodded and began to explain, "Well, it all began with the induction of some engineering graduates fresh out of University. The first task we usually give them is to go through our corporate technical design archives and note down anything from the past that we can make use of today. It's a process we call *'retrospective innovation'* or *'technology revival'*, and sometimes our new graduates actually find useful, relevant technology. We usually allow them a fortnight for the task."

Harmony paused to gather her thoughts, "About a year before the War started, one particular graduate was doing just that and he had noted down a dozen or so mediocre technologies. Well, anyway, it was just before noon on a Friday and he was going to go for an early lunch and basically end his assigned task early. What he later recalled to me was that he was walking out of the archive's terminal room door and was about to close it when he stopped. Instead of leaving, he turned around, closed the door and took one final look into the archives. He opened up a forty-year-old file with an innocuous name and found those base ship designs, which he then quickly noted down. He'd actually found technological gold!"

"What made him turn back around and give it another go?", Danica enquired.

"When I asked him that, he told me that he didn't know why. Apparently, he just had a feeling in his gut, a gut hunch", Harmony admitted.

It was President Reinhardt's turn to look bewildered, "So, all of those ships are forty-year-old designs?", he asked in sheer bewilderment.

Daniel chimed in, "Don't get us wrong, Mr President. That technology is Dumas technology. It is just forty years old and that was just the base technology. We have modified it significantly. So what's coming off of our construction lines is a far cry from the original base designs they came from."

"So, what is different about them?", the President enquired.

"Well, the base designs had the weapons pods with their dual laser beams and dual particle beams on the bow and along the port and starboard hulls, but we added far more firepower", Daniel began explaining, "We added quad pulse plasma cannon turrets along the dorsal and ventral hulls. We added two missile launch tubes and their storage silos up in the bow. We also added double-barrelled electromagnetic rail guns and their feed lines to the bow section as well. To fit that all in, we had to scale up the size of the ships as well. Those forty-year-old base designs gave our engineers ideas around which we could innovate."

Harmony chimed in, "My Husband has left a few things out. The base designs were created with plasma thrusters in mind. The most efficient plasma thrusters of their day, yes, but the new designs, they are designed for the latest fusion drives that roll off our construction lines", then she paused before noting, "I almost forgot. We also incorporated the latest Slayers, Eramis and Iraps technology."

Daniel almost laughed, "Darling, you and I both forgot. The Armoured Supply Tender Craft. They are completely new. There was no real base design for that one. They're based on the newly redesigned Armoured Refuelling Craft."

Harmony nodded, she wasn't perfect and she understood that.

"Not to mention all of the other latest spacecraft technical innovations developed over the past forty years", Connor commented, noting, "The thing is, Dieter, we didn't just use forty-year-old designs, we built on them and made them into something new. They were just a starting point."

Danica asked, "Yes, but who created those base designs in the first place? Why were they made and how were they lost?"

Harmony smiled, "Danica, honey. They weren't lost. They were simply stored away in an archive and forgotten. Of course, with our company's *'retrospective innovation'* and *'technology revival'* policies, it was only a matter of time before they came to light once more."

"As for why they were created", Daniel began, "We aren't sure. It may have been for a military contract that was cancelled. That is the most likely reason, but to be honest, we don't actually know at this stage. It was four decades ago, after all."

Connor nodded and noted, "The important thing is how serendipitous this all was. To find those base designs, which we were then able to upgrade into our newest warship designs, right before the Horridian regime started their War. Serendipitous is an understatement."

Danica nodded, "That timing is just so eerie!"

Harmony mentioned, "More eerie than you might think, Danica. There were aspects to those old designs, technologies, that even our best engineers couldn't understand. Those have been pushed sideways onto the back burner for now. Our scientists and engineers need time to comprehend them."

And then a message came through from Connor's and Carmelita's personal assistant, Shelly Shiraz.

Connor read the message and then exclaimed, "Holy crap!", before asking, "Dieter, you need to put your screen on and call up the news channels."

Ever since the Jovian nuclear missile attack on Earth, the local news services had been keeping a close eye on the Earth's weather satellites. That was how the Jovian attack was first detected and the news services all wanted to be the first to get the scoop on any future attacks. They even went so far as to program triggers into the data streams to notify them if any nuclear detonations were detected. The notifications would yield data on location and explosive yield. Like vultures looking for a corpse!

A detonation event had triggered notifications and the news services scrambled to get the news out first with their *"special breaking news"*.

As President Reinhardt switched on his office's main screen and called up one of the popular news channels, messages came through on the other personal communicators in the room. The messages all stated the same thing. Check the news feeds. The news channel that came online had three anchors, a man and two women.

"Breaking news, viewers. Breaking news", the man was saying, "A nuclear detonation has been detected over the North Pole. That's right, a nuclear detonation was detected over the North Pole. A two-megaton blast was detected just minutes ago, fifteen thousand feet above the North Pole. "

One of the female news anchors, a blond-haired woman in her forties, questioned, "What on Earth has Godric Horridian got against Polar Bears? I mean, seriously!"

The other female news anchor, a dark-haired woman of African American descent, questioned, "Polar Bears?", before continuing, "Sheila, Godric Horridian is insane. For all we know, he's targeting Santa Claus and his Elves. Insane people be like that!"

"Oh, wait, viewers, we appear to have detected a second one. I'm just reading the data ticker now", the male news anchor announced, "This was another two-megaton blast over the South Pole. This one is serious, I believe we have a research station down there."

Sheila, the blond-haired news anchor, replied, "Liz, you're the sciency one. What's the name of that research base? Can we expect casualties?"

Liz, the African American news anchor, checked her information and replied, "Yes, Sheila. That's the Amundsen-Scott South Polar Research Station. It's almost summer down there in Antarctica right now, so that research station has around five hundred people working down there."

"Five hundred people!", Sheila replied, her voice laden with concern.

Liz's face looked serious, "Sheila, Tommy, Viewers. They are gone. Instantly vaporised. They were directly under that blast."

"Yet, another War crime racked up for the insane despot, Godric Horridian", Tommy announced.

"Damn!", Tommy exclaimed, "We've just detected a third detonation. Same altitude, same yield, it's above Point Nemo in the middle of the Pacific Ocean!"

"Point Nemo?", Liz queried rhetorically, "There ain't nothing down that but water. That place is so remote that it was where the old satellites used to be deorbited, back in the days before recycling."

"I don't see any sense to this at all, Liz. Do you see any pattern?", Sheila asked.

"Maybe, maybe, but I can't be sure just yet", Liz replied.

"Holy hell! There's another one", Tommy noted, informing his viewers, "We've detected another detonation in the South Atlantic Ocean. Same altitude, same yield. Right in the middle of nowhere!"

"And there we have it", Liz announced, "North Pole, South Pole, the centre of the Pacific, the centre of the South Atlantic. That crazy despot is precisely targeting out-of-the-way places. A show of force!"

And then, as if to confirm Liz's theory, Tommy announced, "And another one. We have detected our fifth detonation. Same altitude, same yield. This one's in the middle of the North Atlantic Ocean."

Liz's ears perked up, "The middle of the North Atlantic. That's major shipping lane territory."

"Shipping lanes?", Sheila questioned.

"Give me a sec or two, Sheila", Liz replied as she performed searches on her data tablet, "Just as I thought, at least five container ships went dark after that nuclear flash. I can't access their crew manifests, so there's no telling how many more lives have been lost."

Tommy sighed a loud sigh, "We've detected another one, number six. Same altitude, same yield. This one is almost over the centre of the Indian Ocean. Nine hundred and thirty miles northeast, directly above the Chagossian Island of Diego Garcia."

Liz looked up from her data tablet, "That has to be deliberate. Definitely deliberate. The Horridians targeted the military base at Diego Garcia deliberately."

Sheila asked, her voice meek and laced with concern, "How many people, Liz?"

"At least five thousand. Personnel from the United States and the United Kingdom", Liz replied, noting, "They no longer exist, Guys. They're gone. Vaporised!"

Tommy's face took on an ashen colour, as he noted, his voice almost dry, "Guys, I think we've run out of Oceans."

It wasn't over, "Holy crap!", Tommy exclaimed, "We've detected strike number seven! Same altitude, same yield. This one was over the centre of Australia", his east coast US accent drawing it out.

"The centre of Australia?", Liz queried, noting, "That's over the Alice, the town of Alice Springs."

Sheila looked at Liz, not wanting to ask and Liz provided the data after checking her data tablet, "At least fifty thousand people are gone, Sheila. It's best not to dwell on it."

"Oh my God! There's another one over Africa. Same as the others. Over a place in the Central African Republic along the Ubangi River", Tommy announced.

Liz checked her data tablet yet again, "Another thirty thousand or more innocent souls cut down by that Godless bastard."

And then there was another flash over North America, "No one is safe", Tommy announced, "We've just detected another detonation over the centre of North America. Directly above the small town of Rugby in North Dakota. I guess that small town and its folk have been wiped off the map."

Before anyone could react, there was another, "Oh my God!", Tommy exclaimed, "We've just detected detonation number ten over the centre of Europe. Directly over the city of Vilnius in Lithuania. I think that's the Capital of Lithuania!", he exclaimed.

Liz noted solemnly, "The Lithuanian Capital and their largest city. As of the census of twenty one eighty, nine hundred thousand people were living there."

Sheila placed her head into her hands and burst into tears. One of their news crew members had to help her off the set. She was too distraught to continue with the broadcast.

The horror wasn't over, another strike quickly followed, Tommy rubbed his forehead, "Will they ever end. We have another detonation over the centre of South America, a place called Cuiabá in Mato Grosso in Brazil. I have no idea if I even pronounced that right", he admitted.

"I'm just checking the data, Tommy", Liz replied, before informing the viewers, "At their last census, that town, more of a small city really, had over seven hundred thousand people living there."

And then there was another one. Tommy was looking shell-shocked and his pallor had taken on an almost green complexion.

"We've detected another detonation in the centre of Asia. In China, in their Xinjiang province. It's directly over the city of Urumqi. Did I pronounce that right? I feel ill", Tommy reported.

Liz's face looked horrified, "Oh my God! If this census data is right, over eight million people were living in Urumqi. This is truly awful!"

The news anchors fell silent, bracing themselves for the next round of detections, but they didn't come. It appeared the attack was over. Twelve devastating detonations. Random in their violence and destruction, yet not random at all. They targeted the centres of places, places all over the globe. Poles, Oceans and Continents. A very deliberate campaign of terror.

At that point with the attack was completed. One of the Jovian operatives on Earth released a prepackaged speech into the news networks. It was targeted at every news network on Earth and in Cis-Lunar Space. Tommy saw a notification pop up on his ticker and he quickly recomposed himself.
"Viewers, we have just been informed that a speech by Godric Horridian has been received by our network. This is breaking news and we will play in full", Tommy told his audience.

Godric Horridian was standing behind a lectern on a raised podium. He was smiling, with a smug expression on his face. He looked into the camera, his face showing little if any concern for the millions of people he had just murdered, just erased. When he spoke, it was like acid in their ears.
"By now, you will have received my 'gifts'. By now, you will fully comprehend my reach. I can strike the Earth anywhere, wherever I wish. This is nothing you can do about this situation. There is nowhere on the Earth that you can hide, any of you", High Prince Godric informed the viewers.

"The complete annexation of the Earth and Cis-Lunar Space will happen. Why do you resist the inevitable? This is a future that cannot be changed. This is a future that is set in stone. The Horridian Imperium is coming. You, the people of Earth and Cis-Lunar Space, can join the Horridian Imperium of your own free will or not. If not, then what remains of you, what is left of you, will be forced to join the Horridian Imperium by the Jovian Armed Forces. Willingly or unwillingly, you will join the Imperium. In that, you have no choice. The only choice you have is whether you join willingly or unwillingly", the High Prince paused.

High Prince Godric smiled at the camera, "When you have joined the Horridian Imperium, you will find that very little has changed. Your Governments will swear allegiance to the Horridian Throne and bow down before me. Your Governments will pay tributes, tithes and taxes to the Horridian Imperium. You will be given the choice to convert to Christianity, if you are not already a Christian and life will continue almost as normal. So, it is time to make your choice. Are we going to do this the easy way or the hard way? You have six hours to decide", and then the screen went blank.

President Reinhardt looked around his conference room, "If Godric Horridian thinks we will bow down before him, then he is insane."

General Brennan Chives noted, "Dieter. After today's attacks, I believe there is no doubt about Godric Horridian's insanity."

"What did he mean about conversion to Christianity?", Danica Thomlinson enquired.

Connor frowned and replied, "That hearkens back to his Grandfather's day. The Horridians treat all non-Christians as Slaves. Indentured servitude and Slavery are common Horridian practices."

"That's horrible. Absolutely horrible", Danica responded.

"Which is why we must fight them tooth and nail. We cannot let them win", Daniel chimed in.

Connor picked up his communicator and called his personal assistant, Shelly Shiraz, "Shelly, I take it you've seen the news."

"Yes, Sir. I have", Shelly replied.

"Notify our production managers. The Earth urgently needs missile defence platforms. Tell them to make it a priority", Connor instructed her, noting, "I know that they won't be happy, Shelly, but we have no choice. The Earth was just caught with its pants down and we cannot let that happen again."

27. Saturnian Convoy.

The meeting continued into the afternoon along a different tack. They were now discussing the latest atrocities inflicted on innocent civilians by the Horridian Regime. Earth had been at peace for so long that its defences had atrophied. Even the military and refuelling bases on the Martian moon Deimos had been allowed to atrophy over the decades. Of course, now there was a Carrier Strike Group, the Indomitable Wyvern Strike Group, at Deimos to protect Mars and the colonial infrastructure in orbit around it. The Earth, however, had no such defences and Godric Horridian had just shown that his Jovian Armed Forces could target the Earth whenever and wherever he liked with impunity.

In discussions between General Brennan-Chives and the Cis-Lunar Space Defence Minister, Tripp Carlson, it was decided that the Colonial Fleet would second fighters to the Earth's Defence Forces. The Earth's own fighters were only atmo-rated and could not actually fly in space.

As Earth was over three hundred and eight four thousand kilometres away, they had to send long-range fighters. Two squadrons of twenty four fighters each were dispatched to defend the Earth well before Godric Horridian's six-hour deadline was up. A squadron of Talons and a squadron of Gull Wing Interceptors. Their brief was simple. Interdict anything hostile that approaches the Earth.

As the order to dispatch the fighters was given, Harmony noted, "Those fighters can't stay in Earth orbit indefinitely. They will need somewhere to dock. Somewhere for maintenance. Somewhere for refuelling. Pilots do need rest periods as well."

Her Husband, Daniel, was already on it.

He brought up an image of a Stanford torus in high Earth orbit and recommended, "The High Hotel in high Earth orbit. It is a civilian facility, but it does have everything a couple of fighter squadrons could use. One small problem. It is also full of guests and tourists."

General Brennan-Chives replied as she took out her communicator, "Not a problem, Mr Dumas. I'll have the hotel evacuated of its guests and commandeered for use by the Earth Defence Forces", and then she began discussing the issue with her people back on the Earth, with its tedious three second communications latency.

President Reinhardt queried, "Godric Horridian gave us a six-hour deadline and that will be up in two hours. Do you think he's bluffing? What more could he possibly do?"

Connor Dumas looked the President squarely in the eyes, "Dieter. Godric Horridian does not give me the impression of a man who bluffs. As for what more he could do, his last attack killed millions. That bastard could have more missiles en route. He could target major cities next."

The head of the Cis-Lunar Bureau of Investigations, Danica Thomlinson, suggested, "When the deadline is breached, don't send a reply, Mr President. Not you or President Guang Hui of Earth. Let him stew. Make him wait for your answer. Make him wait hours, days, if you can. Make him stew."

Connor's Wife, Carmelita, asked in her Brazilian Portuguese accent, "What will you tell him? When you give him your answer?"

President Reinhardt's eyes took on a coldness, "I can't speak for President Guang Hui, but I personally will tell Godric Horridian to go to hell."

Carmelita had once been destined to be amongst the first colonists in the Uranian Federation in the colony of Oberon Central Command, at Oberon L-Five. However, she and Connor had become involved and eventually, they married. A simple proposal of marriage had changed her entire life.
Carmelita remained in Cis-Lunar Space as the spouse and partner of the elder of the two Dumas Brothers, who managed the vast Dumas Corporate business empire. They had nine children together.
Carmelita knew the distances across interplanetary space very well.

"This attack", Carmelita began, "It cannot be a reprisal for the battle that took place in Jovian L-One. That was just yesterday. Those cold-fusion missiles had to have been launched weeks ago."

Connor replied in agreement, "You are correct, Carmelita, those missiles had nothing to do with the Jovian fleet losses at Jovian L-One. This attack is likely a reprisal for the loss of their three Missile Cruisers and the loss of their Deimos expeditionary force, those seven Destroyers."

Daniel nodded in agreement, "The order to launch was likely given nearly fourteen weeks ago. Assuming that they were launched from Jovian orbit."

Daniel's Wife, Harmony, noted, "Those warhead yields were two megatons each and it takes around one hundred million kilometres to ramp up to that yield. So they had to have been launched from at least a hundred million kilometres out. So at the very least, six weeks out at the edge of Martian Orbit."

"We destroyed their warships. They retaliate by killing civilians", Carmelita noted in reply.

Harmony frowned and replied, "Barbarians do that, Carmelita. That's just what they do."

Godric Horridian's timeline had not been a hollow threat. More cold-fusion missiles had been launched and they were already underway. Godric could send a kill order, or he could let the missiles fly to their designated targets, Los Angeles, New York, London, Paris, Moscow and Beijing. With a combined population at their last census in twenty one eighty of over one hundred million. The result would have been devastating.

As it was, those six deadly cold-fusion missiles were picked up on approach by the two squadrons of Talon and Gull Wing Interceptors and obliterated before reaching the Earth. The Earth had been lucky, very lucky indeed. Had the two squadrons of Interceptors been dispatched just fifteen minutes later, it would have been too late to stop them. Explosions of blue-white light lit up the skies above the Earth, but too far away to have any effects on the world below.

That those missiles had been launched already and were well underway hardened the resolve of both President Reinhardt and President Guang. Godric Horridian's missiles had been launched weeks in advance, making his six-hour deadline completely meaningless. Godric Horridian's word was likewise completely meaningless, painting him as an untrustworthy liar! Someone with whom negotiation would be a fruitless waste of time.

High Prince Godric's ultimatum and deadline had passed three days earlier and yet, he still had no reply to his demands for the surrender of the Earth and Cis-Lunar Space. By now, his cold-fusion missiles with their two-megaton yields should have obliterated six major cities on Earth and yet, there was nothing, nothing at all in the news feeds about any destruction beyond his original attack. Now, however, three days later, his Ministers had news.

"Your Majesty", Security Minister Miles Morton began, "I have received news from one of our assets in Cis-Lunar Space. Our last six missiles did not reach their targets, Sire. They were intercepted whilst on approach to the Earth."

"Minister Morton. I was told that the Earth had only atmospheric fighters", the High Prince noted.

"Yes, Sire, that is correct. However, the Cis-Lunar government sent them a squadron of Talons and a squadron of Gull Wings", the Security Minister informed him, noting, "And our operatives have also informed us that Dumas Colonial Constructions is now building anti-missile orbital defence platforms for the Earth's government."

Defence Minister Peter Macron chimed in, "Your Majesty, we have received word from the governments of Earth and Cis-Lunar Space. Although their response is not what you wanted, Sire."

"Spit it out, Minister Macron!", the High Prince demanded.

"Your Majesty. This is the response from President Reinhardt of Cis-Lunar Space. *'Go to hell.'* The response from President Guang of Earth was in Mandarin and I had to get it translated. Her response was, *'To hell with you.'* Sire, these are, of course, their words", Defence Minister Macron replied.

"Well, isn't that just great!" High Prince Godric spat, "We have one of their Carrier Strike Groups operating in our territory, right in our own backyard! Four days ago at Jupiter L-One, we lost two dozen warships and four colonies. Our missile strike against Earth was meant to break their resolve.
Why are they not breaking?"

Science Minister Peter Patronis cautiously replied, "Sire. We are beyond the point where they will break. This is going to be a long, protracted and drawn-out war, Sire."

After their victory at Jupiter L-One and the destruction of four Stellar Class Missile Cruisers, ten Nova Class Destroyers and another ten Jovian Destroyers of an unknown class, the Spitting Witch Carrier Strike Group re-grouped at rendezvous point alpha. The rendezvous point was on the far side of Jupiter beyond the Jupiter L-Two Lagrangian zone. They were well inside the shadow of Jupiter and rendezvoused with a second Carrier Strike Group, the Eternal Ring.

Motto:
We Come From Out of Left Field with Fists of Iron.
We are the Hammer and the Anvil.

- An Interplanetary Fighter Carrier, the Eternal Ring, Captained by Mr Hiroshi Tanaka,
  - with forty Bat Wing Interceptors aboard.
- A Dreadnought, the Birmingham Kiss, Captained by Ms Amina Yusuf.
- Three Battle Cruisers, the Fists,
  - The Haymaker, Captained by Mr Carlos Mendoza.
  - The Roundhouse, Captained by Mr Jean-Baptiste Moreau.
  - The Uppercut, Captained by Ms Mbali Dlamini.
- An Armoured Refuelling Craft, the Corner Man, Captained by Ms Irina

Petrova.
- An Armoured Supply Tender, the Cut Man, Captained by Mr David Goldstein.

Fleet Captain Nicholas Nikolaidis and Captain Hiroshi Tanaka put together a simple plan. Both Strike Groups would approach the Jovian L-Two zone from within Jupiter's shadow, scan for enemy warships, take out as many as possible and then disappear back within Jupiter's shadow once more.

The situation in the Jupiter L-Two zone was somewhat different to the one in the Jupiter L-One zone. They were both fifty four million kilometres from Jupiter, one in front of Jupiter and one behind Jupiter. The Jupiter L-One zone was in constant sunlight, whereas most of Jupiter's L-Two zone was in Jupiter's shadow and in darkness. The colonies in the L-Two zone were on inclined halo orbits, five million kilometres from the zone's gravitational sweet spot. That meant the civilian colonies would be, hopefully, well out of harm's way.

The refuelling ships, Cauldron and Corner Man, along with the supply tenders, Hearth and Cut Man, hung back in safety, flying from rendezvous point alpha to rendezvous point beta, while the two Strike Groups flew towards Jupiter L-Two.

Upon approaching the L-Two zone, both Carriers, the Spitting Witch and the Eternal Ring, began cautiously using their long-range sensors to locate any Jovian military assets. They found the zone to be almost a mirror of the Jovian L-One zone.

There was an accumulated asteroidal mining mass, the primary mining resource, in the central gravitational sweet spot. That was surrounded by typical mobile mining stations in close orbits or mining the resource's surface. Beyond that, in halo orbits were the ore processing stations and beyond those were the manufacturing stations. They were all in darkness, within Jupiter's shadow.

The main difference was the colonies. Jupiter L-Two Colonial Central Command and its retinue of smaller twin-cylinder O'Neil-style colonies were all grouped together in highly inclined halo orbits five million kilometres from the zone's gravitational centre. That orbit gave those colonies eternal sunlight, weak though it was, while the rest of the zone was in near complete darkness.

If nothing else, the Horridians were consistent. This zone also contained ten Nova Class Destroyers, four Stellar Class Missile Cruisers and ten other Destroyers of an unknown classification. Fleet Captain Nikolaidis and Captain Tanaka quickly agreed to the old divide-and-conquer scenarios.

The ships of the Spitting Witch Task Group targeted the ten Nova-Class Destroyers, knowing that they were all armed with Wild Weasel two-kiloton warheads. The ships of the Eternal Ring Strike Group targeted the ten newer

Jovian Destroyers of the unknown class.

Each of the Colonial Fleet capital ships targeted the Jovian Destroyers with cold-fusion warheads. At the targeting distance, they expected their yields to ramp up to twelve kilotons each. Their two carriers prepared two extra cold-fusion missiles each for the Stellar Class Missile Cruisers.

Undetected and unseen, they simultaneously launched their missiles and waited for the results. Fifteen minutes later, the depths of deep space within the shadow of Jupiter lit up with intense blue-white bursts of pure thermonuclear devastation. Over the space of fifteen seconds, one Jovian ship after another was engulfed in blue-white heat and when the bursts of light dissipated, there was nothing left of the two dozen Jovian capital ships. It was fast, it was clean, it was deadly and it was final.

Fighters immediately launched from the civilian colonies. Star Fires, Talons and Gull Wings. They flew out in confused patterns, not knowing where their enemy was. The two Colonial Strike Groups peeled away, ignoring the Jovian fighters completely and simply melted away into the darkness of the void within Jupiter's shadow. Their destination, rendezvous point beta.

On approach to rendezvous point beta, the four Colonial logistics ships detected something that should not have been there. It was a very large convoy and it was on the approach to the Jupiter L-Two zone. Reverse tracking of the convoy's trajectory showed it was en route from Saturn, from the Saturnian Demarchy.

Captain Ishmael Sardesai of the Armoured Supply Tender, Hearth, contacted his Strike Group's Captain, "Fleet Captain Nikolaidis. We have a Saturnian Demarchy convoy on approach to Jupiter L-Two. At least twenty hauliers are towing extended chains of cargo pods. Please advise."

"Captain Sardesai. Approach the Saturnian convoy with all due caution. Bring the ASTC Cut Man along for the ride", Fleet Captain Nikolaidis instructed and then he noted, "If the convoy is armed or travelling with escorts, withdraw immediately and wait for our main Strike Forces."

"Captain, and if the Saturnian Convoy is unarmed and unescorted?", Captain Sardesai queried.

"Then you order the haulier Captains to cut loose their cargo pods and continue on their way to Jupiter L-Two. As for their cargo, download their cargo manifests. Take what you can make use of and destroy the rest", Captain Nikolaidis ordered, before noting, "Make sure that the haulier Captains fully comprehend that they are aiding and abetting a criminal regime that has committed numerous War crimes. Crimes against Humanity."

The ASTCs Hearth and Cut Man flew to intercept the Saturnian convoy en route to Jupiter L-Two. As they approached, they could easily detect that the convoy was neither armed nor escorted. The two ASTCs approached closer and Captain Sardesai hailed the convoy.

The Captain in charge of the Saturnian supply convoy picked up the hail, "This is Captain Gillian, Gig, Mutton and I'm in charge of this convoy. We are an unarmed civilian convoy on civilian business. Please state your purpose."

"Captain Mutton, I am Captain Ishmael Sardesai, Captain of the ASTC Hearth, of the Eternal Ring Carrier Strike Group. Your convoy is destined for Jovian L-Two space. The Jovian Realms is currently in a state of War with the inner system worlds", Captain Sardesai responded.

"We are travelling en route to Jupiter L-Two under the auspices of the Quadripartite Outer Satellite Agreement. Our convoy carries no weapons. We are not involved in the War", Captain Mutton replied.

"Sadly, that is not the case, Captain Mutton. You are providing materials and supplies to our enemies. Those materials and supplies will be used by the Horridian Regime to build yet more weapons with which they will continue to mass murder our innocent civilians", Captain Sardesai informed her.

"That is not my concern, Captain Sardesai. We are not involved in your War", Captain Mutton insisted, "We have orders to deliver these supplies to Jupiter L-Two Colonial Central."

"Captain Mutton. Perhaps the news travels slowly out this way. Are you aware that the Horridian regime has killed Eros, the World within the Rock? Are you aware that the Horridian Regime has wiped the Argentine city of Buenos Aires off the map, killing over twenty four million people? Or perhaps you haven't heard that their most recent attack on the Earth has killed over eight million more people in the Chinese city of Urumqi? Captain, just this year, the Horridians have murdered over thirty eight million people. You are aiding and abetting mass murderers and War criminals!"

The communications channel went dead silent.

Captain David Goldstein of the ASTC Cut Man hailed the Hearth, "Captain Sardesai, whatever you told them has them rattled. We are picking up a shit ton of comms chatter between their ships."

"I just told their Lead Captain Mutton the truth, Captain Goldstein", Captain Sardesai replied.

"That would do it, Captain. Sometimes the truth cuts sharper than any blade",

Captain Goldstein replied before dropping the line.

A few minutes later, Captain Mutton hailed the Hearth, "Sorry about the delay, Captain. We've just had quite a discussion over here. We had heard about Eros. We had not heard about Buenos Aires or Urumqi. We certainly had not heard about the nearly forty million dead. News does travel slowly in the outer system as you mentioned, especially when on long-haul runs."

"Yes, I thought that might be the case, Captain", Captain Sardesai replied.

"Captain Sardesai. Your ships have my haulier captains all nicker twisted. Your ship's tags read as Supply Tenders, but their sheer size and weapons systems clearly state otherwise. The Hearth and that other ship, the Cut Man, are clearly predators", Captain Mutton remarked, before requesting, "Where do we go from here?"

Captain Sardesai chuckled, "We are rather large Supply Tenders with sharp teeth, Captain", and then he got down to brass tacks, "If you can change course and return to the Saturnian Demarchy, by all means, do so. If you can't change course, then you'll need to cut loose your cargo pods and continue to Jupiter L-Two without them. Your cargo is to be confiscated and/or destroyed."

Captain Gig Mutton frowned, "And by the looks of your ship's weapons pods and turrets, we can't say no, can we?"

"That is correct, Captain. No is not an option. Either return to Saturnian Demarchy territory or cut loose your cargo pods for confiscation", Captain Sardesai reiterated.

Captain Mutton informed Captain Sardesai, "It isn't possible for us to return to Saturnian space, Captain. We need to continue to Jupiter L-Two to refuel before we can return home."

"Understood, Captain Mutton. That just leaves option two", Captain Sardesai responded.

Captain Mutton nodded, "Option two, cut loose all cargo pods and continue on course."

"Correct, Captain Mutton", Captain Sardesai confirmed.

Captain Gillian Mutton sent a broadcast across the convoy's comms channels, "All haulier Captains. All haulier Captains. We have a situation that requires that we cut loose our cargo pods and continue to Jupiter L-Two without them. I recommend compliance. Resistance would lead to the unthinkable."

"I expect you'll be wanting our cargo manifests, Captain?", Captain Mutton queried.

Captain Sardesai looked at his Communications Officer, who simply gave him the thumbs up.

"We already have your cargo manifests, Captain", Captain Sardesai remarked, admitting, "Our Communications Officer downloaded those during our discussion."

Captain Gillian Mutton nodded in understanding and the channel cut out.

The haulier captains released their cargo pod couplings and slowly pulled away from their chains of cargo. Captain Gillian Mutton sent one final message to Captain Sardesai.

"All cargo pods jettisoned. All hauliers en route to Jupiter L-Two", it read.

Captain Sardesai of the ASTC Hearth and Captain Goldstein of the ASTC Cut Man watched as the twenty hauliers flew off to their destination, minus their cargo.

Captain Goldstein asked over his comms, "Captain Sardesai. What are we going to do with this lot? We now have twenty chains of cargo pods to deal with."

"Our orders were to take what we can use and destroy the rest", Captain Sardesai replied, but then noted, "I'm a logistics man, Captain Goldstein. I've got a better idea."

When both Carrier Task Groups finally reached rendezvous point beta, the ASTC Hearth and ASTC Cut Man were both towing ten chains of twenty cargo pods behind them. A total of four hundred cargo pods. Rendezvous point beta was eighty million kilometres behind Jupiter and still just within Jupiter's umbra, its shadow.

"Captain Sardesai. Your instructions were to take what you can use and destroy the rest", Fleet Captain Nikolaidis reminded him, before asking, "What's your logic here?", he questioned with regard to the long chains of cargo pods they were hauling.

"It's all useful stuff, Captain. I couldn't see the sense in destroying perfectly good cargo", Captain Sardesai explained, noting, "Captain Goldstein and I will have it all coupled together into nice, accessible stacks. If we impart the whole thing with just the right orbital velocity, it will co-orbit with Jupiter in its shadow for as long as we want. A nice accessible little warehouse, if you will."

Fleet Captain Nikolaidis shook his head in disbelief. It was, however, a sound idea, just so long as the Horridian Regime didn't know it was there and couldn't use it.

"Okay, Captain Sardesai. We'll *'warehouse'* the cargo pods here for future use", the Fleet Captain replied, "Now send me the coordinates where you intercepted that convoy. I need to set off a nuke at that intercept location to make it look like all of that cargo was destroyed."

"Sending you those coordinates now, Captain", Captain Sardesai replied.

28. Sheer Stupidity.

Defence Minister Tripp Carlson entered President Reinhardt's office. He took note mentally of the fact that General Brennan-Chives was already present. Something that he had noticed of late was that the General and the President seemed to be getting close, definitely professional, but perhaps even romantically. Tripp pushed the thought aside.

"Mr President", Tripp began, "We've received news from the Spitting Witch and Eternal Ring Carrier Strike Groups."

"Good news, I hope?", Camilla asked as she sat on the low couch that was against one wall, gently stroking her German Shepherd, Payback.

"Yes. Good news", Defence Minister Carlson confirmed, informing them, "The Jovians have lost another ten Nova Class Destroyers, another four Stellar Class Missile Cruisers and another ten of those new Jovian Destroyers. The ones we have little information on as yet. From their Jupiter L-Two zone."

Camilla nodded, "The Dumas Corporation's engineers are poring over our scan data. They're most likely Guided Missile Destroyers. Although we'll have a better understanding of those new Jovian Destroyers soon enough."

"So we've cleared out their armed forces from Jupiter L-One and Jupiter L-Two", President Reinhardt noted and then enquired, "Is there anything else, Minister Carlson?"

"Yes, Mr President. Our Carrier Strike Groups have intercepted a Saturnian Demarchy convoy en route to Jupiter L-Two. They've confiscated all four hundred cargo pods and sent their hauliers on their way", Tripp informed them both before smiling broadly and remarking, "They set off a nuke to give the Horridians the impression that the cargo was destroyed."

Camilla Brennan-Chives looked at President Reinhardt, "There will be blowback from the Saturnian Demarchy, Dieter. We need to keep on top of that."

"We'll speak to the Dumas Brothers, Camilla. We can use their Administrator back channels to keep a dialogue open", the President noted.

"Defence Minister, The Saturnian Demarchy, the Uranian Federation and the Neptunian Commonwealth all have that agreement with the Jovian Realms. Their Quadripartite Outer Satellite Agreement. That means that there will be more convoys, probably many more", Camilla explained.

"Yes, I am aware of that, General", Tripp replied, mentally noting how both the President and the General were on a first-name basis, of course, that was none of his business.

"I have instructed the Spitting Witch and Eternal Ring Carrier Strike Groups to blockade the Jovian Realms from all external supply. The Horridians are going to find their Quadripartite Outer Satellite Agreement is of little benefit to them", Tripp Carlson informed them.

General Brennan-Chives nodded, "We have them boxed in from both sides. They can't move into the inner solar system without coming across our first line of defence in the Belter Nations. Now, they can't get resources and supplies from the outer satellites. Make sure our Carrier Strike Group Captains understand to tread softly with convoy interdiction. No casualties, that is important. We do not want the outer satellites entering the fray on the Jovian side."

Tripp Carlson nodded, "Agreed, General. I have already issued those instructions."

"Boxed in on both sides. All we need to do is keep them in that box and intercept any missiles they through at us. The Jovian economy is no match for ours. It will buckle of its own accord, given enough time", President Reinhardt noted.

"Defence Minister. Ensure your ship captains understand. If the Jovian Armed Forces pop their head out of our box, it does not matter which way they go, take their heads off", General Brennan-Chives instructed, "However, when it comes to civilians, treat them with 'kid gloves', no casualties."

President Reinhardt agreed, "The important distinction here is that we are not Horridians."

The Defence Minister also agreed, "While we take the moral high ground, the Horridians will not. Once they realise that they're boxed in with an economic blockade, they will more than likely lash out."

President Reinhardt nodded, "Defence Minister Tripp, we just need to make sure we are ready for whatever they throw at us."

The General noted dryly, "We have Cruisers coming off both of our construction lines. Heavy Cruisers. I'd recommend that we have a half dozen of each, Earth Defence Force and Colonial Fleet, prowling deep space between the Belter colonies. Further bolstering our first line of defence."

"And in deep space between Jupiter and Saturn, Camilla?", President Reinhardt enquired, noting, "We have two Carrier Strike Groups out there, but are they enough?"

"For now, yes, Dieter, but in the long run, we will need to second some of our Heavy Cruisers to our Carrier Strike Groups. Our forces out that way need bolstering as well", the General replied.

"Our Carrier Strike Groups are quite formidable, General", Defence Minister Carlson noted and then he agreed, "Of course, a couple of our Heavy Cruisers for each of our Carrier Strike Groups won't hurt. We can't be sure what's coming out of those Jovian construction yards at Ganymede L-four."

"New Destroyers at the very least and I expect they'll be launching Dreadnoughts. They already have older models, so we can expect new models to appear soon", General Brennan-Chives predicted.

"I'll start working with Colonial Fleet Command on ship deployments. We'll have something for you to review by the month's end", the Defence Minister replied.

Prime Minister Quintus Malbeck of the Saturnian Demarchy entered Administrator Swenna Goodchild's office. His demeanour showed that he was somewhat out of sorts. The Prime Minister was a popular politician, but not a brilliant one, nor was he that good at handling stress. Which was why he had his advisers and bureaucratic administrators handle the heavy lifting. Swenna Goodchild was his go-to adviser and head administrator.

"Prime Minister Malbeck, I have been expecting you. Please take a seat", Swenna greeted.

The Prime Minister sat down in the offered seat and asked, "You always know when to expect me?"

Swenna Goodchild smiled, "Prime Minister. A part of my job is to keep my fingers firmly pressed on the pulse of the Demarchy. Everything imaginable crosses my desk first."

"Then you are aware of the fact that the Cis-Lunar Colonial Fleet is intercepting our convoys to the Jovian Realms?", he enquired, knowing, of course, full well, that the answer was yes.

"Yes, Prime Minister. Three of our convoys thus far and one each from the Uranian Federation and the Neptunian Commonwealth", Swenna informed the Prime Minister.

"These interceptions are flagrant acts of aggression. The hawks want to declare War", Prime Minister Malbeck replied, his face showing serious concern.

Swenna smiled and shook her head, "Ignore the hawks, Prime Minister. They are outnumbered by the doves, twenty to one."

"Prime Minister. I have access to all of the other Administrators in the network across the solar system. We are all of the opinion that the Jovian Realms under Godric Horridian are disastrous for everyone, everywhere. That one man has presided over thirty eight point five million deaths. You are aware of that, yes?", Swenna noted.

Prime Minister Malbeck nodded, "Yes, Ms Goodchild. I am aware of the death toll. It is horrendous, absolutely horrendous."

"Yes, you could even say it is Horridious!", Swenna commented in agreement, before noting, "We have to comply with the Quadripartite Outer Satellites Agreement, yes, but only to the letter of that agreement. Nothing beyond what we signed up for. Nothing beyond what is written down."

"And we are, but with these convoy interceptions, the Horridians will arc up. They are bound to", Prime Minister Malbeck now showed his primary concern.

"Yes, Prime Minister, that was always going to happen. Convoy interceptions or not", Swenna confirmed and then asked, "Did you read the latest demands from Godric Horridian? You know, the ones in that speech he made straight after bombing the Earth with cold-fusion warheads and killing over eight million innocent people?"

"Yes, Ms Goodchild. He wanted the Earth and Cis-Lunar Space to surrender and join his so-called Horridian Imperium without going through a bloody War", Prime Minister Malbeck confirmed.

"Yes, but you don't see it yet, do you?", Swenna replied and then she explained, "The War is already bloody. There are nearly forty million dead, along with Eros, an entire world. When Godric has locked in and annexed the inner solar system, he will then turn on the Belters and conquer them."

Swenna paused to let that sink in, "Then she dropped the bomb shell. Once Godric Horridian has achieved that, that little snake will turn on us. And not just us here in the Demarchy, but the Federation and the Commonwealth. With the inner system under his control, it will be easy for him. Like stepping from one island in the ocean of space to the next. Imagine the inner system resources at his disposal."

Prime Minister Malbeck ran his hand through his hair as he began to fully comprehend the madness of the Horridian Imperium, "Holy fuck, the Horridian Imperium is a creeping pan-solar annexation!"

"And one that is based on Slavery to boot", Swenna confirmed, "Re-read, Godric Horridian's speech transcripts. He wants to convert all non-Christians to Christianity and those that refuse, well, they will become his Slaves."

"Swenna! We must not let this happen!", Prime Minister Malbeck exclaimed.

"It won't, Prime Minister and fortunately for us, the Colonial Fleet has given us an out", Swenna informed him.

"An out?", Prime Minister Malbeck questioned.

"We have to comply with the Quadripartite Outer Satellites Agreement, but is it our fault if those crucial supplies never reach their destination? No. It is not our problem", Swenna almost laughed.

"But all of those resources are being wasted. Destroyed", the Prime Minister lamented.

"Here's a secret for you, Quintus", Swenna replied using the Prime Minister's first name, "You can't tell anyone this, but those convoys. No lives are being lost. No resources are being destroyed. The haulier crews are allowed to go on their way and their cargoes are simply confiscated."

Prime Minister Malbeck looked at Swenna curiously as she continued, "Those cargo shipments are being stashed, hidden away, at secure locations in the outer Jovian Trojan asteroids and other places beyond Jovian-controlled territory. No one is dying. Nothing is being destroyed. Nothing is being wasted. Godric Horridian is simply being denied those resources for his War machine. We could send him hauliers without any cargo pod chains and he would not know the difference."

"Those clever Colonial Fleet bastards!", the Prime Minister exclaimed in realisation.

"Yes indeed, Quintus, yes indeed and we in the Administrators network are privy to it all", Swenna commented, before finishing off with, "Godric Horridian has painted himself into a corner and the inner system powers have boxed him in. Godric Horridian is just a foolish little snake."

High Prince Godric was in his throne room, sitting on his gold-gilded throne. His Brother's thrones, equally gold-gilded, although still less ornate, were on Godric's right. Prince Aluric, Godric's mentally ill, debauched younger Brother, was not present. That was not unusual. His youngest Brother, Prince Friederic, was still on Io Prime in his own palace and not interested in Godric's War. In fact, Friederic refused to have anything to do with Godric's disastrous War.

Only his other Brother, Prince Emeric, was present. His throne was between Aluric's and Friederic's, and even he did not really want to be there. With Prince Aluric being mentally ill, Prince Emeric was ostensibly the next in line to the throne. Prince Emeric did not want it.

Prince Emeric looked at his Brother Godric, who had taken to biting his nails, *"That fucking throne is cursed! I have absolutely no intention of sitting on it!"*, he thought to himself.

The High Prince commanded, "Tell me again. Our situation. How bad is it really?"

Prince Emeric replied, "Brother, we've heard this four times already. Do you really want to hear it all over again?"

High Prince Godric turned to his Bother, "Brother Emeric, I need to get my head around this!", his voice was sharp but laced with fear, almost bordering on dread.

Defence Minister Peter Macron cleared his throat, "Ah, hum! Sire, our forces in Jupiter L-One and Jupiter L-Two have been eliminated. In Jupiter L-One, we have lost four colonies and Jupiter L-One Colonial Central has suffered major devastation. That was caused by friendly fire, Your Majesty."

The High Prince frowned, "Spin that as a deliberate strike by the Colonial Fleet. Why do I not have a new Communications Minister?"

Miles Morton, his Minister of Security, cautiously replied, "Sire, after what happened to Temu Trump, nobody wants the position. We are having trouble finding suitable, qualified volunteers."

High Prince Godric looked at his fingernails, which were already chewed down to the quick.

Defence Minister Peter Macron cleared his throat once more, "Ah, hum! Sire, it is not all bad news. While the Colonial Fleet does have two Carrier Strike Groups operating close to our territories and have eliminated our Armed Forces at Jupiter L-One and Jupiter L-Two, they are not occupation forces."

That did little to alleviate the High Prince's concerns. He looked to his Brother, Emeric.

Prince Emeric had nothing. How could he help? There was nothing he could do!

Prince Emeric just asked, "These Carrier Strike Groups. Do they have designations?", as if that might help.

Security Minister Morton responded, "Yes, Your Highness. Our assets at Cis-Lunar L-Five tell us that they are the Spitting Witch Strike Group under the command of Fleet Captain Nicholas Nikolaidis and the Eternal Ring Strike Group under the command of Captain Hiroshi Tanaka."

"Fuck!", the High Prince exclaimed, "Do they name their Carrier Strike Groups just to taunt me?", his paranoia was growing.

The Defence Minister stepped back in, "Sire, Captains Nikolaidis and Tanaka appear to have orders to blockade our system. None of the supply convoys from our QOSA allies are getting through."

Commerce Minister Devlin Dervish chimed in, "Sire, Defence Minister Macron is correct. All convoys from the Saturnian Demarchy, the Uranian Federation and the Neptunian Commonwealth are being intercepted. They are allowing the hauliers to continue, but all of the cargo pods are being destroyed. And as we are all aware, the Belters have already stopped all trade with us."

"We need to strike at the Belters and take one or two of their colonies. If we do that, we can use them as bases of operations to project our power into the inner system", the High Prince considered out loud.

Defence Minister Macron cautiously responded, "Sire. That would be very unwise. All thirteen Belter Nations currently have three capital ships protecting them. One of those new Dumas-designed Battle Cruisers, a Colonial Fleet Destroyer and an Earth Defence Force Destroyer", and then he paused.

When the Defence Minister continued, he was cautious, "To make matters worse, Sire. There are Earth Defence Force and Colonial Fleet Heavy Cruisers, six of each, patrolling the space lanes between the Belter Nations. Every ship that I've noted has the latest Dumas-manufactured upgrades as well."

High Prince Godric stared at his fingers. There was little left of his fingernails to chew.

"What about the mining colonies in the Martian orbital zones? Surely we can take those? Make use of them? They'd make good forward operations bases", he demanded.

"Sire, the Martian Trojan mining zones have the exact same protection as the Belter Nations", his Defence Minister replied, cautiously explaining, "Even Mars itself is protected. They have a third Carrier Strike Group stationed at the Deimos military base. The Asteroid Belt and the Martian Orbital zones are effectively their first and second lines of defence."

Security Minister Miles Morton chimed in, "Sire, that would be the Indomitable Wyvern Strike Group under the command of Captain Janice Whatley."

High Prince Godric glared at Security Minister Morton. He could have him disembowelled, like his former Communications Minister, Temu Trump. However, his Security Minister was his new enforcer. He could not very well command his new enforcer to disembowel himself.

"Okay. So if I understand our position correctly, we are boxed in by two Carrier Strike Groups on our outer frontier and our enemy's first and second line of defences in the Asteroid Belt and Martian orbital zone", High Prince Godric summed up and then he demanded, "Find me a way to strike at the Earth and Cis-Lunar Space directly. I will burn them into submission. Those peasants will obey me!"

High Prince Godric had looped back into his previously failed terror tactics.

The High Prince's logic was circular and going nowhere fast.

Defence Minister Peter Macron was extremely cautious with his response, "Sire, any attempt to send our cold-fusion missiles through Belter territory would likely lead to their interception. Our enemies have built up enough forces there to be able to do so."

Security Minister, Miles Morton, added his assessment, "Sire, even if we could get through. The colonies of Cis-Lunar Space now have formidable anti-missile defence platforms."

"The Earth doesn't", the High Prince countered.

"Sire, the Earth didn't. Things have changed somewhat. Our spies in Cis-Lunar L-Five inform us that in addition to seconding two fighter squadrons to the Earth Defence Forces, that damnable Dumas Corporation has begun building anti-missile defence platforms specifically for the Earth", the Security Minister cautiously informed.

Science Minister Peter Patronis chimed in, "Sire. I have seen the photographs. Based on my people's analysis, those missile defence platforms use a combination of anti-missile missiles, high-powered laser beams and high-powered particle beams."

High Prince Godric stared at his Science Minister coldly, "You are my fucking Science Minister! You find me a way to get my missiles through the Asteroid Belt to strike the fucking Earth!", he shouted.

At that precise moment, Science Minister Peter Patronis wished that he'd kept his big mouth shut. None of his fellow Ministers were his friends. Each and every one of them would betray any of the others in a heartbeat. In the High Prince's cabinet, there were only survivors with clever language, hoping not to be the next to die.

Peter Patronis had noticed, Security Minister Miles Morton was standing, his hand resting on the hilt of his sheathed K-bar knife.

Would Peter Patronis be the next Jovian Minister to find himself gutted and disembowelled like former Communications Minister, Temu Trump?

At least with Roberta Nummus or Aurange Sheergibbon, the execution was a swift beheading. Now, however, Sheergibbon was dead. Roberta Nummus had killed him and then beheaded the previous High Prince with a gruesome chop, chop rip of his head and fled off into deep space. Miles Morton, though, was a butcher who enjoyed his brutality. That toothy grin he displayed as he stabbed people with his K-bar knife. Slicing and disembowelling his victims was epic in every possible wrong way. He'd even been known to murder his sex Slaves after they'd performed their duties on him.

The Jovian Realms bred monsters and they were in charge, each feeding off the others under the High Prince's reign.

Peter's very next words were a matter of life and death.

Cautiously, very cautiously, Peter Patronis answered the High Prince.

Science Minister Peter Patronis stood up and bowed slightly as he carefully crafted his reply.

"Your Highness. We all forget that this solar system of ours is not a flat two-dimensional plane. All of the major planetary orbital zones lie in the plane of the solar system, the ecliptic. However, space has three spatial dimensions", Peter Patronis explained as he kept Miles Morton in his peripheral vision.

Peter Patronis continued, "Sire, if we cannot punch through their defences in the Asteroid Belt, then we must go over them or under them. Perhaps even both. We must use trajectories that rise above and below the solar system's ecliptic."

Defence Minister Peter Macron caught on, "Yes, yes. We do what they might not expect. Rain cold-fusion missiles and merry hell down upon them from above and below the ecliptic. Minister Patronis, that is genius. Pure fucking genius. You are right, this is a three-dimensional battle space. Four, if you consider the temporal aspect. How bleeding obvious!"

Peter Patronis replied cautiously, "If and only if they don't detect them, Minister Macron. It is only a good plan if it works", and then he cautiously sat back down with a silent sigh of relief.

The Science Minister had to be extremely explicit in allowing for the possibilities of failure. His very life might depend on that later.

The High Prince looked at his Security Minister and shook his head. Mile Morton sat back down, his face showing signs of severe disappointment. He was looking forward to some fun.

High Prince Godric von Horridian had been presented with a straw and he grabbed it gleefully with both hands. Like a drowning man breathing through a thin reed, he grabbed at that straw. If he couldn't punch through the enemy's defence lines, he would go around them. Over and under the Asteroid Belt, above and below the solar system's ecliptic. It all seemed so simple!

"Defence Minister Macron!", High Prince Godric was almost shouting, "Hit those insolent, quisling, unruly peasants with fifty fucking cold-fusion missiles. Send them arcing above and below the ecliptic. Hit them hard and force them to obey me! I will be obeyed!"

His Defence Minister replied cautiously, enquiring, "Do you have any particular targets in mind or would you prefer our defence department personnel to select the targets, Your Majesty?"

Godric von Horridian laughed loudly and responded, "No, Minister Macron. I have no targets in particular in mind. Just Wild Weasel those missiles and let them select their own fucking targets at random. I don't particularly care what they hit, just as long as those quisling peasants understand terror! Sheer fucking terror! They must fully understand the price to be paid for their defiance!"

"Fifty cold-fusion missiles auto-targeting on approach. Maximum yield. Twenty five above and twenty five below the ecliptic", Minister Macron noted down on his data tablet and then he cautioned, as he must for his own survival, "Sire, as we are Wild Weaselling these missiles, they will strike whatever they randomly target. That may have unintended consequences, Sire."

Godric von Horridian snorted, "Like I give a flying fuck about what happens to quisling peasants."

Defence Minister Macron nodded, "Your will be done, Your Majesty."

High Prince Godric stepped out of his gold-gilded throne and strutted out of his throne room.

Prince Emeric watched him leave, thinking to himself.

"Did that just happen?"

"Random Wild Weasel auto-targeting with two megaton cold-fusion warheads?"

"What could possibly go wrong with that? Fucking everything!"

Prince Emeric stared at his Brother's Throne, *"Everyone who sits there goes insane! I seriously need to avoid my Brother's and my Father's fate"*, he silently thought to himself.

High Prince Godric von Horridian's latest plans were sheer stupidity!

29. Venus Enters the Fray.

Prince Emeric returned to his apartments in Ganymede Prime. It was nowhere near as spacious and opulent as his palace on Europa Prime, but it was comfortable. It was also independent of his Brother, Godric's, palace. It was a place where he could relax in privacy. Emeric contacted his Brother, Friederic, the Prince of Io. He understood that the conversation would be slow, with a lot of time lag, due to the more than two-second delay between the mega colonies of Ganymede Prime and Io Prime, but he did it anyway. It took many long seconds before Prince Friederic answered the call.

"Brother, Emeric, you don't normally make these long-distance calls", Friederic greeted him, "What's gone wrong?"

"Friederic, our Brother, Godric. He's completely lost the plot", Emeric informed him, "His War is going very badly and his moves are becoming increasingly desperate."

Friederic nodded and replied, "I know. I've been watching the news feeds. Not just our internal ones, but the external news feeds as well."

"You still have access? I thought Godric had your access revoked?", Emeric replied in surprise.

"Godric tried, but I just rerouted my access in a way that they can't block", Friederic smiled, noting, "That is what happens when loyalty is valued more than competency."

Emeric nodded in understanding, "Temu Trump is gone. Mile Morton gutted him, disembowelled him with that K-bar knife he carries."

"That was bound to happen. Temu Trump's lies and manipulations were bound to catch up with him", Friederic understood all too well how quickly a Minister could lose favour and then he asked, "That's not what you're calling about, though, is it?"

"Godric is insane, Brother. He has ordered another missile strike on Earth and Cis-Lunar Space. Long-range interplanetary missiles. Fifty of them", Emeric informed Friederic.

Friederic smiled a wry smile, "I've read their so-called top secret briefs. Doesn't our Brother understand, those missiles won't get through the Asteroid Belt and even if they do, the missile defences in Cis-Lunar Space will take them out."

Emeric frowned, "The Asteroid Belt is going to be bypassed, Friederic", then he paused slightly, "And those missiles, they are going to be auto-targeting!"

Friederic was the smartest of the Horridian Princes and quickly put two and two together.

"So they're lobbing those missiles above and below the ecliptic. That is clever. Even I have to admit that, but auto-targeting? That is not going to work. Interplanetary missiles require specific targets to be assigned at their destination. Then their A.I. targeting systems lock on using all available information and data, and then they make precise targeted strikes. Auto targeting interplanetary missiles isn't a thing", Friederic replied, he had a deep understanding of how they worked.

Emeric shook his head, "Our Brother, Godric, in his wisdom has ordered those interplanetary missiles to be '*Wild Weaselled*'. Godric wants them to target whatever they lock onto first at random."

Friederic blinked, not because it didn't make sense, that was his Brother, Godric's, logic. Strike fear and terror into his enemies. Using missiles raining down from above and below the ecliptic and targeting at random was just Godric's style.

"Emeric. That means the missile A.I. targeting systems have to be removed. They'll be putting in cheap and dirty Wild Weasel auto-targeting systems in their place and that, my dear Brother, is very, very bad", Friederic explained.

"I know, Friederic, but our Brother, Godric, he won't listen to reason", Emeric replied, the frustration showing clearly on his face.

"Look, Emeric, they are taking the flawed auto-targeting systems out of a two-kiloton tactical nuke and placing them into a two-megaton interplanetary missile. The only way that works is if they launch those missiles on ballistic trajectories above and below the ecliptic towards Cis-Lunar Space", Friederic explained, noting, "They are relying on those missiles picking their own targets upon arrival. Some may overfly Cis-Lunar Space completely and become rogue missiles. They could end up anywhere, targeting anything. It's very possible that unintended targets could get hit with unintended results."

"I know that, Brother, I know that", Emeric replied, his voice exasperated, "Yet, our Brother, Godric, simply does not listen."

"My advice to you, Emeric. Walk away from Godric's court. Come here to Io Prime. Minerva and I would be happy to host you", Friederic offered, before dangling the cherry, "Your Wife, Chastity, is staying with us and you do need to make up with her."

"Chastity won't take me back. Not after this horrendous War and all of Godric's atrocities", Emeric replied, he was truly upset with the state of his marriage and it showed on his face.

"Incorrect, dear Brother, in so many ways", Friederic replied, "I can assure you that Chastity does not blame you for our Brother, Godric's, excesses. If you grovel at her feet long enough, she will take you back", and then he laughed, "You will need to grovel, Emeric. Chastity is still pretty pissed!"

"And I will do that, Friederic, but not now. Godric's court and his cabinet are all in a state of fear. They may turn on Godric and I have to be there to prevent that", Emeric explained, but he also noted, "I also need to be there to witness Godric's decisions first-hand. Someone has to!"

"Then you are a better man than I, Brother Emeric. I could not sit there and watch Godric's descent into madness. I had to leave his court. I could not stand the insanity of it all", Friederic admitted.

"Know this, Brother Friederic. If Godric falls, I will refuse the throne. It is cursed, evil and I will not sit on it", Prince Emeric announced.

"You put me in a difficult position, Brother Emeric. With Brother Aluric being mentally unstable, you are the next in line to the throne. If you abdicate your responsibilities, you will be forcing me to take up the cursed throne and I'm not so sure that I want it either", Prince Friederic replied.

First, High Prince Albert descended into senility and madness. Now, High Prince Godric follows the same path. The throne must never be empty, yet nobody wants the evil curse that goes with it!

It was a fourteen-week flight for the Jovian interplanetary missiles. Twenty five above and twenty five below the ecliptic. During those fourteen weeks, the War grew slow with little more than careful posturing by both sides. The Belters had reluctantly accepted the protection of Earth and Cis-Lunar Space. To them, it was the lesser of two evils. They couldn't stand alone, but that didn't mean that they wanted Colonial Battle Cruisers and other warships on their doorsteps. It was simply expedient.

The Belters had little choice in the matter. Without actual defence forces of their own, they would have been easy pickings for the Horridian Regime. They also fully understood that projecting power into the inner solar system would require the Jovian Realms to invade their territories. To set up forward operating bases. The Belters knew both sides and the greater evil to their minds was the Six Jovian Realms and their Horridian Regime.

High Prince Godric's Armed Forces continued to probe the Asteroid Belt. It was a distraction, a feint. So long as the Jovian Armed Forces probed the inner system's outer defences in the Asteroid Belt, their enemies weren't looking above or below the ecliptic.

The High Prince's armed forces also probed deep space beyond Jupiter's orbital zone. They were hoping to escort the Saturnian Demarchy, Uranian Federation and Neptunian Commonwealth convoys in their traversal of interplanetary space to Jovian territory. However, that was in itself problematic.

The Spitting Witch and Eternal Ring Carrier Strike Groups, with their Refuelling and Supply Tender craft, could operate further out in the deep void between Jupiter and Saturn. The Jovians had no equivalent craft and always required courses and trajectories to account for refuelling stops within their own realms. The convoy interceptions were taking place well outside of their reach.

"Why haven't you broken their blockade? Why are we still boxed in?", High Prince Godric demanded to know.

"Your Majesty", Defence Minister Macron began, "The enemy's Carrier Strike Groups operate in the deep void between our Jovian Realms and the Saturnian Demarchy's territory. Those Carrier Strike Groups operate outside of our reach, Sire."

"I understand that, Minister Macron. I am talking about the Asteroid Belt. We need forward bases of operation. We need to take and occupy Belter territory", the High Prince replied, his eyes showing dark shadows from lack of sleep.

The Defence Minister was about to reply, but Prince Emeric cut him off. Peter Macron sighed with relief. He had not wanted to give the High Prince bad news. Prince Emeric gave him a subtle nod.

"Brother, Godric", Prince Emeric began, "For us to take one or two of the Belter colonies would require that we send in our main fleet. We could do that, but it would be costly, very costly, Brother. It would also leave our outer defences wide open."

Having delivered the bad news, Defence Minister Macron stepped back in, "His Highness is correct, Your Majesty. We have run battle simulations for taking one or two of the Belter colonies. Our best simulations indicate our Jovian Fleet losses at forty percent. We would win the day, but at a great cost and as Prince Emeric has noted, we'd leave our outer defences woefully wide open."

Defence Minister Macron looked to Prince Emeric for confirmation or validation. Anything at all!

Prince Emeric commented, "Brother. We can take one or two of the Belter Nations, but at an enormous cost. After which, the chessboard changes. Their

Carrier Strike Group at Mars will regroup with their surviving forces and simply retake those Belter colonies. Those two Carrier Strike Groups that they have out there in the deep void would then punch through our outer defences and challenge us here in our own system. Our own backyard."

Defence Minister Macron then noted further bad news, "The Dumas Colonial Construction shipyards are also producing more of those Carrier Strike Groups, Sire. Although we do lack intelligence on those at present, Sire."

High Prince Godric shook his head in despair, "Is there nothing we can do?"

"Brother", Prince Emeric began, "The blockade stops us from projecting power beyond it, into the inner solar system. It also blocks supplies and raw materials from reaching us from the other outer satellites. However, that is all it does. Our enemies seem unwilling, or at the very least, overly cautious, about bringing the War to us here directly in Jovian Cis-Lunar Space. They may have contested our L-One and L-Two zones, but they haven't bothered to contest either of our two Jovian Trojan Realms."

"What are you getting at, Emeric?", High Prince Godric enquired.

Defence Minister Macron chimed in against his better judgement, "Sire, I believe what Prince Emeric is alluding to is that the blockade, although annoying, is having little effect on our internal operational abilities."

Prince Emeric nodded in agreement, "Brother, they have boxed us in, sure, but we have all the resources we need here in Jovian Cis-Lunar Space and our Leading and Trailing Trojan Realms. Honestly, as long as they stay in the periphery at the edges of their box, their blockade is a nonsense."

"A nonsense?", Godric von Horridian enquired, "How can their blockade be a nonsense?", he asked.

Science Minister Peter Patronis responded, "Sire, our manufacturing stations and shipyards in Ganymede L-Four are still churning out weapons and ships. New Destroyers and Dreadnoughts, all with fusion drive systems. All we need to do is keep doing what we're doing. Build up our forces and basically outwait them. They think they have us, but do they really?", he asked tentatively.

Godric turned to his Brother, Emeric and Emeric replied to his look, "They may have controlled the early stages of this War, Brother, but in the long run, unless they are willing to take the fight into our own backyard, we will simply grow stronger over time."

High Prince Godric smiled for the first time in many weeks, "So it's not all lost!", he exclaimed, before commenting, "All we need to do is wait them out and keep lobbing missiles at them!"

Prince Emeric sighed a deep internal sigh, thinking, *"That is not what I meant, Brother Godric! That is not what I meant!"*

High Prince Godric's newfound cheer simply turned his mind back towards the infliction of terror!

Above the Earth in Cis-Lunar Space, Human infrastructure was everywhere. Not just in the Earth's orbit, but farther afield as well. On the Earth's Moon itself, there was the Lunar Mining Consortium's mining complex and its many mining zones. Helium three mining was particularly profitable. Off-world in Cis-Lunar Space, organised in Lagrangian Gravitational zones, was the bulk of the colonial infrastructure.

Cis-Lunar L-One, which was fifty eight thousand kilometres from the Moon in the direction of the Earth, contained Lunar transfer stations, way stations, orbital hotels and a handful of smaller, boutique colonies. Equidistant on the other side of the Moon was Cis-Lunar L-Two. A zone that contained not only orbital hotels but also civilian research stations, military surveillance stations and the Dumas Astro Resource Corporation's research stations.

The most important of the Cis-Lunar gravitational zones were Cis-Lunar L-Four and Cis-Lunar L-Five, which were a little over three hundred and eighty four thousand kilometres ahead and behind the Moon in its orbit around the Earth.

Cis-Lunar L-Four contained the industrial heart of the Cis-Lunar Space colonies. That was the zone in which all of the mining catchalls, ore processing stations and manufacturing stations were. Amongst these were the Cis-Lunar Space Government's space ship construction yards, the Dumas Colonial Constructions facilities and the Himmelstaff Interplanetary Constructions facilities. It was also where the Cis-Lunar Space Colonial Fleet's military training cylinders and the Cis-Lunar Space Government's correctional facilities, Stamford Toruses, were located.

Cis-Lunar L-Five was the residential hub of Cis-Lunar Space and it contained hundreds of colonies in halo orbits, all orbiting the zone's gravitational sweet spot. There were smaller Bernal Sphere and Stanford Torus colonies, but most of the colonies were of the twin-cylinder O'Neil-style. Of course, the largest colonies, including the twenty four kilometre long mega-colony of Colonial Central Command, were of the single-cylinder variety.

However, the Earth also had its own Lagrangian points. Sixty degrees ahead and behind the Earth in its orbit were Earth's L-Four and L-Five zones. These contained the Dumas Earth Trojan Mining Corporation's accumulated asteroidal masses, mobile mining stations, ore processing stations, and manufacturing and warehousing stations.

In each Lagrangian zone, there were also six twin-cylinder O'Neil-style residential colonies for the Dumas Corporation's employees. In the Earth's L-Five zone, in a high halo orbit, was also the dead World within the Rock, Eros, previously a paradise. The very first victim in High Prince Godric von Horridian's War. A world murdered! Both of the Earth's L-Four and L-Five zones were farther afield and now very well protected.

The other two Lagrangian zones, the Earth's L-One and L-Two zones, were in line with the Sun. One point five million kilometres in front of and behind the Earth. The L-Two zone is in the Earth's shadow and contains civilian research stations, military surveillance stations and more Dumas Astro Resource Corporation research stations. In a higher halo orbit, in constant sunlight, there were also several twin-cylinder university colonies.

Of these two particular zones, the most active was the Earth's L-One zone. In this zone, there were vast solar power arrays that continuously beamed energy back to the Earth. As with Venus L-One, in the Venusian orbital zone, there were also twin-cylinder colonies, although somewhat less than at Venus. What was of note was the orbital way station in the centre of the Earth's L-One gravitational zone. It was the way station for the Venus cycler system. A massive transportation hub.

There were eight cyclers in all and each carried passengers and cargo between the Earth's and Venus's L-One zones. The cyclers, known as Venusian clippers, did require electric propulsion to keep them on track, but otherwise, they worked as a typical interplanetary cycler. Cargo and passengers would be offloaded on approach. Refuelling would take place after offloading. After which, new cargo and passengers would be taken aboard for the trip back to Venus L-One and the Venusian colonies.

Once on the cycler way station, the passengers and cargo would be processed by immigration and customs and then ferried to the Cis-Lunar colonies. The cycler way station itself also contained major hotels, restaurants and boutique shops. Passengers often stayed at the hotels for several days before travelling to their destinations. The restaurants and the duty-free shopping were particularly popular.

The cycler system did not rely purely on gravitational ballistics. Rather, it relied on electric propulsion and stable L-One rendezvous points. Each of the eight Venusian clippers flew the same corridor between Earth-L-One and Venus-L-One every fifteen weeks like clockwork. They were more like interplanetary liners with atomic-powered VASIMR drives than simple ballistic cyclers. The Venusian cycler system had been in continuous use without a single incident, since not long after the Venusian colonies had been constructed over a century earlier.

They were sleek and painted the same colour as the void of space, a deep inky black. For fourteen weeks, they'd been on their ballistic trajectories. There were fifty of them in all, twenty five above and twenty five below the solar system's ecliptic. They were all converging on the one region, Cis-Lunar Space. As above and so below, at five million kilometres out, their auto-targeting systems kicked in.

High Prince Godric had thought to catch the Earth and Cis-Lunar Space defences off guard. He actually thought that the Earth and Cis-Lunar Space authorities were two-dimensional thinkers. The High Prince was wrong, so very wrong. No sooner than the Jovian cold-fusion missiles had switched on their auto-targeting sensors and began to thrust manoeuvre, they were detected. The battlefield was a four-dimensional chessboard and the Cis-Lunar Space authorities knew this all too well.

The cold-fusion missiles picked their targets at random. It mattered not what the targets were. Perhaps a construction shipyard or two, perhaps the Cis-Lunar Mining Consortium's mining complex. Perhaps a civilian colony here or there, maybe even Colonial Central Command itself. It mattered not, High Prince Godric wanted random terror and he cared not one whit for the life or limb of his enemies. As above and so below, the cold-fusion missiles fell upon their auto-selected targets. Raw two-megaton cold-fusion might held in abeyance until their strike!

Laser beam cannons lanced out with their superheated coherent blue light. Particle beam cannons blazed with their powerful orange beams of particles. Plasma cannon spat balls of plasma so hot they'd melt through iron and steel ship hulls. Electromagnetic Rail Guns spat out explosive tungsten rounds in rapid succession.

As above and so below, there were immense, brilliant bursts of blue-white light as two-megaton cold-fusion warheads exploded prematurely, well away from their auto-selected targets. The night skies of the Earth lit up with short-lived new stars that blinked in and out of existence in a handful of seconds. The explosions were far more visible and visceral for the colonists living in Cis-Lunar L-Five and working in Cis-Lunar L-Four. The gut-wrenching fireworks didn't last long and when it was over, not a single target in Cis-Lunar Space had been struck.

Except, of course, these cold-fusion missiles had been fired on simple ballistic trajectories and a handful of them had overshot Cis-Lunar Space completely. Four of the cold-fusion missiles had Wild-Weaselled and gone rogue. When they auto-selected their targets, it was well clear of Cis-Lunar Space. There were no anti-missile defences in the region they'd targeted. There was nothing to stop them and they fell upon their targets with the pure thermonuclear obliteration of two-megaton strikes.

Four immense flashes of blue-white light lit up space a million and a half kilometres from the Earth. When the flashes of light had dissipated, two major solar power arrays, one outbound Venusian clipper full of passengers and the immense Venus cycler way station, with all of its workers and travellers, were no more. They'd all been vaporised in an instant. Thousands of souls burned to ashes, erased, their lives snuffed out!

The two solar power arrays could be construed as *"economic"* targets and perhaps justified. The Venusian Clipper and the Venus Cycler way station, however, could not. They were a shared, civilian resource, jointly owned by both the Cis-Lunar Space Government and the Venusian Government.

The Venusians, of course, had remained steadfastly neutral since the beginning of the War. Strongly denouncing the Horridians, yes, but still steadfastly neutral. Now, however, that would change. There had been Venusian civilians, tourists, returning to the Venusian Republic on the outbound Venusian Clipper. New colonists, emigrating from Earth to the Venusian Republic, were also onboard that Venusian Clipper.

And then there was the Venus cycler way station itself. A large contingent of the passengers who had just disembarked from that same Venusian Clipper, when it was inbound, were in the way station. Venusian citizens, including a large contingent of Venusian diplomats, all with their diplomatic immunity. A little over fourteen weeks earlier, Jovian Science Minister Peter Patronis had mentioned to High Prince Godric von Horridian something about unintended consequences.

As above and so below, retribution was coming.

Within twenty four hours, President Bradley Klein of the Venusian Republic released a statement to the media. It was a written statement, not a speech. The President's office had stated that Godric Horridian did not deserve spoken words, only responses and that they would be coming.

The President's statement simply read, *"I, President Bradley Klein, as the duly elected President of the Venusian Republic, hereby exercise my power under the Venusian Constitution and with the full backing of the Venusian Congress and Senate, hereby declare that a state of War now exists between the Venusian Republic and the Six Jovian Realms. The unlawful and illegal attack and murder by the Jovian Realms of the peaceful citizens of the Venusian Republic will not, I repeat, will not go unanswered. The Venusian Armed Forces are henceforth mobilising for War!"*

Within seventy two hours, six Venusian Heavy Dreadnoughts had been dispatched towards Jovian space. These were neither the stretched triangular nor the stretched rectoid-shaped ships like those of the Cis-Lunar Colonial Fleet or the Earth Defence Forces. Nor were they like the stretched ovoid-shaped Dumas-designed and built Dreadnoughts that literally bristled with weapons.

No, the Venusian Heavy Dreadnoughts were unique, stretched, conical-shaped ships, bristling with laser beams and particle beam cannons, with a single powerful electromagnetic rail gun running the full length of their interior hull. They could punch holes through another ship, unseen, from ten light seconds away with explosive tungsten slugs travelling and ten percent the speed of light! The defences on the Venusian ships included specialised titanium alloys designed to withstand intense radiation and their ships hulls were painted in a thick ceramic coating that could dissipate the strikes of both laser beams and particle beams.

No one knew that the Venusians had these Heavy Dreadnoughts. It had been a state secret. Now, that secret was going to come to the light of day. The Venusians had been peaceful, yes, but they had a simple philosophy. *"Better to have it and not need it than need it and not have it."* These were just the kind of unintended consequences that Jovian Science Minister Peter Patronis had been warning about.

The Venusian Republic was entering the fray!

30. Ice Pick.

Before the Jovian Republic had fallen and became the Six Jovian Realms, in the preceding year in twenty one seventy seven, the two Trojan Republics had been annexed. The then High Prince, Albert von Horridian, had sent three Dreadnoughts to each of the Trojan Republics, which, having no Armed Forces of their own, capitulated straight away. That was quickly followed by the deployment of loyal Jovian Shock Troopers. After which, the Jovian Dreadnoughts returned to their normal patrol duties.

With the onset of the first Horridian War in twenty-one eighty two, which became known as the Outer Satellite Insurrection due to the Quadripartite Outer Satellite Agreement, the QOSA, the new High Prince Godric von Horridian, had considered it prudent to send three Jovian Dreadnoughts to his two Trojan Realms to ensure that his holdings were adequately protected.

This had occurred almost immediately after the signing and ratification of the Quadripartite Outer Satellite Agreement and could have been seen as a harbinger of what was to follow. The Horridian's first strike, against Eros, the World within the Rock. No one put two and two together until after Eros had been thoroughly destroyed.

It was now twenty one eighty three and the War was already well into its second year. Through the miscalculations of High Prince Godric von Horridian, the Venusians had entered the fray. Six Venusian Dreadnoughts had been launched. Three towards Jupiter's Leading Trojans and three towards Jupiter's Trailing Trojans. After more than twelve weeks of flight, they approached their respective destinations.

The Captain on the bridge of the Jovian Dreadnought, Calliope, was watching his main screen. The Calliope's Sister ships, Polyiope and Thessiope, were clearly visible as the three ships sat on station watching over the Hector Colonial Central Command colony. The massive twin-cylinder capital colony of the Jovian's Leading Trojan Realm. It was a peaceful Sunday and all was well.

As the Calliope's Captain drank his coffee and looked at his main screen, the Calliope's Sister ship Polyiope convulsed and ripped into two in a massive explosion that was so sudden that he dropped his coffee cup to the floor in shock. It shattered on the ship's deck.

"What fuck just happened?", he questioned in alarm.

Then, before anyone could answer, the Calliope's other Sister ship, Thessiope, also convulsed and ripped into two in another massive explosion. One exploding Dreadnought might have been a malfunction, a catastrophe, but two, that was definitely an attack.

"Battle stations", the Calliope's Captain shouted out and then before he could issue another command, his own ship erupted with explosions and tore itself apart.

The Captain of the Venusian Dreadnought, Sunfire, hailed the other two Venusian Dreadnoughts, "Sunburst, Sunflare. Excellent work. Alter course for rendezvous point gamma. Repeat. Alter course for rendezvous point gamma."

The unintended consequences of the random missile attacks on Cis-Lunar Space, which took out a Venusian clipper and the Venus Cycler Way Station, were coming back to haunt Godric von Horridian.

At almost precisely the same moment, one hundred and twenty degrees away on the other side of Jupiter's orbit, in Jupiter's Trailing Trojan zone, the same military action was taking place. A peaceful, tranquil Sunday. Three Jovian Dreadnoughts, Mnesiope, Euthiope and Xanthiope, three more Sister ships of the Calliope. They all sat watching over their charge, the massive twin-cylinder capital colony of the Jovian Trailing Trojan Realm, Patroclus Colonial Central Command colony.

Then, from out of the void, launched from over three million kilometres out, three long explosive tungsten slugs travelling at ten percent of the speed of light struck without warning. The three Jovian Dreadnoughts were ripped in two and the Mnesiope, Euthiope and Xanthiope all exploded before they even knew what had hit them. The Venusian Dreadnoughts, Sunblazer, Sunspark and Sunlight all altered course and proceeded towards rendezvous point gamma.

In both cases, no mayday was given out. The Venusian Dreadnoughts had launched their tungsten slugs from over three million kilometres away. The Jovian Dreadnoughts had not detected them and were caught completely by surprise. The first thing that High Prince Godric heard of the disaster was from the public operations report released by the Venusian Armed Forces over the public news networks. Confirmation from his own sources, from Hector Central and Patroclus Central, came later, much later, several hours later.

The High Prince's gaze was like venom, "How has this happened?", he demanded.

Defence Minister Peter Macron first glanced at Security Minister Morton, before he cautiously replied, "Your Majesty, we had no idea that the Venusians had any Dreadnoughts. All of our current information is that they had nothing more than a handful of short-range Missile Destroyers."

High Prince Godric looked towards his Security Minister with a definite snarl on his face, "Minister Morton, how is it that the Venusians have Dreadnoughts that we did not know about?", he demanded.

Security Minister Miles Morton glanced at the Defence Minister before responding, "Your Majesty, we currently have no assets in Venusian space."

"No assets in Venusian space? Why? How is that even possible?", the High Prince questioned.

Security Minister Miles Morton replied with a clever lie, "Sire, we were in the process of transferring some of our assets from Cis-Lunar L-Five to the Venusian colonies in Venus L-One. Sadly, Sire, our operatives were onboard the Venusian clipper that was destroyed during our missile attack."

The lie worked. It now appeared that the cause of the problem was thrown back to the missile attack.

"So, Minister, this is all my fault, is it?" High Prince Godric asked directly.

"No, Sire", Security Minister Morton replied, quickly glancing at Science Minister Patronis, before continuing, "It is merely an unintended consequence as Minister Patronis once mentioned."

Science Minister Patronis quickly added, "This could not have been foreseen, Your Majesty. We could never have known that a handful of our missiles would go so rogue and draw the Venusians into the conflict. It was an unfortunate and unintended consequence, Sire."

"So we've lost six of our Dreadnoughts! Six of our best and they never even got a look at the enemy's ships!", High Prince Godric shouted and then he questioned, "How is that even possible?"

Science Minister Patronis replied, his scientific mind caught off guard and scrambling, "Your Majesty, the only possible method I can think of would be long-range electromagnetic rail guns."

"Oh, really, that's fucking great! Not only can the Venusians have their Dreadnoughts in our territory in twelve weeks, they have long-range fucking electromagnetic rail guns!", the High Prince shouted.

No one said a word.

Prince Emeric chimed in, "Brother, this does pose us with a problem. We have no naval assets in our Trojan Realms. Our L-One, L-Two, L-Four and L-Five zones are all completely undefended."

High Prince Godric smiled at his Brother, "You are stating the bloody obvious, Emeric. I think the Venusians wanted payback and they got it!"

The High Prince turned back to his Ministers, "So, where are those fucking Dreadnoughts now?"

"We can't know for sure, Your Majesty. However, they may join those Carrier Strike Groups and reinforce the outer blockade", Defence Minister Macron suggested.

"That would make logical sense, Sire", Science Minister Patronis agreed, citing, "They've had their payback, now they'll likely join the blockade."

"You cannot be certain of that", Security Minister Morton argued, he really wanted to gut Minister Macron like a fish, "They could just as well start picking off our outer defences with those long-range electromagnetic rail guns!"

Science Minister Patronis disagreed, "No. That is very unlikely, Minister Morton."

"Explain your logic, Minister Patronis! Explain it!", Security Minister Morton demanded.
High Prince Godric turned to his Science Minister in anticipation.

Science Minister Peter Patronis explained, "We should have received word from our Trojan Realms about this disaster first. We didn't. We heard about it first on the external news feeds. That means that the Venusians publicly released their operations report in advance, even before their Dreadnoughts had started their attack. This whole thing was choreographed for maximum humiliation."

Prince Emeric chimed in, "If that's the case, then they are likely to join the blockade."

Science Minister Patronis smiled and nodded, "Precisely, Your Highness", and then he turned to Defence Minister Macron, "Although we should definitely intensify our deep scans around Jovian Cis-Lunar Space, just to be on the safe side."

"Agreed", Defence Minister Macron replied as he quickly typed into his data tablet, "I will organise that immediately."

High Prince Godric doubled down as was his way, "Defence Minister Macron. Just how many cold-fusion missiles do with have up our sleeve?"
"We have plenty of cold-fusion missiles, Your Majesty", the Defence Minister confirmed.

"Good, then. Send another hundred to Earth and Cis-Lunar Space. Wild Weasel them just like before. Above and below the ecliptic, just like last time. Let's overwhelm them and see how many missiles it takes to break their defences", the High Prince ordered.

Prince Emeric sighed internally. He would have shaken his head in disgust, but that would have appeared too obvious.

High Prince Godric added, "And send a couple of dozen missiles to the Venusians as a gift."

"Yes, Your Majesty", Defence Minister Macron replied, adding, "Your will be done!"

And that was how the First Horridian War, the Outer Satellite Insurrection, progressed. High Prince Godric von Horridian had his cold-fusion missiles Wild Weaselled. He launched them above and below the ecliptic on ballistic trajectories, self-targeting at random on their final approach. Godric targeted Earth, Cis-Lunar Space. He even targeted Venus. He even targeted Mars. All thoughts of preserving the living worlds, Earth and the newly terraformed Mars, were completely forgotten. Godric took on a new madness and that was the order of the day. He was relentless!

However, after the destruction of the Venus cycler and one of its clippers, anti-missile defence platforms were placed everywhere across the colonies, protecting lives and infrastructure alike. They rolled off the Dumas Colonial Construction lines hand over fist. They were shipped out to the Venusian Republic to protect their colonies. They were also shipped out to the Martian colonies that were not yet independent and heavily reliant on the Earth and Cis-Lunar space.

The six Venusian Dreadnoughts, Sunfire, Sunburst, Sunflare, Sunblazer, Sunspark and Sunlight had all rendezvoused with the Spitting Witch and Eternal Ring Carrier Strike Groups at rendezvous point gamma. The Venusians had orders to join the Carrier Strike Groups and bolster the outer blockade. Nothing moved between Jupiter and the other Gas Giants in the outer solar system.

In between launching volleys of his cold-fusion missiles at the inner solar system worlds, Godric would order his fleet to test the borders of his Jovian territories. Always at the very edge of their long-range scans, his Dreadnoughts would detect enemy ships. Inside Jupiter's orbit, there was an ever-growing presence of Colonial Battle Cruisers and beyond Jupiter's orbit, the Colonial Carrier Strike Groups and the almost certain death that they brought with them.

There were skirmishes and ships on both sides were being destroyed, albeit at a slow rate of attrition. Smaller ships, Corvettes, Frigates and Destroyers mainly. Even some of the older Cruisers and a handful of newer Heavy Cruisers. The

Dumas-designed Battle Cruisers and Dreadnoughts could take a punch and still keep on striking back. Any damage they received was repaired by their Armoured Supply Tenders. And those Venusian Dreadnoughts, those sleek, stretched cones of pure death, plied the spaceways like ethereal wraiths, killing the Jovian ships at a distance with impunity! The War dragged on with both sides almost stalemated and soon the First Horridian War, the Outer Satellite Insurrection, was approaching its eighth year and increasingly looking to be endless.

Roberta Nummus had spent the intervening years since arriving on Mimas being healed by the Martians. With their telepathic abilities, they carefully removed the layers of conditioning and the triggers that had been programmed into her during her specialised, experimental military training at the hands of the rogue Cis-Lunar Colonial Marine Generals nine decades earlier.

Beyond that, Roberta Nummus honed her martial skills even further, both hers and those of her adopted Daughter, Lina Mitchel. Elaine Haynes was truly proud of how far her Wife, Roberta, had progressed. However, at the back of Roberta's mind was her failing and the continuing Horridian War.

Would the War have even happened at all had she beheaded Godric von Horridian?

Had she taken Godric's life when she had the chance? Roberta did not know! It was a heavy burden!

One thing Roberta Nummus did know was that stalemates were inherently unstable and that meant at some point, the stalemate would break. Roberta didn't know when the stalemate would break, but she knew for sure that it would. It was only a matter of time before Godric von Horridian broke it.

Roberta Nummus convened a meeting with her friends inside Mimas.

Gideon Reas and his three Wives, Winchilly, Sandra Danker and Freyja, were already present when Roberta, her Wife, Elaine Haynes and her adopted Daughter, Lina Mitchel, arrived.

The first thing Sandra Danker noticed was the way that Roberta was dressed, "Why are you wearing full tactical body armour, Roberta?", she asked curiously.

Roberta's face looked serious, "Because when this meeting is over, Sandra, you and Gideon are going to teleport me over to Ganymede Prime."

Elaine Haynes chimed in, "My Wife, Roberta, wants to end this War once and for all. To do that, she needs to go to Ganymede Prime."

Gideon Reas replied calmly, "We are not going to jaunt Roberta over to Ganymede Prime so that she can assassinate Godric Horridian. That is simply not happening!"

Sandra Danker agreed, "We don't do assassinations, Roberta."

Winchilly also agreed, "We Martians cannot condone assassinations either, Roberta."

Freyja played the devil's advocate, "We should at least hear what Roberta has to say. What's your reasoning, Roberta Nummus?"

Roberta explained her reasoning, "This War is currently in a stalemate. Godric Horridian attacks with missiles and the inner solar system Allies defend against them. The Jovians probe the Allies' first line of defence and the Allies repulse them. Over and over it goes, on and on, never ending."

Sandra replied, questioning, "As long as the War remains in stalemate and the Jovian Armed Forces remain boxed in, that's a good thing, isn't it, Roberta?"

"No, it's not, Sandra. Stalemates are inherently unstable. They break and when they do, the result is usually devastating", Roberta assured her, before noting, "Godric will break this stalemate. It is only a matter of time. Just a matter of when!"

"If he does, he is going to run into a lot of Colonial Fleet and Earth Defence Force ships. Not to mention the Venusians", Gideon noted, adding, "Even Godric Horridian can't be that stupid."

Roberta sighed, she was talking to intelligent people, yes, but when it came to War, they were like small children. They simply didn't understand the mind of a Warmonger.

"I've been to the same meetings that you have. We have all discussed the War and what's happening with Swenna Goodchild. Earth is building ships. Cis-Lunar Space is building ships. Hell, even the Dumas Corporation is building ships", Roberta explained and then she added, "Guess what? So is Godric Horridian. The Jovian shipyards at Ganymede L-Four will be working overtime and Godric has endless Slave labour at his command. He doesn't have to worry about safety regulations or labour laws. He can work his Slaves around the clock until they drop. He can literally work them to death! Those Jovian shipyards are churning out Destroyers, Cruisers and Dreadnoughts, and while they are older designs, they all have the latest fusion drive technology. The former Colonisation Committee of Sol, may their souls rest in peace, gave that technology to Godric. That was a mistake!"

Sandra Danker nodded in understanding, "While the Earth and Cis-Lunar Space have to worry about regulations and safety, the Jovians don't. They can cut corners and work their Slaves right down to the bone. They'll be out producing the allies with sheer numbers, inferior, yes, but numbers have a quality all of their own."

Roberta pointed to Sandra, "Exactly, exactly, Sandra!", finally someone understood!

Roberta began to explain how things would pan out, "At some point in the future, which we cannot determine, Godric Horridian will decide that he has enough ships to defend the Jovian core systems and enough ships to launch an attack on the inner system's first line of defence. The Asteroid Belt."

Roberta paused before commenting, "It is completely irrelevant who eventually wins in the Asteroid Belt. If Godric wins, his forces will plunge into the inner solar system. They'll burn the Martian Trojan Mining Corporation's colonies, the colonies in high Martian orbit, Port Phobos and even the Deimos Military base. Then, they'll move onto the Earth. The Earth Trojan Mining corporations will burn and that will be followed by the colonies in Cis-Lunar Space itself. Hundreds of millions will die!"

Roberta paused and Sandra was about to speak, but Roberta raised her hand and cut her off, "If the inner system Allies win in the Asteroid Belt. Their forces will plunge into the Jovian Realm's core systems in Jovian orbit. The Jovian colonies will burn. At least five mega colonies and hundreds of smaller colonies. Again, hundreds of millions will die!"

Sandra finally got to speak, "We've already seen nearly forty million dead, Roberta. I cannot imagine the Earth Defence Forces or the Colonial Fleet burning the Jovian Realms."

"This is War, Sandra and once the bloodletting begins in the Asteroid Belt, it will not stop. Whoever wins in the Asteroid Belt will burn their enemy to ashes. That is precisely how this will play out", Roberta counted and then she explained, "And even before we consider who prevails in the Asteroid Belt, understand this, Belter civilisation will be the first to burn. Those thirteen Belter Nations, tens of millions of people living peacefully in the Asteroid Belt, will die first. Belter civilisation will die first!"

Roberta had explained this to Elaine and Lina already, Gideon and his three Wives were hearing it for the very first time. They all sat back in silent shock.

Could Roberta Nummus be right? How the hell could one woman change all of this?

"And you think killing Godric Horridian will prevent this from happening?", Gideon asked.

"No, Gideon, that won't be enough. I have to do something much, much worse", Roberta admitted.

"What could be worse than assassinating Godric Horridian?", Freyja enquired.

"I need to disable Godric Horridian. He has to be disabled permanently, so that he cannot remain as the High Prince of the Jovian Realms and yet still remain as a permanent reminder of what I can do", Roberta explained, noting, "I will then convince the next Horridian Brother that's in line to the Throne, which is Prince Aluric, to end this War."

"And if Prince Aluric ignores you?", Sandra Danker enquired.

"I will inform him that if the War hasn't ended, that I will be back to do the same thing to him and that there is nothing, nothing at all, that they can do to stop me", Roberta announced, remarking, "I will repeat the process until one of those Horridian Brothers actually listens and ends this War."

"And you can do this?", Gideon enquired.

"Yes, Gideon. I can do this. As horrible as it sounds, I can do this", Roberta admitted.

Gideon and his three Wives discussed Roberta Nummus's plan for over an hour. If disabling one man could prevent the fall of the Belter civilisation and hundreds of millions of deaths, Freyja was all for it. Winchilly, being a Martian, could not condone such an action under any circumstances. To her Martian mind, there simply had to be another way.

Gideon and Sandra were unhappy at being forced into having to make a decision that was just so morally repugnant and yet, they were leaning towards Freyja's position. One man balanced against hundreds of millions of men, women and children. In the end, Gideon, Sandra and Freyja all agreed. Winchilly, in her Martian way, agreed to disagree.

"Roberta, Freyja will jaunt you to Ganymede Prime", Gideon finally announced.

Roberta declined Freyja's offer of help, "I'm sorry, Gideon. It cannot be Freyja. Apart from my Wife, Elaine, Freyja is my best friend. She is a member of the Council of Shadows and it would dishonour her Cousin, Orpheus's memory, for her to be a part of this. I will need you and Sandra to assist me."

Gideon ran his hands through his hair, "Roberta, both Sandra and I are also Council of Shadow operatives. We have been for more than forty five years."

"Yes, but you are not scions of Folcrom Tafazah. You do not have a familial tie to Folcrom Orpheus. Freyja does! She cannot assist me!", Roberta explained.

Gideon and Sandra both shook their heads, as Sandra responded, "Okay then, let's get this done!"

Elaine Haynes hugged Roberta Nummus and kissed her deeply before commenting, "If you die, Roberta Nummus. I will never forgive you."

Lina leaned in and hugged them both, "That goes ditto for me, too."

Roberta chuckled, "I am not that easy to kill. Seriously, I am very difficult to kill."

Elaine and Lina stepped back as Gideon and Sandra took Roberta's hands in theirs. Slowly, Gideon and Sandra linked their minds together and reached over the void of space. First, they astral projected to Jovian Space, before locating Ganymede Prime in its orbit about Jupiter at Ganymede L-Five. Their linked minds astral projected into Ganymede Prime's northern end cap and quickly located the High Prince's palace, with its ornate gardens and high stone walls.

The palace itself was set inside parklands and Gideon and Sandra picked out a spot, a small clearing surrounded by trees. Sandra and Gideon focused on that small clearing and with Roberta Nummus in tow, they jaunted across the void of space and materialised inside Ganymede Prime. They were unseen and completely undetected.

The twenty-foot-high walls of the palace grounds were less than a hundred yards away. Roberta Nummus nodded to Gideon and Sandra before checking her kit. Then, without a word, Roberta bolted off towards the palace walls. Neither Gideon nor Sandra had seen Roberta Nummus run before.

Roberta was fast, very, very fast. A blur of motion. Roberta was across the intervening space and at the wall to the palace grounds within mere seconds. With two quick movements, Roberta was up on top of the palace wall and over it. Gideon and Sandra looked at each other in disbelief and then raised their psychic obscuration fields.

Once within the palace grounds, Roberta unsheathed her Katana, *the Harōingu*. Roberta Nummus burst into full speed, her Katana, the Harrowing, cutting imperial guards down in her wake. Within seconds, she was inside the palace and the imperial palace guards were dropping like flies under her blade. Roberta scoffed. The palace had been rebuilt after the last time she'd been there and all but destroyed it, yet it had been rebuilt in exactly the same style as before. No imagination whatsoever! After carving through three dozen palace guards, Roberta burst into High Prince Godric's throne room.

"Well, hello boys, I'm back", Roberta Nummus announced, *the Harōingu* still dripping with blood.

Security Minister Miles Morton pulled out his K-bar and advanced on Roberta. He wasn't anywhere near quick enough. Roberta shook her head and sighed before slicing off the Security Minister's right hand with a flick of her blade. The blade's movement was so quick that it was barely noticeable. Miles Morton's K-bar clattered to the throne room floor, still clasped in twitching fingers. Roberta punched the Minister in the face with a right cross and sent him to sleep, a crumpled mess upon the palace floor.

"If anybody else moves, I will start taking heads", Roberta warned the other Ministers as she walked up to Godric Horridian.

"Godric Horridian", Roberta greeted, before denouncing him, "You have been one horrible, evil little shit! I could even say, you've been a horrible little cunt!"

"That's High Prince Godric von Horridian to you, quisling peasant!", Godric sneered back, spitting, "Get down on your knees before me, traitor and beg for my forgiveness!", he shouted.

Roberta had no time for chatter. She simply grabbed Godric by his throat with her left hand and lifted him up. Then she wiped her bloodied Katana, the Harrowing, off on his royal robes before re-sheathing it. Godric struggled under her grip, but he could not get free. Roberta reached down to her utility belt with her free hand and pulled out an ice pick. It was one of two that she always kept on her person.

With one deft motion, Roberta Nummus rammed the ice pick straight up into Godric's left nostril while he squirmed in her grip. Godric squealed in alarm! He sounded just like a stuck pig! Roberta twirled the ice pick left three times, then twirled it right three times, before repeating three twirls to the left. Maximum non-lethal damage! Roberta withdrew the ice pick and released Godric from her grip.

High Prince Godric slumped into his throne. He'd pissed himself and he'd released his bowels.

Blood trickled from Godric's left nostril and he began to drool.

He was alive, he was lobotomised, he was no longer fit to be the High Prince of the Jovian Realms.

Roberta Nummus surveyed the throne room. All of the Jovian High Ministers sat quietly, all averting their eyes. They all knew Roberta Nummus's reputation. Stare at her overly ample breasts for too long and your head is forfeit. She would take it off with a single slice of her blade and keep it as a trophy.

They had no idea that that particular trigger no longer existed. That was the old Roberta Nummus.

The new Roberta Nummus scanned the thrones in the throne room. Two of them were empty.

"Where the fuck is Prince Aluric?", she demanded.

Prince Emeric replied sheepishly, "Prince Aluric is in his own palace on Callisto Prime", there was a slight pause before he added, "My Brother, Aluric, is mentally ill."

"So, Prince Emeric, you are next in line to the throne", Roberta surmised, before announcing, "The High Prince is incapacitated", she then pointed to Prince Emeric, announcing, "Long live the new High Prince, for the throne must never be empty."

The provisional new High Prince, Emeric, shouted back, "No fucking way! I don't want it!"

Roberta stared coldly at Prince Emeric, "Really, Prince Emeric! Then that leaves Prince Friederic."

"Yes, my Brother, Friederic", Prince Emeric stammered.

"Prince Emeric. Give your Brother, Prince Friederic, my ultimatum", Roberta told him, her cold, steely eyes locking onto his, "This War ends when I leave this palace. Got that?"

"Yes, yes, I will explain that to my Brother, Friederic", Prince Emeric stammered once more.

"Good. Because I'm telling you this now. If this War does not end, then I will be back and I will lobotomise every little cunt that sits on that fucking throne until it is", Roberta Nummus threatened, declaring, "And by all the Gods of the Greater Way, there is nothing, nothing at all that any of you little whelps can do to stop me!"

Roberta Nummus walked towards the throne room door. Before leaving, she made one more request.

"Prince Emeric, please pass on my apologies to Princess Valeria for me", Roberta requested, noting, "I did not want to lobotomise her Husband, Godric, but had he been a more reasonable Human being, it would not have become necessary."

And then she left just as quickly as she'd come, in a blur of fluid motion.

Gideon and Sandra watched as Roberta Nummus came flying over the palace wall. How Roberta managed to leap over a twenty-foot wall was unfathomable to them. Roberta most certainly could not levitate. Her abilities were purely physiological, albeit augmented by experimental scientific processes and procedures that were completely unknown. All knowledge of those procedures was destroyed when Roberta Nummus and Aurange Sheergibbon had broken out of the experimental military training facility where they had been conditioned.

Within seconds of clearing the wall, Roberta was back by their sides. Gideon checked his wristwatch. Less than fifteen minutes had passed.

Gideon asked Roberta incredulously, "Is it done?"

Roberta smiled, "Yes, I've lobotomised Godric Horridian. He is now unfit to be the High Prince."

"And Prince Aluric? He'll end the War?", Sandra enquired.

"No. Prince Aluric is mentally ill. His Brother, Prince Emeric, has declined the throne as well. The next in line is Prince Friederic", Roberta explained.

"And Prince Friederic will end the War?", Sandra queried.

"Prince Friederic is the smart one and after today, he won't have any choice in the matter", Roberta replied and then she smiled, "I've put them all on notice. I'll keep lobotomising everyone who sits on that fucking throne until one of them finally ends this War. And they all know I'll do it too."

Both Sandra and Gideon nodded in understanding before jaunting back to Mimas with Roberta.

31. It's Cursed. I don't want it.

There was chaos in the palace on Ganymede Prime. All of the palace servants had retreated upstairs away from the carnage and chaos. Some had even retreated up to the third level, where High Prince Godric and Princess Valeria had their personal rooms and living quarters.

One of the servants, actually one of the palace Slaves, had mumbled something about a blurred devil that moved almost too fast to be Human, carving its way through the Imperial Palace Guards.

Princess Valeria thought back several years to twenty one eighty one and the regicide of former High Prince Albert. A devil that moved in a blur too fast for the eye to register. That was precisely how they'd described Roberta Nummus, only she was at the Mimasian colony on the Saturnian Ice Moon Mimas.

Had Roberta Nummus returned to Ganymede Prime?

When she went downstairs to the throne room, would her Husband, Godric, still have his head?

Had Roberta Nummus done her, *"Chop, Chop, Rip",* and left Godric's headless body behind?

Had Roberta Nummus claimed yet another head as a trophy and carried it away?

After waiting for several tense minutes, one of the palace servants checked downstairs and reported back to the Princess that the demon had left the palace and was last seen crossing the palace grounds.

Princess Valeria cautiously descended downstairs, worrying about how to bury her Husband's headless corpse. Princess Valeria would be shocked by what she found. It was far worse than death!

Princess Valeria stepped into the main hallway that led to the throne room. The first thing that she noticed was that there were a lot of corpses. The bodies of Imperial Palace Guards lay everywhere. Many were without heads, many had bled out from severed limbs and some had been cleanly cleaved in two. This was most definitely the work of Roberta Nummus.

There were only two people the Horridians knew who could cause such carnage and only one of them, Roberta Nummus, was still at large. The other, Aurange Sheergibbon, was dead. At the hands of Roberta Nummus, of course!

Princess Valeria and her retinue of servants and Slaves found themselves stepping over corpses, but when they reached the throne room itself, they noticed a complete contrast. Security Minister Miles Morton was unconscious, lying on the throne room floor, his right hand was missing, severed at the wrist. Yet, there was no further visible carnage to be seen, at least not at a glance.

Princess Valeria simply pointed to him and one of her servants went to his side to attend to his severed right arm. All of the other Ministers sat quietly, their faces all ashen in colour. Prince Emeric sat on his throne, feet drawn up, arms wrapped around his legs and face buried in his arms.

Her Husband, High Prince Godric, sat on his throne. Godric's body was slumping, his face was expressionless and his jaw was slack. Godric's eyes stared into space and showed no signs of recognition, not of his Wife, the Princess, not of anything.

Princess Valeria noticed a trickle of blood flowing from High Prince Godric's left nostril. It soaked into his tunic. Godric sat there, not moving. He was just drooling. There was a slight smell of piss and excrement in the air. Whatever had happened had caused Godric's bowels and bladder to involuntarily release themselves. Princess Valeria's eyes brimmed with tears and her lower lip began to quiver.

"What in the name of Jove has that bitch done to my Husband?", Princess Valeria demanded as she quickly walked over to Godric, "Someone fucking answer me!", she demanded once more.

No one answered. They were all still in shock!

Princess Valeria looked into Godric's expressionless eyes, "It's going to be alright, Godric, my love. Whatever Roberta Nummus has done, we will fix this", she said softly and then she demanded once more, "Emeric, what did Roberta Nummus do? Answer me, God damn it!"

Prince Emeric looked up, his face was ashen with fear and his hair had turned white at the temples.

Prince Emeric stammered, "She, she, she. Roberta Nummus, she stuck Godric with an ice pick. She, she, lobotomised my Brother", then he began shaking his head and repeating, "Ice pick. Lobotomy. Ice pick. Lobotomy", several times over.

Realisation dawned on Princess Valeria's face. There was no coming back from an ice pick lobotomy.

Prince Emeric stopped mumbling and repeating himself, noting, "Roberta Nummus offered you her apologies, Princess. She didn't want to do this. She said it was necessary."

Princess Valeria slumped into the empty throne beside Godric's, Prince Aluric's throne. She took Godric's right hand in hers and tears welled in her eyes once more.

"Someone call the Court Physician", Valeria demanded, "Someone call the Court Physician, now!"

The Court Physician arrived. He gave Security Minister Morton a cursory glance and directed a nurse to attend to him. The nurse bandaged the Minister's severed wrist and he was then taken away on a stretcher along with his severed hand. The Court Physician assessed High Prince Godric very carefully, checking the ice pick's entry point. It was clean, it was precise, the flow of blood had already started to clot, but it was very clear what had been done.

Then the Physician checked Godric's responses, flashing the light of a small torch into his eyes and watching the results carefully. The Court Physician sighed. Godric von Horridian was stable, but there was nothing that he could do. The Court Physician directed a pair of orderlies to take the High Prince to the palace infirmary and then he turned to Princess Valeria.

"Your Highness, Ma'am. We will need to take some brain scans, but I suspect that what has been done is irreversible. Your Husband, the High Prince, has been lobotomised with surgical, almost clinical precision", the Court Physician delivered the bad news before noting, "Your Husband is no longer capable of continuing his duties as the High Prince of the Jovian Realms", it was now official.

The Court Physician bowed to Princess Valeria and then he followed his orderlies and the High Prince out of the throne room.

Princess Valeria sat there on Prince Aluric's throne. Her Husband, Godric's, throne to her left smelled of piss and excrement. Godric had been taken away to the palace infirmary, but the smell still remained. Godric von Horridian would likely be transferred to Ganymede Prime's hospital for brain scans.

There was blood on the floor where Security Minister Morton had lain, his right hand severed at the wrist. Miles Morton and his hand were also taken away to the palace infirmary. No doubt, he too would end up in Ganymede Prime's hospital to have his hand sutured back on.

The other Ministers all just sat there, all ashen-faced and silent. Prince Emeric sat on his throne to her right, all curled up as if the universe was about to open up and swallow him. Beyond the still-open throne room doors, Princess Valeria could hear the emergency response teams attending to the corpses of the dead. It was a mess, a bloody fucking mess! For the second time in less than nine years, Roberta Nummus had murdered her way through the palace of the High Prince. Nothing was sacred anymore!

Princess Valeria stood up from Prince Aluric's throne and surveyed the throne room. Princess Valeria felt like fainting. She was a noble princess after all. It might even have been expected of her, but how could she faint when all of the men in the throne room behaved like frightened, bloody sheep?

"What is Prince Aluric's status?", Princess Valeria enquired, needing clarification.

"Prince Aluric has been diagnosed as mentally ill, Your Highness", Science Minister Peter Patronis cautiously confirmed.

"So I take it that Prince Aluric will not be able to ascend to the throne?", Princess Valeria queried.

The Science Minister confirmed, "No, Your Highness. Prince Aluric's condition makes him entirely unsuitable. The Prince is mildly medicated and being managed at his palace on Callisto Prime."

Defence Minister Peter Macron chimed in with brutal honesty, "Everyone in Prince Aluric's court has been placed there by Prince Friederic specifically to manage him, Your Highness. Ma'am, they keep the Prince happy and distracted, but his life is more like a circus than a royal court. Prince Aluric cannot ascend to the throne."

Princess Valeria nodded, she could see where this was going, but needed the Ministers to confirm it officially before taking things further.

Princess Valeria asked softly, "So, am I correct in assuming that my Brother-in-Law, Prince Emeric, is now the next in line to the High Throne?"

Defence Minister Peter Macron confirmed, "Yes, Your Highness. Prince Emeric is the next in line to the High Throne. He has been since Prince Aluric's official diagnosis."

Princess Valeria turned to her Brother-in-Law, Prince Emeric. He was still curled in upon himself, but did appear to be listening, nonetheless.

"My Husband, High Prince Godric, has been lobotomised. There is no coming back from that", Princess Valeria clearly stated, her own words cutting her like a knife, making her want to scream.

Fighting back tears, the Princess announced, "My Husband, High Prince Godric, can no longer serve as the High Prince of the Six Jovian Realms. Godric has been rendered unsuitable", and then she gestured to Prince Emeric, "The throne must never be empty. Prince Emeric is now the new High Prince! Long live the new High Prince!", and then she bowed to him.

Prince Emeric uncurled in an instant and was on his feet. The Prince pointed to his Brother, Godric's throne, his face contorted in abject horror.

"That fucking thing! It's cursed. I don't want it. You cannot force me to sit on a cursed throne", Prince Emeric spat out vehemently.

Prince Valeria closed her eyes and sighed internally, "*Not now, Emeric, please grow some fucking balls*", she thought to herself.

When Princess Valeria opened her eyes once more, she could see the look of abject horror in Prince Emeric's eyes. The Princess thought quickly before enquiring.

"Ministers. The throne of the High Prince has been tainted by blood, Albert's and is now defiled by piss and shit, Godric's", she named the problem as she saw it and then asked, "Those secondary thrones in the palace's operations room. Are they identical to these thrones?"

Science Minister Peter Patronis replied, "Yes, Your Highness, they are essentially identical in most aspects. What differences there may be can be corrected as necessary."

"Excellent!", Princess Valeria exclaimed, before requesting as she gestured to the throne of the High Prince, "Have this throne incinerated. Bring in the secondary throne from the operations room. Better yet, just to be on the safe side, incinerate all of these fucking thrones and replace them with the ones from the operations room."

Science Minister Patronis queried, "Your Highness?"

Princess Valeria rolled her eyes before explaining, "I've never understood the logic of having two sets of thrones. One set here in the throne room and another set in the operations room. It makes absolutely no sense at all. So, since the thrones in this room are apparently cursed, we should incinerate them all and replace them with the thrones from the operations room. It is that simple! Make it so!"

Princess Valeria turned to Prince Emeric, "Your Majesty", she addressed him as the new High Prince with a slight bow, "All of the cursed thrones will be disposed of and replaced. Now, please, Sire, accept your inheritance and take up the mantle as the new High Prince. Take up the High Throne!"

Prince Emeric shook his head, "You cannot cleanse a cursed position by simply rearranging the fucking chairs, Princess! It is the position of the High Prince itself that is tainted, that is cursed. It is cursed and I do not want it", he reiterated.

Princess Valeria rolled her eyes once more, thinking to herself, *"Well, I certainly don't want it either"*, before responding, "Sire, you are the next in line to the throne. Are you telling us, everyone here present, that you are abdicating your rights as the heir to the High Throne?", she queried.

Prince Emeric was quiet for a long moment and then he responded in very carefully measured words, "The position of High Prince is cursed and I don't want it. Everyone who takes up the mantle of the High Prince is likewise cursed. I have no intention of being cursed. I hereby and henceforth abdicate my rights to the High Throne of the Six Jovian Realms. It is cursed and I don't want it!"

Princess Valeria sat back down on Prince Aluric's throne and sighed deeply before shaking her head and slumping forward with her head between her hands. This was becoming all too much for her to bear. Her Husband, Godric, had been violated, lobotomised and all she wanted to do was collapse and cry like any normal person.

Didn't she have the right to grieve?

Defence Minister Macron noted at the forming power vacuum, "The High Throne sits empty!"

Science Minister Patronis commented, "The High Throne must never be empty!"

Princess Valeria stood up and announced, "Prince Emeric has abdicated his rights to the High Throne of the Six Jovian Realms. That leaves only one other Brother, Prince Friederic!"

The Defence Minister remarked, "Prince Friederic is at his palace on Io Prime, Your Highness. Assuming that he does take up the mantle of High Prince. The High Throne will remain empty until Prince Friederic arrives here to sit upon it."

As the discussions about who would take up the mantle of the High Prince were taking place, Princess Valeria's servants had been carrying out her instructions. The four secondary thrones from the palace's operations room had already been brought into the throne room. The servants lined three of the thrones up against a wall, while two servants replaced Godric's defiled throne. While the Princess, the Prince and the Ministers all talked, the palace servants quietly went about their duties.

Princess Valeria nodded to the Defence Minister, before replying, "Apprise Prince Friederic of the current situation. Inform him that Prince Godric is no longer fit to sit on the High Throne. That Prince Emeric has declined to sit on the High Throne and that he, Prince Friederic, is now the new High Prince. Inform Prince Friederic that his presence is urgently required on Ganymede Prime."

Science Minister Patronis commented, "Your Highness, Princess Valeria, the High Throne will still be empty in the interim. The situation is still intolerable!"

Princess Valeria nodded, she understood, "Technically speaking, the High Throne is not empty. Prince Friederic is the new High Prince, whether he is here on Ganymede Prime or not."

Prince Emeric murmured, "Unless, Brother Friederic declines the High Throne as well."

Princess Valeria glared at Prince Emeric, wanting to tell him to shut the fuck up, but instead she replied calmly, "Let's hope it doesn't come to that, Prince Emeric."

Princess Valeria looked to Defence Minister Macron, "The Jovian Realms need certainty, Minister. When you inform Prince Friederic of his new responsibilities, make sure you get his response. We need to know if he is willing to accept the mantle of High Prince. We need to know urgently!"

Defence Minister Peter Macron nodded, "Yes, Your Highness."

Commerce Minister, Mr Devlin Dervish, who had been quiet during the proceedings, requested, "Your Highness, the optics of the High Throne being empty is not good for public perceptions. It might take days for Prince Friederic to arrive here on Ganymede Prime and officially take up the mantle of the new High Prince."

"Just where is this going, Minister Dervish?", Princess Valeria enquired.

"The High Throne has just now been replaced, Your Highness. The defiled throne has been removed from the throne room, Ma'am", the Commerce Minister replied, before requesting, "Princess Valeria, would you be so kind as to sit upon the High Throne as Princess Regent, until your Brother-in-Law, Prince Friederic, arrives?"

The other Ministers all agreed, with some nodding in agreement and others shouting, "Hear! Hear!"

Princess Valeria reluctantly stood up from Prince Aluric's throne and sat herself back down upon the High Throne. She, herself, did not want to be Princess Regent. All Princess Valeria wanted to do was to go upstairs to her bedroom and grieve!

"Defence Minister Macron. Inform High Prince Friederic that his throne is not empty. I will keep it warm for him as Princess Regent until such time that he arrives on Ganymede Prime", Princess Valeria instructed, before noting, "I do not want to sit on this thing any longer than is necessary."

And as Princess Valeria sat upon the High Throne as Princess Regent, her servants quietly went about the business of replacing Prince Aluric's and Prince Friederic's empty thrones. Then they waited patiently and silently for Prince Emeric to stand before replacing his throne.

Of the four Horridian Princes, it was the youngest, Prince Friederic, who was the smart one. Prince Friederic did not believe in curses. He was both eclectic and pragmatic. Prince Friederic had always been against the War. He had predicted with fair accuracy how disastrous it would become.

Prince Friederic did not need any warnings from Roberta Nummus to end the War. Although he knew that any warning coming from Roberta Nummus was far from hollow. It was a simple matter of fact, Prince Friederic's ascension to the High Throne was always going to end the War. Sadly for Prince Godric, it took his forced lobotomy and Prince Emeric's abdication for Prince Friederic to become eligible for ascendancy to the High Throne.

Prince Friederic accepted the mantle of High Prince and so the throne was not going to be empty, much to the relief of Princess Valeria. However, even before leaving for Ganymede Prime, the Prince sent an urgent message to the Saturnian Demarchy. Prince Friederic was pleased to end the War, yes, but was exceedingly unhappy that Roberta Nummus had somehow broken confinement on Mimas and once again butchered her way through the palace of the High Prince to lobotomise his Brother, Godric. High Prince Friederic's first official act was to demand an explanation. That explanation would come from Saturnian Demarchy's Bureaucratic Administrator, Ms Swenna Goodchild.

Finally, when High Prince Friederic flew from his palace on Io Prime to Ganymede Prime, he took two ships. The first was his private space yacht, the Ionian Wanderer, in which his family, including his Wife, Princess Minerva and their two Sister-in-law Princesses, Serenity and Chastity, travelled to Ganymede Prime.

The second was his personal Jovian Dreadnought, the Ionian Fist. The new High Prince intended to swiftly consolidate power. He was taking his own personal Imperial Palace Guards with him, along with his own trusted personal advisers. When he arrived at Ganymede Prime, he fully intended to clean house and that meant all of Godric's dross had to go!

32. Ascendancy.

Prince Friederic entered the palace on Ganymede Prime with his advisers and personal Imperial Palace Guards. The Prince instructed them to wait in the throne room's antechamber while he entered the throne room with his Wife, Princess Minerva and Princesses Chastity and Serenity.

It had been four days since Roberta Nummus's little visit and the atmosphere in the throne room was still quite tense. The Jovian High Ministers were all seated when Prince Friederic entered. Prince Friederic noted that Security Minister Miles Morton's right hand and forearm were covered in a medical regeneration sheath. Prince Friederic had read all of the reports and he was surprised to see that Minister Morton was present. He was even more surprised that the medical staff had saved his hand.

Prince Emeric sat on his throne, while Prince Friederic's and Prince Aluric's thrones remained empty, which was quite normal. Princess Valeria sat upon the High Throne. Immediately upon seeing Prince Friederic enter the throne room, Princess Valeria stood up from the High Throne and curtseyed. It had been a stressful four days and the Princess just wanted to weep, which she did, almost bursting into tears as she greeted High Prince Friederic. The Princess was grief-stricken but was unable to grieve.

"Friederic, Your Majesty. It has been so horrible. Thank God you're here", Princess Valeria greeted the new High Prince with tear-laden eyes.

High Prince Friederic placed one hand on each of Valeria's shoulders and held her gently for a long minute, before taking her into his warm embrace, "I've read all of the reports, Valeria. How you're coping with all of this, I cannot fathom. You need some time out to grieve. I'll take over from here on."

"Thank you, Your Majesty", Princess Valeria replied as she stepped back from his embrace.

The High Prince gestured to his Wife, Minerva and the other two Princesses, "Please, go and relax with my Wife, Minerva and the Princesses. I'm sure you have much to catch up on. You do what you need to do, Valeria. I'll keep you abreast of any further developments here."

Princess Minerva took Princess Valeria by the arm and, with Princesses Chastity and Serenity in tow, they walked out of the throne room. Then, High Prince Friederic sat down on the Jovian High Throne.

"Security Minister Morton. I am very surprised to see you here, considering your injury", High Prince Friederic greeted, "Now, tell me, Minister Morton, how the hell did Roberta Nummus get inside Ganymede Prime? This is an orbital colony after all, a sealed bottle, so how the hell did she get in?"

It was straight to business and Security Minister Miles Morton had no answer, "Your Majesty, Sire. We have no knowledge or understanding as to how Roberta Nummus arrived, nor how she left for that matter", his voice was shaky, clearly he was on painkillers.

"So, Roberta Nummus just magically appeared inside Ganymede Prime, waltzed into the royal palace and lobotomised my Brother, Godric? And then she just vanished into thin air, just like that!", High Prince Godric questioned, clicking the fingers on his left hand.

It had been a rhetorical question, however, Defence Minister Peter Macron answered, "Your Majesty, Sire. Roberta Nummus did not arrive on any ship. She does not appear on any security camera records beyond the palace. The woman appears only on the security records within the palace grounds and inside the palace itself. Nowhere else, Sire. Roberta Nummus has left us with a mystery, Sire."

"It's like she was a ghost, Brother", Prince Emeric chimed in, "Just like a ghost. In and out without leaving a trace, just bodies and mayhem in her wake! They've just finished cleaning and repainting!"

"And you don't know the half of it, Brother Emeric. You have no idea how strange this gets. This rabbit hole gets very deep indeed!", High Prince Friederic replied.

"Are we even certain this was Roberta Nummus?", High Prince Friederic questioned, remarking further, "I have seen the palace security footage. On that security footage, it looks like Roberta Nummus, it moves like Roberta Nummus and the results, the results are exactly what you'd expect from a visit by Roberta Nummus."

Prince Emeric looked confused and every one of the Jovian High Ministers looked confused as well. There was no doubt that it was Roberta Nummus, absolutely no doubt whatsoever! All eyes in the throne room fell upon the new High Prince in utter confusion.

"Brother, it was definitely Roberta Nummus. There is absolutely no doubt about that", Prince Emeric replied with a confused tone, "She stood right there, Brother. Right in front of where you're sitting and lobotomised our Brother, Godric, with one of her ice picks. You know, the ones she keeps on her utility belt. Roberta Nummus even spoke to me. She gave out an ultimatum and a warning. She even asked me to pass on her apologies to Princess Valeria. There is no way it could have been anyone else but Roberta Nummus!"

High Prince Friederic frowned as he looked at his Brother, "I know, Brother Emeric. I have seen the security footage. Clearly, it was Roberta Nummus, but here's the problem. I've been in contact with the Saturnian Demarchy and things simply do not add up!"

The new High Prince informed everyone present, "Before I left Io Prime, I sent a communique to the Saturnian Demarchy. I demanded to know why they had allowed Roberta Nummus to leave Mimas. Why had they not stopped her? Why had they not apprehended her? I received their reply during my transit from Io Prime to Ganymede Prime and what they've said is confusing, to say the least."

Prince Emeric queried, "Confusing? Why, Brother?"

"I received the reply from the Saturnian Demarchy's Bureaucratic Administrator, Ms Swenna Goodchild", High Prince Friederic stated, commenting, "Swenna Goodchild states that no ships have left Mimas since the arrival of the Dark Angel, with its passengers, Roberta Nummus, Elaine Haynes and Lina Mitchel onboard. They still have Mimas boxed in and blockaded with four Dreadnoughts."

"That's impossible, Brother", Prince Emeric replied, the incredulity clearly in his voice, "Swenna Goodchild must be lying! There is no other answer!"

Security Minister Morton stepped in, his voice showing subtle hints of pain, "Sire, we do have a folio on this, Ms Swenna Goodchild. The woman is known for her honesty and forthright manner. Her file shows no history of deceit or lying. She is, according to our own records, an honest person."

"I've seen her file, Minister Morton. Which makes her reply all the more confusing. I queried her in a follow-up communique", High Prince Friederic replied, noting, "She confirmed her previous statement and sent me their complete surveillance logs and recordings of Mimas going back one year. She even offered to send me their older logs if I required them. All of them, every damned log!"

Science Minister Peter Patronis chimed in, "Sire, Saturn is on average six hundred and fifty million kilometres from Jupiter. At high delta-v, Nummus's ship, the Dark Angel, would take four months to fly here and another four months to fly back to Saturn."

"And yet we are to believe that she got here without a ship because I've had my people research those surveillance logs and records. Not a single ship has left Mimas, not on the logs we've received at least. And no ships were detected at the time of Nummus's infiltration either!", the High Prince replied.

High Prince Friederic shook his head, "It gets even weirder though", he stated and then he continued, "I informed Ms Swenna Goodchild of what had happened here. This was in my third communique to Ms Goodchild. Up to that point, I had not told her the specifics of Roberta Nummus's infiltration. I then told her everything and even gave her the date and timestamps of Nummus's attack."

Prince Emeric interjected, questioning, "And her reply, Brother?"

High Prince Friederic looked at his Brother, frowning, "Brother Emeric. Four days ago, less than one hour after Roberta Nummus's attack, Swenna Goodchild was in a teleconference meeting with the Mimasian authorities."

"And so?", Prince Emeric queried, wondering where his Brother was taking this.

"During that meeting, they were discussing Roberta Nummus", the High Prince replied, noting, "The Mimasians are considering making Roberta Nummus one of their diplomats with full diplomatic immunity", then he paused, "Roberta Nummus was present in that damned meeting!", he exclaimed.

Science Minister Peter Patronis chimed in, "Wait? What? Sire, that is simply impossible!"

"Tell me about it, Minister Patronis", the High Prince replied, noting, "Ms Swenna Goodchild even sent me the video footage and the minutes of the meeting. Roberta Nummus was clearly present and engaging in the discussions! I have even checked all of the metadata involved myself!"

Prince Emeric got up from his throne and began running his fingers through his hair, "That's simply impossible, Brother", he declared, questioning, "How can Roberta Nummus be here in this very throne room, lobotomising our Brother, Godric and then within an hour be back on Mimas in a teleconference? That is simply fucking impossible!"

"You notice that, did you, Brother?", High Prince Friederic replied, adding, "And the Mimasians want to make Roberta Nummus one of their diplomats", he just started shaking his head in disgust.

Administrator Swenna Goodchild had been completely honest and forthright in her communications with Prince Friederic. No ships had left Mimas and the Saturnian Demarchy's blockade of Mimas was ongoing and remained unbreached. All of the evidence, the surveillance logs and the video footage supporting this claim had been provided to the High Prince. There was no evidence of any deception.

The video teleconference that allegedly happened less than one hour after High Prince Godric's unfortunate lobotomisation did indeed happen. During that video conference, Roberta Nummus's new position as a Mimasian diplomat with full diplomatic immunity was discussed, along with other less contentious points of discussion. Again, Ms Swenna Goodchild provided all of the video evidence and the meeting notes to support this claim. Again, there was no evidence of deception. Roberta Nummus was an active participant in that meeting. There was no refuting that fact.

One detail stood out. Among the three other participants in the teleconference were Doctor Gideon Reas, Sandra Danker and a woman named Freyja. Freyja had been seen before, in Roberta Nummus's earlier confession video released in twenty one eight one, shortly after the regicide of former High Prince Albert.

Freyja still radiated power, subtle, sublime and unnervingly refined. It was a presence both unmistakable and almost impossible to pinpoint. What was more intriguing was that Gideon Reas and Sandra Danker projected the same kind of aura. All three of them were different, something more than ordinary humans and yet paradoxically, they remained entirely human at the same time.

What was also confusing was that both Gideon Reas and Sandra Danker were well-known people. They were both retirees, now in their early eighties. Gideon Reas had been the Lead Terraformer Scientist working on the Mars Terraforming project, as well as the Administrator of the Martian orbital colonies. While Sandra Danker had been the Lead Engineer working on the same Martian Terraforming project. What they were both doing at the reclusive Mimasian colony was completely unknown and yet, for some reason, they were both there. Not only were they there, but they were involved with Roberta Nummus and high up in the Mimasian authoritative apparatus.

Everything that Ms Swenna Goodchild had told the new High Prince was the truth. Every piece of evidence that she provided was also the unadulterated truth. However, there was something that Ms Swenna Goodchild held back, simply because she herself did not know of it.

Gideon Reas, Sandra Danker and Freyja were all members of the Council of Shadows and they could jaunt, teleport across interplanetary distances. They were supramundane and could even take other people, ordinary folk, mundanes, like Roberta Nummus, along with them!

The Council of Shadows was occult. It was hidden and no one knew of its existence except its own members. Not even the Earth's Psi Corps, of which the Council of Shadows was ostensibly a part, knew of its existence. With the exception of Gideon Reas and Sandra Danker, all Council of Shadow members were scions of Folcrom Tafazah. They all had psychic potentials of level ten or higher!

Gideon Reas himself had timed their little impromptu meeting with Swenna Goodchild with absolutely perfect timing. Deliberately to confuse the Horridians. Even the purpose of the meeting, to discuss Roberta Nummus becoming a Mimasian diplomat, was part of their plan to confuse the Horridians. The whole thing was working beautifully. The Horridians were both baffled and confused.
Confusing the Horridians was considered a very good thing!

High Prince Friederic had already wanted to end the War, but now, with Roberta Nummus's seeming ability to appear at two places separated by hundreds of millions of kilometres of deep space at the same time, gave her threats a gravity that simply could not be ignored. Failure to comply with Roberta's demands would lead to further lobotomisations. Of that, High Prince Friederic had no doubt.

The new High Prince pressed a button on his communicator. The doors of the throne room opened and his personal advisers walked in. They were followed by his own personal Imperial Palace Guards.

The Jovian High Ministers looked around in stunned silence as heavily armed guards with Ionian Military insignia positioned themselves around the throne room.

"Ministers. Would you all kindly stand up and move away from your seats to the centre of the throne room, please?", High Prince Friederic requested in a soft, almost pleasant voice.

Prince Emeric enquired of his Brother, "Friederic, what are you doing?"

The High Prince raised his right hand to silence his Brother, "Guards, arrest the Jovian High Ministers. Take them all into custody. Their ministerial privileges are hereby revoked and they are to be shackled and treated as prisoners henceforth. My personal advisers will take their place."

The now former Jovian High Ministers all stood there with their mouths agape, opening and closing like fish trying to breathe in shallow water. While Friederic's personal Imperial Palace Guards placed handcuffs on the former Jovian High Ministers, his personal advisers took their seats. The new High Prince had already appointed his new Jovian High Ministers even before leaving Io Prime.

"Guards! Take the prisoners to the brig on my Dreadnought", High Prince Friederic commanded.

And that was that. All of High Prince Godric's former Ministers were taken away in handcuffs.

Prince Emeric finally found his voice after being silenced, "Brother!", he almost shouted.

The new High Prince smiled and turned to his Brother, "Emeric, you didn't think I was going to let those untrustworthy snakes remain at their posts, did you?"

Prince Emeric shook his head, "You might have told me, Friederic. You know, a little heads up."

High Prince Friederic smiled, "Brother Emeric, it was better this way. Quick and clean."

Prince Emeric nodded. He understood. Friederic was not like Godric.

Friederic was a thinker and left nothing to chance. Friederic always planned ahead like a three-dimensional chess master.

"What will you do with them now, Brother?", Prince Friederic enquired.

"They will remain in my ship's brig until I need to deal with them", the High Prince responded.

"And then, Brother?", Prince Friederic enquired further.

"Emeric, you know that I never wanted this War to start. You also know that I've always wanted this War to end", High Prince Friederic replied, noting, "With Roberta Nummus's threat hanging over my head, I now have no choice in the matter. That damned woman can be in two places at once across vast stretches of the void and that makes her ultimatum the most real and honest thing in this entire solar system. Roberta Nummus simply cannot be ignored. This War must end!"

"And the former ministers, Brother Friederic?", Prince Emeric enquired, he had not yet caught on.

"Nearly forty million dead, Emeric. Nearly forty million! This War has been ridiculously lopsided, with most of the dead on the inner system side!", High Prince Friederic spat out, explaining, "They will want justice. They will want payback. How am I to end this War without giving them something?"

"You're going to give them the ministers", Prince Emeric nodded, he finally understood.

The new High Prince nodded, "Of course I am, Emeric. I'm not going to give them Godric. What would be the point? I've read his medical report. Roberta Nummus did a right number on him. He's not even cognitively aware of his own existence."

"What about our Brother, Aluric and myself?", Prince Emeric enquired with serious concern.

"Aluric is mentally ill. I doubt he even knows we're at War. And as for you, you've always been against this War. This is Godric's War. This entire debacle rests squarely on Godric and those spineless snakes that encouraged him. I'm not giving either of you to them", High Prince Friederic reassured.

"So what are you going to do then, Brother?", Prince Emeric asked.

"I'll work it out, Brother. I'll work it out. I always do", High Prince Friederic replied.

High Prince Friederic announced to his newly appointed Jovian High Ministers, "What our realms need now are certainty and continuity. As High Prince of the Six Jovian Realms, I hereby and henceforth decree that should I die or fail in health so as to become incapacitated, then my Wife, Princess Minerva, will replace me as Princess Regent. That if my Wife, Princess Minerva, should die or fail in health so as to become incapacitated, then my Sister-in-law, Princess

Valeria, will replace her as Princess Regent. Until such time as my own children reach the age of inheritance. My children are to begin training for future royal duties immediately."

One of the new Ministers, the Jovian Minister of State, a new Department, noted everything down on his data tablet, "So noted, Your Majesty. Our people will organise everything."

One of his other new Ministers, the new Security Minister, queried, "Sire, what if both your Wife and Sister-in-law should pass or become incapacitated?"

"Then the line will be Princess Minerva, Princess Valeria and then Princess Chastity. Is that sufficient?", High Prince Friederic replied, questioning.

"I believe so, Sire", his new Minister of State replied, taking down some more notes.

"You have excluded Princess Serenity, Sire?", his new Security Minister questioned.

"After what my Brother, Aluric, did to her, Princess Serenity is far too timid for the post", the High Prince responded, noting, "Princess Serenity's emotional healing is ongoing. We need to look after her, not put her in a pressure chamber and expect her to function."

The new Security Minister nodded in understanding.

High Prince Friederic then turned to his Brother, "Now, Emeric. Get your royal arse upstairs. Find your Wife, Princess Chastity, and sort out your bloody marriage. Grovel at her feet if you have to, but fix your marriage. Princess Chastity is a good woman and to be quite honest, you need her. Now go upstairs and sort out your marriage. That is my royal command!"

Prince Emeric stood up, nodded to his Brother and quickly left the throne room to find his Wife.

"Right then, Ministers, you have a coronation to organise", High Prince Friederic von Horridian announced, "Nothing fancy. Just keep it simple. Nothing ostentatious and no over spending."

High Prince Friederic was seated in an ornate gold-gilded throne in the Jovian High Church's Cathedral in Ganymede Prime's northern end cap. The Cathedral was packed with carefully selected citizens, who were all seated in the nave of the Cathedral. In the centre between the seating, the nave was left clear and open. Each of the audience members was carefully checked for weapons as they entered, which was the usual procedure for a royal coronation. Off to the sides in the aisles were a hundred fully armed Jovian Shock Troops from Io Prime, to ensure that the ceremony proceeded without incident.

The Pope of the Jovian High Church moved to Prince Friederic and a Cardinal dressed in red passed him the royal crown. The crown was the same crown used in the coronation of Friederic's Brother, Godric and his Father, Albert, before him. It was by far the most ornate of crowns ever made by man. It was truly magnificent and even that word was insufficient to describe it.

The golden crown glinted softly in the candlelight of the Cathedral. Its polished gold surfaces caught every glimmer like flickering fire. The thick circlet of heavy gold, shaped perfectly round. Along its rim rose eight elegant spires, tapering, regal, each crowned with a gleaming gemstone. Deep red rubies and cold white diamonds alternating in perfect balance.

Between each spire were delicate golden filigree twists like vines, etched with patterns too fine to trace at a glance. At its centre, a soft, rich velvet dome, deep crimson in colour, with peeks between the arches, bordered with a thin trim of the purest, whitest fur. It was beautiful and to call it magnificent was an understatement. It was beyond magnificent. The crown commanded a presence all of its own.

The Pope of the Jovian High Church took a deep breath. He could not mess this up.

The Pope held the ornate crown high above Prince Friederic's head as he declared, "By the powers invested in me by God almighty, I hereby declare, Prince Friederic von Horridian, Prince of the Jovian Realm of Ganymede and all of its domains", then he paused and took another deep breath, "High Prince of the six Jovian Realms of Ganymede, Callisto, Europa, Io, the Leading Trojans and the Trailing Trojans", and then he slowly, carefully placed the crown upon Friederic's head.

The Pope stepped to one side and the entire Cathedral erupted in applause. The Horridian High Prince had been crowned and the Six Jovian Realms now officially had a new High Prince.

The entire Cathedral began shouting, "Long live High Prince Friederic", and they did so over and over and over.

The Pope of the Jovian High Church smiled, thinking to himself, *"Three for three. Nailed it again"*, it was, after all, his third coronation.

The most important part of the whole coronation was that it was video recorded and played live over both the internal and external news networks. The entire solar system now became aware that a High Prince Godric von Horridian was no longer in power and that Godric's youngest Brother, Friederic von Horridian, was now the new High Prince of the Six Jovian Realms.

The news ticker at the base of the screen stated clearly that the coronation was live. It also stated that High Prince Godric von Horridian had suffered a major health issue requiring that he step down as the High Prince. It also made note of Prince Aluric's ill health as a cause for his non-suitability in exercising his rights to the High Throne and Prince Emeric's abdication of his rights to the High Throne as well. Thus necessitating that Prince Friederic, the youngest Horridian Brother, take up the mantle as the new High Prince.

This led to some confusion in the audience until the new High Prince, Friederic von Horridian, stood up from his throne. High Prince Friederic walked over to a nearby podium and stood behind its lectern. High Prince Friederic then removed his crown, passed it to the Pope of the Jovian High Church and delivered his first speech then and there. It was so unusual, no one had expected there to be a speech.

High Prince Friederic began speaking, "Citizens of the Six Jovian Realms. Citizens of the entire solar system. For those of you who may have missed my coronation, I am Prince Friederic von Horridian and I am the new High Prince of the Six Jovian Realms. My Brother, Prince Godric, the former High Prince, has suffered a neurological disorder, a disorder that is severe enough that he was unable to continue his duties as the High Prince. My Brother, Prince Aluric, was also unsuitable to take up the mantle of High Prince, as he too has his own health issues. My other Brother, Prince Emeric, although more than capable, has declined the Jovian High Throne and, of his own free will and volition, abdicated his rights to the Jovian High Throne. That left it to me to take up the mantle of the Jovian High Prince."

The High Prince paused, it was a long pause as he gathered his thoughts, "As the new High Prince of the Six Jovian Realms, I swear to be a just and fair ruler. As such, my first duty is to end this disastrous War. The cost of lives, economic losses and sheer destruction is simply unacceptable. I have always been against War in any of its many forms and personally, I had advised my Brother, Godric, against this War and even warned him of how disastrous it would become. Now, I am in a position where I can end it. I hereby decree that henceforth, the Six Jovian Realms will be implementing a unilateral ceasefire. All Jovian Armed

Forces are to stand down and cease-fire immediately. This disastrous War must end. The Jovian Realm's diplomatic channels are now open for discussions with the inner system powers regarding the cessation of all conflict and how we can establish a lasting peace. Thank you."

High Prince Friederic bowed to the cameras and his audience before stepping down from the podium and leaving the stage.

There was immediate clapping and cheering throughout the Cathedral and the streets outside.

33. The Council of Shadows.

The impromptu meeting in President Dieter Reinhardt's office was to discuss the recent development concerning the coronation of High Prince Friederic. Namely, the unilateral ceasefire declaration. General Camilla Brennan-Chives, Defence Minister Tripp Carlson and Bureau of Investigations Chief Danica Thomlinson were present.

The Dumas Brothers, Connor and Daniel, were also present. As the Chief Executive Officer and the Chief Operating Officer of Dumas Incorporated Industries, Connor and Daniel had back-channel access to a great deal of otherwise unobtainable information via the *"Administrator's"* Network.

A network of Bureaucratic Administrative Heads from across the entire solar system that kept in regular contact with each other and shared information as necessary. The central repository for all of this shared information was not a government agency,. It was Dumas Legal Incorporated Ltd, one of the many Dumas Incorporated companies and organisations.

President Reinhardt thanked everyone for coming and began his meeting by querying his Defence Minister, "Tripp, just how real is this unilateral ceasefire?"

Defence Minister Carlson replied, "As far as we can tell, it's very real. The Jovian Armed Forces are no longer probing our defence lines in the Asteroid Belt and we have not detected any further missile launches from Jovian Space either. Their ships are all pulling back to their own Jovian territories."

General Brennan-Chives chimed in as she stroked her German Shepherd, Payback, who was lying on the office floor beside her, "More importantly, Dieter, the Jovians have given us a heads up on the missiles that were launched while Godric Horridian was still in power."

"So we have our scopes on those missiles then, Camilla?", the President enquired.

"We did have, right up until we detected them exploding in deep space above and below the ecliptic. There were around five hundred missiles in all this time. Fortunately, though, it appears that Friederic Horridian ordered their self-destruct sequences to be triggered", the General replied.

"So, this ceasefire is real", President Reinhardt noted, "Tripp, Camilla, put out the word. We are implementing our own ceasefire. Keep an eye on the Jovians, mind you, if they break their ceasefire, we need to be ready", President Reinhardt informed them both.

"I have also received a private communique from Friederic Horridian. In that Friederic tells me that Godric's neurological disorder was caused by Roberta Nummus", President Reinhardt informed them, adding, "Roberta Nummus infiltrated Ganymede Prime, broke into the royal palace and lobotomised Godric with an ice pick."

"How did she even get to him?", Danica Thomlinson asked.

"Roberta Nummus slaughtered her way through three dozen palace guards and then delivered the coup de grace", President Reinhardt replied, noting, "In that same communique, Friederic was quite forthright. Aluric Horridian is apparently mentally ill, which takes him out of the line of succession and his other Brother, Emeric, has abdicated his rights to the throne. That is why Friederic now sits on the Jovian High Throne. Aluric has no idea that there is even a War and both Emeric and Friederic have always been against it. I am very surprised at how candid Friederic has been."

"That would be highly unusual for a Horridian, Dieter", Connor Dumas replied.

"Yes, I know, which is why you are all here", the President informed them.

"Danica, what can you tell me?", the President enquired.

"Not a lot, I'm afraid. Most of the Jovian spies we have in custody don't have any knowledge of Jovian palace intrigues", Danica Thomlinson replied.

"I need to understand this Horridian, this Friederic. Just how honest is he being, or is he just tapping us along?", President Reinhardt asked.

Connor Dumas stepped in, "I think my Brother and I can help you there, Dieter", and then he turned to Daniel and nodded.

"We have information from the administrator's network and other sources that both corroborate and confuse what Friederic Horridian has told you, Dieter", Daniel commented.

"Corroborate and confuse?", Danica Thomlinson questioned, "That does not make any sense."

Daniel explained, "The Saturnian Demarchy's Administrator, Ms Swenna Goodchild, was in a teleconference meeting with Gideon Reas, Sandra Danker, a woman named Freyja and Roberta Nummus, less than one hour after Godric Horridian's lobotomisation. They were on Mimas at the time. That is what confuses the issue, Danica. Swenna is one of the most honest people you could meet. She provided me with the complete video, including timestamps and metadata, everything. Roberta Nummus was in fact on Mimas, less than one hour after the alleged attack!"

General Brennan-Chives shook her head, "Guys, Jupiter and Saturn are almost at their farthest distance from each other at the moment. So we are talking about something north of two billion kilometres. There is absolutely no way that Roberta Nummus could be in both Ganymede Prime and Mimas one hour apart. That would contravene the laws of physics!"

Connor stepped back in, "Correct, Camilla. Which is why we checked our other sources", he then nodded to his Brother once more.

Daniel looked around the room at the other faces present, "What I'm going to tell you must not leave this room. Not under any circumstances. Are we all agreed on this point?"

Everyone in the meeting agreed.

Daniel nodded and continued, "The original capital of the old Jovian Republic was Himalia Central and the Administrator of Himalia Central was part of the Administrator's Network. When the capital changed to Ganymede Prime, our contacts at Himalia Central had to become exceedingly cautious. We still receive information from them. I sent them a coded enquiry and they sent me a coded reply. Roberta Nummus was on Ganymede Prime and Roberta Nummus did lobotomise Godric Horridian with an ice pick. Now, this is not common knowledge. The ordinary Jovian public doesn't know this. And naturally, the Horridian Regime does not know that we have contacts inside their Realms."

"So, we now have confirmation of an impossibility", General Brennan-Chives announced, noting, "Roberta Nummus was on Ganymede Prime and less than an hour later on Mimas, over two billion kilometres apart. Daniel Dumas, that defies logic. It defies physics. Right now, even at the speed of light, Jupiter and Saturn are close to two hours apart!"

"Yeah, I thought that might be obvious. So I went straight to the source. Straight to Mimas and sent them a communique", Daniel informed them all in reply.

The General then asked, "Well, Daniel, don't keep us all in suspense."

"You won't like the answer", Daniel replied, before telling them, "The reply came from Doctor Gideon Reas. You know, the former Lead Terraformer Scientist working on the Mars Terraforming project and the former Administrator of the Martian Orbital colonies. Doctor Gideon Reas confirmed that Roberta Nummus was on Ganymede Prime lobotomising Godric Horridian and that she was also at the meeting less than one hour later on Mimas. As impossible as it is, Doctor Reas says both are true!"

The room went silent, dead silent, as they digested this new information.

President Reinhardt stepped into the silence, "Friederic Horridian was also in contact with Ms Swenna Goodchild. He said that no ship left Mimas, that it's still under blockade and that no ship arrived at Ganymede Prime either. Daniel, you are talking about superluminal travel without a ship!"

General Brennan-Chives added, "Faster than light travel without a ship. Daniel, that is impossible. Did you point that out to Doctor Reas? Did the man give you any explanation for this?"

Daniel smiled, "Yes, I did, Camilla. I absolutely did query him", then he went silent for what was a very long moment.

When Daniel continued, he stated, "As I said, you won't like the answer. Doctor Reas just said it was a Mimasian state secret and I should not ask any more questions about it. That I, or now, we, should just accept it and let it go. I can only assume that the Mimasians have some kind of new teleportation technology. Something that we've never seen before or even considered, for that matter."

The General blinked, the answer was absurd, "How are we just going to accept that? Ask no questions? Accept the impossible and just let it go? That is simply ridiculous?"

"General, I said you won't like the answer", Daniel reminded her and then he smiled a wry smile, "And we shouldn't ask either. We just need to accept that Roberta Nummus can be anywhere she wants, anytime she wants and that the last time she went to Ganymede Prime, she lobotomised High Prince Godric to stop a War. Let's just let this sleeping dog lie, yeah?"

Connor chimed in, "Daniel and I have asked our engineering department to look into teleportation."

Daniel smiled, "Our lead engineer just asked us how we'd like them to break the laws of physics and then he told us that they weren't just suggestions."

President Reinhardt chimed in, noting, "At least one mystery is solved."

"What mystery is that, Dieter?", the General enquired.

"Doctor Gideon Reas and Sandra Danker", the President replied, "After they retired, they just disappeared, they fell off the radar. Now, we know that they went to the Mimasian colony and they've been there all of this time."

Connor Dumas added, "Sandra Danker was the Lead Engineer on the Martian Terraforming Project. Most of the ships used in the project were her designs."

Daniel Dumas chimed in, "You might remember that at one of our previous meetings, we mentioned that the base designs for the warships coming off our production lines were from the twenty one forties. We now believe that those were also Sandra Danker's designs."

"So, what are you saying, Daniel? Has Sandra Danker cracked interplanetary teleportation?", Danica Thomlinson enquired.

"Yes, I'd like to know that one as well, Daniel. Has Sandra Danker created some form of faster-than-light, superluminal transport?", General Brennan-Chives agreed.

"We don't know. We have no idea. All we know is that Sandra Danker was a master engineer. One of the best ever. All of the base designs that we used for our latest warships appear to be her handiwork. Her design philosophy is all over those blueprints. It's like her design dna", Daniel replied, knowing that any speculation on superluminal travel was just that, speculation.

"Perhaps that's a second mystery solved", President Reinhardt noted, "Where those old blueprints and designs originated. They were Sandra Danker's handy work."

"Discussions about superluminal transport aside, we do have other political problems with this ceasefire", President Reinhardt commented.

Defence Minister Carlson enquired, "Political problems? I thought we were just going to match their ceasefire with one of our own?"

Connor understood and he stepped in, "The Godric Horridian problem."

"Yes. We would ask for Godric Horridian's extradition, but he's been lobotomised", the President noted, adding, "Godric Horridian no longer has the mental faculties to understand what he's done, let alone stand trial. My understanding is that he's catatonic and not even aware of his own existence. He has no self-awareness. His frontal lobes have been completely scrambled."

Danica Thomlinson added, "And his Brothers. Aluric is mentally ill and doesn't even know there is a War, and both Emeric and Friederic have always wanted to end it. With Godric incapacitated, Friederic finally got his chance. Not that Friederic would hand over any of his Brothers anyway. So, who exactly do we put on trial for all of these deaths and all of the destruction?'"

President Reinhardt smiled, "Friederic Horridian has even thought of that one, too. Godric's Ministers were all enablers. Godric was surrounded by people who egged him on and agreed with everything he came up with. Friederic has arrested them all and put them in prison."

Defence Minister Carlson enquired, "And Friederic has offered to hand them over to us for trial?"

"In a heartbeat, like sacrificial lambs to the slaughter. Friederic understands that the costs in terms of deaths and destruction were completely disproportionate. He will ship them to us if we request it", the President confirmed and then noted, "I already have made that request."

"So we put Godric's fleas on trial instead of the dog", the General noted wryly.

"Better his fleas than no one at all, Camilla. We need peace. This War has to end", the President replied and then he noted, "I'll be handing the negotiations over to our diplomats. If all goes well, perhaps, just perhaps, we can achieve a just and lasting peace."

"Still though, nearly forty million dead, Dieter, forty million!", Camilla reminded him.

"We have to let that go, Camilla. What's the alternative, continue this disastrous war in an attempt to make the deaths balance out?", President Reinhardt replied, noting, "It's not a perfect peace, but it is still peace and right now, the solar system needs peace."

Camilla nodded, she understood, "After any war, peace is never perfect, yet always preferable."

While the meeting continued, three unseen people watched. They weren't physically present, only there in astral form, their bodies sitting cross-legged in lotus posture in Gideon's house inside Mimas. Gideon, Sandra and Freyja watched curiously as the meeting unfolded. They were fortunate. There was no need to tweak anything. Which was good because to alter memories and tweak decisions, they would need to be physically present, albeit psychically obscured. Something that they could not do with Payback, General Brennan-Chive's dog, in the room.

Psychic obscuration only worked on sapient beings. It did not work on animals. So companion animals like dogs, cats or even ferrets could see straight through it. Dogs would stand and bark, and a well-trained dog might bark and point. A guard dog might even attack. It had been a pack of palace Doberman Pinschers that had almost mauled Freyja's cousins Tina and David to death back in seventy seven. Freyja remembered all too well. After the mauling, her cousins were beaten unconscious and then hanged whilst barely conscious by the Albert Horridian's Imperial Palace Guards.

As for cats, they would either stand and hiss or take cover under something and then hiss. Ferrets would run around in circles making *"Dook Dook"* noises to draw their owner's attention to something in the room that they could see, but their owners could not.

Gideon, Sandra and Freyja adjusted their awareness from Colonial Central Command in Cis-Lunar L-Five to the Earth, specifically a place buried under the sandstone of the South Australian outback fifty kilometres from the town of Coober Pedy. Once their minds were present and they were astrally there, they jaunted across the vastness of space and appeared inside a large dugout cavern.

There was a podium to one side, upon which there was a lectern. To the right side of which was a comfortable chair. That chair was empty. That had been Freyja's cousin, Folcrom Orpheus's favourite chair. No one sat there. It remained empty in memory of and honour of old Orpheus, who had passed away back in twenty one eighty two at the age of one hundred.

Off to the left of the podium was a series of desks. Some Council of Shadow members were seated, reviewing reports. Two of them had stopped what they were doing and watched as the trio approached.

Dante Reas stepped out from behind his desk and wrapped his arms around Freyja, "Mother!", he exclaimed as his Sister, Divine Reas, also got up from her desk.

Divine wrapped her arms around her Freyja, "Mother!", she also exclaimed before noting, "You should visit more often. What's kept you away this time? And don't say the War, we heard that's over."

"Only because of us, my dear child", Freyja responded.

Sandra Danker clarified, "Or more correctly, because of Roberta Nummus."

"Roberta Nummus?", Divine questioned and then asked, "What has that assassin got to do with it?"

Freyja leaned in and pressed her forehead to Divine's and shared her memories and Gideon's memories with her. The process took many long seconds before Freyja stepped back.

"Divine, honey. Share those memories with Dante and bring him up to speed", Freya instructed.

Divine did as instructed and shared the memories with her Brother, Dante.

"Father", Dante began, "Are you sure that's wise? Allowing the mundanes to know about jaunting."

"They don't know anything about jaunting, Dante", Gideon corrected, explaining, "They think Sandra has crafted some sort of superluminal teleportation technology. It's actually a good thing."

Divine questioned, "Father, you must be getting old or something. How does having the mundanes think you have teleportation technology play to our advantage?"

Gideon smiled, "They now think Mimas is a technological powerhouse. Those base ship designs that the Dumas Corporation has been using were Sandra's. Now they know that as well. Now they also think that Mimas has superluminal teleportation technology. With Roberta Nummus able to appear anywhere she wants, anytime she wants. It will keep them all on edge and for quite a while. Especially considering that Roberta Nummus may be ageing at a rate as slow as one year in ten."

"And at bay", Sandra Danker added, noting, "Let's not forget that. Anything that protects the Martians and the Thols is a very good thing."

Divine nodded. She understood, it was pure subterfuge and bluffing. A common tactic.

Dante questioned, "Roberta Nummus lobotomised Godric Horridian with an ice pick! Are we condoning that sort of behaviour now? I mean, seriously, Dad, that's not setting a good precedent."

Gideon frowned, "Look deeper into those memories, Son. Then you will understand the necessity of it. It was not a decision that was taken lightly."

Dante closed his eyes and allowed his mind to rifle through his Mother's, his Father's and Sandra's memories. Deep within them, he found Roberta Nummus explaining how things would pan out if Godric Horridian had not been stopped.

"Lobotomise one to save a hundred million or more", Dante noted softly.

Divine had been doing the same and added, "And the whole of Belter civilisation!"

"And you Guys thought you had it bad with all of those reports", Freyja scolded gently.

"Anyway, enough of all of this Council of Shadows nonsense, tell me how my

Grandchildren are doing? Come on, I need to know?", Freyja requested.

Dante chuckled, "Well, my eldest, Raphael, he's now on the Flinders Psychic Academy's Grey Council. He thinks he might be dean someday. Dean Folcrom Raphael", his pride in his Son showed.

Not to be outdone, Divine noted, "My eldest, Genevieve, is high up in the remote viewing teams. She's a Snake on the Serpent Council and manages six Wyvern Covens. She also has the ear of the Viperous One!", she exclaimed.

Freyja frowned and raised her hand, "Guys, it's not a competition."

Sandra, although involved with the Council of Shadows, had zero knowledge of the remote viewing teams, "Snakes? Serpent Councils? Wyvern Covens? The Viperous One?", she questioned.

"I'll explain it all in detail later, Sandra. For now, the Viperous One is the head of the remote viewing teams. He or she heads the Serpent Council. The members of which are titled Snakes and each Snake manages six Wyvern Covens. There are seventy two Wyvern Covens and each is run internally by a Dragon, just another title. At any given time, there are nine hundred and thirty six active remote viewers in those Wyvern Covens, not including the Serpent Council, which adds another thirteen. Remember, though, to the mundanes, they are just called remote viewing teams. We don't want them to freak out", Freyja quickly explained.

"That sounds complicated", Sandra responded, "Crazy complicated."

Freyja shrugged, "It works. Has done for over a hundred and fifty years", and then she laughed, "And Psi Corps has no idea that the Council of Shadows even exists. Even with all of their remote viewing teams."

"And Folcrom Tafazah set it all up", Sandra asked rhetorically.

"Yeah, he sure did. Tafazah set all of it up. The Academies, the Old Scholars Outreach, the Remote Viewing Teams and even our Council of Shadows", Freyja confirmed and then she asked her children, "Okay, so your eldest are both doing really well, great, what about the others?"

Dante smiled and replied, "A couple of Psi Corp teachers and a freelance psychic. They're all generally doing quite well. Of course, they all work for us when we need them to."

Divine also smiled, "Same with my lot as well. A couple of freelancers and a Psi Corp teacher. And of course, all of our Grandchildren are studying at the Flinders Psychic Academy."

"I'm just happy that they're all doing well", Freyja smiled back.

Sandra asked the most important question that had not been asked, "Dante, Divine, just how many of the scions can jaunt?"

"Well, that's a bit of a problem, Aunt Sandra", Dante admitted.

Divine stepped in, "There's Mum and then, of course, there's you and Dad, but neither of you is actually a scion."

Sandra nodded, "Can you tell me, how many Council of Shadow members are actually psychics with level ten or higher potentials?", she was becoming concerned.

Dante replied slowly, "Well, as you know, we are all supposed to be level tens or higher, but as the gene pool has become diluted, we've had to induct level nines. As you are aware, Divine and I are both just level nines."

"Guys, all of the other level tens who could operate off-world and jaunt have either retired or passed on. Gideon and I have been doing this crap for what, forty eight years? Your Mother, Freyja, has been doing this for what, probably sixty years?", Sandra informed them.

Freyja interjected, "About sixty years, Sandra, maybe a little more."

Sandra continued, "Thank you, Freyja. My point is, Guys, we three aren't getting any younger. We are tired. So, if you have few level ten psychics, no one who can jaunt and no one who can operate off-world, then just how is the Council of Shadows going to continue?"

Divine frowned, "Well, we are still working on that, Auntie."

Dante chimed in and clarified, "We have a plan, or at least the concepts of a plan. We are all going to follow your example, Aunt Sandra."

"Our example? What example?", Sandra questioned.

"Well, the problem, the dilution of our gene pool, was caused by us scions marrying with the mundanes and not other psychics. Had we predominantly married other psychics, we would not be in this predicament. We would have far more level tens and they'd be able to use the gifts off-world and even jaunt. They followed love and not duty", Divined explained.

Dante carried the explanation forward, "Our generation has vowed to fix this. We are going to marry for duty going forward, as in marrying other psychics. If that coincides with love, then so be it."

"And if they marry for love and that happens to be a marriage to a mundane?", Gideon enquired, "Because that is bound to happen. You guys do know that, yeah?"

"Then in that case they'll follow your example, Dad", Dante announced.

"Again, our example? What is our example?", Sandra circled back.

"Aunt Sandra, Dad married both you and Winchilly. Then later, he married Mum", Divine replied, noting, "That is the example. Your example!"

Dante chimed in, "If one of our scions marries a mundane for the reasons of love, they must also marry a psychic for the reasons of duty."

"Polyamory", Freyja chuckled and then she smiled broadly, "Look at what we've been teaching our Children, Gideon. Polyamory!"

"Now, Freyja, don't get cocky. It was you who insisted on marrying into an already polyamorous family", Gideon reminded her.

"I'm not complaining, Gideon. It's just ironic that we've set an example that we had no idea that we were setting. Winchilly will find all of this so amusing", Freyja responded.

"Here's the problem with your plan, Guys. It took four or five generations to get into this situation. It will likely take another four or five generations to get back out of it", Sandra noted, her voice taking on a serious tone once more.

"Yes, Aunty", Divine agreed, commenting, "By my own calculations, it took five or six generations and nearly one hundred and fifty years to get to where we are today and it will likely take just as long to get back out of it. Unfortunately, there are no quick fixes."

"And in the interim?", Sandra enquired.

"We have been looking into our history and trying to understand Folcrom Tafazah's intent", Dante replied, "This situation shouldn't have arisen for another five decades. Tafazah even predicted this genetic dilution issue. What he didn't take into account was our lack of concern for duty."

Divine interjected, "Tafazah could not have predicted the Mimasian War either, nor could he have predicted the Horridian War. We were never intended to work off-world. Tafazah's intent was purely to keep Psi Corp honest. That was essentially our entire purpose. We took it up ourselves to branch out into space and work off-world. That was beyond our intended purpose, our mandate."

Gideon laughed, "So, as I see it, for the next five or so generations, the Council of Shadow will be going back to its roots, its core purpose. You will all be Earthbound."

"Yes", Divine agreed, "Perhaps in a hundred and fifty years or so, one of us will master jaunting once more. Until then, we will be, as you said, Father, Earthbound."

"Gideon, this is really bad. What if Friederic Horridian turns out to be as bad as his Brother, Godric?", Sandra queried.

"Well then, Sandra, you, Freyja and I, we'll just have to hang around as long as we can just in case Friederic Horridian turns rogue", Gideon replied.

Freyja noted wryly, "And if Friederic Horridian does go rogue like his Brother, Godric, and starts another War, Roberta Nummus will have an ice pick with his name on it."

"Mother!", both Dante and Divine exclaimed in unison.

Epilogue.

It took two years for the armistice to be agreed upon. Two years of diplomatic discussions followed High Prince Friederic's unilateral ceasefire decision. It wasn't perfect, but it did end all of the hostilities on a more permanent basis. Certain weapons systems were banned under the agreement. The flash vaporisers that were so devastatingly used against civilians in Cis-Lunar Space and the Wild Weasel tactical nuclear missiles, amongst others.

As predicted by Swenna Goodchild, the Saturnian Demarchy's Administrator, the inner system allies considered the outer satellites, Saturn, Uranus and Neptune, all complicit. And so it got recorded. The Quadripartite Outer Satellite Agreement (QOSA) had ensured that it would come to pass.

The Belters were also unhappy. They had been pleased to have inner solar system allied protection, yes, but the fact that they were the meat in the middle between two warring sides rankled them no end. Had things escalated into an invasion of the Asteroid Belt, then the Belter civilisation would have come to an end. That was what was remembered down the decades and well into the future.

It would take decades, perhaps centuries, for trust to be rebuilt, if at all and for the most part, it didn't. There was always the thought at the back of people's minds in the inner solar system that at some point in the future, another Horridian High Prince would go rogue. Even in peace, there was fear.

Time passed and Roberta Nummus's adopted Daughter, Lina Mitchel, married one of Winchilly's and Gideon's Grandsons, her Daughter, Weehalani's eldest Son. He was one-quarter Martian and, like all Martians and most hybrids, did not use a surname. Lina's children all went by the surname, Mitchel. Some of Lina's children married the great-grandchildren of Gideon, Sandra and Freyja. Their lineages all became entwined with one another.

Roberta Nummus herself could not have any children and so neither could Elaine Haynes. Instead, they took delight in Lina's children and grandchildren, along with those of their friends, Gideon and his three wives, Winchilly, Sandra and Freyja. Apart from her Wife, Elaine Haynes, Freyja was Roberta's best friend. Roberta even kept detailed genealogical records. Of course, those were the good times.

Gideon was in his mid-nineties when he retired as the Mimasian Administrator. Technically, he was in charge of all Human society within Mimas, those of Earth descent. He had also controlled foreign affairs, defence and communications with the colonies beyond Mimas.

The Martians had their own Council of Elders and the Thols had their

Matriarch and Patriarch. Winchilly had been a Martian Elder and had stepped down a decade earlier in favour of her Eldest Daughter, Weehalani.

Upon stepping down as Administrator, Gideon appointed Roberta Nummus, who immediately refused the post. That was to be expected. Roberta still considered herself to be a monster.

"My past makes me completely unsuitable", Roberta had said.

Gideon had smiled back and told her, "Roberta, it is your past that makes you the most suitable candidate", and he would not accept no for an answer.

Roberta reluctantly took up the post. Roberta was now a part of the Administrator's network.

It was around that time that Elaine Haynes remarked, "Roberta, I don't think you're ageing at all. Not one year in ten, you've simply stopped ageing."

Lina had chimed in, "Elaine is right, Roberta. I don't think you're ageing either."

After that, Roberta stared into a mirror for a long time and she even poked her face occasionally. They were correct, she was not ageing at all and appeared to be about twenty nine years old, not quite yet thirty. Roberta Nummus was simply not ageing.

Of course, the good times with young ones being born and families growing are only half of the story of life. The sick, the elderly and the infirm eventually pass on. First, Gideon passed away. He was a hundred and six. A good age, he'd lived a long life. This affected Roberta, yes, but far more so Sandra, Winchilly and Freyja. Roberta, Elaine and Lina all found themselves consoling the three women, who themselves had always been so strong and there for them. Roles had reversed completely.

About a year later, Sandra Danker passed away and that was followed by Freyja less than three months later. Freyja's passing hit Roberta hard, like a kick in the guts. Roberta cried for days afterwards. Elaine and Lina found themselves not only consoling Winchilly but also Roberta. In her life, Roberta had had very few friends and Freyja had become one of her closest.

Winchilly had become frail and Roberta, Elaine and Lina all took time to look after her. Winchilly finally passed away several years later. She was one hundred and nine. Winchilly had been a Martian Elder for most of her adult life and the whole Martian community mourned her passing, all eight million of them. Even the Thols, with their much smaller community, mourned and grieved.

The old guard had passed on and now there were Roberta Nummus, Elaine

Haynes and Lina Mitchel left behind. These were, of course, the bad times and Roberta took down detailed notes, recording them meticulously in her genealogical records. And via the Administrator's Network, Roberta even kept track of Freyja's children and descendants back on Earth.

As bad as losing Gideon, Sandra, Freyja and Winchilly was, there were worse times yet to come. When Elaine Haynes was in her nineties, she passed away suddenly in her sleep. One morning, she simply did not wake up. Roberta Nummus was distraught with grief and inconsolable. Even Lina and her children were unable to console her. Lina did the only thing she could. She asked the current Thol Matriarch, Yeelahwah and one of the Martian Elders for help. The Martian Elder, it turned out, was a great-grandchild of Winchilly, named Weesahani.

The first thing that Yeelahwah did was something that would have been done for a distraught Thol. It was something that was not done outside of Thol families. It was something intimate and reserved for close family and friends. Yeelahwah crawled into bed behind Roberta and gently wrapped her arms around her and then she unfurled her great leathery wings and encapsulated Roberta in a Tholish double-hug. Yeelahwah began singing softly, cooing and trilling into Roberta's ear in ancient Tholish.

Weesahani watched, understanding that Roberta Nummus was so well regarded amongst Thols that the matriarch herself was bestowing upon her a great privilege. Roberta Nummus was no longer considered the monstrous assassin that she had once been.

Weesahani sat down on the bed beside Roberta and gently stroked her hair. Roberta was quiet, crying and did not respond, so Weesahani climbed into the bed and looked directly into her eyes.

Weesahani gently entered Roberta's mind and looked into her grief processing.

Roberta had once been conditioned, both physically and mentally, to be a weapon. What had been done to her had left her in a psychotic state that had lasted more than eight decades. Weesahani's people, the Martians, had healed her. However, they had forgotten one major point. Weapons were never designed nor meant to grieve.

"This is our fault, Roberta", Weesahani began telepathically transmitting, explaining, *"My people were so intent on healing you, removing all of your psychological conditioning and those awful psychoses and triggers, that we didn't see it. You were conditioned to completely ignore grief. In removing all of that conditioning, we left you open to grief in a way that left you with no ability to process it. Even we Martians aren't perfect. Sometimes we Martians make mistakes."*

Roberta stared back blankly, not responding, her tears still flowing freely. Yeelahwah and Lina both heard Weesahani's thoughts as well, as they were not meant to be private.

Weesahani frowned and placed her forehead to Roberta's, transmitting, *"Roberta Nummus, I, Weesahani, Martian Elder, share with you a piece of my mind."*

After several minutes, Weesahani pulled her forehead back from Roberta's.

Roberta Nummus slowly and carefully sat up in bed. Yeelahwah unwrapped her great leathery wings.

Weesahani sat up as well, asking telepathically, *"How do you feel now, Roberta?"*

Roberta's tears had stopped, she sniffled and wiped her eyes, "What did you do? I feel different."

"That little piece of me that is inside your mind has turned off the valve on your grief. That should give you time to breathe and compose your thoughts", Weesahani explained, noting, *"It will release the grief trickle by trickle, allowing you to process it more slowly without overwhelming you."*

Yeelahwah spoke in English with her Tholish trills, clicks and barks lacing it, "Martian mind share is good in many ways. Help you, it will, Roberta Nummus."

Weesahani smiled, transmitting, *"Yes, it can be helpful. If you need a second opinion on anything or even just information for that matter, look within you, Roberta Nummus. Look for a small, almost infinitely small, purple patch with golden threads and direct thoughts at it. It will be like you are talking to me, with me giving you advice and any information that it knows."*

"For how long does it work?", Roberta enquired.

"That's up to you, Roberta. You may ignore it or you may not. It will help you with your grief, regardless. The sharing lasts as long as you last, even beyond my lifetime", Weehalani explained.

"Weehalani, I do not age. I may live for a very long time, maybe even forever", Roberta replied.

"Then, I will be with you maybe even forever, even after I'm long gone. My Mother, Weehalani and even my Grandmother, Winchilly. We will all be with you", Weesahani noted in reply.

"Wait! What! Winchilly's inside my head?", Roberta queried.

"Yes. Winchilly shared with Weehalani often and my Mother and Winchilly both shared with me. So all of those Martians in the chain of sharing are with you", Weesahani explained, adding, *"We share very often, it is the Martian way. It is very likely that Gideon,*

Sandra and Freyja are there as well."

Roberta Nummus closed her eyes and there, deep within her, Winchilly smiled back.

Roberta burst into tears and Weesahani had to explain to everyone present, *"Tears of joy!"*

In the due course of time, even Lina Mitchel passed away and even though Lina was Roberta's adopted Daughter, the grief she felt was carefully modulated by Weesahani's sharing. It was felt, yes, it was painful, yes, but it was not so overwhelming. Roberta was able to process her way through the grief. Roberta felt happy about that. She did not want her beautiful memories of Lina torn apart by an uncontrollable, overwhelming grief.

Time passed slowly and as the Mimasian Administrator, Roberta Nummus spent her days managing Mimas. Roberta spent quite a lot of her time documenting the genealogies of the descendants of her friends and Daughter. Roberta kept tabs on everything that was happening across the solar system as well. The news feeds always had information, but they were chaotic and sensationalised, whereas her primary source of information, the Administrator's Network, was not. It was from a combination of both that Roberta learned that something interesting had arisen. Something very interesting indeed.

It was in the mid twenty three fifties that a pair of powerful psychics came to light. As Psi Corp also kept an extensive genealogical database, Roberta took full advantage of it. It was an amazing resource. The lineage of Folcrom Tafazah, the first of the Folcrom, could be traced back into deep antiquity for five thousand three hundred years. Roberta downloaded the entire database and strangely enough, Psi Corp allowed her to do so. A Flinders Psychic Academy Grey Council member, called Lord Folcrom Mandrakus, personally signed off on it.

The pair of psychics Roberta was studying were powerful, at least level nines and likely much, much higher. They were both distant cousins and scions of Folcrom Tafazah. The first was a young woman called Lady Folcrom Selene. The other was called Lord Folcrom Forkbraid, obviously not his original name. Roberta quickly found out that Forkbraid had named himself in the ancient Viking fashion. He'd named himself after a prominent facial feature. His braided beard that was long and forked at the end, a Forkbraid! Roberta looked up his birth name in the Psi Corp database.

Forkbraid's Father was in fact Lord Folcrom Mandrakus, the very man who'd approved Roberta's access to their database and his Mother was one Lady Folcrom Cybilla. Their surname was Reas and they had named their firstborn Son, Gideon, Gideon Reas! Forkbraid was not only a scion of Folcrom Tafazah, but he was also a scion of the Lady Folcrom Freyja, Roberta's long-departed friend.

Mandrakus wanted her to know! He had personally approved Roberta Nummus's access!

Forkbraid, upon his graduation as an apprentice at the Psychic Flinders Academy, had changed his name so as not to be confused with and compared to his long-deceased ancestor who shared the same name. They were namesakes separated across the centuries. Roberta Nummus followed Selene's and Forkbraid's careers with a newfound glee.

Roberta had followed the pair's exploits. They both became Flinders Island Psychic Academy Grey Council members. The youngest Grey Council members ever. Gideon himself became the head of the Psi Corp remote viewing teams and he became the Viperous One!

In the year twenty three sixty, Lord Folcrom Forkbraid left the Earth for Cis-Lunar L-Five. Forkbraid was tasked with tracking down terrorists after an attack on Earth at a Flinders Island Psychic Academy psychic induction ceremony. Scores of young children, all psychic inductees, had been killed. What Roberta understood from that, was that Forkbraid could use his gifts off-world!

Around the same time, Lady Folcrom Selene had travelled to Mars, now terraformed and open to colonisation. Selene's task was to set up the new Elysium Colony and the New Flinders Psychic Academy on the Martian subcontinent of Elysium. A thousand psychic couples travelled with her to Mars. Again, what Roberta realised, was that Selene could also use her gifts off-world as well.

More importantly, Forkbraid chased the terrorists from the colonies of Cis-Lunar L-Five all the way to Mars. Interestingly, the first ever, off-world born psychic, a young girl named Miranda, had been kidnapped by the terrorists and taken to Mars as a hostage. Which was the very reason Forkbraid was chasing after them. The terrorists, once defeated, eventually fled from Mars to the Jovian Realms. Meanwhile, back on Mars, both Forkbraid and Selene ended up together as a couple.

Forkbraid and Selene were both different kinds of Psi Corps operatives. Unlike Gideon, Sandra and even Freyja, who all rejected violence as much as possible. Forkbraid and Selene would do what needed to be done and if that meant being violent, then so be it. Forkbraid was even known to execute the worst of the terrorists. To them, he became judge, jury and executioner. The psychic couple did not flinch when it came to evil and its irradiation. They were relentless! That was something that Roberta Nummus understood.

It was disappointing to see a second Horridian War break out in the year twenty three sixty two. Like the previous War, there were four Horridian Brothers, except this time there was also a pair of Sisters. This time around, the instigator was one Heinrich von Horridian and he began his War with a decapitation strike. Two thousand two hundred interplanetary missiles, each armed with ten cold-fusion warheads with yields of two megatons apiece. Most of the missiles were targeting the Earth, a couple of hundred targeted Cis-Lunar L-Five, while ten targeted the official Martian colonies. The outcome should have been devastating!

Wipe out the Martian colonies, making a terraformed Mars far easier to occupy. Cause damage to the colonies of Cis-Lunar L-Five, sowing fear and doubt. And, of course, bombing the Earth back into the Stone Age, removing all resistance. It was a typical Horridian gambit. Roberta was incensed by this repeated stupidity and yet, all she could do was sit back and hope for the best. Heinrich von Horridian's gambit should have worked and yet it failed!

On Mars, Forkbraid had commissioned a ship. It was of a new design and the man who built it was often described as the man who could build anything, one Varakhan Utana. The ship's computer and control systems were designed and built by a positronic matrix engineer named Peter Swann. Both men were brilliant in the extreme with intelligence quotients left and right of three hundred. The ship that they built was extraordinary, with multiple methods of motility, including the first-ever slipstream drive. Roberta, of course, found out about those things long after the War had concluded.

Forkbraid, his crew and his ship, the Solstice, had destroyed the missile en route to Mars and then later, they had destroyed thirty percent of the missiles bound for the Earth and Cis-Lunar L-Five. The efforts of that one ship and its crew alone had enabled the Earth's orbital defence platforms, the Earth's Defence Forces and Cis-Lunar Space's Colonial Fleet to take down the rest. There were missile strikes on Earth and in Cis-Lunar L-Five and there were millions of deaths, although far, far less than in the first Horridian War.

One side called Forkbraid and his crew heroes. The Horridian labelled them as pirates!

The Solstice itself as a ship was a thing of beauty, of an unusual disk and sled design with slightly downward curved delta-shaped wings and topside stabilisers. The ship had no less than thirty six weapons systems. Eight phased laser arrays, four twin particle disrupter beams, a quad pulse laser cannon, two twin high-powered, rapid-fire pulse plasma cannons, three double-barrelled electromagnetic rail guns with a two seventy degree sweep and three double torpedo launch tubes.

The Solstice was a ship designed for her times and her times included a devastating and bloody conflict.

The Solstice's hull was made of a single piece of polyceramalloy laid down molecule by molecule using highly precise industrial-sized three-d printers. The Solstice's defences not only included standard deflector shields but also an eight-by-eight layered, impenetrable defence grid. Its eight-by-eight layered defence grid could also bend light around the ship and cloak it entirely. The outer skin of the Solstice's hull could be skinned in passive camouflage, usually the inky black of deep space. The Solstice was a ship that could travel unseen like a ghost.

The Solstice contained advanced micro-fusion stealth thrusters, a Levity disc and two Hamel thrusters, in addition to its Slipstream drive. Its power source and fuel storage were a controlled Quantum Singularity and the entire ship was controlled by an advanced three-laws safe, three-o-three model positronic brain. Its weapon systems, however, were controlled by a separate system, a clustered matrix of seventy two positronic assemblies, called the Hornets Nest, which was not three-laws safe.

Forkbraid, his crew and the Solstice played a large part in the Second Horridian War. Along with the Earth Defence Forces, the Cis-Lunar Colonial Fleet and the Venusian Defence Forces. The war ended quickly, within two years. With his decapitation strike thwarted and the Solstice working unseen within Jovian Cis-Lunar Space itself, Heinrich von Horridian watched as his terrible War came crashing back down around him. His decapitation strike had been his Hail Mary and it had failed.

Once the inner system allies destroyed and routed the Jovian's outer defence fleet and entered Jovian Cis-Lunar Space, the end was nigh. The Jovian's inner defence fleet quickly fell and the colonies of the Jovian Realms were left vulnerable and undefended. High Prince Heinrich, two of his Brothers and their families fled into exile along with the other Jovian nobles and all of their followers. Four interplanetary push ships departed the Jovian System for the distant Dwarf World, Eris.

The remaining Brother, Prince Leopold, became the new High Prince. The cost had been high and the Six Jovian Realms had lost their Trojan territories. The Trailing Trojans became a Constitutional Principality, with his Sister, Princess Luisa, becoming a figurehead. The Leading Trojans became a Constitutional Republic, his other Sister, Princess Sofia, having been murdered during the rebellion.

High Prince Leopold quickly ended the War, acknowledging that his Brother's disastrous War had been lost, although Leopold did manage to win the peace.

Leopold was a reformer. He ended Slavery and all forms of indentured servitude across the four remaining Jovian Realms. He even restructured the Jovian High Churches and introduced a true parliamentary system with upper and lower houses.

The power of the High Prince was no longer absolute. Prince Leopold had power, yes, but tempered by parliamentary and judicial processes. It was after the Second Horridian War that the solar system entered a period of true peace. A true Golden Age. The previous first Golden Age had been destroyed by Godric von Horridian with the first Horridian War one hundred and eighty years earlier.

After the Second Horridian War had ended, Roberta sent a message to the New Flinders Psychic Academy on the Elysium subcontinent on Mars. The message was sent via the Administrator's Network and crossed the desk of the Martian Administrator, the Elon of Mars. Governor John Anderson of the Chryce Colony had never heard of Mimas. Mimas was an obscure colony moon within the Saturnian system and had never been on his radar. The Governor sent the encrypted message directly to Lady Folcrom Selene, who was not only the Dean of the New Flinders Psychic Academy but also the Governor of the Elysium Colony.

Sadly for Roberta, she did not receive any reply. It had been a simple message, introducing herself, but the message did request clarification of both Selene's and Forkbraid's abilities. Roberta needed to know if the old Council of Shadows was reaching off-world once more. Roberta did not know it, but her query had raised two pairs of eyebrows. What the hell was the Council of Shadows?

A mysterious spaceship appeared in the vicinity of Mimas. It was outside of the twenty five thousand kilometre exclusion zone. It was a design that the Saturnian Demarchy Authorities had never seen before. The ship ignored all hails sent to it and then it went dark. It just disappeared right off the Saturnian scopes and radars. It had simply vanished as if it had never been.

Inside Mimas, Roberta Nummus was visiting the graves of her dear friends, especially the graves of Elaine Haynes and Lina Mitchel. Roberta had just laid flowers down on each grave and then stood back up. Her eyes caught a mysterious couple standing by the graves of Gideon Reas and his Wives, Sandra, Winchilly and Freyja. Roberta could not remember seeing them before, which was fair enough, over twenty million people were now living inside Mimas.

The woman turned around. She was tall and thin with pleasant facial features, not overly beautiful, but certainly far more than plain. Her hair was long and dark, with a single long lock of pure white hair to the right of her forehead. She had a curious aura about her, something that reminded her of Sandra and Freyja. She also appeared to be pregnant. Then the man turned around. He was taller than the woman and his hair was long, light brown and parted in the middle. Roberta immediately noticed his beard, it was a goatee, long, braided and forked at the end. Roberta Nummus almost fainted.

Roberta felt a gentle warmth supporting her legs. The man, obviously Forkbraid, had his hand slightly outstretched. Forkbraid smiled at Roberta and tilted his head slightly as if reaching down into deep memories.

"Are your feet steady, Roberta Nummus?", the thoughts entered her mind.

Roberta nodded and the gentle warmth supporting her legs dissipated.

Lady Folcrom Selene's thought entered Roberta's mind, *"I am Folcrom Selene and this is my Husband, Folcrom Forkbraid."*

They both walked over to Roberta and Forkbraid asked, vocally, "Now, Roberta Nummus, what is this Council of Shadows you messaged us about?"

Roberta didn't answer straight away, she merely walked over to the graves of her friends, Gideon, Sandra, Winchilly and Freyja.

Roberta places a single red rose on each of their graves before stating, "You look remarkably like your namesake, Forkbraid. Gideon, of course, didn't have a beard. Neither Sandra, Winchilly, nor Freyja, for that matter, were big on beards."

Selene smiled warmly, "Funny that, Roberta. I prefer my man with a beard."

And that was that the ice was broken.

In order to exchange knowledge most efficiently, Selene requested access to Roberta's memories. At first, Roberta was taken aback, after all, they had only just met, but then again, Selene had asked when she could have just taken them. Roberta allowed Selene to access her memories, which she did in precisely the same way as Winchilly, Freyja or Sandra had done in the past. A direct touch of Selene's forehead to Roberta's forehead. Roberta nodded to Forkbraid and he accessed her memories in the same fashion. It took them mere seconds to come up to speed.

Selene's and Forkbraid's eyes opened wide in wonder. The interior of Mimas had been an eye-opener. No one outside of Mimas knew of this vibrant, living World within the Ice moon. It was huge, far, far bigger than the ruined world of Eros of old. Like living on the inside of an immense terrarium. Now, however, things were far more fascinating.

When they'd jaunted into Mimas, they had both searched for Human minds, specifically for the mind of Roberta Nummus. They had already read Roberta's file. The mind of an immortal should not be too hard to locate. Such a long-lived person would have a depth of memories that stood out like a beacon and they were correct. Roberta's mind was like a massive ball of memories and knowledge. They found her easily. A simple task.

Now, however, they'd retrieved Roberta Nummus's memories and the grand scale of everything was falling into place. There were Humans inside of Mimas, sure, but holy fuck! There were other Humans as well. A subspecies called Martians. And then there were the Thols, an alien species of what could only be described as angelic beings. Not just that either. Roberta's memories also contained the shared memories of other people, Winchilly, Weehalani, Weesahani, Sandra Danker, Freyja, Gideon Reas and many, many others. Both Selene and Forkbraid sat down on the cobbled stone path of the graveyard.

Roberta enquired with concern, "Are you both okay? Did I do something wrong?"

Selene smiled, shaking her head, "No, no, Roberta Nummus. You did nothing wrong at all."

Forkbraid added, "We just need five or ten minutes for your memories to collate. We should have been far more cautious when absorbing the mind of someone who could potentially live forever."

And that was that Selene and Forkbraid both had the full knowledge that Roberta Nummus had. They now knew of the Council of Shadows, the Great Conceal and the Mimasian War. Of Tarlaks, Thols and Martians. All of the details of the First Horridian War. It was all there, swimming around in their minds, slowly being collated and assimilated.

Forkbraid thought to Selene, *"Perhaps we were too eager to share memories with an immortal. We should have done this at her home with a couple of cups of coffee."*

Selene and Forkbraid explained how they'd arrived in the Saturnian Demarchy by Slipstream drive aboard the Solstice. That they'd jaunted from the ship to Mimas and that they'd also return to Mars the same way. They also informed Roberta that they could jaunt directly to and from Mars and Mimas, however, they did need to test the latest changes that Varak had made to the Slipstream drive system. Killing two birds with one stone, so to speak. The trio found their way back to Roberta's modest house and they spent the whole of the day talking about what Roberta's memories had revealed and their future ramifications.

Selene and Forkbraid found themselves inexplicably drawn to Roberta and jaunted to Mimas quite often to visit her. Over time, the trio all became good friends. Seven months later, when Selene's pregnancy was coming to its end, Forkbraid jaunted Roberta to the New Flinders Psychic Academy on Mars to be there for the birth. Selene and Forkbraid had a baby Daughter and they gave Roberta the privilege of naming her.

"Can we call her Elaine?", Roberta suggested.

"Of course, we can", Selene replied, cradling her newborn Daughter, "Elaine, it shall be."

Time passed quickly and Selene produced five more children with Forkbraid. All up three Daughters and three Sons. Roberta was asked to name their second and third Daughters as well and she chose the names Lina and Sandra. Roberta had wanted to name their next Daughter, Freyja, but alas, the other three children were all born as Sons.

While Selene raised their Children at the New Flinders Psychic Academy on Mars, Forkbraid spent a lot of time jaunting back and forth to the underground caverns outside of Coober Pedy on Earth. As Selene and Forkbraid were both scions of Folcrom Tafazah and well above level ten in their psychic potentials, they were quickly inducted into the Council of Shadows.

There, Forkbraid shared with the other Council of Shadow members the methodologies that he, Selene and a handful of others used to jaunt across interplanetary distances. Towards the end of the year twenty three seventy, the Council of Shadows was now off-world capable once more. Council of Shadow members tested their newfound abilities by jaunting to Mimas and back and Roberta Nummus documented them all with meticulous detail.

Of course, time stops for no one and eventually, both Selene and Forkbraid passed away. In the mid-twenty-sixth century, the Council of Shadows decided it was time to end the Great Conceal. Roberta Nummus was the Administrator of Mimas and everyone living inside Mimas was her responsibility, Humans, Martians and Thols alike. Roberta was completely against ending the Great Conceal. It would endanger the Martians and the Thols, she had explained.

The Council of Shadows representative, who frequently jaunted, albeit clandestinely, around the solar system, explained to Roberta that it was time and that the Great Conceal was never meant to be forever. They told her that its end was well overdue and that it should have been done when Selene and Forkbraid were still alive. Telling that to Roberta simply hardened her heart!

That all changed when the Martian Elders and the Tholish Matriarch and Patriarch visited Roberta. They were representative of the very people that Roberta was protecting. Amongst them was another Martian, not from Mimas. This one was a representative from the Elders of the Martians of Mars itself. They each reminded Roberta that the Great Conceal affected not just Mimas and its people, but also the Martians living on Mars as well. They explained it was more than just about people, but about memory, history and the truth.

Finally, the Thol Matriarch spoke in English, laced with her Tholish trills, clicks and barks, "All things have their time and in time they have their ending. The ending of the past sorrows is nigh."

It had been a long time since Roberta had turned within, to get advice from her old friends, Winchilly, Weehalani and Weesahani, centuries in fact. Were they still there? Would they respond?

As the Martians and Thols watched, Roberta Nummus closed her eyes, looked within and sought their shared memories.

Winchilly's smiling face appeared almost immediately, *"Listen to the Matriarch of the Thols, dear Roberta. It is time."*

Weehalani and her Daughter Weesahani both appeared and nodded in agreement.

They replied in unison, *"Winchilly is right, dear Roberta. It is time for the veil to lift. This charade must end. The Great Conceal must end."*

Roberta thanked them all and then opened up her eyes, "It is time. The Great Conceal is over."

The Martians had all witnessed the ancient memories speak. They already understood.

What followed happened almost overnight. The Council of Shadows had prepared for the Great Reveal for centuries. The Great Conceal was always going to end and now, after long centuries, that time had come. Long-hidden computer records were released and almost immediately appeared in the public domain, placed in their correct chronological sequences. Centuries-old hard copies of files and records magically appeared on the desks of the appropriate clerks. The locations of indisputable evidence appeared, including where to find the bodies of the deceased Tarlaks from the long-ago Mimasian War. News feeds were all abuzz with more information than they knew what to do with. It was chaos, sheer organised chaos and it was everywhere.

In a single night, the entire solar system found out about the Mimasian War, how the Earth had nearly been conquered by the Tarlaks. The sheer magnitude of deaths that the Colonial Troops sustained to end the War and all about the Martians and the Thols. It read like fiction and yet it was all real. All of the evidence had been released along with the data. Tarlak bodies and even the locations of hidden Colonial Troop cemeteries.

For the next decade, the Great Reveal caused pure chaos as two sets of histories sat side by side. The Decade of Great Confusion! The Great Conceal, with no supporting evidence, had long been assumed to be real and the Great Reveal, with all of its supporting evidence galore. And along with the bodies of aliens, the Tarlaks, was the living proof, the Martians and the Thols. There was even detailed biodata released for each of them. Martians, a subspecies of Human, Homo sapiens martialis and a completely unknown alien species, Tholus sapiens mimasensis. The proof was all there and in the end, that was what won out.

The Great Reveal and its subsequent Decade of Confusion created no end of headaches for Roberta Nummus. Roberta was the Administrator of Mimas and the requests kept rolling in and landing on her desk. Engineers wanted to see the inside of Mimas, most especially its environmental control systems and its enormous ion drive systems. Roberta stamped every one of those with a simple stamp, REQUEST DENIED. Roberta was NOT handing sophisticated ancient Tholish technology to people who had, within her long lifetime, fought two disastrous Horridian Wars. Let Humanity continue to grow up a bit more first was her simple logic. Humanity was not yet ready!

When the Tholish Matriarch had queried the rejections, Roberta had replied, "Honey, my people are little more than hairless, upright walking apes with attitude. We simply aren't ready for this yet."

The Tholish Matriarch and Patriarch both deferred to Roberta's wisdom.

It wasn't just engineers either, there were a lot of requests for access to the interior of Mimas coming from biologists, anthropologists, zoologists, geneticists, ecologists, evolutionary scientists and even archaeologists. This was the major headache. Engineers wanting ancient alien technology, sure, no problem, just deny them access. That was easily fixed.

Martians, Thols and the environment they lived in, the interior of Mimas, that was not in her purview. Roberta passed those requests onto the Martian Elders and the Tholish Matriarch and Patriarch, recommending only the most well-considered proposals and even then, giving them limited access. They all agreed.

They would let some of them in based on the merit of their proposals, along with strict guidelines as to how and what they could study. They would also be carefully supervised. Especially where actual people were involved. Everyone else with failed proposals would have to work with what the Martians and the Thols released publicly themselves.

Then, of course, came the request for samples! Roberta was really pissed off at seeing those. Various so-called *"sovereign"* governments on Earth, all under the United Nations and Earth's Government, wanted actual alien samples. Their scientists could not get inside Mimas, so they demanded that Mimas send them samples instead!

Roberta, through the Martians and Thols, organised samples to be shipped to the Earth. Plant samples, dna samples and even, where appropriate, animal carcasses. That was all that was going to be permitted. Of course, then the requests came in for Martian and Thol samples. What the fuck! These were people, not just animals! Actual sentient, sapient people! Roberta was disgusted, thoroughly disgusted! Out came her REQUEST DENIED stamp once more.

The Martian High Elder and the Thol Matriarch approached Roberta. They had concerns, serious concerns. They had seen all of the requests for actual Martian and Thol specimens. Roberta explained that all such requests would be automatically denied as unacceptable. Which the Martian High Elder and Thol Matriarch both agreed, but there was a pattern to the problem.

"They don't see us as people, Roberta. Only curiosities to be studied", the Matriarch explained, her voice laced with trills, clicks and barks.

The Martian High Elder agreed, *"They need to see us as people. Then they will understand."*

And so it was decided that Mimas needed an embassy, two to be precise, one on Earth and another at Cis-Lunar L-Five. As the gravity inside of Mimas was set to point four gs, they would purchase a large Bernal Sphere colony in Cis-Lunar L-Five.

In a Bernal Sphere, the gravity changed from zero gs at its rotational axis, gradually to one g along its main living surface. That would allow the Mimasian Thols, Martians and other Mimasian Humans to acclimate gradually to one standard gravity. Those who were fully acclimated to one standard g could then go to the Earth and stay at the Mimasian Embassy there.

Roberta was more cautious and made two requests. Everyone from Mimas, who went to these *"Embassies",* must be issued with full diplomatic credentials and full diplomatic immunity. That would protect them from a diplomatic standpoint. The next part hearkened back to her previous history. Roberta Nummus could not protect those diplomats if she were not there.

Roberta Nummus then proposed that she stand down as the Mimasian Administrator and requested that she be put in charge of the Mimasian Embassy's security. Roberta herself already had diplomatic status and diplomatic immunity, granted to her at the time of the first Horridian War. Roberta had already chosen her replacement, a non-psychic descendant of Gideon Reas and Sandra Danker.

The first Mimasian embassy opened in Cis-Lunar L-Five. It orbited in a halo orbit centred on L-Five's gravitational sweet spot, one of a cluster of embassy colonies that did so. The Mimasian colony was just a short shuttle ride from the Colonial Central Command mega-cylinder. Always willing to help, the Dumas Corporation's Dumas Colonial Financial Ltd had provided the finances for its construction at discounted rates. At the same time, Dumas Colonial Constructions Ltd had built the actual Bernal Sphere colony.

The Mimasian personnel who arrived first were of Earth Human descent. They were just ordinary staff to maintain the colony and required no diplomatic status or protections. The next to arrive were the diplomatic staff, a mixture of Humans of Earth and Martian descent, along with Thols. They all had full diplomatic status and immunity. The Mimasians used long-range ships, retrofitted military transports from the long-ago Mimasian War era of twenty one forty two to bring them to Cis-Lunar L-Five. There were a thousand of those military transport craft still on Mimas's northern hemisphere.

Security staff, all Humans of Earth descent, travelled with them. The security staff had all been personally trained by Roberta Nummus. The first transport with the workers flew to Cis-Lunar Space without an escort. The diplomatic transport that followed was escorted by Roberta Nummus herself, flying alongside in her ship, an ancient, although heavily upgraded, Tristar Interplanetary Stealth Ship, the Dark Angel. Alongside the refurbished military transport, the Dark Angel was almost invisible.

Everything was going to plan. The Human workers from Mimas, who were of Earth descent, quickly acclimated to the embassy's one standard gravity areas. As did the Human diplomats of Earth descent. The Martians, who, although Human, were a subspecies of Human and used to roughly point four gs, took longer to acclimate, as one might expect. The Thols, who were physiologically designed for flight and had hollow bones like birds, took somewhat longer. They gradually moved from the lower gravitational zones of the embassy to the higher gravitational main living areas over the course of a year. During this gravitational acclimation period, all of the diplomatic work was performed in the Bernal

Sphere's lower gravitational zones. It was slow and laborious, but the process of acclimation was working.

During this period of time, no one noticed the presence of Roberta Nummus. She was just another Human of Earth descent, even though she had been born in a Cis-Lunar L-Five colony and never actually been to the Earth. Roberta acclimated to one standard gravity with ease, within hours of entering the Bernal Sphere embassy colony. It was two years after the opening of the Mimasian embassy in Cis-Lunar L-Five that the Mimasian embassy on Earth was ready for opening and occupation. By then, all of the Martians and Thols had acclimated to one standard gravity and those assigned to Earth, were all ready to make the move.

When the day finally came, one-third of the Mimasian diplomatic staff were transported to Earth. They used the same refurbished military transport as they'd used to arrive in Cis-Lunar Space two years earlier. Roberta Nummus escorted them to Earth in her ship, the Dark Angel.

As these were both essentially military vessels, they had to get special clearance. Especially for the Dark Angel, which was formidably armed. Both ships landed in the sprawling embassy grounds. The transport ship dropped off its diplomatic passengers, their luggage and cargo and then returned to the other Mimasian embassy in Cis-Lunar Space.

Roberta Nummus's ship, the Dark Angel, remained in the embassy grounds. It had all gone like clockwork, like a military operation. Roberta took no chances and had her security teams make a thorough sweep of the embassy before the disembarkation of passengers.

The Mimasian embassies proved exceedingly popular with diplomats. With leaders from across the Nations of the Earth and Cis-Lunar Space wanting to meet the Martians and Thols. Up till now, their only knowledge of them had come from information provided in the form of physiological reports. Now, they were here in Cis-Lunar Space and even on Earth and people actually wanted to meet them.

It was even debatable as to which species was the more popular. The Martians, a subspecies of Humans who were non-verbal telepaths with their golden-hued skin tones, their golden-blond hair and those vibrant emerald green eyes. Or was it the Thols, a completely alien species, with their alabaster white skin, powerful leathery creamy white wings and tails? Hands that had six fingers set in three pairs, the outer pairs being opposable.

The Thols had the faces of angels, with the most enigmatic purple eyes and white blond hair. Both Martians and Thols, as it turned out, were the gentlest of species, with the Thols being described as absolutely *"Angelic"*. The first thing people noticed about Thols was that they did not wear shoes. Their feet had the same arrangement of toes as their hands and fingers. They were designed to grip branches, not for walking, flight being their natural mode of motility.

People everywhere wanted to meet them. They had become very, very real. Even Flat Earthers wanted to meet them. After all, their very existence blew their conspiracy theories right out of the void! Both Martians and Thols were constantly in the news and the paparazzi hung around the outside of their embassy with the cameras fitted with telescopic lenses like vultures.

The Mimasian embassy on Earth had only been open for two weeks when the Earth Defence Forces turned up. They had taken note of the Dark Angel, a warship belonging to the notorious, violent criminal, Roberta Nummus. On checking their data, they found an issue. Roberta Nummus was listed not only as the embassy's head of security, but she also had full diplomatic status and, along with that, came diplomatic immunity. The Earth Defence Forces wanted answers and after conferring with their colleagues at the Cis-Lunar Colonial Fleet, so did they.

Without any invitation or prior arrangement, the Earth's military deployed outside the Mimasian embassy. Two full platoons of Marines. They did not enter the embassy grounds. The Marines all deployed around the outer perimeter wall. The paparazzi, vultures that they were, began snapping photos like there was no tomorrow.

Four men arrived in a military vehicle. An Earth Defence Force General and a Field Marshal, a Colonial Fleet Captain and an Admiral. They pulled up to the embassy gate, stepped out and demanded entry. One of the gate sentries, one of Roberta's security men, was handed a document. It was a military arrest warrant for Roberta Nummus. The man laughed, he laughed loudly and passed the document to his colleague. That sentry also laughed loudly.

The first gate sentry enquired, having seen the marines deploy, "How many troops did you bring?"

"Two full platoons", the General replied.

Both sentries laughed once more, "You'd better fuck off then. A hundred men won't be enough. You could double that number, even triple it, multiply it by ten, even, and it still wouldn't be enough. They'll be just lambs for the slaughter for the boss Lady. All just dead men walking."

The other sentry added with a wry smile, "The boss Lady has diplomatic immunity anyway, General. So get on your bike and leave. You ain't getting in!"

The four men just looked from one to the other.

The General scoffed, "You think you guards could take on a thousand marines and triumph!"

Both guards blinked and then laughed, then one of them explained, "You misunderstood me, General. The boss Lady would tell us to take a nap on the embassy lawn over there while she deals with your men herself."

The other guard chimed in, "The boss Lady is like that, General. Real hands-on. We'd take a nap on the lawn over there while she gives your men a bloody good spanking."

A voice crackled over the gate sentry's intercom, "Guys, I am listening to this conversation. Seriously! Just let our new guests in. I deal with them myself."

"And their dogs, Ma'am?", one of the gate sentries enquired.

"Their dogs get to stay outside. They can wait around pissing on the perimeter wall for all I care, just let their brass in. I probably have much to discuss with them", Roberta replied.

"Yes, Ma'am. Brass in, dogs out", the gate sentry confirmed, then he noted to their guests, "The boss Lady says you may enter", and they let them in, but only the four of them.

Roberta Nummus met the four military men at the main embassy door and ushered them inside to a conference room. Inside the conference room were the lead Martian and Thol diplomats, both Ambassadors. One was a Martian Elder, the Thol was an appointee of the Thol Matriarch. They were not happy with this military encirclement.

Roberta Nummus was wearing full tactical body armour, there were weapons placed strategically on her utility belt and about her person. A long-bladed katana, *the Harōingu*, was sheathed and strapped to her back. This was the Roberta Nummus they had been briefed about. A deadly, ageless assassin. Roberta politely introduced her colleagues because that was precisely who they were.

"This is the Mimasian Ambassador of the Martians of Mimas, Ambassador Myral. This is the Mimasian Ambassador of the Thols of Mimas, Ambassador Yyltrac. I am the Mimasian Ambassador of the Humans inside of Mimas, Earth descended, of course. Roberta Nummus", she announced, "Please, take a seat and then you can explain yourselves."

That caught all four guests off guard. Roberta Nummus was not just any diplomat. She was an Ambassador. They had really fucked up!.

The four men took their seats. The Earth Defence Force Field Marshal apologised. They had not known that Roberta Nummus was actually the new ambassador to Earth. They thought that she was just some low-level diplomat, whose diplomatic status could be revoked with the presentation of an arrest warrant. Roberta had chuckled at their confusion, shaking her head in amusement. Ambassadors Myral and Yyltrac were somewhat less amused. Diplomatic immunity was expected to be respected.

The General passed the arrest warrant across the conference table to Roberta, who looked at it. Her face was expressionless as she read through the very, very long list of charges. When she passed it to Myral, the Martian Ambassador and then finally to Yyltrac, the Thol Ambassador, they both just laughed. Myral laughed telepathically and Yyltrac laughed in lyrical trills, clicks and soft barks.

"Every single charge after twenty one ninety is complete rubbish", Roberta announced and then she continued, "And half of the charges up to twenty one ninety are complete rubbish as well."

The four men all looked at each other in confusion.

The Field Marshal spoke up, "And you have proof of this, Ms Nummus?", he could not yet bring himself to address her as Ambassador.

"Gentlemen. I have lived inside Mimas since the year twenty one eighty one. I did leave Mimas once in twenty one ninety to ice pick Godric von Horridian and end the first Horridian War", Roberta informed them all, adding "From then up until two years ago, I hadn't left Mimas and I've only been on Earth for two weeks. Ninety percent of the crimes on that list of yours, you've just blamed on me instead of tracking down the real criminals. Shit! There are even crimes on there that happened on Earth and this is my first fucking visit! You've all been scapegoating me for your own investigative failures!"

All four military leaders looked at each other in confusion. Had they really been attributing crimes to Roberta Nummus that had nothing to do with her at all?

Myral telepathically added confirmation, *"Ambassador Nummus is correct, Gentlemen. I can vouch for her personally"*, her words entered their minds loud and clear.

"As can I. Roberta Nummus has only just left Mimas in the last two years", Yyltrac added in perfect English laced with trills, clicks and barks.

That just added to their confusion.

Roberta took to the list of crimes recorded on the warrant, all four hundred of them, with a red marker. One by one, she struck them from the document. When she was finished, there were only twenty left that she knew were definitely hers. There were a lot of others that were missing, not recorded, Roberta ignored those. Fully ninety five percent of the charges had been misattributed to her. When Roberta passed the document back to the General, he passed it to the Field Marshal, who, in turn, passed it to the Admiral and the Fleet Captain. They all looked confused and astonished.

"The remaining crimes are mine, I will admit that. They all occurred between twenty one hundred and twenty one ninety. So four hundred or more years ago", Roberta admitted, and then she noted, "Those last two. The regicide of Albert von Horridian. That was in self-defence. Albert sent an assassin after me and my family. I responded with main force. Chop, chop, rip as one does. And as for Godric von Horridian, while I did lobotomise him with an ice pick, that was to end the first Horridian War and save hundreds of millions of lives across the solar system. I will not apologise for either of those."

Ambassador Myral chimed in telepathically, *"That was all before my people healed Roberta Nummus. We removed her military conditioning, removed all of her triggers and cleared up her psychoses. The Roberta Nummus who sits before you today is not the same woman as the psychopath who committed those crimes. You cannot hold her accountable."*

Ambassador Yyltrac agreed, her voice trilling, clicking and barking in English, "You cannot hold this Roberta Nummus accountable and we will not allow it. Roberta is a Mimasian Ambassador."

The Admiral replied, his voice showing he'd been rattled, "We will take this back to our people. Obviously, there is much in this document that is in error and needs correcting. As for the remaining charges, it is not up to us as to whether they are dropped or not."

The meeting then ended and as the four men left, the Fleet Captain enquired, "Ambassador Nummus, could you really have taken down a hundred of the Earth Defence Force's finest?"

Roberta smirked and looked at her watch, which showed the embassy's perimeter wall.

After less than twenty seconds, Roberta replied, smiling, "In five minutes, Fleet Captain. In five minutes. That's all it would have taken."

Roberta left it at that as the Fleet Captain left, his face showing sheer astonishment.

Roberta didn't hear from the military after that incident for another six months. The same four military brass, the General, the Field Marshal, the Fleet Captain and the Admiral booked an appointment for their second visit. They sat in the same conference room, with Roberta, Myral and Yyltrac. The meeting was far more cordial than the first one. Roberta was informed that all of the incorrectly attributed charges had been struck from her file. It had caused issues, of course, as now they had no idea who'd committed those crimes. Investigative failures at their finest!

Roberta was also informed that the regicide of High Prince Albert was indeed self-defence and that the Jovian authorities had agreed to drop the charges. The lobotomisation of High Prince Godric with an ice pick was a contentious issue. However, as it was directly responsible for ending the first Horridian War. The Jovian authorities had agreed to drop those charges as well.

The remaining charges, which Roberta had fully admitted to, had also been dropped. They were over four hundred years old and no one, absolutely no one, not a single prosecutor, wanted to reopen those cases and attempt to try them. Especially considering that the current Roberta Nummus was no longer the same psychopathic woman who'd committed them. All charges had been dropped. Roberta Nummus was now entirely free.

Roberta thought it was all over. However, the Earth Defence Force General and Field Marshal, the Cis-Lunar Colonial Fleet Captain and the Admiral, could not let things lie. They could not let things go. Roberta Nummus was an enigma. The woman was born in the year twenty eighty, making her over five hundred years old.

Roberta Nummus had joined the Colonial Armed Forces at eighteen years of age and was trained as a Special Armed Forces Operative. Then, having completed her training, she volunteered for what turned out to be rogue military experimental conditioning, physical, psychological and even genealogical conditioning. That had caused more than eight decades of psychoses, and yet, here she was, a survivor and an immortal. What does one do with an immortal with her training, her abilities?

More importantly, Roberta had overcome her psychoses and become a functional member of Mimasian society. The Martians and the Thols trusted her implicitly with their very lives. Roberta had also worked as the Mimasian Administrator for over four and a half centuries.

Roberta Nummus was highly skilled, highly trained and her resume, albeit tainted by her past psychoses, actually glowed with capabilities. Capabilities that the military, Earth's or Cis-Lunar Space's, could use. At least once a week, one of the four military brass would drag out her file and re-read it. What to do with Roberta Nummus?

Roberta Nummus had been an Ambassador for four years, two of them on Earth, when the same four military brass booked an appointment to see her. It was unusual, everything, all of her charges had been cleared up. So, what could they possibly want?

At the meeting, Ambassadors Myral and Yyltrac were present once more. Roberta felt a certain comfort in having them with her. For this meeting, Roberta was actually dressed like an ambassador. No body armour and no weapons were visibly present on her person, but nonetheless, they were there. They were just hidden. Roberta was not one to ever be fully unarmed.

The General, the Field Marshal, the Fleet Captain and the Admiral all sat there stone-faced and not showing any emotion. They were completely unreadable.

The Field Marshal spoke first, "Ambassador Nummus, you pose us with a problem. You have certain military skills that make you one very dangerous woman. Yet, you also have skills that are highly sought after. Centuries of experience as a Colonial Administrator, for instance."

The Admiral chimed in, "What the Field Marshal is trying to say, Ambassador, is that someone with your resume, your particular skill set, belongs in a military command position. Ambassadorial duties, although no doubt you are good at them, seem somewhat out of place."

Yyltrac stepped in, "Making Roberta an Ambassador gave her diplomatic protections", her melodic trills and clicks interspersed with her English.

The General enquired, "Ambassador Nummus, why are you really here?"

"Gentlemen, to be entirely honest. I am here to keep my people, the Martians and the Thols, safe. That is it in a nutshell. Being an Ambassador has kept me safe as well. It has been convenient for all of us involved", Roberta explained honestly.

The four men looked at each other. Roberta Nummus showed such loyalty. Yet another quality that they all actually admired in the woman, as dangerous as she was.

Roberta looked at the men with cold, steely eyes, "Gentlemen, you either cut to the chase or this meeting is over!"

"Roberta Nummus, we are offering you a job", the Admiral announced.

"What kind of job?", Roberta enquired, they had just piqued her curiosity.

"That all depends", the Field Marshal replied, explaining, "If you join the Earth Defence Forces, then we are offering you a commissioned officer position with the rank of Colonel."

The Admiral stepped in, "And if you choose to join the Cis-Lunar Colonial Fleet, we will be offering you the commissioned officer position of Captain with your own ship, of course."

Roberta stared at the four men in disbelief, the questioning thoughts, *"Colonel? Captain?"*, running through her mind.

The General noted, "These are, of course, brevet ranks. However, they do have all the same remuneration and privileges."

Roberta replied wryly, "I don't need money! I have more credits at my disposal than you can imagine. Besides, I've been there and done that. I was betrayed the last time, or have you forgotten?"

The Fleet Captain replied, "Ambassador Nummus, we have not forgotten, but please understand, the Colonial Fleet is nothing like the old Colonial Armed Forces. A lot has changed in five hundred years."

The General interjected, "And besides, Ambassador, what better position to be in to protect your people than as a Colonel in the Earth Defence Forces or as a Captain in the Colonial Fleet?", and then he gestured to the Martian and Thol Ambassadors.

Roberta shook her head, these people simply didn't get it, she doubled down, "Gentlemen, Colonels and Captains only protect what they are ordered to protect. Nothing more. Nothing less. In case you had not noticed, I am not one to take orders. I am one to give them."

All four men went quiet, as Myral sent Roberta a private message, *"You have them rattled, Roberta. Completely rattled. They don't know what to make of you."*

Yyltrac spoke out with her trill and click-laced English, "Roberta Nummus has integrity, she does. Not one to take bribes. Bribes she will not do. You waste her time!"

The Field Marshal asked, his voice lower, more contrite, "We offered you a position in our Armed Forces. You've rejected that position. We get it. Where do we go from here?", he questioned.

"Gentlemen. My people are my family. I will protect them above all else and a mere Colonel or a Captain would never be in a position to allow that", Roberta replied.

"What are you suggesting, Ambassador?", the Admiral asked.

"Obviously, you all want me on your team, so to speak. And honestly, I cannot see the point if I cannot protect the people I love", Roberta was speaking from her heart and then she dug in, "If you want me on your team, you need to step up your game. I give orders. I don't take them."

The Fleet Captain could see where this was going and repeated the Admiral's question, "Roberta Nummus, precisely, what are you suggesting?"

Roberta smiled, a broad, wry smile, "If you offer me the position of General or Admiral, I will consider your offer", she replied in jest.

Myral gave off a quiet, private telepathic chuckle that only Roberta and Yyltrac could pick up. Yyltrac, on the other hand, burst out in Tholish laughter. Roberta was messing with their heads!

All four men looked from one to the other and their faces could not hide their shock. Was this woman being serious?

Offer her upper-level command positions and she would merely consider their offers. The meeting ended abruptly. The General, the Field Marshal, the Fleet

Captain and the Admiral all left. They were not one bit happy at all.

"What if?", Yyltrac queried, her voice laced with trills and clicks, "What if they make you those offers, Roberta Nummus?"

"They won't, Yyltrac. There is no way in hell that they'll offer me upper-level command ranks", Roberta replied, noting, "I just told them that to put the wind up them."

Myral had been lost in thought for a long moment, *"Roberta Nummus. The Field Marshal and the Admiral were actually both considering doing just that"*, she transmitted.

"Really, Myral. That does not seem very likely", Roberta replied.

Myral tapped her right temple, *"Telepath, remember. They were all upset that you pushed them so hard, yes, but the Field Marshal and the Admiral were taking you seriously. They just need to consult the powers that are above them. I believe the term is, it is above their pay grade."*

Yyltrac began trilling and clicking, "If they offer you such positions. You should take up their offers, whichever is best, Roberta Nummus. Protect us best from a high position, from the highest rank!"

Myral agreed, telepathically noting, *"As a General, you can protect our people anywhere on Earth. As an Admiral, you can protect our people right across the entire solar system."*

Myral and Yyltrac were both right. What if they came back with actual offers?

Nothing was heard from the four military commanders for four months and then two letters arrived. Actual old school letters, no emails, no messages, no electronic communiques, just two letters. They were even delivered by registered post, requiring Roberta's actual signature. The Field Marshal, Hans Norbit, had been authorised to offer her the position of General under the Earth Defence Forces. The Admiral, actually High Admiral Montague Montgomery, had also been authorised to offer her the position of Admiral under the Cis-Lunar Colonial Fleet.

Roberta's immediate thought to herself was, *"What the fuck is the matter with these people?"*

And then she realised that they had been authorised to make those offers. This was all coming from higher up. Much higher up, non-military, it was political.

There were people in the Earth's Government and in the Cis-Lunar Government who wanted her in their Armed Forces. And they were even willing to give her the rank of her choice to do so.

Roberta Nummus replied to both letters with letters of her own, two simple words, "Under consideration", after all, this was something that she needed to discuss with Myral and Yyltrac.

On the third level of the Mimasian embassy, Myral and Yyltrac both tried to convince Roberta of the merits of accepting one of the offered positions. Her colleagues pointed out that being a General in the Earth Defence Forces would probably limit her protective scope to just Earth. That would be like being in the Venusian Defence Forces or in the Martian Defence Forces, limited to just one orbital zone.

Roberta's colleagues were of the opinion that by being a Colonial Fleet Admiral, she could expand her aspirations, not only protecting the Thols and Martians inside Mimas, but also the Martians who still live on Mars itself. Yyltrac even pointed out that Roberta's own people also needed her. That all of the people of the solar system needed her. That they were, in fact, all her people.

Yyltrac had even quoted Roberta herself, "The needs of the many, sometimes require the actions of just the one", her voice as always a melody of trills, clicks and soft barks.

Myral had agreed, transmitting, *"With this position of Admiral. You can help to protect everyone."*

Roberta was still unsure. She still had very vivid memories of her *"experimental"* training and the abuses she had been put through. The memory of an immortal was long and Roberta's early lessons were learned the hard way. They had been brutal. She had been brutalised and, in turn, she had brutalised others.

Roberta Nummus could not ever forget the past.

They had been discussing the pros and cons of accepting an Admiralty for most of the morning and it was now midday. Roberta sensed a change in the room. Did that chair at the other end of the table just move ever so slightly? Then there was the squeak! It was almost inaudible, except Roberta Nummus had heightened senses and she'd heard it. Roberta looked quickly at Myral, who showed no signs of reaction and then she turned to Yyltrac. Yyltrac had heard something with those Tholish ears of hers, although it must have been subconscious. No conscious reaction was noticed. Then there was another almost inaudible squeak from the empty chair across the other side of the table.

Roberta stood and walked over to the window. A long, seamless length of clear, crystalline plasteel. Roberta stared out the window with her back to the empty chair that tickled her senses.

"Is there anything wrong?", Yyltrac trilled and clicked.

Yyltrac had sensed it too, she just didn't register it consciously.

Roberta answered carefully, trying not to give anything away, "No, nothing is wrong, Yyltrac. It's just such a nice day outside. Do you remember the skies of Mimas? That concave curvature was like living on the inside of a fish bowl. It's the reverse here. The curvature is all convex. It's the complete reverse. It is, nonetheless, beautiful, of course. Absolutely breath taking, in fact."

And then there was that slight squeak once more. Roberta swung around in one fluid motion, her left hand reaching out and across to the empty chair. It was not empty. With a swift blur of motion, Roberta's left hand swept upward to what should have been a throat. Her left hand tightened and her left arm raised. There was a shimmering in the air and then a person appeared out of nowhere. It was a young woman wearing a hooded, black cloak that shimmered like raven feathers, and Roberta had her firmly by the throat.

Roberta shook her head, "I knew it. Council of Shadows, I presume?", she enquired.

The woman in the black cloak nodded slightly and Roberta released her grip.

"I'm Folcrom Celestia", the woman replied and then she asked, "How did you detect me?"

Roberta pointed to the chair, "It squeaks, not a lot, but just enough for me to hear it. Young Lady, if you had not sat down, we would not have known you were there. Remember that for next time. Sometimes chairs squeak. Otherwise, your psychic obscuration field was working fine", and then she walked back to her seat.

Almost in unison, Myral transmitted and Yyltrac trilled, *"Council of Shadows?"*

"Yes", Roberta replied, noting, "We haven't seen them for a while. Not since Lord Folcrom Forkbraid and his Wife, Lady Folcrom Selene. That was a long time ago."

Celestia was quite young, she giggled, "They were my ancestors", then she paused as she approached a closer chair and sat down, "Oops! I screwed up. You weren't supposed to detect me. This was my first solo observational jaunt. My Mentor will be most displeased."

Roberta smiled at the young Council of Shadows operative, "Then don't tell him. I know we won't."

Yyltrac enquired, trilling and clicking, "Child, you said it was your first solo observational jaunt. Why were you observing us?"

Celestia frowned and lightly bit her lower lip before replying, "I am not a child. I'm twenty six years old", and then she explained, "I was sent here to observe Roberta Nummus's decision. My Mentor believed that there was a ninety seven percent chance of her accepting the Admiralty position and a twenty three percent chance of her accepting the position of General. I was supposed to report back on which choice Roberta made. It is a very important matter!"

Yyltrac noted with a trill and a few clicks, "That does not add up to one hundred percent."

Celestia simply replied, "They're not supposed to. The choice is more complex. It's a nexus point."

"A nexus point?", Yyltrac trilled questioningly.

"Yes, a critical juncture where the happen tracks can branch into three major, distinct and important directions, each with its own probability. General, Admiral or neither", Celestia tried to explain.

Roberta just shook her head.

"So, your mentor gave you a simple, cherry assignment, and you made one simple mistake. Tell your Mentor that I'd grade you with a B+. Now, Celestia, what has the Council of Shadows got to do with any of this?", Roberta replied with more critique before asking what mattered.

Celestia frowned once more, "Roberta Nummus. The Council of Shadows has determined that you are needed in a more appropriate position. Being an Ambassador is all well and good, but as a General or an Admiral, you could do so much more."

It was now Roberta's turn to frown, "So, the Council of Shadows has orchestrated all of this? They've just been tweaking away behind the scenes?"

"Ah, yeah, of course, we have. That's kind of what we do. We maintain order and balance", Celestia replied matter-of-factly.

Myral chimed in, in her telepathic way, questioning, *"So, even the Council of Shadows sees merit in Roberta taking up the Admiralty offer?"*

"Of course, General, Admiralty, we would not have set them up if we didn't see the merit of them", Celestia confirmed, noting, "However, it must be Roberta's choice. Roberta Nummus is the nexus point and her choice matters. I can observe, but I cannot interfere."

Yyltrac, in her Tholish wisdom, needed more than just words, "Young, Celestia, you have proof of this? You have proof that you are really from the Council of Shadows? We need more than just words, young one", she trilled, clicked and barked softly.

Myral agreed with her, telepathically transmitting, *"Yyltrac does have a point. Can you prove that you really are from the Council of Shadows?"*

"Guys, if it looks like a duck, quacks like a duck, swims like a duck and flies like a duck, then it's a duck. Every single thing about Celestia simply oozes Council of Shadows operative", Roberta disagreed, as she had had far more interactions with them.

"No, Roberta. They're right. I could be a rogue psychic causing mischief. Although I must admit. I've never heard of such a thing. Psi Corp would never allow it and the Council of Shadows most certainly wouldn't. Such a person would be psychically demolished and reconstructed", Celestia replied.

"So, Celestia, what do you suggest?", Roberta enquired.

"Simple, Roberta Nummus", Celestia replied, smiling as she dragged her chair closer to Roberta, "I'll share my memories with you. Then you can see for yourself."

Celestia leaned in towards Roberta, gave her a quick peck on the lips and then touched her forehead to Roberta's. Roberta allowed the sharing to occur and it took several minutes.

When Celestia withdrew her mind, she noted, "I am a scion of Folcrom Tafazah. I have memories from Selene and Forkbraid, going back even further to Gideon Reas and Freyja. They shared with Sandra and Winchilly, so their memories are all in there as well. I've given you the full package, Roberta Nummus. You can access them with just a little bit of concentration."

Roberta did. She accessed the memories and Celestia had spoken the truth. All of the shared memories were there. They crossed linked with shared memories that Roberta had received in the past, many centuries ago and Winchilly's face appeared once more, as the memories all collated.

Winchilly's memory smiled at Roberta, *"Follow the path of the greater good"*, she implored.

Celestia smiled at Roberta, "So, Roberta Nummus. What do you choose? General? Admiral? Perhaps neither, perhaps even your own path? There is actually a small, non-zero chance that you'll do something right out of left field. A wild card choice! It is so exciting!"

Roberta smiled back, "I'll take Winchilly's advice. I'll choose the path of the greater good."

Celestia's face took on a disappointed look, "The path of greater good?", she questioned and then asked, "Is that your own path?"

Roberta continued to smile, "As a Mimasian Ambassador, I serve only Mimas and keep my people safe. As a General in the Earth's Defence Forces, I'd serve Earth while keeping my people safe. As an Admiral in the Colonial Fleet, with an expanded scope, I'd serve the entire solar system. I'd keep everybody safe. That seems to me to be the greater good."

Yyltrac trilled in agreement, trilling and clicking, "It took you long enough, Roberta."

Myral told Celestia telepathically, *"And now you have your answer, Celestia."*

"Brilliant!", Celestia exclaimed, adding, "That is just the happen track we need. It's perfect."

Then Celestia leaned in to Roberta and impetuously kissed her on the lips. Surprisingly, Roberta didn't resist and the passionate kiss lasted a full minute. Myral and Yyltrac looked on in shock.

When Celestia finally pulled back, she noted, "I've always liked older women. I'm going to visit you more often, I think. When I'm not on the job, of course."

Roberta smiled and replied, "You remind me of Freyja. Highly impetuous, except, of course, Freyja didn't swing that way. Freyja was a very good friend to me."

"I know, Roberta. I have Freyja's memories as well", Celestia replied as she stood up, "I'll definitely see you later", she told Roberta and then she vanished in a small flicker of blue light.

Roberta sent off two letters that day. One to Field Marshal Hans Norbit, officially declining his offer. The second, more important letter, was to High Admiral Montague Montgomery. It was Roberta Nummus's letter of acceptance to the position of Admiral in the Cis-Lunar Colonial Fleet.

The very place where she could do the greatest good.

Roberta Nummus's choice paid off, in more ways they one. After centuries of being alone after the passing of Elaine Haynes, Roberta found love once more. And although Roberta was over five hundred years old, she did have the appearance of a woman not yet thirty. The apparent age difference, with Celestia being only twenty six, made it seem natural. Folcrom Celestia, the Council of Shadows operative, became Roberta Nummus's second Wife and they were very happy together.

The wheel of time was ever turning and the years passed by. Within two years of being an Admiral, Roberta Nummus went from being an Admiral at her desk to her first command. She was given command of her own Carrier Strike Group based around the Interplanetary Fighter Carrier, the Celestial Protector. Roberta named the ship herself. As it was peace time, officers were allowed to have their spouses aboard the ship.

No one knew that Celestia was a psychic, let alone a Council of Shadows member. Of course, the wheel of time kept turning and in due course, young Celestia grew older and eventually, she too passed away. It was another sad time for Roberta Nummus. Such was the curse of immortality.

It was after the passing of Celestia Reas, yes, that was her surname, that the psychics from the New Flinders Psychic Academy on Mars allowed the Slipstream drive to be released and developed. It had been developed back in Folcrom Forkbraid's day, but was not allowed to be released, as the second Horridian War had just ended and Humanity was far from ready.

Humanity's first interstellar destination was Proxima Centauri and much to their surprise, the second planet, an eyeball world, already had a thriving Human population. They were all psychics and they called their world Twilight. Like all eyeball worlds, it had an extremely hot side, an extremely cold side and in Twilight's case, a habitable zone encircling the terminator, along with seas and oceans.

It turned out that Folcrom Forkbraid and his Wife, Folcrom Selene, could not only jaunt across interplanetary space but across interstellar space as well. With the aid of Psi Corp, the pair had set up colonies right across the Alpha Centauri system. Along with Twilight, they had colonised the third planet of Alpha Centauri A, a world, an Earth analogue, that was called Gaia. They'd also colonised the second planet of Alpha Centauri B, another Earth analogue, that they'd named Odhinn.

There were also Mars analogues in the Alpha Centauri system. The fourth planet of Alpha Centauri A, named Aires and the third planet of Alpha Centauri B, named Thor. Both were super Mars analogues and eminently terraformable. The supramundane psychics even had research bases on them. There was a whole civilisation in the Alpha Centauri system, waiting patiently for the mundane Humanity to catch up and arrive. And so they did.

The initial greeting was, *"What kept you so long? We've been waiting here for you for centuries."*

The wheel of time was relentless, turning ever onward and Roberta Nummus was eventually promoted to Fleet Admiral. Her promotion had taken longer than most, as she was an immortal, but that did not bother Roberta. She had plenty of time. All of time, in fact!

It was in the year thirty four fifty that the Tholish holy grail was located. The homeworld of the Thols. It was in the Xi Bootis system, twenty two light years from Sol. Xi Bootis A Secundus. A world festooned with life, much like the Earth. Unlike Twilight, Gaia and Odhinn, only the Earth and Secundus possessed true sapient beings! Secundus was home to five sapient species: Thols, Carlins, Harricks, Tarlaks and Chitten, the last two being violent and deadly. Each of the five species had a different name for their world, although only three were known.

Orbital research stations were set up and the world was studied intensively via stealth drones for two decades. Humanity knew exactly what to expect in terms of sapient biology. They already had the detailed information provided by the Mimasian Thols from Sol.

A second habitable world was also found in the Xi Bootis system. Xi Bootis B Primus. It was another eyeball world, very much similar to Twilight. It too was festooned with life, but not as we know it. Multiple Sapient beings that were neither animal, plant, nor fungi, but instead a combination of all three, lived there.

Their heads had the appearance of Earth flowers and so they were named after those flowers. Chantrieri and Simianthus were given the Taxonomic Kingdom of Floravitae. There were two species. The Chantrieri had three subspecies: dark, golden and light. There was only one species of Simianthus.

Each lived in its own region. The dark Chantrieri lived in the hot sunward side, the light Chantrieri lived in the cold night side, while the golden Chantrieri lived in the terminator zone, with its planet girdling ocean full of islands. The Simianthus lived on a single large island in the terminator zone.

Homo sapiens sapiens, Earth humans, Sol - Earth.

Homo sapiens martialis, Martian humans, Sol - Mars & Sol - Saturn - Mimas.

Tholus sapiens mimasensis, Mimasian Thols, Sol - Saturn - Mimas.

Tholus sapiens arbormundensis, Homwol Thols, Xi Bootis A - Secundus.

Carlinus sapiens vallimundensis, Vale Carlins, Xi Bootis A - Secundus.

Harrickus sapiens occultomundensis, Harricks, Xi Bootis - Secundus.

Tarlakus sapiens robustus, Tarlakan Tarlaks, Xi Bootis A - Secundus.

Chittenus sapiens formicus, Chittens, Ant-Like, Xi Bootis A - Secundus.

Chantrieri sapiens obscurus, Day side, Xi Bootis B - Primus.

Chantrieri sapiens aureus, Terminator Coast & Islands, Xi Bootis B - Primus.

Chantrieri sapiens lucidus, Night side, Xi Bootis B - Primus.

Simianthus sapiens floridus, Terminator Islands, Xi Bootis B - Primus

And so, the Sol and Xi Bootis systems stood revealed, not as barren outposts of dead rock, nor as simple worlds with simple life, but as orchards of intelligence, each blooming, shaped by time, environment and memory.

In the year thirty four seventy, Roberta Nummus requested command of the colonisation fleet to Xi Bootis A Secundus. Her request was granted and along with it came her promotion to High Admiral of the Colonial Fleet. The reason for Roberta's request was simple. On board the twelve interstellar colonial push ships were at least two direct descendants of Lina Mitchel and a descendant of

Freyja, a scion of Folcrom Tafazah. The system of Sol was a safe place and the frontiers of deep interstellar space, not so much. Roberta Nummus was always driven to protect those she loved and their descendants and so she had made the request.

Also aboard the twelve push ships were, of course, nearly twelve thousand Humans and a handful of Martian colonists. Martian colonists were not so unusual. Some had hybrid ancestry and the Human wanderlust that went with it. Mimasian Thols, however, had never colonised anywhere beyond Sol.

It was only because Xi Bootis A Secundus was their original and ancient homeworld, a world they called Homwol, that they were going at all. Many of them clamoured to be the first to go *"back home"*. Their numbers amongst the colonists were not insignificant. A lucky two hundred were allotted positions as colonists. Roberta Nummus needed to keep them all safe, each and every one of them.

Xi Bootis A Secundus had a single large moon called Luns and with it came five Lagrangian points. Roberta's tasks were clear. First, use the resources of Luns to build colonies and infrastructure in Cis-Luns L-Five and L-Four. Second, set up a surface colony on Secundus. Both were to be developed simultaneously. The planet had a single large continent and that continent had a broad river valley running almost its full length from East to West. The surface colony was to be on the land midway between the villages of the Carlins in the valley and the villages of the Indigenous Thols in the tall trees in the mountains to the north.

By slipstream drive, the Xi Bootis B system and their new home, Secundus, were less than three days away. The interstellar push ships flew as a fleet to the outskirts of Jupiter, just beyond Callisto's orbit, where they activated their Slipstream drives. Two minutes and ten seconds later, they were on the outskirts of the solar system well beyond the orbits of Neptune and Pluto.

Once all twelve push ships had arrived, they performed their precautionary system checks, which they did after every Slipstream jump. Then, once their system checks came back okay, they activated their Slipstream drives yet again and two minutes and ten seconds later, they were in the far outskirts of the Xi Bootis system. The two stars, a small yellow G-type star, slightly smaller than the Sun, and an even smaller orange K-type star, were clearly visible on their scanners in the distance.

They performed their precautionary system checks once more and after they came back okay, they activated their Slipstream drives yet again and two minutes and ten seconds later, they were in Xi Bootis A Secundun Cis-Luns space, looking at the blue planet in the distance.

A large blue-green orb, almost the size of the Earth, nearly all ocean, with one very large continent, Masula and its large moon, as big as the Earth's Moon, called Luns. The twelve interstellar push ships slowly flew to Cis-Luns L-Five using their fusion drives and immediately placed themselves in high Halo orbits. Now, they begin planning to build the two colonies.

A twenty four kilometre long, four kilometre wide, single cylinder, O'Neil-style mega colony and a planet-side colony in the Northern Masula Valley on the Masula Continent, between the Indigenous Thol villages in the tall Jula Jula forests to the North and the picturesque Carlin villages to the south.

High Admiral Roberta Nummus, now thirteen hundred and ninety years old, watched silently as her fleet of twelve colonial push ships settled into orbit.

Planet Fall had arrived and this was their new home!

Time observes and space abides, with the immortal Roberta Nummus now amongst the stars!

www.ingramcontent.com/pod-product-compliance
Lightning Source LLC
Chambersburg PA
CBHW050841030726
47503CB00007BA/2268